S0-CFX-466

THE COMPLETE

INDEPENDENCE DAY

OMNIBUS

NOVELIZATION

SILENT ZONE

WAR IN THE DESERT

ALSO AVAILABLE FROM TITAN BOOKS

Independence Day: Resurgence
The Official Prequel (May 2016)

Independence Day: Resurgence
The Official Novelization (June 2016)

THE COMPLETE

INDEPENDENCE DAY

OMNIBUS

NOVELIZATION

SILENT ZONE

WAR IN THE DESERT

TITAN BOOKS

The Complete Independence Day Omnibus
Print edition ISBN: 9781785652011
E-book edition ISBN: 9781785652028

Published by Titan Books
A division of Titan Publishing Group Ltd
144 Southwark Street, London SE1 0UP

First edition: March 2016
3 5 7 9 10 8 6 4 2

INDEPENDENCE DAY

OFFICIAL NOVELIZATION

DEAN DEVLIN & RONALD EMMERICH
AND STEPHEN MOLSTAD

Special thanks to
Elizabeth "Little Bit" Ostrom
and Dionne McNeff
for their invaluable assistance.

The sea of tranquillity was an eerily still wasteland, a silent crater-shaped outdoor tomb of ashes and stone. Two sets of footprints were etched into the powdery gray soil surrounding the landing site, each one as freshly cut as the day it was made. On the horizon, a curved sliver of the bright earth was rising into the sky, the vivid blue of its oceans a stark contrast to the colorless valley. Hammered into the lunar surface were the sensor rods of a seismometer, a square box capable of detecting the crash of a sea-sized meteor at a distance of fifty miles, and on the far side of the camp, an American flag waving proudly in a nonexistent breeze. The entire site was littered with debris: scientific experiments and the cartons which had carried them, the unused plastic bags used to gather soil samples, and a handful of commemorative trinkets. This equipment, carelessly scattered around an area the size of a baseball infield, had been imported by the astronauts of Apollo 11, the first two humans to set foot on the moon. When they left, they jettisoned everything deemed nonessential for the ride back home. Armstrong and Aldrin had taken one giant step for man, and left behind a ton of garbage for moonkind.

Their decades-old footprints marched fifteen paces out toward the horizon in every direction before turning back to the center of the camp. Seen from high above, they formed a pattern in the sand like a large, misshapen daisy. At the eye of this flower stood the gleaming Lunar

Landing Platform, a four-footed framework of tubes and gold foil which looked like a jungle gym on a hastily abandoned campground. Marooned deep in a sea of silence, the spot had the creepy aspect of a long-ago picnic which had come to an abrupt and terrifying end, as if there had been no time for the visitors to pack up their belongings. Only enough time to turn and run for safety. Nothing, not a single grain of sand, had moved in all the years since the earthlings' departure.

But something was beginning to change. Gradually, an infinitesimal churning began to engulf the area. For many hours, it was nothing more perceptible than the disturbance caused by the fluttering of a moth's wings at a distance of a thousand paces. But it grew steadily, inexorably, into a tremble. The electric needles inside the seismometer skittered to life. The machine's sensors shot awake and began to scream their warning to the scientists on earth. But the moon's extremes of heat and cold had disabled its radio transmitter within days of it first being planted. Like a night watchman with his tongue cut out, the small device struggled hour after hour to sound the alarm as the rumbling grew. A single grain of sand tumbled down the edge of a footprint, then another, and another. As the quaking blossomed into a deep rumble, the stiff wire sewn into the bottom seam of the American flag began to wobble back and forth. The footprints began to shake apart and disintegrate in the vibrating sand.

Then a vast shadow moved across the sky. It passed directly overhead, eclipsing the sun and plunging the entire crater into an unnatural darkness. The moonquake intensified as the thing moved closer. Whatever it was, it was much too large to have been sent from earth.

The rocky flatlands of the New Mexico desert could feel as alien and inhospitable as the moon. On a dark night when the moon was new, this was one of the quietest places on the planet: a thousand miles of blood-red desert, its clay hills baked hard and smooth. At one o'clock in the morning on July 2, jackrabbits and lizards, drawn by the warmth of the pavement, were gathered on a thin strip of asphalt in a valley where a dirt road snaked its way out of the foothills and down to the main highway. The only discernible movement came from the incredible profusion of insects, a thousand species of them that had adapted to this harsh environment.

Where the dirt road ran up toward the crest of some hills, there was a wooden sign half-hidden in the sagebrush. It read "NATIONAL AERONAUTICS AND SPACE ADMINISTRATION, SETI." Those who followed the road—with or without permission—to the top of the rise were rewarded with a spectacular sight. On the other side were two dozen enormous signal-collecting dishes, each one well over one hundred feet in diameter. Precision-built from curved steel beams painted white, these giant bowls dominated a long narrow valley. Because the moon was new, the only light on them was the red glow of the beacon lamps attached to the collector rods suspended over the center of each dish. The beacons were a precaution against curious or hopelessly lost pilots hitting the equipment with their planes and tangling themselves into the steel beams like flies caught in the strands of a spiderweb.

SETI, the Search for Extra-Terrestrial Intelligence, was a government-funded, NASA-administered scientific project and the field of giant radio telescopes was its primary laboratory. Far from the noise pollution that blanketed the cities, scientists had erected this mile-wide listening post to search for clues that would help solve a riddle almost as old as human imagination: Are we alone in the universe?

The telescopes picked up the noise emitted by a billion stars, quasars, and black holes, sounds that were not only very faint, but mind-bogglingly old. Traveling at the speed of light, radio emissions from the sun reach the earth after a delay of eight minutes, while those coming from the next nearest star take over four years. Most of the cosmic noise splashing into the dishes was several million years old, with a signal strength of less than a quadrillionth of a watt. Taken together and added up, all the radio energy ever received by earth amounted to less energy than a single snowflake striking the ground. And yet, these giant upturned steel ears were so exquisitely sensitive they could paint detailed color pictures of objects far too dim and distant for optical telescopes to perceive. They twisted slowly in the moonlight like a field of robotic flowers opening to the faint moonlight.

Tucked between these giants was a pre-fab three-bedroom ranch house which had been converted into a high-technology observatory. A skyful of data was gushing down into the telescopes, zipping along fiber optic cable into the house where it was sliced up, sorted, and analyzed by the most sophisticated signal-processing station ever built. All of this technological wizardry operated under the control of a master computer monitoring the entire system, which meant guys like Richard Yamuro had very little to do.

Richard was an astronomer who'd made a name for himself with his work on "the redshift" phenomenon associated with quasars. Six months out of graduate school, he'd landed a position at the prestigious Universita di Bologna in northern Italy. When SETI called two years later to offer him a job, he'd leapt at the chance to exchange his swank downtown apartment for a tiny cabin in the arid backcountry of New Mexico.

SETI was founded in the early sixties by a handful of "crackpots astronomers," who just happened to be some of the world's top research scientists. Their idea was simple: radio is a basic technology. It is easy to send and even simpler to receive. Its waves travel at the speed of light, effortlessly penetrating things like planets, galaxies, and clouds of gas without significant loss of strength. If an advanced civilization were attempting to communicate with us, these scientists argued, they would never be able to cross the infinite distances of the universe. The only realistic way to establish communication with earth would be to send a radio message. After years of lobbying in Congress, SETI won the funding for a ten-year exploration of the skies over the northern hemisphere. Under the guidance of NASA, the small staff had set up two other installations, one in Hawaii and the other in Puerto Rico. If intelligent life existed somewhere in the universe, the small band of SETI astronomers were the people most likely to find them.

Richard had pulled the overnight observation shift, which in most jobs would be the least attractive, but among the handful of scientists stationed in New Mexico, it was the most sought-after time to work. At four A.M. the night-watch commander could override the scanning system and use one of the large telescopes for his or her own projects. Which meant Richard still had two hours to kill before he had anything interesting to do. In the meantime, he was brushing up his golfing skills. Going down to one knee, he pictured himself lining up his birdie putt on the eighteenth green at Pebble Beach.

"The entire tournament comes down to this one final shot," he whispered like a television commentator. "Yamuro's left himself twenty feet from the hole. Normally, that would be no problem for a golfer of his amazing skills, but he'll be putting across the roughest, most wicked section of turf, the uneven stretch of green called 'the walkway.'"

"That's exactly right, Bob," he murmured, becoming the second announcer, "it's an almost impossible shot. The pressure is really on Yamuro at this point. It's a make or break situation, but we've seen him come through situations like this a hundred times before. If anyone can do it, he can."

At the far side of a room jammed with expensive electronic gadgetry, he'd laid a crinkled paper cup on its side. The golfer got to his feet and took a series of practice swings as the huge imaginary crowd looked on in perfect silence. Then he lifted his eyes to survey the scene. He glanced toward the tall narrow machine nicknamed "The Veg-O-Matic" for its ability to slice and dice the random noise of the universe into computer-digestible morsels. In its place, he saw his family biting their nails as the tension mounted. His mother, a grim expression on her face, nodded her head to show her son she believed in his ability to sink the putt, thereby bringing honor and glory to the Yamuro name. The golfer looked behind him and spotted a familiar face. "Carl," he said solemnly to an autographed photo of the popular astronomer Carl Sagan mounted on the office wall, "I'm gonna need your help with this one, pal."

At last, Yamuro stepped up to the ball, brought his club back, then, with a crisp and confident stroke, sent the ball sailing toward the hole. It moved unevenly over the worn spots in the office carpet until it reached the paper cup and clipped the edge of it before rolling off to one side. He had missed the shot! The golfer collapsed in agony to the floor. He had failed himself, his army of fans and, worst of all, his mother. While he was down on both knees, clutching at his heart and trying to find the words which could express his feelings of sorrow, the red phone rang.

The nightwatch commander's heart jumped into his throat. The red phone was not an outside line. It came directly from the master computer and was the signal that something unusual had been picked up on the monitors. Leaving his club on the floor, Yamuro snatched up the phone and listened carefully to the computer's digitally sampled voice reading off a string of coordinates. Blinking red lights began erupting all over the main control board.

"This isn't really happening," he muttered as he wrote down the time, frequency, and position coordinates of the disturbance onto a pad of paper. When the red phone rang, which it very rarely did, it meant the computers in the next room, the ones sorting through the billion channels of shrill, random bursts of space noise, had detected something out of the ordinary, something with an intentional pattern. With a sense of dread and a rising pulse rate, Yamuro slipped into the chair at the main instrument console and reached for the headphones. He slipped them over his ears and listened, but heard nothing unusual, only the usual hiss and crackle of the universe. Protocol, at that point, called for him to alert the other scientists, some of them sleeping in their cabins scattered around the grounds. But before he became a member of SETI's False Alarm Club, Yamuro wanted to check it out more carefully. It was probably nothing more than a new spy satellite, or a lost pilot calling for help. He punched some numbers into the keyboard of the computer and took over manual control of dish number one. Reading the input data, the scope swiveled back to the exact position it had been in when the disturbance began.

Then he heard it. Startled by the sound, he jerked backward in his chair, eyes the size of pancakes. Over the usual popping, fizzling background noise, he heard a tonal progression coming through loud and clear. The resonant sound oscillated up and down inside a frequency window known as the hydrogen band. It sounded almost like a musical instrument, an unlikely cross between a piccolo and a foghorn, and vaguely like a church organ in dire need of a tuning. It was like nothing he'd ever heard before, and he recognized it immediately as a signal. Slowly, something like a shocked smile crossed his lips and he reached for the intercom.

Ten minutes later, the small control room looked like a high-tech pajama party. Sleepy astronomers in robes and slippers crowded around the main console, taking turns with the headphones, all of them talking at once. By the time SETI's chief project scientist, Beulah Shore, came stumbling through the darkness from her cabin, her staff was already convinced they'd made contact with an alien culture. "This is the real thing, Beul," Yamuro told her.

Shore looked at him dubiously and plopped herself down in a chair below a poster that read "I BELIEVE IN LITTLE GREEN MEN," which she herself had posted. "This better not be one of those damned Russian spy jobs," she grumbled as she slipped the headphones on and listened with no visible change of expression. Two things were running through her mind: *This is it! We've found it!* There was no mistaking the slow rising and falling of the tone for anything accidental. But at the same time, her scientific training and her need to protect the project forced her to be skeptical. There was already a buzz of excitement among her co-workers and she had seen the ruinous effects of disappointment set in after previous false alarms.

"Interesting," she allowed, poker-faced, "but let's not jump the gun, people. I want to run a source trajectory. Doug, get on the phone to Arecibo and feed them the numbers."

Arecibo was a remote coastal valley in eastern Puerto Rico, home to the largest radio telescope in the world, one thousand meters in diameter. Within five minutes, the astronomers there had shut down their own experiments and wheeled their big dish around to the target coordinates. On a separate telephone line, high-speed modems transferred the data feed instantaneously. As the results of the Arecibo scope came over the line, the normally polite scientists jostled one another for a first look at the printout as it came spitting out of the machine.

"This can't be right," one scientist said, puzzled and somewhat frightened.

Yamuro tore the page from the printer and turned to Beulah. "According to these calculations, distance to source is three hundred eighty five kilometers," he said in confusion. Then he added what everyone in the cramped room already knew, 'That means it's coming from the moon."

Shore walked over to the room's only window, pulled back the curtain a few inches and scrutinized the crescent moon. "Looks like we might have visitors." Then, after a moment of reflection, she added, "It would've been nice if they'd called first."

Just across the Potomac River from the White House, the Pentagon was the largest office building in the world. The giant five-sided structure was home to the byzantine bureaucracies of the United States Armed Forces and was a small city unto itself. Even two hours before sunrise, when its workforce was reduced to the few thousand souls who pulled the graveyard shift, it was a bustling place. An armada of semis were lined up near the building's loading docks to deliver everything from classified documents to restaurant supplies, while dozens of trash trucks hauled away the previous day's mountain of waste.

Speeding across the southern parking lot, an unmarked late-model Ford sedan was headed directly for the building at seventy miles per hour. A second before it rammed into the side of the edifice, it broke into a long skid and fishtailed perfectly into the parking space closest to the front doors.

Seconds later, General William M. Grey, commander in chief of the United States Space Command and head of the Joint Chiefs of Staff came up the steps into the lobby, the steel taps on the soles of his shoes clicking an angry rhythm across the tiled floor. Forty-five minutes earlier, he'd been dead asleep when the phone rang. Nevertheless, the stocky sixty-year-old arrived at the office looking every inch the five-star general, all spit and polish. Without breaking stride, he was joined by his staff commander, Colonel Ray Castillo. The lanky young science officer followed his scowling boss to a fleet of elevators and opened a set of doors with a swipe of his identity card. The doors swooshed open and the two men stepped inside. The instant the doors were closed, the men knew it was safe to talk.

"Who else knows about this?" the general demanded.

"SETI out in New Mexico phoned about an hour ago. They picked up a radio signal at approximately one fifteen A.M. The thing is emitting a repetitive signal, which we're trying to interpret." Castillo answered nervously, trying to sound professional. He knew how little tolerance Grey had for sloppy work.

"They tell anybody else? The press?"

"They agreed to keep quiet about it for the time being. They're afraid of losing credibility if they announce anything prematurely, so they're going to run additional tests."

"Well, what is this damn thing? Do they know?"

Colonel Castillo shook his head and smiled. "No, sir, they're clueless, even more confused than we are." Grey swiveled his head around and impaled his assistant with a disapproving grimace. The men and women who worked for the United States Space Command, an autonomous division of the Air Force, were not permitted to be confused about anything, not while Grey was running the show. Their job was to know all of the answers all of the time. Castillo winced and studied the stack of papers he was carrying. "Excuse me, sir."

The doors opened onto a clean white basement hallway. Castillo led the way down the corridor and through a thick door. He and the general stepped into a plush, cavernous underground strategy room, with a big screen computerized map dominating the main wall. Designed and built in the late seventies, the room was a large oval space with the primary work area, sixty radar consoles, sunk three feet below a 360° perimeter walkway. Three dozen high-security-clearance personnel were down in the pit monitoring everything that moved through the sky: every satellite, every reconnaissance mission, every commercial passenger flight, and every moment of every space shuttle mission. In addition, a network of specially dedicated surveillance satellites kept an eye on each of the thousands of known nuclear missile silos worldwide. With its thick carpeting and colorfully painted wall murals of space flight, it always reminded Grey of "a goddamned library," as he had called it on more than one occasion.

"Take a look at these monitors," Castillo said, pointing to a row of ordinary televisions tuned to news broadcasts from around the globe. Every few seconds, the picture quality would suddenly disintegrate into a rolling blur, different from any sort of picture distortion they'd seen before. "Satellite reception has been impaired. *All* satellite reception, ours included. But we were able to get these shots."

He led the way to a nearby glass table which was lit from below and showed Grey a large photographic transparency. Taken with an infra-red camera, it showed a blotchy, orb-like object set against a background of stars. The image quality was too grainy and distorted for the general to make either heads or tails of it. Several members of the Space Command staff joined them at the table.

Grey, the only non-scientist in the group, wasn't about to start asking a bunch of asinine questions. Instead, he glowered down at the blurry image for a moment before announcing his opinion.

"Looks like a big turd."

Castillo was about to laugh when he realized his boss wasn't trying to be funny. He continued his presentation by laying down a second, equally turdlike photo of the object. "We estimate this thing has a diameter of over five hundred and fifty kilometers," he explained, "and a mass equal to roughly one-quarter of the moon's."

"Holy Mother of…" Grey didn't like the sound of that. "What do you think it is? A meteor, maybe?"

The entire clique of officers glanced around at one another. Obviously, Grey hadn't been completely briefed about the nature of the object they were looking at. "No, sir," one of the officers piped up, "it's definitely not a meteor."

"How do you know?"

"Well, for one thing, sir, it's slowing down. It's *been* slowing down ever since we first spotted it."

Grey's trademark scowl melted temporarily into one of bewilderment as the implications of what he was being told began to register. If it was slowing down, it could only mean the object was being controlled, piloted.

Without a moment of hesitation, he marched to the nearest phone and called the secretary of defense at home. When informed by the man's wife that he was sleeping, Grey barked into the receiver, "Then wake him up! This is an emergency."

Thomas Whitmore, forty-eight years old, was one of the first people awake in a city of early risers. Still in his pajamas, he lay on top of the covers with a pair of bifocals perched at the end of his nose thumbing through a stack of newspapers. It was a sweltering, muggy night in the District of Columbia, and even with the air-conditioning running, he was too uncomfortable to fall back asleep. The phone rang at a few minutes past 4 A.M. Without lifting his eyes from an article about international shipping policy, he reached over to the nightstand, picked up the receiver, and waited for whomever was calling to begin speaking.

"Hello, handsome," a female voice purred into the phone.

That captured his attention. Recognizing the voice, Whitmore tossed the paper to one side. "Well, well. I didn't expect to hear from you tonight. Thought you'd already be asleep. How may I assist you?" He smiled.

"Talk to me while I get undressed," she replied.

"I think I can help you with that request," Whitmore said, arching an eyebrow. He didn't get an invitation like that every day. He glanced around the sumptuously appointed bedroom, making sure no one was around except the small figure beneath the sheet at the other side of the bed. Glancing up at the clock, he noticed, "It's past four in the morning here. Are you just getting in?"

"Yes, I am." She didn't sound too pleased.

"You must want to strangle me."

"That possibility has crossed my mind."

"Honey, federal law specifically prohibits attempts to cause me any bodily harm," he informed her. "Why are you so late?"

"The party was out in Malibu and they closed the Pacific Coast Highway. The waves were crashing all the way up onto the highway. They think there must have been an earthquake somewhere out at sea. Anyway—"

"So, what did Howard say?" Whitmore asked anxiously. He had sent her to Los Angeles on a not-so-secret mission, hoping to recruit Howard Story, a super-rich Hollywood entertainment executive with a Wall Street background, to join their campaign.

"He's on board," she reported.

"Excellent! Marilyn, you're amazing. Thank you. I'll never ask you to do this kind of thing again."

"Liar," she crooned with a smile. One of the things Marilyn Whitmore loved the most about her husband was his inability to lie. She shut off the light in her hotel room and slipped into bed. She hated those glitzy West Coast movie people and their lavish garden parties, everyone trying to impress everyone else with their name-dropping and tedious descriptions of their next big project. She'd rather have been in bare feet and jeans hanging around "the house."

"In that case, I have a confession to make," Whitmore told her. "I'm lying in bed next to a beautiful young brunette." As he said this, the small figure on the other side of the bed stirred slightly, vaguely aware she was being talked about. Whitmore pulled back the sheet to reveal the sleeping face of his six-year-old daughter, Patricia, who had graced her pillow case with a tiny drool mark.

"Tom, I hope you didn't let her stay up watching TV all night again."

"Only part of the night," her husband admitted.

Patricia recognized something in her father's voice and, without opening her eyes, lifted her head off the pillow. "Is that Mommy?"

"Uh-oh! Somebody's waking up," Whitmore said into the phone, "and I think she wants to talk to you. When exactly are you flying back here?"

"Right after the luncheon tomorrow."

"Great. Call me from the plane if you can. I love you. Now, here's the wee one."

He passed the phone to his daughter and found the remote control for the television. He turned the set on and surfed through a few channels until he ran across a political talk show, a panel of pundits pontificating on politics. The first thing he noticed was the picture distortion. Every few seconds, the screen split into vertical bars which then rolled and collapsed to the side. Although it was distracting, it didn't prevent him from listening to the crossfire argument.

"I said it during the campaign and I still say it today," a bald man in suspenders declared, "the brand of leadership the president provided during the Gulf War bears no relationship to the kind of savvy insider politics needed to survive in Washington. After a brief honeymoon period with the congress, his inexperience is catching up with him. His popularity numbers continue to decline in the polls."

A woman with smart hair and a sharp tongue waved her hand in the air, dismissing the bald man's ideas. "Charlie, you remind me of a broken clock—you're only right twice a day. But this is one of the few times I agree with you. The current administration has gotten bogged down in the swamp of D.C. deal-making. In recent weeks, the president has waded into the murky waters of pragmatic backroom politics, only to find the sharks of the Republican party biting at his ankles."

Whitmore rolled his eyes at the overwrought prose. "Where in the world do they find these people?" Simultaneously disgusted and entertained, he got out of bed to see if he could adjust the set. As he began working the knobs, the channels began flipping one after the other. He stared at the set confused until he turned around and discovered that Patricia had picked up the remote control he'd left behind. After saying good-bye to her mother, she was hunting for the morning's first cartoons. Every station had the same picture distortion.

"Honey, it's too early for cartoons. You need to go back to sleep for a little while."

"Yes, I know, but…" The little girl paused to think, hoping she might be able to negotiate a compromise. Then she tried a different strategy. "Why is the picture all messed up?"

"It's an experiment," her father informed her. "The people at the television stations want to see if they can make little girls watch really boring shows all night so they miss everything fun during the day."

Patricia Whitmore wasn't buying any of it. "Daddy," she tilted her head to one side, "that's preposterous."

"Preposterous?" Whitmore chuckled. "I like that." Nevertheless, he switched off the television and put the remote out of reach. "Get some sleep, sweetheart." He put on his robe, gathered up his newspapers, and slipped out the door.

In the hallway, a man in an expensive suit was sitting on a chair reading a paperback novel. Startled, he snapped the book closed and jumped to his feet. "Good morning, Mr. President."

"Morning, George." Whitmore stopped and handed him a section of the newspaper. "I've got one word for you: the Chicago White Sox!"

"They won again?"

"Read it and weep, my friend."

In truth, neither man cared very much about sports, but both of them paid enough attention to give them something to talk about when they were together. George was from Kansas City and Whitmore from Chicago. Last night's victory put the Sox half a game ahead of the Royals in the pennant race. George, the Secret Service agent who protected the president from midnight to six, pretended to study the paper until Whitmore was a polite distance down the hallway. He then pulled out his walkie-talkie and whispered a message to his fellow bodyguards, alerting them that their workday had begun.

The breakfast nook was a cheery room decorated with yellow wallpaper and antique furniture collected by Woodrow Wilson in the early years of the century. At the long table in the center of the room was an attractive young woman in a white blouse and tan skirt. Her shoes were sensible and her hair was perfect. She'd already finished her breakfast and was elbow deep in a mound of newspapers and press releases by the time her boss joined her.

"Connie, you're up early."

"This is disgusting, reprehensible," she growled without looking up, "the lowest form of bottom-feeding scum-sucking journalism I've ever seen."

She was beautiful, intelligent, and always ready for a fight. Constance Spano, President Whitmore's communications director, had started out as a campaign staffer during his very first run for political office and, over the years, had developed into his most trusted adviser. The two of them had reached the point where they could finish each other's sentences. Although she was in her late thirties, she looked much younger and was a very visible symbol of Whitmore's "baby-boomer" presidency. She made it her job to aggressively defend her boss against an increasingly hostile and irresponsible press. The object of her wrath this morning was the editorial page of *The Post*.

"I can't believe this crap," she said slapping the paper with the back of her hand, "there are a hundred bills before Congress right now and they devote their Friday op/ed column to personality assassination." Without looking up, she cleared some room for him at the table.

"Good morning, Connie," her boss said again pointedly, as he poured himself a cup of coffee.

She looked up from the paper. "Oh, right, sorry. Good morning," she said before launching off once again on the crimes of the city's conservative newspapers. "Tom, they've spent all week taking cheap shots at your health care and energy proposals, but today they're attacking your character outright. Just listen to this: 'Addressing Congress...'" She paused long enough for the butler to serve the chief his omelet. "'...Addressing Congress earlier this week, Whitmore seemed less like the president than the orphan child Oliver holding up his empty bowl and pleading, "Please sir, I'd like some more."'" Connie stared across the table, outraged. "Am I missing something here, or is that just old-fashioned mud-slinging?"

Whitmore, an unusual politician, never took the papers too seriously. He left that part of the job to Connie, knowing that before the day was done, she would strike back at anyone who had dared to attack him. "He deserved it," the president said between mouthfuls.

"Who did? Deserved what?"

"Oliver. A hungry kid asking for a second helping of gruel from the stingy master of the orphanage. I think it's kind of flattering."

Connie disagreed. "The point is, they're attacking your age. Trying to spread the idea that you don't have enough experience or wisdom. And the only reason it's working for them is because of the perception that you've hung up your guns, set aside your ideals. When Thomas Whitmore is fighting for what he believes in, the media calls it idealism. But lately, there's been too damn much compromising, too much you-scratch-my-back, I'll-scratch-yours business." She shut up and reached for her coffee, realizing she'd overstated her case. But somebody, Connie thought, needed to have the guts to say it out loud.

Whitmore stabbed another bite of his omelet, chewing it thoroughly before he responded. "There's a fine line between standing behind a principle and *hiding* behind one," he said calmly. "I can tolerate some compromise if we're actually able to get some things done around here. The American people didn't send me here to make a bunch of pretty speeches. They want results, and that's what I'm trying to give them."

As far as Connie was concerned, he was missing the point. Real accomplishments, she believed, weren't born from a spirit of muddling through. She feared Whitmore was losing his fire, his vision. Until recently, everything about his presidency had been different. They'd campaigned on the themes of service and sacrifice, an "Ask not what your country can do for you..." message that all the experts and operators told them was sure-fire political suicide. They said nobody wanted to hear about doing more and having less. But in Whitmore's awkward-charming way, he'd made the message real to millions of Americans, and he had easily beaten his Republican opponent. In his first year, he'd introduced major legislative initiatives to reform everything from the legal system to health care to the environment. But for the past few months, the programs had been stalled in committees, held hostage by lawmakers who all wanted something on the side for their districts. Against the advice of Connie and many of his advisers, the young president had spent most of his time and energy shepherding his bills through the process, allowing himself to get bogged down by first-term representatives he could have steamrollered. All of them were willing to cooperate, but only in exchange for one favor or another. In the meantime, his prestige and popularity were down among the voters. Connie considered Whitmore not only her boss, but her friend and her hero. It killed her to see him bleeding from the thousand small wounds inflicted on him by other politicians, and the summer session was only beginning.

"Speaking of getting something accomplished," Whitmore grinned, showing her the front page of the *Orange County Register,* "I've been named one of the ten sexiest men in America! Finally, we're getting somewhere on the *real* issues." That broke the mood and both of them enjoyed a laugh as they began reading through the article.

They were interrupted by a young man who poked his head in the doorway. "Excuse me, Mr. President?"

"Alex, good morning," he said to the staffer. "What is it?"

"Phone call, sir. It's the secretary of defense with an emergency situation," he reported nervously as Whitmore made his way to the breakfast room phone.

"What's going on?" Whitmore asked. For the next two minutes, he listened, walking over to the window and peering outside. Whatever it was, Connie already knew from the expression on the chief's face that it was serious. Serious enough to change the day's whole schedule.

One of the amazing things about humanity is how often and how effortlessly we ignore miracles. The strangest, craziest, most sublime things happen around us all the time without anyone taking much notice.

One such miracle used to take place at Cliffside Park in New Jersey. For a few glorious moments every summer morning, as the sun began rising out of the Atlantic, great slabs of light sliced between the skyscraper canyons of Manhattan, mixing with the mist coming off the Hudson. It was a scene made famous on postcards and television commercials, but the men who gathered in the park every morning before dawn almost never gave the sight so much as a quick glance. They were mostly older gentlemen who had come to play chess on the long rows of stone tables near Cliffside Drive. For every man playing a game, there were three others standing about watching. In hushed murmuring voices, they exchanged gossip and news, announced the births of grandchildren and the deaths of long-time friends. Except for their sneakers and sweatshirts, they could have been the ancient Greeks conferring in the agora.

The largest group of these men were gathered loosely around two expert chess players, David and Julius. They seemed to be unlikely opponents. David was tall, gaunt, and intense, with a mop of curly black hair. Although he was in his late thirties, he played with the concentration of a child building a house of cards. His fingers smooshed his face into strange expressions and his long limbs coiled around one another at odd, uncomfortable looking angles. Completely focused on the game, he was totally unaware of looking like a human pretzel. He knew he needed to concentrate if he hoped to beat a wily opponent like Julius.

Julius, on the other hand, had only one way of sitting. At sixty-eight years old, he often said, his ass was too fat to squiggle around like David's. Once he had plopped himself down, that's how he stayed. His legs, stuck straight out, were barely long enough to rest his heels on the ground. His meticulously ironed slacks were jacked halfway up his calves, exposing the white socks he didn't think anyone could see. Under his windbreaker, he wore one of the two dozen white shirts he got from his brother-in-law when he retired from the garment business five years ago: *Hey, why not? They fit perfect!* To complete his look, the old guy was working a half-smoked cigar around the side of his mouth.

These opponents had faced one another many times, usually drawing a sizable crowd. This morning's match had begun with a flurry of standard moves until the older man, a speed player, began a blitzkrieg with his bishops. Since then, David had had to think about every move very carefully. Julius, always a showman, went to work on David psychologically, loud enough for everyone to hear. "How long are you gonna take? My social security will expire and you'll still be sitting here."

David pulled his fingers slowly across his face. Without

looking up, he said, "I'm thinking."

"So think already!"

Still thinking, David lifted his queen's knight and moved it tentatively forward. The moment his fingers lifted off the piece, Julius responded like lightning, pushing a pawn forward to challenge. David glanced up for a moment, genuinely puzzled, before looking down to study his options.

"Again he's thinking," Julius announced, reaching into a carefully folded paper bag to retrieve a Styrofoam cup full of coffee.

David shot him a disappointed look. "Hey, where's the travel mug I bought you?"

"In the sink, dirty from yesterday."

"Do you have any idea how long those things take to decompose?" David reached across the table to take the cup, but Julius drew back, protecting his caffeinated treasure.

"Listen, Mr. Ecosystem, if you don't move soon, *I'll* start to decompose. Play the game."

Disgruntled, David countered the challenging pawn with one of his own. Then Julius really gave him something to think about. Without hesitation, he slid his queen into the middle of the battle. "So," the old man leaned in over the board, "if I am not mistaken, a certain someone left a message on your answering machine yesterday." Julius sat back and took a sip of his coffee. David merely grunted. "Furthermore, I understand that this person is single after an unfortunate divorce, that she has no children, that she has an interesting career, that she's educated and attractive. All good things."

"You're doing it again," his opponent complained with a growl. At some point, Julius would invariably bring up something uncomfortable, some emotionally-charged issue that made it difficult to continue with the match. David was pretty sure there was no malicious intent, that the old guy was just worried about him, wanted to see him happy. Then again, maybe he was just trying to win at chess. He protected his bishop by advancing his king's knight.

"So did you call her back I'm wondering," Julius said, casually advancing another pawn.

"Look, I'm sure she's a beautiful and sophisticated woman, but she invited me to go country line dancing. I can't really see myself doing that, and besides, I'm convinced those tight cowboy jeans can do permanent damage to one's reproductive organs."

"What, so you can't even call the poor girl back and spend five minutes on the phone? After she worked up the chutzpah to call you, you can't just maybe be polite and call her back?"

"Dad, I'm not interested," David said flatly. "Besides, I'm still a married man." He held up the wedding ring on his finger to prove his point. He pulled one of his bishops back to safety.

Suddenly, Julius felt embarrassed by the presence of the crowd, the old-timers who were his friends and confidants. They knew the whole sad story of David's broken marriage and his refusal, or inability, to let it go. He glanced around at them, hoping they'd take a hint and make themselves scarce. Not a chance. They were more interested in the conversation than in the game. As he usually did, Julius went ahead and said what was on his mind anyhow. "Son, I'm thankful you spend so much time with me. Family is important. But I'm only saying, it's been what, four years? And you still haven't signed the divorce papers?"

"Three years."

"Three, four, ten, what difference? The point is, it's time to move on with your life. I'm serious—this is not healthy what you're doing." As if to prove his point, Julius reached across the table and captured a knight with his queen.

"Healthy? Look who's talking about healthy." He pointed at the old man's cigar and coffee. "We're exposed to so many carcinogens in our environment and you make it worse by—" The frantic chirping of David's pager interrupted him. He glanced down at the number display and saw that it was only Marty calling from the office for the third time that morning.

"That's about six times they've called you. Are you *trying* to get yourself fired? Or maybe you've decided to get a real job." David moved his bishop to take one of the pawns guarding Julius's king.

"Checkmate," he announced matter-of-factly. "See you tomorrow, Dad." He untangled his limbs, hopped up, and planted a kiss on his father's cheek, then grabbed his fifteen-speed racing bike.

"That's not checkmate," Julius roared, "I can still take your... but then you can... oh." He yelled across the park as David began to pedal away, "You could let an old man win once in a while, it wouldn't kill you!" But secretly, Julius Levinson loved the fact that his son could swoop in whenever he felt like it and beat almost anyone in the park.

A rush hour jam session was underway. Grumbling across the George Washington Bridge, blaring bumper to bumper traffic mingled its noise with the honking and screeching of ten thousand hungry seagulls to produce an early morning orchestral cacophony over the Hudson, the whole mess pouring itself into Manhattan. David, on his bike, shot through the gridlock and hung a hard right onto Riverside Drive. Five minutes later, he turned onto a street full of old warehouses and coasted to a stop in front of an aging six-story brick building. Foot-high stainless steel letters anchored into the bricks spelled out the name of the site's present occupant: COMPACT CABLE CORPORATION. Outside the front doors, a man with a picket sign was marching back and forth, protesting.

David dismounted and wheeled the bike over to the man. "Still planning to shut us down, huh?"

"You got that right, brother," the man answered. King Solomon was a slight, hyperalert black man in his fifties. As usual, he was dressed up in a crisp suit and a bow tie. His sign read, "Unchain the Airways, Cable Companies have NO RIGHT to charge you."

"Haven't seen you for a couple of months. Everything all right?"

King looked both ways then leaned closer, conspiratorially, "Been at the library, doing research. I found a ton of good stuff for my show." King had a half-hour slot on the public access channel where he went head-to-head with the giant communications conglomerates like AT&T. In addition, he'd been picketing around town for years, explaining his idiosyncratic theories, a mix of socialism and anarchy, to anyone who would listen. "Hey, Levinson, you got a minute?"

David pictured Marty stomping around the office in a ballistic frenzy over some minor technical glitch, pulling his hair out. "Sure, I got a minute."

"Okay, the subject is phone calls, but it applies to the legalized extortion of the cable television companies as well, 'cause both move through satellites. Because you guys control these satellites, you can charge little guys like me outrageous prices to do things like watch a football game or make a call to my lady friend who lives in Amsterdam, right? Now the same thing was going on in England way back in the 1840s. The government was trying to regulate communication so they could make extra money. If somebody wanted to send a letter, they had to go to the post office and hand it to a clerk. The farther the letter was going, the more this clerk charged you. Long distance rates, see? The whole thing was so expensive and such a damn headache, nobody wrote letters. Then this one dude came along, I forget his name right now, who figured out all the work, all the labor, was done at the beginning and the end of the process, sorting out and then delivering the letters. All the costs along the way, the shipment, remained the same whether there was one letter or a hundred. So this guy goes to the king and says, 'This is bullshit, baby. Let's have one low price for all letters, wherever they're going.' The king said okay, and do you know what happened?"

"Everybody started writing letters?"

"Exactamundo, mon ami. All over Europe folks started expressing their feelings and communicating scientific ideas, and shazam! we had the Industrial Revolution. That's why I'm out here every day. If y'all would quit monopolizing the satellites sent up there at taxpayers' expense, I could be on the phone to my lady friend in Amsterdam and my show could be seen in China. The common people could have a renaissance, an information revolution. Whaddaya think?"

Somewhere in the middle of King's speech, David's pager had buzzed again. This was absurd, even for the eternally panicked Marty. He began to think something serious might be happening. "As usual, King, you're convincing. Have you ever played on the World Wide Web, the Internet?"

He hadn't. Didn't own a computer. David told him where to find a public terminal and suggested that he check it out. It was the closest thing he knew to unrestricted communication. Then it was time to go into work and face Marty.

Inside the revolving doors was a completely different world. Compact Cable's front lobby was a graceful, marble and mahogany environment with a ceiling three stories tall. A swank, low-slung reception desk stood in the middle of the room guarding the entrance. With his bike hoisted onto one shoulder, David strolled past the receptionist and into the main office space, a beehive of partitioned work areas with a huge bank of television monitors mounted to the southern wall. The minute he walked in, he knew something big was up. The room was much louder than usual, the activity more frantic. Before he could put down his bike, he was confronted by a one-man electrical storm. Marty Gilbert, a heavyset man with a lascivious goatee, blasted out of his office, waving his arms and shouting.

"What the hell is the point of having a beeper if you never turn the damn thing on?" Steaming mad, Marty stopped in the middle of the room waiting for an answer. He was armed with his two favorite weapons: a can of diet soda in one hand, a cordless phone in the other.

"It was turned on," David explained matter-of-factly. "I was ignoring you."

"You mean to tell me," Marty screamed, "you got every one of those pages and you didn't call in? Did it occur to you that maybe, just maybe, something critical was going on?"

David was used to Marty's apoplectic, foot-stomping shit fits. He had one every couple of days and they usually lasted about ten minutes. The man lived in a perpetual state of high anxiety. He was constitutionally high-strung and had compounded his problem by taking on the incredibly stressful job of operations manager for one of the largest cable providers in the nation. His job was, in his words, "to be in charge of every little thing." In a complex operation like Compact Cable there were a thousand little things that could go wrong, and enough of them did every day to keep Marty hopping from one crisis to another.

This morning's run-in was a perfect example of why he hated David's guts and loved him like a brother at the same time. Marty knew beyond any shadow of a doubt that David was the best chief engineer in the country. He was so overqualified for the job, so good at handling all the hypertechnical stuff, that Marty knew he'd never be able to replace him in a million years. David was his secret weapon, the ace-in-the-hole that kept him in front of the competition. Now that he had finally shown up, Marty knew it was only a matter of time before he could phone corporate headquarters with the good news that they were the first ones to restore service to their customers. But it drove him bonkers how flamboyantly casual David was about everything. If he didn't return phone calls or answer his pager, Marty could huff and puff all he wanted, but there wasn't much else he could do about it. The quirky technical wizard made his own hours and operated independently of Marty's control.

"So what's the big emergency?"

"Nobody can figure it out." Marty calmed himself with a long gulp of soda. "Started this morning around four A.M. Every channel is making like it's 1950. Picture's all messed up. We're getting static and this weird vertical roll problem. We've been down in the feed room all morning trying everything."

David stashed his bike next to the vending machines in the employee kitchen and was about to head off for the feed room when Marty, expressing his frustration, slammed his empty soda can into the trash.

"Damn it, Marty, there's a reason we have bins labeled 'Recycle,'" David said loudly, turning back. The company's recycling program had been instituted largely due to David's insistence. He was a one man posse for the eco-police. More disturbing still, when he bent down to fish the can out, he found six more identical cans at the bottom of the bin. Appalled, he asked, "Who's been throwing their aluminum cans in the garbage?"

"So sue me," Marty hissed back. Then, before David could launch off into one of his save the earth speeches, his boss took him by the arm and forcibly helped him down a short hallway and through a door marked TRANSMISSION FEED.

Inside were the mechanical guts of Compact Cable. Hundreds of flat steel boxes, signal modulators, were stacked in tall steel racks along the back wall. A long console with mixing and switching panels stretched the length of the room below several television monitors. Taped to the walls were technical charts showing satellite positions, vertical and horizontal transponder polarizations, the different commercial licenses within the megahertz bandwidth and an ancient poster of four hippies in San Francisco with the words "Better Living Through Chemicals" above their heads. And cable. Miles of coaxial cable, the backbone of the industry, snaked off the overhead shelves and ran everywhere underfoot. Like a thousand black asps writhing around an Egyptian tomb, the flexible cord connected every piece of machinery to all the others.

"Okay you guys, make room," Marty squawked as they came in. "The Amazing Dr. Levinson has agreed to grace us with a demonstration of his skills." Paying no attention, David walked over to the mixing board where a technician was fiddling with some knobs. The monitor above his head showed a transmission of the *Today Show*. Like Marty said, the picture was disintegrating into rolling vertical bars every few seconds.

"Looks like somebody's scrambling our satellite feed," David mumbled, thinking for a moment of King Solomon marching around outside.

"Definitely," one of the two technicians told him. "We're pretty sure it's a satellite problem."

"Have you already tried switching transponder channels?"

"Oh, puleeeeze!" Marty howled. He was up on tiptoes looking over their shoulders. "Of course we tried that. What do we look like—idiots? Don't answer that."

David pulled a chair up to the control board and sat down. Almost immediately, his long limbs began to coil around one another. "Bring up the Weather Channel." The technician plinked a command into the keyboard. A text display popped up on the television monitor. "Experiencing Technical Difficulties. Please Stand By."

"May I?" David asked, moving the technician out of the way, "I wanna try something real quick here." His fingers whizzed across the keyboard, switching the monitor over to broadcast reception—regular antenna-on-the-roof reception. Suddenly, the *Today Show* looked fine, then fuzzy, then fine again. "Oh my God, you're a genius," Marty gushed, "how did you do that?"

"Not so fast, Marty." With his legs woven into a lotus position, David hunched over the board working in trance-like concentration. The *Today Show* was replaced by a computer bar graph. After entering a last few commands, David came up for air. "You're right, it's definitely the satellite. That good picture was a local broadcast. I pointed our rooftop dish over toward Rockefeller Plaza. They're putting out good signal."

"And what's this computer caca on the screen? We're not sending this out to the customers, are we?"

"Will you relax already? No, it's not going out. I'm running a signal diagnostic." David studied the test results on the screen, then sat back, perplexed.

"According to this, the satellite signal is fine. It's coming through at full power. Maybe the satellite itself is fritzing out."

Turning to Marty, he came up with a plan of action. "I'll get up to the roof and retrofit the dish to another satellite. You get on the phone and rent some channel space. SatCom Five has plenty of space available."

A self-satisfied grin spread across the heavy man's face. He didn't understand all the technical stuff, but for the time being, he had the jump on David. "Already thought of that," he announced proudly. "I called SatCom, I called Galaxy, and I called TeleStar. Everybody in town is having the same problem."

"Everybody in town?" David asked, incredulous. "If those guys are having this same problem, it means the whole country—no, the whole hemisphere—is getting bad pictures." David thought it over for a moment then added, "That's impossible!"

"Exactly," Marty shot back. "Now fix it."

CRASH! Miguel sat bolt upright out of a deep sleep and tried to focus his eyes. He had been dreaming a flying dream. A beautiful girl with pale skin and luminous dark eyes had taken him by the hand and showed him how to lift himself into the air. At first he was afraid of falling out of the sky, but once he got the hang of it and the two of them began looping and diving like a pair of dolphins, his only fear was that the girl would disappear.

CRASH!

He pulled back the plastic windowshade. A squad of fearless soldiers, the seven- and nine-year-olds from next door, were shooting it out with squirt guns. They looked like the Ninja Turtles at the OK Corral. Once they were shot, they died in ostentatious flailing body slams against the back of the Casse's Winnebago.

"*Vayanse!* Quit hitting our damn trailer!" he yelled. The warriors looked up at him then squealed away as a group, fanning out across the Segal Estates, which is what the owner had the nerve to call this place. An RV campground that had gone downhill, it was now a sort of flophouse on gravel and asphalt. Half of the tenants were Mexican migrant laborers, *campesinos,* who pooled their money to buy a mobile home so they could bring their families north. The other half were white folks who had "retired" out to the desert. It was half a mile from the highway, and cyclone fencing on three sides separated it from the surrounding alfalfa fields. Miguel, along with his sister, his half-brother, and his stepfather had been renting space at the Estates for about three months. They'd been living in the Winnebago for almost a year.

Two weeks before, Miguel had graduated from Taft-Morton Consolidated High School, but refused to go through the ceremony. He hardly knew any of the other kids and was afraid Russell, his stepfather, would show up and embarrass him. That evening, Alicia organized a cake and soda party for just the four of them. Halfway through it, Russell, who was drinking something stronger than soda, went off on a drunken, teary-eyed speech about how proud he was and how he wished Miguel's mama was still alive so she could see this. It ended the way so many of their conversations did, in an ugly shouting match with Miguel slamming the door on his way out.

At the front of the trailer, eleven-year-old Troy sat in the "kitchen" slapping the side of the television set. They were about forty miles north of Los Angeles, and the broadcast was being relayed through satellites to improve its signal strength, but it obviously wasn't doing much good.

"What are you doing?" Miguel hollered from beneath his pillow.

"The TV's all blurry and messed up."

"Hitting it isn't going to help. It's probably a problem at the station. Just leave it alone." But Troy didn't have much patience. When the picture failed to improve after ten seconds, he smacked the set again. Miguel threw back the sheets and came to see what was going on. It was already eight A.M. and he should have been gone out looking for a job by now.

"See?" Troy gestured toward the rolling picture. "Should I whack it again?"

"No, Mr. Kung Fu television repairman, I told you. It's not the set, it's the... whatevers, the airwaves." His younger brother was unconvinced, so Miguel changed the subject. "Have you taken your medicine?"

"I'll take it later." Troy was born with adrenal cortex problems, the same condition that killed their mother. He was supposed to take a small dose of hydrocortisone every morning, but because of the expense of the medicine, his family allowed him to skip a couple days a week. As long as he ate right and wasn't under a lot of stress, missing the medicine wasn't any big deal.

"Have you eaten anything yet?"

"Nope."

"Alicia, what are these dishes doing?" Obviously, they were sitting in the sink waiting for someone to wash them. She'd made herself breakfast, leaving the boys to fend for themselves. She was up front, stretched out in the Winnebago's passenger seat clipping photos out of a fashion magazine. When she heard Miguel yelling at her, she raised the volume on her Walkman. She was fourteen, bored, and developing a gigantic attitude problem. Since her hormones had started to kick in that spring, she'd taken to wearing makeup, skimpy cut-offs and tight white T-shirts, which had become the unofficial uniform among the ninth-graders at her new school.

Miguel came over and was about to give her hell for being so selfish when a red Chevy truck skidded to a halt in the gravel at the end of their driveway. The driver sat inside for a moment angrily talking into a cellular phone. His name was Lucas Foster, a local farmer who had hired Russell Casse to do some emergency crop dusting this morning. Plant-munching moths had invaded the desert croplands north of LA, just in time for the Casses, who were dangerously low on cash.

The farmer stomped up the driveway with a head of lettuce in one hand. Miguel knew his morning was about to get off to an ugly start. He went to the side door and opened the screen. "Good morning, Lucas. What's going on?"

"Your dad in there?" Lucas Foster, a muscular young man, was steaming mad.

Alicia slipped past her brother out into the sunlight. "He went to spray your fields," she said. "He left a long time ago."

"Well, where the hell is he, then?"

Miguel created a story about how Russell's plane had a mechanical problem the day before, but the other man didn't let him finish. "It's one damn thing after another with that jackass. He's sitting around somewhere with eight hundred dollars of insecticide while these damn moths are eating my crops!" Lucas heard himself shouting and quickly regained control. He was only a couple years older than Miguel and felt sorry for him. Now he was cursing himself for making a business decision based on sympathy for these kids and their crackpot dad.

"Maybe he had to refuel and he's there now," Miguel said hopefully.

"Naw, I just called my dad and he's not in the air," Lucas replied. "He'll probably get there about the same time the wind kicks up. Then we'll have to wait until tomorrow, while these moths eat our entire crop."

Humiliated, Miguel wanted to crawl into a hole and die. His stepfather, a notorious drunk around town, had put him through some embarrassing moments, but nothing like this. Miguel didn't blame Lucas for being mad. Behind him, Troy was still slapping the side of the TV. "Troy, stop it!" Miguel warned.

"If he's not in the air by the time I get back there, I'm going to call Antelope Valley Airport and get somebody else. I can't wait another day."

"Yeah, okay, that's fair. I'll go out and look for him right now." He grabbed the keys to his motorcycle and headed out the door. As he walked with Lucas down to the end of the driveway, Alicia called after them, asking Lucas for a ride down to the Circle K Market. "No!" Miguel exploded, wheeling around to face her. "You get in there and make Troy some breakfast before you go anywhere."

Miguel kick-started his bike, an old Kawasaki, and sat in the driveway wondering where to look first.

Colonel Castillo and his crew at the Pentagon had determined that the giant object had taken up a fixed position and parked itself less than 500 kilometers behind the moon. As the moon moved through space, the object moved with it, hiding behind the white orb like a shield. After repositioning three of their satellites, U.S. Space Command was able to get a pretty decent look at the object. They had three live cameras beaming infrared pictures of the object back down to earth, where they were keeping it under constant surveillance.

"Colonel!" one of the soldiers called loudly. "You better take a look at this!" Castillo sprinted across the floor and looked over the man's shoulder at the composite infrared picture. The area under the massive object was undergoing some kind of disturbance.

"Looks like it's exploding," Castillo observed.

"More like a mushroom dropping its spores," the man at the monitor said.

Large segments of the thing were detaching themselves and twirling away into nearby space. After watching the process for a few more minutes, and seeing the way the pieces arranged themselves in a circle, Castillo and the others realized what they were watching. It was time to call General Grey, who'd gone across the Potomac to the White House.

Connie tried sneaking out the side door of her office, but it didn't work. Members of her own staff, along with a dozen White House pages, were milling around in the hallway, and they pounced on her the moment she came through the door. Each one of them had a notepad full of urgent questions. All morning the phones had been as hot as teakettles, ringing off their hooks with one heavy hitter after another: senators, foreign ambassadors, queens and kings, Whitmore's family, network anchors, prominent businessmen that would normally be put straight through to the president. Nobody knew what to tell these people, each one calling with some crisis on their hands.

Connie knew her people needed answers, but didn't have the time to talk to them. She was already five minutes late for the presidential briefing, something that had never happened before. She'd been on the job long enough to know the best way to handle a stressful situation: wear a charming smile, ignore everyone, and bull your way through the crowd. Fran Jeffries, her chief lieutenant, saw what she was going to do. She stepped right in front of her boss and spoke fast.

"CNN says they're going to run a piece that the United States may have conducted an open-atmosphere nuclear test at the top of the hour unless you call to deny."

Connie shrugged, "Tell them to run with it if they want to embarrass themselves."

Everyone started shouting their questions at her. "NASA's been up my butt all morning," a harried aide complained. "Can you read their position statement? It's short and they need approval."

"Our official position," she told him, "is that we don't have an official position."

Constance, still smiling, pushed through, focusing on the portrait of Thomas Jefferson at the end of the hallway. When she got there, she surprised them by turning left, away from the stairs, where more people with more questions were waiting. She pushed the button for the old elevator, the clunky antique installed for Franklin Roosevelt.

When Gil Roeder, a top operative, saw she was about to escape, he yelled over the others. "Connie, what the hell is going on?"

Perfect timing. Just as the doors were sliding closed, she tried to look as if her feelings were hurt by the question. "Come on, people. If I knew anything, would I keep you out of the loop?"

Outside the doors, she could hear them answering in unison, "Definitely!"

In the Oval Office, the president had already called the meeting to order. He sat with his chief of staff, Glen Parness, the head of the Joint Chiefs, General Grey, and Secretary of Defense Albert Nimziki. For very different reasons, Whitmore trusted each of them.

"But I want to remind everyone," Grey was in the middle of saying, "that our satellites are unreliable at the moment. It's not clear whether this thing wants to or will be able to enter the earth's atmosphere. It's still possible it won't come any closer. It might not want to deal with the force of our gravity, for example."

"That's true, Mr. President," Nimziki allowed, "this object might, as the commander suggests, pass us by. But our responsibility is to prepare for the worst-case scenario.

Having no information, we must assume the object is hostile. My strong recommendation is that you retarget several of our ICBMs and launch a preemptive strike."

Nimziki was a tall, gaunt man of sixty who had earned the nickname, "the Iron Sphincter." He was a rarity in Washington, a cabinet-level appointee who kept his job through changes of administration. Whitmore was his fourth president, his second Democrat. He was not a likable man, but when he spoke, everyone felt obliged to listen. Some years back *The Post* had written about him: "Not since J. Edgar Hoover has a government official amassed so much power without ever having stood for election." An intensely political animal, Nimziki always managed the appearance of staying above politics. He never let them see him pull the strings. He was, in a word, Machiavellian. His suggestion was precisely the kind of shoot-first-ask-questions-later style of thinking everyone else in the room was trying to avoid.

"Forgive me," Grey broke in, "but with the little information we do have, firing on them might be a grave error. If we're unsuccessful, we could provoke them, or it. If we are successful, we turn one dangerous falling object into many. I agree with Secretary Nimziki about retargeting the missiles, getting them set, but—"

Constance came in the door, but stopped short when she saw all the brass.

"What's the damage?" Whitmore asked her, beckoning her to join the discussion. "How are people reacting?"

"Hello, gentlemen." She nodded around the table as she took the seat next to Nimziki. "The press is making up their own stories at this point. CNN's threatening to plug in a segment suggesting we're covering up a nuclear test. I've scheduled myself a question-and-answer session for six o'clock, which should keep them on ice until then. The good news is nobody's panicking, not seriously."

Nimziki, impatient with the interruption, spoke across the table to Grey. "Will, I think it's time for you to contact the Atlantic Command and upgrade the situation to DEFCON Three."

The others jumped on him at once, telling him that was premature. The majority opinion was that sounding an alarm and causing panic before they even knew what they were up against would be a mistake. Nimziki defended his position, but was eventually talked down. At the end of the flare up, the chief of staff, Parness, was still talking.

"Furthermore, we're two days out from the Fourth of July and fifty percent of our forces are on weekend leave. Not to mention all the commanders in Washington for the parade on Sunday. The only quick way to call our personnel back to their bases would be to use television and radio."

"Exactly," Constance seconded. "We'd be sending up a major red flag to the world."

The door opened again. One of General Grey's men, his liaison to the Pentagon, came in carrying a bombshell. "Our latest intelligence tells us that the object has settled into a stationary orbit which keeps it out of direct sight behind the moon."

"Sounds like it's trying to hide," Grey remarked.

"That sounds like good news for the time being," Parness said, hopefully. "Maybe it just wants to observe us."

Grey's liaison wasn't finished. "Excuse me, but there's more. The object established its orbit at 10:53 A.M. local time. At 11:01 A.M. local time, pieces of the object began to separate off from the main body."

"Pieces?" Whitmore asked, not liking the sound of it.

"Yes, sir, pieces," the man continued. "We estimate there are thirty-six of them, roughly saucer-shaped, and small compared to the primary object. Still, each craft is approximately fifteen miles in diameter."

"Are they headed toward earth?" Whitmore asked, already knowing what the answer would be.

"Looks like it, sir. If they continue along their current trajectories, Space Command estimates they'll begin entering our atmosphere within the next twenty-five minutes."

The president stared back at the young man in the Air Force uniform, dumbfounded and more than a little frightened. For a moment, he thought this must be some kind of joke everyone else was in on, an elaborate piece of theater staged to get a reaction from him this very moment. Then the grim reality of the situation began to sink in. What had seemed so laughable, so far-fetched a few hours before, was coming horribly true. One of the primal fears of mankind, a fear buried under mountains of denial, was coming to pass. The earth was being visited, and perhaps invaded, by something from another world.

Nimziki broke the stunned silence. "Thirty-six ships, possible enemies, are headed this way, Mr. President. Whether we like it or not, we must go to DEFCON Three. Even if it causes a panic, we must recall our troops and put them on yellow alert immediately."

No one in the room could disagree.

An alarm went off, a red light flashing in time with a piercing beep. A door opened and the alarm died. David's arm reached through the door and pulled out his Cup-O-Noodles. It was lunch hour at Compact Cable. David had hardly left the feed room. As if there wasn't enough equipment in there already, he had gone and retrieved two additional suitcase-sized machines and his laptop computer. They were set upright in the middle of the floor. David was sloppy when he was concentrating. He sat with his feet under him in the chair, elbows between his knees, coiled in concentration. He stared intently at the screen of his laptop computer, watching a visual display that repeated itself about every twenty seconds.

"Hello, you handsome genius." Marty peeked around the corner, all smiles. "I'm not here to pressure you. I'm just checking to see if there's anything you need." Which was, of course, a bald-faced lie. Whenever there was a problem, a mother hen like Marty *had* to be there.

"Marty! Old pal! Have a seat, relax."

Marty tiptoed in like a leper trying not to scratch. David had already kicked him out once for looking over his shoulder and asking too many questions. He had promised himself that he wasn't going to bug David, and for the first ten seconds he didn't. Then his willpower broke down. "David, tell me you're getting somewhere. I'm begging. Say you've got it figured out."

"Well," David said, very leisurely, "I've got good news and bad news. Which would you like to hear first?"

"What's the bad news?"

"The bad news is you're in meal penalty for disturbing my lunch."

Marty put a hand on his hip and got sarcastic. "Don't tell me. The good news is: you're not going to charge me."

"Actually," David took a last spoonful of soup, "the good news is I found the problem."

Marty clutched his heart and took a few deep breaths, hamming it up. "Thank God. Okay, so what exactly is the problem?"

"There's a weird signal embedded in the satellite feed. A signal within a signal. I have absolutely no idea where it's coming from. Never seen anything like it. Somehow, this signal is being cycled through every satellite in the sky.

Marty stared back at him, mouth agape. "And exactly *why* is that supposed to be good news?"

"Because the signal is following an exact sequence, a pattern. So the rest is simple! We just generate a digital map of the signal frequency, then translate it into a binary strand and apply a phase-reversed signal with the calculated spectrometer I built you for your birthday, and bingo, we should be able to block out the overlay completely."

"Block out the overlay?" Marty looked confused. "Does that mean we get our picture back?"

"You're quick."

"Does that also mean," Marty asked slyly, "that we'll be the only guys in town who are putting out a clean program?"

"Unless we share what we have learned," David suggested, angelically. He knew Marty was hypercompetitive with his fellow station managers and would luxuriate, wallow, and bask in this moment of triumph over them.

"Ha-ha, I love it!" Marty erupted with savage glee. "Our secret weapon! The phase-reversed spectrometer calculation analyzer thingee! This is turning out to be a wonderful day."

When Miguel finally found him, Russell had sprayed about a quarter of a 1000-square-yard tomato field. A group of field hands was gathered around their cars, unable to work while the spraying was going on. The field was about a mile long and bordered on one side by a row of giant eucalyptus trees that ran right up to the road. Instead of spraying parallel to the trees, Russell was flying straight down the rows and pulling up at the last possible moment, straining the old Liberty engine to clear the tops of the trees. Miguel couldn't tell if he was drunk or crazy, but if this was like most mornings, Russell was both.

The plane was a gorgeous old de Haviland biwing, a bright red two-seater built the same year Lindbergh crossed the Atlantic. The retractable wings were made of cloth stretched tight over wooden frames. The U.S. Post Office had used de Havilands to open transcontinental airmail service in the twenties. The machine belonged in a

Saturday air show, not out dusting crops. It was too heavy and hard to maneuver to begin with, but to make matters worse, Russell had an extra 200 pounds of spray equipment strapped to the back with twine and bungee cords.

As Russell dove over the tops of the trees to begin another pass at the tomatoes, Miguel yelled and waved, calling for him to land. The farm workers understood what the boy was doing and a few of them joined in. The plane's pilot waved back stupidly.

"Come on, Russell, wake up," Miguel pleaded. Over the last two years, Russell had been going downhill fast. He was drinking himself to death and losing all sense of responsibility for his kids. He'd straightened up for a while when the neighbors had reported him to the police, who in turn had called in the social workers. He'd always been crazy, but when Miguel's mother got sick and finally died, Russell had plunged totally over the edge. He'd developed a death wish. Every few days, he'd snap out of it and promise to make a new start. Which meant that Miguel was usually the one left to take care of things like paying the rent, getting Troy's medicine, and buying the groceries. That was one thing nobody could take away from Miguel: he was responsible. Russell was less like a parent to him than a burdensome roommate.

As the plane circled around for another pass, Miguel suddenly started up his motorcycle and tore straight across the field, uprooting plants and splattering tomatoes as he bounced over the irrigation ridges. He stopped right in the path of the plane, which raced toward him, a white cloud of liquid poison misting out the back. Luckily, Russell saw him in time and shut off the feeder. As he passed, he focused his eyes and saw that the boy was waving him down. He turned around in his seat and smiled to Miguel, raising his thumb to show he understood. He could see the boy was pointing, trying to tell him something, but he didn't understand until he turned back around in his chair and found himself face-to-face with a picket fence-lined row of hundred-foot-tall eucalyptus trees, and it was way too late to pull up.

"Whoa, Lordy!" he screamed over the sound of the motor. Luckily, for Russell, there was no time to think. Acting purely on reflex, he rolled the plane ninety degrees onto its side and sliced through a narrow gap between trees. He had less than a foot clearance on either side. Rather than kicking himself for being so stupid, or thanking heaven for being so lucky, Russell let out a long, blood-curdling victory whoop, delighted with his own skills.

A few minutes later, the plane coasted to a stop on the remote highway. When Miguel raced up and skidded to a halt, Russell was just climbing awkwardly out of the cockpit. "Did you see that?" he yelled. "That was a damn trip!" He pulled off his leather aviator's cap and lowered himself carefully onto the lower wing. At fifty-one, Russell Casse looked like a big little boy. He had full, round cheeks and a bush of curly blondish hair. He was large, over six feet tall and broad across the shoulders. Over the last couple of years, his drinking had turned his complexion from rosy to ruddy, and he'd started to develop a gut.

"What the hell are you doing over here?" Although there was a sharp tone to Miguel's voice, it didn't penetrate his stepfather's thick skin.

"I'm bringin' home the bacon," Russell sang proudly, "Earnin' my keep. And, if I do say so myself, doing a pretty fine job of it."

"This isn't Foster's place. It's the wrong field," Miguel told him. "You're supposed to be on the other side of town."

Russell, still perched on the plane's wing, took a long look at the field and the farmhouse down the road. "Are you sure?"

"Damn it, Russell. He was doing you a favor. He was

just at the trailer asking where the hell you were. And he's gonna make you pay for the spray you wasted."

Russell climbed down to the pavement and stood there, a little wobbly, shaking his head. *No use in getting upset about it now,* he told himself. But this was the first work he'd had all season, and Lucas was about the only farmer in town who was on his side. He looked at his son, but couldn't think of anything to say.

"Do you know how hard it is to find someone who doesn't think you're totally crazy?" the boy hissed. "Now what are we supposed to do? Where are we supposed to go now?"

Russell didn't have any answers. He badly wanted to promise Miguel things were going to start changing right then and there. But he knew the boy wouldn't believe him and he wouldn't have believed himself. So he stood mutely in the center of the road until Miguel kick-started the bike and drove away in disgust.

Russell brought a flask of Jack Daniel's out of his jacket. He was pretty sure something had just ended. Maybe it was just the end of him pretending to put up a fight. The last few years had broken him. His wife's degenerative illness and eventual death, the night he was abducted, the news that Troy had inherited his mother's adrenal cortex deficiency. Screw it. If life was going to be that painful, he didn't want any piece of it. If it weren't for his kids, he would have climbed back into the old plane, flown it to its top altitude, then cut the engine and let her freefall back to earth. Instead, he uncapped the flask and took a long swig of whiskey.

Deep in the desert of Northern Iraq, Ibn Assad Jamal squatted before a small campfire, preparing his morning coffee. A Bedouin, he'd been forced off the land his tribe had claimed as their own for countless generations and had been herded into a squalid, crowded tent city along with several other Bedouin clans. It was still an hour before the first light of dawn, but by force of habit, the whole makeshift village was stirring to life.

He reached into the fire and retrieved his grandfather's coffee jar, boiling a thick brew of Arabian coffee. As he was waiting for the grounds to settle to the bottom, he heard a single scream pierce the night air. A second later, many people were screaming and calling out in a panic.

Jamal stood paralyzed from the sounds. At the top of the dunes, he saw the outlines of a dozen figures rushing toward him. His first thought was that the camp was being attacked by the army, but as the people came sprinting past him, shouting and whimpering, he saw what they were running from.

"*Ensha'allah,*" he muttered to himself. He saw something that knocked his knees out from under him. A giant piece of the sky was on fire. A mountain-sized fireball, flaring orange, white, and gray, was plunging through the sky like a flat rock splashing into a river. The fire cast a dark reddish glow on the sand as it sank deeper in the sky. Jamal stared up at the phenomenon for several moments as a pounding terror grew in his heart. Finally, he got back to his feet, stammered something unintelligible then turned to run, screaming just like the others.

A few hundred miles away, in the approximate center of the Persian Gulf, the nuclear-powered submarine USS *Georgia* was plowing along the surface of the dark water, its antenna array rotating atop the conning tower. Inside the sub's radar room, all hell had broken loose. A loud klaxon alarm was blaring, triggered by unusual readings on the radar scopes. Jittery crewmen, who'd been sleeping only moments before, poured through the bulkheads to their combat stations. The sub's commander, Admiral J. C. Kern, stepped through the forward hatch and yelled over the noise for a report. "Ensign, status?"

A sailor wearing a headset wheeled around in his chair. "Sir, we have a total radar blackout over a seventeen-kilometer area." The admiral moved to the main radar map and studied the incoming signal. A large portion of the upper screen was blank, but it was obviously not an equipment failure, because the blank ellipse on the screen was *moving*.

"Admiral." One of his officers stepped closer. "I've ordered a complete diagnostic run. The auxiliary radar units—"

"Sir, excuse me, sir," shouted another sailor from the opposite side of the cramped room. "Radar may be malfunctioning, but infrared is completely off the map. No reading at all." He pushed away from his monitor to give Kern a view of the infrared tracking system. The entire screen was a bright pool of red light.

"Lieutenant," Kern barked, almost amused at the chaos.

"Yes, sir?"

"Get Atlantic Command on the line."

The Oval Office was crowded with military leaders and the president's advisers. Thirty phone calls were taking place at once, but the noise level stayed at a hushed murmur. Extra tables had been carried in and there was a constant stream of foot traffic in and out of the room. The joint chiefs had arrived an hour earlier having recalled the nation's armed forces. The fleet of nuclear submarines was maintaining launch readiness, and battleships were deployed along both coasts. Civilian advisers had taken over the sofas, and the president sat under the north windows behind Resolute, the impressive desk given to

Teddy Roosevelt by the Queen of England. There were also representatives from the Atlantic Command, NATO, and military attaches from the British, Russian, and German consulates.

This impressive collection of decision-makers, one of the most powerful groups ever to assemble at the White House, had adopted a wait-and-see attitude. Many of them had advocated a preemptive strike against the object lurking behind the moon. NASA engineers had been consulted as to the feasibility of sending the space shuttle to attack with nuclear weapons, but, for many reasons, they had eventually arrived at an uneasy consensus not to do so. They waited tensely for the thirty-six segments to enter the earth's atmosphere. When the line from the Pentagon rang, all the major players in the room fell silent.

General Grey, as commander of the joint chiefs, stepped forward to answer the call. "This is Grey," he growled into the receiver, his face as expressive as chiseled stone. "Where in the Pacific?" he asked. After listening for a moment, he turned to the president. "They've spotted two coming in over the west coast, both over California."

"Send the plane from Moffet Field," Whitmore ordered. The plan had already been set in motion. An AWACS aircraft from the facility near San Jose was already in the air, waiting for the order to begin a close-up inspection of the incoming craft.

The door flew open and Connie marched toward the president's desk. "CNN is doing a live shot from Russia. They've got a picture of this thing."

"Put it on," Whitmore said, glancing at Lermontov, the worried Russian ambassador. One of the staffers pulled open the armoire doors and switched on the television.

The broadcast was coming live from Novomoskovsk, an industrial town two hundred miles south of the Russian capital. A local reporter stood at the edge of a wide boulevard which ran through the city's most fashionable neighborhood, shouting over the mayhem that surrounded him. Although it was just past six in the morning, the street was choked with panicked residents, running headlong in every direction. Cars sped past the camera, swerving to avoid pedestrians. The reporters words were being translated by someone in CNN's Atlanta studio.

"...sightings of this atmospheric phenomenon have been reported here in Novomoskovsk and other parts of Russia. Again, this phenomenon is moving too slowly to be a comet or meteor. Astronomers can't explain this baffling occurrence."

The camera then panned away from the reporter and upward. In the distance, it showed the grainy image of a fireball hanging in the early morning sky. As the camera zoomed in, the flame-spitting giant filled the screen, towers of fire erupting in all directions as the surface of the speeding object moved against the sky, its friction burning up huge amounts of oxygen.

Everyone in the Oval Office stared at the television, grimly transfixed by the strange spectacle. The boiling cloud of fire looked like God announcing himself in an old Charlton Heston movie.

"As you can see from our live picture," one of the CNN anchors broke in, "a sense of panic has gripped the people of Novomoskovsk. We have learned this same type of reaction is happening in all parts of the city. The Russian equivalent of the Red Cross reports there have already been scores of injuries, most of them traffic-related as citizens scramble to get as far away from this strange phenomenon as possible. The situation is even worse in Moscow, where the craft is thought to be headed."

"Mr. President," General Grey interrupted, "our AWACS from Moffet Field has an ETA of three minutes with the contact point. We can put a line from the cockpit through this phone."

"Put it on the speaker phone." Whitmore saw no reason for the others not to hear the report.

Worried faces gathered in a rough circle around the president's desk, looking at the phone and one another as the sounds of the AWACS's cockpit were radioed to the Oval Office, three thousand miles away.

The plane was flying south, several miles off the California coastline. The AWACS, Airborne Warning and Control System, was capable of scanning a four-hundred-mile area and tracking five hundred enemy planes simultaneously. But the state-of-the-art radar system, like so many of the earth's communications systems, was malfunctioning.

The calm, professional voices of the aircraft's crew came murmuring over the phone line. "Radar Two, I'm drawing a blank. Forward radar doesn't see a thing and side radar is impaired—what's your status? Over."

"Absolutely correct, sir. Forward radar is totally gone. We're flying IMC blind. Over."

Inside, the aircraft was packed with wall-to-wall computers, instrument banks, radar scopes, and other intelligence-gathering equipment. Technicians in headsets and orange jumpsuits were talking frantically to one another, trying one experiment after another, racing to adjust the navigation systems.

"Little Pitcher," a voice came over the radio, "we're tracking you down here at Ford Ord and you're looking all clear. Are you out of those clouds yet? Over."

"Negative," replied the pilot, squinting out the front window, "we still have zero visibility." A tropical storm had blown unusually far north from Mexico, leaving a thick mass of clouds hanging over the California Coast. "Fort Ord, what's your best estimate on our ETA? Over."

"Sorry, Little Pitcher, we just lost our angle. We can't see you any longer. You're into the blackout zone on our screens. Maybe San Diego can still see you."

After a tense moment of silence, a new voice came onto the line. "This is San Diego. Negative on that. We've got the same problem. Little Pitcher is inside the disturbance field. Sorry, Pitcher. We'll stand by."

Blasts of sunlight came through gaps in the clouds and into the cockpit, only to vanish a split second later. "Ground Control, this is Pitcher. We're starting to experience general instrument malfunction. Our altimeter and environment controls are gone. We're still moving through zero visibility and can't get any kind of reading on what's in front of us. I'm going to climb a little higher and see if we can't get clear over the top of this cloud cover."

"Roger, Pitcher," came the reply from Moffet Field. "It's your call at this point. You are totally manual."

"Don't climb," the president whispered. A former fighter pilot himself, he was imagining himself at the helm of the plane, "just keep it level." But the phone hookup was a one-way transmission.

"That's looking a little better," the AWACS reported with relief. "I think we've found a clearing."

Growing louder, a sonic disturbance, the cracking hiss of static interference, growled over the speakerphone. Then, just as the AWACS broke free of the clouds, the pilot's voice screamed over the noise, "Jesus God! The sky's on fire!"

In front of him was a solid wall of flame five miles high and twenty miles long, a majestic and fearsome sight. Roughly disk-shaped, it was shedding altitude, dropping down right on top of him. The pilot jerked back on the controls, forcing the plane into a steep climb. But when they came too close to the fireball, the plane suddenly shattered like a lightbulb crashing against an anvil.

There was a sharp crack on the speakerphone before

the line in the Oval Office went dead. "Get them back," General Grey snarled to one of his men, even though he, like everyone in the room, suspected the plane was lost.

The commander in chief of the Atlantic Air Command stepped closer to a stunned President Whitmore. "Two more have been spotted over the Atlantic. One is moving toward New York; the other is headed in this direction."

"How much time do we have?"

"Less than ten minutes, sir."

With this news, Whitmore's civilian advisers began pushing their way through the ring of military men that circled his desk. The first one through was Nimziki. He spoke very precisely in a voice loud enough for the entire room to hear.

"Generals, we must move the president to a safe location at once. Organize a military escort to Crystal Mountain." General Grey agreed completely. He leaned close to the president's chair and urged him to move immediately to a secure location.

As orders began to fly around the room, the president reached across his desk and put a hand on Nimziki's shoulder. The gesture took the secretary quite by surprise. He froze in place, staring at the hand as if at a tarantula. President Whitmore used the moment to confer with his most trusted adviser.

"Connie, what's your take? Can we expect the same kind of panic here as in Russia?"

"Probably worse than what we just saw," she said.

"I agree," Whitmore said. "They'll start to run before they know which way to go. We'll lose a lot of lives."

Nimziki could see where the president was heading. He stepped backward, out of the president's grip. "Mr. President, you can discuss these secondary matters on the way. But the situation demands that you, as the commander in chief—"

"I'm not leaving," the president announced.

Nimziki was stunned, as were most of the people in the room. Several top-ranking officers stepped closer to the president, urging him to come to his senses and evacuate to a protected location.

"We must maintain a working government in a time of crisis," one of them reminded him loudly, making no attempt to disguise his frustration. A dozen men were all shouting at once, concerned for the president's safety. A pair of Secret Service agents pushed their way close and stood at his side.

With a long, glaring look, the president silenced the room. Slowly, he issued a set of commands. "I want the vice president, the cabinet, and the joint chiefs taken to a secured location. Let's get you men to NORAD. For the time being, I'm going to remain here in the White House."

Nimziki bristled, "Mr. President, we all—"

"I understand your position," Whitmore cut him off, "but I'm not going to add to a public hysteria that could cost us thousands of lives. Before we take off running, let's find out whether these things are hostile and exactly where they're headed."

Nimziki stared icily back at the president. He had hoped Whitmore would be different from the other presidents he had served, that his military training would keep him cool in an emergency. Even though this was a totally new situation, there was still a protocol to be followed. But Whitmore was trying to write his own script. Nimziki still had a few aces up his sleeve, but knew it was too early to play them.

"Connie," Whitmore continued, "initiate the emergency broadcasting system. I'll do an announcement as soon as you can set it up. Write a brief speech advising people not to panic, to stay home if possible. Can you do that in twenty minutes?"

"Give me ten," she said, already on her way out the door.

The joint chiefs were still standing in the office, confused, not quite willing to leave their posts here in what had become the command center.

"All right, people, let's move," Whitmore commanded, "I want you to get to NORAD as quickly as possible." The six generals exchanged glances with their staffers, then began moving reluctantly toward the exits. General Grey broke away from the pack and stood in front of Whitmore.

"With your permission, Mr. President, I'd like to remain by your side." As chairman of the joint chiefs, it was an unusual request, but given the long friendship between the two men, it came as no surprise.

"I had a feeling you would." Whitmore smiled. "And you, Mr. Nimziki?" The tall, brooding man replied without hesitation, "NSC directives require that the secretary of defense make himself available to the president at all times." Then, after a beat, he tried changing tones. "It's my job to stay." He tried to make it sound friendly, but it came out like most of the things he said: vaguely menacing.

General Grey turned to Whitmore and asked the grave question that had been gnawing away at all of them for the past hour. "Mr. President, what happens if these things *do* become hostile?"

Whitmore thought for a second. "Then God help us."

Like the cob-webbed entrance to a forgotten tomb, the feed room door creaked open very slowly. David, his mind wandering through some parallel universe, his nose buried in a computer printout, shuffled absent-mindedly into the central office of Compact Cable. The single-spaced print out was sixteen pages in length and contained only one thing: a single, incredibly long number, a continuous mind-numbing strand of ones and zeroes, a binary mathematical representation of twenty minutes worth of the mysterious, disruptive signal. His custom-built phase-reversed spectrometer had done its job. The device had compiled a precise numerical "portrait" of the oscillating frequency and specified the mirror-image signal that could be broadcast to cancel out the interference. Marty was going to be very happy. He could start pumping a clear picture out to their subscribers then get on the phone and taunt the competition. But David wasn't finished: as soon as he'd figured out a way to block the signal, he started asking himself where it was coming from and *what it meant.*

He was halfway across the office before he noticed it was empty. David glanced at the wall clock. *Way past lunch time,* he told himself. Jack Feldin, an old-timer who worked in sales, was at his desk sobbing like a baby into a telephone. In a vague way, David realized something was wrong, but he was so focused on solving the puzzle he ignored everything else. He was an obsessive puzzle-solver, had been since he got hooked on the *New York Times* Sunday crossword at age twelve. When the "Genius Puzzles" came out in the Mensa magazine each month, he'd plow through them one by one until, an hour or a few days later, he'd cracked them all. This business about the repeating signal in the satellite feed was a real-life riddle David was uniquely qualified to decipher. After all, how many engineers were there with his practical and theoretical skills who could also put their hands on fifty million dollars worth of high-tech communications equipment any time they liked?

He took the pages to his cubicle, slipped a disk into his desktop computer, and brought a sequence analyzing program up on the screen. With a few flicks of his fingers, he created a representation of the transmission. On a hunch, he asked the program if the repetitions of the signal were precisely equal. Negative. It was getting shorter, slowly reducing itself down to nothing. But *it wasn't losing any strength* and television reception was in the same sad shape it had been in all day. Curious. Assuming the signal was being sent for some intelligent purpose, why would it fade to zero? Very weird.

It took David about sixty seconds to do the algebra. According to his calculations, the signal would cycle down to extinction and disappear at 2:32 A.M. EST. *Okay,* he said to himself, *so what*? Because he'd been locked away in the crypt of the feed room all day, he had no idea where the signal might be coming from. After deciding he probably wouldn't learn anything else until that night, he stood up and left the cubicle. It was time to deliver the good news.

Marty's office was, as usual, a disaster area. Yellowing newspapers, take-out lunch containers, extra copies of the latest shareholder's report, and great heaps of unopened mail were piled on top of overflowing file cabinets. In addition to all the mess, there were five bodies crowded into the room, their attention glued to the television.

David barely noticed them. He did, however, spot the only unoccupied seat and slid into it like someone might beat him to the spot at the last minute. He casually draped a leg over the arm of the chair. It took him a moment to pick up on the mood of frightened anxiety in the room.

"I've got a lock on the signal pattern," he announced, "and we should be able to filter it out."

"Huh?" Marty realized he was being spoken to. Then, absently, "Oh, good, good."

"But here's the strange thing. If my calculations are right, and they usually are, the whole thing's gonna disappear in about seven hours anyway." When he didn't get any reaction, he looked up and said with emphasis, "The signal reduces itself every time it recycles. Eventually, it will disappear. Hey, are you listening?"

"David, my God," Marty realized, "haven't you been watching this? This is horrible, David."

"What are you talking about?"

"Look, it's right there."

David wheeled around in his chair and saw a live picture from Australia. A giant plate of fire, fifteen miles wide, was hanging in the sky over Melbourne. David's first thought was that there had been some sort of ecological disaster, the ozone reaching a critical state of frailty and erupting into spontaneous combustion. But a moment later, he asked the same question everyone had when they'd first seen the thing, "Is there a war going on?"

"They don't know what the hell these things are," somebody said. "*Atmospheric phenomena* is the term they keep repeating."

"It's probably some kind of debris from an asteroid," a coworker suggested. "These things are falling all over the earth."

"Oh, will you please wake up and smell the coffee," Marty snapped at the man. "They've said it about a hundred times: *they're not falling objects!* They're moving too slowly. And some of them have started moving sideways. They're flying. They're fucking flying saucers and this is the fucking invasion of the earth, okay?"

David hesitated for a moment, not knowing whether to laugh or shit his pants. The distressed faces of the others in the room confirmed that Marty was serious.

"Whoa! Wait a second." David stood up unconsciously waving the idea away. A sharp chill ran up his back, lodged itself in his brain, then erupted into a creepy variety of terror. Marty came around the desk and put a concerned hand on David's shoulder, then began filling him in on what little was known about the thirty-six "phenomena."

Suddenly, he pointed at the TV screen. "David, look. Isn't that Connie?" Following the strictures of the Emergency Broadcast protocol, every channel switched over to a live picture of the White House press room. An attractive woman in a white silk blouse stepped up to the microphone and began taking questions from the press. The sight of her immediately wrenched David out of one drama and hurled him into another, more personal one. The woman was none other than Constance Marianne Spano, his estranged wife.

"...emphasize that so far this phenomenon, while it has disrupted our televisions and radios, hasn't caused any lasting damage and we have no reason to assume that it will."

David watched her lips moving, but hardly heard the words. They had spoken only a few weeks before, but watching her now made him realize they hadn't actually *seen* one another for a year. Even through all the signal disturbance, he knew she looked different: a little older, a little more polished, and much further away.

"The president is in an emergency planning meeting at the moment, but he wanted me to assure each and every American, as well as all of our allies, that we will be prepared for any possible outcome. The important thing now is for people not to panic."

A reporter shouted up at her, "Why did you initiate the EBS?"

Connie, composed, congenial, responded. "We have instituted the Emergency Broadcast System. As anyone who has called long distance or anyone who is watching us now understands, we're getting a lot of interference. The system helps ensure reliable communication links between government and military installations, that's all." David was the only person in the world who knew exactly when Connie was and was not bullshitting. She was telling the truth on this one.

"We have a fix on four different occurrences," she continued, "that will soon appear over American cities. Two are headed toward San Francisco and Los Angeles.

The other two are on our Eastern seaboard moving toward New York and Washington, D.C."

Marty smiled at Pat Nolan, an enthusiastic new employee who poked his head into the office. "You guys, we found an old bomb shelter in the basement of this building. If any of you care to join us down there, we've got room for a few more. But I wouldn't wait too long." With that, he turned and walked out. Jeanie, one of Compact's copywriters, bolted out the door after him, trying to beat the others in the room downstairs for a spot.

When she was gone, Marty shook his head. "This is going to get very, very ugly."

Burlie's was a depressing, dilapidated beer joint just across the highway from the tiny local airport. The felt on the pool table was frayed, and the thumbtacked posters of busty chicks caressing power tools hung on nicotine-encrusted walls. Russell Casse was perched on a bar stool, staring at his second scotch and water, waiting for a man to walk through the door and hand him ten thousand dollars.

As soon as he'd landed the de Haviland, he'd gone to the office to find Rocky, the owner-manager of the two-bit landing strip. Rocky was a terrible name for this obese, oily man, so obscenely overweight he looked like a prize hog.

"How much'll you gimme for that old plane?" Russell asked.

"Ten thousand bucks," Rocky replied, half joking. Both of them knew an available 1927 de Haviland could probably fetch seventy-five grand.

"All right, I'll take it," Russell said softly, "but I need the whole thing in cash. I'll wait for you at Burlie's." With that, he had turned and walked away, knowing Rocky would pour himself in his Lincoln and race to the bank.

But it had been well over an hour since their conversation, and Russell was ready to order another drink, even though he couldn't pay for the first two if Rocky didn't show up with the cash. The television set at Burlie's was switched off and Russell was the first customer of the day. Neither he nor the bartender knew about the catastrophe taking place in the skies around the planet. Nevertheless, the topic of conversation turned to UFOs when a trio of greasy mechanics from the airport walked into the bar.

"Well, well, well, speak of the devil," said the largest and dirtiest of them. "We heard you had a little trouble this morning, Russ. Went up and dusted the wrong field?" The other two guys cracked up. Russell faked a smile and kept his eyes on his whiskey. "Don't laugh, you guys," the big man continued, "it ain't Russ's fault. He's still a little confused from his hostage experience." Once again, his two pals began to cackle like a pair of hyenas in coveralls.

One of them stopped abruptly and asked, "Hostage experience? What happened to him?"

"Let the man drink in peace, fellas," said the bartender without much conviction as he slid their beers across the bar. But the leader of the grease monkeys was just getting started.

"You mean he ain't never told you? Well, a couple years back, our boy here got himself kidnapped by aliens and taken up to their ship. And the little fellers did all kinds of nasty experiments on him. Tell him, Casse."

"Not today, guys. Okay?"

"He's not talkin' now," the guy brayed, "but you just wait till he has a couple more drinks in him. We won't be able to shut him up. Hey, Russ, could you do us a favor?" he asked, glancing at his watch. "Would you get stinkin' drunk *before* we head back to work?" That brought on another round of laughs from his buddies.

When the bartender went into the back room for something, Russell stood up quickly and started for the door. As he passed the mechanics, their leader reached out and clasped him by the shoulder. In a mocking whisper, he said, "Hey, Russ, tell us the truth. When they took you up in their space ship, did they do... you know... any sexual things to you?"

The blast of laughter that erupted from all three of the airport workers brought the bartender into the front room. Russell, no small man himself, was calmly preparing to knock the mechanic's teeth down his throat when the long neon lights hanging from the ceiling began to shake back and forth. A deep rumbling noise, growing louder, came through the building's walls. Beer bottles began to dance across the bar, and the sound of glasses and bottles tinkling against one another grew louder in the dingy barroom. In California, that could mean only one thing: an earthquake.

Their differences suddenly forgotten, the men ran out of the dark bar into the blinding midday glare of the parking lot. Something was wrong. Something about the *way* the ground was shaking, something about the evenness of the noise. It wasn't like any tremor they'd experienced before. It was too smooth.

Russell glanced up, but the sun immediately stabbed into his eyes, causing him to look down at the dusty asphalt. The dark border of an enormous shadow moved toward him across the parking lot. As it passed in front of the sun, the men were able to see what was coming. All at once, the mechanics screamed and took off running in different directions.

Russell stood his ground, his hands clenching into tight fists. One of the thirty-six phenomena was rumbling through the air only a mile or so off the ground. He studied the enigmatic pattern of the object's lower surface, knowing exactly what was happening and exactly who was inside the monstrous rumbling craft: the same frail-bodied, fast-moving freaks who had ruined his life years before.

When Troy was still a baby, and Russell was still in the business of restoring old planes, he'd stayed late at the hangar one night rebuilding an engine. It was a hot July night, so he'd left the rolling doors wide open. All of a sudden, he felt the strength go out of his body. His arms dropped to his sides and the wrench in his hand clattered to the ground. He couldn't understand what was happening to him, thought he might be suffering a heart attack. His whole body had gone numb, paralyzed, except he was still able to move his eyes.

A noise came from the open doors. Glancing in that direction, Russell saw a strange little figure leaning around the corner. It couldn't have been more than three and a half feet tall. This creature had a large head like a yellow lightbulb and two black eyes as lifeless as coat buttons. Gripped by a sudden animal terror, Russell struggled against his rigid body, trying to make it run, but his limbs wouldn't respond. He looked back at the creature peering in at him, and after a few moments, his panic began to subside. *All of this is quite normal, no reason to be alarmed,* Russell told himself, *you will not be harmed.* This idea repeated itself continuously in his brain until he realized that it was a message, a form of mind control, being communicated to him by mental telepathy.

The next thing he knew, he was sitting on the floor, leaning against something. The creature from the door was sitting directly in front of him, its sinewy arms wrapped around its bent knees while others, perhaps a dozen of them, flitted in and out of his peripheral vision. They were doing some sort of work, moving with astonishing speed. The creature seated before him continued to cloud Russell's mind with reassuring feelings. This succeeded in keeping him calm until he noticed something glinting in a narrow container. It was a needle, about six inches long, which was apparently going to be inserted into his skull. As clearly as if it were spoken aloud, one of the creatures told him, *There will be no pain, no damage.*

At that point, Russell remembered thinking of his family, struggling to form the words that would allow him to beg for his life. Then, blackness. The next thing he remembered was being far out in the desert, lifting off the ground. The landscape corkscrewed away as he lifted higher and higher into the air. Then the floor of a ship closed like an iris beneath him. He was in a small, dingy chamber. The dark walls around him glistened with moisture, creating the sensation of being inside the body cavity of a very large animal. He felt their tiny hands moving everywhere over his body. Only then did he notice he was stripped naked. Again he tried to plead with them, mentally howling to be released.

Then the experiments began. Unable to resist, Russell lay stretched out on his back while they invaded his body with several instruments that resembled medical probes. At some point, he remembered one of them lifting his head and laying it on its side so he could look out a window cut into the bottom of the ship. He recognized the vague outline of hills far below and remembered tears pouring off his face as the experiments continued until the whole side of his head was soaking wet.

He was found the next afternoon wandering through the parking lot of a supermarket ninety miles from the airport, suffering from amnesia. He couldn't remember his name or his address, and it took him almost a week to recognize his own wife, Maria. When asked what had happened to him, he said that he'd been chasing a brace of jackrabbits through the desert and had gotten lost. It didn't take him long to figure out this was only a screen memory planted in his mind to camouflage what had really happened.

He never fully recovered. Over the course of the next several months, irritable and depressed, he developed an obsession about reconstructing the events of that night, spending all his money and energy pursuing those fugitive fragments of memory. He put himself in psychotherapy, underwent hypnosis, and traveled to meet others who claimed to have been taken. It was during these months that Maria began to get sick. Her skin turned blotchy and, at night, she'd get terrible headaches that sometimes developed into trembling seizures. By the time Russell looked up from his own problems long enough to realize how sick she was, and drove her into LA for testing, it was too late. The same day she was diagnosed with Addison's syndrome, an easily treated deficiency of the adrenal cortex, she died in her sleep.

As the vast coal-black ship rumbled past overhead, Russell clenched his fists tighter. He wanted nothing more than to murder a few of the shifty little runts he thought were inside the ship. The object was moving north at about two hundred miles per hour. By the time it had moved past, allowing the sun to beat down once more on the parking lot of Burlie's, Russell was gone.

In Washington, D.C., the first people to make a visual sighting of the oncoming ship were the tourists crowded into the observation platform at the tip of the Washington Monument. They began a stampede down the stairwell of the 555-foot structure, trampling everyone who didn't get out of their way. The first casualty was an eleven-year-old girl visiting from Lagos, Nigeria. Although her father had to shelter her body under his, someone had stepped on her back while her head was resting on one of the steps. She was limp and unconscious when he finally got her outside, the last two people out of the building. The

National Park rangers, not knowing they were still inside, had already gone.

The man looked down the grassy hill and saw people running as fast as they could in every direction. In the sky behind Capitol Hill, one of the huge black disks, still trailing wisps of smoke, was looming over the Maryland state line, rumbling closer. In vain, the man shouted to the people running past him, asking them where he could find a hospital for his daughter. No one stopped, or even slowed down.

Thousands of confused visitors were pouring out of the Smithsonian and the other museums lining the mall. As they came outside and saw the disk-shaped gargantuan crawling along the sky, most of them panicked. Great herds of frightened humans were running in all different directions, crashing blindly into one another. Mothers separated from their children stood amid the chaos screaming over and over again the names of the little ones they'd lost. Some froze in their tracks, uttering profanities or calling out the name of God. Here and there, groups of strangers had clustered around trees at the sides of buildings, staring mutely upward. Many others had collapsed to the ground, some praying, others cowering with their arms thrown over their heads. Thousands more, armies of federal employees, came tearing down the granite steps of their workplaces, sprinting, elbowing their way toward the entrances to the underground Metro system. The thing in the sky inspired an immediate, all-consuming sense of dread, an angel of death grinding inexorably closer.

Less than a mile away, at 1600 Pennsylvania Avenue, Whitmore was on the phone with Yetschenko, the Russian president. "Yes, I understand," he said to the translator on the line with them. "Tell him we'll keep him informed and that Russia and the United States are in this together." While his message was being translated into Russian, he looked up at Connie and rolled his eyes. "Okay, and tell him I said good-bye. *Das vedanja*."

"What was that all about?" Connie asked.

"I don't know. I think he was drunk."

Suddenly the doors flew open and a frightened staffer bolted into the room. "It's here!" the woman shouted, leading the way to a set of tall windows that opened onto a balcony. Whitmore and Grey shared a look, then stood up and followed the excited woman to the windows.

"Daddy!" Patricia Whitmore came tearing across the carpet toward her father with tears in her eyes.

"You're supposed to be downstairs," her father snapped at her. But the next moment, realizing his mistake, he was down on his knees to catch the girl as she threw herself into his arms. Alarmed by the tense mood that had seized the White House, Patricia had escaped from her baby-sitters. Whitmore picked the girl up and carried her to a quiet corner of the office, consoling her.

When he turned around again, he noticed his entire staff standing frozen in place on the balcony. Still holding his little girl, he walked out to join them.

The black mass of the ship was prowling low over the capitol, almost on top of them. Its front edge came sweeping over the Anacostia River, casting a circular shadow fifteen miles in diameter. Unconsciously, Whitmore tightened his grasp on his sobbing daughter, pulling her closer to his chest to shield her from the awesome, terrifying sight. Without realizing it, Connie and the others had taken hold of one another, hands and arms laced together in order to keep their balance and stave off the deep dread the ship inspired. Only the Secret Service agents patrolling the edge of the roof remained detached, focused on the job of protecting their leader.

"Oh, my God, what do we do now?" Connie whispered.

"I've got to address the nation," Whitmore said. 'There

are a lot of frightened people out there *right* now."

"Yeah," she looked at him, "I'm one of them."

Having communicated nothing to the people of earth except their arrival, the three dozen ships fanned out over the globe's most populated and powerful cities including: Beijing, Mexico City, Berlin, Karachi, Tel Aviv, and San Francisco.

In Japan, the citizens of Yokohama had watched the fireball splashing out of the heavens then level off at six thousand feet, a cauldron of boiling smoke. Out of the dense clouds, the clean front edge of the ship came plowing forward. The audacious scale of it staggered the thousands of people watching from the docks, then turned them into a screaming mob as the endless bulk of the ship continued to emerge. It had moved directly over their heads, plunging the great port into a quaking artificial twilight for several minutes until it moved away to the north. It was still visible from the rooftops, hanging in the air forty miles away over the nation's capital, Tokyo.

In Yokohama's central train station, the mood had calmed considerably once the object was no longer directly overhead. People loaded down with personal belongings jammed onto the platforms, waiting impatiently for the trains they hoped would carry them off to the safety of the countryside. Transit officials in blue uniforms and white gloves stood on crates above the throng, blowing whistles and urging the crowd to cooperate. Visible through the Plexiglas walls, a battalion of American soldiers from the nearby base were trotting down the street in formation toward an unknown destination. For the moment at least, the evacuation was proceeding in an orderly fashion.

The same scene was repeating itself in cities around the world. One of every five people on earth found themselves trying to get out of the cities, great hives of humanity, only to learn what a tiny fraction of them could be accommodated by all of their roads, trains, and subways. As they stood waiting, sardined onto loading platforms, crowded at bus stops, or stacked into the backs of pickup trucks, they were having the same conversation in every conceivable language: Who or what was inside these gigantic ships, and what were their intentions? Their sinister exteriors convinced the vast majority of people that they had not come for an exchange of gifts and ceremonial handshakes. Still, many remained optimistic. The advanced technology of the ships, they argued, suggested a correspondingly high degree of evolution. Perhaps the extraterrestrials inside were representatives of a higher form of civilization. They would certainly be able to teach us many things about the universe. The optimists compared their situation to that of Stone Age humans on some undiscovered island who looked up and saw an airplane circling overhead. Terrified, they might naturally assume the world was ending when the crew of the airplane was there merely to satisfy their curiosity and thirst for discovery.

Arguments such as these usually led to the depressing admission that humans had never gone anywhere new merely for the sake of curiosity. The people who first populated North America had slaughtered the American Indians. The Spaniards wiped the Incas out with prisons and disease. The first whites to visit Africa were slave-catchers. Whenever humans had "discovered" a new territory, they had turned it into a conquest, subjugating or killing those who were already there. Everywhere, the prayer went up that the newcomers would treat humans in a more civilized way than they had treated one another.

One of the fifteen-mile shadows swallowed New York Harbor, dimming the Statue of Liberty. It was moving directly toward Manhattan. Sporadic clusters of New Yorkers littered the banks of the Hudson, hundreds of frightened strangers, most of them poor, who'd come to see with their own eyes the grim spectacle they'd spent the day following on their TVs. The mood of hushed anticipation ruptured into a wave of human screams rushing north along the river when the dark ship came into view. Long before the craft's low rumble could be heard over the growl of traffic, the city's collective anxiety swelled to a crescendo. Given their visual cue, the riverside crowds bolted off in separate directions, running for home, the subways, their cars, or wherever they instinctively felt they would be safe.

Over the Bowery and Wall Street, the sky disappeared and a bone-rattling vibration began pulsing through Lower Manhattan. Taxi fenders crashed like cymbals. Pedestrians walking along the avenues cleared the sidewalks, hiding themselves in doorways and behind corners when they saw the giant swooping above the city. Everywhere, as car horns blared, people ran out of their houses to watch the ship pass overhead, or ducked into offices and restaurants to get away from it. And everywhere, it seemed, people were screaming.

David's legs churned through the pitch blackness, taking the stairs three at a time. He came to the top, rammed the door open with his shoulder, and stepped outside. The rooftop lay beneath a web of thick cables connecting the satellite dishes and transmitters with the offices below. A moment after he stepped into the sunlight, it was obliterated. Midtown Manhattan was plunged into the same semidarkness the earth usually experienced during a total eclipse.

"God help us," David muttered, face-to-face with the low-flying colossus. His first, irrational reaction was to stoop down, physically oppressed by the sheer weight of the thing rolling over him. The underside of the ship was an endless black-and-gray surface stretching away into the distance. Like the computer-designed tread on a knobby tire, it was studded with sharp outcroppings, building-sized projections arranged into complex patterns. Although the thing was well above the city, its overwhelming size was much larger than the island on which David stood. Its western edge protruded well into New Jersey while the other end was still over Long Island. It seemed to be crushing down on top of him, a mosquito facing the front bumper of a semi. Around him, the equipment on the roof began vibrating, adding its rattle to the steady rumble pulsing through the city. He ran to the north side of the building and watched Central Park fall under the blanket of artificial night.

David imagined his father, terrified and alone in his brownstone. He knew Julius would never in a million years abandon his home. He was probably boarding up the windows and barricading the doors, preparing for another Masada. Yet, for some strange reason, the picture in David's mind changed to Julius calmly playing chess at the kitchen table. He flashed back to that morning's match in the park and then, all at once, a horrible realization unfolded in his mind. He made the connection.

"Oh my God, the signal!"

In the middle of the Los Angeles basin, the Baldwin Hills were an awkward mix of derelict oil fields and million-dollar homes. Many of the houses commanded views which stretched from downtown all the way out to the ocean at Santa Monica. Magazines called it the "most affluent Afro-American neighborhood in the country." Lots of Jaguars and circular driveways. At the top of Glen Clover Drive, sandwiched between a pair of traditional four-bedroom houses, was a narrow piece of property with a bungalow built on the bluff. This red-and-white cottage with a neatly manicured yard featured a redwood deck hanging over the city. The rent was obscenely reasonable, making it one of the best rental deals in all of LA. The tenant was a young woman named Jasmine Dubrow who had moved west from Alabama only two years before.

A minivan pulled into her driveway. Its driver, an energetic housewife, "Joey" Dunbar, unbuckled her passenger's seat belt and helped him open the door.

"Here's your key, Dylan," she warbled.

"Thank you, Ms. Dunbar." Dylan, Jasmine's six-year-old son, accepted the house key, then slid down the seat until his feet reached the sidewalk. He was dressed in Oshkosh overalls, Nike sneakers, and a You & I backpack, the fashion statement of choice among the neighborhood's younger set.

"Everybody say good-bye to Dylan!" Ms. Dunbar chirped. The three kids strapped into the backseat waved over the top of the seat. Dylan could see nothing but their hands, but he waved back anyway. "Remember, tell your mommy you can sleep over next weekend, okay? Bye-bye, I'll wait for you to get inside."

A Mercedes-Benz convertible came tearing down the street at fifty miles per hour. It flew over a bump, then bottomed out on the pavement. Joey, outraged, turned to see who was driving like that through her quiet neighborhood and noticed the neighbors standing on their roof looking through binoculars. A busybody, she whipped around the other way to see what they were looking at.

"What? What's so interesting?" she asked, scanning the block in exasperation. Then she saw the thing in the sky and fell quiet. She stared westward over the housetops, unconsciously baring her teeth. She remained frozen until the squealing of tires broke her concentration.

Another neighbor had jerked his car into reverse down his driveway, leaving behind rubber as he sped away around the corner.

Before Dylan was halfway to the house, his baby-sitter hit the gas and fishtailed away, leaving the confused boy staring skyward.

"Mommy, wake up! Look at this," he cried, coming through the door. Making a bee-line for her room, he jumped on the bed. "Mommy, come outside and see."

Jasmine quickly covered her naked body with the bedsheet, but remained otherwise immobile. "See what, baby? It's too early."

"A spaceship!" Dylan had seen similar situations on cartoons and knew exactly what to do. Wasting no time, he sprinted back to the front windows intending to shoot the thing down.

"What's with your dog?" a man's groggy voice asked.

Boomer, Jasmine's golden retriever, had started barking and whining a few minutes before Dylan came in. After following the boy into the front room, he returned carrying a high-top basketball sneaker in his mouth and deposited the shoe at the head of a large lump under the sheet next to Jasmine. The lump turned over and threw back the cover. "You're just not gonna let me sleep, are you?"

Steven Hiller, a handsome, muscular man in his late twenties, pushed himself reluctantly into a sitting position and stared back at the excited dog. The sour expression on his face showed he needed another hour of sleep. He and Jasmine had been out late last night, closing down Hal's Restaurant after hopping between nightclubs.

"He's trying to impress you," Jasmine said into her pillow.

Groggily, Steven surveyed the scene around him. Large dolphins splashed and smiled on a poster while several smaller ones, statuettes, were arranged on the dresser and nightstands. A trail of hastily removed clothing led from the hallway to the bed. A framed snapshot of Steve in the cockpit of a fighter jet winked back from the top of the dresser. His and hers robes hung on the hook near the bathroom door. He listened to the dog and the kid in the other room and, for a moment, was surprised to find himself in such a domestic situation. *This is the way married people live,* he thought. If that same idea had occurred to him a few months earlier, he would have dressed quickly and hit the road ASAP. But now, slumped against the headboard, he only smiled. *I think I like this.*

He and Jas had been seeing each other exclusively, passionately, exhaustively for half a year, whenever Steve could get into town for the weekend. But he didn't realize he'd fallen in love with her until a pair of experimental F-19 bombers landed at El Toro Marine Air Base, where he was stationed. Normally, the arrival of such planes would have kept a gung ho pilot like Steve hanging around the base for a chance to fly them. When he chose to spend the time with Jasmine instead, he knew his priorities were changing.

Since graduating from the flight academy, he'd learned to fly every kind of aircraft the service had. When a new airship came through the base, whether it was an old World War II bomber or a highly classified spy plane, Steve always managed to win permission to take her up. On dry weekends, he'd jump in his red Mustang convertible and rip north along the 405 Freeway to LA, his hometown. He'd party all weekend, crashing at his parents' house, or at one of his girlfriends' places. He had the reputation of a lady's man, a smooth operator. Then one night, his parents twisted his arm into going with them to one of their stodgy dinner parties, where, much to his surprise, he became smitten with one of the female guests, the drop-dead gorgeous woman now lying beside him. He turned and examined the perfection of her mocha-colored skin and the graceful way her shoulder curved down to her chest.

Boomer continued to whine. He was whimpering and turning in circles with his tail tucked between his legs. Steve knew there was no use in resisting any longer; he was awake for the day. He stood up and padded into the bathroom. While taking his morning leak, his noticed a tall glass jar set on the back of the toilet. Was it his imagination, or was the bath oil inside vibrating slightly? He knew he didn't pee *that hard*. The sound of a low-flying helicopter caught his attention, a Marietta, judging from the sound of the engine. When he was finished doing his business, he looked out the bathroom's narrow window. He couldn't see the helicopter, but he got a damn good view of the neighbors. A man and wife ran to their Range Rover, flung a few things into the backseat, then tore off in reverse down the driveway.

"Kinda weird," he said to his reflection in the mirror. He looked down at the oil in the tall jar. No doubt about it: it was shaking ever so slightly. He stood absolutely still for a moment. Between the gunshots of Dylan's shoot-out in the living room, Steve thought he heard a low rumbling noise. He hurried out to the bedroom and searched for the remote control.

"Whatcha doing, baby?" Jasmine's Alabama accent was stronger when she was tired.

"I think we're having an earthquake and I wanna put on the TV."

"Where's Dylan?" Jasmine sat up, suddenly wide awake. "Dylan, come here, baby," she shouted into the other room. The television snapped to life, showing a local newscaster reading from her notes.

"...through the Southland, but so far there are no reports of injury or property damage. Eve Flesher, a spokesperson for the mayor's office, issued a statement from the steps of city hall only moments ago urging people not to panic." As tape of the news conference began to roll, Dylan burst into the room, Rambo-style.

"Hey, Steve!"

"Hey, Dylan!" The men hugged good morning. "What've you been shooting at, outlaws?"

Dylan looked at him like he was crazy. "What outlaws? I'm shootin' at the aliens."

"Aliens?" Steve and Jasmine exchanged a knowing glance. Dylan had a vivid imagination and they loved encouraging him to spin out his fantasies.

His mother asked him, "Did you get any of them?"

Dylan only stared back at her, perturbed. He was old enough to know when adults weren't taking him seriously. "You think I'm pretending, but I'll show you."

"I'm going to see the space ship," Jasmine said to Steve as she was being tugged out of the room. "Want some coffee when I'm done?"

"I'm coming, too. This might be a job for the Marines." On his way to the door, he glanced once again at the television. As they did almost monthly, whenever a small tremor rattled the city, the station cut to a shot of the seismometers at Cal Tech in Pasadena. A true Californian, Steve had learned to ignore earthquakes. But when he switched off the set, the rumbling was still there, growing louder.

Plates crashed to the floor in the kitchen and Jasmine shrieked at the top of her lungs. Steve ran out and found her pulling Dylan away from the window. She was scared out of her wits by something outside. Steve threw open the front door and marched on to the porch, prepared to confront whoever or whatever was out there. Or so he thought.

One of the ominous ships was surging toward downtown like a poisonous thundercloud. On this nearly smogless morning, the Santa Monica and San Gabriel Mountains surrounding the city seemed puny, dwarfed by the stupendous size of the object in the air. The entire LA basin resembled a giant stadium with a mechanical roof slowly rolling closed.

"What is it?" Jasmine called from inside. Steve moved his lips, but no explanation came out. He cleared his head and made a careful observation.

The top of the ship was a low curved dome, smooth except for a craterlike depression a mile across at the very front of it. Jutting out of this hollowed area was a gleaming black tower roughly the size and shape of a skyscraper. It was perfectly rectangular, except where its back wall followed the curve of the depression. The tower was as black as wet tar. Irregularities on its surface suggested doors or windows behind concealing black screens.

The bottom was essentially flat and had a distinct pattern to it. It resembled a perfectly symmetrical gray flower with eight petals. These petals carried a blue tint and ran seven full miles out to the upturned edges of the craft. Seen from a distance, they had the same vein-laced shimmering transparency of an insect's wings. Each "petal" appeared to be built of eighteen thick slabs, planks laid down in long rows that overlapped to create a jagged surface. Crowded onto them was an array of industrial-looking structures. They looked to Steve like cargo bays, docking equipment, storage containers, observation windows, and other large-scale mechanisms. These structures were not separate pieces bolted individually to the underbelly, but parts of the body, protruding like innumerable hard-edged tumors just below a glistening skin. Further away from him, the eye of the flower was a smooth steel plate with deep lines etched into a simple geometric pattern. At first, he thought these lines might be some kind of hieroglyphic decoration, but when they passed overhead, they looked more like the seams to a set of complicated doors. There was nothing decorative about the ship. It was a floating barge, obviously designed to do a job, not to look pretty.

Steve's first reaction was revulsion. It was not only the sheer volume of the thing hanging over them, or the instinctual dread of feeling trapped beneath a potential predator. There was also something disturbing about the design of the craft, something built unconsciously into its architecture. There was a sinister, joyless necessity to it that revealed something ugly and starkly utilitarian about the personalities of its builders. As if all the industrial waste ever produced had been mixed together into one vast sludge heap and transformed into this stunning, intricate, terrifying machine. Still, there was a certain dark magnetism about it, like microscopic photographs of fleas or fungus that reveal a certain hideous beauty.

When David returned to the ground floor, the office was completely empty. The wall of television monitors played for no one. Adjusting the volume on one of the sets, David listened for any information that might confirm or deny his new theory. CNN, still distorted, had pasted together a flashy letterbox logo—a bold graphic that twirled toward the viewer until it filled the screen: "Visitors: Contact or Crisis." Wolf Blitzer, looking frazzled, was standing in the false night outside the Pentagon.

"Officials here at the Pentagon have just confirmed what CNN has been reporting. Additional airships, like the one hovering directly above me, have arrived over thirty-six major cities around the globe. No one I've spoken with here is willing to make an official comment, but speaking off the record, several people have expressed their dismay and frustration that our space defense systems failed to provide any warning."

A graphic superimposed on the screen. It was a world map showing the locations of the spaceships. David nodded. It was exactly what he had expected to see. He heard a voice coming from Marty's deserted office and walked closer.

"Yes, I know, Mom. Calm down for a second, will ya?" Marty had crawled under his desk and was yelling into the receiver. When David stuck his head in the doorway and said hello, Marty got such a scare he banged his head hard against the underside of his desk. "Ow! Nothing, I'm fine. Somebody just came in. Well, of course he's human, Mother, he works here."

"Tell her to pack up and leave town," David said.

"Hold on, Mom." Marty covered the phone. "Why? What happened?"

"Just do it!" he yelled.

"Mom, stop talking and listen. Pack up a few things, get in your car, and drive to Aunt Ester's. Don't ask. Go. Call me when you get there." Marty hung up and crawled out from under the desk. "Okay, why did I just send my eighty-two-year-old mother to Atlanta?"

David was pacing around the cluttered office, thinking. "Remember I told you that the signal hidden inside our satellite feed is slowly cycling down to extinction?"

Marty suddenly recalled the television disruption he'd been so worried about a few hours ago. "Not really. *Signal inside a signal,* that's all I remember."

"That's right, the hidden signal. Marty, it's a *countdown.*"

"Countdown?" That didn't sound too good. Marty parted the shades and peeked at the dark shape outside. "Countdown to what?"

"Think about it. It's exactly like in chess. First you strategically position your pieces. Then, when the timing's right, you strike hard at the opponent's major pieces.

You see what they're doing?" David motioned toward the television picture of a ship parked above Beijing, China. "They're positioning themselves over the world's most important cities and they're using this signal to synchronize their attack. In approximately six hours, it's going to disappear and the countdown will be over."

"What then?"

"Checkmate."

Marty took a minute to digest the information, then he started having trouble breathing. He opened a can of soda and picked up a phone. "I gotta make some calls. My brother Joshua, my poor therapist, my lawyer... Oh, fuck my lawyer."

David grabbed a second phone and punched in an eleven digit number he'd rarely called yet knew by heart. While the phone was ringing, every television in the office switched to the same image.

The president of the United States approached the podium in the White House press room, doing his best to project calm and confidence. *Everything is under control, no need to panic.* While a number of people, including Grey and Nimziki, joined him on the small stage, Whitmore smiled tensely around the room.

"My fellow Americans, citizens of the world, a historic and unprecedented event is taking place. The age-old question as to whether or not we humans are alone in the universe has been answered once and for all..."

"Communications." The voice on the phone was curt, all business.

"Yeah, this is David Levinson. I'm Connie Spano's husband. This is an emergency call. I need to talk to her right away."

"I'm sorry, she's in a meeting," the man answered, "can I take a message?"

"No. I need to speak with her *right now*. I know she's

busy, I'm watching her on the television. This is more important, believe me. Now go get her." David's voice was full of command.

"Hold please."

David turned his attention back to the president's speech. Connie was standing with a group of people near the stage, just inside the doorway that led into the White House offices. A young man, probably the guy he'd spoken to, came to the door and whispered something in her ear. A moment later she slipped discreetly, professionally through the guarded entrance. David felt a wave of relief. He hadn't been sure Connie would take the call.

"What do you want?" she hissed into the phone.

Taken completely aback, David sputtered, "Connie, listen, you have to get out of there. The White House, I mean. You have to leave the White House." Neither of them knew what to say for a second. It sounded like David was rehashing an unpleasant conversation they'd had countless times before. Aware that he wasn't communicating what he had to say, he bulled forward. "Wait, you don't understand. You've got to get out of Washington all together."

Connie, angry with herself for leaving the press conference, tried to get off the line. "Thank you for being concerned, but in case you haven't noticed, we're in a little bit of a crisis here. I've got to go."

Realizing she was about to hang up on him, David yelled into the phone. "I've been working on the satellite disruption all day and I've figured it out. They're going to attack," David blurted.

The line went silent for a moment. David thought she must be thinking over what he'd said but soon realized she was only covering the receiver while talking to one of her assistants. "They're going to attack," she repeated, "go on."

That made him angry. He was calling to try and save her life, and the last thing he needed was for her to speak to him in a condescending tone. "That's right, *attack*," he said with an edge to his voice. 'The signal is a countdown. When I say signal, I mean the signal that's causing all the satellite disruption." He could sense her impatience. He knew the information wasn't coming out in order, which only made him more nervous. "I just went up on the roof and it hit me. This morning I... Connie?"

She'd hung up. He hit the redial button on the phone, but realized that wouldn't do him any good. She wouldn't take another call. He looked up at the snowy image of President Whitmore.

"...My staff and I are remaining here at the White House while we attempt to establish communication..."

When he heard that, David knew what he had to do. He packed up his laptop and a few diskettes, then grabbed his bike and headed for the door. "Marty," he called across the office, "quit wasting time and get out of town right now."

Marty, still on the phone, listened to the end of Whitmore's address. "...so remain calm. If you are compelled to leave these cities, please do so in a safe and orderly fashion. Thank you."

Slam! A taxicab trying to drive along the sidewalk crashed into a delivery truck doing the same thing. David, pedaling furiously, weaved in and out of the thick traffic. Everywhere around him, the streets were in total gridlock. Even when he got onto the bridge, the people crossing on foot were making much better time than the cars.

Fifteen minutes later, he coasted up to a row of tidy brownstone houses in Brooklyn. He swerved at the last second, narrowly avoiding a mattress being tossed out a second-story window. All up and down the street, residents were packing up whatever they could, preparing to evacuate.

He banged and banged on his father's front door until suddenly it flew open and David found himself nose to nose with a pump-action shotgun. "Whoa! Pops, it's me."

Julius lowered the gun, peering both ways down the street and dragging his son through the doorway. "Vultures. They said on the TV they've already started with the looting. I swear before God, if they try breaking in here, I'll shoot."

"Pop, listen, you still got the Valiant?"

Julius arched an eyebrow, suspicious. "Yeah, I still got it. What do you care? You don't even have a driver's license."

"I don't need a license." He looked the old man in the eyes. "You're driving."

Steve stood by the bed, repacking the weekend clothes he hadn't had a chance to wear. Wearing his officer's uniform and a cocky grin, his movements took on a disciplined intensity and athletic grace that showed how anxious he was to get back to El Toro and, if need be, teach the uninvited guests a lesson. Jasmine leaned against a wall chewing on a fingernail, visibly upset.

"You could say you didn't hear the announcement," she told him.

He just chuckled and kept on packing. "Baby, you know how it is. They're calling us in, and I've got to report."

"Just because they call... I bet half those guys don't even show up."

"Whoa." He stopped her. "Jazzy, why are you getting like this?" She looked like she was about to start crying, and Steve moved to comfort her. He reached to put his arms around her, but she slapped them away, accidentally knocking one of her dolphin figurines off the nightstand.

"I'll tell you why I'm getting this way," she shouted, tearing the curtains back to show him the sky, "because that thing scares the hell out of me!" She slumped against the closet door and let herself slide to the floor.

"Listen to me." Steve squatted down to face her and picked up the glass dolphin, which was still intact. "I don't think they flew ninety billion light years across the universe just to come down here and start a fight. This is a totally amazing moment in history."

It was a corny thing to say, but Steve meant it. He feared nothing. Not in a tough-guy-with-a-death-wish way; he just didn't understand letting yourself get frightened. He knew lots of people who let themselves be crippled by a thousand small fears, who let fear become a habit. They were so afraid of failure or humiliation or physical pain they stopped taking risks, stopped living large. What he had always admired most about Jasmine was her bravery. Like everyone else, she lived with uncertainty, but never seemed to sweat the little things that kept other people in straight jackets: money, schedules, what other people thought of her.

He reached for her hands again, and this time she let them be held. While they were looking into one another's eyes, the big question suddenly appeared again. The same one they'd been doing their best to ignore for the past couple months: what they meant to one another and whether their relationship had a serious future. Steve gulped. He had a small box in his pocket that he wanted to take out and show her, something he'd had custom made several weeks ago. His lips tried unsuccessfully to form the words that would let him broach the subject. He wanted to ask her a question, *the* question. But the consequences of asking would be devastating to his career. So, unable to choose between the two things he cherished most, he executed an evasive maneuver.

"C'mon, walk me out to the car."

Jasmine was brave, but she wasn't fearless. She'd been

abandoned too many times and lost too much to meet this situation with Steve's breezy confidence. She felt like she had finally put her life in order, that for the first time everything was working out for her, and now, with the arrival of the ship, it all threatened to come unraveled at once. Intellectually, she knew Steve was under orders to return to the base, and it didn't mean he was abandoning her. But at the same time, this was a crisis, and Steve's first move was to pack his bags.

"Can I take this?" He held up the little glass dolphin. "I'll bring it back, I promise."

She smiled and nodded. She had no choice but to try and believe him.

He'd left his Mustang's top down all night, and when he came outside, Steve found Dylan behind the steering wheel. After lifting the boy out of the car, he reached into the backseat for a bag he'd left there.

"I've got something for you, kiddo. Remember I promised to bring you some fireworks?" Steve turned over custody of the package, adding, "But you've got to be real careful with them."

Dylan tore back the wrapping to reveal a bundle of brightly colored paper tubes with sticks attached. They looked like overgrown bottle rockets and the name FyreStix was printed on each one.

"Wow, fireworks!" the boy said in awe, holding the sacred objects out for his mother's inspection. "Cool big ones."

Jasmine shot Steve a look: *Oh, thanks a lot!*

"I was gonna set 'em off myself in the park tonight, but... You're supposed to plant 'em in the grass, and they shoot off a bunch of pretty colors straight up about twenty feet."

Jasmine was half listening, distracted by the sight of the

huge ship, which had parked itself over downtown LA's tallest building. Soon after it had ceased to move forward, it started rotating very slowly and the rumbling disappeared.

Steve reached into his jacket pocket and fingered the small box inside. It was hard for him to see Jasmine feeling scared. "I was thinking," he began thoughtfully, "why don't you and Dylan pack up some things and, you know," he looked up and down the street, "come stay with me on the base tonight?" The invitation took Jasmine by surprise. He'd never invited her anywhere near the base and she'd never asked to come. She knew he had good reason for not wanting to be seen with her. Suddenly she was concerned for him. "You sure that's okay? You don't mind?"

"Well," he moaned, "I *will* have to call all my other girlfriends and put the freaky-deaky on hold till later, but no, I don't mind."

She punched him in the arm. "There you go again, thinking you're all that. Let me tell you something, Captain, you're not as charming as you think you are."

"Yes, I am." He grinned, hopping into the car.

"Dumbo ears."

"Chicken legs," he shot back, firing up the engine. Then, after a final kiss, he drove off, calling over his shoulder, "I'll see you tonight." Watching them wave good-bye in his rearview mirror, he wondered if he'd done the right thing, inviting Jasmine to El Toro. It was only a compromise solution.

For her part, Jasmine felt elated and terrified at the same time. She and Dylan stood in the street waving until the red convertible disappeared behind the crest of the hill, then looked once more at the slowly twirling cancerous daisy blotting out the sky. She picked up her son and carried him toward the house, snatching the package of FyreStix from his hands. "I'll take those, thank you."

"Mom, come on!"

Julius's '68 Plymouth Valiant was in mint condition. He kept it under a tarp inside his garage and most of the miles he put on the car were his once-weekly drives to the grocery. His top speed on the highway was usually a maddeningly slow forty-five miles per hour, even during out-of-town drives, which helped explain why David had never applied for a driver's license. But, because this was an emergency situation, the old man tore down the highway at the blistering pace of fifty-five. The highbeams of faster cars bore down on them like the eyes of mechanical wolves. Many of these cars were stuffed to the windows with people and suitcases and boxes of food. Some had mattresses lashed non-aerodynamically to their roofs and when they zoomed past, the passengers would all turn and stare at the two men in the midnight blue classic who were tooling along like they were out enjoying a Sunday drive. The faces behind the windows were hardened into masks of fear by the first twelve hours of the invasion.

"Slow down, you ding-a-ling!" Julius waved a fist and shouted as a van whizzed past at double the Valiant's speed.

"Fifty-five, Dad, please," David said, calling the old man's attention once more to the speedometer. "You're dipping."

"I'm dipping?"

"Dipping below fifty-five. Keep your speed up." David would have liked to be passing every car on the road, but he knew his father's limits, and fifty-five was one of them. Any faster, Julius felt, and the car would self-destruct beneath them. David bit his tongue and tried to relax. There was still time. Besides, he couldn't push too hard after the way Julius had accepted the mission.

David had expected him to put up a fight, to rant and rave for at least half an hour about what a ludicrous idea it all was. But as soon as he'd explained why he *had* to get there in one breathless tumble of words, Julius had leaned close and stared into his child's eyes for a long moment as if searching for something in particular. Something he saw convinced him. "Fix me a sandwich," he said, shrugging. "I'll get my coat."

Thirty minutes later, they were out of town, thanks in large part to David's incredible prowess at navigation. Having spent a good deal of his life in the back of a taxicab, he knew every short cut there was. Once they were out on the highway and pointed for D.C., David broke out his laptop to learn more about the signal, still surprised that his plan had met with so little resistance from his usually resistant father.

"It's the White House, for crying out loud," Julius suddenly erupted, as David stared at the numbers on his computer, "you can't just walk up and ring the doorbell. 'Good evening, hey, let me talk to the president for a minute.' You think they don't know what you know? Believe me, they know. They know everything."

"This they don't know, trust me," David said, trying to concentrate.

"If you're so damn smart, explain me something. How come you went ten years to MIT, graduated with honors, and won all those awards just so you could become a cable repairman?" The question, like many Julius asked, hit below the belt.

"Please don't start in on me about that," David muttered in a way he hoped would close the subject. It was one of his sorest spots, what everyone else referred to as his lack of ambition. He was grossly overqualified for his position at Compact and had been headhunted by research labs all over the nation. He still got occasional letters asking if he'd be interested in working for scientific projects as diverse as the super collider in Texas or the Biosphere in Arizona. He could have pretty much written his own ticket in jobs like those, but he preferred to stay where he was. He loved his city, his job, his father and, until she left to work for Senator Whitmore, his wife.

Stung by the question, David pretended to work at the computer. He couldn't have cared less what other people thought of him, but his father's disappointment was a thorn in his side. "Seven years," David grumbled.

"Seven years? What are you saying?"

"I was only at MIT for seven years, and I'm not a cable repairman, I'm the chief consulting systems engineer."

"Excuse me, Mr. Bigshot," Julius said derisively, leaning close to the steering wheel. "All I'm saying is: they've got people to handle this kind of thing. If they want HBO, they'll call you."

Another low blow. David bit his lip and checked the speedometer again. "You're dipping."

The first lady had the swank hotel lounge to herself. Her retinue of assistants and Secret Service agents had backed off to give her some privacy while she telephoned her husband. Whenever the door opened, she could see the herd of reporters waiting for her out in the main lobby. A handful of LAPD cops had corralled them behind velvet ropes while they waited for her to emerge and hold the press conference they'd been promised.

"Mare?"

"Tom, hello. How are you holding up?" she asked.

"Considering the circumstances," Whitmore answered, "pretty well." It was 11 P.M. his time, and his voice sounded weary.

"Where are you?"

"In the bedroom. I thought I should try and lay down for a while."

"Good idea. What's the mood like back there?"

"Listen," he changed the subject, "I'm arranging to

send a helicopter to the Biltmore. There's a helipad on the top of the building. I want you out of Los Angeles as soon as possible. If these things decide to get ugly on us..." He didn't finish the sentence.

Marilyn smiled. "I thought you'd say that, but I just saw Connie's press conference. Tom, I'm proud of you for staying in the White House. I think it's the right thing to do. But the statement you're trying to make isn't going to be very convincing if they watch me hightail it out of here."

"You're directly below that thing, aren't you?" Indeed, her hotel, the historic and luxurious Biltmore, was only two blocks from the old First Interstate Building. The center of the slowly spinning craft was directly overhead. Downtown LA, usually crowded on a Friday night with an incongruous mix of stretch limousines and promenading Centroamericanos, was nearly empty, a ghost town.

"Yes, it's still up there," she allowed, "but I've got a dozen news crews waiting in the lobby. Johanna's out there setting up a news conference and then a few interviews. I'll leave as soon as they're finished. I promise."

"No way. I appreciate what you're trying to do, but we have no idea what these ships have planned. I'm going to—"

"Tom, listen to me." She cut him off sternly. "I know you're worried. But I have a responsibility here, too. People will listen to me."

He couldn't argue with that. In one public opinion poll after another, Marilyn Whitmore had proven to be the single most popular figure in all of Washington. What Jacqueline Kennedy had done with glamour, Mrs. Whitmore had done with her down-to-earth style. She had won the heart of the nation by being the First Lady to wander the halls of the White House in blue jeans and bare feet. She had the simple, heroic beauty of a pioneer woman and a no-nonsense manner of speaking to the public that inspired trust. The political establishment disliked her, but for ordinary Americans, she was a symbol of hope; their representative-at-large in the corridors of power. As her husband's presidency had floundered over the previous several months, she had become the administration's most potent political weapon. She felt it was her duty to get on the airwaves and try to keep the evacuation of the cities as orderly as possible.

There was a long pause on the phone line. "Oh, all right," her husband relented, his tone making it clear how little he liked the idea. "But I want you on the roof in ninety minutes. I'll have a helicopter waiting to fly you to Peterson Air Force Base in Colorado."

"Make it two hours and you've got yourself a deal." Then, switching gears, she asked about their daughter. "How's the munchkin?"

"Good. She'll be airlifted out of here and meet you at Peterson. We had a little jail break this afternoon. She got away from the nanny and ran into the Oval Office just as the ship was coming in over the city."

"Oh God," the girl's mother moaned, ' how did she react?"

"Like the rest of us. It scared her half to death. She's conked out right next to me. Want me to wake her up?"

"No, let her sleep. But I'm worried about her making that trip by herself. Will you make sure there's a phone on board so I can talk to her?"

"Of course. But she won't be alone. In exchange for staying on at the White House, I'm letting the staff evacuate all their kids to Peterson. I think I'd have a mutiny on my hands if I didn't." A soft knock came at the president's bedroom door. "Just a second," he called across the room before returning to his conversation. "I've got to go. I'll probably see you at NORAD in the morning." Neither one of them wanted to get off the phone, but both felt the tug of their responsibilities. "And, honey…"

"Yes?"

"I love you."

"I love you, too. Very much. And I'll see you in a few hours."

"Bye."

Whitmore, still wearing his slacks and dress shirt, walked across the room and opened the door. Standing in the dim hallway were General Grey and Chief Nimziki.

"We have the report you asked for, sir," Grey said, handing over a fax. "There are still only thirty-six of the ships. We haven't spotted any more entering our atmosphere for several hours now."

"And these are the affected cities?" Whitmore asked, studying the report.

"Yes, sir."

Whitmore took his time studying the data. He could see that Nimziki was edgy and seething, chomping at the bit to say something. When the president finally handed the sheet back to Grey, the defense secretary could contain himself no longer.

"Excuse me for saying so, but this is insane," he said between clenched teeth, "absolutely suicidal. By sitting on our hands like this, we're giving away our first strike capability. We've come here to urge you to take action, to initiate nuclear attack."

The word "we" took Whitmore by surprise. He looked at Grey and asked for his opinion. "General?"

"As you know, Mr. President, I'll support whatever course of action you choose. This is a tough call, whether to fire first or sit tight. But I'm inclined to agree with A1 on this one. Perhaps we should strike first." It was a surprising answer coming from Grey. There was no love lost between him and Nimziki, but they'd joined forces to present this plan to their leader.

Whitmore leaned against the doorway and rubbed his eyes. He thought about it for a few moments. "I don't think so," he finally announced. "You don't punch the biggest kid in school till you're damn sure he's the class bully."

Nimziki was about to press his argument further, but a sharp look from Grey shut him down. *The president has spoken,* the look said, *and that ends the discussion.*

"What about our attempts to communicate with them?" Whitmore asked.

Grey filled him in. "Attempts on all frequencies have led nowhere. Atlantic Command is trying to rig up a kind of visual communication we can put right in their backyard. They'll have to answer us."

"Let's just hope we like what they have to say."

No one noticed what a gorgeous night it was, a million evening stars washed by a comfortably warm breeze. The nervous souls in the trailer park were completely absorbed with questions of safety and survival. That afternoon, neighbor after neighbor, people who had lived there for years, had packed up their belongings and driven away, many without any specific destination. At the same time, new arrivals, mostly dilapidated RVs on the verge of engine failure, were pulling up to the gates, where the manager had erected a flimsy road block. An obese woman in a floral muumuu collected what she considered a fair price before allowing the refugees, their pitiful faces cowering behind the windows, to roll past and claim one of the narrow dirt lots. Field workers stood around their battered Fords listening to Spanish-language radio stations, deciding which way they should run. Anxious women peered through their screen doors every few minutes for signs of danger before locking themselves inside once more. Everybody was on edge, keyed up like high-stakes gamblers hanging around a casino waiting for the rules of a strange new game to be announced.

Barefoot and cross-legged, Miguel surveyed the whole scene from above. He'd climbed onto the roof of his family's trailer bringing their small television with him, hoping to get some decent reception. After several experiments with wire coat hangers and wads of tin foil, he achieved the best picture quality he was going to get. He leaned back on his hands and watched the news, the warm wind playing through his shoulder-length hair.

There had been no word from Russell since their confrontation alongside the tomato field that morning. *Typical,* he thought, *whenever there's any kind of a crisis, he evaporates.* Like he'd done a thousand times that day, Miguel glanced in the direction of Los Angeles. The dark hump of the mysterious ship was visible above the foothills separating the city from the desert. The rising sliver of moon cast a shadowy gloss along the eastern edge of the craft. Just below the ship, miles of headlights snaked through the canyon as thousands of motorists continued to escape from the city. Watching the lights come toward him down the highway then change into glowing red tail lamps speeding away to the safety of Bakersfield, Fresno, Bishop, and points beyond, Miguel thought again about his plan. All afternoon, he'd been turning it over in his mind. He had to get Troy and Alicia out of the area, away from the danger of the ship. The only place he knew to run was a relative's house in Arizona. The Casse family had burned all their other bridges over the last couple of years.

Flipping channels, he thought about how he would propose the idea to Russell, if and when he ever returned. Then he saw something on the screen that stunned him almost as much as his first glimpse of the spaceship. One of the local channels was running a story supposedly showing the lighter side of the invasion. With a smirking, ironic tone, the anchorman read from the TelePrompTer.

"...a local man who works as a crop duster was arrested today after he flew over parts of the San Fernando Valley in an antique airplane tossing thousands of leaflets over the side." Miguel moaned out loud when he saw the videotape of his stepfather, feral and handcuffed, being escorted into the Lancaster police station.

"You people better do something," Russell snarled at the news crews. "I was abducted by these aliens ten years ago, and nobody believed me. They did all kinds of tests on me—they've been studying us for years! We've got to do something. They're here to kill us all!" One of the deputies dragged Russell away and pushed him through the front doors of the stationhouse.

Back in the news room, the anchorman's eyebrows lifted. "A rather unique reaction. The man, a drifter identified as Russell Casse, is being held at Lancaster police station for further questioning. The handwritten, photocopied leaflets claimed—"

"Whatcha watching?" A voice from behind startled Miguel, who instantly switched the channel. It was Troy, climbing up the ladder to see what his brother was doing.

"Nothing." Miguel's voice was strangled with emotion. He cleared his throat and spoke again. "Hey, Troy, you remember Uncle Hector, from Tucson?"

"Of course. He's got that SEGA Saturn CD, sixty-four bits. Remember?"

"Yeah. What would you think if we went there to stay with him for a while?"

The younger boy nodded his approval. "That'd be pretty cool."

Miguel looked at the highway for a minute, thinking. Then he made a decision. "Start packing up. We're going." On the television, First Lady Marilyn Whitmore was making a speech, another plea to remain calm. Miguel unplugged the set and brought it carefully to the edge of the roof.

"We're leaving now?" Troy asked from the ladder, confused.

"Right now."

"What about Dad?"

Miguel jumped off the side of the trailer, landing softly on his feet in the dirt. He stepped up onto the tire to retrieve the television. Noticing his little brother hadn't moved, he snapped angrily, "You heard me, Troy, get your stuff ready to go." Then he stomped off into the darkness of the trailer park to find his half sister. He had a pretty good idea where he would find her.

"But we can't leave without Dad," the boy complained. Miguel didn't look back.

He slipped his hand under her shirt. "This could be our last night on earth," he whispered. "You don't want to die a virgin, do you?" He tried to make it sound half joking and half serious, rolling the dice to see how far he could get. The question made Alicia nervous. She bought some time. Her mouth opened onto his for yet another long, hot, grinding, twisting kiss that pushed him backward against the driver's door. On top of him now, she came up for air and stared down at him. The yellow glow of a porch light seeped through the windows of the truck.

"What makes you think I'm still a virgin?"

The question embarrassed and encouraged him at the same time, made him think that tonight, after weeks of making out, he would finally have her. Alicia was no mind reader, and she didn't have to be one to know exactly what he was thinking. She could feel his excitement in the arch of his back, the way his fingers dug into her hips.

Living in a twenty-two-foot-long travel trailer with

three other people was like spending an endless weekend in hell. Alicia, almost fifteen, wanted out. And the only way she could see that happening was for a man to take her away. The guy she was kissing wasn't exactly a man, but he was as close as Alicia had come to finding one. Andy was eighteen, and around the trailer park, he felt like a pretty big wheel. He and his mom, the manager, shared the largest permanent trailer in the park. He had a steady job, a new Toyota truck with a killer sound system, and plans for getting his own apartment. Alicia liked him, but at the same time, she wasn't ready for sex. She knew she'd allowed the conversation to go too far and found herself trying to figure a way out of the situation without looking like a big tease.

Andy was still thinking about the virginity question when the door he was leaning on suddenly opened. The young lovers nearly toppled out onto the ground. Alicia's brother stood looking down at them.

"What the hell are you doing, Miguel?" Untangling herself from Andy, she sounded angry and embarrassed, but was secretly relieved.

"Come on, we're going to Tucson."

"Right!" She rolled her eyes. "Like I would go anywhere with you."

Without further discussion, Miguel reached past Andy and put a vise grip around Alicia's wrist. He pulled her out of the truck, bringing Andy with her. She landed outside with a thump and a growling scream.

"Hey, dude, take it easy," Andy demanded.

Miguel prepared to take him out with one skull-crushing punch. The savage look in his eyes paralyzed Andy, making him sit back down muttering, "Whatever, it's cool."

Alicia, fuming, shouted as she stomped across the dusty yard, "Miguel Casse, you are such an ass. You're a psycho who needs help. I'm telling Dad what you just did, and I hope he whips the hell out of you." Then she took off running, disappearing into the shadows.

While Alicia pouted inside, the two boys grabbed flashlights and went to work. Twenty minutes later, they'd disconnected the water, electrical and sump lines, strapped the bicycle and the motorcycle to the back frame, brought in the folding chairs and the hibachi. The Casse trailer was ready to roll. Miguel buckled himself into the driver's seat, fired up the engine, and muscled the column shift into Drive. But he did not move.

Standing in the glare of the headlights, wobbling slightly, like an overweight, retarded elk, was his stepfather. Russell was out of jail, just in time to make their lives even more miserable. Miguel's first impulse was to hit the gas and run him over, slam into him and run over his flabby drunken ass. Instead, he shifted into neutral and waited, eyes straight ahead.

As carefree and cheerful as ever, Russell shuffled over to the driver's side window. "All right, kids! You read my mind. Let's get as far away from that thing as we can." He looked toward the dark shape over Los Angeles and shook his head. "Nobody understands, Miguel. Nobody believes me, but that thing is going to turn LA into a slaughterhouse, mark my words."

Miguel only looked back at him, a blank and hostile stare. Ignoring it, or not noticing, Russell told the boy to open up and let him get behind the wheel. Instead, Miguel slipped out the door and closed it behind him.

"They let you out?"

It never occurred to Russell that he ought to feel guilty or embarrassed. "You're damn right they let me out! Since when is it a crime for a man to exercise his right to free speech? Whatever happened to first goddamn amendment? Anyway, they've got bigger fish to fry right now, believe me. Come on, let's go." When Russell started toward the trailer, Miguel stepped in front of him, trembling.

"We're leaving without you, don't try and stop us."

Finally, he had his stepfather's full attention. "What are you talking about?"

"We're sick of it," Miguel said as calmly as he could. "We're sick and tired of picking up after you, of carrying your dead weight around." The boy took a breath, keeping his eyes on Russell's hands. "We've got enough money to make it to Tucson and stay with Uncle Hector for a while."

Russell stared at him as if it was the craziest thing anyone had ever said. "The hell you are," he thundered loud enough for the entire park to hear. "I'm still your father, boy, and don't you forget it!"

That was the last straw. Miguel's fuse had burned all the way down and now he exploded, going off like a rocket.

"You are not! You are not my father. You're just some drunken fool that married my mother. And she took care of you like you were a stinkin' baby and when she got sick you did *nothing*! You're a lunatic, Russell, and you are *nothing* to me. Now please," he said more calmly, "move out of the way. I'll take care of us and you take care of you."

Russell took a long, deep breath, thinking it over. He was always half expecting something like this to happen, but now that the moment was here, it felt like being stabbed in the heart. "What about Troy?"

"That's exactly what I'm talking about! You're so damned selfish. Try, for once in your life, to think about what's best for him. Who's the one who actually takes care of him? Who has to go around begging for money and jobs and medicine? Huh? Who? Every time you screw up, *I'm* the one. I'm the one who has to do all the dirty work. I'm the one who has to get out there and scrape together enough to buy that damned medicine." Miguel could have gone on and on, but the sound of shattering glass stopped him.

"Stop it! I'm not a baby!" Troy screamed. He had come outside and was breaking vials of his medicine on the pavement. "I don't need this stupid medicine!" he yelled, hurling another one against the ground. "I don't need anyone to take care of me."

As soon as he realized what was happening, Miguel darted through the headlights and grabbed his brother before he could throw the last vial, but as they struggled, Troy managed to drop the bottle and crush it under his sneaker. Furious, his brother grabbed a handful of the boy's hair and shook him.

"You know how much that stuff costs? Now what happens when you get sick again? Answer me!"

He waited for an answer, but his anger changed suddenly to sadness, and then to crushing despair. He'd tried. He'd taken a stand against his stepfather and tried to engineer an escape. All at once, he realized that he had failed. And failed miserably. Speechless, thoughtless, Miguel turned and disappeared into the trailer.

"Sorry," Troy said softly.

"C'mon, let's get going, Troy-boy." Russell led the way to the idling vehicle.

David kept reminding himself that the gentleman seated behind the wheel was his father, a man to whom he owed love, patience, and filial gratitude. On the other hand, Julius was driving him absolutely berserk. The Levinson men hadn't spent so much time in a small space together since the summer David turned thirteen and the family had taken that hellish road trip down to Florida to visit Aunt Sophie who was ill and couldn't make it to David's bar mitzvah. As they drove, Julius, always a kibitzer, seemed less interested in traffic than in his nonstop conversation. He'd been talking since they left New York, jumping from one subject to the next, analyzing, criticizing, posing questions then answering them. Twice a week over a game of chess in the park, it was fine. But confined to the cabin of the antediluvian Plymouth, bobbing along on bad shocks like an ocean liner at fifty-five miles per hour, his constant chatter was pushing David to the brink of insanity. For the last twenty miles Julius had been pouring over the plotlines of some of the most recent movies he had seen, such as 1959's *The Blob* and the earlier *War of the Worlds*. There were too many similarities for Julius, amateur conspiracy theorist, to believe somebody somewhere hadn't known all this would come to pass. The only time he was quiet was when he was listening to some strange new noise coming from the engine compartment.

David bit his tongue and stayed quiet. This was, after all, the only way he had of getting himself to D.C. Every couple of minutes he would glance over at the speedometer, then check his watch.

"Fifty-five!" Julius would boom when he noticed his son checking the speed. "I'm going fifty-five miles per hour. Any faster and the engine will blow up. Trust me."

There was nothing for David to do but sink back in the seat and try to remain patient. Every mile or so they shot past another vehicle pushed to the side of the road, out of gas or radiator hissing hot jets of steam into the night air. Traffic was backed up all the way to Washington, forty miles away. David thought it was only a matter of time before the frustrated motorists knocked down the meridian barriers and took over the southbound lanes as well. That was exactly what was happening, under police supervision, further up the highway. But for now, the boxy chrome-and-steel Valiant had the highway all to itself. David turned and looked out the rear window.

There were no headlights behind them, only open empty road. He looked ahead. No taillights either, except for a seemingly abandoned police car parked sideways in the fast lane. The lights were flashing and both doors stood wide open, but as they sped past, there was no sign of the Maryland State trooper who had stopped the car there.

"We must be getting close," David said. "We're the only ones on this road."

"The whole world is fighting each other to get *out* of Washington, and we're the only schmucks trying to get *in*!" The highway led up a hill and around a long bend. As they came to the crest of the hill, they had their first direct line of sight toward the District of Columbia. Both men stared wide-eyed at the sky ahead. The lights of the nation's capital, rising into the night sky, reflected off the underbelly of a giant dark shape hovering over it: a spacecraft identical to the one they'd seen in New York. The city lights were just bright enough to show the massive gray outlines of the ship's dark flower design. Neither man uttered a word as they coasted down the hill. When a stand of pine trees blocked the view, Julius cleared his throat.

"David, I suddenly have a strong desire to visit Philadelphia, where there aren't any flying saucers. What about we turn around and just—"

"Check your speed, please." Without realizing it, the old man had slowed to thirty-five miles per hour.

Now that they were approaching the city, David's manner became more urgent. Quickly, he reached into the backseat, retrieved his laptop computer, and booted it up. From a plastic file sleeve, he extracted a CD-ROM and popped it into the computer's external drive slot.

Julius knew what a CD was, but he'd never seen one in person before. "What the hell is that thing?" he wanted to know.

David held up the companion disk, volume two, waving it around with a fair amount of showmanship. "On these two little disks, Pops, is every single phone book in America."

"On two little records?"

"Incredible, isn't it?" David's fingers darted around the keyboard, punching in commands.

Julius wasn't going to admit it, but he was impressed. He leaned over and watched the names scroll by on the screen. "Let me guess. You're looking up her phone number."

"Precisely, Sherlock."

"One problem. What makes you think an important person like Constance is going to be listed in the phone book for every crackpot to call her?"

"She always keeps her portable phone listed, for emergencies. The problem is figuring out which name she's put it under. Sometimes she uses only her first initial, sometimes her nickname..." He began trying various options while Julius looked on trying to keep up. After twenty or so possible names failed to yield a match, David started to show his frustration.

"Not listed, huh?"

"I'll find it." David's voice sounded almost convincing. "I just haven't figured it out yet. It's usually under something like C. Spano, Connie Spano, Spunky Spano..."

"Spunky?" Dad was obviously amused. "I like that one. Try Spunky."

"Spunky was her college nickname."

"Have you tried Levinson?"

David frowned. "Please. She didn't take my name when we were married. Now that we're separated she's going to start calling herself Levinson? I'm sorry, but I don't think so."

Julius shrugged and looked away. So what if his ideas

weren't worth trying? What did he care? Eventually, David gave in.

"Oh all right, we'll try Levinson." Julius leaned over and watched the names zip past as avidly as if he were watching a roulette wheel. Abruptly, the names stopped and the machine beeped to signal a match.

"So what do I know?" the old man asked sarcastically.

A loud piercing scream made them glance up simultaneously. Headlights flashing and siren wailing, a police car was speeding down the wrong side of the road. Worse, it was leading a highwayful of traffic, hundreds of stressed-out drivers determined to get away from Washington.

"*Oy, mein gott!*" Julius pushed his glasses higher on his nose, bent closer to the wheel, and prepared for the inevitable.

As soon as David realized they were too close and moving too fast to avoid the oncoming traffic, he did the only sensible thing: he let loose a bloodcurdling scream. Julius jerked the car to the left, narrowly avoiding the lead car's front bumper, then to the right just before they went head-on with a station wagon. A pair of sedans locked up their brakes, fishtailed into a collision, then bounced apart. Julius split the narrow gap between them, inches to spare on either side.

"*Slow down!*" David yelled, his face as white as the headlights bearing down on them.

Julius, leaning over the steering wheel, chewing on his lip, hardly touched the brakes. As car after car crashed around them, spinning like bowling pins, the Mario Andretti of the over-seventy set swooped between them skillfully and, from the looks of it, fearlessly. Two hundred yards from where the mayhem began, there was an off-ramp. With one long tire-squealing tug on the wheel, Julius pulled the car from the fast lane to the right shoulder and then up the ramp.

Adrenaline pumping, mouths open, knuckles gone bloodless white, the two of them stared straight ahead until Julius rolled the car to a gentle stop. Awed by what his father had just done, David turned and stared at him.

"Dad! Nice driving, man." Without knowing why, he started laughing.

Julius was breathing pretty hard. He took out a handkerchief and wiped his forehead. "Yeah. Not bad, eh? I didn't even scratch the paint job." Then, although there was nothing funny, he too started chuckling. It was the nervous, triumphant laughter of two men who had just lived through what should have killed them.

For a few moments they forgot about getting to Washington and simply sat there in the car laughing their heads off, the vast, dark ship looming in the distance.

Jasmine didn't know why she was about to walk out on stage, she just wanted to get it over with. The whole day had been a slow walk through a brightly lit nightmare. Even now, adjusting the straps on her silk bikini, she felt as if she were floating.

The advent of the giant ships had plunged the entire globe into a deep state of confusion. Some believed they were the black angels of the apocalypse, come to drown God's green earth in flood, famine, and fire. Others anticipated a beatific ceremony announcing intergalactic harmony and cooperation. While many were scrambling desperately to escape the city, others, like the man who owned the shoe store at the base of Jasmine's hill, were keeping to their regular schedules. All the rhythms of the workaday world, the infinite number of small routines which had seemed so real the day before, turned out to be no more solid than reflections on the surface of still water. The arrival of the ships dropped a large stone into the center of the pond, turning daily life into a rippling, distorted dream. Robbed of its rules, the world didn't know how to behave.

The only reason she'd gone in to work was to pick up her paycheck. It was supposed to be a fifteen-minute stop on her way down to El Toro. But then she'd run into Mario. Fifty, expensively tailored, hair slicked straight back, a notorious name-dropper, he was the very picture of a middle-aged Mafioso wannabe. His club, the Seven Veils, was all he had in the world, and his reaction to the crisis was to insist that the show must go on. Many people over the years had accused him of being a vampire, draining the life out of his girls, sucking every nickel from their bodies before tossing them out for dead. When Jasmine came in for her paycheck, he begged, cajoled, and threatened until she agreed to perform that night. If her head had been clearer, she would have laughed in his face, told him where to shove it, and disappeared. But no one's head was clear.

After all, what if the ships turned around and left? What if Steve decided a woman with a checkered past and a six-year-old son were more than he wanted to handle? Where else was she going to find a job that let her choose her hours and paid her so generously? She desperately wanted to believe Steve wasn't going to let her down and was fairly certain he wouldn't. But she and Dylan had had the rug pulled out from under them before, and Jasmine was nothing if not protective of her son.

Mario took full advantage of her history while trying to convince her to stay and work. He'd known Jasmine for a long time, knew all about her life before Dylan in her native Alabama. She'd started dancing in some podunk club in Nowheresville before being "discovered" and brought to Mobile. That's where Mario had found her. One night after a show he bought, her a drink and listened sympathetically to her entire life story, then convinced her to head out west, where she could put her past behind her, start over, and make some very serious money.

The good thing about Mario was that he never tried to get her into bed. He maintained a professional relationship with Jasmine and respected her work ethic. She showed up on time, steered clear of the drugs most of the girls took, and never dated the customers. The bad thing about him was that he knew all the right buttons to push when he wanted something out of her. That's exactly what he'd done when she walked in asking for her paycheck. He reminded her of the men she'd trusted, including the one who had left her with a child and no way to support herself. When he figured she was feeling vulnerable, he switched gears and threatened to fire her if she wouldn't help him keep the club open, a pathetic tyrant desperate to keep control over his little fiefdom.

The thumping bass line of her song pulsed over the club's sound system and the announcer's taped voice boomed over the top: "Gentlemen, loosen your collars and get ready for something extremely hot. Put your hands together for the lovely... Sabrina!"

She burst through the curtain and into the blinding glare of the spotlight. Twirling gracefully on her high stiletto heels, she circled the stage until she arrived at the polished brass pole. Grasping it a finger at a time, she pressed her entire body against it, then broke away into another set of pirouettes, tossing away her see-through cape.

Suddenly, "Sabrina's" tigress-in-heat expression disappeared. There was no one in the audience. The hundred chairs surrounding the stage were all empty. The only customers were a handful of men clustered around the big-screen TV at the far end of the room. All of them were regulars who had neither homes to defend nor families to rescue, guys who had wandered over to the Seven Veils for the same reason they always did: the company. Four or five of the other dancers sat with them at the bar watching the news.

Without a doubt, it was the worst moment of Jasmine's career as a stripper. She suddenly felt very angry and very stupid. Standing there, nearly naked, in the blazing stage lights, she began to realize why she had really come to the club. She had *wanted* Mario to confirm all her suspicions about Steve, to remind her of all her failures with men, or more exactly, all the men who had failed her. After all, hadn't he taken off, leaving her and Dylan when the spaceship appeared? But what really made her angry was that she had kept Dylan with her, exposing him to danger unnecessarily. It was time to drive like hell down to El Toro and see whether Steve was for real. She slipped out of her high heels and, unnoticed, walked back through the tacky foil curtains.

She came into the dressing room cussing mad. "I can't believe I let that son of a dog talk me into this. I only came here to get my check. What was I thinking?" She collapsed into the chair in front of her dressing table, wiping off her stage makeup in disgust. At the next table, a washed-out girl of nineteen or twenty sat staring at her portable television set.

"Can you even believe this is going on? It is so totally cool." She called herself Tiffany. She had a long, graceful body, enormous boobs, and armfuls of straight black hair pinned haphazardly atop her head. Lighting a fresh cigarette with the butt of another, she spoke in a slow, spacey voice. "I told you they were out there and you thought I was nuts."

On the television screen, between static interruptions, a pair of newscasters with serious expressions were reading the news. "This next story comes from the 'It Could Only

Happen in California' file. Hundreds of UFO fanatics have congregated on the rooftops of several skyscrapers in downtown Los Angeles. Soon after the craft parked at ten A.M. yesterday, with its center positioned directly above the old First Interstate Building, sign-toting individuals made their way to the rooftops, apparently to welcome the ship's occupants. Gordie Compton is live and on the scene in the Nose for News CamCopter."

The screen cut to an unsteady helicopter shot, its powerful search beam like a shaft of lightning in the night sky, swooping over the crown of the LA skyline, the First Interstate Building. Crowded onto the helipad atop the building were fifty or sixty people. When the light hit them, they went mad, shouting and waving hand-painted signs. Some held up signs like "TAKE ME!!" and "EXPERIMENT ON ME."

"Oh, signs, I forgot," Tiffany remembered. "Look at the one I made." She reached into a shopping bag and took out the side of a cardboard box. In loopy, girlish letters were the words "WE COME IN PEACE" and a crayon drawing of a space alien.

Jasmine gripped Tiffany's arms. "Don't even dare!" she hissed. "Girl, listen to me. You're not thinking about *joining* those idiots, are you?"

Tiffany rolled her eyes and blew smoke at the ceiling. "I'm going over there as soon as I'm off work," she admitted. "Wanna come?"

"Look at me." Jasmine took hold of Tiffany's chin and lifted it until they were eye to eye. Like most of the dancers who worked there, Tiffany was a mental and emotional basket case. She had a drug habit plus an addiction to abusive men. As soon as they'd met, Jas had taken the girl under her wing. "Tiffany, I don't want you going up there," Jasmine continued. "Promise me you won't." A pair of puppy dog eyes looked back until

Jasmine snapped, "Promise me!"

"Oh, all right, I promise." Tiffany pouted, tossing the cardboard sign over her shoulder and onto the floor.

"Thank you. Look, I'm going out of town for a while, and I need you to stay out of trouble until I get back."

Jasmine checked her watch. Steve was probably starting to wonder where she was. She didn't want to leave Tiffany, but she had to get on the road. She had changed into her street clothes when Mario barged into the dressing room, heading for his office. He pulled the door open and stared into the room.

"What the hell is this kid doing in my office?" he bellowed. "And why is there a damn *dog* in here?" Dylan was inside watching a video on Mario's set. Jasmine pushed past Mario and gathered her son up in her arms.

"How many times I gotta tell you damn broads, *no kids* at the club!"

"You try finding a baby-sitter today," Jasmine shot back, grabbing her bag with her free hand and heading toward the exit.

"Whoa! Stop right there, young lady. Where do you think you're going? You promised me you were gonna work today. You leave, you're fired."

Jasmine paused for a moment at the door, glancing back for a last look around. "Nice working with you, Mario."

The mood in the pilots' locker room at El Toro was serious, pensive. Captain Steven Hiller strolled in and noticed most of the men were sitting by themselves, or huddled in quiet, brooding conversations. Turning a corner, he found his squad in a very different mood. The men of the Twenty-Third Tactical Air Wing were relaxing in groups, talking, flipping through magazines, kidding around. "The Black Knights," the squad's official nickname, was emblazoned on lockers, T-shirts, and jackets. There were even a couple of tattoos.

Steve's flight partner and best friend, Jimmy Franklin, was kicked back with his feet up on a locker door, arms behind his head, listening to a portable radio. Without turning around, he knew Steve had come in. The two of them had spent so much time training and watching each others' backs, both in the air and on the ground, they automatically knew where the other one was.

"Where the hell you been, Captain?," Jimmy called out. "Wait, don't tell me. Traffic was a bitch, right?"

Steve dropped his bag in front of his locker and moved into the group of leathernecks. "I bet you guys have been sitting on your butts all day waiting for me to get here, right?" Steve asked facetiously, knowing the group would have spent the day running through one emergency drill after another. The marines responded by pelting Steve with half a dozen towels. Grinning, Steve strolled back to his own locker. Jimmy got up and followed him.

"This is some real serious shit, Stevie. Mucho serious. They've recalled everybody on the base, and we spent the whole day on yellow alert."

Steve opened his locker and saw the mail had been delivered, stuffed through the vent. He flipped through the stack until he came to a legal-sized envelope with the blue NASA insignia printed on one corner. He picked it out of the pile like a negative out of developing fluid and tossed the others aside. He stared at it for a moment before handing it to Jimmy.

"You open it for me. I can't."

"You're turning into a real wuss, you know that?"

If Steven Hiller was the most talented and hardworking pilot on the base, Jimmy Franklin was the most fearless. Nothing scared him, and he'd prove it to you any time you liked. He tore the letter open and read it aloud so only Steve could hear.

"It says here, 'Dear Captain Hiller, Marine Corps blah blah blah. We regret to inform you that despite your excellent record of service...'" Jimmy's voice trailed off. He knew the news would knock the wind out of his pal. "Listen, buddy boy, I've told you this before. It don't matter that you've learned to fly everything from an Apache to a Harrier to a dang hang glider. If you want to fly the space shuttle, you're gonna have to learn to kiss a little ass."

That was the third time they'd turned him down. Disgusted, Steve reached into his locker and ripped down a glossy photo of the space shuttle *Columbia* landing at Edwards AFB. Hanging right beside it was a snapshot he'd taken of Jasmine.

Jimmy made it his job to cheer Steve up. "Let me explain my personal technique. The first thing is to get the right ass-kissing height. When I see a general coming, I get down on one knee, see? This puts me at a perfect level with the ass that needs kissing."

Steve felt like he'd just swallowed a dagger, but he tried to look amused. As he stuffed his jacket into his locker, something fell out of the pocket and on to the floor. Before Steve could grab it, Jimmy snatched it up. It was a small jewelry box, which Jimmy immediately opened. Inside there was a beautiful diamond engagement ring. The sparkling white stone was set in a gold band shaped like a dolphin jumping out of the water.

For the first time in many weeks, Jimmy was rendered speechless.

"Jasmine has this thing for dolphins," Steve told him, a little embarrassed.

"This is a... is this a wedding ring?" Jimmy asked, still on his knees.

"Engagement." Steve heard an edge of accusation in his friend's voice. They'd talked many times about Steve's goal of flying the shuttle into space, and every time they did, Jimmy gave him the same advice: dump the stripper.

"I thought you were going to break it off, man," Jimmy growled.

Just then, some guys from another flight team walked by. They saw Jimmy down on one knee, holding out an engagement ring to Captain Hiller. A couple of them did a double take. Realizing how queer it must look, Jimmy and Steve jumped away from one another in a panic. Steve snatched the box back and put it away.

"Steve, listen to me. Them boys at NASA are real careful about their public image. They want everything to be wholesome, all-American apple pie. You've already made one mistake: being born black. If you go ahead and marry a stripper, you will never ever in a million years get to fly that shuttle. And you know I'm right."

Steve knew it was all true. As soon as Jasmine signed in at the guardhouse as his overnight guest, his hopes of flying the shuttle would probably die forever. He pressed his head against the row of lockers, the metal cool against his forehead.

The powerful klieg lights that would normally have been shining on the White House were blacked out for security reasons. A pair of tanks and a platoon of rifle-bearing Marines were posted at the front gates on brightly lit Pennsylvania Avenue. Hundreds of Washingtonians were there with them. Along with the reporters, and those who were simply too nervous to sleep, were small groups holding candlelit prayer vigils. A bunch of militant pacifists paraded back and forth holding signs with slogans such as "DON'T PROVOKE!" and "VIOLENCE BEGETS VIOLENCE." The police, uniformed and plainclothes, were everywhere.

When a pair of cops pulled a road block aside to allow a line of news vehicles on to the street, Julius cut into the line and drove past the road block like he was Walter Cronkite. Even after years of studying him, David couldn't tell when his father was being sneaky and when he was simply blundering along. When the Valiant lurched to a stop, Julius turned and dryly addressed his son.

"Okay, we're here. You want to ring the doorbell or should I?"

David shot his father a Clint Eastwood stare as he flipped open his cellular phone and dialed Connie's number from his computer screen. He got a busy signal. "Perfect, she's on the phone right now."

Sometimes David made no sense. "How," his father wanted to know, "can it be perfect if you need to talk to a person and her line is busy?"

"Because," David explained, his fingers issuing commands across the keypad, "I have a service that allows me to triangulate her signal and establish her exact position. Even inside the White House."

Julius started to say something else, then stopped short, realizing what David had said. "You can do that?" he asked, honestly curious.

David answered with a diabolical grin, "All cable repairmen can."

Inside the White House, Connie was in one of the hallways taking care of some personal business. She had called her friend and neighbor, Pilar, who was just about to leave for her parents' place in New Jersey. The woman promised to take Connie's cat, Thumper, with her. As soon as the two of them said good-bye, the phone rang again.

"Yes?"

"Connie, don't hang up."

Her eyes rolled toward the ceiling when she heard

David's voice. She leaned against the wall. "How did you get this number?"

"Walk to the window. There should be a window right in front of you." Reluctantly, she looked around. Sure enough, there was a window only a few feet away. She walked over to the tall windows and pulled back the white lace curtains to peer outside.

"All right, I'm at the window. Now, what am I looking for?"

There was no need for more explanation. As soon as Connie looked up at the street, she saw a tall, awkward figure climb up onto the hood of an old blue car and start waving wildly in the air.

Secret Service men quickly surrounded the car and "helped" David down. Filtered through the phone, Connie could hear him telling the men he was talking to someone *inside* the White House.

A moment later, an all-business voice came on the line. "Who is this?" Connie identified herself and, despite her own doubts, assured the agent that the man on the hood of the car wasn't a lunatic. She checked her watch and decided she could come down and talk to him for a minute or two.

A shower of sparks from a welder's torch bounced off the helicopter and onto the tarmac at Andrews Air Force Base, then fizzled away. The hooded man was putting the final touches on something called "Operation Welcome Wagon," a hastily organized attempt to communicate with the visitors. Portable work lights, designed for nighttime road construction, had been trucked onto the runway along with a fleet of loudly chugging generators needed to power them. Scores of news crews from around the world moved as close to the scene as the soldiers would let them.

The center of all this attention was a sixty foot long,

thirty foot high, eighteen-ton piece of machinery, the most advanced instrument of its kind: an Apache attack helicopter. A special steel frame was fitted into the copter, designed to hold a giant light board.

Searching for some way to communicate with the mute Goliaths hovering over the world's capitals, the army engineers had finally seized on a plan. They'd descended on RFK Memorial Stadium, home of the Washington Redskins, and dismantled a large section of the ballpark's message board. The aluminum box, forty feet tall, had 360 lights that could be programmed by computer to display just about any kind of pattern or message. Once the box was delivered to Andrews AFB, it was mounted to the floor of the Apache, extending like a pair of bulky wings from the doors on either side.

A thousand cameras began to flash when the long rotor blades started to turn. Reporters shouted questions at the soldiers and press officers assigned to keep them at a distance, rushing to their positions to do stand-up remotes. Within seconds, they were patched in to live network broadcasts and millions of people around the world were watching the beginning of Operation Welcome Wagon.

"What you see behind me," a CNN reporter shouted over the din, "is an Apache attack helicopter refitted with synchronized light boards. Pentagon officials hope these lights will be our first step in communicating with the alien craft. But what message will we be sending? And in what language? We spoke with one of the men responsible for designing earth's first message to these inscrutable visitors just a few moments ago. He told us that it would be a message of peace sent in the language of mathematics…"

As soon as the blades were at full speed, the ground crew moved away and the pilot lifted off, careful to keep his craft level so that the light board wouldn't slip out.

It rose straight up, then began moving toward the dark metallic menace slowly turning in the night sky. A swarm of smaller helicopters, equipped with cameras, followed it away from the base.

People everywhere followed the scene on their television screens. Even in the White House, a large contingent of military personnel and civilian advisers watched as the tense drama unfolded.

"Where are we?"

Suddenly half the room jumped up and saluted as the president strode into the room.

"We're in the air," General Grey reported, "ETA approximately six minutes." As he said these words, the pounding *thwack* of the Apache was audible over the city. Several officers went to the windows and watched it lifting higher and higher as it flew to the rendezvous point at the tall tower which seemed to mark the front of the ship. President Whitmore stood shoulder to shoulder with the rest of the room, watching in grim silence.

Just down the hall, the doors of the old executive elevator rolled open and out stepped an unshaven Julius Levinson, his trousers wrinkled from the long drive. He made no secret about being impressed with his surroundings. As Connie and David headed down the hallway speaking in urgent whispers, Julius stopped to inspect his appearance in a mirror.

"Oy! If I had known I was going to meet the president," he said loudly, "I'd a worn a tie. Will ya look at me, I look like a schlemiel."

Without a word, Connie hurried back, hooked her father-in-law's arm in hers, and tugged him along until the three of them were standing in the Oval Office. The room was empty, but to Julius it felt as if all the great names of American history were in there with him. He couldn't believe where this strange day had taken him. As a reflex, he combed his fingers through his hair, trying to make himself look presentable.

"You two wait right here. I'll be right back," Connie told them. Before she left the room, she warned David, "I don't know how happy he's going to be to see you."

"Connie, we're wasting time," David urged. "I'm about the last person he's going to listen to."

"Of course he'll listen," Julius erupted, suddenly ready to defend his son, "why shouldn't he listen?"

"Because the last time I saw him I punched him in the face."

Julius gasped and clutched his heart with his hands. He looked at Connie, then at David. "You actually *punched* the president? My son punched the president?"

Connie paused at the door. "He wasn't the president then," she explained. "David was convinced I was having an affair with him, which I *wasn't.*"

With that, she closed the door and walked down the hall to the briefing room. A smile crossed her lips as she heard Julius raising his voice, incredulous, in the room behind her.

Connie stopped outside the door to the briefing room. She was taking an enormous personal and professional risk, pulling the president out of a high-level meeting for a conference with her erratic ex-husband. But David had managed to convince her that he was on to something real, something she thought the president ought to know about. She took a deep breath and plunged in, walking straight up to Whitmore and whispering something into his ear.

"Right now?" he asked, incredulous.

His communications director nodded. Everyone in the room had turned to watch this conversation. The timing couldn't have been worse. The welcome wagon would reach its destination in just over three minutes. But Whitmore was accustomed to relying on Connie's good judgment. Without another word, he turned away from the window and walked to the door.

"You aren't going to leave *now*, are you?" Nimziki made sure everyone in the room was aware of the president's curious decision as Whitmore ignored him and left the room.

"Ugh! How in the world do you put up with that cretin?" Connie asked once they were out in the hall.

"He ran the CIA for years. He knows where all the bones are buried. It comes in handy," Whitmore told her. "Now, exactly who is this I'm going to talk to?"

Rather than answering him, Connie ushered him into the Oval Office. The moment Whitmore saw David, he froze in place. "Damn it, Connie, I don't have time for this!"

Anticipating exactly that reaction, she had shut the double doors and stood in front of them. There was an icy silence.

Julius, understanding the situation better than he let on, broke the tension by marching up to Whitmore, hand extended. "Julius Levinson, Mr. President. An honor to meet you."

"I told you he wouldn't listen," David said, pouting at Connie.

"This will just take a moment of your time," Julius assured him.

President Whitmore shot a dumbfounded look at Connie, amazed that she had dragged these two weirdos into the White House at a moment like this. As he moved to leave the room, David finally spoke up.

"I know why we have satellite disruption," he said calmly.

Whitmore turned and looked back at him. "Go on."

"These ships are positioned all around the globe," he began, coming around to the front of the president's desk and drawing a circle on a notepad. "If you wanted to coordinate the actions of ships all over the world, you couldn't send one signal to every place at the same time." He drew lines between the ships showing how the curve of the earth would block their signals.

"You're talking about line of sight?"

"Exactly. The curve of the earth prevents it, so you'd need to relay your signal using satellites—" David added a pair of orbiting communications satellites to his sketch "—in order to reach the various ships. I have found a signal embedded in our own satellite network, and this signal is actually—"

Before he could finish, the door was forced open behind Connie. An aide poked his head in the door with an urgent message. "Excuse me, Mr. President. They're starting right now."

So far, David hadn't told Whitmore anything he didn't already know from intelligence reports coming out of Space Command earlier that day. The president picked up a remote control and switched on the television. The Apache had just reached the front of the huge spaceship and turned on its light boards. The powerful lights began to flash on and off, creating a repeating sequential pattern. The staff at SETI, after several hours of furious on-line discussion and a blizzard of faxes, had come up with a simple mathematical progression, a message written in what they hoped would be a universally comprehensible language. The entire sequence would repeat every three minutes, followed by a display of the word "peace," written in ten different earthly languages. It wasn't much, but it was a beginning. The message spelled out by these flashing lights was utterly incomprehensible to most humans, including the president.

He turned back to David. "So, they're broadcasting to one another using our satellites?"

David had turned on his computer. He showed Whitmore the graphic he had created to express the signal.

"This wave is a measurement of the signal. When I first found it, it was recycling itself every twenty minutes. Now it's down to three. It seems to be fading out, losing power, but the broadcast power remains stable. It's like they're slowly turning down the volume, shortening it down to zero. It has to be some sort of a countdown."

The president stared back at the television, lost in thought.

"Tom, these things are—" David caught himself and started over with greater composure. "Mr. President, these things are using our own satellites against us, sending out a countdown. And the clock is ticking."

"When will the signal disappear?"

David opened a window on his computer screen. 'Thirty-one minutes."

Whitmore stared at the television. The giant helicopter looked like a mosquito beside the endless gray bulk of the intruder ship. What David had told him made sense, confirmed his worst suspicions. Until then, he'd taken a wait-and-see attitude, but if David was right about the countdown, it was time to spring into action. He nodded his head and walked out of the room, down the hall, and came into the briefing room with a whole new battle plan.

"General Grey, I want you to coordinate with Atlantic and Southwest Commands. Tell them they have twenty-five minutes to get as many people out of the cities as possible."

"But Mr. President—"

"And get that chopper away from that damned ship. Call them back immediately."

Grey picked up the direct line to Andrews AFB and relayed the commander in chief's orders. Nimziki, on the other hand, used the moment as an opportunity to advance his career and accumulate personal power. With a series of glances around the room, he tried to cement the impression that Whitmore was cracking under the pressure, reversing himself for no apparent reason.

"Mr. President," his tone was full of false civility, "why are we pulling back now? What changed your mind?"

Whitmore ignored him. "We're evacuating the White House, effective immediately. Let me have the two choppers on the lawn in five minutes. Somebody go downstairs and get my daughter." Advisers and staff broke into thirty separate conversations, scrambling to execute their new marching orders.

"Sir," Grey held a hand over the phone, "I've got General Harding of Atlantic Command on the line. Just how orderly should this evacuation be?" Grey was as confused as anyone by Whitmore's sudden change of direction. But there was no time to answer the question.

"They're responding!"

All the movement and chatter stopped abruptly as everyone turned toward the bank of television screens. A thin shaft of green light, two inches around, sprouted from the base of the tall tower on the alien ship. Almost like a long finger extending through the darkness, it grew in length until it reached out and poked against the helicopter, a mile away. The Apache, moving sideways through the air to keep itself in front of the tower as the giant ship spun slowly through the air, reacted visibly, jolting backward several feet when the light nudged against it. The beam, bright enough to be visible from the ground, was the pale color of milky jade. The millions watching on television could see that the helicopter was struggling to maintain its position relative to the vast, menacing ship.

The pilot's cool voice came over the radio. 'This ray of light seems to have some type of mass or energy to it. We're experiencing some turbulence, getting knocked around pretty good up here."

As he spoke, a huge screeching noise drowned out his words. A pair of huge armored plates concealing the source of the mysterious pole of green light had begun to grind open with an earsplitting squeal.

"Sounds like God's fingernails on a big chalkboard," the pilot purred in a southern accent.

As the panels pulled open, the light from inside the big ship overpowered the 1500-watt bulbs of the light board. The men inside the helicopter shielded their eyes, still struggling to maintain position. Then the president's order reached them. The lead pilot flipped the switch on his radio, his voice broadcast to millions worldwide.

"We have received orders to return Operation Welcome—"

He never finished. A spike of green light suddenly streaked across the night sky and smashed against the helicopter, shredding it in a single burst. It looked like a dragonfly being taken out by a .22-caliber shell. After the brief explosion lit up the sky, everything was suddenly dark once more. The bright light coming from the spaceship was gone. All that remained were a few pieces of smoking debris drifting earthward like fiery snowflakes. The doors at the base of the tower rolled closed and the huge saucer covering the sky went back to sleep.

A phone rang in the Los Angeles hotel room. Then rang again. Marilyn Whitmore was too stunned by what she had just seen to answer it. She had been packing a few last things into her briefcase when the helicopter exploded. The television was showing it again in slow motion. Grainy enlargements of the pilot showed him covering his head in the last frame of videotape before the blast hit him. Marilyn sat down on the bed feeling sick for the man and his family, but even worse for what the extraterrestrials' response meant to the human race as a whole. When the phone rang again, one of her Secret Service escort picked the cellular up and identified himself. He listened carefully, saying, "Yes sir, I understand," and "Yes sir, immediately. She's right here, do you wish to speak with her, sir?... Yes, sir, I understand."

He clicked the phone off and turned to Mrs. Whitmore. "That was the president, ma'am. He said he loves you very much and gave me orders to evacuate you from Los Angeles at once. We have the southern stairwell secured. We'll take it up to the roof."

"Okay, let's rumble," she said, pulling herself together and heading out the door.

As they came out on the roof, an army transport helicopter was fifty feet above them, coming in for a landing on the rooftop helipad. Mrs. Whitmore wondered aloud whether getting into a helicopter was such a good idea. The city-sized spaceship overhead might have developed an appetite for them. As the whirring blades stirred up the warm night air, Marilyn scanned the city's skyscrapers and noted something curious happening on one rooftop after another: helicopters buzzing around, shining search beams down on the tops of the brightly lit buildings.

Jasmine opened the door and stepped onto the asphalt. She was in the fast lane on the old Pasadena Freeway. Traffic on her side of the road was jammed solid, crawling along at one mile per hour. Just over the guard rail, things were moving much faster. Drivers pushing to get north out of the city had taken over the empty southbound lanes. Just ahead was the mouth of a tunnel cut into the side of a steep hill. The idea of being inside a tunnel while the ship was overhead gave Jas the creeps.

Frustrated, she got back into the car. As soon as she was beyond the tunnel, she told herself, she'd find some way to get across the center divider and make some time, even if she had to ram her way through the guard rail. At the rate she was going, she wouldn't make it to El Toro until next month. Dylan and Boomer were both starting to get bored and restless. Jasmine switched on the radio for another traffic report.

"...authorities have called for a complete evacuation of Los Angeles County. Motorists are being urged to avoid the freeways wherever possible and take surface streets instead. You'll make much better time that way."

"Now he tells us," Jasmine looked over at Dylan and shook her head in exasperation. The boy just shrugged his shoulders. Traffic advanced another thirty feet.

The president and his entourage were moving fast. At the bottom of the stairs, they met an aide who had brought Patricia out to meet them. From there it was out onto the lawn and into the waiting helicopters. The twenty men and women, all looking sharp and polished despite being in their twenty-first consecutive hour of work, jogged across the lawn, up the stairs, and into the big blue-and-white choppers with the presidential seal emblazoned upon the door.

General Grey had already boarded and was on a telephone when the president entered. "Is my wife in the air?" The edge in the chief executive's voice told Grey the answer had better be yes.

"She'll be in the air at any moment. They're loading right now."

Connie was the last one in the door. She looked confused and she was. The Marine guards controlling access to the helicopter had stopped David and Julius behind the cordon. They couldn't come along. There were a couple of unoccupied seats on the chopper, but the president had his nose buried in a fax from the State Department and Connie couldn't imagine asking him to bring David along with them. Besides, it was too late. The ground crew was closing the door and the Air Force pilot was revving the blades up to liftoff speed. Somehow, David and Julius would have to make it out of the city by themselves. Connie knew if David's theory about the countdown were correct, they only had about ten more minutes to do so.

"Tom..." The sound of the voice surprised her, even though it was her own. When President Whitmore wheeled around to face her, Connie found herself at a loss for words. Instead, she pointed out the window to where the Marines had detained David and Julius.

As soon as the president saw them standing out there, he stood up and moved to the door, pushing it open again. Over the roar of the copter blades, he yelled something to the men outside. One of them immediately turned and ran across the lawn, bringing the Levinsons back with him. As the two of them came up the stairs and into the cabin, the expression on Whitmore's face let them know they were expected to sit down and shut up. That's exactly what they did. Finding seats next to Connie, David had his laptop up and running before the copter lifted off. Looking over his shoulder, Connie could see the display on the computer screen ticking down.

11:07 11:06 11:05...

As the helicopter lifted quickly away, Connie looked out the window, watching the people below on the White House lawn. None of them looked like people about to die. They were all so busy, so focused on properly executing their individual responsibilities. Somehow, Connie felt, their concentration made them seem safe, protected. They still had so much work to do. For a moment, she thought she was watching a scene like the one she had imagined taking place at the gates of heaven: some were allowed to pass toward salvation while others were left outside to perish. She shook it off. Certainly, these people, these hard-working background players she had worked side by side with for the last three years would be there as always when the chopper returned.

11:01 11:00 10:59...

She was lifted up the last several flights as if by magic, drawn upwards toward the sounds of the party raging above. At last, she pushed open the fire door and stepped into the open air. Hundreds of laughing, shouting, drinking people were dancing to the blaring cacophony produced by three competing stereo systems. Some were waving signs, others lighting fireworks. A group of women who looked like secretaries had dressed themselves up in "alien suits," white body stockings with tall cone head caps strapped under their chins. One couple, taking themselves a little too seriously, came as the king and queen of a distant galaxy, complete with velvet robes, elaborate crowns, and jeweled scepters. They sat stoically amid the mayhem as if waiting for a messenger to arrive from the ship. The birthday suit was another popular costume. In the big dance circle at the center of the roof, a bunch of young hippies, Deadhead types, had stripped off their clothes and were entranced in a writhing naked group dance. A rumba line was snaking its way through the crowd, and as they passed, one of the dancers shoved a bottle of tequila into Tiffany's hands. She felt as if she'd come home. As if she'd finally found the wildest, coolest, craziest spot on earth. The one she could never find or get invited to. And the ironic thing was that most of the people atop the old First Interstate Building shared one important characteristic in common: they were nerds. Tiffany laughed out loud then gulped down a long slug of tequila.

More amazing than the party was the view of the ship. The dead center of it was directly overhead. *I'm at ground zero,* she thought. She took a long look at the lustrous surface of the craft. The long silver streaks, the ones people said looked like insect wings, were actually a whole network of lumpy projections, warehouse-sized tubs, tanks, and docks that made the thing look like a city hanging upside-down. It was certainly large enough to be a city. Gaping up in awe, she pictured what the inside of the ship must look like, imagined herself whisking around inside doing some important business. A tug at her arm brought her back to earth. An older guy with a beard was working on a joint. Pointing toward the naked snake dancers not far off, he told her a little story over the noise.

"In the last days of the Third Reich, as the allies advanced on Berlin and everybody knew it was all over, that their world was about to end, they started having wild orgies. It's how they dealt with the stress of the situation." He reached out and stroked her arm. It was the lamest come-on line she'd ever heard.

"Whatever!" Tiffany laughed in the guy's face, handed him the tequila, then waded deeper into the thick of the party, pulling her WE COME IN PEACE sign out and waving it to the spaceship. It was crowded, far too many people for the small rooftop. Some of the "alien lovers" were only a few feet from the edge, sixty-five stories straight down without a guard rail.

All of a sudden, a police helicopter lifted over the side of the building, its bullhorn turned to full volume. "You are commanded to leave the roof at once. The president of the United States has ordered the evacuation of Los Angeles. Make your way to the stairs immediately in a safe and orderly fashion."

The crowd reacted predictably, booing and throwing whatever they had in hand. Most of them had already defied the police to get up here, pushing through the cordon they'd set up at ground level. The chopper circled the building once, repeated the order, then peeled away toward the next rooftop.

A tremendous noise erupted overhead, a low, steady rumble like the sound of a hundred thousand timpani drums. Everyone stopped and craned their necks back to witness the amazing spectacle unfolding overhead. The center of the ship was opening. The aliens were preparing to communicate. Huge interlocking doors began to tilt downward. The entire mile-wide center of the ship, the dark circle at the center of the flower, slowly broke open to reveal the dimly lit interior. At the absolute center, one small area didn't move. This was the tip of a long needle-like structure. As the doors around it continued to drop away and apart, the needle began to lower itself over the city. It was long and thin, except near the bottom, where it flared out into a diamond shape, like a snake swallowing an apple. This shaft had a quality to it which made it look both biologically natural and utterly repulsive at the same time. The long neck of it poked below the bottom of the ship, dangling into the night sky like a newly budding flower while the doors continued to lower themselves, spreading apart like the bloom of a black steel rose. When the doors were perpendicular to the ground, the rumbling noise ceased, but the shaft of the needle continued forcing its way deeper into the sky until the tip of it was only two hundred feet above Tiffany and her new friends.

The First Lady's helicopter darted between the skyscrapers, moving at its top speed. The pilot had seen what happened to Operation Welcome Wagon and was anxious to get his passengers out of harm's way. Although their destination lay to the northeast, the pilot took off south, the fastest way out of downtown.

"Maybe it's some kind of observation tower," one of her aides said of the hanging needle.

Then the green light began. From the tip of the needle,

a wide glimmering ray lit up downtown, the light the same milky jade that had annihilated Operation Welcome Wagon. From the ocean to the foothills, everything human stopped to gasp at the light's eerie beauty. The soft beam was so lovely, so peaceful and magical, it seemed to be a sign of friendship. For a few minutes it seemed everything was going to be all right. There wouldn't be a confrontation after all. The light made it seem obvious earth was about to experience a harmonious close encounter. The parties on the several rooftops fell quiet. The history of the planet was about to change forever, and they knew they were right at the heart of the action. Holding their signs skyward, they waited for the communication to begin.

Outside Washington, at Andrews Air Force Base, the door of the helicopter was kicked open before the runners touched down on the tarmac. David's theory about the countdown was being taken very seriously now and there wasn't a moment to lose. Secret Service agents hustled President Whitmore and his entourage out the door, across the open runway, then up the boarding ramp into Air Force One. The 747's turbine jet engines were already revved up to full power, ready to launch the plane down the runway. Like clockwork, the boarding ramp was disengaged, and the pilot released the brakes, sending the airplane lurching forward into its take-off run. As they gained speed down the runway, the flight crew was buckling Julius, the last person up the stairs, into his seat. David, flipped open his laptop and watched the last few seconds tick off on the screen.

00:25 00:24 00:23…

A white tracer beam shot straight down through the center of the green light onto the old First Interstate

Building. Every alien lover within fifty feet wanted to claim the spot where the beam touched the roof, believing perhaps that one of them was about to be selected and lifted into the ship. They fought each other like wild dogs for the privilege of being earth's ambassador.

While they pushed and wrestled, Tiffany retreated to the mellower energy of the area near the stairs. Lots of portable televisions were plugged in, all showing the same sharp white ray was coming from the other ships around the world. In Paris, the beam was on top of Notre Dame cathedral; in Berlin it fell on the old Reichstag building; in Tokyo, the Emperor's Palace; the convention center in San Francisco; Central Park in New York; the Forbidden City in Beijing; the enormous dome of Tel Aviv's Great Synagogue; the statue of Nelson in London's Trafalgar Square, and, in Washington, D.C., the beam was fixed at the very tip of the Washington Monument.

Then the waiting was over. The white beam amplified noticeably. It turned brighter, much too bright to look at. Everyone within two miles turned away, burying their faces in their arms. Those who didn't felt their retinas begin to burn and warp. A whirring hum like a dentist's drill grew louder and louder until it was a piercing thunder. Terrified people on the rooftops fell to their knees clutching their overburdened ears and eyes, screaming silently into the sea of noise. Then, for a brief moment, everything stopped.

For the space of two heartbeats, the light disappeared and everything was quiet once more. The stunned believers had just enough time to uncover their eyes and look upwards for an answer.

WHAM!! A streak of blinding white light slammed down out of the needle. All at once, the old First Interstate exploded from the inside out, shattering into a billion fragments, none larger than a playing card. Tiffany never had time to scream. The thundering light poured down with unbelievable force, and within two seconds, the civic center was gone. A tidal wave blast of fire flared up, then began rolling outward, spreading in all directions at once. A wall of destruction, an awesome sea of fire, crashed through the city, taking everything in its path. Every wall of every building, every tree, every street sign, even the asphalt of the streets was burned up and blown away. A hurricane, a flood, and an atomic bomb blast all rolled into one, the wall of destruction hurled cars high into the air, shattered buildings like scarecrows in a tornado, and smothered the city under a thick layer of fire. The wall of destruction rolled outward from the epicenter, scouring the City of Angels off the planet.

Perhaps the most horrible aspect was how slowly it moved. An atomic blast would have incinerated its victims instantly, before they realized what was happening. But this fireball rolled through the city like a flash flood, allowing its victims plenty of time to see it coming. Everyone turned and ran, but there was nowhere to hide. The few people who managed to make it belowground, into cellars and bomb shelters, were suffocated. The firestorm sucked the oxygen right out of their lungs and cooked them where they hid.

In Washington, the White House and all the buildings flanking the mall area—the Lincoln and Jefferson Memorials, the Smithsonian museum complex—were instantly torn to shreds, decimated. From there, the blast materialized into a tidal wave of fire rushing outward. In the blink of an eye, it blew apart and instantly consumed the Capitol Building, taking most of the hill with it. In the other direction, the Pentagon was flattened, blown to smithereens.

The same grisly scene was repeating in cities around the world, everywhere the giant ships were stationed. Thirty-six of humanity's proudest creations, home to millions upon millions of people, were swiftly and systematically obliterated.

The digital display on David's laptop had ticked to zero six seconds before the rear wheels lifted off the runway. The savage burst of light which signaled the obliteration of Washington, D.C., had already flashed through the windows. David dug his fingers into the cushioned armrests of his chair and looked at the ceiling, waiting.

Julius was the only one who wasn't sweating. He understood there was nothing left to do except hope it wasn't his time. As the plane began to climb, everyone in the cabin took a relieved breath and allowed themselves to believe they'd survived. A second later, the wall of destruction reached Andrews AFB, still a hundred feet high. It tore through the base, ripping it to shreds as it chased the plane down the runway. The 747, slowly lumbering upward, was five hundred feet off the ground when the wall of fire caught up and shot past below. Although they were above the brunt of the blast, the air pressure at the front of the wall swelled up under the tail of the big plane and gave it a violent shove. Bottles shattered in the service area and luggage toppled into the aisle, but Air Force One narrowly escaped.

The tunnel was a long gloomy concrete tube built back in the twenties. Narrow walkways on both sides gave way to alcoves with grime-caked wooden doors every few hundred feet. Along with her fellow drivers, Jasmine was listening to live news reports on the radio. The announcer's descriptions of the enchanting green light lured many drivers out of their cars. They took their keys and ran to the end of the tunnel, where they could stand on the cliff and witness the phenomenon for themselves. Jasmine leaned on her horn. She was only ten car lengths from the end of the tunnel and didn't care about any damned green light. Eventually, realizing she was pinned in, she cut the engine to save gas.

She listened with concern as the man on the radio described the blinding white ray cutting through the soft green light. Then, as the blast pounded down on the city, turning it to an inferno, the newsman began shouting hysterically.

"My God! My God! It's destroying everything. Widening—" Abruptly, the voice was gone.

Jasmine's instincts took over. She reached across and picked up Dylan, hoisting him out of the car. He had just enough time to grab his backpack with the precious fireworks Steve had given him. With her child in her arms, Jasmine broke into a sprint for the mouth of the tunnel, glancing over her shoulder as she went. Already, the sky behind her was burning orange and white. Needing somewhere to hide, she ducked into one of the maintenance alcoves cut into the rock wall. She tried the handle of the flimsy wooden door, but found it was locked. She turned around and checked the tunnel. The wall of destruction was speeding straight toward her. Terrified people bolted out of their cars and ran; others rolled up their windows and cringed.

All the lights in the tunnel suddenly went dark. She was out of time. She turned once more and kicked blindly at the door. The howling firestorm reached the mouth of the tunnel, gushing into the narrow opening with a deafening boom. Anguished screaming and the thunderous noise of cars being swept up and torn apart blasted toward her. Jas put Dylan on her hip, lowered the other shoulder, and rushed the door. The flimsy wood splintered and she crashed through to the other side, landing in a heap.

"Boomer!" she called, quickly scanning the inside of the workroom, lit by the approaching fire. She had landed on top of a wire mesh grating that opened onto an engineer's tunnel and the city's vast network of drainage canals. Boomer leaped off the hood of a car into the room, just as the fire tossed the vehicle away.

She rolled on top of Dylan, shielding the boy's body with hers. As the firestorm raged through the tunnel, a stiff wind came shooting upward through the wire grating. The stone walls of the alcove protected them from the brunt of the blast, but the fire had instantly consumed all the available oxygen. Now fresh air was sucked through the grating, creating a wind tunnel strong enough to blow Jasmine and Dylan into the fire. With Dylan locked under one arm, Jasmine put her fingers through the grating and held on for dear life as the fire fed itself. Without the steady rush of cool air moving over their bodies, the three of them would have been incinerated by the heat.

Then, suddenly, it was over. Thousands of tons of boulders and loose earth clogged the tunnel at both ends. The hillside had collapsed. Jasmine, still trembling, rolled over on to her back. She knew she was lucky to be alive. What she didn't know was that the three of them, the only ones still alive inside the tunnel, were buried under millions of pounds of dirt.

Tokyo sustained the highest number of casualties. More than anywhere else, the Japanese had tried to go about their business as usual without panicking. Once the intricate train scheduling system had gotten knocked out of synch, the stations turned into madhouses. Half of those who did manage to get out of the city in time did so on foot or on bicycles. The destruction of the high-rise city, until then the world's most expensive real estate, was utter and complete. The area leveled by the blast was four times as wide as the H-bombs exploded over Hiroshima and Nagasaki decades earlier. The wall of destruction ended every human life within a twenty-mile radius. As far away as Yokohama and Omiya, half the population had been killed.

Manhattan was gone. The island was transformed into a barren shelf of land, swept clean of buildings all the way up to Yonkers. Amid the choking swirl of dust and smoke, natural gas lines shot towers of flame into the sky. Twisted brick and concrete foundations showed where the buildings had been torn away. Only a few hundred people, mainly those in deep sections of the subway system, had survived. On the south side of Staten Island and deep into New Jersey, those who had not been killed outright by the wall of destruction lay trapped beneath their collapsed homes, their bodies blistered with severe burns.

There was not a single human survivor anywhere on earth close enough to watch the long, needle-shaped firing cones retract into the ships. The petal doors raised slowly to form an impenetrable, airtight seal. The huge ships, the city destroyers, were ready to move on to the next set of targets.

"God damn. I knew it. I knew it! I've been trying to warn everybody about these suckers for ten years." Russell lowered the volume on the radio without taking his eyes off the road. "Kids," he yelled over his shoulder, "haven't I been trying to warn people?"

Liquored up, he had no inkling of how distressed and traumatized his children were by what they'd heard on the radio. Alicia was sobbing, her face resting on the linoleum tabletop. Miguel, his arm around her, stared blankly out the window at the Joshua trees passing through the headlights.

"Where's Troy?" Russell asked into the rearview mirror.

The youngest member of the Casse clan called from his

bed at the back. "You guys," he said in a weak voice, "I don't feel so good."

Russell looked over his shoulder. "When's the last time you had any medicine?"

"I can't remember," the boy moaned. "I think about three or four days ago."

"That's not true," Miguel said, "I gave you some this morning."

"I know, but I didn't take it. I thought I didn't need it anymore."

"What did you do with it, Troy? Where's the medicine?"

Instead of answering, the boy stood up and moved to the door, gesturing that he needed to go outside. Russell pulled to the side of the road and Troy ran outside. A moment later, he was vomiting into the weeds while Alicia helped him keep his balance.

Russell wandered away down the road a bit, far enough to sneak a swig of whiskey without hearing it from the kids. They were in the middle of Death Valley, somewhere near the Nevada border, and it was a spectacular night. A billion stars burned in the sky. Russell strolled along with his head rolled back on his shoulders. At the crest of a small hill, he noticed something odd, a different sort of constellation.

"Miguel!" he called quietly. "Come take a look at this!"

Spread across the floor of a shallow desert valley, a thousand campers, trailers, RVs, and passenger vehicles had congregated at a rest stop in the middle of nowhere. The shimmering lights coming from this makeshift refugee city echoed the stars above. In a way, it was a beautiful scene.

"Ain't that somethin'?"

"Maybe somebody down there's got some medicine," Miguel said. "Let's go ask."

* * *

At the beginning of the end of the world, Steve was in the empty cafeteria building trying to make a call. Over and over, he dropped the quarter into the slot and carefully pecked out Jasmine's telephone number. And every time, a mechanical voice answered: "All circuits are presently busy. Please hang up and try your call again later."

Fishing the coin out of the cradle, he dumped it right back in. He knew the base commanders were itching to order a counterstrike, but until they got the go-ahead from Washington, there was nothing for Steve to do but imagine all the horrible things that might have happened to Jas and Dylan.

"All circuits are presently busy. Please hang up and—"

"*Damn it!*" Steve slammed the phone down on the hook just as Jimmy turned the corner and came sprinting down the hallway.

"Let's roll, daddy-o," he shouted. "Orders just came in." Jimmy, already in his flight suit, was pumped full of adrenaline, but he calmed himself when he noticed Steve was torn up about something. "Wassup?"

Steve didn't try to hide his feelings. "I can't get through to my parents' house or to Jasmine. She was supposed to be here *hours* ago, man."

Jimmy approached his friend carefully, as he would a spooked thoroughbred race horse. "Hey brother," he said laying a hand on Steve's shoulder, "didn't you hear what happened? These freakazoid spacemen took Los Angeles out. Blew it up. Did the same thing to Washington, San Francisco, and New York. They're packing some very serious firepower, bro."

When he heard the news, he pressed his hands to his head. "No," he moaned, "don't tell me that, man. Oh, I fucked up, Jimmy. I fucked everything up. Why didn't I just put her in the car and bring her with me?" Steve kicked a nearby vending machine a couple of times, then punched himself in the forehead. "What the hell was I thinking?"

Jimmy grabbed him by the shoulders and slammed him up against the wall, shocking him temporarily out of his anger. "Listen. She might still show up. If she was on her way here, maybe she got out in time. But either way, don't you go ballistic on me. We still have a job to do." He let go of his friend's uniform and backed away. Steve was looking straight at him, but his mind was obviously elsewhere. Jimmy didn't know what else to say, so he decided to give him some space. "There's a meeting in J201 in five minutes. Be there."

Fifteen minutes later, Steve stood outside the briefing room. After a deep breath, he threw the door open and sauntered in, his old cocky self. In all, there were thirty-five pilots sitting at school desks listening to Lieutenant Colonel Watson feed them intelligence about the enemy. Watson, muscular and fifty, was one of those spit and polish marines who expected everything to be by the book and wasn't real bashful about criticizing you if you did it differently. He never knew exactly what to think of the Hiller/Franklin team. They were his best pilots, his aces. But they were also a pair of jokers who were constantly bending the rules.

When Steve walked in, one look at Watson stopped him dead in his tracks. The colonel wasn't in uniform. He was wearing Levi's and a black crew shirt, the clothes he'd rushed back to the base in. Caught up in the crisis, none of the other men had commented on the boss being in civvies. But when Steve walked in, the whole atmosphere of the room changed. He gave Watson a long, dead pan stare, then let his jaw drop wide open as he turned to the roomful of pilots. They had to laugh.

"Captain Hiller, you found time to join us!"

Steve knew what that meant and quickly found the seat his boys had saved him. Watson described how the mother ship was lurking behind the moon, well out of missile range, and how the city destroyer ships had detached themselves for the flight down to earth. He showed them the piss-poor satellite photo faxed to him by Space Command, but there was little he could tell them about it.

It didn't take long for Steve to figure out that Jimmy had said something to the other guys. He felt them looking at him, searching his face for signs of distraction. But Steve was too good, too smart, too much of a pro to show the slightest hint of doubt to the men he expected to follow him into battle. While Watson lectured, he leaned over real slowly and, with a sideways glance at Jimmy, asked, "You scared, man?"

"No," he whispered. "You?"

"Naw." Steve dismissed the idea, but then twisted his face up as if he were about to cry. "Actually, I am. Hold me!" That was it. The Black Knights burst out laughing in the back of the room.

Watson was just about finished when the laughter erupted. Normally he'd be angry, but he knew why Steve was acting the way he was. Besides, he didn't know if any of these boys were going to live past lunchtime.

"Captain Hiller," he asked sarcastically, "did you want to add something to the briefing?"

"Sorry, sir. It's just that we're all real anxious to get up there and kick us some alien ass."

Watson smiled. "Then let's do it."

The Black Knights marched to their planes, clearly in possession of something no amount of equipment or training could give them. They had the supreme confidence that only comes from knowing you are the very best. They came striding across the airfield in a loose cluster around their leader, Captain Steven Hiller. As they approached their fortified hangar, the huge doors rolled open exactly on cue. Inside were thirty-five F/A-18s, the USMC's elite air-fighting equipment, the gleaming planes surrounded by technicians making last-minute adjustments.

"Now remember," Steve shouted to his men before they scattered, "we're the first ones up there, so we're just gonna check 'em out. See what they got. If we run into anything real hairy, we'll break it off and regroup back here. All right, let's fly." The men broke ranks and headed for their individual planes. As their boots squeaked across the polished concrete, Steve asked over his shoulder, "Jimmy, you bring the victory dance?"

"That's a big affirmative, Captain." He pulled a long Cuban cigar out of his breast pocket, popped it in his mouth, and sparked up his lighter. It had become a ritual with them to light up these expensive, smuggled cigars after every successful mission.

"Don't get premature on me, Flash Gordon," Steve called out, climbing into the cockpit. "Remember, we don't light up till the Fat Lady sings."

"Gotcha, cap," Jimmy answered, feeling good that Steve had bounced back from the loss of his girlfriend.

As soon as Steve was alone in his plane, he doubled over in pain. He couldn't stop thinking about Jasmine and Dylan. The pilots strapped themselves in, ran through their equipment check, then fired up their engines and taxied out to the runway.

The president sat by himself in one of the conference areas, lost in thought. Connie slipped into one of the big leather chairs next to her boss. For a few moments, the two of them sat there listening to the muted roar of the engines. Everyone on the plane was suffering through their own personal state of shock, but it troubled her to see the president sitting motionless, staring blankly at the palms of his hands. She didn't need to ask what he was thinking. She already knew his conscience was torturing him. Millions of Americans had died within the last hour and he took personal responsibility.

"You played it as well as anybody could, Tom. You saved a lot of lives. There's no use in second-guessing yourself."

Whitmore didn't look up at her, didn't move a muscle. "I could have evacuated the cities hours ago. I should have." He sighed deeply. "Everything was so simple when I flew in the Gulf War. We knew what we had to do, and we did it. Nothing's simple anymore. A lot of people died today, Connie." He looked up at her for the first time. "How many of them didn't have to?"

Connie realized he was in no mood to be comforted. Instead, she showed her support by staying with him, sitting quietly until General Grey came down the walkway. Before he could deliver his news, the president looked up and asked eagerly, "Is there any news on my wife?"

Grey's face lost all its strength. He hesitated for a moment before delivering the blow. "The helicopter still hasn't arrived at Nellis and there's been no radio contact. I'm very sorry." The general looked down at the tops of his shoes and added, "I've instructed the tower at Nellis to send out a search plane to look for the beacon signal." Each of the presidential helicopters was equipped with an isotope-powered signal beacon allowing the authorities to trace it in the event of a highjacking, but so far nothing had shown up on the radar screens. Either the cloud of debris and smoke in the air around Los Angeles was blocking the signal, or, as Grey suspected, the machine had been hit so hard that everything, including the titanium casing around the transmitter, was blown to shreds.

All three of them were positive now that the First Lady

had been killed in the blast. The president's face lost all its color. He felt like he'd just been kicked in the gut. But he was still the leader of his nation and he responded by quickly refocusing on his duty. "What other news have you got?"

"The fighters are in the air."

Whitmore took a deep breath, got to his feet, and followed the general to the rear of the plane. Everything had just gotten a lot simpler. It was time to make war.

The two men stepped into the military command center set up aboard Air Force One. In sharp contrast to the muted colors and executive comforts on the rest of the aircraft, the command center was a tight space crammed to the gills with sophisticated equipment that hissed, blinked, oscillated, and scanned. From floor to ceiling, the narrow room was buzzing with radar screens and multichannel radio consoles, technicians in headphones working at computers, maps, and a small glass war table along one wall on which they could keep track of enemy positions.

Nimziki was already inside, staring down into the lights of the war table, studying the movements of the city destroyers. The expression on his face was somewhere between sorrow and disgust. Without being able to pinpoint what it was in Nimziki's attitude, Whitmore knew at a glance that the man was acting a role, trying to convince the others in the flying fortress their president was incompetent. Right from the start, he'd been using the crisis to chip away at Whitmore's self-confidence.

And it was working. Although he despised the secretary of defense on a personal level, he began to wonder whether this kind of situation would be better handled by a stone-hearted tactician like Nimziki. Whitmore felt like perhaps his instincts were beginning to fail him. His political instincts, he knew, were already in sad shape, but he was also starting to lose confidence in his combat instincts. He knew beyond question that he was a warrior, but the business of commanding whole armies was another matter. He strode over to the war table and looked into it, assessing the depth of the catastrophe.

"All satellites, microwave, and ground communications with the target cities are gone. We believe we're looking at a total loss," Grey explained in hushed, somber tones. Another slug in the president's gut.

Maintaining his composure, Whitmore looked up at one of the several tracking screens.

"Where are the fighters?"

Grey checked with a technician quickly before calling out, "ETA with target is four minutes."

Nimziki crossed the room and sat down at one of the radio consoles, putting on a set of headphones for a phone call to NORAD and the joint chiefs.

Flying through pockets of mild turbulence over the Midwest, the 747 experienced some slight shuddering. The unsteadiness went completely unnoticed by the men inside the command center, but out in the passenger area, David suffered through each lift and fall as if it was the Coney Island Roller coaster. His face was covered with sweat and he had a barf bag, emblazoned with the presidential seal, lying ready on his lap. Connie sat nearby, making a string of phone numbers on her cellular. Julius kept a watch out the window, trying to enjoy the view, but David's behavior was becoming an embarrassment.

"It's Air Force One, for crying out loud," he said in disgust, "and still you get airsick?"

"Dad, please. Don't talk."

Either Julius didn't hear him, or he didn't care. "Look at me," he stood up in the aisle and pounded his fist against his stomach, "solid as a rock. Good weather, bad weather, doesn't matter." Then, with David looking weakly up at him, he used his hands to illustrate his story. "We can go up and down, up and down and it doesn't get to me. Back and forth, side to side…"

David's eyes went wide and watery as he watched his father show all the ways a plane ride could make you sick to your stomach. Suddenly, he and his barf bag hightailed it toward the restrooms at the rear of the plane. Julius looked at Connie. "What did I say?"

Connie slid into the seat beside her father-in-law. "He still gets airsick, huh?"

"Hodophobia. Fear of travel, that's what he calls it."

"Listen," Connie reached across the seat and took the old man's hand, "in all the excitement, I haven't had a chance to thank you two. You saved a lot of lives. Mine included."

Julius leaned closer and smiled mischievously. 'Think nothing of it, *Spanky*."

"You mean *Spunky*." She laughed. "Haven't heard that in a long time. He told you about that?"

He checked to see who might be listening, then confided a secret to her. "As soon as he figured out this thing with the signal, all he could think about was getting to you. There's still love there, I think."

Connie sighed. "Love was never our problem."

"'All you need is love,'" Julius quoted. "That's John Lennon, a smart man. Shot in the back. Very sad."

Connie nodded in agreement, trying to conceal a smile.

Four hours after the blast came ripping through the tunnel, sealing them inside a vast tomb, Jasmine thought she had finally found an exit.

She had lifted the wire grating and climbed down into the labyrinth of storm drainage pipes that crisscrossed the city. The concrete passageways had flat floors, twelve-foot ceilings, and absolutely no light. There was the sound of trickling water and the faint smell of oil. At first, Jasmine tried to convince Boomer to lead the way through the pitch darkness, but the dog was a coward, leaving it to her to feel their way along. The moist walls were full of damp, slimy surprises. They had moved slowly along for a few hundred feet, when Jasmine heard something that sounded like footsteps. Her heart turned to stone as the idea occurred to her that the invaders might already be in the sewer with her.

She knelt down and put her hand over Dylan's mouth, whispering very low, "Listen."

The smell of the gunpowder in Dylan's fireworks reminded her there was a book of matches in his backpack. As quietly as she could, she unzipped the pencil pouch, found the matches, and lit one. The chamber was empty in both directions. The match burned low and was extinguished by an imperceptible breeze. Realizing a breeze must mean an opening to the outside, she led her family forward as quietly as possible, listening for more footsteps. She picked her son up and could feel how scared he was becoming.

"You're doing a great job, baby, keep quiet." Any other six-year-old kid would be bawling his eyes out by now, Jasmine thought.

Creeping steadily along the wall, Jasmine's senses were on full alert. Several times, she thought she heard the footsteps again. Each time, she lit another match and saw nothing. Then she sensed a faint flow of air brushing across her face. She set Dylan down and searched the walls with her hands until she found an opening. It was a small square gap about four feet off the ground. Cautiously, she reached an arm through the hole and explored what lay beyond. She was half expecting her fingers to find something from another, unfriendly galaxy. Suddenly she gasped and pulled her hands back. She had seen something moving through the darkness. It took her a few moments to realize it had been the faint outline of her own hands. There was light seeping through the opening which connected to another tunnel above, a way out of this watery indoor grave.

"Baby, I think there's a way out of here. I'm gonna lift you up and you tell me if you can see anything, okay?"

As soon as Dylan's head was through the opening, he yelled, "I see a light! It's outside light!"

A few minutes later, Jas was walking toward the sunlight at the open mouth of the upper tunnel. An overturned car was smoldering just outside. With Boomer in the lead, they picked their way between dangling electrical cables and hunks of mangled automobiles, crumpled like wads of used tin foil.

When they came to the mouth of the tunnel and looked out into the blinding morning light, they saw a new world: postapocalypse LA. Eighteen miles from the epicenter, the neighborhood into which the Dubrows emerged looked like Nagasaki after the bomb. Most buildings, especially those along the east-west streets where the firestorm had moved fastest, were gone, kneecapped at their foundations and blown away. The ground was the gray color of ashes and the sky was a sickly off-white color, swirling with a mixture of dust and ash. There was no sign of life, and for a moment Jasmine wondered if she and Dylan might be the last two people on earth.

The boy reached for his mother's hand and without knowing why began to cry. "Mommy, what happened?"

Jasmine picked him up and stepped out of the tunnel. "I don't know, Dylan. Mommy doesn't know."

High above, the roar of engines punished the sky. A squadron of thirty-five jet fighters was flying north, toward the spaceship over Los Angeles.

"Is that Steve in the planes?"

"It might be. I hope so. Why don't you wave, just in case."

* * *

Hugging the Orange County coastline, the Black Knights thundered toward the battle at an elevation of eleven thousand feet. The missile fields at Seal Beach looked to be operational, but inland the destruction was complete. The wall of fire had cut a large circle of devastation into the area. All around the perimeter, fires continued to burn, lit by the flaming debris the blast had sent flying through the air.

The spaceship was visible on the horizon, hanging like cast-iron doom over the ring of mountains surrounding Los Angeles. Towering columns of black smoke roiled upward from the remains of the oil refinery at Wilmington, causing the Knights to swerve a few miles out over the postcard blue Pacific, its shoreline awash with a million tons of spilled oil and twisted wreckage. Steve studied the destruction, stone-faced. It was now clear to him that Jasmine must be dead. If she had made it beyond the reach of the blast, she would have reported to El Toro long ago. He muttered something in frustration and punched the wall of the cockpit.

"Don't you sweat it, daddy-o," Jimmy's voice came through the earphones in stereo. "I'm sure she got out in time." The line stayed quiet for a long moment until Steve spoke to the entire squad.

"Here we go, boys. Time to lock and load."

Steve reached forward to the computer screen set into the instrument panel and entered a series of commands. Immediately the cantilevered doors along the belly of the fighter dropped open ready to dump their AMRAAMs (Advanced Medium-Range Air-to-Air Missiles). At the same time, a mechanical arm inside the cockpit brought a sighting device to within inches of the pilot's headgear. This was the scope on the plane's FLIR (Forward-

Looking InfraRed) targeting system. Looking through the eyepiece, the sky in front of him was transformed into a pulsing gray-and-yellow computer world. He brought the crosshairs down on the image of the spaceship, adjusting them until the tower was in the bull's eye.

The technicians aboard Air Force One took over the air waves. "Los Angeles attack squadron has AMRAAM missiles locked on target."

"New York and Washington squadrons also reporting lock on."

A new voice came over the radio. "Gentlemen, this is Air Force General Grey, Chief Commander of Allied Space Command. On behalf of the president of the United States, who is here aboard Air Force One, and the joint chiefs operating out of NORAD, I want to wish you all a successful mission. Godspeed. You may fire at will."

The Black Knights were still ten miles away, thirty seconds out of firing range, but the sheer enormity of the ship made them feel much closer. As the details of the ship's exterior grew clearer and more defined, so did the lump in each pilot's throat. The normally boisterous radio communication between the Knights was grimly silent.

"Hold tight," Steve told everyone, "fifteen seconds."

"Looks like one of those seventeen-year ticks we get down in Charlotte," drawled one of the pilots, trying to lighten the mood.

"We'll let's do a little exterminating," Steve held them steady, "five more seconds... and... *fire!*"

The AMRAAMs dropped away and went sprinting out ahead. Radar targeted, they banked slightly toward the target area like a school of minnows swooping to attack a giant gray whale. With their payloads away, the F-18s began to pull up. Few of the pilots seriously expected a ship of this size to go down all at once. The mission called for them to hit the ship in several different areas, reconnoiter to see which type of strike had done the most damage, then provide intelligence to the next wave of attack planes, already sitting on the runway at El Toro. As the F-18s banked away, they kept a careful watch on their missiles. Suddenly, a quarter mile from their target, they all exploded at the same time.

"Damn it!"

"I didn't even see them fire," Jimmy said, obviously impressed. When the smoke began to clear, it was obvious that the alien ship had sustained no damage.

Steve radioed back to Air Force One. "Command, this is Knight One. The target appears to have shot our AMRAAMs down. Zero damage to target. Repeat: zero damage. We're going to switch over to Sidewinders and take it in a little closer."

"Good call, Knight One," Grey replied. "Spread formation."

"Six times five, fellas. Six times five."

The smaller Sidewinder missiles were short-range munitions that would give the spacecraft a tougher test of its air-to-air defense capabilities. This time, instead of thirty bombs, the Knights would give them one hundred and eighty to shoot at. The squadron broke into six separate groups, roaring off in different directions to surround the fifteen-mile-wide disk. It made sense that if the aliens had air-to-air defenses, they'd be located in the tower at the nose of the craft. When everyone was in position, Steve gave the order to charge.

"Everybody check your radar, we're starting from seven miles out. Let's bring it in closer this time. Launch at one mile."

One mile? That's a comfortable distance when you're standing still, but when you're streaking along at four hundred miles per hour on a collision course with something a hundred times larger than the Superdome, it doesn't leave much margin for error. Steve knew that was shaving it pretty close, but he was hungry to inflict some damage on the craft before they headed back to the base.

"Attack!"

At the signal, all thirty jet fighters wheeled in unison and rocketed toward the spaceship, moving in from all sides. Looking through the scopes on their FLIR systems, the pilots nervously watched the numbers count down on their "Distance to Target" displays, the yellow sky disappearing into a growing blot of gray. When it felt like they were right on top of the craft, the one mile marker clicked in, triggering the Sidewinders to fire automatically. Six missiles blasted forward from each ship, their solid rocket fuel leaving a thin contrail in their wake. Almost at once, they reached the same quarter-mile perimeter and, like the AMRAAMs, exploded as a group.

"Pull up! Pull up!!" Steve screamed. 'They got a shield!!" From his front row seat, he suddenly realized why the missiles weren't hitting. Yanking back on the controls, Hiller threw the plane into a right angle turn straight up, the kind of turn that holds you against a seat as if an elephant was sitting on your lap. Twenty-nine Knights made the turn in time. The last man, Zolfeghari, came in too fast. Trying to duck under a slower plane ahead, the hull of his jet did a belly flop against an invisible force field, splattering his plane into an explosion of jet fuel that spilled down the side of the invisible shield.

Steve's group streaked vertically up the face of the tower. "They must have some kind of protective shield surrounding their hull. Let's head home."

But it wasn't going to be that easy. As the squad continued up the face of the tower, a set of massive doors were opening. They pulled back fast, as if yanked open by the strong hands of a giant, and from the opening came a storm of small attacker planes. Forty or fifty pearl gray ships came darting out of the port, single file. They were exiting the city destroyer through the exact airspace Steve and his men had already committed to using.

As he headed into the cross-fire intersection, Steve looked toward the open door and saw the next attacker speeding toward him, the face of the plane almost at his canopy window, bearing down like a huge, hungry insect. By the time he braced himself for the impact he was already one hundred yards beyond the danger point. The next three pilots made it through, but the fourth, a man called "Big Island" Tubman didn't. His jet collided head-on with one of the disk-shaped ships, causing a thunderous explosion right at the city destroyer's front door. While Tubman's plane fragmented on impact, the enemy fighter remained intact. It wobbled forward, as if momentarily stunned, before regaining its balance and flying off as if nothing had happened.

On his way through the cross-traffic, Steve had glimpsed a massive staging area inside the city destroyer. The ship's attack bay looked like an indoor airport, with hundreds of the small attackers parked in clusters along the walls. The monumental architecture of the room reminded him of some sort of hive or nest. Adjusting the yaw to flip his F-18 upside-down, Steve watched the gray planes pour into the sky. Instead of moving in a stable formation, the pack, now perhaps one hundred strong, bobbed up and down, weaving from side to side. Seen from a distance, they seemed to flutter like a swarm of bats. Without warning, they broke off in different directions to answer the attack on their ship.

"Mayday! Mayday! Enemy planes in the sky. Coming out of the tower." A shriek of light whizzed past Steve's plane, then another. "What the fudge?" He craned his neck around and saw one of the hungry-looking gray ships had come out of nowhere and slipped in behind him.

"Check six," Jimmy warned him. "Check your six, Stevie."

"I see him." Steve knew he had to think fast. The whole group of American planes was still moving toward a rendezvous over the top of the city destroyer and the faster enemy ships were surrounding them. Should he have the squad meet at the top where they could defend one another, or would that make them sitting ducks in a shooting gallery? He'd never seen a situation like this and didn't know which tactic to order. Multiplying his confusion was the fact that he had been made by the alien pilot in no time flat. Steve considered himself the craftiest pilot he knew, and to be outfoxed at the very beginning of a dogfight was another new experience for him.

"Evasive maneuvers!" he yelled, jamming his own plane into a sudden sideways loop only milliseconds before a barrage of laser shots sailed by. "Stay in your groups! Keep your spacing."

The gray enemy planes, gliding like metallic stingrays, were firing pulses of super-condensed energy, deadly balls of light that screamed as they sizzled through the sky, leaving a bright white trail. Trying to lose his pursuer, Steve bobbed and weaved his way toward the edge of the black city destroyer. In the commotion, he saw a pair of abrupt explosions as two of his team were blown away. At flight school, they'd emphasized over and over how quickly air battles were won or lost, how drastically they could change in only a few seconds. Here was the proof. The proud Knights, champions of the sky a moment before, were now having their asses handed to them, hunted down and killed. Disorganized and on the run, they broke into pairs, covering one another as they ran for cover.

Steve plunged into a nose dive, accelerating straight toward the ground. His attacker followed. As the blackened earth that had been Los Angeles rushed closer,

Steve fought the impulse to slow down. He remembered what happened to the Apache helicopter during Operation Welcome Wagon and increased his speed. In the next ten seconds he would be either very lucky or very dead.

"Where you at, Jimmy?"

"Right where you need me, Stevie, on this motherfucker's tail. If you can straighten him out for me, I'll waste him."

Steve ceased evasive maneuvers and flew in a straight line for as long as he dared—a total of about 1.5 seconds. Fortunately, that was all Jimmy needed.

"Away!" he yelled. As Steve peeled away into a starboard bank, Jimmy's Sidewinder shot forward and overtook the alien attacker. Five yards before the missile reached the surface of the ship, it exploded. The ship flipped over in midair, staggered forward for a moment, then zipped back into action as if nothing had happened.

"Shit! These little guys got shields, too!"

Steve came out of his dive and looped upward, ready to take a shot at the disoriented attacker plane. In the distance, he watched two more of the American fighters shredded by tracer fire. By the time he was in position again, Jimmy had an enemy on his tail.

"Jimmy, roll right. I'll cover."

Jimmy barrel rolled away just in time to avoid a new burst of tracer fire. Steve brought the crosshairs down on one of the gray stingray planes and fired another sidewinder. The alien pilot banked away, but the tracking system inside the missile chased him down and detonated against his rear protective shield. Radar-guidance was about the only hardware advantage the humans had in this dogfight, and it wasn't buying them much time. For a few seconds, Hiller and Franklin flew unmolested along the crest of the Hollywood Hills. Above them, they watched the fluttering gray ships hunting in packs, tearing the F-18s, and their brother pilots, to ribbons. The sky was littered with tracer fire and the fiery wreckage of America's elite air strike force. A new pair of attackers came racing toward them from above the ship, unleashing a hailstorm of firepower.

"Maybe we can outrun them. Follow my lead."

"Let's run, then. Here they come at two o'clock, Stevie."

The powerful jet engines of the F/A-18s surged into a higher gear when the Americans hit the SuperCruise control. They shot forward, speeding east over the mountains and leaving the enemy aircraft far behind. Or so they thought. As the planes accelerated, both pilots experienced the phenomenon of "pulling a few gees." One gee is equal to the force of gravity at sea level. Moving from below Mach speed all the way up to Mach 2 in a matter of a few seconds was something like being strapped to the nose cone of a moon rocket. It was the extreme physical discomfort of feeling your organs crash backwards against the seat as the plane rocketed forward. Ears, lips, cheeks—everything tried to slide backwards off their faces. The landscape below them rushed past in a blur. When they were up to speed, both men felt dizzy and slightly nauseated. Steve struggled to get a look behind them. The stingray ships were close behind and gaining.

"Jimmy, kick it, man. They're gaining on us."

"We're already over Mach Two." Jimmy sounded woozy.

"So push it!" Once again, the two pilots were flattened against the backs of their cockpit chairs. The instrument panels showed that they were pushing their planes way beyond the intended limits, zooming out across the California desert at twice the speed of sound.

"Gotta get off the ground, partner. I'm… uh, I'm feeling… I don't know." Jimmy was losing consciousness. He knew increasing his altitude would make the landscape, now flashing by at a dizzying pace, appear to move slower.

Steve thought the attackers showed some reluctance about getting too close to the ground, but Jimmy was already building altitude, so he followed.

"Keep it straight, Jimmy, you're veering right."

"You get out, Stevie."

"Don't start that crap on me. We're together all the way, you hear? But you gotta keep your speed up, man."

Steve slowed to keep him in sight, watching his jet continue to drift right. The attackers began to close in.

"We gotta go, Jimmy! Gotta push it!"

It was no use. The attackers were tucked in tight behind them, tracer fire whizzing past. Steve screamed into his microphone, begging Jimmy to wake up, but it was no use. He took a quick glance backward and saw his partner's silver jet flying itself, already miles away. Just as he was about to turn and follow, he saw the flash of light. The enemy planes had split up and the one following Jimmy had shot him down.

Steve screamed with his whole body and began shaking the controls, making the plane convulse with his anger. He rammed the engine thrusters forward so hard he bent the shaft against the stop, and still screaming, he pushed the plane to the very limit of its speed. At Mach 2-plus, the desert was a fast blur of brown scrub hills crossed by flashes of highways and small towns. It felt like being in the flight simulator with the pursuit speed setting stuck on "Impossible." For a couple of minutes, anger and pain still clouding his mind, Steve flew in a straight line without checking behind. Given the opportunity, he would have flown kamikaze, head-on into any attacker in his way. His rage subsiding, he finally checked behind and found he had a single attacker at five o'clock, trailing him patiently. He knew there was no way he could win a firefight. Escape was his only hope. But, as he flew through a cloudless sky over the vast empty stretches of Death Valley, there weren't too many places to hide. Something glinted far out on the white horizon of the desert, a city rising out of nowhere. He banked north and flew that direction. Within seconds, the distant city was beneath his plane. Steve could see enough, just enough, to tell him the city was Las Vegas.

The engines were feeling the strain. Their whining told Steve they wouldn't take this kind of punishment much longer. Still running north, he flew past what looked like a small airbase with a pair of crisscrossed runways built on a dry lake bed. A pair of radar dishes were pivoting on their towers, and it looked like there were camouflage trucks parked next to a couple of hangars. His eyes searched for any sign that they knew what was happening to him and were sending help. He didn't recognize the place at all, didn't know of any base this far north of Vegas.

Then, all at once, he knew exactly what he was going to do. He pulled a hard right over the airbase and lifted over the chain of hills that had created the lake bed ten thousand years before. He checked his compass for due east and turned in that direction. In less than two minutes, he found what he was looking for, his secret weapon: the Grand Canyon.

He cut his engines without warning. The stingray ship, surprised, sailed past as Steve executed a soft dive over the edge of the canyon wall. He drove the plane deep between the red rock walls until he was almost low enough to fish in the Colorado River, the body of water which, over millions of years, had cut this awesome, jagged wonder out of the hard desert floor. The attacker followed him down and caught up in no time.

"Okay, jerk-off. Let's have some fun."

Weaving at high speed through the twisted, eerie rock formations, Steve put on a clinic in advance aerobatics, banking, diving, and swerving like mad. The much larger attack plane followed clumsily behind, the tips of its wings chipping spires of rock into the abyss below. The alien's protective shield allowed him to make mistake after mistake and survive. Not only that, but he seemed to be getting the hang of flying through this obstacle course, managing to get off a few shots at Steve's F-18.

Feeling the pressure, Steve ducked into a much smaller side canyon. Here there was almost no room for error. The serpentine path narrowed in some places to only twice the jet's wing span. Steve knew better than to fly defensively at a time like this. He hit the gas and attacked the turns, climbing and falling with grace. He felt certain that if he kept this ballet going long enough, his clumsy dance partner would eventually plaster himself face-first against the rocks. Then a sensor on the instrument panel began flashing on and off. His fuel tank was almost empty.

"Damn it! You're really starting to burn me up, you damn Darth Vader wannabe."

Not far ahead, a massive wall of stone stood where the canyon came to a dead end. Knowing that once he was out of the canyon he was a dead man, Steve decided to go for broke. He eased off on the speed and hit a switch labeled "Fuel Drop." Reserve fuel in both tanks spewed into the air behind him, splattering the gray ship. Then he hit the afterburners, igniting the fuel in the air, leaving a trail of superheated fire in his wake. Steve looked back just in time to see the attacker burst through the wall of flame, undaunted.

"Damn you! Okay, if you're the sucker who's gonna take me out, I want to see if you can fly under cover."

Pulling the cord marked "drag chute," a large parachute suddenly shot open behind his fighter. With a lightning reflex, Steve hit the release, detaching the cords from the plane before he was rear-ended. As he hoped, the chute fluttered shapelessly in the air for a second before the attacker ran into it nose first. The alarm buzzer was now ringing in Steve's earphones, the signal that his fuel was completely gone. He felt the engines hesitate as pockets of air came through the fuel lines.

"Now let's see if you're fully equipped."

Steve unplugged his headset, tightened up his seat belt, and pointed his plane right at the dead end wall. Behind him the attacker brushed against the side of the gorge tearing the parachute away. He accelerated hard to catch the F-18.

Two hundred feet from impact, Steve shut his eyes and yanked up hard on a cord running down to the bottom of his seat. A moment later, there was an ear splitting *thwack* as the plane demolished itself against the precipice.

The alien pilot saw what was coming and swerved violently upward. He came within ten feet of cleanly scaling the wall, but instead, the stingray ship went nose to nose with a boulder one hundred times its size and lost. Sending a shower of dust and splintered rock into the air, the craft plowed into the rock, then glanced away, flipping end over end over end, crashing across the rocky desert floor until it finally came to rest, looking like a coin bent almost in half.

Still strapped in his pilot's chair, Captain Hiller laughed as loud as he could at the broken UFO. He was slowly falling through the hot Arizona morning beneath the shade of his open parachute. When he finally hit the ground, it was a quick, hard landing. Rolling over, he popped the buckles on the chair and freed himself. Wasting no time, he marched across the sand and rock toward the nearby attacker, the cicadas chirping a strange high pitched tone in the scrub brush. He was dazed, maniacal, angry.

The closer he came, the more menacing the fallen attacker appeared. It was protected by a dozen plates of armor. One of these had torn partially loose where the tail of the ship had bent upward. Beneath the gray plate, it had the raw look of a freshly skinned animal. The ship's muscles, tendons, and ligaments were actually thousands of tiny interlocking mechanical pieces. A delicate, ghastly white, they lay exposed to the sun, embedded in a thick layer of transparent, sticky gelatin.

Steve took the last few steps toward the ship slowly, hands out in front of him, feeling for the invisible protective shield. It was down. Spotting what looked like a hatch that had been broken open, he hoisted himself up onto the wing, and after seven full strides, he came to the center of the craft. With all his might, he yanked the door fully open.

Immediately, he screamed and jumped backwards. Just inside the door, struggling to pull itself out of the plane, was a living creature, an alien. A large shell-like head emerged unsteadily into the sunlight. Beneath deep empty eye sockets, the creature had a protruding snout, a tangled mask of cartilage jutting forward like the oily white roots of a tree. Moist tentacles ran off the chin and ears, feeling the edge of the escape hatch. Its thick bony neck flared outward before tapering to a point at the top of its head. A deep gash ran right up the center of the face from the chin to the tip of its pointy head, where the two halves of the skull had fused together. It looked like the result of a crossbreeding experiment between a fully armored medieval warrior and a cockroach.

After watching the repulsive animal struggle toward the sunlight for a moment, Steve performed his sworn duty. With one savage punch, he clocked the alien square in the face. With a sickening crack, the monster's bony head bounced off the side of the hatch then collapsed, knocked unconscious.

He stood over the alien's limp body until his anger and fear subsided. Eventually, he sat down and reached into his breast pocket, withdrawing a slightly damaged Victory Dance cigar. He bit off one end and spit it into the face of his unconscious enemy. Then he lit it up and took a long, angry puff.

"Now that's what I call a close encounter."

In Death Valley, the refugees spent the night milling about under the stars, locked in a thousand grim strategy sessions. They were gathered in a bone-dry valley, their RVs and trailer homes parked at odd angles to one another. All night long, groups of people congregated in the dusty glare of headlights, silhouettes holding coffee cups and shotguns, ready to defend their campground against unwanted visitors, terrestrial or otherwise. Dead Joshua trees were collected to fuel a central of bonfire around which one plan after another was proposed, hashed out, and agreed to, until some new motorist arrived with a fresh supply of rumors. Then, all their arrangements fell apart and had to be renegotiated from scratch.

Russell, for once, had done well. Not once did he mention his famous abduction, and he helped keep the others in his group focused and steady. He held fast to the very first plan they had made: drive into Las Vegas for gasoline and supplies, then get into the open space of Arizona.

By midmorning, the fifty or so trailers the Casses planned to travel with were in the final stages of preparing to leave the campground. Some were already parked alongside the road, their motors idling while the drivers stood around in weekend T-shirts and baseball caps waiting impatiently for the others. The Casse family, however, was distracted by Troy's condition. He was getting worse, the way he did when he'd had his first seizures. Blotches were coming out on his skin and although he wasn't in convulsions yet, he was starting to get awful shaky.

Miguel decided to try once more. For the third time since they arrived, he went through the camp, going door to door asking for medicine. He knew he was unlikely to find any hydrocortisone, but hoped someone might be a diabetic who could spare some insulin. Lots of people offered hydrocortisone cream, an anti-itch medicine, and were a little put off when Miguel didn't stay to explain the difference.

The morning was turning hot outside, but Troy lay in the bed shivering under a thick pile of blankets. Russell sat next to him, wiping down his forehead with a cold compress while Alicia made him some more sweet tea.

"You know, you're just like your mother used to be. She was stubborn too. She was a sweet, sweet woman— rest her soul—but when it came time to take her medicine, she'd get ornerier than a mule."

Troy was scared. "I'm sorry, Dad. I shouldn't have wasted the medicine. I'm sorry."

"Hey, that's past history, Troy-boy. We'll find some more, you'll see."

"I'm not going to die like Mom, am I?"

The question caught Russell by surprise and hit him hard. Before he could dismiss the idea and reassure his weakening son, he remembered sitting at Maria's bedside telling her the same thing.

"You're going to be fine," Alicia was adamant. "Of course you're going to get better. Don't even say that."

Miguel returned to the trailer, empty-handed. "I tried everyone. I couldn't find anything. And now everybody's packing up to leave. Some guy drove by yelling that a spaceship is heading this way."

The family looked at one another, startled by this news. "Then we'd better make ourselves scarce. We need to leave anyhow," Russell said with a nod toward the boy.

"Don't let the spaceship get us, Dad. Let's go. I'll get better."

"Our group's headed south. We're going to take back

roads the whole way, but we'll pass a hospital near Las Vegas. It's only a couple hours away, so I think we should leave now."

Russell agreed. Then a knock came on the door. Alicia edged past Miguel and stood in the doorway. On the other side of the screen was someone she recognized, a handsome boy of sixteen, with a mop of reddish hair. He had something in his hand.

"Penicillin," he announced, holding up a bottle of pills.

"Hello, Penicillin. My name's Alicia."

When he realized he was being teased, he broke out in a warm grin. "Oh. I'm Philip. Philip Oster. You remember me from last night?"

A sudden rustling noise behind her in the trailer made the boy realize his question could be taken the wrong way. He raised his voice a notch and hastily added, "You told me your little brother was sick."

That was true. After noticing each other several times during the long evening and engaging in several bouts of significant eye contact, they'd finally found the nerve to approach one another. They had a brief conversation about Troy's condition, and Philip had promised to try to help. And now there he was with a vial of penicillin.

"Anyway, I know this isn't exactly what he needs but it should keep his fever down."

Alicia glanced down at the ground, blushing. "It's really nice of you to help," she said softly, opening the screen to accept the medicine. Behind her she could feel her father looking over her shoulder. Philip took a full step backward when he saw the large, unshaven Russell staring down at him.

"I wish I—I mean, my family wishes we could do more," he stammered, "I mean, like, if—well, anyway, we're leaving in a few minutes."

Alicia's face brightened when she heard that. A little

too eagerly, she told him, "Us, too. We're going with you!" Then, hearing her father groan behind her, she added, "I mean, we're leaving, too."

"Cool." Philip smiled warmly. "That's a great old plane you guys are towing. Does it work?"

Russell had had his fill of this tender little balcony scene. "That's enough," he grumbled. "Thanks for the medicine. Now quit sniffing around and get back to your own trailer."

"Dad, please!" Alicia said through her false grin. But Philip didn't seem to mind very much. With a charming smile, he backed away from the doorstep. "So, talk to you at the next stop?"

Smitten by this gallant young man, Alicia watched him jog back to his parents' fancy RV. When he was gone, she turned around and found the Casse men, even ailing Troy, staring at her expectantly. "What?" she demanded. "I was just being nice to him because he brought us some medicine."

"Yeah, right."

NORAD, the North American Aerospace Defense system, was the safest spot in the world. Built deep within Cheyenne Mountain near Colorado Springs, it was an impregnable underground military command post, a high-tech sanctuary for the nation's leaders—the president in particular—in the event of nuclear attack. The walls of the bunker were designed to withstand the force of a nearby nuclear blast by themselves. Buried, as they were, deep below the surface of the earth, they offered even greater protection. Everything could be controlled from the giant war room, which was at the heart of the facility. Even if every city in the U.S. were to be wiped out, the technicians in Colorado would be able to track enemy movement, coordinate troops stationed overseas, and launch several different kinds of missile attacks. The vice president, the joint chiefs of staff, their advisers and families were already safely sheltered in the mountain, waiting for the president to arrive. NORAD computers were linked to those aboard Air Force One.

Approximately twelve minutes into the bloody, one-sided dogfights in the skies over New York, Los Angeles, San Francisco, and Washington, the technicians crowded into Air Force One's command center began losing the ability to coordinate the nation's military response. First, they lost radio contact with the surviving F-18s. Next, global radar capability was interrupted. Finally, they lost their links with NORAD and had to switch over to microwave telephone.

"They must be targeting our satellites. We're losing all satellite communication, tracking, and mapping."

They switched over to Air Force One's ULR (UpLooking Radar) then, and watched a sweep screen showing the positions of the most important Comsats. One by one, they were vanishing. The only explanation was that the invaders were up there, 33,000 miles into the heavens, the altitude where a satellite could stay in geosynchronous orbit over a fixed spot on earth. As the awkward multimillion dollar transmitters floated past, they were being blasted out of the sky.

The military had satellites stationed in different orbital paths at other altitudes, but switching over required ground crews in several locations to retarget receptor dishes. Before that work could even be ordered, the bases themselves came under massive, virulent bombardment. The last thing Air Force One heard from El Toro was the flight tower screaming, "Incoming! Hostile incoming!" Before a single plane could get off the ground, the base was transformed to a smoldering ruin. Slowly, the president's flying fortress was being cut off from the rest of the world.

Moving to the circle of chairs just outside the command center, Whitmore and his advisers discussed their dwindling list of response options. Connie and Julius sat within earshot, listening carefully to the tense conversation.

General Grey spoke to one of his aides. "I don't care how you do it, but I want the line to NORAD reestablished as quickly as possible. Get it done!"

"Yes, sir," the soldier said crisply before returning to the squawking mayhem of the control room.

"What's the report from Peterson?" the president asked, referring to Peterson Air Force Base near Colorado Springs, where they were scheduled to land in less than thirty minutes, the base closest to NORAD.

The demoralized expression on Grey's face told more than his words. "We're continuing to evacuate as many of our forces from the bases as possible, but we've already sustained deep losses."

"Damn it." The president slammed his fist down on the arm of the chair. "Not only do they know *where* to hit us, they've got the order of priorities down. They're moving right down a damned checklist."

"Yes, sir," Grey allowed, "it's an extremely well-planned attack. They seem to understand our defense system."

David came stumbling out of the bathroom with a sickly look on his face. He overheard the conversation and stopped in the passageway, hoping for more. What he heard next made him forget about his queasy stomach. Nimziki stood up and walked to the center of the conference room, speaking in his imperial tone.

"As you know, I've been speaking directly with Commander Foley and the other joint chiefs since they arrived at NORAD." His every sentence was apparently calculated to make the president look bad. "We agree that there is only one sane and prudent course of action. We must launch a large-scale counteroffensive with a full nuclear strike. Hit them with everything we've got."

It was another Nimzikian moment of badly executed theater. He was trying to force the president's hand by presenting the plan as if it were a foregone conclusion. Whitmore resented the attempted manipulation, but was too interested in the idea to criticize the man.

"Above American soil? You understand the implications of that move? We'd be killing tens of thousands, maybe hundreds of thousands, of innocent American civilians."

Utterly calm, almost amused, Nimziki had already planned his answer. "To be perfectly honest with you, Mr. President, I expected you'd balk at the idea. But if we don't strike back soon, there won't be much of an America left to defend. In my conversations with the joint—"

"Sir," General Grey's aide interrupted, returning from the tank.

"It can wait, soldier," Nimziki shot back, although technically he had no authority to do so.

"It's NORAD, sir," the man continued, his face white with fear. "It's gone, sir. They've taken it out." It took a moment for the idea to sink in. The group went from confused to stunned to mortified.

"That's not possible..."

"My God, the vice president, the joint chiefs."

"Perhaps their communication systems are out, but all of NORAD can't be *gone*."

The aide explained more fully. "I have it from pilots out of Peterson. They were in the sky when alien attack planes massed over NORAD and began firing continuously for several minutes. Eventually, the entire complex was exposed and destroyed. Shortly thereafter, Peterson itself came under attack and they lost radio contact."

"Isn't Peterson where we're heading? We need a new destination!"

"Mr. President, we must launch a nuclear attack,"

Nimziki insisted, highly agitated. To make sure his message got through, he hit below the belt, adding, "A delay now would be even more costly than when you waited to evacuate the cities."

The president shot out of his chair and stood nose to nose with Nimziki. 'That is *not* the issue here." He was on the verge of punching the taller man when they were interrupted.

"You're not serious!" David came around the corner, outraged. 'Tell me you're not considering firing a bunch of damn nuclear weapons at our own people." Connie reacted immediately. She bolted toward her estranged husband and tried to move him backwards, "David, don't…" she warned, remembering the time he'd slugged Whitmore. If he did that again, it would be a federal crime. She knew it took a lot to get David riled up, but once his fuse was lit, he almost always exploded.

"If you start detonating nukes," he went on, shouting, "so will the rest of the world. Do you have any idea what that amount of fallout will do to the planet? Think! Do you know what the long-term consequences will be? Why don't we just blow our brains out right here?"

David, slim but deceptively powerful at six feet four inches, easily brushed Connie to one side and advanced across the floor. General Grey quickly put himself between the hysterical computer genius and his president. Although he was the much smaller man, he was fully prepared to knock David to the carpet if necessary.

"Mr. Levinson," his voice was controlled, stern, "let me remind you that you are a guest here."

Ignoring him, David raged on. "This is insanity! We don't even know if nuclear explosions will dent their armor, but we know for certain it's going to kill *us*. There won't be anything left!"

Nimziki had suffered this idiot long enough. Accustomed to being obeyed, he pointed at David and boomed, "Shut your damn mouth and sit your ass down this instant!"

His insulting tone of voice backfired on him. It brought Julius into the fray. "Don't you tell him to shut up! You'd all be dead right now, blown to high heaven, if not for my David."

The old man shook a finger in the face of the secretary of defense. Connie, sensing all hell was about to break loose, ran back across the room and grabbed her father-in-law. The septuagenarian stood his ground, giving the Washington hotshots a piece of his mind.

"I blame all of you for what's happening. You did nothing to prevent this! You knew! You knew it was coming and yet you did nothing! Now you attack my son."

Julius's strange outburst probably prevented an all-out fist fight aboard the presidential aircraft. Like so many things he did, it was impossible to know how much was accident and how much was by design. The image of him shaking a bony finger in Nimziki's face while being dragged backwards by Connie temporarily distracted everyone from their anger. The president knew it was time to get back to business. He took a breath, regained his composure, and answered the old man's charges.

"Sir, there wasn't much more we could have done. We can be blamed for a lot of things, but in this instance, we were taken totally by surprise."

"Don't give me that taken-by-surprise crapola. Since nineteen-fifty-what-ever you've had that flying saucer, the one that crashed in New Mexico."

"Oh, Dad, please!" David was trying to make an impassioned plea to save the planet, and his father was starting in with the UFO hogwash he got from watching too much TV.

"What was it," Julius kept right on talking, "Roswell?

That's right, Roswell, New Mexico. You found the spaceship, the three alien bodies, the whole schmeer. Then everything got locked up in a bunker, the... oh, what was it?... fifty-one. Area Fifty-One! That was the name. Area Fifty-One. For years you knew and you didn't do *nothing*!"

For the first time in a long while, President Whitmore smiled. Every month or so, he'd be shaking hands with some citizen who'd ask him about the notorious Area 51. He'd looked into it, and learned that it was all mythology, an elaborate conspiracy theory concocted by UFO nuts.

"Regardless of what you've read in the tabloids, Mr. Levinson, there were never any spaceships recovered by the government. You can take my word for it: there is an Area Fifty-One but there are no secret flying saucers." The president looked around the room, sharing his amusement with the others. It didn't last long.

"Uh, excuse me Mr. President," Nimziki said, swallowing hard, "but that's not entirely accurate." Shocked, everyone looked at the former head of the CIA, the man who knew where all the skeletons were buried, waiting for him to explain.

As soon as Jasmine Dubrow came out into the bright dusty air of the ruined city, she told Dylan to wait with Boomer, then climbed an earthen embankment up to what remained of the freeway. From this vantage point she surveyed the damage, and what she saw sent a long chill down her spine. Everything was gone, pulverized down to a smoking gray rubble. The massive black ship still hung in the air, a tranquil death angel cloaking the city with its wings. Downtown Los Angeles had been scoured completely away by the blast. The ring of skyscrapers and historic buildings where a multitude had worked each day was now a blackened depression in the earth. She looked away and felt the delicate ocean breeze on her face. In the distance, buildings still stood, their windows blown out and dwindling fires trailing rags of smoke into the morning air.

Studying the pattern of destruction, she suddenly understood how very lucky she had been. For miles in every direction, the devastation was nearly absolute. Houses built along the freeway had been torn in half, and everything inside, furniture, water heaters, photographs, half-read books, the dishes in the sink, and sleeping children had been vacuumed out into the firestorm and incinerated. A refrigerator, one of the old-fashioned kind with rounded corners, had landed upright in the middle of the freeway, badly warped by the heat. Absently, Jas looked inside and found a jar of mustard still in its place on the door shelf. *Strange,* she thought, *what survives.*

She hurried back down the slope and found Dylan examining something on the ground. When she came closer, she saw it was some sort of animal, probably a dog, its body torn apart and still smoking. Dylan wanted to know what it was, but Jasmine picked him up and carried him away without a word. With Boomer leading the way, they scouted around for a few minutes, until they found a parking garage full of utility vehicles. The garage was built into the sheltered side of the freeway, and the dump trucks, bulldozers, and mobile cranes were still where they'd been parked for the three-day holiday weekend. The vehicles closest to the outside had been charred in the firestorm, tires and wires melted away. But deeper inside the cavernous structure, Jasmine found an old eight-wheeler, a flatbed truck with the emergency red paint job still in mint condition. She climbed up into the cab and searched around until she hit the jackpot. The keys fell into her lap when she lowered the sun visor. She yelled for Dylan and Boomer to get in, then she fired up the engine and barreled toward the barrier of equipment and a collapsed tin roof. She slammed through the debris and into the sunlight.

Within a few minutes, she had found what remained of a wide boulevard and was bumping along in a southerly direction, swerving around collapsed storefronts and driving over half-incinerated telephone poles. Every few minutes she came to a road block the old truck couldn't clear. She would stop and climb up onto the hood, searching for a clear path through the debris. It was like trying to get out of a labyrinth.

After three or four miles, she found her first survivor, a man about fifty years old dressed in what was left of a three-piece suit. She found him sitting quietly by the side of the road. He had been cut up pretty badly, probably by flying glass. She couldn't tell for sure because the man wouldn't say a word. She helped him into the back of the truck, where he sat down quietly. They drove on. Over the next half an hour, she found six more survivors. Three of them accepted her offer of a ride, glad to be with someone who knew somewhere else to go. She put the passengers in the back, while Dylan and Boomer rode up front in the cab.

In time, they found their first street sign. A steel traffic light, knocked flat against the earth by the blast, had a blue shingle still attached. Jas jumped down and used her boot to wipe away the dust and ash: SEPULVEDA BLVD. That gave her a better idea of where she was. She looked up at the sun, then out toward where she guessed the ocean would be, trying to get her bearings.

"Repent, sinners!"

Jasmine spun around, heart pounding. Not far off, a derelict-looking man was standing on a giant pile of bricks, the collapsed side wall of an aging movie theater.

Somehow, he'd found a piece of unburned cardboard and scrawled a biblical quotation onto it. In the other hand he held a tire iron, the kind with four prongs, brandishing it like a crucifix. From Jasmine's point of view, the crumbling interior wall of the movie house was directly behind him. Painted with a lavish mural of cowboys in old Western scenes, it made an eerie, incongruous backdrop.

"The end hast come! Almighty God speaketh his word and the end hast come!"

"I'm headed down to El Toro. Hop in the back, if you want to come."

"He has spoken in tongues of fire," he screamed toward the sky. "Yours is the torment of the Scorpion, it is the end!" The tortured creature, still shouting into the void, turned his back on the people in the red truck.

Reluctantly, Jasmine left him there. She decided it wasn't her business to try and save any more of these people. But she hadn't driven a city block when she spotted another possible survivor. An olive drab army helicopter, belly up, lay smoldering in what was once the parking lot of a minimall.

Jas and the silent man got out of the truck and approached the wrecked chopper. Dangling in their shoulder harnesses, the pilot and copilot were both dead, crushed to death. But laying on the ceiling of the smashed machine was a woman in an expensive blue dress. Jasmine crawled inside and dragged the woman out. Dried blood was streaked all around her nose, mouth, and ears, sure signs of internal hemorrhaging. Laying her gently on the ground, Jas and the silent man looked at each other. They both recognized the woman as First Lady Marilyn Whitmore.

As they were preparing to lift and carry her back to the truck, Dylan came jogging toward them, "Hey," Jasmine shouted, "I thought I told you to stay in the truck."

Then the unmistakable sound of a pump-action

shotgun being cocked sliced through the silence. Jasmine wheeled around to see a beer-bellied white man in a hunting jacket approaching. Two more men, dressed in filthy camouflage gear, trailed along behind him, one of them pushing a battered shopping cart piled high with treasures they'd scavenged from the rubble. They looked like a trio of greasy vultures who had come in after the blast to pick through what little was left.

"Looks like we've solved our transportation problems. That's a damn nice truck you got there. Are the keys in it?" the armed man demanded, speaking with a mountain accent. An angry white redneck threatening her with a gun was the last thing Jasmine needed right now. Somehow, she forced herself to smile warmly. "Hey, you're welcome to come with us. We're leaving here anyway, headed south down to—"

"Keep your damn mouth shut, you black bitch," he screamed, training the gun at her head. His partners ran over to the truck like overgrown children. While the larger one began dragging the injured out of the flatbed, the other one checked the ignition switch. Boomer, still in the cab, nuzzled up to the intruder, hoping to get petted.

"Keys aren't in the truck," he yelled to the man with the gun.

"All right," he turned to Jasmine and the silent man, "I'm gonna ask nicely once more, and then I'm gonna blow your brains out. Which one of you has the goddamn keys to the goddamn truck?"

"Repent, sinners! The end has come!" The crazed preacher had followed the truck down the street. "Almighty God's judgment is upon you!"

"Back off, mister. This ain't none of your business," warned the lead vulture.

As the preacher stalked forward, Jasmine pulled her son close to her, easing one of the FyreStix out of his backpack.

"You cannot go against the will of God," the ragged

evangelist frothed, "you cannot resist His word!"

"Sure I can." The hunter laughed, pulling the trigger.

A load of buckshot knocked the preacher backward with a hole in the middle of his chest. The explosion echoed across the empty, ruined landscape. Jasmine had sparked one of the matches, but when the rocket wouldn't light, she quickly pinched the match out between her fingers. The man with the gun looked as surprised as anyone by what he'd done. He'd obviously never shot anyone before. His buddies looked on nervously.

"Now you'd better hand over those keys, bitch."

Boomer, the world's worst guard dog, had been making nice-nice with the rednecks until the gunshot sounded. Suddenly he came charging from the direction of the truck, snarling and barking at the man with the gun. Perhaps the guy was a dog lover, or maybe he felt guilty about having killed an innocent man. For whatever reason, he hesitated to shoot the dog.

"Call off the dog," he shouted, the barrel of the shotgun inches from the retriever's bared teeth. "Call him off, or I'll shoot him, I swear to God."

Jasmine reached down and lit the FyreStix. The blast of brightly colored gunpowder shot out the end with more force than she expected. She pointed the ten feet of sparkling fire right at the gunman, moving in on him at the same time. The burning sulfur stuck to his face and hands. Involuntarily, he dropped the gun as his arms went up to protect his face. Jasmine picked up the gun, broke open the breech to check the cartridges, and snapped it back closed before the redneck had quit screaming. When he looked up again, the tables had turned.

"This *bitch* was born down in Alabama with a daddy who loved to hunt." She worked the pump action on the gun. "So don't you think for a minute I don't know how to use this thing." She squeezed the trigger, sending a shot sailing past the fat man's ear. She pumped the gun again, the spent shells twirling to the ground, new ones moving into the chambers. "Now why don't you take a nice long walk back the same way you came."

The three vultures were only too happy to oblige. They jogged away over a short hill, turning to curse Jasmine before disappearing for good.

As she and the silent man carried the unconscious Mrs. Whitmore back to the truck, the First Lady's mouth opened. Quietly, almost choking, she said with a smile, "That was brave."

Steve lowered his shoulder and strained against the weight of the straps. He'd wrapped the unconscious alien in his ejection seat parachute and was towing him across the scorching sand, muttering the whole way.

"Ya know, this is supposed to be my weekend off. But nooooo! You had to come down here with an attitude, and now you got me out here pullin' your potato-chip munchin', slime-drippin' ass across the burning desert with your dreadlocks hanging out the back." The creature's long tentacle arms had worked their way free and were dragging limply behind. "Think you can just come down here, acting all big and bad, and mess with me and my guys?" He turned around like he was expecting an answer. His anger rising, he screamed, "I coulda been at a barbecue, you freak!" He staggered toward the orange nylon chute and delivered one vicious kick after another to the lump of comatose biomass wrapped inside until he had to stop for breath. Panting, he added, "but I'm not mad."

Drenched in sweat, Steve knew he was going to need water pretty soon. Leaving his package behind, he grunted up a short hill and surveyed the desert. Empty brown hills stretched away to infinity beneath powder blue sky. Heat lifting off the desert floor shimmered like silver ocean waves. Just before he trudged back down to gather his prisoner of war, a glinting light caught his eye. It came from the top of a hill several miles away. Soon he realized what it was: traffic. There was a road less than a thousand yards in front of him. He dashed back for his cargo and began a furious charge toward the road. He arrived a few minutes later, sat down at the edge of the old two-lane highway, and watched in amazement as an armada of a hundred trailers, campers, vans, and trucks rolled steadily closer.

"Hey, mucous-head, our ride's here." Steve put a big fat grin on his face and stood in the center of the road, waving his arms. "Gonna have to run me over if you won't stop."

Fortunately, the mile-long caravan rolled to a gradual halt. Steve walked up to one of the lead vehicles, the one towing an old biwing airplane behind it. "Captain Steven Hiller, United States Marine Corps."

The driver, a big curly headed guy with a sarcastic sense of humor, leaned out his window and asked, "Need a lift?"

Two minutes later, Steve was surrounded by two dozen curious members of the caravan. He took a long slug of water before explaining what he had in the parachute. That got their attention. He told them he needed to get into Las Vegas, to Nellis Air Force Base, that it was a matter of urgent national interest.

"Sorry, soldier," an old guy with a rifle on his hip said, "they told on the radio that Nellis got all shot up. It's wiped out."

Steve walked over to the parachute and gave it two more swift kicks. "All right, then, when I was flying past here, I spotted an airbase next to an old lake bed. I need somebody to take me over there."

Several people produced maps of the region. Although some were quite detailed, none of them showed an airbase.

According to the maps, the whole area was nothing more than a missile testing area, off-limits to civilians. To make matters worse, there was not one, but *four* dry lake beds.

"Trust me, it's there," Steve told them.

The whole thing was too spooky for most of them. They wanted to *get away* from the aliens, not chauffeur them around. The leaders of the group were willing to take Steve and his package with them, but they weren't going to waste precious fuel on a wild goose chase through a restricted military area.

That's when the guy with the sarcastic attitude came to Steve's defense. He pushed a couple of the map readers aside and stepped to the center of the blacktop conference.

"Groom Lake," he said to Steve. "Groom Lake Weapons Testing Facility is the base you saw. Pair of runways crossing in an X, four or five real large hangars up against a mountain, right?"

"That's right." Steve and the others listened as the big man explained exactly how to get there, drawing in roads the map-makers had left off. When the man was done, Steve asked, "How come you're such an expert on this place?" The man's son, a long-haired kid about seventeen years old put in, a little too quickly, "Because we live around here."

"My name's Russell Casse," the man said in a low, almost conspiratorial voice. He shook Steve's hand and continued, "About ten years ago I had a run in with these little blood suckers, and I'd do anything to help you kick their nasty little asses. You mind if I take a look?"

Steve didn't care if the man was crazy, as long as he was willing to help. "Not at all," Steve said, "but it's not a real pretty sight."

"I've seen 'em before," Russell assured him. "Big black eyes, puckered little mouth, white skin." His son, Miguel, followed close behind and seemed to be less than enthusiastic about cooperating with the Marine pilot.

Even from twenty feet away, Russell knew something was wrong. The long tentacles hanging out of the parachute had nothing to do with the aliens he "remembered" taking him from the airfield almost a decade ago.

Steve tore back the nylon material. The motorists who had followed them to the parachute jumped back in visceral disgust. Russell stared down at the creature, horrified for a completely different reason. The creature was too large, too bony, and too fearsome to be one of the delicate little monsters who had kidnapped him a decade earlier. *Could this be a completely different species of alien?* he wondered. *Or did I imagine the whole thing, make it up?* Suddenly, the most real thing in Russell's past, the moment that ruined the rest of his life, didn't seem very real at all. He felt himself getting a little bit dizzy and put a hand on Miguel's shoulder to steady himself.

"Dad, don't forget about Troy. We need to get to that hospital."

Russell stared at the boy for a moment, trying to focus his mind. Then he nodded and turned toward the trailer.

"So, sir," Steve called to his ally. "are we headed to Groom Lake or what?"

Russell had already forgotten about his promise to Steve. "Look, friend, I'd like to help you, but I've got a sick boy in the back of my rig over there. He's going to die in a few hours if we can't find the medicine he needs. You just follow those directions I gave you. Take you about two hours from here."

"We'll get you over there," a tall, sunburnt man said. "Philip, clear everything out of the pickup, put it in the RV." The redheaded boy shot a sad look at Alicia before running off to follow his father's command.

"Hey, Mr. Casse, wait up." Steve jogged up to Russell, who appeared to be in pain. "Your boy needs medicine, I understand that. Look, a base that size will have a complete clinic with everything you need. You said it's two hours from here."

Russell looked at his son, "Your call."

Miguel thought about it for a moment. "Let's try to make it in an hour and a half."

Soaring over the endless Nevada desert, Air Force One's pilot. Captain Birnham, announced that the Nellis Range could be seen off to the left. Peeping out the little opera windows, the passengers were disappointed by the sight of a small- to medium-sized air base in fairly shabby condition. On the surface, Area 51 consisted of one very large airplane hangar surrounded by several smaller ones, a pair of crossed landing strips, plus a smattering of radar dishes and bunkhouses. Here and there, scattered around the wide open desert, they spotted other buildings, but the unspoken consensus among the passengers was that there was nothing especially interesting about this secret facility tucked against a set of steep brown hills.

By agreement, there was no ceremony to welcome the president. As soon as the big bird touched down, Captain Birnham was directed toward the largest hangar, the doors of which rolled open as they taxied up. As a small contingent of soldiers pushed mobile stairs toward the blue-and-white Boeing, Whitmore and his entourage crowded the doorway, waiting impatiently to be let out. Sheepishly, Nimziki came forward from the command center, where he'd been contemplating his next move. Everyone did their best to politely ignore him until the doors were thrown open.

At the bottom of the gangway, they were met by the base's top administrator, Major Mitchell. He had fifty or so of his soldiers lined up for the president's inspection.

"Welcome to Area Fifty-One, sir," he said with a crisp salute.

Whitmore returned the salute, explaining, "We're in a hurry."

"Right this way." Mitchell didn't need to be told why the president of the United States had decided to visit his backwater base in the middle of a global catastrophe. He had come for the ship. And, although technically speaking, it was a violation of federal law for him to show it to anyone, even the president, he led the way without the slightest hesitation.

Mitchell was a large, intimidating presence, handsome in the way square-jawed prize fighters are handsome. Although he was young, just shy of thirty, he was a climber, moving quickly up the ranks. His superiors at Fort Cayuga, impressed with his work, had steered him into his current position of supervising operations at Area 51. He was responsible for everything that happened on the base except research. If something was happening, Mitchell always knew about it and was most often standing right there to watch it happen. He was well aware that the job was only a stepping stone to something higher up, something in Washington. But he also knew that any breach of security, whether it was an infiltration from the outside, or information leaks coming from within, anything at all that put Area 51 into the newspapers, would get him swiftly busted back to a desk job in rural Idaho. He took his job seriously.

He ushered the group into a drab dead-end hallway with locked office doors on either side. At the end of the room there was a water cooler and a few wilted plants. Mitchell stepped inside and closed the door behind him.

"Stand clear of the walls," he warned, unlocking a cover plate and flipping a switch.

Suddenly there was a loud hydraulic hum and the whole room began to sink into the ground. The office doors appeared to climb the walls, as the floor lowered down a concrete shaft. The entire room was an enormous elevator.

While the others gaped around them, impressed, the president's anger slowly boiled over.

"Why the hell wasn't I told about this place?" he demanded, staring at Nimziki for an answer.

"Two words, Mr. President." For once Nimziki appeared humble and earnest. "*Plausible deniability.* The decision was made way, *way* before my time to keep this thing under wraps. Hoover knew it would be turned into a political football, so it was classified 'need to know,' and until today—"

"Enough!" Whitmore snapped. Nothing Nimziki said could erase the harm he had already done. "Plausible deniability, my ass," he muttered.

What Nimziki failed to mention was that one of the reasons the army, CIA, and the FBI had conspired to keep the crash secret was to gain advantage over the Russians in the Cold War. They slapped a twenty-five-year gag order on the project at Area 51. Both the Cold War and the secrecy order had expired under Nimziki's tenure, but he hadn't made the discovery public. He had ambitions of running for national office, maybe even the presidency, and the way he saw it, he had everything to lose by admitting he'd kept the thing secret and everything to gain by keeping control of the whole project to himself.

Metal doors slid open onto what looked like a scrubdown area in a research hospital. Dozens of masks and white coveralls hung on hooks near a series of sinks. Proceeding through this area, the group came to a set of Plexiglas doors. Beyond them was a partial scene of a busy workspace, several workers dressed from head to toe in sterile white overalls, masks and hair caps were moving in and out of view.

"This is our static-free clean room," Mitchell announced proudly, giving them a moment to gawk before showing them the way to the next exhibit on his tour.

"Well, let's see," the president said.

Mitchell didn't know exactly what to say. There wasn't much of interest in there and he was sure if Whitmore knew how many hundreds of thousands of dollars it would cost the American tax payers to decontaminate the facility, he wouldn't insist. "Actually, sir, entrance to this room requires—"

Whitmore heard the wrong answer coming out of the soldier's mouth. He explained what he wanted in a way that left no room for interpretation. "Open this goddamn door right now."

Suddenly Mitchell couldn't get the door open fast enough. He slid his magnetized ID badge through the scanner lock and the glass doors whisked apart with a smart hum. The group, eleven strong, marched into the state-of-the-art, dust-free research facility. Once they were inside and turned the corner, they realized they had only been able to see a tiny slice of it from the scrub room. The chamber was at least a hundred yards long with a raised walkway, two and a half feet higher, running straight down the center. On either side, like astronauts in their white suits, bonnets, and shoe bags, the staff was busy with a number of projects on either side of the aisle.

They moved around their workstations tweaking robotic arms, conducting laser experiments, studying graphs and charts, or sitting around doing nothing. But all of them stopped what they were doing when President Thomas Whitmore unexpectedly walked past. Mitchell stayed a step ahead of the others, explaining in a word or two the work being done at each station. The quality and sophistication of the equipment was astounding, and in many cases it was *beyond* state-of-the-art. In every detail, the lab was well staffed, well supplied, and well organized.

"Where the hell did all this come from?" the president

whispered to Grey without breaking stride. "How did this get funded?"

Doddering along at the back of the pack, seemingly out of earshot, Julius overheard the president's question. "You didn't think they actually spent ten thousand dollars for a hammer and thirty thousand for a toilet seat, did you?" The old guy gave a little laugh, not realizing he was partly correct. Military procurement officers had been funneling money to Area 51 for decades by padding other expenses, but the bulk of the funds came straight from the American congress. Part of the national budget was always listed as "the Dark Fund," money for projects deemed too sensitive for the lawmakers to know about, usually R&D on new weapons systems for the military.

A steel ramp at the far end of the room led up to a thick titanium and steel door. An electric motor shook the door to life, lifting it straight up. Ducking underneath and starting down the elevated walkway to meet the president came a pair of scientists dressed in white lab coats.

Dr. Brackish Okun was the director of research at Area 51. About forty-five years old, Okun had a full head of wild gray hair falling to his shoulders. He had an unmistakable hippie bounce in the way he walked, hands thrust deeply into the pockets of his lab coat. He was smiling one of those uncontrollable, ear-to-ear smiles the president often saw on the faces of kids when they walked up to meet him.

"Oh God, what now?" the president muttered under his breath. He'd already had so many strange encounters over the last thirty-six hours, and here came another one.

Mitchell did the honors. "Mr. President, I'd like to introduce you to Dr. Okun. He's been heading up our research here for the past fifteen years."

Okun was an odd, hyperenergetic man who had obviously spent too much time in underground isolation.

He stood nodding and grinning for an awkward moment, his wrinkled gray and yellow tie blending with his pale skin, before suddenly reaching out and shaking the president's hand with too much enthusiasm.

"Wow, Mr. President, it is truly an honor to meet you, sir. Oh, and this is my colleague Dr. Issacs." Issacs, a handsome man with close-cropped hair and a goatee, appeared to be the normal half of the team.

As Issacs leaned forward to shake hands, Okun turned to one of the researchers and whispered, "This is so cool." Whitmore shot him a disapproving look, which Okun seemed to recognize. "If any of us seem a little odd down here, it's because they don't let us out much," Okun said in apology.

"Yes, I can understand that," the president said, barely disguising his irony.

"So! I guess you'd like to see the Big Tamale," Okun surmised. "Follow me."

Every member of the group glanced around in befuddlement. They did, however, follow the odd scientist toward the next room. Leaving the long research hall, they walked up a ramp into a tight space between concrete walls. Inside, there was a small, level area and then another steel door. Issacs swiped an access card through the magnet lock, took a quick breath, then slapped a large button on the wall. A small red siren light began twirling to the sound of a buzzer as the wall in front of them lowered like a drawbridge, revealing a spectacular sight.

On the other side was a huge, dimly lit concrete chamber, five stories deep and just as wide. Armed guards patrolled a series of steel catwalks high above, automatic weapons at the ready. But the centerpiece of the room, perched on a custom-built platform and dominating the rest of the space, was an alien attack plane, its armored exterior a lustrous midnight blue beneath the work-lights. It was a replica of the ships that had laid waste to the Black Knights. The members of the president's entourage were suitably impressed. Mouths agape, they came down the ramp.

It was unlike anything they'd seen before and not at all what they had expected. The basic shape was familiar, like two saucer plates stacked rim to rim. That explained the thousands of descriptions of UFOs people had registered over the years, but it was the details of the sixty-foot craft that made it compelling and fascinating. Along the spine of the ship, starting at the crown, then tapering to a sharp point at the tail, was a tall, bony, six-foot-tall projection that the scientists called "the fin." The surface seemed to be made of large, armored plates connected at the seams by countless pieces of intricate machine tooling, tiny metallic gadgets set in place with the same precision as the muscles in a human hand.

The group moved onto an observation platform, face-to-face with the darkly fascinating bird, displayed like a sleeping stegosaurus in a hushed museum. At the front of the machine was a sort of cockpit with broad, flat windows. Below these, at the very nose of the plane, curved projections came forward to form sharp tips, almost like the mandibles on a huge insect. More than one of the amazed visitors imagined being squeezed between those powerful claws before being consumed.

A score of scientists and technicians moved around the ship, taking readings, making minor adjustments, scanning the surface with curious blue lamps, their equipment on portable tool carts, making them look like high-tech auto mechanics. In several places, long gray scars zigzagged across the surface, showing where the scientists had patched the craft up after it cracked apart in the New Mexican desert.

"She's a beaut, ain't she?" Okun wiggled his bushy eyebrows.

Julius whispered loud enough for everyone to hear, "Ha! Never any spaceships recovered by the government?"

Whitmore brushed past Okun to get a better look. He walked directly under the spacecraft and reached up to touch the surface. Etched into the surface of the plate armor were thinly cut grooves arranged in patterns.

"These designs," the president asked, "what do they mean?"

"We have no idea," Okun replied, as if he'd never thought about it. In fact, he'd thought about the markings obsessively. He'd even managed to arrange a security clearance for one of the world's leading cryptographers, Dr. D. Jackson, who had once spent three frustrating weeks trying to figure the markings out before being called away to another government project.

"Are you telling me we've had one of their ships for forty years and we don't know anything about them?" Whitmore asked testily.

"No, no, no, no, no," Okun assured the president, "we know *tons* about them. But the supercool stuff has just started happening in the last couple days. See, we can't duplicate their type of power, their energy. But since these guys started showing up, all the little gizmos inside have turned themselves on. The last twenty-four hours have been wild—really, really exciting."

The president exploded. "Millions of people are dying out there! I don't think *exciting* is the word I'd choose to describe it!"

The cavernous room echoed the words as everyone fell silent, letting the president blow off some steam. Whitmore walked to the far edge of the ship, trying to gather his thoughts, but a single image had plastered itself like a billboard to the inside of his forehead: his wife Marilyn being overwhelmed by a sea of fire. Staring blankly into the dim recesses of the room, his eyes began to fill with tears. He wasn't going to cry, wouldn't allow himself that kind of personal indulgence. He sucked in a long stiff breath, then wiped his eyes, trying to make it look like he was massaging a headache.

General Grey took over, filling the silence. "Doctor, I'm sure you understand we're in the middle of a very severe emergency. Now, what can you tell us about the enemy we're facing?"

Beginning to appreciate the urgency of the situation, the long-haired scientist answered more soberly than before. "Well, let's see. They're not all that dissimilar to us. They breathe oxygen and have similar tolerances to heat and cold... That's probably why they're interested in our planet."

"Whoa! Why do you assume—" David started to blurt out a question, then stopped to check if that was okay. Grey and Whitmore both signaled it was. "What makes you think they're interested in our planet?"

"Just a hunch," Okun said, cleaning his glasses with his tie. "They're animals like us and they have a survival instinct. Perhaps some catastrophe drove them from their home planet and now they're wandering around. Also, I'm guessing they need space because they're ranchers or farmers; they do some sort of animal husbandry."

"How do you know that?"

"You're standing under the answer. Those large plates, the ship's armor. If you examine them under a microscope, you'll find hairline striations and even pores!" Okun saw that none of the visitors understood the implication. "That means, of course, that the plates are *grown* rather than forged. Each one is as individual as a human fingerprint. We don't know how they do it. I think it's done through bioengineering, manipulating the DNA so that the shells grow to precisely the same size. But Dr. Issacs believes they grow the animals in molds, the way the Chinese used to bind women's feet to keep them under a certain size. As to their age, we can't be entirely sure. We've developed a variation of the carbon fourteen test which indicates the plates take about eighty years to grow. And, if our methods are reliable, the plates on this ship are between three and nine thousand years old." Okun, still a geeky college boy at heart, looked around at the visitors mischievously. "Hey, you guys wanna see them?"

Reports of UFOs hovering in midair for several moments then darting off at unbelievable speeds were not uncommon over the southwestern desert of the United States. Nearly all of these sightings were made by unreliable witnesses who say they were alone at the time. Inevitably, reports filed by highly credible sources, such as the one made by former President Jimmy Carter while governor of Georgia, inspired dozens of copycat observances.

But on the night of July, 4, 1947, something happened that no one could explain away. Hundreds of citizens in and around the town of Roswell, New Mexico, claimed to have seen a glowing, disk-shaped object, about sixty feet across, streaking northwest across the sky. Immediately, they flooded the local sheriff's office, radio station, and newspaper with a deluge of phone calls. Certain the thing they had seen was not of this earth, the entire town spent the night gathered in restaurants and the parking lots of supermarkets trading accounts of what they had seen and nervously watching the sky for signs of unusual movement. Public reaction bordered on near-hysteria at times: It was still the main topic of conversation when, a few days later, the United States military issued a press release: they had recovered the wreckage of a crashed flying saucer which they believed to be of extraterrestrial origin. This startling announcement was made by Colonel William Blanchard of the 509th Bomb Group at Roswell Field, who later went on to become a four-star general and vice chief of staff of the United States Air Force.

The afternoon after the mass sighting, a local rancher, W.W. "Mac" Brazel, had found the wreckage of an unusual aircraft on his property. The pieces were made of a material he'd never seen before and some of them had markings on them, something like hieroglyphics. Mac followed the trail of debris out to where he found the ship—and the body he would never admit to seeing later. Figuring it was one of the experimental aircraft from the nearby army airfield, he drove into town and called the base at Roswell, seventy-five miles away. A squad of intelligence officers hurried to the scene to examine the wreckage. That night they broke the story to the press.

Then, just as surprisingly, they denied their own story. Following visits to the site by one high-ranking military delegation after another, a second news conference was called. They said it was a weather balloon. A strange new type of weather balloon, possibly put up by our dreaded enemies, the Soviets. No one believed a word of it, but the army stuck to its story. The reporters who had descended on the scene were not allowed to examine the evidence. It had already been airlifted out of Roswell to an undisclosed location, where it would undergo "further testing."

The glowing object observed that night over Roswell was a scout plane that had broken off its much larger parent ship, which was hovering at the edge of earth's atmosphere. Like hundreds of flights before and after it, the ship had conducted several hours of research and observation. It was only moments away from completing its mission when the parent ship was suddenly threatened with discovery and bolted away. The scout ship had wandered further than it should have and now lay behind the curve of the earth, preventing the energy flowing from the parent craft from reaching its engines. The occupants of the craft, realizing they only had a few minutes of reserve power, panicked.

Rather than raise their ship higher into the air, they darted northwest, back to the area they were assigned to explore. As they tore along, their sensors screaming of imminent engine failure, a shield of negative ions covered the ship and, reacting with the ship's own strange form of energy, created the soft moon-bright glow seen from the ground. Too late. The left engine exploded into a thousand fragments, and a moment later, the ship bottomed out on the desert.

Two of the aliens inside had survived the crash; the third was dead. The stronger of the two survivors struggled for over an hour before finally opening the hatch and pulling himself outside. He dragged himself off the edge of the ship and 120 feet across the sand before he was attacked by a pack of coyotes. As they nipped and gnawed him to death, his comrade inside the ruined ship felt every hideous bite and heard every soundless scream. He sat paralyzed inside the vessel until, the next morning, the earthlings began arriving. The surviving alien was airlifted by helicopter to Roswell Field, then flown by an army medical plane to a new super-secret facility, Area 51.

Okun led the way to a door as thick as a bank vault. Using a distinctive triangular key, he opened it. Issacs slipped into the pitch-black room and fumbled around until he found the light switch. Once a high-security lecture hall with theater chairs facing a podium, the room had become, over the years, a graveyard for Okun's obsolete scientific equipment. The president and his entourage stepped over and between the piles of expensive junk, moving to the front of the room. The focal point of the space was a trio of metal cylinders, five feet wide, running from floor to ceiling.

"Is everybody ready?" Okun asked like a barker outside a circus tent. "This, ladies and gentlemen, is what we affectionately refer to down here as the Freak Show."

He was on the verge of saying more—he had a whole routine he usually went through—but a frown on the president's face made him cut it short. He entered a sequence of numbers into an old-fashioned security keypad and the three cylinders began to lift upward into the ceiling.

Behind the cylinders were three glass tanks, each one containing the body of a dead alien floating as peacefully as mermaids in a murky solution of formaldehyde. Their long frail bodies, orange and yellow under the lights, were in various states of decay. Their spindly bodies hung like kite tails from large bulbous heads. Gentle black eyes the size of eight balls on either side of a tiny beaklike nose gave the faces a startled expression, as if they were just as surprised as the earthlings on the other side of the glass.

Okun studied the faces of the visitors and noted all the usual reactions. Some looked frightened, some lit up with curiosity, and others turned away in revulsion.

"When my predecessor, Dr. Welles, found these three, they looked a whole lot different. They were wearing biomechanical suits, horrible looking things with long tentacles coming off the back and shorter ones on the face. The two on the sides died in the crash, and it was only during the autopsies that Welles discovered the creatures inside. Once the suits were off, we were able to learn a great deal about their anatomy. Their senses are many times more sensitive than ours. The eyes, as you can see, are much larger than ours and have no irises to limit the amount of light they can receive. The auditory nerves and olfactory organs are coterminous, ending here in the nose. Our theory is that they can not only hear sounds, but also smell them. The same goes for odors; they must be able to 'hear' the scent and smell it at the same time. Cool, huh?"

Oops, he'd done it again. Okun held up his hands, apologetically, but the president was too involved with learning about the aliens to pay much attention.

"Continue."

"Okay, let's see. Circulatory system. They don't have a central organ, a heart, like we do. The blood is kept moving through their bodies by the peristaltic motion of the muscles. They have no vocal cords, so we're assuming they communicate with each other through other means."

"What kind of other means?" David broke in. "Obviously you're not talking about hand gestures or body language."

"No. They seem to use some kind of extrasensory perception."

"Telepathy," Issacs put in bluntly. "They read each others' minds."

"Well, now, Dr. Issacs," Okun looked up at the ceiling, a sarcastic tight grin smeared across his face, "as we have discussed many times, there is still no trustworthy scientific evidence to support that claim. I don't want to start engaging in speculation and give our visitors the impression that we're a bunch of crackpots." He shot a dagger glance at Issacs, who stared back just as icily.

"What the hell are you two talking about?" demanded the no-nonsense Grey.

Issacs came forward out of the shadows and explained. "The one in the middle survived for eighteen days after the crash. Dr. Welles did everything he could to save the creature's life. On the tenth day, he reported having the sensation that the thing was reading his mind. On the eleventh day, he claims that he and the creature 'spoke,' not with words, but in images and feelings. These conversations continued until the creature became too weak and eventually died. The sense he took from these 'conversations' was that these beings meant us no harm, that their intentions were peaceful. That's why we didn't warn anyone. We had no idea anything like this was going to happen."

When the bearded doctor finished speaking, everyone looked at Whitmore for his reaction. If they were expecting him to forgive the scientists for not alerting the world to the danger of invasion by these powerful predators, they were wrong. Instead, he turned again to Okun.

"I'm still thinking about something you said out there by the ship. You said 'that's probably why they're interested in our planet,' and then you said they raise other animals. Do you know what these things eat?"

The image of humans being herded together in pens, fattened outside the doors of the slaughterhouse, naked and crowded, occurred suddenly to everyone.

Julius couldn't bear the thought of it. "That's revolting. Are you saying these things are going to make us into sausage?"

"I don't know. That's what I'm asking the doctor," Whitmore replied.

Okun was visibly disturbed out by the idea. The way his face twitched, he must have been imagining it pretty vividly. For the first time, he started to understand just how serious the situation was.

"They do have mouths, very small ones right there under the beak, but they're nothing more than slits in the skin. The autopsy also found a set of digestive glands that secrete a highly corrosive substance. Nothing was found in any of the stomachs, so we don't know what they eat."

"One more question." The president walked closer to Okun. "How can we kill them?"

"Geez, that's a toughie," he said, lacing his fingers on top of his head to help him think. "Of course, their bodies are even more frail than ours. The real problem is getting past all the technology they've developed to protect themselves. And judging from the little bit of it we've seen, that technology is far more advanced than ours."

David had wandered around to the other side of the

glass tubes and was making a close inspection of the sinewy corpses when his nation's leader called on him.

"David, you've already unlocked one part of that technology. You cracked their code, translated their signals in a relatively short time."

David hadn't realized that he and the president were on a first name basis. With the curve of the tube distorting his face, he answered, "Oh, I don't know about that, *Tom*. All I did was stumble onto the signal because it was disrupting the... I don't know how helpful I can be."

"Show them what you've discovered. I want the two of you," he meant Okun and David, "to put your heads together and, hopefully, come up with some answers." Then he leaned close enough for David to know it was a challenge. "Let's see if you're really as smart as you think you are."

UNAUTHORIZED VISITORS SUBJECT TO
IMMEDIATE ARREST.
TRESPASSING ON THESE GROUNDS IS A
FEDERAL OFFENSE PUNISHABLE BY UP TO THREE
YEARS IN FEDERAL PRISON.

The signs were posted every five hundred feet beside the single lane of asphalt leading toward Groom Lake. Other signs warned of hidden cameras and radar observation. All the warnings were real. They were put in place to discourage the intrepid UFO fanatics who were always trying to infiltrate the area for a look at the flying saucers the government had either developed or captured, depending on whose story you believed. If this were like any other day, two teams of military police would have been lurking in the sagebrush, waiting to make arrests. But it was like no day the earth had ever known.

Steve was riding in the back of a pickup truck with his prisoner and four men carrying shotguns. They kept a close watch on the thing beneath the orange parachute. If it woke up, they were ready to open fire. It seemed to take forever before they reached the tall chain-link fence with the barbed wire looped around the top, and the guardhouse that stood at the main entrance.

Two enlisted men, unfortunate enough to draw gate duty on the day the world was ending, shut off the news and came outside holding some serious-looking assault rifles. When Steve stood up in the back of the pickup, one of them hollered to him.

"Sorry, Captain. We can't let you through without clearance."

"You wanna see my clearance. Come over here, Private, I'll show you my goddamn clearance."

The soldier reluctantly came toward the bed of the pick up truck. Steve grabbed a fistful of the guard's collar and tore back the parachute, holding his face inches away from the ghastly exoskeleton.

The guy jumped back, shitting in his pants.

"Jesus Mary Joseph! Let 'em through," he yelled to the other guard. "Let 'em through."

When David's head popped up through the floor, he experienced the sensation of entering a strange, darkly exotic galaxy. The interior of the attacker was a dim, oppressive chamber. Its rounded walls, dripping with creepy, semiorganic technology, felt more like the inside of a crypt than a flying machine. His first impulse was to call the whole thing off and climb back down the ladder. Okun, already inside, made matters worse by grinning maniacally through the gloom and saying, "I think you'll find this supremely cool. I do."

David squeezed his tall frame into the honeycomb cabin, then made his way to the front of the craft, where at least he could look out the dark windows at the "normal" environment of the concrete bunker. As Okun had promised, the cockpit was alive with a mad assortment of gizmos and flashing lights. There was a main control panel, but David hardly recognized it as such. Swollen irregular lines that resembled veins ran through the dashboard, and the lights of the instrument panel didn't flash on and off; they throbbed brighter then relaxed, like a beating heart. The whole place made him feel like he'd crawled inside some prehistoric insect.

"We've had people in here working around the clock trying to get a fix on what all this crap does. Some of it, we figured out immediately. Like this whole clump of stuff." He picked up a tube that looked like a piece of dried intestine. "This is part of the life-support system for the cabin. It runs back to a set of filters. This do-hickey over here," he pointed, "is a governor for the engines, either a manual override or the accelerator pedal."

"Did these seats come standard?" David asked planting himself in one of the leather chairs bolted to the floor.

While Okun told him the whole story of how the chairs got there, replacing a set of slimy "body-pods," David took an interest in one of the instruments. It was some type of screen that seemed to be composed of a translucent membrane, possibly the thin amber shell of some animal, with green patterns of light dancing through it. He stared at the strobing green light for several moments, then started tapping his foot to keep time. Okun was asking him something, but getting no response.

"Hello! Earth to Levinson!"

"Sorry. What did you say?"

"I asked if you'd found something interesting?"

"Maybe. Excuse me," David said absently, still transfixed by the pattern emerging on the screen. "Connie," he called out, "are you still out there?"

"Yes, I am." Her voice came in through the open hatch.

"Are you still holding my laptop?"

"Yes, I am."

"I need it."

Before she could answer, David realized how he sounded. Just like he used to when they lived together, like a spoiled genius who thought the world had to revolve around him. He jumped out of his chair and came to the hatch. Connie had already kicked off her heels and was climbing the steel rungs of the ladder. David's face at the hatch so suddenly surprised her.

"Ms. Spano, have I told you recently that you're a hell of a good sport?"

Connie handed the computer up to him at a loss for words. "No, you haven't."

"Thank you." David smiled down at her before disappearing again. There was something vaguely familiar about the green light on the screen, something similar to the broadcast signal he'd found. He flipped open the computer and booted up, explaining to Okun as he worked, "These patterns here on the, er… I think you called it the do-hickey."

"No, this is the thingamabob," Okun said wryly. "Please keep it straight. We're trying to be scientific."

"A thousand pardons, Doctor. The patterns here on this instrument, they're repeating sequentially, just like—" he spun the machine around so Okun could see the screen "—just like their countdown signal. I think they're using this frequency for some kind of computer communications. It might be how they coordinate their ships."

Okun nodded, but still had questions. "Let's say you're right. Two problems: what's being said over the computer, and second, so what? What do we *do* about it? Where'd you go to school, anyway?"

"What I did with the countdown signal was apply a

phase-reverse transmission to cancel out the signal."

"Did it work?"

David frowned. "Well, it didn't stop them from firing on the cities, but it cleared up the satellite reception problem I was working on. I went to MIT. Why? Where'd you go?"

"Cal Tech. No reason, I was just wondering."

Just when David was starting to doubt that Okun knew anything at all, the oddball doctor showed that he understood the situation.

"Okay, we still have two problems. First, we don't know what's being sent on this frequency. Could be attack plans, or it could be classical music. Maybe it's their version of an FM radio. Second problem: with the satellite disruption, you had a way of transmitting the countervailing signal, but this instrument here looks like a receiver. How are we going to send a canceling signal?"

David collapsed into the chair, all the steam taken out of him. "Another slight problem is that I ran out the door and left my phase-reverse spectrometer behind."

Okun impishly comforted him. "Luckily, you've come to the right place. Not only do I have a spectrometer, but I also have another piece of technology which I think we're going to need. Feast your eyes on this." From his pocket, he withdrew a $1.98 screwdriver. "Let's take this screen apart and see if we can jerry-rig it to act as a transmitter."

"Cal Tech, huh?" David was learning to like this guy, up to a point.

It only took the pair of brainiacs a few minutes to solve their first problem. They tore the green screen loose and delicately attached a pair of alligator clamps to the sinewy wiring on the back. Although the machine had been built thousands of years before in another part of the universe, the data feeding into it was arranged in a binary system, a continuous string of ones and zeros, or whatever the alien equivalent was. Neither Okun nor David cared at that point, just as long as the little laptop could read the sequence.

A crew of technicians hauled Okun's spectrometer out of storage and brought it into the cockpit. As they were leaving the ship, planning to sneak back into the "freak show" room for another look at the dead aliens, David hit the enter key and applied the reversed sequence. For a moment, nothing happened and the two technical wizards felt the sinking feeling of disappointment. Then, cursing and shouting erupted outside the ship. Through the cockpit windows David and Okun could see the group of technicians laying flat on their asses. The men stood up and tried to walk away, but bounced off some unseen force field.

"Hey," Okun said, "we got the force field to work! I guess we must have put something in backwards when we repaired it the first time."

David sank back, depressed and deflated. He had been sure the amber screen was the way in to some kind of central command structure, but now he realized that he'd just spent a couple of hours making an insignificant repair. Disgusted with himself, he looked around the instrument panel. There were at least forty more gizmos to work on and no assurance that any of them would lead anywhere.

He shut off the force field signal when he saw Major Mitchell come racing across the concrete hangar toward the ship. The major spotted Okun behind the windows of the attacker and yelled up at him.

"They've got one! And it's still alive!"

As soon as the elevator doors slid open, Mitchell took off at a dead run, leaving Doctors Okun and Issacs to jog along by themselves. Issacs, who had once run an emergency room in Boston, had the presence of mind to grab his black bag.

As they ran toward the crowd gathered just inside the giant hangar doors, Okun's lab coat gave up a steady stream of pens, electrical caps, hand tools, including the slide rule he'd been using since high school, and several stray pieces of the attacker's instrument panel. By the time they crossed the hangar, someone had handed Mitchell a bullhorn.

"All nonmilitary personnel step away from the stretcher," he yelled at the hundred or so civilians who were helping deliver the creature. "Clear out of this hangar immediately. Step behind the doors and wait outside."

Okun shoved his way through the dispersing crowd and found a large body wrapped in a parachute strapped tight to a medical gurney. He pulled enough of the nylon material free to recognize the surface of the biomechanical suit.

"Who found this thing?" he yelled.

"I did, sir. Captain Steven Hiller, U.S. Marines. His ship went down in the desert."

"Alone? Weren't there others?"

The question took Steve off guard. "As a matter of fact, there were two more. Both killed in the crash," he reported. He looked the long-haired doctor over carefully and couldn't help asking, "How'd you know that?"

"How long has this one been unconscious?" Issacs asked.

"Since I kicked the—" Steve decided not to tell them how the creature got to be unconscious. Instead, he finished, "About three hours."

The gurney was on the move, soldiers wheeling it fast across the smooth hangar floor. All the civilians had obeyed the command to return to their vehicles outside, all except two.

"Doctor, excuse me," Russell said for the tenth time, his arm around Miguel's shoulder. Steve remembered that the big red-headed man needed to find some medical help for his son and, from his position on the far side of the stretcher, tried to get Okun's attention. It was no use; everyone was completely focused on the alien specimen.

"Let's get him down to containment, stat," Okun yelled. Then, to his colleague, "Is it still alive?"

Amidst the turmoil of the speeding gurney and people shouting in every direction, cool-headed Issacs had put a stethoscope to the monster's chest. "Still respiring," he reported.

"Listen, doctor, my boy is very sick. He needs immediate attention."

Okun seemed to look up at Russell as they entered the elevator hallway, but he was only searching for the button that would take them down to the operating room. "He's drying out. Let's have some saline solution ready by the time we get down there."

Okun pushed past Russell and moved to the switch. He touched the button and the room began its hydraulic, humming descent. But before the elevator had moved a foot, it suddenly lurched to a halt.

Russell slammed his fist against the emergency stop button, then grabbed a fistful of the first thing that looked like medical help. He came up with Dr. Issacs's white lab coat. He pinned the man so tightly against the elevator wall that the doctor's toes were off the ground and stared at him with furious bloodshot eyes.

"My boy has a problem with his adrenal cortex. He's going into adrenal shock and collapse. If he doesn't get some medicine right now, he is going to die." Issacs could smell the stale liquor on the man's breath.

Miguel, for once, felt proud of his father. "He needs an injection of cortecosteroid, or at least some insulin."

Issacs, unflappable, spoke calmly to his burly attacker. "Sounds like Addison's syndrome. I've got some cortecosteroid right there."

Russell followed the doctor's eyes down to where his

black bag rested beside the gurney. Issacs didn't like the idea of missing any part of this history-making medical procedure, but he knew Okun could handle the OR until he got there.

"O'Haver, Miller, come with me." Then to Russell, "Take us to him."

Near Anaheim, Jasmine found the freeway and headed south. Because she had the First Lady bumping around in the back of the truck, she couldn't go any faster than thirty miles per hour. As the sun began to set, turning the sky a thousand hues of orange and purple through the smoke on the horizon, it was almost possible to forget the destruction behind them. The electricity was out, but otherwise the neighborhoods surrounding the freeway seemed fine, normal. There was light traffic headed in both directions, and the heat of the day was relaxing to a warm evening.

She followed the signs and took the El Toro exit. Miles before, still driving over and around the rubble, she met several people who told her that the base had been hit. They advised her not to waste her time, but the news only increased Jasmine's anxiety to hurry up and get there. No matter how much damage the base had incurred, she assumed she'd be able to find medical attention for Mrs. Whitmore and, if she were lucky, find Steve. She imagined herself driving up to his broken plane out on a runway where he was working on it, determined to patch it up so he could join the fight.

As soon as she was off the freeway, the signs of destruction were all around her. Soon she found herself driving through low, rolling hills along a road that disappeared into giant potholes every few yards. She spotted a group of kids poking through the smoking remains of a building further up the road. She drove up the hill onto a level plain and yelled to them.

"Hey, you guys, you know where El Toro is? The Marine base?"

"This is it, lady," one of them yelled back.

Jasmine drove another hundred yards through the wreckage before coasting to a stop and suddenly turning off the engine. She stepped down out of the truck and walked a few feet to the collapsed facade of a building.

WELCOME TO EL TORO
MARINE CORPS AIR STATION
HOME OF THE BLACK KNIGHTS

Nothing was left standing. The whole area had been pulverized under a hailstorm of laser blasts until not a single building was left standing. Instead of a thriving military base, the area looked as flat as freshly plowed farmland interrupted by a few piles of charred rubble. Jasmine sat down and cried until the last light of evening faded from the sky.

The nation's official military headquarters had transferred from the Pentagon to a noisy, makeshift office 150 feet below the floor of the Nevada desert. The experiment control room at Area 51 was designed to monitor test flights by prototype jets and other experimental aircraft. It was well stocked with electronic gadgetry, everything from old rotary dial phones on up to worldwide radar tracking screens, but almost none of it was working. The earth's great communications networks had all been torn apart, and the damage was getting worse by the hour.

Major Mitchell's men were joined by the crack squad of communications specialists from Air Force One. They'd requisitioned three CB radios from the horde of RVs parked outside and were busy gathering information from guys that said such things as, "10–4, good buddy." The second wave of cities had already been destroyed and the big ships were moving on, apparently firing at will. Even deep in the earth, hundreds of miles from the nearest city destroyer, people were scared. They were starting to realize that even if the destruction were to stop immediately, the country and the world they had known would never be the same. Not even close. They knew they were totally at the mercy of the creatures in the huge ships.

Nimziki was scared, too. He wasn't afraid of dying physically, but the idea of political death terrified him. He'd spent his whole life working harder than anyone else to grab and keep control, never leaving tracks, never leaving his back exposed, making himself indispensable to others in power. He'd risen to the top, being appointed the chief of the CIA, then becoming Whitmore's secretary of defense, and even that didn't give him enough control. 'The Iron Sphincter" was losing his grip. He knew that beating these invaders was a real long shot, but by force of habit his mind planned on being back in Washington, picking up the pieces, reestablishing his network of allies and, most of all, trying to beat the rap he knew he was going to take for withholding the Area 51 secret too long. He came into the war room, as they were calling it, and picked up one of the phones.

"Got any other secrets up your sleeve that might help us win this fight?"

"That's a cheap shot, General, and you know it." Nimziki knew Grey, doggedly loyal to Whitmore, would come after him sooner or later.

"I seem to remember a staff meeting yesterday in Washington. You sat there on that damn couch while we presented options to the president on a code yellow emergency and you didn't say anything about this place."

"I gave President Whitmore my best advice: hit them with nuclear weapons. That is still my recommendation, and if he had followed it, we wouldn't even be here right now. Besides, all I knew was that there was some old spaceship down here."

"Don't feed me that line of crap. You keep your fingers up more asses than a proctologist, so don't claim you didn't know everything about this place. When were you planning on informing the rest of us?"

"Look, The whole project was deemed classified, black shelf."

Grey didn't pretend to hide his disgust. "Christ, why didn't you say something when they first arrived? You could have saved the lives of over a hundred American pilots." Grey stared at him, trying to fathom the man's banal form of evil. He knew full well that Nimziki had sat on the information as long as he did to save his own political hide.

"Look, don't lay the lives of those pilots at my doorstep. Knowing—" Everything changed when President Whitmore came through the door. Nimziki and Grey turned away from each other and the dozen technicians manning the communications equipment went back to work. Connie led the way over to a paper map of the United States that was taped to the wall, the destroyed cities circled in black.

"Oh my God." She gasped when she saw the update.

"Are these confirmed?" Whitmore asked, staring at the bad news on the map. "Atlanta, Sacramento, and Philadelphia?"

"Yes, sir. Those sites are confirmed hits. We're also hearing of several raids on isolated targets, mainly military air bases."

"Which way are they heading?"

Grey answered. He walked over and used the map

to illustrate. "It looks like their plan is to send the Washington ship down the Atlantic coast, then possibly head in over the Gulf states. The Los Angeles craft looks like it's going to continue up the West Coast, while the New York ship is moving toward Chicago right now."

The president moved to the conference table, took a seat, and poured himself a glass of water while Grey went on.

"They're actually attacking corridors, sending out those little attack fighters as they pass through an area to hit specific targets. They aren't moving around blindly, that's for sure. We heard from Europe that the ship over Paris moved immediately to Brussels and hit NATO headquarters while the smaller planes picked apart Western Alliance installations." Then, with an accusatory glare in Nimziki's direction, he added, 'They've obviously scouted us, planning this attack for some time. The shits know exactly where and how to hit us."

Seething with anger, the president turned toward his secretary of defense ready to unload on him. Then, just as quickly, he turned away. There was no time to dwell on his treasonous behavior now. He would deal with Nimziki in the future, if there was one.

"What about our forces? What kind of capability have we got left?"

"We're down to approximately fifteen percent, sir." Grey gave him a moment to soak that in before spelling out the dreadful consequences. "Calculating the time it's taking them to destroy a city and move on, we're looking at worldwide destruction of every major city within the next thirty-six hours."

Whitmore took a long, calm drink of water. "We're being exterminated." That was an ugly way to describe the situation, one that made the players in the room bristle uncomfortably, but no one could think of a more accurate term. A knock came at the door.

"Mr. President." Major Mitchell entered. "I have that pilot you wanted to meet."

"Show him in."

Whitmore stood up and straightened his tie as Mitchell waved Steve in the door. Still wearing the same sweat-soaked undershirt and combat pants he'd marched across the desert in, Steve didn't feel ready to meet a roomful of powerful white people, especially the president.

"Captain Steven Hiller, sir," he announced with a ramrod salute.

"At ease." The president smiled without returning the salute. His enthusiasm immediately put Steve more at ease. "It's an honor to meet you, Captain. You did one hell of a job out there today."

"Thank you, sir. Just trying to do my job."

"You're out of El Toro, aren't you?"

"Yes, sir. Black Knights, first squadron."

"Have you ever heard of the Hellcats out of Fort Bragg?"

Steve couldn't repress a quick smile. He knew Whitmore had been a fighter pilot, of course. During the Gulf War, the Hellcats had become a household word. But he hadn't expected any pilot talk during a meeting with the commander in chief. "I've heard of them," he said.

"What have you heard?" Whitmore pressed him.

"Second best unit in the whole damned armed services, sir. Right behind the Knights."

Now both of them were grinning in mutual admiration. "Where's that prisoner you brought in?"

Mitchell saw his opening and jumped in. He wanted to get over to the operating theater and observe. "He's in a medical containment area, sir. The doctors are optimistic that he'll survive."

"I don't know if that's cause for optimism," the president said, "but I'd like to have a look at this thing."

That was the cue for the president's staff to snatch

their papers off the table and prepare to move. General Grey stepped forward and expressed his misgivings about the plan, but Whitmore was determined. "See to it this man gets whatever he needs," he said, pointing to Steve before leaving the room at the head of his entourage.

"Excuse me, General." Steve caught Grey's attention as he was about to leave for the medical area. "I'm real anxious to get back to El Toro."

Now that he'd turned the alien over, there wasn't much reason for him to stick around. And he kept hearing Jimmy's voice in his head telling him Jasmine might have survived the blast. If she had, there was only one place he knew to look for her. He asked the general if he could have some time on one of the radios or if a message could be sent.

Grey stopped dead in his tracks and put a hand on Steve's shoulder. "I'm sorry, son. I guess you haven't heard. El Toro was destroyed this morning in the attack."

Shattered, Steve stood still, trying to breathe as the general hurried off to join the others.

A blood orange moon lit the path through the ruins. An hour after they'd left to search for supplies, Jasmine and Dylan came picking their way through the dark toward a roaring campfire. Each of them carried a box loaded with cans of food salvaged from the remains of the base's cafeteria. Dylan's box held an industrial-sized can of baked beans that weighed half as much as he did and a bunch of bent spoons they'd found in the dirt. Before they left the pantry, they'd thrown boards over the opening and covered them with dirt.

"Okay, folks, dinner is served." Jas set the box down and then took a set of steak knives from her pocket. "We'll use these for can openers."

The quiet man had taken charge in Jasmine's absence and done quite a job. The First Lady was laying on a bed of cardboard and folded clothes, his jacket neatly folded under her head as a pillow. Jas had started a small fire before she left, but he'd improved it considerably, building a neatly stacked bonfire straight off the cover of a scouting magazine.

"Hey, you did a nice job. I hardly recognize the old place."

She went to check on the president's wife, who tried to sit up when she saw Jasmine coming. The effort cost her a great deal of pain. She went into a coughing fit, her lungs filling with fluid.

When Jas got her settled down again, she scolded, "Don't move like that. I'm serious. You keep as still as you can tonight, and in the morning we'll get you some help."

She helped the injured woman sip some pineapple juice. Then the two of them stared into the fire for a long time without saying anything.

The quiet man had opened a can of frankfurters for Dylan who was doing the Dance of Happiness while he ate. The dance consisted of staring at the sky and wiggling his butt back and forth to express how good the food was. The motion was repeated with each mouthful. Jasmine watched him gyrate, stonefaced. Tonight they would feast, but in the days to come she knew there would be famine. Where would tomorrow's meal come from?

"Your son," Mrs. Whitmore said weakly, "he's beautiful."

Jasmine was about to scold her again for not resting, but instead, she allowed, "He's my angel."

"Was his father stationed here?"

Jasmine let out a deep, resigned sigh. "Well, he wasn't his father. I was sort of hoping he'd want the job, though." She threw a pebble into the flames. She was about to start bawling her eyes out again, but forced herself not to.

The other woman could sense it was time to change the subject. "So, what do you do for a living?"

"I'm a dancer."

"How wonderful. Modern? Ballet?"

Jasmine smiled at the flames. "No, *exotic*," she announced, glancing at the president's wife, wondering how many strippers she'd ever met and whether that wouldn't be a bee in her high-class bonnet.

"Oh... sorry."

"Don't be," Jas told her, "I'm not. It's not where I thought I'd end up, but the money's real good, and besides," she lifted her chin toward Dylan, "he's worth taking good care of."

Jas didn't usually go around telling people what she did for a living. She wasn't ashamed of it, but she wasn't proud, either. When the subject came up, she'd sometimes lie, sometimes tell the truth, and sometimes give no answer at all. This was one of those times she wished she hadn't told the truth, because she was pretty sure a respectable gal like the president's wife wasn't going to have a whole lot to say to her afterward. She wanted to say something else, something like "Don't worry, just cause I'm a stripper. I'm still going to find you a doctor in the morning." But that would have sounded stupid.

"And what are you going to do when the dancing's over?" Marilyn asked. "What about your future?"

Jasmine smiled again, this time because the First Lady's question was one she'd asked herself a million times. It had been a monkey on her back from which she suddenly felt herself released. "You know, I used to ask myself that question every day, but you know what? I don't think it matters anymore."

"Mommy, can I have some more weenies?"

"Sugar, come over here to mama for a minute. I want you to meet the First Lady." Dylan, hoping it might lead to more weenies, came over to be introduced.

"That's funny. I was sure you didn't recognize me."

"Well, I didn't want to say anything. I voted for the other guy."

Dr. Okun put his face close to the lens of the video camera. "This recording is being made on July Fourth at six forty-five P.M. The alien sustained a violent plane crash this morning at approximately nine o'clock. As you can see—" he stepped away revealing the eight-foot-long creature strapped down to an operating table "—the thing appears to be very weak." Indeed, the only signs of life came from the short tentacles on the face which twitched and twisted sporadically. The four longer dorsal tentacles, measuring between six and twelve feet, had been tucked haphazardly under the thick retaining straps and remained motionless.

The operating theater, as this tiled room with stainless steel trimmings was known, had several tall windows of reinforced glass looking out onto the storage/lecture room Okun had called the Freak Show. The great tubes holding the bodies of the three dead aliens were visible in the darkened chamber beyond. Three assistants moved efficiently about the room: a woman anesthesiologist and two male orderlies. One of the men made adjustments to a complicated piece of machinery connected by a series of flexible hoses to a large vat of formaldehyde. The other orderly handed Okun a set of tools, a mallet and a chisel as thick as a railroad tie. Okun, ever the showman, held them in the air, pretending to be Dr. Frankenstein in an old movie.

"All the life-support monitors are recording?" The anesthesiologist nodded her head then the doctor continued speaking to the camera. "We're going to split the skull open and peel it back in order to reach the living creature inside. This," he said, rapping on the yellowish exoskeleton, "is only a suit of armor. The animal you are seeing now is actually a completely separate species which the aliens raise to maturity, slaughter, then gut. The internal organs are scooped out, but the musculature is preserved. The skull and chest have a seam down the middle allowing the aliens to slip in and out. So they wear the body of this other creature, sort of like crawling inside a zombie. Then, by a process we may never understand, the physical impulses of the frail creature inside are carried out by the corpse of this much larger, much stronger animal. Notice how the tentacles seem to flop around with little control. As you will see in a moment, the animal inside has no tentacles, so it may be that they are not able to manipulate these extra arms. Alas, until we find a healthy specimen to study, this bio-armor will remain a mystery. Gentlemen, are you ready?"

His assistants were more than ready; they wanted to get this business done and get out of there. While Okun hammed it up for the video camera, the others were keeping tense eyes on the bony leviathan strapped to the table, half expecting it to roar to life at any moment.

Working the chisel into the seam of the skull, Okun delivered a few sharp whacks, each one causing the gruesome sound of cracking bones. The men, Colin and Patrick, tugged in opposite directions until the skull gave way. They peeled the meat and ligament back until it lay flat on the table.

"Oh, Jesus!" The smell coming from the inside of the suit backed the four humans away. "Stinks like ammonia," said Patrick, his eyes watering up. "We gotta open the door." He was already at the security keypad when Okun realized what he was doing.

"No!" the doctor shouted. "We can't risk releasing an airborne virus. Turn up the ventilation system. Jenny, stand by with one hundred cc's of sodium Pentothal just in case our little friend here decides to get rowdy."

While the others gagged on the fumes and tried to clear

their eyes, Okun returned to examining the creature. The crown of the alien's head was visible tucked into the chest cavity of its host animal. He ripped open the throat and upper chest of the armor until the fleshy, bulbous head of the alien lay exposed. The huge lidless black eyes stared back up at him. Okun bent close to examine the creature's face, slathered in a thick coat of gelatinous slime, the material that passed the alien's impulses out to the armor-body. The eyes showed no response, but the beaklike nose began to twitch as Okun hovered over it. One of the facial tentacles curled towards the eyes, moving weakly back and forth. Okun poked at it once before letting it curl around the finger of his gloved hand with the strength of a newborn baby. It seemed to be the same kind of friendly gesture he had read about in the extensive notes left by his predecessor, Dr. Welles.

"Damn!" Colin returned to the table as the ventilation system began filtering out the worst of the powerful, pungent odor. "They've conquered space travel but not BO."

"Release me," Okun said softly to no one in particular.

"Pardon?" Everyone looked up at the doctor for an explanation, but he seemed not to realize he'd said anything.

"Okay, let's pull him out of there. I'll—" He broke off in midsentence, staring out into space.

"Doctor? Doctor Okun, you all right?"

He stared back at them for a moment as if he were having trouble remembering who they were and where he was. Then, just as quickly, he snapped out of it. "Yeah, I'm fine. I think the fumes are starting to get to me a little."

"The tentacles are showing increased activity, doctor. Shall I go ahead and inject the Pentothal?" Jenny asked.

Sodium Pentothal, most famous as a supposed "truth serum," was a common barbiturate used to tranquilize patients during medical procedures.

"No. Bad idea. No injections." Okun was staring

straight ahead once more, talking in a calm, almost slurred voice. "Remove the restraints."

His assistants were accustomed to Okun acting strangely, but they'd never seen him do anything downright spooky. Seemingly disoriented, his head slowly swiveled around on his shoulders while his eyes darted from one thing to the next, investigating the room around him. Then he reached up and grabbed his head with his free hand, obviously in agony. He shouted once, gripped by a vicious pain coursing through his head. Jenny nudged the orderly standing next to her, using her eyes to call attention to the doctor's wrist. One of the tentacles from the creature's back had slipped free and wrapped itself around Okun's wrist just above the rubber glove.

"Let's stick him," she ordered.

Patrick pulled back the thick flesh of the armor-body and wiped at the alien's neck with an alcohol swab. Jenny stabbed the hypodermic needle into the translucent flesh and began to squeeze the plunger. Before anyone had time to flinch, the tentacle holding Okun's wrist flashed over the table and whipped Jenny across the face, knocking her across the room in a spatter of blood. Lightning fast, the same powerful arm tore the restraining belts away, breaking them off where they were bolted to the steel frame, then cracked down savagely on Colin's head as he turned to run for the door. Patrick picked up a surgeon's scalpel, waving the small weapon threateningly, as if that would be enough to protect him from this ferocious, overpowering beast. It stood up, its sharp claw-like feet clacking on the clean linoleum floor, and charged across the room. Two of the tentacles pinned his arms while a third impaled him, stabbing into his heart and coming out the other side. Patrick's body smashed into the formaldehyde tank, shattering it. As the contents of the tank flooded onto the floor of the operating theater, one of the vacuum tubes was torn loose, gushing great quantities of steam into the air.

The vaultlike door pushed open and Mitchell showed the president, his advisers, and bodyguards into the storage vault. The operating theater was completely hidden by a thick cloud of steam. When Mitchell saw this, he reached down and unsnapped the flap on his pistol. Before he could withdraw it, one Secret Service man had pulled the president away and the other had a revolver pointed directly at the major's head. The big soldier never noticed. Realizing something had gone wrong, he rushed to the window and activated the intercom system.

"Dr. Okun, can you hear me?" he called. "If you can hear me, sir, say something so we know you're all right." There was no response. The clouds of steam rolled silently behind the glass. Mitchell turned to the president. "Sir, there's a—"

Slam! Okun's blood-smeared body smashed violently against the glass, a thick tangle of quivering tentacle wrapped around his throat. It was impossible to know if he was dead or alive. Camouflaged by the thick fog, the alien forced the scientist's face tightly against the glass, pushing it out of shape. Okun's mouth opened and words came out, but the voice was not his. The words were barely intelligible, like a dead man's last breath passing over his vocal chords.

"Lelethe meh. Lelethe meh," the voice croaked.

"We've got to get him out of there," Mitchell yelled. "I'll go around and open the door."

"Stay where you are," General Grey ordered. He stepped closer to the window. "Doctor Okun, can you hear me?"

Slowly, Okun's lips opened again, and this time the words were more intelligible. "...will kill... release me. Now!"

Grey and the others began to understand what was happening. The alien was speaking through Okun, controlling his body like a ventriloquist controls a wooden dummy. The formaldehyde tank had shut itself off and the ventilation system was slowly clearing the atmosphere inside the room. Slowly, they were able to see where the tentacle holding Okun to the glass came from. It led up to where the creature hung from the ceiling, frantically clawing at an air duct in an attempt to escape. Frustrated, the animal dropped to the floor, then advanced toward the windows through the swirling steam.

Its indistinct outline stood writhing at the center of the clearing room. Okun had been half right about the tentacles. The creature inside had no corresponding limbs to control those on the suit. They danced and jangled without direction until the alien, by force of concentration, made them do its bidding.

They were, in fact, the alien's weapon of choice, having trained with them from birth.

Whitmore and the others could see how the torn skull and chest of the suit flopped lifelessly from the rigid backbone. The larger animal had been gutted, sliced from navel to forehead, providing a sort of open hood for the creature within,

Once more, it punched at the window with Okun's limp body. It was quickly learning how to work the speech organs of the man's not-quite-dead body. This time the words were clear and loud. "Release me!"

Whitmore came halfway to the windows. "Why have you come here?" he demanded. "What do your people want?"

The pulsing, livid crown of the alien's skull appeared from between the hip sockets of the suit. Black eyes peered over the wall of flesh. Then with an audible slurp, the creature raised up out of the suit's lower abdomen to face his captors. Its yellow skin glistened in the dim light under a thick slather of clear jelly. Its huge, startled eyes gave it the look of a naturally meek animal surrounded by predators.

Okun, under the creature's control, gasped suddenly for breath. "Air. Water. Food. Sun."

"Yes, we have all of these," Whitmore replied through the intercom. "Tell me where you have come from. Where is your home?"

"Here," it said slowly, "our new home."

"And before here, where did you come from?"

"Many worlds."

"We have enough air and water and sun. We could share them. Can we negotiate a truce? Can your people coexist with us?" There was no answer, but the president persisted. "Can there be peace between us?" A voice behind him suggested that the thing might not understand the word peace, so he tried a different angle. "What is it that you want? What do you want our people to do?"

The alien answered the question. This time it did not use the humans' clumsy grunting form of communication. It "spoke" in its natural language, free of sound, gesture, and emotion. Perhaps the sodium Pentothal was taking effect, or perhaps the alien had read their minds and learned he could not escape. It began a high-speed telepathic communication with Whitmore. It was a language of images and physical sensations, a lightning fast download of a virtual reality rocket ride through the alien's entire memory. The exchange of information was happening faster than the synapses of Whitmore's brain could fire. The result was that the president fell over backward clutching at the left side of his brain, screaming in pain.

In a few seconds, he moved through battles on other worlds, learning how the aliens had conquered planet after planet, flying from place to place like a swarm of locusts, feeding on an environment, expanding their population, until its resources were ruined, exhausted. Provisions would be made for the journey to the next feeding ground, and they would all board the mother ship, the temporary hive. All the creatures would sleep during the long journey and awaken famished, warriors ready to do battle for new food. He understood there would be no mercy, that the concept of it was nowhere in the alien's mind, as foreign to him as it would be for us to spare the lives of roaches. To him, we were vermin, filthy little things that needed to be exterminated. And that was their plan, to wipe humanity off the face of this small planet. The objective of the initial wave of attack would be to exterminate the largest nests of humans, disable their weapons, and establish beach heads, room for the aliens to establish their colonies. Then, for many years, they would live and breed here, developing new tools, until it was time to travel, stronger and more numerous, to the next home.

"Kill it!" Grey shouted.

Mitchell and both of the president's bodyguards spun around and started blasting, shattering the window, squeezing off every round of ammunition they had. The bullets tore into the alien's delicate white body, smearing him against the shell of his armor like thick gops of paint. The armor-body collapsed backward with a crash onto the wet tiles, both creatures dead. Okun slid down the window and collapsed in a pile.

"Stand back," Grey yelled, returning to the president, "give the man some air."

Woozy and disoriented, Whitmore lay on the floor breathing hard. When he sat up, he was still holding the side of his throbbing head. "Wanted me to understand… communicated with me. They're like locusts," he said. "They travel from planet to planet. The whole civilization moves. After they've consumed everything, the natural resources, they move on."

As if slowly untangling himself from a strong dream, Whitmore sat on the floor piecing the images together. He wanted to explain it all to the others, but there was only one conclusion to draw from the experience. He stood up the best he could and turned to Grey. "General, coordinate a missile strike. I want a nuclear warhead sent to every one of their ships. And I want it done immediately."

Grey looked the president in the eyes to make sure he realized what he was saying. The poisonous fallout from that number of simultaneous explosions would cripple the planet and every creature on it. Satisfied that Whitmore was lucid, he nodded.

"It'll take some time, maybe an hour." Under the weight of this order, Grey started off toward the war room. On the way, he passed Nimziki, who had remained silent until then.

As Grey passed him, Nimziki smirked. *I told you so.*

Steven Hiller was a hero to the horde of people parked outside the hangar. He was also someone they could talk to, a member of their group. The guards outside the hangar were tight-lipped and unfriendly; as far as they were concerned, these campers weren't welcome. Their orders were to keep the people supplied with fresh water and let them use the bathrooms two at a time, which meant the bushes off in the distance were getting most of the business. It was night when Steve walked out, telling the guards at the gate that he was sent by Dr. Issacs to check on the sick boy. Steve never made it to the Casse trailer. A bunch of people waiting in line to use the restrooms recognized him and walked with him as he disappeared into the thicket of vehicles.

Steve moved through the trailers shaking hands and answering the same questions over and over again. Was the ET still alive? What were they doing with it? Were there any spaceships coming this way and why couldn't they come inside? Why were they being made to sit out there like sitting ducks? They made him promise to ask whoever was in charge if they could come inside.

Steve moved among them, listening and smiling, but he hadn't come out there to fraternize. His concentration was on a pair of Hueys, fat gray transport helicopters standing outside another hangar three hundred yards from the perimeter of the trailer camp. Steve watched for a few minutes, until he decided they were unguarded. Excusing himself from the conversation, he strode across the tarmac trying to look like he was on official business. He kept expecting someone with a bullhorn to stop him, but to his surprise he made it all the way unchallenged, climbed into the pilot's chair, and switched the systems on. There was plenty of gas, so he reached for the switch that fired the motor. A split second after the twin rotors, front and back propellers, came groaning to life, Steve had an M-16 rifle pointed at his chest.

"What are you doing? Get out of there, this minute."

The soldier on the other end of the rifle looked to be no older that eighteen. Dressed in camouflage fatigues, his desert helmet fit him like an old wash pail bouncing loosely around his head. Although he was the one holding the weapon, it was clear from the start who was afraid of whom. Steve decided to brazen it out. He reached back and pulled the seat belt forward, locking himself in.

"Captain Hiller, Marine Corps. I'm going to borrow your chopper for a couple of hours."

"You can't just—" The kid looked around for help, but they were alone. "The hell you are... sir."

Steve figured there was a fifty-fifty chance the kid would shoot. He decided to gamble. Reaching up, he switched on the lights and prepared the craft for liftoff.

"Soldier," he shouted over the blades, the air knocking the kid's desert helmet around, "I know you don't want to shoot me, but if you're gonna do it, do it. right now, because otherwise I'm leaving."

The kid stared unblinking at him for a minute. Without lowering his gun, he yelled, "You're gonna get me into a world of trouble, Marine."

"We're both in one already." A jeep was barreling toward them on its way across the tarmac from the main hangar. "I'll be back in a couple hours and explain everything." Then the big bird thumped into the air and twisted away to the west.

News of Whitmore's decision to launch a nuclear attack spread through the underground scientific complex, plunging the place into a deep silence. Work came to a standstill as people huddled into groups, most of them sitting silently, resigned to their doom. No one was happy with the decision, but neither could they suggest a workable alternative. There was nothing to do now but wait.

Connie, on the verge of tears, slipped away from the oppressive gloom of the war room, where Whitmore sat drumming his fingernails on the tabletop, while the strike was prepared. She came into the echoing concrete hangar, keeping one eye on the stingray attacker. Through a set of windows, she could see David pacing back and forth in an office lounge, talking to himself. She came up the stairs and into the room to discover he wasn't talking to himself. He was speaking to a bottle of scotch he'd found in one of the closets.

"I take it you've heard," she said, closing the door behind her.

"Ah, Ms. Spano, you're just in time!" His voice was too loud. He was already drunk. Hoisting the bottle into the air, he declared, "A toast! I would like to propose a toast to the end of the world." He threw back his head and took a long slug of whiskey before handing her the bottle.

"He didn't come to this decision lightly, David." She

felt guilty, complicitous in his eyes.

"Connie, honey, come on! Don't tell me you still believe in this guy."

"He's a good man."

"He must be." David laughed, flopping into a swivel chair and pushing himself in a circle. "After all, you left a gem like me for him. No. Excuse me, not for him. For your *career*." David knew how to be nasty, but Connie wanted to explain herself.

"It wasn't just a career move, David. It was a once in a lifetime opportunity. It was a chance to make a real difference, to make my life mean something."

"And I just wasn't ambitious enough for you," David said casually. It was an idea that had crippled him with pain for the last few years, but now it all seemed rather humorous. "I couldn't get the lead out of my ass and start climbing up the ladder."

"You could have done anything you wanted," she yelled, "research, teaching, industry. You've got so much talent."

David broke out into a vicious imitation of the familiar voices: "Oh, that David Levinson, so much potential and all he does is work for that silly old cable company. All that brain power going down the drain. What a shame." That attitude disgusted him. "What's the matter with being happy right where you are?"

"But didn't you ever want to do something more? Didn't you ever want to be part of something really meaningful, really special?"

Those last few words mixed with the scotch to punch David square in the solar plexus. He leveled a wounded stare at Connie and told her the plain simple truth. "I felt like I *was* part of something special."

She immediately realized that the whole time she'd been talking about their careers, he'd been thinking about their marriage. She could see that she'd hurt him. He came across the room and took back the bottle.

"If it makes any difference," she said softly, "I never stopped loving you."

"But that wasn't enough, right?" he spit back. He returned to his chair and took a good long swig of whiskey.

Connie suddenly realized why she'd come to find him. She wanted to make peace with a man she still loved. Somewhere in the back of her head she thought they might forgive each other, renounce their anger, and try to find some comfort in one another now that the end of their lives was clearly within sight. But instead, she'd encountered a venomously angry boy. As he did so often with her, David's way of coping with pressure was to retreat into himself, or his work, or whatever was close at hand and offered escape. Tonight it was a bottle of Johnny Walker.

She left him there, spinning around in the swivel chair, singing to himself. With tears in her eyes, she slipped out the door, closing it quietly behind her.

Grey was able to orchestrate the nuclear strike in less than a quarter of the time he'd anticipated. Returning to the war room, he got the good news that military radar and radar capabilities had been partially restored thanks to some quick thinking in San Antonio. The cluster of Air Force bases surrounding the city had scrambled two dozen AWACS into the skies over the United States. The large spy planes, with their trademark radar dishes whirling on top and sophisticated eavesdropping equipment within, took over the job orbiting Comsats had done so reliably for decades. Their multichannel switching relays allowed military personnel to begin communicating once again. One of the first messages they broadcast came from Area 51. There was to be a simultaneous nuclear strike against all the ships over American airspace.

Within minutes, a quartet of B-2 Stealth bombers was in the air, streaking toward their targets. They flew "dark," meaning their radar-deflecting systems were up and their radios were switched off, hoping to avoid detection by the city destroyers until they came within striking distance. The president was in the infirmary being examined by Dr. Issacs when word came that the B-2s were airborne. Without hesitation, Whitmore pushed the doctor aside and hurried to the war room.

"Which target are we going to reach first?" he demanded, barging through the door.

A soldier turned from one of the monitor consoles. "The ship approaching Houston. Approximate intercept time is six minutes. We can't say for sure because the B-2s are flying dark."

Whitmore thought for a minute before issuing a change. "Wake the B-2s up. I want to make sure we all stay on the same page."

The soldier spun back to his console and typed in the code word that switched the B-2s' radios on automatically. Instantly, the radar scans spotted them and the four planes blipped up on the screens. The Houston plane was easily the closest to its target.

"All right, here's what I want," Whitmore explained to the room, "one plane, one bomb. Let's see what happens in Houston. Maybe we can hit that one before it arrives over the city. If we're successful, we'll go ahead and fire on the others right away." He looked at Grey, who was scowling over a computer printout.

"General, has there been any word from our friends?" At the same time he was authorizing the use of an atomic weapon, he was trying to restrain their use by the rest of the world. ICBMs in many locations were programmed to respond automatically to radar-perceived attacks. The last thing the earth needed was a chain-reaction nuclear launch initiated by computers.

"We have commitments from most of our friends. They'll wait to see our results," Grey said. "But I think we're too late to save Houston."

"That's affirmative, sir," a voice rang out from the consoles. "The enemy ship is already over the city."

The president didn't flinch. He knew Houston would be lost one way or the other. He sent orders to the other B-2s that they were to hold their fire until the Houston bomb's impact on the invaders' ship could be assessed.

Grey had arranged for observers in armored tanks to position themselves around the perimeter of the expected blast area. One of the San Antonio AWACS spy planes also positioned itself over the Gulf of Mexico at high altitude.

The people of Houston had wasted no time. With only a few hours of warning, the city was almost ninety percent vacant by the time the ground began to tremble under the approaching ship. The evacuation had turned ugly, causing almost two thousand casualties and countless injuries as escapees were trampled under foot or hit by speeding vehicles. Similar frenzied exoduses were underway in Kobe, Brussels, Portland, Chicago, and all the other major cities standing in the paths of the great black ships.

Whitmore called for a moment of silence. After whispering a brief prayer, he ordered the strike with a simple nod. "May our children forgive us."

The B-2's bay doors dropped open, depositing its twelve-foot-long missile into the air. It flew parallel with the batlike plane while the tracking system in its nose cone scanned the horizon and configured its telemetry. A second later, it blasted forward to its rendezvous with the gigantic ship's protective screen.

"Payload is deployed," the pilot reported. He pulled a long U-turn and put distance between himself and the coming explosion.

Everyone in the war room held their breath, following the bomb's approach on their radar screens. As planned, the cruise missile approached the shield on the ship's top side in an attempt to minimize damage to the city below.

From the AWACS plane, there was a violent shock of ultrabright light followed immediately by the sight of suburban Houston vaporizing, folding and collapsing like tall grass in a sudden wind. The destruction traveled outward in concentric circles at an awesome rate of speed. In a few seconds, the racing explosion was over and the entire area was covered with dense smoke. An immense mushroom cloud gathered and floated higher into the sky. In the war room, the destruction showed up as nothing more than a small patch of fuzziness, an atmospheric disturbance bleeding across lower Texas, but no one felt the loss of innocent lives more than the men and women in that small room. With pained expressions, Whitmore and his staff watched and waited.

Minutes later, the AWACS pilot broke radio silence. "Unfortunately, it looks like our target is still in the air."

The team at Area 51 let out a collective groan. After twenty-four hours of shocking disappointments, this one was possibly the worst. This had been humanity's last line of defense, its last chance.

"Yes, that's confirmed," the pilot went on, "we've got a good look now. Target looks to be in good shape. In fact, it's still moving in over Houston. Jesus Christ, we didn't even put a scratch on her."

"Call the other planes back," Whitmore said softly.

Nimziki couldn't believe it. "The other bombers might have better luck," he argued. "One of their destroyers is en route to Chicago. We still have time to intercept it and deliver multiple warheads. We can't just give up!"

"I said call them back."

The president sank into a chair and stared up at the

ceiling. The failure to inflict any damage on the aliens' ship convinced him there was no way to prevent them from landing. Suddenly, he felt like there was plenty of time. Somehow, he knew from his mind-meld experience with the captured alien, it would take them a couple of years to move the entire population down to earth from the mother ship.

In light of what happened in Houston, it seemed to be time now to rethink the strategy of fighting the aliens and time to begin organizing ways to resist them once they began their invasion. The only logical course of action Whitmore could see was to wait for them to establish their cities, then blow the world to smithereens. Mankind was going to be exterminated, he knew, without mercy. *If we're lucky,* he told himself, *we might be able to take them down with us.*

Jasmine, fighting sleep, watched the embers of the dying fire. Although she was exhausted, too many dangers, real and imagined, lurked in the darkness for her to close her eyes. Marilyn Whitmore, near by, seemed to be resting easily. The quiet man wasn't as quiet as before: he was snoring, really sawing some logs.

In the distance, Jas could hear the sound of helicopter blades and wondered if removing the First Lady from the crash site had been the right thing to do. For all she knew, the helicopter in the distance was out there searching for Marilyn. Coming to El Toro, especially after all the warnings she'd heard along the way, felt like a horrible mistake. She would have left immediately to get Marilyn to a hospital, but in her haste to find Steve, she had smashed out the headlights on the truck by crashing through barricades of rubble. Traveling in the dark could be too dangerous.

The helicopter would come closer, scanning the ground with a searchlight. Not until it was half a mile off did Jas think it might actually find their tiny camp. She grabbed a branch and stirred the fire, sending a shower of sparks into the air. The others awoke to see the chopper heading toward them, the blinding searchlight in their eyes. Jas waved her arms and pointed at Mrs. Whitmore. To everyone's surprise, the helicopter began to set down not far off. Jas ran toward the spot, eager to get some help. When she saw who was piloting the big olive green bird she burst out weeping and laughing at the same time. Overwhelmed, she ran to the helicopter and jumped through the door into Steve's arms. She smothered him with kisses, then yelled over the noise of the blades, "You're late!"

He grinned and yelled back, "I know how much you like big dramatic entrances."

Steve brought a stretcher from the helicopter and, together with the quiet man, loaded Marilyn in the back for the ride back to Area 51. It didn't look like she would live to see her husband again. She was coughing badly again, hacking up blood.

Steve pulled the quiet man close and shouted, "We got room for one more, buddy. You wanna take a trip to Nevada?" When the man shook his head no, Steve shrugged, "Suit yourself. Jas, let's go!"

As Jasmine passed the quiet man, she asked, "You're not coming?"

The man just looked at her, droopy-eyed, then gestured toward the band of wounded people they'd collected during the afternoon. He didn't want to leave them. She handed over the keys to the truck and told him where the supply of food was hidden. Before she turned to go, she looked into the man's eyes. "Hey, my name's Jasmine Dubrow. What's yours?"

The man looked at her sadly, as if he hadn't understood.

Steve bellowed, "Jas, let's go. We've got to go now."

Tearing herself away, she trotted to the copter and

strapped herself in, then watched the quiet man grow smaller and smaller as she flew away.

Dr. Isaacs felt like a marathon runner hitting the wall. Thirty hours of nonstop work were taking their toll. Bleary-eyed and sallow, he looked in on Mrs. Whitmore, a fake smile smeared across his face. When he saw her sleeping, his face dropped back into a mask. A moment later, he saw the president trotting down the corridor carrying a child in his arms. Behind him, Connie and a Secret Service agent jogged along on either side.

"How is she?" he demanded.

Issacs gave the president a look that told the whole story. Turning to the little girl riding in her father's arms, he said, "I'll bet you're Patricia Whitmore."

"Hey, how'd you know that?" The six-year-old was always amazed when strangers knew her name.

"Because your mommy is right inside there and I know she wants to see you. But you have to promise to be gentle, okay? She's very sick." The moment she was turned loose, Patricia tore around the corner like she hadn't heard a word.

"I'm sorry, Mr. President," Issacs said. "Perhaps if we'd gotten to her sooner. She's bleeding internally. Even if we had gotten to her immediately, I'm not sure…" His voice trailed off. "There's nothing else we can do for her, sir."

The president put a hand on Dr. Issacs's shoulder before straightening himself up and pushing through the double doors.

"Oh, my munchkin!" Marilyn was doing her best to wrap an arm around her daughter. She looked weak, but not on the verge of death.

Remembering to be very gentle, Patricia reached up and patted her mother's stomach. "Mommy, we were so worried. We didn't know where you were."

"I know. I'm so sorry, but I'm right here now, baby."

Issacs waved the medical staff out of the room. When the last of them were gone, Whitmore walked over to the bed and knelt down next to Patricia. "Honey, why don't you wait outside so Mommy can get some rest."

Reluctantly, the little girl kissed her mother and went outside to wait with Connie. As soon as she was gone, Marilyn's brave smile shattered into tears and whimpers of pain. She reached for her husband's hand.

"I'm so scared, Tom," she whispered, tears pouring freely down both cheeks.

"Hey, none of that," he said bravely, "the doctor said he's optimistic, said you're going to pull through this."

She smiled and rolled her eyes. "Liar," she said, squeezing his hand with fading strength. Then the two of them put their heads together and cried. They cried and kissed and looked into one another's eyes until she fell asleep for the last time.

When the president finally stepped out of the room, his face was drained of color, his eyes bloodshot. A number of people waited at a respectful distance down the hallway, most of them with questions for their leader. They needed his approval on communiques and authorizations for troop movements, the thousand decisions presidents made every day. But the man who stepped into the hallway didn't feel at all presidential. Overwhelmed with grief, he didn't feel capable of acting as the leader of anything. Without a word, he moved through the people in the hall until he came to Jasmine. Before he could find his voice, she reached out and took his hand.

"I'm sorry," she told him. "I'm so sorry." She still felt a lingering guilt about not being able to get Marilyn to a doctor sooner.

Whitmore shook his head. "I just want to say thank

you for looking after her. She told me. You sound like a very brave woman." He turned to Steve and managed a weak smile. "And you again! Thank you for letting me say goodbye to her."

Patricia had followed her father down the hall. "Is Mommy sleeping now?"

He reached down and picked the girl up, realizing he didn't have the strength to explain it all just yet. "Yes, baby," he said, squeezing her in his arms, "Mommy's sleeping."

By the time Connie found Julius and asked him to speak to his son, David had turned the small office space into a disaster area. Acting much drunker than he actually was, he had thrown the chairs against the room and overturned the refrigerator. He was storming around kicking the furniture when Julius saw him through the plate-glass windows and hurried into the room.

"David! David! What in the hell are you doing? Stop already!"

David was just about out of gas anyway. He stopped flailing long enough to explain, "What's it look like I'm doing? I'm making a mess."

"This I can see," Julius assured him. "And why? Why are you messing?"

"We've gotta burn the rain forest, pops. We've got to dump all our toxic waste!" To illustrate his point, he emptied out a waste paper can, then threw it against the far wall. "We've got to pollute the air! Rip us the ozone! Maybe if we screw this planet up badly enough they won't want it anymore." Taking careful aim at a coffee cup someone had left at the edge of the counter, David did his best to kick it. He missed by a mile and ended up sprawled on his ass in the middle of his own litter.

"Well," Julius looked around the room, admiring the

work his son had accomplished, "you've gotten us off to a good start. This room is officially polluted. Now it doesn't matter if the Martians kill me, because when the bill comes for this office I'll die of a heart attack."

He walked over to David, who laid back and put his arms over his head, moaning. Clearing a spot, Julius sat down next to his son. He suspected David's tantrum had more to do with Connie than he was willing to admit. He searched for the right thing to say. "Listen," he began, "everyone loses faith at some point. Take me, for example. I haven't spoken to God since your mother died."

David opened one eye, surprised by his father's revelation.

"But sometimes," the old man went on thoughtfully, "you have to stop and remember all the things you do have. You've got to be *thankful*."

David snorted and covered his head again. "What have we got to be thankful about anymore?"

"For instance…" Julius looked around, searching for an idea. At a temporary loss, he said the only thing he could think of. "Your health! At least you've still got your health." He knew that was a pretty lame argument and didn't blame David for moaning again. Nevertheless, he took hold of an arm and began tugging his son to his feet. "Come on, let's go look for a jacket and a cup of coffee. Drinking weakens your system. I don't want you catching a cold."

Reluctantly, David let himself be pulled to his feet. Then suddenly he stiffened, caught in the grip of a startling idea. Something like a smile twitched across his lips.

"What did you just say?"

"About faith? Sometimes a man can live his entire life…"

"No, the second part. Right after that." David turned and looked through the glass at the alien attacker resting just outside.

"What? That you might catch a cold?"

"Pop, that's it. That's the answer. Sick. Cold. The defenses come down! It's so simple. Pops, you're a genius!!"

Julius gave him a long, suspicious look, wondering if his son had finally gone off the deep end.

When Julius finally persuaded her that David was sober enough to be on to something worthwhile, Connie had gone to the president and asked him to come into the storage hangar where David wanted to demonstrate something about the alien attacker. He claimed to have a plan.

The group had gathered on the observation platform, standing around waiting. "All right, Ms. Spano, what's this all about?" Nimziki demanded, impatient from the second he'd walked in.

"I really have no idea," she said, talking to the whole group. "He wanted everyone here to show us something about the spacecraft."

Nimziki bristled at the idea of being summoned by a civilian and not even being able to get a straight answer. "Well, let's get on with this," he said testily. "We've all got more important things to do."

Connie was fed up with this pompous ass. She put her hands on her hips and was about to lay into him when the president came striding down the steel ramp into the hangar. He called a group of advisers to one side of the ramp and had a quick word with them.

Dylan standing beside Steve, asked loudly, "Does that plane fly in outer space?"

"It certainly does," Steve told him.

David came through the cabin hatch and climbed down the ladder to the large pedestal holding the attacker. He gave a technician inside the ship a few last-minute instructions, then jogged toward the observation platform.

"What have you got for us, David?" This time

Whitmore's use of David's first name implied no challenge. He'd been hit in the gut so hard, so many times over the last two days, he was way too weary to try to pull a power trip on anyone. He spoke as one frightened man to another.

"Ladies and gentlemen, boys and girls," David began, sounding a lot like the late Dr. Okun, "I've worked up a little demonstration. It'll just take a moment of your time."

David reached into a trash receptacle and fished out a soda can. "We'll just recycle this guy," he said to himself, trotting back to the attacker and reaching up to set the can on the tip of the wing. When he returned to the observation platform, he waved a signal to the technician sitting behind the windows of the attacker. The man hit a switch, then gave David a thumbs up. Looking at the crowd on the platform, David could see he'd captured their interest. "Major Mitchell, from where you're standing, do you think you could shoot that can off the ship?"

Mitchell looked at the president, who returned a "why not?" shrug. Unsnapping the flap on his holster, he withdrew his pistol. After a last quizzical look around, Mitchell, a pretty fair marksman, raised his firearm and sighted on the can, slowly squeezing the trigger. With a crack, the bullet blasted out of the gun and crashed against the protective shield. A loud clink sounded when the ricochet struck one of the iron catwalks above. Suddenly everyone lost enthusiasm for the experiment.

"Oops, I didn't think about that," David apologized. "You see, the can is protected by the ship's invisible shield. We can't penetrate their defenses."

"We know that already," Nimziki said. "Is there a point to all of this?"

"My point," David said, getting to the good part of his show, "is that since we can't break through their shields, we've got to work our way around them."

David walked over to a rolling tool shelf where he'd

set up his laptop computer. It was connected to a cable that ran through the shield, into the cockpit of the alien craft, and plugged into the shield receiving unit he'd repaired earlier that day.

"This will just take a second." David typed instructions into the machine, then stared down at his wristwatch, silently counting down.

"Now, Major Mitchell, as far as my assistant sitting in the cockpit is concerned, the ship's shield is still protecting the can. He hasn't made any adjustments. Would you mind trying to shoot the can again?"

Reluctant to send another bullet ricocheting through the concrete bunker, Mitchell looked testily at David. Not until Grey gave him the go-ahead did he unholster his gun.

"Hold on now!" Steve wasn't taking any chances. He carried Dylan to the top of the ramp and got behind the concrete corner. Most of the observers followed him up there. Mitchell took careful aim and shot again. This time, the can flipped over backwards and the bullet clanged off the wall at the far end of the big hangar.

"How did you do that?" General Grey asked, suitably impressed.

"I gave it a cold."

Julius, beaming with pride, nodded to the others in the group. The president, intrigued, moved closer to where David continued working with his computer.

"More accurately," he went on without looking up, "I gave it a virus. A computer virus. Nasty little things, very hard to shake once you've caught one." With a final, artistic tap, he hit the ENTER key, then turned the machine around to show Whitmore and Grey the graphic he'd brought up. The president studied the screen for a moment, nodding in agreement with what he saw.

Grey, who knew computers but hated them at the same

time, kept his eyes on David. "Are you telling us you can send some kind of a signal that will disable *all* their shields?"

David touched his fingertip to his nose. "Exactly. Just as they used our satellites against us, we can use their own shield signal against them... if."

"If what?"

"If we can plant the virus in the mother ship, it would then be sent down into the city destroyers and the attack ships like this one. Okun told us that this ship's power was coming directly from the mother ship, so that must be true of the large ships, as well."

"I hate to poop on your party," Nimziki had snuck to the edge of the observation platform and was leaning over the railing for a look at the computer screen, "but just how are you proposing to 'infect' the mother ship with this virus? They don't have a Web page on the Internet." He looked around for others to share his joke.

David responded without hesitation. "We'll have to fly this attack craft out of our atmosphere and dock with the mother ship." He said it as if it were the most natural, obvious idea in the world.

Steve's ears perked up the way they always did when space flight was mentioned. He set Dylan down and walked down the ramp to hear more. David unrolled one of the satellite photos of the mother ship, the 415-mile-long titan which was waiting patiently behind the moon for the destroyers to pave her way. All concentration, David handed the president one corner of the blurry poster-sized satellite photo.

"Here—" David indicated what looked like a docking bay "—we can enter right here. They seem to follow a certain logic in the design of their ships. If this one is like the city destroyers, this is the front door."

David could sense that the politicians and military bigwigs around him were more than skeptical.

"You know what? He's probably right." Steve surprised everyone, including himself by interrupting the intense discussion. Everyone turned to look at him, so he continued. "When I flew past that door on the LA ship—city destroyer, I guess you're calling them—I could see this big-ass—I mean, this giant docking bay inside. The ships park in clusters around a central towerlike thingie."

"Dr. Okun showed me that the long finlike structure on top of the attacker is full of terminal wiring. He hypothesized that whatever type of computer link they run, the fin is the connector. When one of these attackers docks inside the larger ships, some type of connection is established through the fin."

"Oh, spare me the bad science fiction," Nimziki moaned from his rail. "This plan is so full of what ifs, it's ridiculous."

Ignoring him, Grey asked, "How long would their shields be down?"

"That's anyone's guess," David told him. "Once they discover the virus, it could be only a matter of minutes until they figure a way past it. It's not very complicated, because I don't know enough about their system."

"So you're suggesting that we coordinate a worldwide counterstrike with a window of only a few minutes?" Nimziki shook his head; it was ludicrous.

Grey turned around to face the intelligence chief. "We've got our radio link to Asia reestablished. The signal is weak, but we should be able to send some sort of instructions. If we could get past those damn shields, it might be possible."

Nimziki's mocking grin disappeared. He was angry that this lame brain idea was getting so much attention when the perfectly plausible option of a nuclear strike, *his plan,* had been dumped after a single failure. If he could have, he would have locked the whole group up in the spaceship and ordered the strike himself.

Thinly masking his criticism of Whitmore by seeming to address everyone in the room, he boomed, "I don't believe you're buying into any of this nonsense. We don't have the resources or the manpower to launch that kind of a campaign. If we had two months to plan it, maybe. Not to mention *that* piece of rubbish," he shouted, pointing at the alien ship. "The whole cockamamie plan depends on this untested flying saucer that no one in the world is qualified to operate."

Once again, Steve interrupted. He stepped forward and cleared his throat. "Er... I believe I might be qualified for that job, sir." Nimziki shot him a murderous look, but Steve went on. "I've seen them in action. I know how they maneuver." He looked the president in the eyes. "With your permission, sir, I'd like a shot at it."

"That thing's a wreck. It crash-landed in the forties, for chrissakes. We don't even know if it's capable of flying."

"Aha!" David took center stage once more. He had a group of Okun's staff waiting in the wings. "Release the clamps!" he called out like the ringmaster at a circus. He looked up at Connie standing on the observation platform. She rolled her eyes to show him how crazy she thought he was, and how proud she was. "C'mon, c'mon, remove the clamps."

It took longer than David expected, but once the technicians opened the last of the steel locks, there was a loud clank as it lifted up and flipped over onto the ground.

In a moment, the mass of the sixty-foot ship had lifted into the air, wobbling unevenly above them. At a height of fifteen feet, it stabilized and sat as perfectly still as it had for the last fifty years. Their mouths open in amazement, the gallery of spectators looked at David.

"Any other questions?"

Everyone looked at everyone else. Not even Nimziki knew what to say at that point. Finally, Whitmore broke the silence. He shook his head, showing what he thought of the plan before announcing, "It's a long shot, but let's give it a shot."

Suddenly everyone was talking, asking questions, or, like Nimziki, offering their opinion of why the idea was doomed from the outset. David came to the side of the observation platform, reached up and tugged on the leg of Steve's fatigues. The young pilot quit staring at the alien plane and leaned closer to hear David better.

"You really think you can fly this thing?" he asked, showing a clear lack of confidence in Steve's ability.

Steve returned the favor. "You really think you can do all that bullshit you said you could?"

Within minutes, Connie was escorting General Grey and the president back to Area 51's makeshift war room, all of them talking at once, fleshing out the details of the plan, figuring out some of the tough communications hurdles that a simultaneous worldwide strike would entail. They felt a spark of hope for the first time in what seemed like a long while.

"Hold on!" It was a command, not a request. The three looked back to see Nimziki storming down the hallway after them.

"What now?" Connie mumbled under her breath.

The secretary of defense stepped close to the president, ignoring the two others. There was an iciness in his voice. As usual, his words were calculated to cut as deeply as possible.

"I understand that you're still upset about the death of your wife," he said, leaning over Whitmore, "but that's no excuse for making yet another fatal mistake. An objective analysis of the situation from a military standpoint—"

Nimziki never finished the sentence. Before he knew what was happening to him, Whitmore took him by the lapels of his suit and slammed him against a wall, pinning him. The president put his face close to Nimziki's, an inch away.

"The only mistake I made was appointing a sniveling weasel like you to run a government agency. But that's one mistake, I am thankful to say, I don't have to live with anymore. Mr. Nimziki, you're fired!" With a final shove, he released his grip on the man and took a step backward. Impaling Nimziki with a threatening glare, he added a final warning. "Stay as far away from me as you can get, or I'll have you arrested as a threat to national security."

Nimziki looked for support from Connie, then from Grey, but received none.

Starting once more down the hallway, Whitmore picked up where he left off. "I want Major Mitchell to organize every single airplane he can get his hands on and find us some goddamned pilots who can fly them."

Behind them, they heard Nimziki talking to the walls. "He can't do that!"

Connie couldn't help it. She looked over her shoulder and said, with unconcealed pleasure, "He just did!"

Four British pilots, sweat-stained and unshaven, were doing their best to avoid the oppressive heat of the Saudi summer. They'd pitched a large canvas tent that one of them, a pilot named Thomson, had had in his personal cargo pod, and were sitting around talking to pass the time as they waited for something to happen. One of the men, Reginald Cummins, seemed to be in charge. By no means the senior officer, Reg was nevertheless put in the position of group leader because he was the only one who knew the first bloody thing about the Middle East. The other three men had simply been delivering new planes to the base at Khamis Moushait when all hell had broken loose. Reg was on permanent assignment there. He spoke Arabic passably well and, more important, he knew how to talk to groups of pilots without offending anyone, a tricky bit of business in the Middle East, but even more important given their present situation.

"We listened in to the Americans as we were coming over Malta," Thomson was saying. "They weren't encrypted, scrambled, nothing, and one of them was saying the Syrians still had a squadron intact near the Golan Straights."

"Heights," Reg corrected him. 'The Golan Heights," and he showed Thomson where it was on the map. "If we could get them to cooperate, they'd be in excellent position to reinforce us if it comes to a dogfight. Unfortunately, they're a difficult bunch, not exactly team players."

Suddenly the tent flap tore open in a barrage of shouting. Thomson fell over backwards in his flimsy folding chair, drawing his pistol by the time he crashed to the ground. A tall dark man, with a full beard and mustache, was yelling something unintelligible into the tent. His green jumpsuit identified him as one of the boys from Jordan, probably the only one of them who didn't speak English. Reg never flinched. He looked back at the man calmly until he dropped the tent flap and hurried away.

"What in bloody hell was that all about?" The three tourist-pilots were still riding a shock-wave of adrenaline.

"Seems they're getting a signal. Old Morse code, but they can't read it. He wants us to come and see if it's English."

"Morse code? What have they got out here, old telegraph cables?" Sutton, one of the others asked. With a serious look at Reg, he asked, "Couldn't be some sort of trap, could it?"

Reg shrugged and led the way out into the blinding hot afternoon. Halfway around the world from Groom Lake's Area 51, on the smooth surface of another ancient lake bed, a hundred or so fighter planes had set down out in the middle of nowhere. The jets were parked at odd angles to one another, ready to take off in a hundred directions as soon as the alert came. It was a truly international scene, with pilots from eleven different nations, many of whom would be shooting at one another under any other circumstances, hiding together out in the middle of nowhere. They had become reluctant allies.

"I still can't believe this," Reg said with a smile, enjoying the irony of the situation. "Seventy-five years of frantic diplomacy gets us essentially nowhere, then twenty-four hours after these bastards show up, we're all one happy family"

"That's not exactly how I'd describe it," Thomson said, sticking close to Reg, offering a nervous little salute and smile to a band of Iraqi pilots smoking cigarettes in the shade of their planes. They stared blankly at the Brits as they marched past. "I don't think those chaps have caught the family spirit of the thing."

"How do you think the Israelis feel?" Second only to the Saudi contingent in size, the Israeli planes, the impressive F-15s, sat a short distance away, their planes fanned out at precise angles, prepared for a simultaneous take-off.

"What's up?" one of them called out, an Uzi propped lazily against his shoulder.

"They're getting a signal. Morse code," Reg called back.

The man tossed away his cigarette and came jogging over to join the Brits. "Am I invited?"

Reg smiled without breaking stride. "I don't see why not."

The inside of the elaborate Saudi tent looked like an electronics swap meet. They'd imported a good deal of radio equipment from a nearby air base and had it spread out on an odd assortment of carpets, parachutes, and tarps. Saudi pilots from a handful of different nations were engaged in a dozen conversations. Everything ground to a halt as the visitors came into the tent. There was a tense moment as the pilots from enemy nations stared each other down. The Arabs seemed particularly nervous about an armed Israeli coming into their space. For a tense moment, no one took a breath, let alone said anything. Finally, Reg broke the ice.

"*Latuklaka ya awlad enho nel mohamey betana,*" which translated roughly to "Don't worry, boys, he's our lawyer."

Suddenly the whole tent broke into hysterical laughter, everyone except the three visiting English pilots. They smiled along, though, anxious to help alleviate the tension.

"*Ana shaif ho gab mae kommelhaber betae,*" (I see he brought along his fountain pen,) one of the Arabs cracked, causing another laugh.

The Israeli surprised everyone by playing right along. In Palestinian slang, he joked that it was a "*Wakeh el-police Israeli ala estama rat el-ehtafalat elmausda ra,*" a ceremonial document-signer issued by the Israeli secret police. They were laughing so hard, other pilots poked their heads in to see what was going on.

"So where's this Morse code?" Reg asked in English.

One of the Saudis handed over the headphones. Instead of the dots and dashes he'd expected, he heard a voice that seemed to be making an urgent announcement. But there was too much static coming over the line. Reg signaled for quiet and the men in the tent complied. The broadcast was originating from the war room at Area 51. By the time it reached Ar-Rub Al-Khali, it had been relayed so many times Reg couldn't make heads or tails of it.

"Wait, you will hear," one of the Saudi Royal Air Force pilots told him. Sure enough, as soon as the muffled, inaudible voice finished the announcement, it was repeated in Morse code, loud and clear. It took a few minutes for Reg to get the whole thing written down, then a few more for him to decipher his own writing.

"It's from the Americans," he announced. "They want to organize a counteroffensive."

"It's about bloody time. What's their plan?" Thomson asked.

"It's... well, it's damn creative." He grinned before going on to explain the particulars.

A squadron of twenty-four Russian MiGs were parked in pairs on a vast sheet of ice. They'd been ordered into the air for an attack on the city destroyer that had already blown Moscow away and was at that time en route to St. Petersburg. When other planes began splattering themselves across the ship's protective force field, the mission was aborted. On their way back to their base at Murmansk, they listened in horror as the base was overrun and destroyed by a swarm of stingray attackers. Murmansk lay above the Arctic Circle, and the squadron flew even further north to hide among the glaciers they knew so well. They crossed the eighty-fifth parallel and set down between the rocky islands of Franz Joseph Land, where the ice hadn't thawed yet.

They arrived in the morning and had been sitting tight waiting for orders ever since. During the daylight, the sun coming through their glass canopies had warmed the cockpits, but the temperature at night was numbing cold. Miserable and starving, they sat in their planes waiting hour after hour.

Around nine o'clock, one of them was fiddling with his radio and found something at the low end of the dial. At first he thought it was the ETs talking to each other in clicking voices, but eventually he realized it was Morse code and called it to the attention of the other pilots. Fortunately, the message repeated itself several times. Almost two hours after they'd run across it, the squadron's leader, Captain Tchenko, talked to the others by radio.

"The Americans say they can bring down the shields for at least five minutes."

"*Da, da! Maladietz!*" The others endorsed the plan enthusiastically. Any plan sounded better than spending the rest of the night in the ice fields.

"When do they want to attack?"

In Sapporo, on Japan's northernmost island of Hokkaido, some of the world's most powerful civilian signal receivers and transmitters dotted the mountainsides. A thousand miles from the television and radio headquarters in Tokyo, the sensitive machines were the information link between the provinces and the capital. The engineers had come to work as usual and stayed late when they realized they might be able to help. Along with them, several members of the volunteer army were crowded around radio and television transmitters. Although Japan had no more than a symbolic air force, mainly cargo and munitions transport planes, they were determined to participate. They broadcast the message in several different languages to most of Asia.

"The attack will begin in thirteen hours," their message said, "at nine P.M. GMT."

As confirmation was received from various governments or scattered battle forces around Asia, the Hokkaido station relayed the information to Hawaii via short wave radio. From there it was sent to the USS *Steiner*, 200 miles off the Oregon coast, which bounced the signal up to the 747s out of San Antonio. As confirmations trickled back to Area 51, the data was recorded on the foldout map of the world taped to the wall of the war room.

"How are we doing?" the president asked.

"Better than we thought." Grey nodded, showing him the map. Hundreds of tiny stickers, each one representing a combat-ready air squadron, littered the map. "We're still taking inventory, but it looks promising. Europe is being hit almost as hard as we are, but the Middle East and Asia seem to have fifty percent of their capabilities intact. Plus, we still have our aircraft carriers."

"What about our troops here?"

"Unfortunately, we're the weak link. The bastards have taken out almost every air base west of the Mississippi. A handful of pilots escaped from Lackland and they're headed this way. Plus, we've got a shipment of munitions flying down from Oregon, but..." The general shook his head.

"But what?"

"Mitchell's got plenty of planes stashed around the base, but we haven't got the pilots to put them in the air."

"Then find them," Whitmore ordered, as if it were only a matter of Grey trying a little harder.

Thirty minutes later, Miguel stepped into the Casse trailer as quietly as he could. All the lights were out and he didn't want to wake up Troy. He pulled the door closed and began to kick off his shoes.

"Where the hell have you been?" Russell's voice boomed out of the darkness. "And where's that sister of yours?" The voice startled Miguel, who switched on a light. Russell was sitting on the bed at the rear of the narrow space, next to a sleeping Troy.

"Yow, you scared me!"

"Answer me!"

Miguel thought they'd gotten past all the bullshit this afternoon when they'd teamed up to save Troy. He didn't know why Russell was acting like this all of a sudden. "Alicia's talking to that kid, Philip. That's where I was. He's a pretty cool guy." Before Russell could comment on that, Miguel took him in another direction. "How's Troy?"

It worked. Russell looked down at the sleeping kid, his mouth pushed into a strange shape by the pillow, and smiled. "He's out solid. Watch this." He tapped the boy's cheek hard with his finger. "See that? He's a log. I think he's gonna be fine. What a relief, huh?"

"Yeah," Miguel agreed, even though he was starting to sense that something was wrong. Not with Troy, but with their father. "Can I ask you something and you won't have a cow about it?"

"Shoot."

"Have you been drinking?"

Russell smiled his guilty little boy smile. He'd taken a solemn oath just a few hours before that he wouldn't take another drink until this whole mess was over, since he was out of booze anyhow. "I couldn't help it, man, I forgot about the little stash I had in the plane." The cockpit of the old biwing had more Jack Daniel's bottles rattling around than a liquor store in an earthquake.

"Hey, why don't you join me in a little celebration." He waved the bottle in the air as if it might tempt the boy.

Crestfallen, Miguel grabbed his shoes and headed out, slamming the door behind him.

"Miguel, get back in here," Russell called, stumbling to the door. "Don't be mad. Come on, Miguel!" He watched the boy storm away into the refugee camp. Determined to explain himself, Russell took off after him. The hard-packed sand was still hot under his bare feet. Turning a corner, he arrived at the center of the temporary village.

A Jeep with speakers attached to the back was parked near a large camp-fire. One of Mitchell's soldiers was standing in the back compartment of the vehicle talking into a microphone.

"…which is when we plan to launch the counteroffensive. Because we're in a situation of depleted manpower, we're asking for anyone with flight experience, anyone at all who can pilot a plane, to volunteer. Military training is preferable, but anyone who thinks they can handle a plane would be useful."

"Hey! Me!" Russell yelled to the officer, pushing people out of his way in a hurry. "I fly. I mean, I'm a pilot. I got a plane, too!" In his enthusiasm, Russell pointed back toward his old de Haviland biwing, the bottle of J.D. still in his hand. Some of those in the crowd laughed.

"I'm sorry, sir, I don't think so," the soldier said, trying to be polite.

When Russell heard that, he got mad. Sloppy drunk and smelling like it, he moved in on the officer, vaguely threatening. He didn't notice the MPs sliding their clubs free from their holsters. "You don't understand, mister. I gotta be part of this. They ruined my whole life, and this is my chance to get revenge on those shitty little... things, guys, whatever they are."

"Get rid of this joker," the officer said quietly. A pair of military police grabbed Russell under his arms and escorted him roughly back the way he'd come, ignoring his blubberings about being abducted years before.

"You're unfit to pilot a plane," one of them said, turning him loose with a shove. "Go sleep it off somewhere. Maybe when you're sober they'll still need pilots."

Russell watched them walk away, then lifted the bottle to his lips for another drink. Realizing what he was doing, he spit the booze out and threw the bottle hard against the ground, spraying shards of glass around his bare feet.

The big circular door to the storage lab was left ajar. Connie pushed it all the way open and found Julius sitting inside. The old guy faked a big smile.

"There you are, I've been looking for you," she said, but her father-in-law only nodded and smiled back at her. She sniffed at the air and asked him, "Are you *smoking* in here?" Busted, Julius exhaled a big puff of smoke and brought the cigar out from behind his back.

"A little," he admitted. "Don't mention it to David.

He's such a health nut, he always gives me grief about my cigars."

David's health was precisely what she'd come to discuss. "I hope you're not planning on letting him go through with this idiotic scheme of his, are you?"

"Letting? You see me *letting* him do anything? He's a big boy."

"A big baby is what he's acting like. He's going to get himself killed."

Julius shrugged and glanced toward heaven. He knew there was no fighting David on this one. He was already committed.

Not finding the kind of support she was hoping for, Connie stomped away, frustrated, to the door. She turned back to say, "I don't think you're supposed to smoke in there."

Stepping out of the Freak Show, Connie found David standing under the wing of the attack plane. Along with Steve Hiller and General Grey, he was listening to one of the staff scientists explain a last-minute addition to the ship. He was showing them the work his team had done to one of the gun turrets that hung like jet engines from the bottom of the spaceship, the one that had been torn away during the crash. They'd emptied out the six-foot-long structure and inserted a cylindrical frame. While that was going on, a crew of mechanics was very gingerly wheeling a two-ton bomb across the floor, a big baby in a steel cradle. Connie noted that these mechanics, in blue jumpsuits, were new faces, not part of the Area 51 staff. They were ground crew specialists who'd flown the bomb in from Arizona.

"We've done what we could to disguise it," the scientist was saying of the hollowed-out turret, "but it's not going to pass a real close inspection. The missile's nose cone is going to protrude somewhat."

The mechanics worked the crane dolly, keeping the bomb perpendicular to the floor as they lifted it up to the underside of the attacker. When the tail fins of the bomb were even with the cylindrical frame, the mechanics began the delicate process of loading it into the chute.

"Don't anybody sneeze," the chief mechanic told David and the others. "We had to put the warhead on there before we loaded it. If my boys drop that thing, it'll be all she wrote."

"Pretty powerful bomb, huh?" David asked, clueless.

All the military men turned and looked at him, surprised he hadn't been informed.

The chief mechanic filled him in. "This, my friend, is a laser-guided cruise missile with a thermonuclear warhead slapped on the front end. If we drop that sucker, we all go boom, big time. And that's why our man, Captain Hiller here, is going to be extra careful getting this ship out the door."

David looked over at Steve, too surprised to actually form words.

Steve flashed him his trademark grin. "Piece of cake, Dave." The young pilot's audacity went a long way toward calming David's nerves.

Before he had a chance to think twice about what he was getting himself into, the staff scientist went on with his lecture. "We found some room in the ship's manifold and that's where we hid the launcher. As you can see, we didn't have any way to disguise the wiring, so we just welded it down to the surface. If you stand way back, you can't even see it."

General Grey stepped to a nearby table and picked up a small black box. "This will be attached to the ship's main console."

"It's just like an AMRAAM launch pad on the B-2 Stealth," Steve noted.

"That's exactly right. Use it the same way. There'll be one difference. We've programmed the nuke so it won't detonate on impact. You'll have another thirty seconds to get as far away as you can."

David felt himself getting lightheaded. All the talk about nuclear explosions was going to make him pass out if he didn't get his mind on something else. "I think I'll go see how they're doing with the radio transmitter." As he started to stagger away, Steve checked his watch.

"Holy smokes, David, we're late!"

David and Connie were the only two who knew what he was talking about. They told him not to worry, that they'd be there in time, as Steve jogged out of the hangar. David started toward the attacker to check on the progress his assistants were making inside when Connie stopped him.

"Thirty seconds? Maybe I'm a little dim or something, but isn't thirty lousy seconds cutting it a little close when you're trying to run from a nuclear explosion?"

"Not really. We're not going to fire the bomb until we're on our way out the door. Beside, that Hiller is supposed to be an amazing pilot." A shower of sparks rained onto the platform as one of the technicians began welding a device to the bottom of the ship. When David looked his way, the man pulled off his welding mask.

"This is the strongest UHF transmitter we could get our hands on. It'll tell us when you've uploaded the virus."

"Right. Then we all cross our fingers and pray the shields go down."

"Why you?" Connie wasn't finished. "Why does it have to be *you*? I mean, isn't it just a matter of pushing a button once you're connected? Can't you just show someone else how to plant the virus, somebody trained for this kind of mission?"

David wondered what she meant by trained for *this*

kind of mission. "I don't think there's ever been a mission like this. And if anybody's trained for it, it's me, because I designed the virus. What if something goes wrong, or doesn't match the way I think it will? I'll have to think fast, adjust the signal, or... who knows?" He walked over and picked up a soda can Mitchell had knocked to the floor. "Con, you know how I'm always trying to save the planet? This is my chance."

He tossed the can into a government-mandated RECYCLE container, planted a kiss on Connie's forehead, then rushed toward the attacker's cockpit.

Connie watched him go with mixed emotions. Speaking out loud to no one in particular, she said, "*Now* he gets ambitious."

When Jasmine asked where she could borrow a dress, everyone in the labs gave her the same hesitant response. "Try Dr. Rosenast," they suggested, making it clear this was a last resort, something to be done only in the case of severe emergency.

After knocking repeatedly at the indicated door, Jas could hear someone muttering and cursing on the other side. Just as she was about to give up, the door was yanked open and she was confronted by a huge pair of bifocals with the face of a sixty-year-old woman behind them. She looked like a sweet old thing, round rosy cheeks and big blue eyes magnified even larger by her glasses. Her gray hair was carefully coifed into a towering hairdo, and beneath her lab coat, she was dressed to the nines in a forest green blazer and matching skirt made of high-quality silk. The crowded room behind her was a combination office/laboratory/living quarters, every inch of space crammed with scientific equipment and the woman's personal effects. To Jasmine, she looked more like Santa Claus's wife than one of the world's leading electrical engineers.

"Dr. Rosenast, I hate to bother you but—"

"I already told that other son-of-a-bitch, *it's not ready*," she snapped.

The rebuilt alien attacker was scheduled to lift off in less than half an hour and she still hadn't finished a crucial piece of technology: a combination wattage booster/power transformer that would run off the ship's energy. Without it, David wouldn't be able to use his computer to upload the virus and infect the mother ship's signal.

"I'd be done already if it weren't for all the fuckin' interruptions!"

"I need to borrow a dress," Jasmine interjected, "something to get married in."

The old woman looked both ways down the hall as if to make sure she wasn't on *Candid Camera*. When she was satisfied that Jasmine was serious, she pulled her inside and brought her to a closet overflowing with the outfits she'd collected during the dozen years she'd been living underground. "I live for mail order," the woman admitted guiltily. "I think your tits are too big for what I've got here, but go ahead and borrow anything you like. I've got to get back to work."

Jasmine rifled through the closet as the doctor went back to work on the transformer. The doctor was a real clothes horse, with a penchant for Chinese dresses with slits running dramatically up the sides. *When does she wear these things?* Jasmine wondered. Then her search came to an end with the discovery of a simple red sun dress with a pattern of white and yellow flowers. On her way to the door, Jas planted a kiss on the surprised woman's cheek, then dashed off to the women's locker room. Eight minutes later, she was showered, powdered, rouged, and wriggling into the dress. It fit the curvaceous Jasmine snugly.

"Dylan, zip me up."

After struggling for a minute to bring the zipper to the

top, the boy gave up. "It's too tight."

"Okay, I guess that's good enough. Let's go, kid, we're late!"

It had been a long time since the men she passed in those hallways had seen anything like Ms. Dubrow. They were accustomed to seeing their female coworkers covered from head to toe in sterile white cotton. From the looks she was getting, Jasmine knew the dress was too tight, especially in the chest. Beginning to feel self-conscious, she asked Dylan, "How do I look, kiddo?" The boy put his hand out and wobbled it back and forth: so-so. "Oh, thanks," she said, "you're a lot of help." They turned a corner and arrived at the chapel.

The space was a combination house of worship and recreation room. Stained glass windows with fluorescent lights behind them shone down on felt-covered poker tables. Area 51's multidenominational minister, Chaplain Duryea, an elderly gentleman with an Einstein hairdo, had come in and pushed a Ping-Pong table out of the way. He shook hands with Jasmine and they stood talking for a few minutes until the others arrived.

"Somebody call the fire department before I burn to the ground!" Steve stood in the doorway, palms pressed to his cheeks. Admiring the way Jasmine looked in the dress, he came down the aisle and planted a kiss on her cheek. "You look... Jas-alicious."

"You're three minutes late," she chided, showing him her wristwatch.

"You know me. I like—"

"I know, I know," she finished the sentence for him, "you like to make a dramatic entrance."

The chaplain put himself behind a lectern and made sure everything was ready. "Steve, do you have the ring?"

"You bet." From the pocket of an Air Force jacket he'd borrowed, he produced the same leaping dolphin ring

Jimmy had caught him with the day before.

"Witnesses?"

Just as he asked the question, David and Connie came through the door, both of them working feverishly on the necktie David had borrowed seconds before. They never did get it right and finally just let it dangle in a sloppy knot. They came forward and took their places on either side of the happy couple. When he could see that everything was set, Chaplain Duryea smiled and said, "Then let's get this show on the road."

The short ceremony proved to be as meaningful and as moving for the two witnesses as it was for the bride and groom. During the vows, Connie reached for David's hand and toyed with the wedding ring she had given him years before.

The team of mechanics making repairs to a line of ten F-15s were putting on quite a show. Shouting instructions to one another, calling for tools to be handed up, they moved with the frantic grace of an Indy 500 pit crew. They were racing against the clock to make the sleek jet fighters air worthy. The sounds of rivet guns and pneumatic wrenches echoed off the walls. Similar work was going on in every corner of the gigantic hangar, which now stood packed to the gills with aircraft of every description.

As soon as the orders came upstairs around midnight, Major Mitchell's crew had worked feverishly, scouring not just their own hangars, but the entire Nellis Weapons Testing Range, an area of approximately six hundred square miles, to gather up every working and half-working plane. Since Area 51's ostensible purpose was R&D of experimental aircraft, they had accumulated quite a collection of planes over the years. Most of them were early models of standard American transport and attack planes, but there was also quite a number of specially-built prototypes, exotic ships that never went into production. Planes like the wedge shaped Martin X-29 and the awkward MSU Marvel Stol, with its turboprop engine set into a wind cone above the tail. These planes had been "liberated" from America's enemy or "accidentally misdirected" from her allies.

The most exciting find had been the fleet of F-15s, stored in one of the half-underground storage hangars surrounding the "minibase" at Papoose Lake, nine miles to the north. Like many of the planes they found, the F-15s had missing parts, having been cannibalized over the years for the sake of other projects. A radar system was missing from one, while the tail fins had disappeared from another. Still, these planes were legitimate, state-of-the-art fighting machines that had one great advantage over almost all the others: there were missiles for them to fire. The five that could move under their own power taxied back to the main hangar; the other five were towed. The lead mechanic figured eight of them would be ready by the time the counteroffensive was scheduled to begin.

The base had received much-needed reinforcements, and quite a scare, when a score of F-111s arrived without warning at approximately two A.M. They were a group of foreign pilots-in-training and their army instructors who had been stranded at a proving grounds in the California desert when the invaders began to arrive. They had no way of responding to the message being broadcast from Area 51, so they decided to come and join the crowd. Only three of the pilots were experienced instructors. The other seventeen were trainees from allied countries: Czechs, Hondurans, and a group from Nigeria. Like most pilots around the world, they spoke English, the international language of aviation. There were no lights on the runways and they were fortunate not to have lost anyone during the landing.

Everyone in the hangar knew both the plan of attack and their odds of surviving it. Mitchell had made no bones about it, bluntly explaining that even if the shields came down, the aliens would still have them outnumbered and outgunned. At *best*, they could expect an aerial dogfight with the faster, tighter-turning attackers, the swarming flock which had downed thousands of jets worldwide while suffering only a single casualty. When Mitchell was done, he looked around and asked if anybody wanted out, told them it was better to quit now than once they were up in the air. No one said a word. "Good," he told them, "because we're going to need all the help we can get."

The Jeep with loudspeakers was parked between the huge rolling doors. Mitchell got up on the back of it to assign the pilots to their planes. While the men were crowded together in a group, they were noisy, macho, and fearless, bragging to each other about all the ways they would crush their foes. But an hour later, the only noise in the room was the buzz and thump of mechanics' tools. A few of the warriors spoke quietly to one another in groups, but the majority of them had wandered away to private corners, isolating themselves with their thoughts.

This was the scene the president found when the elevator doors slid open an hour before the makeshift air force was to head north and engage the West Coast city destroyer. Instead of his usual entourage, Whitmore brought only General Grey and one of his Secret Service agents along.

"Where'd they dig up some of these contraptions? It looks like the Smithsonian's Air and Space Museum in here."

"Beggars can't be choosers," Grey reminded him. "I think Mitchell might have gone a little overboard, but the order was to bring in everything that could fly."

"How many planes can we put in the air?" Whitmore asked.

"If you're asking me how many combat-ready pilots we can put into planes in decent working order, the answer is thirty. But we're going to lower our standards and stretch it to one hundred and fifteen."

Whitmore had come up top to review the troops before they left for battle. He hadn't expected to find so quiet, so desolate a scene. These people, unexpectedly pressed into service, weren't exactly fired up. The worried, defeated expressions on their faces made them seem like a football team down 211–0 at halftime. Whitmore wished there were something he could say, some ringing motivational speech he could deliver, but he knew he wasn't a talented improviser. He always knew the ideas he wished to convey, but relied heavily on Connie and his staff to script the actual words for him.

He began to walk down the long aisles of planes, stopping here and there to offer a word of encouragement or inspect an airplane. Many of the men hardly glanced up at him as he passed, so deep were they in their personal reflections. Whitmore imagined George Washington moving among the freezing, starved, troops at Valley Forge, quietly measuring their morale and their will to fight. He came upon a man sitting cross-legged on the floor who seemed to be talking to himself. Closer inspection revealed he was praying, whispering hurried incomprehensible words to heaven, aware there wasn't much time left. Around the next corner, he came upon a muscular young man wearing nothing but a pair of jeans. He was sobbing uncontrollably. All the photos were out of his wallet arranged in a neat row on the concrete. Wiping away his tears, he was taping them one by one to the side of his plane, an old P-51 Mustang. Whitmore realized they were snapshots of his dead, loved ones he'd lost to the blasts. The young man's grief was hypnotic, and as Whitmore watched, he couldn't help thinking about the way Marilyn's hand had gone limp in his. Suddenly, Grey's hand took hold of his arm and pulled him away from the scene. Without realizing it, Whitmore too had begun to tear.

From a military standpoint, the new recruits were a pitiful sight. A frowning man of sixty sat in the cockpit of a Russian MiG studying an impossibly thick operating manual, badly translated from the original Russian. Whitmore exchanged a few words with him and discovered he hadn't flown any kind of plane since the Korean War. Still, he was the most experienced pilot in his flight group. Most of the others had never flown at all. A group of them was standing on the wings and fuselage of a plane while one of the California flight instructors sat in the cockpit giving them a "crash course" on how to keep a plane in the air. This group had volunteered for the last, and the ugliest, assignment Mitchell had handed out. Their task during the battle would be to fly the planes for which the base had no ammunition. They would act as distractions and decoys, something for the aliens to shoot at while the more experienced pilots attacked the larger ship. Whitmore interrupted the training session for a moment to greet these doomed young men and women, then moved on.

Eventually, he came to the front of the hangar and the row of F-15s. Whitmore knew the vessel well. He had logged many an hour in the sleek jet before being promoted to flying Stealths. Among the men assigned to pilot this elite weapon, he was surprised to find the captain of Air Force One, Captain Birnham. Even more surprising was the fact that Birnham was listening intently to a stick-thin man with a bushy beard named Pig explain certain features of the plane. Pig had a hog, a motorcycle he rode with his gang, an off-shoot of the Hell's Angels, every weekend. He wore black leather pants, a denim jacket with his name in gothic letters over an obscene cartoon logo, and a bandanna tied around his wild red hair. Whitmore joined their conversation and learned that the biker had been a navy master chief mechanic stationed for years in San Diego. Whitmore refrained from asking how Pig had learned to fly an F-15, positive he didn't want to know the answer.

Many of the nervous pilots had followed Whitmore and Grey toward the front doors, and news of his presence had already leaked outside into the campground beyond the hangar doors. Lights inside the tents and vehicles switched on as the displaced civilians began coming out into the night air. The president stepped up into the back of the Jeep with the loud speakers, tapped the microphone a couple of times then spoke into it.

"Good morning," he said uncertainly. Everyone inside the hangar quickly came out from behind their planes to assemble in the open space near the line of F-15s. Turning around to check the night sky for signs of the approaching dawn, Whitmore watched the bedraggled refugees marching toward the hangar doors. For several moments, he stood quietly at the microphone, staring awkwardly into the expectant faces of his audience, not knowing what he would say to them. Then, without knowing where to begin, he began.

"In less than an hour from now, over one hundred of you will fly north to confront an enemy more powerful than any the world has ever known. As you do so, you will be joined by pilots from around the world as they launch similar attacks against the other thirty-five ships attacking the earth. The battle you will join will be the single largest aerial conflict in the history of mankind." He paused to consider that idea.

"Mankind," he repeated, allowing the word to hang in the air. "The word takes on a new meaning for all of us today. If any good has come from this savage and unprovoked attack on our planet, it is the recognition of how much we humans share in common. It has given us a new perspective on what it means to live on this earth together. It has shown us the insignificance of our thousand petty differences from one another and reminded us of our deep and abiding common interests. The attack has changed the course of history and redefined what it means to be human. From this day forward, it will be impossible to forget how interdependent the races and nations of the world truly are." As he spoke, Whitmore began to feel less self-conscious. He knew what needed to be said and began to trust his instincts. The words felt like they were being drawn out of him.

"I think there's a certain irony that today is July the Fourth, America's anniversary of independence. Perhaps it is fate that once again, this date will mark the beginning of a great struggle for freedom. But this time, we will fight for something even more basic than the right to be free of tyranny, persecution, or oppression. We will fight against an enemy who will be satisfied with nothing less than our total annihilation. This time we will be fighting for our right to live, for our very existence."

His voice grew stronger as the words took on a life and momentum of their own. "An hour from now, we will confront a strange and deadly adversary, an army more powerful than humanity has ever faced. I'm not going to make any false promises to you. I cannot offer any guarantee that we will prevail, but if ever there were a battle worth fighting, this is it. And as I look around me this morning, I realize how extraordinarily lucky I am to be here, at this critical moment, surrounded by people like you. You are patriots in the original and truest sense of the word: people who love their home and are willing to lend their talents, skills and, in some cases, even their lives to the task of defending it. I consider it an honor to be allowed to fight alongside you, to raise my voice in chorus with yours and declare, whether we win or lose, *we will not go quietly into the night!* We will not vanish without a fight, but struggle fiercely for what is rightfully ours, our heads held high until the very last moment.

"And if we succeed," he said, smiling into the mic, "if we somehow accomplish this thing that seems so impossible, it will be the most glorious victory imaginable. The Fourth of July will no longer be known only as an American holiday, but as the day when all the nations of the earth stood shoulder to shoulder and shouted: 'We will not lay down and die. We will live on! We will survive!' Today," he thundered, "we celebrate our Independence Day!"

Whitmore stepped back from the microphone as a tremendous roar of approval swelled through the crowd. Deeply moved by his words, the men and women surrounding him forgot their fear and pumped their fists into the air and cheered, ready to fight. They would have followed their leader anywhere.

As the applause and the shouting continued, Whitmore hopped down from the Jeep and made his way to the line of F-15s. Grey watched as he exchanged a few quick words with Major Mitchell and the pilot of Air Force One, Bimham. The general had noted with disapproval the shift from *you* to *we* midway through the speech. When he saw Bimham hand over his flight jacket and helmet to the commander in chief, Grey began pushing his way through the crowd.

"Tom Whitmore," Grey rasped, playing the incensed mentor, "what in hell do you think you're doing?"

Whitmore was already suiting up and inspecting one of the jets. He smiled at his old friend and explained. "I'm a pilot, Will. I belong in the air." He pulled his helmet on, adding, "I'm not going to ask these people to take any risks I'm not willing to take myself."

"Think about what it would mean for people to learn the American president was killed."

"Will, I believe this is probably our last chance. If I don't come back, it won't matter tomorrow if there's a president or not."

Grey wanted to argue, but saw the man was determined. He appealed to the Secret Service agent, but the man only shrugged and wagged his head. He didn't officially support what the president was doing, but he sure had to admire him for doing it. When Grey looked back, Whitmore was already climbing into the cockpit locked in conversation with the man wearing a jacket that said PIG. Spitting mad, Grey marched away to take his position in the war room.

In the frantic few minutes before takeoff, the technical staff checked and rechecked the equipment. They had festooned the cockpit with a dozen scraps of paper, each hanging from a different place on the instrument panel, with operating diagrams printed on them in marker. Not exactly professional, but it got the job done.

Just outside the ship, people were trying to figure out how to say good-bye. No one said it out loud, but they were all thinking the same thing: Steve and David had a million chances to fail and only one to succeed. They were probably going to die and that made saying good-bye more difficult, more final.

"When I'm back we'll light the rest of those fireworks," Steve told Dylan.

Jasmine rolled her eyes a little and tried to smile. She draped her arms over Steve's shoulders and put her lips to his ear, whispering something that put a dopey grin on his face. When she was done, she kissed him on the cheek, picked up Dylan, and went up the stairs of the observation platform.

A voice came booming over the loudspeakers. "One minute to scheduled lift-off. Clear the area."

"Pssst. David, over here."

It was Julius, hiding something under his sportscoat he didn't want the rest of them to see. He pulled his son off to one side, and with a glance to make sure no one was looking, he pulled back the coat.

"Here, take these. Just in case." Tucked into his belt were a couple of pilfered "barf bags," souvenirs of his ride aboard Air Force One. Each of the starch white receptacles was emblazoned with the presidential seal. David smiled when he saw the gift.

"You're the greatest, Dad. I've got something for you, too." He dug around in his computer case for a second before pulling out a yarmulke and a small leather-bound Bible. Julius made a long face, amazed. A Bible was about the last thing he would have expected David to be carrying. Leaning in close, David whispered, "Just in case."

Julius looked him up and down, then said, "I want you should know, I'm very proud of you, son." Those words meant more to David than his father knew. Julius stepped aside to let his son say farewell to one last person.

Connie's smile wobbled like a house of cards, threatening to crash into tears at any second. She and David had so much unfinished business between them, so much still to say. Now it appeared they would lose one another again, this time for good. With a thousand things left to say, they both felt incapable of words. Nevertheless, the look between them, a look of mutual acceptance and love, seemed to sweep all the residual pain away in a single moment.

"Be careful," was all Connie could say. David turned to follow Steve up the ladder.

"No, no, no. We can't go yet." Steve suddenly started frantically searching the pockets of his uniform. He'd lost something. "Cigars, man. I gotta find some cigars."

Steve was ready to bolt out of the room. He wasn't superstitious about too many things, but without a victory dance waiting for him at the end of the ride, he knew something bad would happen.

Julius grabbed him by the arm and retrieved two cigars from his coat pocket. "Here you are. With my blessings."

"You're a lifesaver," Steve told him, and Julius hoped he was right.

A few seconds later, Steve was scampering up the ladder and into the rebuilt alien attacker. With a last nervous smile, David awkwardly followed him inside.

Connie joined Jasmine and the others behind the glass windows of the observation booth. It was a small room designed long ago to control security and other functions inside the enormous concrete box that contained the attacker. The equipment inside, most of which had sat idle since it was installed in the late fifties, didn't inspire much confidence. Much of it was custom built, and the embossed strips of plastic that labeled the control panels were peeling off. A couple of them fell to the floor as the vinyl dust covers were lifted away.

Fortunately, the lead technician, Mitch, was able to figure it all out. After punching a couple of buttons, the entire room felt a rumbling tremor. High above, an ancient electric motor chugged to life and a large section of the concrete roof began to open, then another, opening an escape route for the attacker. The hole in the roof gave way to a large, slanted shaft which in turn led up to the open air. The shaft was approximately one hundred feet across, giving Steve a few feet of leeway on either side to get the sixty-foot-wide spaceship into the open air. Of course, the designers of the shaft never expected the ship to have to make it through with a nuclear explosive strapped to its hull.

When confirmation came by radio that the ground-level doors had also opened, Mitch gave the all-clear to Steve. The pilot nodded back and gave the sign to release the clamps.

"Now this is important," Steve announced, waiting to get David's undivided attention. He held one of the cigars out across the aisle. "Hang on to this. This is how we're going to celebrate on the way home. It's gonna be our victory dance. But we don't light up till we hear the fat lady sing." As he handed the stogie across the aisle, he noticed the barf bags sitting on David's lap.

"I have a confession to make," David said, strapping himself in. "I'm not real big on flying."

As he spoke, the clamps released the sides of the ship, crashing against the floor loudly enough to be heard inside the spaceship. The attacker lifted into the air, waffling slightly until it stabilized at twelve feet, steady as a rock. A pair of white handles, like the legs of a spider, unfolded themselves from the instrument console, extending until they were within easy reach of the pilot's chair.

"I'm in love with this plane. This is so damn cool, isn't it?"

David forced a smile. "I'll think it's a lot cooler if we leave the building in one piece." He was thinking about the warhead, which was almost directly under his chair.

Following the instructions printed on the duct tape, Steve made the craft float upward higher and higher, until they were even with the escape shaft. David's fingers were leaving permanent grip marks on the arms of his chair. Steve, on the other hand, was elated.

"Are you ready? Okay, then, let's rock 'n' roll!"

Steve pointed the nose of the ship at the escape tunnel and pulled back on the control stick. The machine responded, but not the way he'd anticipated. It shot backwards across the big room, picking up speed until its rear end smashed into a wall. Fortunately, a mass of fiberglass air-conditioning ducts were there to damped the collision.

"Oops."

David, who had just suffered an imaginary heart attack, gasped, then growled. "Oops? You call that an oops?"

Steve reached forward, peeled a piece of tape off the console, and turned it over before reattaching it.

"Let's try that one again." This time he nudged the steering control gently forward, jerking the attacker forward and into the mouth of the escape tunnel. The shaft sloped upward at an angle. Steve knew he'd gotten away lucky with that first crash. He made sure to go real slow through the shaft, scraping the roof as he went to make enough room for the warhead below. As soon as they nosed out of the tunnel, Steve jacked the controls forward. With a whooshing noise, they zoomed out of the underground shaft and soared into the night sky, dawn just beginning to break on the horizon.

Almost as soon as they were out of the gate, the attacker corkscrewed through the air in a wild set of barrel rolls. They straightened out momentarily, then began twisting and looping once more through the sky.

"Uuuuuugh." David invented a new sound, gurgling and moaning at once. "Steve, what's happening, what's going wrong?"

"Nothing's wrong," the pilot assured him, straightening the ship out, "just getting a feel for this little honey. I have got to get me one of these."

"Look, please don't do that. I've got this inner ear thing. Pretty serious." Steve answered by throwing the rocket-fast ship into yet another series of stunt maneuvers.

The president watched the attacker take off from the cockpit of his F-15. A group of forty planes had taxied onto the runway, where the eastern skies were slowly changing from purple to pink. The pilots had their canopies open and were listening to their radios. As Steve and David's attacker shot through the sky, it appeared to them as a dark streak, an unidentified flying object disappearing at a terrific rate of speed into the darkness overhead. It was something of an anticlimax, a shadow only briefly visible against the thin line of pink breaking to the east.

Once the show was over, Whitmore settled into his cockpit. Strapping on his helmet as the canopy lowered over him, he got on the radio and spoke with the war room.

"Grey, do you read me?"

"Roger, Eagle One, loud and clear. Stand by, sir." The edge in Grey's voice told the pilots listening in that something was wrong. A minute later, the general returned with the ugly news. "Eagle One, our primary target has shifted course. We're watching the radar right now."

"Which way is it heading?" The president assumed it was moving out of range and all the preparations he had ordered were about to be proved futile.

"I think our little secret is out. The ship is moving east by southeast and traveling at a pretty fair clip. They're headed right for us, sir. Estimated time of arrival is thirty-two minutes."

Whitmore's plan had been to take his thrown-together squadron into the air and put them through their paces, giving them some desperately needed practice time. Now that part of the plan would have to be scrubbed. Aware that the other pilots were listening in, he tried to put a positive spin on this development. 'That means we'll have the home court advantage. Let's get up in the air and stake out our territory."

Then he switched over to the private channel Grey had opened for him. "Will, do you read?"

"Go ahead, Eagle One."

"Put the word out for reinforcements. Get us any help you can. We're going to need it."

David was collapsed against the back of his seat, his eyes a pair of loose marbles rolling free in their sockets. Between moans, he appeared to be chanting to himself. Either that, or he was about to woof his cookies.

Steve finally took pity on his passenger and straightened the craft out. It was an amazing machine, lightning fast and superbly maneuverable at the same time. It cornered like a dream and seemed to have some sort of gyroscope built into the system so that it came out of any maneuver, no matter how reckless, as steady as a rock. This was no wobbly goblin.

"You still with me?"

David, green in the face, nodded sheepishly.

As the ship began leaving earth's atmosphere, the blue sky darkened to violet, then faded to black. The pilot's mouth dropped open in awe, then blossomed into an ear-to-ear grin. As the last layers of the outer atmosphere brushed past, the attacker suddenly accelerated, liberated. High above the earth, in the eternal night illuminated by the eternally blinding sun, the attacker plunged upward, deeper into the blanket of stars around them. For Steve, it was a moment of wonder and boyish magic, a promise fulfilled at last.

"I've waited a long time for this."

Quietly now, they continued to plummet upward, the sun on one side, the moon on the other. Ahead of them the vast blank wall of space receded to infinity. Steve, joyriding, forgot for a moment what they'd come for. David fought down the stomach acids churning inside him and kept a careful watch on the life-support monitors installed on the floor. He saw something that made him certain he was losing consciousness. The monitors were strapped to the floor with thick strips of woven nylon, heavy-duty seat belt ribbon. One of them seemed to come to life as David watched it, lifting into the air like a tentacle arm.

"Feel it? Zero gravity, baby. We're here!"

Steve had some experience with weightlessness. He'd once finagled an invitation to ride in the cargo compartment of a B-52 flying parabolas through the sky. The plane came to the top of its climb, then began to dive at a carefully calculated angle, producing a simulation of zero gravity which allowed the passengers to float through the air for two or three minutes at a time. For Steve, it was a welcome recognition of a familiar moment. Not so for David. If he had imagined his breakfast worming its way back toward his esophagus before, now he felt it for real.

"Of course," he burbled, "weightlessness. I should've thought of that."

David turned to look out the window, focusing on the moon. Although on earth the moon was a slim toenail shape at this time of month, from David's angle it looked almost full. They were seeing what only a handful of humans had ever seen with their own eyes, the moon's dark side. But what really caught their attention was something no human had ever seen: a black orb lurking in the distance, one-fourth the size of the moon. The mother ship, its smooth surface illuminated by the sun, glinted back at them malevolently. A pair of monstrous prongs, hanging off what looked to be the bottom of the ship like a pair of saber-tooth fangs, curving hungrily through space.

"Thar she blows," David said, coming out of his queasiness. "Head straight for it."

Steve did exactly that. It had been less than five minutes since they'd torn free of the earth's atmosphere and less time still since they'd escaped her gravity. There was no way for them to know, no reference point or speedometer to tell them, that they'd been accelerating the whole time. But as Steve retargeted the ship with a flick of his finger, they were both impressed by the incredible speed at which they rocketed toward the moon. The size of the lunar satellite grew inside the frame of the windows until it seemed to David that they were getting just a little too close.

"You know how to slow this thing down, right?" he asked nonchalantly, trying not to step on Steve's toes.

"Uh-oh," Steve said, suddenly worried.

"Uh-oh? That doesn't sound good," David said, now able to study the individual craters. "What's wrong?"

"Something's happening. Ship's not responding."

David checked his laptop computer. For the first time since the clamps released the ship, David seemed thrilled to be aboard.

"I knew it!" He looked at Steve. "Well, at least I thought it. The way you described the inside of the city destroyer, I thought there must be a tractor beam organizing the flight, a computer-driven air traffic control mechanism. They're bringing us in." David went back to working on the keyboard.

Slightly miffed, Steve asked him, "So when were you planning on telling me about this?"

David looked across the cabin. "Oops."

"We have visual."

Long before the city destroyer was within range of Area 51, its hulking fifteen-mile wide frame was seen cruising above the horizon. The president and the thirty F-15s had ascended to a height of 30,000 feet, high above the approaching warship and the tangle of amateur pilots who were having trouble maintaining their formations. He had three civilian pilots with him who had never flown a war plane before. They were doing remarkably well. Whitmore had them practice using their sighting devices. On these older planes, the HUD gave neither a "God's eye view" of the battle nor a "dream world" display, functions which came standard on later models. To locate the enemy, Whitmore's team, called Eagle squadron, would have to rely on the technicians in the war room and plenty of old-fashioned looking around.

"Basically, boys, we're gonna keep our eyes open," Whitmore announced, then asked Grey, "any word yet on that delivery?"

"Negative." Whitmore could just about see his scowl over the radio. "Do not engage until we've confirmed delivery of the package."

At least a dozen voices came over the radio at once. "Roger!" the pilots acknowledged the order.

"And keep this damn frequency clear!" Grey barked. He turned and watched the radar screen.

In order to avoid crashing into one another, they'd organized themselves into four main groups, flying laps around the desert. Grey watched them merry-go-rounding across the radar screen, then said to Connie and Major Mitchell in disgust, "This whole operation is the damnedest harebrained thing I've ever seen."

Pulling the major aside, Connie asked about something that had been troubling her for a while. "What if that thing, the ship, gets here before David can plant the virus?"

Mitchell was concentrating on coordinating his part of the battle. He figured Connie was putting two and two together and beginning to worry about her own life. There wasn't time for that now. "We're pretty deep underground here. It should give us some protection."

Connie read him instantly. "It's not us I'm worried about. It's all those people outside."

Mitchell remembered what had happened to NORAD and knew Area 51's defenses were flimsy in comparison. If the city destroyer moving toward them fired its big gun, it wouldn't matter if the refugees were up top or down in the labs—everyone would die together. Still, he knew moving the people below-ground would offer them a slightly better chance of surviving.

He pulled one of his men off his tracking assignment and appointed him supervisor. Without a word of explanation, he grabbed Connie by the arm and they dashed out of the room.

The mother ship was the size of a small planet sliced cleanly in half along its equator. The shimmering half dome was protected by a smooth exterior shell over most of its surface, except where it seemed to have been cut away to expose long swathes of a ruddy black surface beneath. The flatness of the underside was interrupted by bulging projections fifteen miles in diameter. They were the domes of city destroyers, identical to the ones attacking the earth. There were at least one hundred of them still locked on to the underbelly of the mother ship like leeches. Thirty-six empty rings showed where the giant warships which were attacking the earth had once docked. Hanging dramatically off the side of the craft was a pair of tusklike projections. Glossy white and at least a hundred miles tall, these enigmatic structures arched through space like a mammoth set of cobra fangs.

The ship was pulled toward one of the dark, rugged strips that lay between sections of the steel blue armor covering ninety percent of the ship's exterior. Drawn closer, the bulk of the mother ship overwhelmed the view from their attacker's windows, until Steve and David could see nothing except the black surface directly in front of them. In contrast to the view from a thousand miles away, a close look at this part of the ship revealed it to be surprisingly primitive. Beneath the thin blue shell, the ship's surface was composed of a material as wavy and jagged as recently cooled lava, like mile after mile of barren Neolithic stone.

A huge triangular portal, one of several earth's recon satellite photos had failed to detect, had been cut through the dense walls. A pale blue light leaked from within the craft. As David and Steve approached this gigantic three-sided entrance tunnel, they noticed dozens of attackers like theirs sitting idly in space. Made to look microscopically small by comparison to the megalith behind them, these attackers were washing in and out of the opening as gently as if riding the tide of an invisible ocean.

The inside of the darkened tunnel put them in a dramatically different environment. The walls and ceiling were covered with sheets of ceramic-like tile that had turned a rusty brown. At sporadic intervals, shafts of light shot out of the walls and into the passageway like solid columns. As they flew past one of them, it seemed to be some kind of holographic torch, the artificial image of an artificial light source, which nevertheless provided just enough illumination to let them see where they were going. The steep walls plunging to a V-shape below them were connected by a series of massive structures crisscrossing the tunnel. Like the barnacle-encrusted strut wires of a sunken galleon, these structural supports were overgrown with irregular, organic bulges. Light seeped out of pinhole windows on these massive cables, indication, perhaps, that there was life inside of them. Although their stingray was moving at over 300 miles per hour, the enormous size of the passageway and the cablelike structures gave them the sensation of drifting slowly along, deep underwater.

The tunnel ended and the tiny ship reached the source of the pale blue light. They entered the central chamber of the mother ship. It was like swimming through milky blue water on a densely foggy day. For several moments, neither Steve nor David could see anything at all. It wasn't until the first of the towers came into view that they realized the soupy atmosphere was limiting visibility to twenty miles or so. The towers were knobby, bulging structures rising through the fog like endless sections of rope tied into thick knots. They were built in piles, like dripping candle wax that grows eventually into a spire. Along the outsides of these towers were clearly defined pathways, access roads perhaps, for repairs. The dizzying height of these towers, disappearing out of sight both above and beyond, made the humans feel like guppies who had wandered into a shark tank.

As they neared the center of the mother ship, they came across something stranger still, what looked like a tip of a screw hanging above a round platform. This circular platform was a level field approximately fifty miles across and fell away steeply on all sides. As the men were drawn closer, they were treated to a horrifying image of several thousand aliens marching in phalanxes towards the edges of the platform. The area was some sort of parade ground and the creatures appeared to be loading themselves into the long boxy ships that were docked around the platform's edges. An invisible energy shield protected them from the vacuum of space.

"What the hell is that?" David wondered, physically repulsed.

"Looks like they're preparing the invasion," Steve answered with a lump in his throat. For the first time in a long while, he felt himself getting scared.

Their attacker was lifted higher, up toward the massive structure hanging directly above the alien parade ground, what had looked like a screw tip from a distance. Like an inverted mountain peak, this structure spread from a sharp point up to a massive base. It was built in thousands of layers or stories, each one containing numerous large windows that showed a brighter source of light behind them. Near each window, stiff beams extending a short distance into the inner space of the central chamber held two or three of the stingray attackers. This was their central docking point, and the nerve center of the entire alien civilization.

David carefully noted that, just as Okun had predicted, the attackers were moored to their host ship by a set of clamps that closed over the rigid fin running along the top of each stingray. The circuit terminals ended in a fingerlike flange, allowing the small ships to connect directly to the computer-compatible command system of the mother. Dangling off the wall beside each of the million windows on the conical tower was a limp tube. As the humans drew closer, they could see that the tubes were made of a transparent material that resembled nothing so much as a very large intestine. Apparently they could be controlled to reach out from the wall and attach themselves to the bottom of the ships, sealing over the hatch to allow the pilots to enter the tower, providing a passageway into the main ship, shielding those who used them from the vacuum of space.

"This isn't gonna work," Steve said, drawing David's attention to the large window they were approaching. "They'll be able to see us before we can do anything." Indeed, through the large plate windows, several aliens were visible inside a well-lit space that appeared to be a control booth. The distance between them was shrinking rapidly.

"Not to worry," David assured him, "this ship comes fully equipped. Reclining bucket seats, AM/FM oscilloscope and," he pressed a button on the console, "power windows!"

Instantly, a set of heavy blast shields began rising along the windows, blocking the aliens' view, but also sealing Steve and David inside. Flying blind the last few hundred feet, they felt the ship lurch violently to a stop, then heard the powerful clamps locking themselves onto the fin overhead. The only lights in the claustrophobic cabin came from the ever-blinking instrument panel and the sickly greenish glow rising from the screen of David's laptop.

"This is getting a little too spooky," Steve whispered.

David didn't hear. He was too deep in concentration, watching the changes flash across his computer screen. The moment the clamps locked them in place, the movements on the screen, which showed the status of the protective shield, reversed their direction. That told David that they were connected to the source. He switched over to another screen, which flashed the words "Negotiating with Host." He held his breath as the signal analyzer program sorted through the billions of possibilities. Then, much sooner than he expected, the machine beeped and displayed a new message, "Connecting to Host."

"We're in! I can't believe it, but we're in!"

"Great, now what?" Steve was less than thrilled about sitting in the creepy box surrounded by a hive of aliens. When David returned to working on his computer without answering his question, the pilot unbuckled his seat belt and moved to the entry hatch, ready to plant his boot into the mouth of the first alien who stuck his head inside.

"Okay," David said more to himself than to his companion, "I'm uploading the virus."

Outside the ship, the lights on a small black box welded to the bottom of their attacker blinked on and off, distinguishing it from the thousands of other ships parked around them.

A technician pulled his headphones off and turned away from his console to face General Grey. "He's uploading the virus."

Grey's scowl suddenly disappeared, temporarily replaced by a look of astonishment. He wasn't expecting any part of this lamebrain plan to work. Then, just as quickly, the furrowed brows and downturned corners of his mouth returned as he picked up a handheld microphone and sent his voice into the sky. "Eagle One, do you read?"

"Affirmative," Whitmore answered, "loud and clear."

"The package is being delivered. Stand by to engage."

Although Grey's furious reprimands had taught the rookie pilots to stay off the airwaves, he imagined their shouts of joy when they heard the news. Even the president could not hide how he felt when he acknowledged the message. "Roger," he said excitedly, "we are standing by to attack!"

There was no such excitement aboveground at Area 51. The effort to evacuate the refugees had begun in an organized fashion. A dozen or so people at a time were ushered inside and took the elevator down to the underground scientific complex, where they were being housed in the long clean room. But as soon as the sinister shape of the city destroyer became visible on the horizon, the camp broke into a panic. People ran into their trailers, searching for one or two last possessions to take with them, the last handfuls of their former lives. The soldiers organizing the elevator shipments were overwhelmed and, in the confusion, precious moments were lost.

Alicia, rampaging through the Casse motor home, couldn't decide what to save. She'd already sent Troy running inside, promising to meet him soon. The door of the trailer swung open. Philip poked his head inside.

"Alicia, let's go! They're coming!"

"I know!" she yelled, picking up the first thing she saw, a large duffel bag filled with dirty clothes. She slammed against the walls trying to drag the heavy bundle toward the door. Philip jumped inside and took hold of the bag, giving her a moment to calm down.

"I'll take the bag," he said soothingly. "This is kind of a crazy first date, isn't it?"

Alicia smiled and took a breath. He'd successfully brought her back to her senses. "Okay, Romeo, where are you taking me?"

Philip hoisted the bag onto one shoulder as they stepped out into the sunlight. Without letting Alicia see him do it, he glanced up to check the position of the approaching warship. All around them, panicked people scrambled in every direction, shouting for family members, sprinting for the open doors of the hangar. Alicia came outside and calmly put her hand in Philip's. She liked this game, pretending this was a normal Sunday afternoon and that this delightful gentleman caller had invited her out for a stroll. While the confusion continued around them, they created a small island of serenity, walking across the sand toward the hangar as if they were strolling along the banks of a springtime river.

Their fantasy was abruptly ended when a hand landed on Alicia's shoulder and spun her around. It was Miguel, covered with sweat from running all over the area. With a wild look in her eyes, he demanded to know, "Have you seen Russell? I can't find him anywhere."

Unseen by any of the people heading toward the shelter, something moved through the sky. Completely invisible, moving at the speed of light, it was picked up by the base's radar dishes. It was a radio signal, instantly decoded by the machines in the war room. Flashing on the screen dedicated to monitoring radio contact with David and Steve's ship were the words UPLOAD COMPLETE.

"Well, I'll be goddamned," Grey said, admiring David and Steve's work. He got on the radio. "Eagle One, this is Base. The delivery is complete. Engage."

"With pleasure, Base."

Whitmore was flying the lead position in a formation of the thirty fighters. When the clearance came, he gave the pilots on either side of him a visual signal, then accelerated. The others followed his example, increasing their speed for a bombing run on the city destroyer and buzzing over the top of many slower planes in the process. The bay doors at the bottom of Whitmore's jet split open, allowing the first of his three AMRAAM missiles to drop down. Still in its launch harness, the laser guided nose cone computed its flight and locked on to the spot Whitmore had selected on his HUD. He punched one of the buttons and the missile blasted away.

Grey's voice came over the radio. He was tracking the flight of the missile on radar. "Keep your fingers crossed," he rasped.

"Come on, baby," Whitmore said, watching the missile speeding away.

A quarter mile from the surface of the megaship, the AMRAAM exploded harmlessly, seeming to detonate in midair. The shields were still in place.

"Nothing," one of the rookie pilots said, breaking onto the airwaves. "It blew up on the shield, didn't make a scratch."

"That's it." Grey had seen enough. "Eagle One, disengage immediately. I want you out of there ASAP."

"Negative!" Whitmore shouted into his radio. "Maintain your formation." Although they were now less than two miles away, the president continued to hold his squadron on a collision course with the side of the vast invader ship. Without announcing what he was doing, he allowed the second of his AMRAAMs to dip into the air. He locked a target area not far from the tall black tower at the front edge of the ship, then launched it. The missile shot away and, within seconds, arrived at the same spot where all the others had met an invisible dead end. Nothing happened. The pilots lost visual contact with the AMRAAM. It seemed to disappear, but there was no time to wonder where it might have gone because the jets themselves were quickly approaching the deadly quarter-mile perimeter. Then something took them all by surprise.

A huge explosion flared up, biting deep into the side of the destroyer. A large section of the ship, the size of a city block, ruptured like brittle clay, then exploded in flaming pieces toward the ground.

The war room erupted into wild cheers. Even General Grey, the model of vigilant self-constraint, swung his fist through the air, delivering an imaginary roundhouse punch to an alien jawbone. For the next thirty seconds, the excited pilots, whooping and hollering, made the airwaves unusable, prematurely celebrating a victory they had not yet achieved.

As order began to restore itself, Whitmore led his squad of fighters in a long downward loop that eventually carried them back to their original attack position, several miles from the front of the still advancing ship.

"We're going back in," he announced. "Squad leaders, take point." As they'd planned, the top pilots spread themselves out in a long line. Then, slowly but surely, the others tucked themselves in behind their group leaders, who led them away to their attack positions.

When the massive ship was encircled, the attack coordinators in the war room sounded the battle cry. From every direction at once, the squad leaders led the charge toward the enemy. Not understanding how to attack, the inexperienced pilots began breaking ranks to "improve" their positions rather than diving or climbing. Bombing an airborne target, even one as large and slow as the destroyer, was trickier than it looked, and three-quarters of the missiles flew wide of their mark. Only about thirty or so of the missiles, mostly AMRAAMs fired by the seasoned airdogs, found their target.

Some of the rookies lifted their planes high above the destroyer while others dipped below it. All of them moving toward the center at once, their main concern became not running headfirst into one another. In their confusion, they spit an orgy of Sidewinders, Silkworms, and Tomahawks into the air. Those with heat-seeking guidance systems locked themselves onto friendly planes weaving through the line of fire, then chased them down and killed them. The aerial battle was quickly degenerating into mayhem. But the true battle hadn't yet begun in earnest.

Then, the moment they all feared arrived. The portal door on the gleaming black tower pulled open and a swarm of the nimble gray attackers belched into the sky. After rising high into the air as a group, they flashed off in different directions to begin hunting down the earthlings.

"RUSSELL!"

The scream traveled as far out into the scrub desert as the distant roar of circling jet engines would allow. Miguel had come to the far end of the parking lot cum refugee camp searching for his stepfather when he heard what sounded like a sonic boom. He spun around to face the approaching city destroyer. Although he didn't know the first thing about air warfare, he was positive the last-chance air force which had recently lifted off the very runway where he now stood wasn't doing it by the book. Looping around aimlessly, swerving at the last moment to avoid midair collisions, flying too slow and too close to the ground, he had little confidence in their ability to repel the city destroyer. But the second he heard the boom, he knew one of the missiles had connected. Within seconds, other missiles began to fly. He would have stayed to watch this awesome and unlikely spectacle, but he had to find Russell before the huge ship was overhead.

Miguel was guessing that his stepfather had found a patch of shade where he could feel sorry for himself without being interrupted. And chances were, he'd brought a bottle to keep him company. He was probably somewhere nearby and probably badly wasted. He might even have passed out. The boy knew he should be angry. Once again, Russell's irresponsibility was forcing the boy to protect a family he was reluctant to call his own, but instead of anger, he felt sure Russell would be killed unless he reached the safety of the underground labs.

His search came to a sudden end once the pearl gray attackers swarmed into the sky. Every instinct told the boy to run for cover, and to run as fast as he possibly could. Throwing a glance over his shoulder, he saw a large detachment of the alien planes break off from the main group and head straight for Area 51. They were right behind him and coming in fast. He sprinted through the camp as laser pulses began tearing it up. RVs exploded and flipped off the ground. At least a hundred people hadn't made it into the hangar. They hid themselves behind their vehicles, or went running in zigzags across the open space separating the last trailers from the hangar doors.

Miguel heard a series of blasts strafing the ground behind him and dodged to one side at the last minute, jumping behind a pickup truck. The doors to the hangar were forty yards away, across a wide open stretch of pavement. Bodies littered the territory he had to cross. Inside, he could see soldiers and a woman in a white blouse, waving people inside. The woman spotted Miguel cowering behind the truck and waved to him frantically, beckoning him inside. She had dark hair and dark eyes, and for a moment, Miguel thought he recognized her. Too frightened to think, Miguel darted out into the open in a mad dash. Weapons fire tearing into the earth around him, he put his head down and ran for all he was worth. Leaping over bodies, he focused on reaching the woman in the white blouse. He made it. He raced through the big steel doors just as the soldiers were rolling them closed. The last one to make it inside, he followed the woman to the elevator, which was crowded with injured people waiting for the ride downstairs. A loud blast rocked the huge steel structure. The front doors had been blown out of existence, taking the soldiers along with them.

Connie, the woman in the white blouse, pounded hard on the button inside the elevator and waited through the eternity it took for the doors to close. Laser blasts were raining down on the hangar, and just as the last bit of light disappeared between the closing doors, the entire structure gave way and began to collapse.

Steve slammed the engines to their highest rev and shook the steering apparatus so hard David was sure he would snap the delicate steering handles out of their sockets.

"Try something else!" David yelled. "Just get us out of here!"

"Can't you see I'm trying? I can't shake her free. These clamps are too strong!"

Steve let go of the handles, stood up, and paced to the back of the cabin, trying to clear his head. By the time he came back moments later, David was putzing around on his laptop, looking for some way to help free them from the docking mechanism. Desperate, Steve began randomly flipping switches on the instruments the scientists had been unable to identify. When he had exhausted all the options, he returned to his pilot's chair and flopped into it, defeated.

"This is not the way I thought it was going to end. I pictured a balls-out dogfight, taking nine or ten of these little weevils down with me, you know?" He glanced over at David, who was obviously disturbed by that vision. "Well," the pilot continued, "at least we got the virus into mama's system." Both men jumped halfway out of their skin when the blast shield growled to life, lowering itself from the windows. "What are you doing? Don't let 'em see us!"

David put his hands in the air. "It's not me. They're

overriding the system." Steve hit the deck, hiding himself behind the instrument panel. David, who had developed an instinct for protecting his computer at all times, slid gently down the front of the chair until he too was on the floor. When the shield was all the way down, the two men stared at one another, wondering what to do next.

"Take a look." David pointed up toward the windows.

"Be my guest," Steve countered. "You take a look. You're the curious scientist."

"I'm a civilian," David declared proudly "I believe it's your duty as a marine to..." he fumbled for the word, "...to reconnoiter the enemy position!"

Steve gave him a look as sour as month-old milk. With deep reluctance, he turned his head sideways and inched slowly higher, determined to poke nothing more than an eyeball over the top of the dashboard. Like the view from a periscope, it took Steve a moment to realize what he was looking at. Standing behind what appeared to him to be a thick sheet of crystal, because of the way it refracted the light, was a group of large-headed, big-eyed aliens staring straight back at him.

"Ahhhh!" He landed on the floor, trying to stay as low as possible. "Damn! There's a whole bunch of them standing around out there."

"Did they see you?"

"Yeah."

"I mean did they really see you, get a good look at you?"

"Yes! There are twenty or thirty of 'em looking this way!"

"Then, Steve," David asked calmly, "why are we hiding?"

Setting his computer carefully to one side and taking a deep breath, David peeked outside. Sure enough, the ghostly creatures were staring back at him with giant black eyes. After peering nervously around for a minute, he uncoiled himself and stood straight up, strangely relaxed. More and more of the aliens were crowding into the control room behind the glass. Soon, he knew, they would come through the tubes to reclaim possession of their long lost ship. He looked down at Steve with a defeated grin.

"Check and mate."

The lights died, then flickered back to life as the energy of another blast shot through the electrical circuits and shook the underground labs at Area 51 like a sharp, two-second earthquake. The muted rumble of more distant explosions pulsed through the earth with a constant roar, terrifying the thousand people crowded shoulder to shoulder in the clean room.

"Julius!" Connie spotted her father-in-law standing to one side of the elevated walkway running the length of the room. She jostled her way toward him through the crowd. "Julius, are you all right?"

"Me? I'm fine." He had appointed himself temporary guardian of a group of children separated from their parents. Connie recognized two of them: the president's daughter, Patricia, and Jasmine's son, Dylan. "Of course, we're all a little scared by the noise," Julius announced loudly, "but we're not too worried because we know we're going to be okay. Right?" he asked the kids.

"Right!" the children agreed in one voice.

Connie couldn't believe it. In the middle of this frantic madhouse, which might have been a scene from London during the worst of the Blitz, doddering old Julius had managed to calm these children who should have been screaming bloody murder. She was more convinced than ever that the man possessed some kind of magic. Another blast plunged the room into a moment of darkness, reminding Connie that she had to keep moving.

"Stay safe," she said when the lights returned. "I've got to…" She pointed off in the direction of her business.

Julius only nodded and gave her the slightest wave of the hand, his concentration on the children. He had work to do also. As Connie left, he unfolded a yarmulke and set it on top of his head. He had the children join hands and asked if they'd like to hear a song one hundred percent guaranteed to keep them safe. They said they would, and he began to recite from memory a prayer from the Torah, singing in fluent Hebrew that would have astonished David had he been there. Opening one eye, he spied Nimziki watching him from nearby. Julius didn't much care for the man, but could sense he was lost.

"Join us," he called to the secretary of defense.

Nimziki, terrified, wanted someone to sit with, but he only shrugged and called back, "I'm not Jewish."

"So what?" Julius chuckled. "Nobody's perfect!"

"Miguel, did you find him?"

Connie, standing on the walkway, looked into the dual pits of wall-to-wall refugees and saw a girl of about fourteen shouting over the top of the noise in her direction.

"I'm still looking!" a male voice yelled directly behind her. Connie spun around and found that the boy with the long hair, the last one to make it inside, was following her through the clean room. "Stay where you are," he shouted to his sister. "I'll come back and find you."

Alicia nodded then sat down again, taking her place under Philip's comforting arm. She lifted her head to look him in the eyes. "If I die today after finally finding you, I'm going to be really really pissed off."

He smiled broadly, leaning down to kiss her.

Connie muscled her way through the room, Miguel shadowing her every step of the way.

* * *

Although its exterior armor had been battered and torn, the giant ship had sustained no significant damage. Scarred and smoking, rocked by the initial round of bombing, it had nevertheless continued inexorably forward, single-mindedly pushing toward Area 51. It was intent on crippling this last remaining pocket of resistance in the western United States. For a brief moment, it had seemed as if the humans might triumph, that their minuscule explosives might peck away patiently at the fifteen-mile wide ship until it came down. But since the stingray-shaped attackers had swarmed out into the electric blue morning, the ship had sustained almost no further damage.

Their hands already full with controlling their planes, many of the inexperienced pilots went hysterical when the alien attackers began systematically removing them from the battle. Despite Grey's pleas for calm, most of them squandered their last rockets with wild shots at the attackers. On the radar screens, the men in the war room watched the last of the missiles sailing away into the desert.

"We're running out of firepower, General," a technician reported, "and we're not causing enough damage to the main ship."

President Whitmore, surveying the chaos from 18,000 feet, concurred with that estimation. His squad of thirty planes was reduced to just eight. A few had been shot down in the first mad moments of the stingray counterattack. The others had been separated from the main group during the retreat. Taking a quick inventory, he learned that the pilots in his group had fewer than ten missiles left between them.

"Let's make 'em all count," he reminded them.

Connie had come into the war room to see if there

was anything she could do. Standing behind Grey, she watched one of the radar screens showing a three-dimensional display of the huge city destroyer. Because some of the base's primary radar receptors had already been destroyed, the image on the screen was incomplete, blinking on and off like a ghost. She felt a long shiver run through her legs up to her scalp when someone reported that the thing was directly overhead, then pointed out to General Grey some aspect of the torn, indistinct image.

Once he understood what the man was showing him, Grey snatched up the microphone and spoke to the remaining pilots.

"Attention! They're opening the bottom doors and getting ready to fire the big gun. Somebody get down there and knock that thing out before they can use it!!"

Dazed and sickened by this news, Connie turned and walked out of the room, moving past Miguel, who had snuck in behind her amidst all the confusion. He stood to one side, keeping out of the way, and eavesdropped on Whitmore's radio communication.

"Roger, Base," Whitmore called. "I've got one AMRAAM left and I'm on my way." He broke into a steep dive, pushing the engines into high thrust. "You boys keep 'em off my tail."

His squad leveled off and cruised along the bottom of the ship. The airspace in front of them was crowded with jets and attackers flying in all directions. Weaving in and out of traffic at high speed, Whitmore angled his attack run so that his missile would slice between two of the huge doors which were lowering themselves over the desert. He activated his HUD and sighted on the tip of the giant gun, the huge diamond-shaped bulb from which the powerful beam was about to fire. Something flashed across his peripheral vision just as the AMRAAM launch mechanism lowered from his jet. Attackers arriving too late, he thought. As he reached forward to fire the missile, the F-15 flying a few yards to his right unexpectedly blew up into a thousand pieces. The explosion rocked Whitmore's craft just as the missile blasted out of the harness, sending it badly off course. For a moment, he watched it speed away toward a collision with the hills.

"Damn it! Eagle Two, take point. I'll drop back and try to buy you some time."

"I'm on it," the pilot returned, moving into the lead position.

Behind him, Whitmore and the other pilots were yelling out the positions of incoming attackers. The opening on the bottom of the city destroyer was apparently a vulnerable point, and as the squad moved in for their strike, a dozen of the stingrays swarmed to the aliens' defense. There was so much confusion over the airwaves that the lead pilot never heard Whitmore warning him to take evasive action. One of the stingrays dropped in behind him, firing a steady storm of laser pulses. Another one of the F-15s, Pig's Eagle Twelve, rushed past the rest of the American pilots until the nose of his plane was practically up the stingray's tail. He pumped the alien plane full of .50-caliber shells, but it was too little too late. Eagle Two burst into flames, then exploded before its pilot could even lock down the targeting system. The wounded stingray peeled away toward the safety of the interior of the ship, but Eagle Twelve swerved with him, firing the whole time, until the ship fell to pieces, ripping apart in midair without an explosion.

"Nice work, Twelve," the president said without much enthusiasm. "Now, does anybody up here have any missiles left?"

Connie stepped through the doors of the infirmary and felt like she'd left the frying pan for the fire. Uniformed soldiers and a few volunteers were still bringing bloodied civilian victims of the air raid on the camp into a room already jammed with people. They were laid out on the floor and propped up against the walls. Their moans were accompanied by the constant rumblings of the bombardment from above. As horrific as the moment seemed, Connie knew it was only a prelude to the catastrophe that was to come. All the screaming would end a split second after the mammoth ship hovering overhead fired its awesome destructive beam.

"Put me to work!"

She grabbed Dr. Issacs's arm as he hurried past, carefully stepping over the bodies of the dead and wounded. By now, the bearded doctor was past the point of exhaustion. The only color left in his face were a pair of dark rings below his eyes. After a confused moment, he pointed into the next room.

"Help her," he shouted to make himself heard. "She's doing pre-op." Then he continued on his way.

Connie moved through a doorway and found Jasmine cleaning up a patient who'd taken some shrapnel right above his groin. Despite the thick flow of blood and the exposed view of the man's intestines, Jasmine was talking to him in a calm, friendly voice. When Connie approached the table, Jasmine immediately put a towel in her hands and showed her where to apply pressure to staunch the man's bleeding. Normally squeamish at the sight of blood, Connie pressed down with the rag, keeping the patient's internal organs from spilling out all over the table. Jasmine picked the last fragments of debris from the wound, cleaning it as she went.

"You're pretty good at this," Connie noted. "Keep it up and you could turn pro."

"Thanks," Jas smiled without looking up, "I like doing it and it's helping me keep my mind off other things." Connie thought she must be talking about the blast that was going to crush down through the roof any second, until she realized she was talking about her new husband. 'This is a hell of a way to spend a honeymoon, don't you think?"

"Huh? Oh, yes. A hell of a way," Connie agreed absently. She looked at the man laying on the table. He kept raising his head to watch what was happening to him, his teeth chattering the whole while.

Dr. Issacs shouted into the room, "Okay, let's get this one into the operating room."

As an orderly took over Connie's job, she smiled weakly at the man on the gurney, telling him without much conviction that he was going to be fine, just fine.

Several pilots answered in the negative. After a quick conference with his men in the war room, Grey returned to the radio. "Eagle One, proceed to Headly Air Force Base in Manitoba, Canada. We believe you have enough fuel left. We've radioed ahead and they'll send an escort out to meet you. This will be your new headquarters, sir."

Whitmore refused to break off the fight. They were so close. "Doesn't anyone have any damn missiles left?"

The green beam that began the ship's firing cycle spilled out of the huge firing pin, scanning its target. Whitmore knew it would only be a matter of seconds until the blast ripped down and chewed a hole in the ground where his daughter was hiding. He felt completely numb except for a wave of queasiness in his stomach. He didn't want to stick around and watch.

"Eagle Squad," he said with great reluctance, "let's head north. Follow my lead, do you copy?"

"Sorry I'm late, Mr. President!" an unfamiliar voice shouted over a background of engine noise on the radio.

"Who is this?"

"I'm just here to help out."

The president turned and saw the damnedest thing: an unsteady old red biwing aircraft that looked like something Baron von Richthofen might have flown during World War I. The ship was sputtering through the air, piloted by a man in a leather helmet. Strapped to the side with bungee cords and twine was something that looked like a missile.

"What are you doing?"

"Don't worry, sir. I'm packin'."

Russell had stolen the heaviest, nastiest missile he could find. It was too heavy for the plane, and every time the wind shifted, it clanked against the flimsy wall of the cockpit with a frightening thud. A red light the size of a button flashed off and on, indicating the weapon was armed.

"What I need from you, sir, is to keep those guys off me for a few more seconds."

Whitmore looked around and saw a fleet of the attackers diving in. The American pilots moved to engage them, laying down a barrage of cover fire to protect the wobbly old biwing. The plane continued lifting uncertainly toward the giant firing pin.

In the war room, all eyes were on the radar model of the ship, a small blip slowly climbing toward the origin of the beam, also visible on the screen. Grey grabbed the radio mike. "Pilot, identify yourself!"

"My name's Russell Casse," the pilot answered, "and I want you to do me a favor…"

"Who is this guy?" one of the technicians wondered.

"Russell!" Miguel rushed toward the soldiers gathered around the monitors. They caught him by the arms and held him back.

"…tell my children I love them very much."

As one of the radio technicians spoke to the president and his squad, keeping them alert to enemy craft positions, Miguel yelled over the open microphone: "Dad! No!"

Russell couldn't help smiling at being called "Dad." He didn't know if Miguel could hear him, but he yelled back over the radio, "I've got to, kid. You were always better at taking care of them than I was anyways." Then he added, "This is just something I've got to do."

He snapped off his radio and pulled the de Haviland into as steep a climb as the engine could bear without stalling out. He had the nose of the plane pointed at the side of the firing pin. The tail of the biwing disappeared into the opening as the president and the remaining fighters banked away, clearing the area. The green light suddenly disappeared. In two seconds, a white light would appear and a massive beam of destruction would fire down on Area 51.

"Hello, boys! I'm back!" Russell hollered at the top of his lungs. "And in the words of my generation: UP YOURS!!"

The old plane flew nose-first into the side of the firing pin, causing an insignificant explosion that puffed out the bottom of the city destroyer without appearing to cause any real damage. But just as the deadly white beam erupted from the bottom of the ship, it abruptly cut off again. The huge ship lifted up and away with astonishing speed. In the same instant, every attacker plane turned on a dime to follow it. The entire swarm raced away over the desert.

None of them got very far.

Beginning at the center of the massive city destroyer, a sharp explosion burst a hole through the domed roof, like a skull exploding outward from a suicide bullet. Russell's bomb had set off a chain reaction that ripped through the body of the fifteen-mile-wide ship, melting the entire vessel from within. One after another, the thunderous internal explosions turned the monster in the sky fire red, exposing its internal architecture like an X-ray. Quickly, it was fully engulfed. Still in midair, it began to implode and explode simultaneously, incinerating itself into fragments, falling in huge flaming chunks to earth.

The chain reaction extended down to the war room, which erupted into a roaring victory cheer. They'd found a way to sink the impregnable alien battleships. Everyone went crazy, jumping into one another's arms, pumping fists in the air, laughing wildly. Everyone, that is, except Miguel. As shouts of triumph filled the room, he quietly opened the door and stepped outside into a corridor full of refugees. They were confused by the discrepancy between his sad expression and the cheering going on behind him. Grey, permanently levelheaded, took one of the celebrants by the scruff of his collar, calming him down instantly.

"Get back on the wire," he snarled, "and explain to every squadron around the world how to shoot these sons of bitches down."

Steve thought he could hear the fat lady singing. Still sprawled on the floor, hiding himself below the dashboard, he reached into his breast pocket and removed the pair of cigars Julius had given him. He held one out to David.

"I guess there's nothing left to do," he said, handing over the smoke, "except nuke 'em before they come in here and do something nasty."

David, still locked in a staring contest with the creatures behind the glass, nodded, coming to grips with the fact that he was about to die. Inspecting the cigar, he mused, "It's funny. I always thought things like *these* would kill me. Okay, let's fire away."

Steve lifted himself off the floor and sat down in his pilot's chair, trying to keep his eyes off the repulsive sight of the creatures straight ahead of him. He opened the cover plate on the black box and punched in the launch code. The LCD screen blinked rapidly, presenting him with two options: LAUNCH and CANCEL.

"Nice meeting you, man." He reached across and shook David's hand.

"Likewise," David assured him. "And we almost got away with it."

"Almost," Steve agreed. "Ready?"

"Bye-bye, Fuzzy. Bye-bye, Blinky." David waved to the aliens, giving them individual names. "See you later, Egghead, and you, too, Froggie."

"Think they know what's coming?" Steve asked, the cigar dangling from his mouth as he reached down to execute the firing.

"Not a chance."

As soon as Steve's finger touched the button, the floor of the tiny cabin kicked violently backwards, knocking both men off balance as the eight-foot-long missile shot away in a shower of rocket exhaust. Fire and shards of glass flew everywhere. By the time Steve and David could look up, the missile had penetrated the crystal observation window, crashed through the back of the observation room, and lodged itself into a distant wall, its rocket engine still spewing a jetstream of sparks.

Their artificially generated atmosphere impeached, the aliens behind the glass began to twist and expand horribly as their bodies were sucked in all directions by the vacuum of empty space. Their bulbous heads burst and splattered like kernels of bloody popcorn.

As this gruesome show, played itself out beyond the windows of the attacker, the clamps holding the ship unexpectedly released and the ship lifted several feet in the air. An explosion in the observation tower knocked the ship backwards. It skittered off an identical craft parked next to it and wobbled out into the open.

"We're loose!"

"Doesn't matter," David said, "the game's over."

Steve checked the data from the black launch pad. Its digital counter showed the time remaining until the nuclear warhead self-detonated: 22... 21...

"I don't hear no fat lady," he said, jumping into the pilot's chair and spinning the craft around. David had just enough time to jump into his chair before Steve yanked back on the controls, jerking the ship into a full-speed getaway.

"Forget the fat lady. You're obsessed with the fat lady. Just get us out of here!"

Quicker that any human pilot could have reacted, a handful of attackers roared into pursuit. Although Steve hadn't mastered his plane's steering mechanism completely, he had no choice but to push it to breakneck speed. Swerving dizzily, he rocketed through the dimly lit maze of the mother ship's interior. The pursuing attackers held off firing at their prey until it came to the mouth of the exit tunnel. Suddenly, they unleashed a flood of tracer fire, but they didn't have the angle they needed, and Steve shot into the triangular passageway toward the exit.

"It's closing," David shouted, "the doors are closing."

"I can see that!" Steve had enough to worry about without a sideseat driver. The exit at the end of the tunnel was growing smaller by the moment as three thick doors moved closer, sealing off their last hope for escape. Straining the controls to the breaking point, Steve milked every ounce of speed from the craft, roaring toward the closing porthole. He checked the black box:... 09... 08...

"It's too late, they're closed." David watched the last few stars disappearing behind the triangular doorway. When he saw Steve meant to try it anyway, he closed his eyes and held his breath.

They shot through the narrow aperture with only inches to spare.

"Elvis has left the building!" he screamed.

"Thank you very much," David chimed in, lamely attempting to imitate The King.

Once they were out in space, Steve located the earth and steered the plane toward it... 01... 00.

The attacker continued to accelerate, streaking through space at several thousand miles per hour as its occupants stared at North America, perfectly clear but so far away. Then there was a flash of light so bright it seemed to come from the rear of their attacker. Steve and David had just enough time to look at each other with concerned expressions before the force of the blast moving through space caught them from behind. Like a loose board caught in the surf, their little ship rode the crest of the explosion, getting knocked ass over teakettle. Steve tried to steer through the wave of turbulence for a moment but then lost control as the explosion engulfed them completely.

The canopy of the president's jet lifted and a gloved fist rose in the air. Whitmore tore off his mask and lifted himself out of the cockpit onto the wing of his F-15. Seven of the Eagle Squad had returned, and thirty or so of the ragtag air force were coming in for their landings. They'd stayed in the air dogfighting with the last remaining attackers until the gray stingrays had started losing power and falling out of the sky. Apparently, they had only limited reserves of onboard energy.

Once his feet were on the ground, Whitmore pointed a finger at one of the other pilots, the long-haired, bearded Pig, acknowledging the credit he deserved. Pig pointed right back at the president. Cheering soldiers ran out to greet the planes. When the president gave them the order, they led the way to a hole in the earth. A stone's throw from the collapsed main hangar, a set of iron doors embedded in a slab of concrete opened onto a stairway. It was an emergency exit leading down to the research labs. Whitmore and his fellow pilots followed the soldiers into the passage.

The stairs ended in the scrub room. When the president turned the corner and stepped into the long clean room, it took a moment for him to recognize it. In place of the hooded workers he'd seen before, Whitmore came face-to-face with hundreds of ordinary citizens, the refugees who, only minutes earlier, had been preparing themselves to die. They erupted into loud, sustained cheering for the crew of heroes who had shot the alien destroyer out of the sky. Overwhelmed by their reception, Whitmore waded through the crowd, shaking hands and letting himself be hugged until he spotted someone he knew a short distance away. Julius lifted little Patricia onto the walkway and she ran toward her father as fast as her feet would take her. Whitmore scooped the girl up, wrapping her in his arms.

A young man with long hair stood nearby, watching the scene without emotion. He felt a hand on his shoulder.

"Dang, Miguel," Troy was back to his ornery self, "didn't you hear us? We've been yelling at you for ten minutes."

Alicia pushed her way through the cheering mob with Philip's help. The expression on Miguel's face told her instantly that Russell was dead. She burst into tears, leaving Philip and throwing her arms around Miguel.

"Hey, what happened?" Troy demanded. "What's wrong?" Without a word, Miguel reached out and pulled the boy close.

Slamming through the door of the war room, Whitmore was greeted with more applause. Grey, scowling at one of the monitors, turned and saw who it was. Something like a smile lit up his expression as he came forward to embrace his friend.

"Damn it, Tom, you trying to give an old man heart failure?"

"How's the attack coming?"

"Excellent. We've already got eight confirmed knock-downs and several more probables."

"Got another one, General," one of the soldiers

yelled. "The Dutch air force just wasted the ship over the Netherlands."

The man's report sent another chorus of cheers through the room, but when Connie came through the door with a sad smile on her face, most of the men in the room quieted down. Jasmine, carrying Dylan on her hip, followed her inside.

"And our delivery boys?" Whitmore asked. "Any word yet from up there?"

Reluctantly, Grey answered, "Unfortunately, we lost contact with Hiller and Levinson about fifty minutes ago, a moment or two after the mother ship exploded."

Whitmore looked over at Connie and Jasmine as they listened to the bad news. Just when he was coming toward them to offer a few words of condolence, one of the men at the monitors shouted.

"Hold on! Something's showing up on radar. Looks like we have another incoming."

Everyone crowded around the monitor, watching the tiny blip move across the radar screen.

An hour later, a Humvee crowded with passengers was speeding across the afternoon desert, kicking up a long trail of dust. Behind the wheel, Major Mitchell steered the transport, half sports car and half tank, toward a towering column of black smoke rising in the distance. The war room crew had tracked the craft moving across their radar screens until it landed about nine miles from the base, deep in the middle of nowhere. In the bucket seat next to Mitchell, Jasmine kept watch out the front window while Dylan bounced around on her lap. Standing just behind her, with their faces to the wind, Connie, President Whitmore, and General Grey held on to the roll bar, scanning the horizon for signs of life. In the roomy cargo area, Julius sat with the president's daughter

Patricia. Another vehicle, a jeep loaded with armed soldiers, followed a short distance behind.

At a distance of three miles, they could see that the ship had crash-landed against an isolated set of rocky hills. There was no evidence to support their hope it was the same ship Steve and David had taken into space, and even less reason to believe the men might still be alive. The ruined attacker was completely engulfed in flame.

Tiny dark shapes appeared on the flat brown horizon. As the Humvee came closer, it became clear these shapes were actually a pair of creatures. They seemed to be standing upright and moving. Grey yelled for Mitchell to slow the vehicle down, then motioned the soldiers in the jeep forward. With several assault rifles trained on the two figures, the caravan rolled forward at a cautious pace.

At fifty yards away, Mitchell brought the vehicle to a stop, switched off the motor, and draped his arms over the steering wheel. "Well, I'll be damned," he said in disbelief. The mysterious figures were smoking cigars.

Hiller and Levinson had done the impossible and lived to tell about it. They'd infiltrated the alien fortress, disabled her shields with a dime store computer virus, blown the planet-sized orb to smithereens, then flown back to Nevada before their attacker's energy supply was exhausted. Now they came swaggering across the sand, casual and confident, as if it were all in a day's work.

Jasmine threw open the door and went sprinting across the hot sand. She didn't stop running until she was wrapped in her husband's arms. Squeezing him like she'd never let go again, her voice choked with emotion, she said, "You scared the hell out of me. We thought you got trapped inside."

Steve looked down at her with that cocky grin of his. "Yeah, but what an entrance!"

Jasmine stared at him, shocked and amused in the same breath. Didn't *anything* scare this man? "There you go again." She shook her head. "I guess your ego's gonna be out of control now, and you'll be impossible to live with, right?"

"Probably. You still willing to find out, Chicken Legs?"

She let out a joyous laugh. "Yeah, I'm willing to give it a try, Dumbo Ears!"

Connie and David approached one another slowly, then stopped to face one another as if one step closer might set off a buried land mine. She was mightily proud of him. For David, the sweetest part of living through his ordeal was being able to see her again. But neither of them knew what the other wanted, so they remained standing three feet apart.

"So," David asked, looking around the empty sky, "did it work?"

The question brought Connie suddenly back to earth. She'd been imagining what it would be like to move across the last small piece of territory separating them and feel his kiss again. But, naturally, he wanted to know whether his brilliant plan had been successful. Embarrassed by her hidden thoughts, she suddenly felt the eyes of those watching from the vehicles.

"Yes, yes," she told him, "it worked beautifully. A couple of minutes after the upload, all their shields went down and we started hitting them with missiles."

She started to tell him how the city destroyer had come toward Area 51 and how Whitmore himself had led the air battle, how the mysterious pilot in the old biplane had arrived in the nick of time, but David held up a hand to interrupt the story.

"No, what I mean is," he pointed to her and then back to himself, "*did it work?*"

The smile that spread across Connie's face was brighter than the afternoon sun. "You bet it worked," she told him. They stepped across the no-man's land between them and into one another's arms, "you bet it did."

When the couples returned arm in arm to the vehicles, Whitmore nodded his head at the two men in begrudging approval. "Not bad," he told them, as if they'd just taken a test and scraped by with a C+. But the next moment, he was grinning from ear to ear, unable to hide his admiration for all that the two heroes had accomplished. "Not too damn bad at all!"

He congratulated Steve with a handshake, then turned to the lanky MIT alumnus who had punched him in the nose years before. "You turned out to be even smarter than I thought you were," he said as they shook hands. "And a hell of a lot braver than I ever gave you credit for. Thank you, David."

"What I would like to know," a loud voice interrupted, "is how come Mr. Healthnut is suddenly smoking one of my disgusting cigars?"

Julius was relaxing on the bumper of the Humvee, his legs not quite long enough to reach the ground. David let go of Connie long enough to wrap his father in a rowdy bear hug, lifting him off the ground.

"Oy, now he's a pro wrestler."

David set the old man down and eyed him suspiciously for a moment. As Julius composed himself, straightening out the hair and clothing his son had mussed, he asked David what he was staring at.

"How did you do it, Pops?"

"Do what?" the old guy asked. "I don't know what you're talking about."

"You know exactly what I mean," David kept at him. "First, you got us to Washington, then to Area Fifty-One, and just when I was about to quit, you gave me the idea for the virus. I suppose you'll tell me it was all just a series of accidents, right?"

For a split second, Julius let a cunning grin play across his face before returning once more to an expression of mock annoyance. "I don't know what happened to you out in space, but I'm thinking those aliens maybe did something funny to your brain."

The two men smiled warmly at each other.

Steve was kneeling down beside Dylan, getting his welcome home hug, when General Grey stepped forward for a word with him. "Well, soldier, you've had quite a weekend."

"Yes, sir, I have," the Marine pilot agreed.

"And you did one hell of a fine job. We're all proud." Grey offered a salute, which both Steve and Dylan returned.

Triumphant, the group began to load into the Humvee for the ride back to Area 51. As they were doing so, Patricia Whitmore pointed up to the sky and yelled, "Hey, what's that?"

The group turned in time to see a fireball, orange and red, streaking overhead like a falling star. Then another trail of light, this one bright yellow, ripped across the aqua blue sky. Wreckage from the exploded mother ship was raining through space and burning itself up at it entered earth's atmosphere. The colorful meteors would go on bursting in the air all through the night.

Steve lifted Dylan into his arms and looked skyward. "You know what day it is?" he asked.

"Yup," Dylan told him, "it's the Fourth of July."

"That's right, son. And didn't I promise you fireworks?"

The battle over Area 51 had ended in a relatively clean and painless victory. Fewer than three hundred people had died. But the situation was far different in other parts of the country and around the world. Humanity had survived, but only at a staggering cost. Millions were dead and millions more were injured. Many would never recover from the wounds, both physical and emotional, they had sustained during the invasion. Even as the survivors began digging themselves out from under the debris, thankful to be alive, they felt the dread of the months and years of rebuilding which lay ahead. The howls coming from the victory celebrations echoed out over a collapsed and blighted world. In most places, the destruction was so severe that the living envied the dead.

More than a hundred of the world's largest cities had been obliterated, among them ancient, irreplaceable treasures such as Paris, Baghdad, New York, and Kyoto. Gone too were the world's finest museums and libraries, its major airports and factories, food processing plants, markets, office buildings, and one out of every three human homes. Refugees, hundreds of millions of them, without shelter or means of feeding themselves, wondered how they would survive. The situation was most dire in the southern hemisphere, where it was the middle of winter. Mass migrations to the temperate zones of the earth began immediately, further taxing already strained ecological resources. The earth's water, land, and air were all heavily polluted in the aftermath of the short but cataclysmic war.

It seemed that everything had been lost and that only one thing had, perhaps, been gained: a wider frame of reference. Along with the certain knowledge that humans were not alone in the universe, the murderous squabbling over petty differences of race and nationality suddenly seemed to be petty foolishness. In the wake of the attack, the people of earth finally realized the things they shared in common far outweighed their subtle differences. There was a worldwide recognition that the human imagination had been fundamentally altered and there was no turning back. In a sense, the species had grown up the hard way, being shoved unwillingly toward maturity. There was also an awareness of a new interdependence: the world would have to prepare for the possibility of a similar invasion in the future. Whitmore's hope had come to pass: July

Fourth would no longer be merely an American holiday.

It was a new future, and leaders like Whitmore were anxious to help shape the new world that would be built upon the ruins of the old. They knew the direction and character of this rebuilding would be determined early, within the first few months. There was every possibility for America, one of the most violent and divided nations in the world, to tear itself apart in a struggle over scarce resources, but there was also the possibility of people coming together, cooperating with one another in a spirit of community that would set an example for others around the globe. Before the dust of the battles had settled, Whitmore would be on the campaign trail once again, making essentially the same call to service and self-sacrifice he had delivered during his run for the presidency. But this time the scope would be international and the risks much higher. What kind of world would he pass on to his daughter?

As the rebuilding began, one fact quickly made itself abundantly clear: the human spirit, like the supple, tenacious weeds already beginning to push their way up through the ruins, would once again reassert itself, tougher, smarter, and more unified than ever.

INDEPENDENCE DAY

SILENT ZONE

CREATED BY DEAN DEVLIN &
ROLAND EMMERICH
NOVEL BY STEPHEN MOLSTAD

To my science advisor.
K.R.W., and his wife.

PROLOGUE

THE BATTLE CONTINUES

On July 5, the worldwide battle against the invaders continued. All thirty-six of the alien city destroyers had successfully been shot out of the sky, but there was no mood of celebration in the below-ground research facility referred to as Area 51. This secret lab, buried below the Nevada desert, had replaced Washington, DC, as the functioning headquarters of the United States. Inside the lab's communications and tracking room, President Thomas Whitmore, his advisors, and a crew of technicians were frantically working to coordinate a counteroffensive. Four city destroyers, along with thousands of smaller ships called attackers, had crashed to earth on American soil—many of them in the scrub desert surrounding the lab—and it was too soon to know how many survivors there might be. President Whitmore, who had first come to national prominence as a fighter pilot in the Gulf War, had personally climbed into the cockpit of an F-18 jet and led the squadron of planes which had scored the first kill against these gargantuan airships. The aliens had apparently detected the radio transmissions coming from the base and broken off another attack to fly toward the spot. They were on the verge of destroying Area 51 when Whitmore's team discovered that it only took a single AMRAAM missile detonating against the giant ship's primary weapon to cause a chain-reaction explosion powerful enough to rip the craft apart. The technicians immediately spread this news around the globe, then waited for reports to filter back.

High above the base, AWACS reconnaissance planes were circling, using their sophisticated electronic equipment to provide Area 51 with cell-phone and radio links to the remnants of America's military. From their perspective, the AWACS pilots had a clear view of the monstrous, fire-blackened hull of the destroyer lying in the desert, a smoldering shell seventeen miles wide. Also visible were the convoys of military vehicles coming from all directions to surround the destroyer. All day long, men and equipment that had survived the devastating attack poured in from military installations all across the Southwest. By midafternoon, the solid ring of soldiers and civilians surrounding the craft was thick enough to be seen from the air. On the ground, the crest of the ruined megaship was visible from as far away as Las Vegas.

Delta Company out of Fort Irwin was one of the first on the scene. This elite squad of soldiers was given the unenviable task of acting as the shock troops for the counterinvasion. They were the first ones in.

It was like storming into an impossibly large church. They entered through a two-hundred-foot break in the exterior wall, advancing quietly, twenty-five yards at a time. The size of the ship's interior spaces was stunning, incredible. Once they had secured and cleared the first thousand yards, armored vehicles, Jeeps, and hundreds of both soldiers and civilians, poured through the breach. Deeper into the ship, the rooms became a labyrinth of smaller chambers, closing down to the size of narrow hallways in some places. Delta Company pushed forward, tensely expecting to encounter hostile survivors around each corner. They began to find fragments of alien corpses ripped apart in the blast. But by the end of the first twenty-four hours, not a single survivor had been discovered.

Helicopters had entered the ship's vast central chamber

through great holes that the explosion had torn through the roof. The pilots had reported "a big barrel of fish," thousands of destroyed attackers lying in a single heap three miles across. Delta Company received orders to spearhead a drive toward this central chamber, where it was thought they might find survivors and take them as prisoners.

Nolan jumped from the surface of one crashed alien attack ship, landed on the hard shell of the next, then sprinted the sixty feet to the edge of another, where he took cover and searched the vast space around him with the barrel of his assault rifle. The central chamber of the city destroyer gave him the feeling of being at the bottom of an underground lake surrounded by blackened vertical walls. He estimated the distance across the chamber to be about three miles. Gray sunlight poured in from where the explosion had torn away a large section of the roof. In the distance, he could hear the sound of a Jeep and the sporadic shouts coming from another recon team working the southern sector of the chamber. The space had obviously been some kind of portable airport, a staging area for the attacker planes, which now lay in a colossal pile, stacked ten deep in some places, after having been knocked loose from their moorings high overhead.

Nolan glanced back the way he had come and gave Simpkins the come-ahead signal. As his partner crossed the open space, Nolan covered him, tensely scanning in all directions for signs of danger. Although Delta Company hadn't heard or seen any live fire, reports had been made in other sectors of alien snipers using handheld weapons. As Simpkins made his dash, the ship under him settled slightly, groaning deeper into the pile of identical ships on which it rested. He was momentarily knocked off balance, recovering just in time to avoid being tossed over the side. Peering over the edge, he looked into the maze of narrow tunnels created by the jumble of saucers. He gulped before backing carefully away toward higher ground.

First Simpkins, then Myers, then Henderson joined Nolan under the ledge where the edge of one ship rested on another. Their objective, a cigar-shaped craft, visibly different from the others, was just on the other side of the ship they were using for cover.

Nolan spoke into his handset, "OK, Captain, we're one ship away from the target. I see some windows, but no doors. Looks like the best way in would be to shoot out one of the windows."

"Roger, team leader. Use your discretion. If you can't find a quick way in, turn around and come back down to base. Over."

"Confirmed." Nolan slipped the walkie-talkie back in his belt. Turning to the other men, he said, "Me and Simpkins go in first. As soon as we get through the windows you two advance and cover. Here we go."

And off he went. At close range, Nolan squeezed off a few rounds from his M-15, and the armor-piercing bullets completely shattered the clear material. Up close, the surface of this long ship had a weathered look. Unlike the others, it seemed to have seen service out in the elements. And this one wasn't covered with any of the strange symbols embossed into the surfaces of the attackers. He ducked and peered through the opening. No sign of movement, but he was only looking into one, mostly empty, chamber. Using his flashlight, he could see there was a doorway leading deeper into the ship.

"Looks like an operating table," Simpkins said sourly, his own flashlight sweeping across the ceiling of the ship. Indeed, since the vehicle was upside-down, there was a weirdly contoured metallic table firmly attached to the ceiling. On what was now the floor of the vehicle, all manner of debris, including several objects that might have been surgical tools, lay in heaps.

"Sick mo' fo's," Nolan snarled to himself. "I'm going in." He fitted his flashlight into the mount at the top of his rifle, rolled through the opening, and snapped to his feet, ready to fire. Once Simpkins had joined him, he signaled toward a doorway covered with some stiff material drawn closed and obstructing the view to the back of the ship.

Communicating by gesture alone, the pair put themselves in position, then Simpkins tore back the curtain. Fingers tense against triggers, the men aimed into the next chamber. It was a narrow corridor with large shelves on both sides. These shelves had been full when the ship turned over, spilling their contents into the narrow aisle between them. Beyond the pile of debris, the space opened again.

"Nolan, check this out. What the hell were they doing in here?" Simpkins's flashlight was focused on the spilled contents of the shelves: a green nylon baseball cap with the Quaker State logo, a prosthetic leg, hunting jackets, shoes, scarves, a rifle, photographs, all manner of human artifacts, the detritus of a thousand abductions.

"All those people who said they got kidnapped by aliens and they stuck probes up inside of them and did experiments, looks like this is where it happened. And this pile of crap is the coatroom."

"...or the lost and found."

Nolan took four measured steps deeper into the room, crunching a pair of eyeglasses under his boot. He reached down and picked through the debris, retrieving an audiocassette. "It's in Japanese," he said, tossing it aside and picking up a piece of paper. He studied it for a second, then reached for a second sheet.

"What is it? You find something?"

"Maybe. You know how people are saying they must have had spies, humans who were helping them?"

"Yeah, I've heard that, but it's bullshit. Like they needed any help."

"Take a look." Nolan shrugged. He handed the pages over his shoulder and picked up a third. The pages had been torn from a blank book, and were full of quick-but-skillful engineering schematics of alien technology. One showed some kind of screen at the top of a wiring chart, another page labeled "aqua box" had a two-second sketch of something that looked like an Egyptian hieroglyph in a six-sided box. Surrounding the picture were equations and notes, all of them completely indecipherable to the soldiers. "There's a whole book of this crud. Let's take some of this stuff down to show the captain and come back with more men."

Simpkins relayed that plan back to Henderson and Myers, then returned to where Nolan was gathering evidence. "How convenient," he said when he noticed that his partner had found a shopping bag and was dumping items into it like this was a rummage sale. Simpkins spotted some poor slob's wallet and started flipping through it when he thought he heard Nolan say something like, *Don't worry. I won't hurt you. Be calm.* He glanced over at Nolan, who looked right back at him.

"Quit messing around, Simpkins."

Don't be afraid. Do not use your weapons. No harm will come to you. This time they were looking right at one another, and nobody's lips had moved. *Do not use your weapons,* the command repeated itself out of nowhere. Both men turned toward the back of the ship, fully expecting to see a tall alien figure step into the murky light. And a second later, that is exactly what happened.

Nolan snapped his rifle up and took aim at the thing's forehead, in the spot above its eyes where the brain was so close to the surface you could literally see it thinking. In the glare of the flashlight, the creature's glistening skin looked ghost white. Long almond-shaped lids blinked over bulging reflecting eyes the size of ripe plums.

Simpkins's first impulse was to shout "enemy in the hole," and open fire. Instead, he froze, staring down the barrel of his rifle, locked on the alien's chest. Then, almost mechanically, he felt himself change his mind. *Tell the others not to fire,* he said to himself. Then, quite aware that he was being manipulated by this bony, snot-shiny, shell-headed crawdad, he felt *the need* to tell the guys outside. Without breaking concentration on his target, he backed into the rounded room with the table on the ceiling and yelled to the others, "We got one. It's alive, but it's not dangerous! He won't attack! Hold your fire."

"It's messing with us, man," Nolan said, visibly trembling—partly from fear, partly because of the effort it took not to lay his rifle aside as the thing was urging him to do. "It's messing with my head."

In this confusing situation, Nolan and Simpkins were, quite literally, of two minds. Without losing any possession of their regular consciousness, they were "mentally listening" to the alien, who had found some way to "speak" to them. They were about to shoot anyhow, but then both men felt something like an emotion, a vibe, which assured them the alien would cooperate. It was a teletactile communication, a skillful imitation of the human feeling of friendship, a trick the creature could only have learned through previous exposure to Earthlings.

"All right, let's try to take this boy prisoner," Nolan relented. "Hands up, asswipe. Hands up." The creature awkwardly complied, lifting its slender, semi-transparent arms away from its sides. Nolan and Simpkins carefully backed into the doorway before signaling the thing forward. Slowly, clumsily, it made its way over the pile of clothing and other objects until there was nothing between it and the men's rifles.

"Hold your fire," Simpkins ordered the two men leaning in the broken window, weapons trained on the doorway. The alien stepped into the open space of the upside-down examining room, its fleshy, two-pronged feet carefully exploring the surface of the debris-littered ceiling for a secure foothold each time it advanced.

From beyond the shattered window, Henderson's voice could be heard as he spoke into his radio. "Cap, we got one. We got a prisoner. Send in some backup."

It took two full hours to march the alien prisoner back to the command post at the western extremity of the central chamber. The hard slopes created by the jumble of ships proved treacherous footing for a creature accustomed to a very different environment. At every fork in the mazelike journey, the soldiers carefully selected the path that would offer the least chance of an escape. By the time they arrived with the Extraterrestrial Biological Entity they were calling "the monster," over a hundred armed men were there, with rifles drawn to greet them.

A Jeep was brought forward to transport the alien outside. By this time, Simpkins had appointed himself the creature's bodyguard and was busy channeling the soldiers' hostilities by reminding them how valuable a prisoner would be for preventing any future attacks. The creature, doing exactly what was required in the situation, remained perfectly docile, even when Simpkins came forward with a large piece of canvas. It was draped over the alien, then tied down in a way that completely concealed its body. This was done more for the creature's security than for fear it might try to escape. Simpkins had already visualized the seven-mile journey to the outside, and foreseen the danger of an angry soldier squeezing off a few rounds in spontaneous hatred. Everyone was anxious to get some payback for what its race had done to theirs.

Bundled like a rolled-up carpet and lying passively

in the back of the Jeep, shotguns leveled at its head, the creature endured the long rough road out of the destroyer without moving a muscle.

Hours later, Simpkins, Nolan, Henderson, and Myers reported to the remnants of Area 51's main hangar. Their prisoner was en route back to Fort Irwin for interrogation, and they had come to deliver the evidence they had gathered from the cigar-shaped craft to General Grey. He had requested to meet personally with these men. They were quickly coming to be known as the guys who brought the only prisoner out of Whitmore's ship. As their story circulated, each retelling added some new detail which emphasized their bravery. In time, their story would join hundreds of others and would be told, in different forms, for many years, as part of the folklore that arose in the wake of the invasion.

While they were waiting, Nolan started thumbing through the sketchbook he'd found. He could see it was the haphazard journal of someone with very sloppy handwriting. Its pages were filled with equal parts of machinery sketches, English sentences, and mathematical equations. He turned to a watercolor painting of the desert and admired the artist's skill. The picture was signed in the bottom corner. The book had belonged to someone named Okun.

1

A NEW ROOF FOR PROJECT SMUDGE

1972

At 5:58 A.M., the hallway leading to the inner ring of the Pentagon complex was busier than usual. Office workers and uniformed officers had come in early to get the latest issue of the *Washington Post* and read about the latest development in the Watergate case, which felt, at least to those in the District of Columbia's political circles, like the end of the world. Slicing through this early-morning mull and buzz, came a tall figure in a conservatively cut suit half a size too small for his lanky frame. Albert Alexander Nimziki stopped briefly outside one of the Pentagon's many coffee shops and studied the headlines shouting back at him from a newspaper rack: COX, SPECIAL COMMITTEE CONSIDER IMPEACHMENT. Of course, that morning's news came as no surprise to him. As deputy director of the Central Intelligence Agency, it was his job to know what was going to be in the newspapers days, weeks, and sometimes years before the papers themselves knew.

Nimziki was the youngest man ever to attain the post of deputy director, but he had gotten a jump on the competition, having been a professional spook since he was sixteen years old. Nimziki grew up in Lancaster, Pennsylvania, where he internalized some of his chilliness of public demeanor from his Amish neighbors. When his agronomist father landed a job with the UN, he moved the family to New York City's Roosevelt Island, into a neighborhood crowded not only with UN diplomats but with the spies sent from around the world to keep an eye on them. Overlooking a busy, upscale intersection, the family's new apartment afforded young Albert the perfect vantage point for watching the endless game of cat and mouse. For two years it had been a spectator sport, with him spying on the spies. But one day he boldly walked downstairs and talked to one of them. Only a day later, he had a parabolic mike and telephoto lens, using them to eavesdrop on conversations transpiring at the posh outdoor cafe across the street. From this early training, he'd moved on to Georgetown U., where he earned a double major in criminology and international relations. Soon after joining the CIA, he proved himself to be not only a daring and talented field operative but also a highly efficient administrator, and it was this second skill which had fueled his steady rise through the agency's ranks. At only thirty-four years of age, he had aspirations to rise higher still.

He found his elevator and rode it down one floor to the building's basement. The heavy doors opened after he inserted a security card into the lock, depositing him into a bare hallway guarded by a pair of soldiers. After glancing at his ID plaque, they waved him through, and he stepped into the Tank, the most secure conference area in the entire Pentagon complex.

Inside, sitting around a long walnut conference table, were a dozen men, all of them white, all of them older than Nimziki. They were elite figures from the U.S. military and intelligence communities, men who had been entrusted, however reluctantly, with "the nation's dirtiest little secret." Collectively, they were known as Project Smudge.

After a brief round of perfunctory greetings, Nimziki sat down, and Bud Spelman, assigned to the Defense

Intelligence Agency, walked to the podium at the front of the room. Serious as a bulldog, the barrel-chested Colonel Spelman had once been an Army drill instructor, and it showed in the blunt way he handled the meeting.

"Gentlemen. The purpose of this meeting is to update you on a series of possibly threatening UFO occurrences and, if warranted, to adopt an action plan. Now I trust everyone has had a chance to review the status report I sent around, so you basically know the situation, but I do want to show you a piece of radar tape shot last month by Northern Tracking Command." After pulling down a retractable white screen and dimming the lights, he moved to a projector set up at the back of the room. As the film began, the screen went black. "You're looking at the night sky over our atomic storage facility near Bangor, Maine. These are enhanced-composite radar images transferred to film to improve their quality. And here comes our visitor."

From the upper corner, an uneven blotch of white light appeared. The pulsing, indistinct shape began a slow and steady descent toward the bottom of the screen, its outline slowly coming into better focus. "In addition to the radar, we had several naked-eye witnesses on the ground who say they got a good look at it. But, as usual, their descriptions are all over the map. Some of them said the thing gave off a golden light, others called it an orange-red light, while another maintains it was bluish in color. The same with engine noise. Some people heard 'a high whine, like an electric motor' while others noted a 'complete absence of sound.' What we know for certain is that this thing hovered directly over our Underground Storage bunkers at an altitude of fifteen hundred feet for approximately two minutes, then—and here comes the reason for showing you the film."

All eyes were turned toward the screen. The UFO suddenly darted straight up, rising another thousand feet above the earth before commencing a series of startling zigzags across the night sky. Whatever it was, it moved with both incredible speed and astonishing agility as it executed a series of right-angle and hairpin turns without significant loss of velocity. Then, as mysteriously as it had appeared, it zipped out of view in one long streak. Spelman stopped the tape and turned to face the others.

"Looks like my wife has been giving driving lessons," an Air Force general quipped, eliciting a polite chuckle from the others.

Spelman didn't change expressions. "No aircraft known to Defense Intelligence has performance capabilities equal to what we just witnessed. After review of the tape, DIA considers it likely that what you have seen is a reconnaissance mission. And where there's smoke, there's fire. This intelligence gathering could be preparatory to some sort of attack, or, in a worst-case scenario, a full-scale invasion."

Spelman paused to let that sink in. His audience was less amazed by the tape they'd seen than by Spelman's ability to make this speech as if it were the first time he'd ever made it. Once a year, he would call a meeting such as this one to present evidence to the members of Project Smudge. And each time, he and Dr. Wells, his sole ally on the committee, would argue that the nation was exposed to a clear-and-present danger. They were the hard-liners who argued that the world was on the brink of imminent invasion by extraterrestrials. Behind their backs, they were known as the crazies, especially Dr. Wells, the only man known to have held a conversation with an intelligent life-form from another world. Eventually, Wells's desperate insistence on the need to adopt his proposals led to his banishment from Smudge. Isolated, Spelman was reluctant to call another meeting, but then had found a most unexpected ally, someone with a daring plan which might finally end the interagency bickering which had crippled the government's research into UFOs for more than a decade—Nimziki.

When it was apparent that Spelman was finished talking, Dr. Insolo of the Science and Technology Directorate was the first to raise a familiar objection, "We've been getting sightings like this for years; why is this one special?"

To Spelman, one of the true believers, the question seemed ridiculous, almost insulting. "First off, *all* of these sightings are significant. What makes this one especially threatening is that it didn't take place over the desert or the ocean. This vehicle buzzed one of our most sensitive and potentially damaging installations. We don't want all that uranium falling into the wrong hands."

Jenkins, subchief of the CIA's Domestic Collections Division, did little to disguise his feeling that this meeting was a waste of time. "Are you proposing that the committee adopt the Wells plan?" The oft-proposed and always-rejected course of action recommended by Wells called for nothing less than a full-scale preparation for war, a series of projects so large that the presence of the aliens would soon become public knowledge. The plan was always rejected by an overwhelming margin. Secrecy was priority number one, and there were two reasons for this. In the wake of every group sighting of a UFO, civilians became hysterical. There was no telling what kind of mass chaos the country would face if the government were forced to confirm the presence of these visitors. The second, related reason, was that no one wanted to take responsibility for having kept the information hidden for over twenty-five years. Secrecy begat secrecy, one denial led to another, until the participating agencies found themselves, a quarter of a century after the crash at Roswell, sitting on a full-blown conspiracy to keep the American public—and the world—in the dark. There was not a chance in hell that anyone in that room was going to commit himself to an effort like the one Wells had envisioned, especially given the present unstable political climate. No one wanted to be caught holding the bag if Congress started one of its investigations into the nation's spy agencies.

Then Nimziki unleashed his bombshell. "I've decided to support Colonel Spelman. After reading through some past reports and looking at the tape we've just seen, I think the time has come to start taking this threat seriously."

Since Nimziki had joined Smudge, he had been the most ardent critic of the Wells plan, arguing that it was a gigantic waste of time and money, that the aliens posed no significant threat. In fact, he had taken a personal dislike to Wells and had not been content with kicking him out of Smudge, but had stripped him of any security clearance and had him run out of the government altogether.

Jenkins grinned across the table. He knew Nimziki well enough to realize there must be some ulterior motive at work. "What exactly does the deputy director have in mind?"

"The plan I'm proposing takes certain elements from the one dear old Dr. Wells drew up. But, as you might expect, it's significantly more low-key. It calls for the formation of a rapid deployment alien-vehicle intercept force, a Special Weapons And Tactics squad capable of getting to one of these aircraft before it gets away. At the same time, I want to revamp and redouble our efforts at Area 51, to see if we can't get some results from the craft we already have. I have some long-term plans to get things moving out there."

"This SWAT team. What would it do?"

"The purpose of this force would be to gather better visual information on these craft, attempt to establish radio communication, and, if possible, to bring one of them down for further study and reverse-engineering purposes."

"You mean you want to shoot them down?" asked one of the Navy guys, visibly agitated by the idea.

"Is that wise?" Dr. Insolo asked. "Let's not forget, these airships are armed. They have laser cannons which, except in the Wisconsin case, they haven't used. We don't want to start a fight we're not sure we can win."

Jenkins nodded. "He's right. Besides, what good will it do to capture one of these rascals? We've already got the one that went down at Roswell, and that hasn't done us a lick of good." One by one, the members of the committee took turns raising objections and pointing out shortcomings of the plan. Then Jim Ostrom, aka the Bishop, asked the question that was on everyone's mind.

"This is an about-face for you, Albert. I remember when Dr. Wells used to make rather similar proposals, and you'd sit there and shoot him down. What's changed? Is it this film we just watched?"

"No, it's a story I heard from your colleague at the NSA, Dr. Podsedecki." Podsedecki, a former Wells-supporter and leader of the Walker Greens, a secret society within the already hypersecret National Security Agency, was a sort of legendary cult figure in spy circles.

"It goes like this. Let's say you're out for a hike in the mountains with some old friends. You're walking down a narrow trail surrounded by tall grass. It's a beautiful day, and you're looking around enjoying the scenery when the hiker right behind you suddenly shouts RATTLER! How are you going to react? Do you stop and consider the credibility of your source? Wait for additional evidence to satisfy your threat-assessment criteria? Or would you go into immediate action, doing everything in your power to locate the threat and determine its precise nature? The tape we've witnessed this morning is one of two things: it's either a snake in the grass, or something that *appears* to be a snake in the grass.

In either case, it's our responsibility to find out."

"Shoot first, ask questions later," Jenkins commented sardonically.

If the comment bothered Nimziki, he didn't show it. "There's one aspect of this plan that doesn't appear in your briefing papers. Given the political climate inside the beltway at the present moment, we all expect to see a slew of new appointees. Even if Nixon weathers this storm, his major appointments are sure to face scrutiny and possible replacement, most likely with a bunch of Midwesterners with spotless records—guys like Jim Ostrom."

Everybody who knew Jim laughed. He was a real Jimmy Stewart-type. "But unfortunately," Nimziki went on, getting to the most delicate part of his presentation, "these people aren't necessarily going to be as good at maintaining secrecy as Jim is. In other words, Project Smudge faces exposure, especially if we go ahead and adopt the proposals we're considering today. Exposure of this information to the public would, of course, be a disaster, especially now. Americans aren't sure they can trust the government at the moment, and we don't want to do anything to exacerbate that perception. Therefore, I propose consolidating these programs under one roof."

"The question is: Whose roof?"

"Mine."

"Yours? The CIA would take control of the project?"

"Not the entire CIA," he explained, glancing at the team from Domestic Collections. "Just me. At least until things settle down."

The generals could hardly suppress their delight. This young hotshot seemed to be offering them a valuable and unexpected gift, a way out of Project Smudge. If they understood him correctly, they would all be able to wash their hands of the government's "dirtiest little secret." After a long moment of silence, Dr. Insolo spoke up.

"The Science and Technology Directorate, for one, would be extremely interested in such a proposal." Knowing that Nimziki would have a price, he went on to ask, "What would a program like this cost?"

Spelman and Nimziki took turns explaining the rather creative funding structure they had devised. It was something of a shell game that would cost each agency less than three million per year. To get out of the project, the agencies would have paid five times that price. Within a matter of minutes, the members of the committee voted unanimously for the official dissolution of Project Smudge. Then, all smiles and handshakes, they began heading out the door, anxious to get on with other business.

Bishop Jim stopped in the doorway and leaned in for a private word with Nimziki. "It's an awful risk you're taking, Albert. All it would take would be for one of these ships to buzz over Cleveland during an Indians game and... well, it wouldn't exactly be good for your career. But I trust you know what you're doing." What Nimziki was doing was following his instinct for accumulating power, for picking cards up off the table and tucking them up his sleeve until he needed them.'

Before he went, Ostrom had one last piece of advice. "I like the idea of getting things running again out at Area 51, but be careful you don't have too much success with it too quickly. If the military finds out you've got that ship up in the air, this committee will come back to life faster than you can say the words 'Soviet Union.' You need to be careful who you select as your new lead scientist out there. Make sure it's someone you can trust."

"As a matter of fact," Nimziki replied, "I think I've already found the perfect guy for the job."

2

RECRUITING FRESH BLOOD

Brackish Okun was a certified, bona fide, clinically tested genius. But this wasn't the opinion most people formed of the twenty-one-year-old science student upon first impression. He was often mistaken for a simpleminded hippie kid with very strange taste in clothings. It wasn't so much the bell-bottom corduroy slacks or the riot of pens, calculators, and slide rules crowding the breast pocket of his Perma-Prest shirts. Nor was it the mop of long hair that straggled down to his shoulders. The thing that most made him appear to be nothing more than a simpering blockhead was his constant nodding. Whether he was concentrating on a lecture, listening to music, or working through a thorny mathematical equation, Okun nodded. His friends teased him about it. His mother tried to get him to stop, telling him it was an obnoxious habit akin to cracking his knuckles. But Okun continued to nod. And those who spent time with him, rather than convincing him to stop, often took to nodding themselves. Although seemingly insignificant, there is a case to be made that, contained in this single quirk of character, this continuous cranial quivering, was Okun's entire orientation to life and the universe. The action signaled a positive and optimistic outlook, an ongoing acknowledgment and approval of the world around him. It was an affirmation of whatever or whomever he was focused on, especially when he nodded in conjunction with one of his favorite phrases, "groovalicious," "I dig," or "cool to the power of ten." His nodding showed him to be fascinated and intimately involved with each of the billions upon billions of details that add up to create a day. But to those who didn't know him well, it just made him look like a dimwit.

In April of '72, staring down the barrel of graduation and, beyond that, the frightening prospect of holding a real job, Okun began having second thoughts about the way he'd spent his years at Caltech. Earlier that semester, recruiting officers from major corporations like Lockheed, Hughes, and Rocketdyne had come to the campus and hired a bunch of numbskulls just because they had good grades. Okun had earned mainly As or Fs, leaving him with a dismal 2.1 grade point average. After a stellar performance in high school, where he'd won several awards and citations, crowned by the achievement of being named the winner of the nationwide Westinghouse Science Talent Search, he'd squandered his time in college. It's not that he'd stopped learning. His mind was still an unquenchable sponge thirsting for knowledge and all of that, but he'd spent way too much time applying his prodigious skills to a series of oddball projects that the school's administration had classified as pranks.

One such stunt, which Okun thought he should get course credits for, happened during Caltech's annual "Hawaii Week." After gaining unauthorized, after-hours access to the chancellor's office, he and his friends— who called themselves "the Mothers" in honor of Frank Zappa's band—carried in a few dozen sandbags, some surplus tubing, and a giant polyvinyl tarp. They set to work constructing a small heated swimming pool right under the noses of the school's founding fathers, whose stem portraits hung on the walls of the office between its floor-to-ceiling bookcases. By the time the campus police arrived in the wee hours of the morning, the stuffy office had been transformed into a tropical paradise. Dozens of undergrads were skinny-dipping in the pool or lounging on the leather sofas sipping Mai Tais and listening to ukulele music. After a stern lecture from the chancellor, the incident was forgotten.

But the incident that was to shape the life and career of this young Einstein-with-a-mood-ring was to involve a flying saucer, and it would take place in broad daylight.

One afternoon, as students and faculty began filling Caltech's central plaza to enjoy the sun during their lunch hour, Okun and the Mothers were holding a secret meeting in the stairwell of an adjacent building that bordered the plaza. After a final check to make sure the plan was ready, they broke off in separate directions to launch the attack. Okun and a couple of other Mothers climbed the stairwell with a box of radio equipment and began setting up their command post on the roof. Peeking out between the balustrades, they could see the unsuspecting crowd below without being seen themselves.

A few moments later, precisely on schedule, a Mother named Chris Winter sauntered into the plaza carrying a nine-foot ladder under one arm and a large cardboard box in the other. Something about the way he walked through the quad announced the fact that something mischievous was afoot. Winter set up the ladder, climbed to the top, opened the box, and removed a perfect balsa-wood replica of a flying saucer. He lifted the twenty-two-ounce vehicle over his head until he could feel it react to the invisible field of energy shooting through the air. Slowly he took his hands away, and a roar of approval erupted from the crowd. He quickly grabbed the ladder and disappeared, leaving the little saucer hovering in midair.

From his hiding place, Okun looked down on his audience and nodded in satisfaction. He tested the joystick on his remote control, and found it worked tolerably well.

The radio waves sent the small ship wobbling first this way, then that. Inside the saucer, a supercharged, plate-sized magnet reacted to his command, causing the saucer to bob and skitter over a strong field of electromagnetic energy being pumped into the quad by a trio of cleverly disguised wave-particle generators the Mothers had liberated from the applied sciences building. Undergrads rushed up to get a closer look at this strange spectacle, laughing, catcalling, and looking everywhere to see who was making it fly. But the fun really started when Okun switched on his microphone and began talking to the crowd via the transistor radio speaker he'd built into the saucer.

"Greetings, Earthlings. My name is Flart. We are from the planet Crapulong. We come in peace. But we demand your cafeteria stop serving those cruddy fish sticks on Friday. This is a crime against the universe. We also demand that the one you call Professor Euben get a new toupee." It wasn't high-caliber comedy, but it put the crowd in stitches. The voice coming from the teetering saucer was distorted and full of static owing to the magnetic energy in the air, which only made Okun sound more "like an alien."

The charge in the magnet should have lasted a full hour, but the flight was cut short when Flart made the mistake of flirting with the wrong earth girl, telling her that he, master of the universe, found her extremely desirable and would she consider spending an intimate evening with a being one-tenth her size? The crowd and the girl found all this hysterically funny, but after a while her boyfriend had had enough. He shouted to the unseen operator of the remote control vehicle to knock it off.

"Lieutenant Zarfadox," came the answer from the saucer, "prepare the anal probe. This Earthling obviously has something stuck up his ass." And so ended the flight of the alien Flart. The boyfriend hurled an apple, which struck the ship broadside just hard enough to dislodge it from the invisible net provided by the three generators. It crashed to the pavement with Flart shouting a long string of expletives. Once the generators were safely back in their labs and the Mothers had sat through a stern lecture from the chancellor, the whole incident should have been forgotten.

But the next morning, a brief account of the event appeared in the *LA Times*. Although the three-sentence article explained it had all been in good fun, it sufficiently impressed one reader, one of the CIA's army of "burrowers," who clipped it out and started a file: "Okun, Brackish (?)" In years to come, this one-page file would expand and multiply until it had become a monster, filling a cabinet all its own.

That April, the file grew considerably when the CIA came visiting. At eight in the evening during midterm week, Okun and the other Mothers had decided not to brave the crowds in the library. Instead, they'd retired to his dorm room, affectionately known as the Pad of Least Resistance, to engage in certain herbal rites. As smoke filled the room, they engaged in what was, for them, a rather typical conversation.

"Dude, you know what we should do?" Winter croaked, struggling to keep from exhaling as he passed the ceramic vase-shaped instrument back to the load-master. "We should put up mirrors in fill the halls so when you're going to class the whole school is like a hall of mirrors at a carnival."

"Cool squared," Okun nodded. "We could invent a new product called Mirror Paint and coat every surface in the room with it."

The Mothers were pleased and showed their approval with a round of silent nods. "Mirror paint. I like."

"What if everything in this room was covered in mirror paint? The walls, the bed, the plants, all these books..."

"And dig this: the final step would be to dip our bodies

in mirror paint so everything in the room, except your eyes, was a mirror."

"Then we could make mirror contact lenses, so we'd disappear completely and you'd have to feel your way around the world."

More nods.

This important research discussion was interrupted by a knock at the door. It was an official-sounding man-knuckle rapping that sent the Mothers into immediate action. While Okun stashed the bag, Winter opened the windows and began fanning smoke out of the room. The knock repeated itself, insistent.

"Just a minute," Okun yelled. "I just need to finish this one thing." Grabbing a textbook off the bookshelf, he opened the door a crack and saw a man in a suit standing in the hallway. He banged the door closed and mouthed the word "NARC!" to the wide-eyed Mothers.

"Excuse me," the voice came through the door, "I'm looking for Brake-ish Okun. My name is Sam Dworkin, and I'd like to speak to him about possible employment."

After a moment of indecision, Okun opened the door six inches and slid through the gap into the hallway, a little puff of smoke trailing him outside. Once he got a good look at the man, he relaxed a little. He was about sixty-five and seemed to be alone.

"Are you Brake-ish Okun?"

"I think so. I mean, yes. It is I. I'm Brackish Okun."

"You're absolutely sure?" the guy asked, seemingly amused.

"I was just, in there reading this"—he glanced down at the page—"this math book. So, you said something about a job? What company are you with?"

The gentleman quickly invented a name, then asked if they could step inside, suggesting that Okun's friends might come back another time.

"Right, good idea." But when he opened the door, he found the room empty. He crossed to the open window in time to see the last Mother jump from the trellis to the flower bed, then sprint away into the night.

"Very cool. I have a fire escape. What was your name again?"

"Dworkin. Sam Dworkin."

Okun offered him the best seat in the house, a beanbag chair, but Dworkin sat down on the unmade bed instead. He looked around the room, dismayed. The cluttered cubicle was a riot of overflowing bookshelves, home-built electronic equipment, and Okun's personal belongings. The ceiling was wallpapered with music posters and schematic drawings. The old man looked a little older once he was inside and seated on the bed. "You're not exactly who I was expecting to meet."

Okun didn't understand.

"Westinghouse Science Student of the Year, National Junior Science Foundation Merit Scholar, eight hundred in math on the SATs. I suppose I expected somebody a little more... square."

"I guess I don't look like my resume," Okun chuckled.

They talked for a while about the pranks Okun and his crew had pulled off, some of the independent engineering projects he'd built—both the failures and the successes. They tossed around a few theories about how such a brainiac could be finishing college with such low grades and finally arrived at a conclusion: *Okun was most motivated when there were obstacles in his path, when what he wanted to build or find was off-limits.* Both of them made silent mental notes to remember that tidbit.

Then the guy got down to business. "Mr. Okun, do you believe in Extraterrestrial Biological Entities? Martians? UFOs?"

So that's what this is all about. Okun quickly came

to the conclusion that his visitor must be some fruit loop from one of those clubs devoted to the study of flying saucers. Feeling considerably more relaxed now that he was sure the guy wasn't a narc, he explained what he believed. "It's all bull, man; it's all made up by people who haven't got anything better to do. Flying saucers, little men from distant galaxies—puleeeez, it's physically impossible. Check it out: Einstein figured out the cosmic speed limit is 286,000 miles per second, the speed of light. Nothing can move faster than that. Now, light from the nearest star where there is even a remote chance of life takes something like a hundred years to get to earth, so, even if you assume that spacemen could travel at the speed of light, which they can't, you're still looking at a trip of hundreds or even tens of thousands of years to get from Planet X to Pasadena." When he was finished with his lecture, he scrutinized his visitor. "Why? Do you?"

The guy only smiled again, asking, "Where do you see yourself working in five years?"

"I dunno. Probably in some company lab, maybe Westinghouse. I've got an interview with them next month and hopefully they'll be able to understand some of my ideas about electromagnetics and superconductivity."

"Superconductors. That's a cutting-edge field of research. They're doing some of that over at the Los Alamos labs. Do you know about the centripetal magnet accelerator? That's the kind of equipment a fellow like you should be using."

Okun, nodding, quickly imagined all the mischief he could do with a machine like that. "Of course I'd love to play around with one of those puppies, but that's all government work, so I don't feel that's realistic for me right now," he said, brushing his hair off one shoulder.

"What if I told you there was a position available with my company that would afford the right person access not only to the centripetal accelerator, but to the entire network of labs at Sandia and Los Alamos?"

"Wowwee! Who do you work for, God?"

The man chuckled. "That's actually not a bad guess. What if I could prove to you that flying saucers really do exist? Would you be interested in working on a project like that?"

Okun just grinned. This after-hours job interview was beginning to smell like a practical joke.

"What if I told you," Dworkin went on, tapping his breast pocket, "that I'm carrying photographs which show an actual flying saucer?"

"You're kidding, right? Did the Mothers put you up to this?"

The man ignored the question. "I'd like to show you these photographs, but before I can do that, I'd need something from you."

This guy is a phenomenal actor, Okun thought. Repressing a smile, he asked what he would need.

"Your solemn commitment not to tell a soul about the photos and what they show."

Okun straightened up and looked at the man through his bloodshot eyes. Deadpan serious, he said, "I swear it."

Satisfied with this response, the man produced an envelope and handed it over to his grinning host. One look at the first photo was enough to melt the smile off Okun's face. It showed a team of scientists in lab smocks lined up for a group portrait in front of what appeared to be a badly damaged flying saucer. The ship looked to have a wingspan similar to a fighter jet's, but it was disk-shaped and looked considerably more menacing than anything he'd seen before. The photograph itself, black-and-white, seemed to be several years old.

"I'm kneeling in the front row," the old man pointed out, "third from the left." Sure enough, it was the same face fifteen or twenty years younger. The corner of an airplane hangar showed on one side of the snapshot, and a couple of uniformed soldiers patrolled the background.

The second photo showed what looked like a cockpit. A pair of tall, arching structures, chairs of some kind, were set before two windows, with an instrument panel below them. The third picture was a close-up of one of the instruments lifted out of the console by a pair of men's hands. Instead of wires, it looked like veins connecting the instrument to the console.

Dworkin waited patiently as Okun went back over the pictures, comparing them, looking, almost desperately, for some evidence that this was indeed a prank. Then, with a stunned expression on his face, Okun looked up at the man, and asked, "What is this? Where were these taken?"

With a gentle smile, Dworkin reached across and took the photos back. "I've said too much already. Of course, if you accept, everything will be explained."

"OK, I accept."

The old guy laughed. "Let's wait until you're in a more lucid frame of mind. Think it over. There are drawbacks. You'd have to leave your family and your friends, the hours are long, and you and your coworkers might not have much in common. Please remember the promise you made. Don't discuss these pictures with your friends, your professors, with your mother, with anybody."

The man got up, leaving a non-nodding Brackish in a state of confusion. As he was about to exit, Okun called after him.

"Hey, wait up a sec. How am I going to find you again?"

Dworkin couldn't resist. "Don't call us, we'll call you."

Three weeks later, Brackish was at home proudly examining his diploma alongside his mother, Saylene. His new employer had arranged for him to take his final exams a month before the semester ended, and Okun had done something he rarely did under normal circumstances: he studied for every class, not just the ones he was interested in. He'd done well on the tests, raising his grade-point average and earning himself a bachelor's degree. But there wouldn't be any time to sit around enjoying this accomplishment. His suitcases were packed and standing by the front door. A young government agent had arrived with an attaché case full of papers, legal documents whereby Okun would sign away his personal freedom in exchange for coming aboard the project. The three of them—Brackish, Saylene, and the man in the expensive suit—sat down at the kitchen table and began wading through the paperwork. Technically, he was being hired by several different entities, each requiring a separate set of applications, background information forms, insurance waivers, tax schedules, retirement plan agreements, and loyalty oaths. At first, Brackish read through each document carefully, asking questions about each one. But as they continued to materialize in thick stacks from the man's briefcase, his caution wore down. Toward the end, Brackish was John Hancocking everything the man laid in front of him without a single question.

Saylene didn't understand why everything had to be so hush-hush. All her son could tell her was that it was an engineering job with the government, and that there was a good reason why it had to be kept secret. But the one thing she understood all too clearly was that she wouldn't get to see her boy for five full years—the length of his contract. He would be allowed to phone home on the first Sunday of each month, and that was it. He was the only family she had left, and she would miss him. Her eyes were already swollen from crying, and she felt the tears rising again when the man announced they had arrived at the last document. His name was Radecker, and she had taken an instant dislike to him. He was too young, too polished, too full of himself and he was taking her boy away from her.

"This is a copy of the Federal Espionage Act," he explained, dropping separate copies in front of each Okun as casually as if he were delivering the monthly phone bill. "Basically, all this says is that you can be prosecuted if you tell anyone about what you know about the project. You should know that the minimum penalty for violating this law is a year in a federal penitentiary."

"Heavy!" Okun sounded impressed. "What's the maximum penalty?"

"Have you ever heard of Julius and Ethel Rosenberg?"

"Oh. Heavier than I thought." Brackish gulped, hesitant to sign something that could land him in the electric chair.

"Don't worry. Just think twice before you go selling any information to the Russians." Radecker grinned.

Nodding, Okun scribbled his name at the bottom of the page.

Radecker turned to Saylene. "Whenever someone asks about your son, you tell them he's taken a job as a safety inspector with the Bechtel Corporation. This job requires him to travel around the world, so you don't know where he is at any given time. Sign here." Reluctantly, she did as she was told.

Then the agent packed up all the documents and told the family, "I'll give you a moment to say good-bye. I'll be outside in the car."

Brackish and Saylene smiled at one another, both calm on the outside, as waves of feeling crested and crashed inside. They spent their last five minutes together crying and hugging. When Radecker tooted the horn outside, Okun looked down at his mom and promised her he'd come back as soon as he could. It was a promise he would keep, however briefly.

3

ARRIVAL AT AREA 51

Life got sweeter and sweeter for Okun. When Radecker told him where they were headed, he had prepared himself for a long ride in the car, but instead they went to Burbank Airport and signed in at the desk of a small cargo transport company, SwiftAir. He'd only flown twice before, once to Chicago when he'd won the Westinghouse competition, and once to New York, for a whirlwind weekend in the Big Apple.

Today they lifted off in a small twin-engine Cessna. Once they got out over the desert, the captain invited him to come up and sit in the cockpit. It was a warm spring day, and, as soon as they left LA's smog behind, the view was superb. Okun pressed his nose against the glass and imagined spotting a crashed UFO. He felt lucky. Radecker had told him they were headed for "a very important laboratory near Las Vegas." Based on what the old man had told him three weeks earlier in his dorm room, he assumed that meant one of the national labs in New Mexico; Visions of sparkling equipment and gleaming multistory buildings danced in his head.

It was a Thursday, and Okun wondered what the Mothers, sitting through Professor Frankel's theoretical physics lecture, were thinking about his sudden disappearance. He would see if there was a way to sneak a postcard out to them once he got settled.

"There she is," the pilot announced forty minutes

into the flight, "Lost Wages, Nevada." Okun had only a moment to study the narrow city built up along both sides of a highway before the plane banked north. A few minutes later, the pilot turned and called back to Radecker over the noise of the engines, "We're coming up to the Nellis Range perimeter, sir."

Okun looked down and saw they were flying over a double fence, one inside the other. *I hope this isn't where we're headed.* The pilot flew over a decent-sized military base, a cluster of a hundred or so buildings and a dozen hangars, but kept going. As Okun's heart began to sink in disappointment, the pilot pointed to a sharp hill rising a thousand feet off the desert floor, and said, "Wheelbarrow Peak." At the base of this, hill was a dry lake bed with a pair of landing strips that formed a big X across the cotton-colored sand. Near the center of the X stood a single airplane hangar and a few dozen small buildings. When Okun realized this was where they were going to land, he immediately marched back and piled into the seat next to Radecker.

"Man, tell me this isn't where we're going, man."

Radecker, who was just as disturbed by what he saw out the window as Okun was, said nothing. Two days ago, before leaving Washington, he'd asked around and learned that Area 51 was "a backwater facility." But the dusty collection of weathered buildings he saw from the plane didn't even deserve the name backwater. It was more like tiny-scuzzy-pond-water about nine million miles from where the action was. This wasn't a promotion; it was exile.

As the plane came in for its landing, they could see that most of the buildings were boarded-up shacks, the sleeping quarters of some long-departed army. A large 51 was painted in black on the doors of the corrugated-steel airplane hangar, before which a contingent of perhaps twenty-five people stood waiting to greet the new arrivals. A pair of antiaircraft guns stood guard over either end of this dusty little ghost town.

"Welcome, gentlemen. I'm Lieutenant Ellsworth," rasped the man who opened the plane's passenger door for them. "I'll be responsible for your security while you're here. My instructions are to escort you directly to the labs and try to answer any questions you might have." Soldiers came forward and helped unload the luggage and other cargo. Ellsworth's tough-customer face was obscured by reflective sunglasses and a baseball cap with a Groom Lake patch sewn on the front. As they marched across the warm tarmac, he explained that the base was under twenty-four-hour guard, and that someone would always be stationed at the phones in case there was any emergency. Everyone who worked in the underground lab was free to come topside whenever he wished, but, for security reasons, would the gentlemen please refrain from fraternizing with the soldiers. When they arrived at the hangar doors, they were met by a group of elderly gentlemen whom Ellsworth introduced as the scientific staff. There were four of them, all about seventy years old, dressed in lab coats and sporting beards. "This is Dr. Freiling, Dr. Cibatutto, Dr. Lenel, and I believe you already know Dr. Dworkin."

Sure enough, standing there with the same avuncular smile Okun recognized from the interview in his dorm room, was Sam Dworkin. Standing next to the sun-darkened soldiers, the quartet of aging scientists looked extremely pale. After a round of handshakes and hellos, the party moved inside.

The hangar was empty except for a few jeeps. They came to a stairwell and began to descend the stairs in silence. Four flights down, it felt like they were preparing to enter an excavated tomb, and Okun could feel himself getting claustrophobic. He took comfort in the sight of telex cables and phone lines snaking up the bare concrete walls of the stairwell. Finally, after six steep flights of steps, they came to a set of heavy steel doors. Okun and Radecker both noticed that these could be bolted closed from the outside.

Okun stopped walking and raised his hand in the air. "I have a question."

"Yes, sir?"

"Is it just me, or is this whole situation starting to feel like an Edgar Allen Poe story? You aren't planning on locking us inside those doors, are you?" Okun chuckled nervously, hoping the others would chuckle with him.

Ellsworth answered mirthlessly. "The doors are never locked, sir. The bolts are there just in case there's an emergency."

"Has there ever been one?"

"Not yet." Ellsworth handed Okun's suitcases over to him. "This is as far as I go. I'm not allowed inside the lab."

"Except in case of emergency," one of the scientists added.

Inside, each of the four elderly scientists carried a crate of new supplies that had been left by the door and led the new arrivals into a long, dimly lit room. Every few paces they moved into a pool of light cast by the lamps mounted on the ceiling. Although half of the lightbulbs had died, Okun and Radecker could see the room stretching out to the length of a football field. Other than a few hundred crates and dusty filing cabinets, it was empty.

"Don't mind this mess," Dr. Cibatutto told them in what was left of his Italian accent. "It's only a storage area for obsolete equipment and a lot of old documents nobody cares about. Someday we'll clean it up, and put in a bowlin galley."

"Put in a what?" Okun asked.

"A bowling alley," repeated Cibatutto, shortest and plumpest of the scientists, enunciating carefully.

"This way, gentlemen." Dworkin turned into one hallway, then another, leading them into the most often used room in this top-secret government lab: the kitchen. In contrast to the murky light and cobwebs of the entrance hall, this room was brightly lit and tastefully decorated. A long table with picnic benches was elegantly set for six diners.

"We take turns cooking down here and, over the years, we've developed into rather adequate chefs, but none finer than Signor Cibatutto," Dworkin told them, setting down the crate he'd carried in. "And, in honor of your arrival, he has prepared one of his most mouthwatering specialties." Cibatutto beamed proudly. "Tonight we're gonna have a mushroom risotto with salmon and a delicious chicken cacciatore."

"Dr. Lenel and I will show you to your rooms," Dworkin said, picking up one of Okun's bags. "We'll give you a chance to relax from your journey, and then dinner will be served."

Radecker wasn't in the mood for a dinner party. "Is it just the four of you down here? Isn't there anyone else?"

All the doctors glanced at one another nervously. "No, just the four of us. Were you expecting others?"

"No, I didn't know what to expect," Radecker retorted.

"I remember now!" Fretting erupted. He'd spent the last few minutes staring at Brackish, scrutinizing him, but now he turned around toward Dworkin. "This is that hippie kid you were telling us about. I been standing here thinking it was a damned girl, but it's not. It's that hippie kid, isn't it?"

Okun grinned sourly at the old man, not nodding.

Dworkin chuckled in blithe amusement and tried to dismiss the incident. "Dr. Freiling's eyesight isn't what it once was."

"Look, gentlemen"—Radecker felt there was too much nonsense going on—"I appreciate the effort you've gone to, but Mr. Okun and I would like to get oriented right away. Why don't you give us a tour."

The old men stared at the young men, their feelings bruised. "Now, now," Dworkin said, "there will be more than enough time for a tour later on. Whenever we show the place to visitors, there are invariably a thousand questions. It takes hours. But first thing tomorrow morning, we'll be sure and—"

"Show us the vehicle!" Radecker demanded with a vehemence that surprised everyone, including himself. He was getting very nervous about the idea of being marooned in this concrete bunker for who knew how long.

The high-spirited mood in the room crashed like a tray full of fine china. The stunned scientists looked at one another. *Who is this guy?*

Dworkin led them through another set of hallways until they came to a steel door with a wheel lock, the same type found at a bulkhead in a submarine. He pulled the door open and stepped into the pitch-black room beyond. A second later, dozens of fluorescent tubes sputtered to life, illuminating the interior of a giant concrete cube, six stories deep. In the center of the room was the alien ship that had crashed at Roswell many years before. Okun's jaw fell open, and his eyes glazed over. In the photograph, the thing had looked somehow ordinary, a machine and nothing more. But now, looking it in the face, there was an animal quality to its appearance, like a great black-gray stingray sleeping peacefully at the bottom of this large concrete tank. It rested seven feet off the ground on a series of wooden trestles. A pair of windows facing the visitors seemed to stare back like sharply focused eyes. Gulp.

They stepped through the doorway and onto an

observation platform, as Dr. Lenel made his way along the underside of the beast and scampered up a ladder into its belly. In a moment, lights came on inside the ship, and Lenel could be seen behind the windows standing in the cockpit.

"This," Okun said to no one in particular, "is far beyond cool." Then, nodding for the first time since he arrived at Area 51, he stepped off the observation platform. Moving closer, he examined the large projection running along the ship's backbone. "The fin," as the scientists called it, started out some six feet tall just behind the windows, then tapered gracefully to a needle-sharp point at the tail. The ship's exterior surface was composed of several armored plates which were etched with thinly cut grooves and embossed designs that looked somewhat like Egyptian hieroglyphs. "I don't recognize this material. Do you know what kind of metal it is?"

"The vehicle's carapace is composed of a very rigid material, but it isn't metal," Dr. Dworkin explained, moving past Okun to reach up and run his hand over the surface. "If you look very closely, you'll notice something curious. Can you see these very small holes? We think they're either pores or hair follicles. This armored plate was once the shell of a living animal."

"Outta sight," the younger scientist commented softly.

Lenel beckoned him even closer to the ship, pointing into the gap between two of the plates. In the crevice, Okun could see countless pieces of intricate machine tooling, tiny metallic gadgets set in place with the same extraordinary precision as the muscles in the human hand. This outstanding workmanship received a large and approving nod.

Mounted on the ship's underside were what looked like a couple of thruster rockets. One of them had been sheared away in the crash and was currently held in place by an awkward network of spot welds and metal plumber's tape.

Radecker, reluctant to move closer to the menacing ship, asked a question from the observation platform. "What about these symbols or designs?"

"They appear to have been pressed into the shells using some sort of mold. We can only speculate as to why they are there. They might be a brand, like the kind we use to identify cattle," Dworkin offered.

"Or they could be technical details for the operation of the vehicle," Freiling countered.

"I personally think they are some kinda heraldic device like the ones you find on a medieval coat of arms," Cibatutto put in.

"We did have one gentleman down here several years ago who had received some training as a cryptographer, but he was not able to decipher their meaning. In short, we don't know."

As far as Radecker was concerned, this whole experience was quickly turning into a nightmare. For the second time since they were introduced, he raised his voice to these mild-mannered scientists twice his age. "Why is this place in such bad shape?"

Cibatutto and Lenel looked at Freiling, who looked at Dworkin. "Bad shape? In what sense?"

"Don't act dumb with me," Radecker shot back. "Look at this dump. It's dark, it's dusty, and it seems like you haven't gotten diddly-squat done on the ship in the last twenty years."

Dworkin, in his refined and gentle manner, offered his new boss some background on the lab. "Since the day the cranes lowered this ship to where it is sitting, no maintenance workers have been allowed access because of legitimate concerns for security. In years past, we did whatever repair work was necessary, but as we've advanced in age, we've been less able to do this work ourselves. And then there is the unfortunate matter of Dr.

Wells, who was, until fairly recently, Area 51's director of research. He was a brilliant man early in his career, but with age he became... oh, how shall I put this?"

"The bastard went crazy," Dr. Lenel mumbled, speaking to the new arrivals for the first time. "Went right off the deep end."

Dworkin attempted a chuckle. "That's not exactly the phrase I was searching for, but it gives you the idea. In the early years, Area 51 was quite an exciting place to work. There were over forty of us on permanent staff, and we had several visitors each year. Perhaps you noticed the old sleeping quarters outside. But then Dr. Wells and his ideas became increasingly unpopular in Washington with the very people upon whom we depend for funding. We've had our operating budget reduced every year for the last seventeen years. When Wells was removed as director four years ago, we were optimistic about getting things back up to speed, but actually conditions have become even worse. Since his departure, we have received no money whatsoever."

"So that's why you guys are so old," Okun blurted out, having put two and two together. "You haven't been able to hire anyone new."

"And that," Dworkin said magnanimously, "is why we're all so excited about your arrival: It represents a new chapter in the history of this project. We haven't seen anything concrete yet, but Colonel Spelman has given us every reason to be hopeful."

When Radecker heard their story he felt sorry he'd yelled at them. "I'll get on the phone with Colonel Spelman this afternoon and see what I can do about this situation. But let's have a look at the inside of this thing."

A steel ladder led to a hatch door twice the size of a manhole cover that lead down to the sewers. And a sewer is what it smelled like as the men climbed up into the ship.

The acrid, penetrating stench of ammonia hung in the air, like old urine.

"The fumes make you crazy after a while." This time, pudgy Dr. Enrico Cibatutto led the way. They climbed the ladder and came through the floor of the small spaceship to examine the spartan interior. There wasn't much to see. The domed interior of the cabin was twenty by twenty at its widest point, and seven feet tall at its peak. The focus of attention was the command console. Two pea-pod-shaped chairs faced the windows, and, below the windows, a bank of instruments was mounted along the front wall of the cabin, in an arrangement the scientists called the dashboard. As Okun stooped over and followed the much shorter Cibatutto to the front of the ship, the scientist warned him, "Mind the pods, they're covered in a thick jelly. Like the tar of a pine, if you get it on your hands, it takes a lot of scrubbing to get off."

Okun regarded the slimy seats in the dim light. They were long arching structures, sticky hammocks connected to both floor and ceiling at forty-five-degree angles and kept in place by means of a web of solid bars. The sight of the chairs reminded the young scientist that spaceships don't crash to earth by themselves. Not sure he wanted to hear the answer, he asked Cibatutto if there had been any bodies.

"Of course. You can see them later."

"So they're, like, down here? Close by?" Goose bumps erupted over most of Okun's body.

The scientist laughed and stroked his short beard. "Don't worry. Not only are they dead, but we have them locked away in a very secure place."

Somewhat relieved, Okun returned to the subject. "I guess the pilot is supposed to sit in this chair, and the gum acts as a seat belt."

Cibatutto politely pointed out that "at several hundred miles per hour, the resin might provide some safety, but its cohesion strength is not as strong as, say, a seat belt."

"Yeah, I guess you're right."

"So, this is the instrument console." It was a mess, showing the signs of having been taken apart and reassembled many times. In an open toolbox, stray pieces of the ship mingled with hammers, soldering irons, screws, and a dozen notepads full of schematic drawings. Cibatutto seemed not to mind the clutter. Okun poked through the box for a moment, then picked up a particularly interesting fragment.

"Cool, an ankh."

"What's an ankh?"

"An ankh is the ancient Egyptian symbol of life, a hieroglyph." He held the half-inch-tall figure up to the light and realized he had been half-right. Like the ancient symbol, the thing between his fingers was composed of a central shaft with a shorter bar crossing it like a stickman's arms and a rounded open head. But this one was 3-D. Instead of two little arms, there were four. Likewise, the hole at the top opened east-west and north—south. *Ankh cubed,* he thought. For whatever reason, it struck Okun as supremely cool, and he put it in his pocket. *It's not stealing,* he told himself. *It's not like I'm going anywhere with it.*

"Here we have the steering controls," Cibatutto continued, pointing to what looked like a tightly folded bundle of greasy bones lying on the floor. "This mechanism goes here, in front of the pilot, and we think it opens outward." It had been removed from its original position and was connected to the console by a series of thin strands that looked like roots or perhaps really hairy veins. "Dr. Lenel went to medical school, so he's the one who sews up our patient after we amputate her a little bit." Indeed, the vein-roots at the bottom of the bony mechanism had been severed and stitched back together using medical sutures. "She looks like a machine," he said, rapping very hard on the dashboard, "but she's actually alive, living tissue. Look closely, and you can see the little tiny scars."

"What does that thing do?" Okun was already on to the next instrument on the dashboard, something that looked like a shell.

Cibatutto said no one knew, but he lifted the thing out of its resting place and held it up to the windows. The yellowish shell plate was thin enough to allow light to pass through, and was laced with a network of very fine veins. There were no dials or switches. As the scientist put it, "She's a mystery."

Cibatutto went on to explain that because the ship was not functioning, it was impossible to say with certainty what the various instruments were and exactly how they worked. Nevertheless, over the course of the years, Area 51's scientists had made a number of highly educated guesses which, in time, would be discovered to have been surprisingly accurate. For Okun, Cibatutto's thumbnail overview of each instrument in the cabin was like the opening pages of a long and fascinating science-fiction novel with him as the hero. He was confident he could figure all these gizmos out. By the end of his quick tour of the interior, he had completely lost his feeling of disappointment about this place. His mind was exploding with questions, possible solutions, and experiments he could run to test his hypotheses.

Radecker couldn't get over the horrible smell of the cockpit. "Why won't this thing fly?"

The question seemed to confuse Cibatutto, and once again Dworkin assumed command of the tour. He was standing halfway up the access ladder, so that only his head and shoulders protruded into the cabin. "Ah, the thorniest problem of them all—the power supply! If you'll follow me, I can show you the aqua-box."

"Here is the main culprit," he said a few moments later, pointing up to it. "Our most insoluble problem, the ship's generator." Dworkin was standing five feet behind the main hatchway, looking up into a square recess in one of the armored plates. The cover, he explained; had been torn loose in the crash, leaving the possibility that the device inside had been damaged or that something had fallen out. Lenel, grumbling about something under his breath, came forward with a flashlight to show Okun and Radecker what was inside. Six dark green walls formed an open hexagon three feet across which tapered slightly toward the top. These walls were the color of dirty jade and appeared to be just as solid. Connecting the six sides were thousands upon thousands of ultrafine strands, thinner than human hairs. They looked like cobwebs pulled taut to form a complex geometric pattern that hugged the walls and left an open space in the center of the hexagon. As the flashlight played over these extrusive threads, it was refracted and splintered, causing tiny dots of light to bounce around the inside of the chamber. *The Mothers would dig this,* Okun thought with a nod.

Dworkin blew a puff of air into the chamber, and, to the visitors' surprise, the rock walls of the hexagon reacted, fluttering like the paper walls of a Chinese lantern.

"No way," Okun said, wide-eyed. "Do that again." Dworkin obliged, and as the long-haired young scientist watched the gossamer walls shudder under the swirl of light dancing through the threads, a word popped out of his mouth, "Fragility."

"Seemingly," Dworkin allowed, "but watch this." He stepped away to give Dr. Lenel center stage. Lenel turned the flashlight around in his hand, reached up into the chamber, and began clanging and smashing it against the walls. Radecker and Okun were horrified, positive Lenel was doing irreparable damage to the device. But a second later the gruff old man showed them no damage had been done. The walls swayed back and forth as serenely as they had before. Dworkin's voice came over their shoulders. "We've tried for years to cut off a sample of this material so we could have it analyzed. Believe me, as delicate as it might appear, it is extremely tough."

"You should see what that sucker does when we pump some juice through the system. It's beautiful," Freiling put in.

Radecker's ears perked up. "What's he talking about? Does that mean you can make it work?"

"Not exactly." Dworkin told them about an experiment Dr. Wells had organized some years earlier, in which the ship was bombarded with a controlled ray of electromagnetic energy. "When we pointed the beam into the aqua-box, we were able to bring the ship's system to temporary life. The instrumentation lit up, and the generator here—we sometimes call it the aqua-box—produced a faint whirring sound. However, the power was purged from the system just as fast as it could be fed in."

"Sounds like your circuit isn't closed," Okun mused. "Maybe there's a wire you didn't connect right and the power's leaching out."

"Exactly." The old man sighed. "We've been searching for that missed connection for years, but because we don't have any blueprints or another ship in working order, we're having to do a lot of guesswork. It's rather like searching for a needle in a haystack with the lights out."

Radecker interrupted. "Wait a second. Let's back up so I can get this straight. You guys brought some kind of generator down here and pumped power into the ship and it *worked* for a second?" He didn't wait for an answer. "Well, I'm not a scientist, but why don't we just get a *bigger* generator and pump in *more* power?"

"Because our power isn't like theirs." This time Lenel

answered. "The most we can do is raise a spark. Even for that we have to use so damn much energy we overheat the circuits and the ship gets hot as an oven. If we gave it more charge, we'd just burn her up."

Okun listened to the explanation, wagging his head deeply. "And I bet you guys tested a whole range of levels."

"Yes, of course. The minimum application of EM radiation required to wake up the system is five thousand volts. We tested up to two hundred thousand volts and found no difference other than the resulting temperature of the ship."

"I see your problem," Okun said, stroking his beardless chin. "That's a toughie, a definite toughie."

Everyone fell silent for a moment. The tour had led Okun through the labyrinth of what was known only to drop him off here at this dead end.

"Another question." Okun's hand was up in the air again. "Aren't we missing something here? Something more important than whether we can get this ship to work. The so-called *bigger picture*?"

"What question are you thinking of?"

"Are there more aliens out there, and are they going to come back?"

4

THE Y

The elaborate dinner the scientists had cooked up was reheated, but by the time the food was actually ready to be served, no one felt like eating after Radecker had gone off like a hand grenade for a second time.

He'd gone down to the director's office to nose around in his new digs and found something that made him very, very unhappy. In fact, after a few minutes of examining the lab's accounting ledgers, he was furious. Everyone in the kitchen stopped what they were doing and listened to the shouts bouncing off the walls. He came storming down the hallway and stopped in the doorway. In his hand he had a stack of receipts. On his face he had an indignant expression, which he focused on Dworkin. "Were you guys thinking I wouldn't turn you in when I found out about this? Have you all gone crazy from living down here so long?"

I can't really believe Spelman has given this barbarous hothead any real power, Dworkin thought, knowing he would have to defend himself against this uppity technocrat.

It hadn't taken Radecker very long to discover some of the creative bookkeeping procedures the scientists had developed to help them through the lean years of underfunding. Among other things, he'd checked the active personnel roster. According to this document, there were supposedly nine old men working at the below-ground facility—one of them 103 years old. Every month, a government paycheck came in for every name on that list. Radecker wanted an explanation. "What happens to the extra paychecks?" he demanded. Cibatutto suddenly remembered an urgent errand over near the oven, so the task of explaining fell to Dworkin.

"We cash them," he explained.

The scheme had been in operation for several years. When it became clear that the flow of money for the project was slowly being choked down to a trickle, the staff had either resigned in protest or received transfers to other places. A hard-core group of twelve refused to leave. They all felt the questions surrounding these visitors were too urgent, too important, to let the lab die. So they dedicated not only their energy, but very often their personal savings as well to the effort. They had pooled their money to pay for new equipment and services such as the chemical tests they'd had done on several alien materials. When the members of this fraternity began to die off, their purchasing power declined as well. They couldn't get at the money in their retirement accounts, so they created a new one. They'd found a small bank in Las Vegas, Parducci Savings, that was known for asking very few questions, and they opened a joint account. Every month the checks were endorsed and deposited.

"I knew something was wrong when I saw all that new equipment in the other room."

"Sam," Freiling whispered loudly across the table, "this young man is angry with us. Who is he?"

"And this is ridiculous!" Radecker blew up again, pointing at Freiling. "The man is senile, totally unfit to be working here. The only reason you're keeping him down here is so you can collect his money. He's leaving on the next cargo plane."

"Mr. Radecker, please. We have maintained very detailed records, which I would be glad to have you examine. They show how every penny of the money was used to further our research efforts. Take a look around the labs, and you'll see we haven't used these funds on any extravagances for ourselves. We have dedicated our entire lives to the task of repairing and studying this vehicle. Area 51 is our home. It's been Dr. Freiling's home since 1951. He has nowhere else to go. We are his family now."

Radecker stood in the doorway, shaking his head at the ceiling. Dworkin's speech seemed to soften his stance, but only slightly. "Do you understand how much trouble you could get into for this? How am I going to explain this to Spelman? I suppose you want me to hide it from him and hang my own ass out on the line." He waved the papers in the air once more. "This is corruption, gentlemen. This is theft, this is tax fraud, this is…" An idea suddenly occurred to him. With a sickened expression on his face, he gazed at Dworkin. "Tell me these dead guys aren't buried down here."

"No, no. We own a group plot at a cemetery outside of Las Vegas."

Disgusted, Radecker marched away back to his office.

"Sam"—Freiling looked up at Dworkin—"don't let him send me away."

Brackish's room was a former office suite on the same corridor with the other scientists. It came with its own bathroom and a plain steel bed with a lumpy mattress. He stretched out in bed that night and told himself he should think about everything that had happened on this, the most extraordinary day of his life. But he found he couldn't stop thinking about the generator on the ship. He hadn't gotten a chance to ask them why they called it the aqua-box despite its decidedly non-aqua color.

On the one hand, it seemed so simple: the ship's power system wasn't holding a charge. There must be a rupture in the circuitry. In that case, it was merely a matter of locating the broken line and stitching it together as

Cibatutto had shown him. On the other hand, it could be some other problem, something totally unrelated to the circuitry, something so exotic no human being could even conceive of its existence. The first possibility was, as Dworkin said, like looking for a needle in a haystack. The second offered even lower chances of success.

Nevertheless, he decided to center on the second possibility. His instincts told him to trust the work the scientists had done over the past twenty-odd years. Not only that. He didn't want to be down there for twenty years himself duplicating their efforts. He decided to assume that the scientists had reassembled every piece of the ship correctly and that it was "good as new." He found himself thinking about the little balsa-wood-and-magnet saucer he'd caused to fly over Caltech. If someone had come along and found that saucer on the ground and started looking for its power source, they could put it together ten million ways and never figure it out. The power wasn't inside the ship. It was in the electromagnetic cannons strapped to the walls. Could the aliens have space-based generators? Of course, they wouldn't be EMFs, or we'd have picked that up as radio and television distortion. He smiled at the ludicrous picture in his head of megamonster power stations circling the earth and beaming power down to the UFOs. But if the power wasn't inside the ship and wasn't being "beamed in" from the outside, there wasn't any place left except for... That was it! In a flash, Okun hit upon, an idea that would obsess him for years to come. The power must somehow exist *between* the ships. Maybe the reason the system wouldn't hold a charge was that it had been designed *not* to. Hadn't Dworkin said something about the energy being drained out of the ship? "Purged" was the word he had used. If the power was being intentionally drained from the system, where did the energy go once the ship spit it out? It had to go to another ship, which would spit it right back. He had a vision of the stingray ships flying in groups, most likely arranged in rigid geometrical patterns. If this was a warship of some kind, it would make perfect sense from a tactical point of view. If every ship were continuously powering all the others, a squadron could maintain the power of its ships even if some of them were lost. There was only one problem: the idea contradicted something Radecker had told him about the so-called bigger picture.

Out in the hall he heard whispering. He got up and went to the door. Three of the scientists were out there holding a conference. As soon as they saw Okun standing in the doorway, they quickly said good night and broke their huddle.

"Pssst, hey, you guys. I think I figured out the power problem."

The men didn't seem to be at all interested and retreated toward their rooms. As Dworkin moved past him, Okun stepped out into the hall. "Sam, I was thinking about the power supply. What if—"

"Young man, I've had a very difficult evening, and I need some time alone with my thoughts." Not only was Dworkin upset about his confrontation with his new boss, he knew from long experience that, newly arrived visitors to Area 51 invariably had a middle-of-the-night epiphany that would miraculously answer, once and for all, all the mysteries surrounding the ship. Right now he was in no mood to listen to the uneducated guesses of this enthusiastic post-adolescent. It didn't help that Okun was standing there in nothing more than his jockey shorts and a pair of mismatched socks when the long-established decorum of the labs called for robes to be worn when using the common areas at bedtime. "We can talk tomorrow."

Dworkin disappeared into his room. When Okun turned

around, both Lenel and Cibatutto were shutting their doors as well. He considered going to see Radecker, but thought better of it. If there was going to be a conflict between the misfit employees and the tight-ass management, Okun knew which side he wanted to be on. It looked like his theories would have to wait for the morning.

He had just resigned himself to going back to bed when old Dr. Freiling came shuffling around the corner. It took Okun about five minutes to explain the idea he'd hit on. When he was done, the old man looked up at him and asked him to say the whole thing again. Even though he thought it was hopeless, Okun knew he wouldn't be able to sleep anyway, so he went through the idea once more. When he was almost finished, Freiling surprised him by saying, "That's a pretty dam good idea. If it were true, it'd explain a lot. But there's a problem."

"I know," Okun said, beating him to the punch. "This ship came alone on a one-time exploration mission."

"That's a bunch of nonsense. Who told you that?" the old man demanded, even though he'd been standing right there when Radecker had explained this to Okun. "Don't start making things up, young man. It's tempting, I know. There are so many questions and so few answers, but you can't start assuming things you have no proof for. We don't know whether this ship came alone or was part of a group."

"But Mr. Dworkin gave me the idea that—"

"Bah! Don't trust everything Sam tells you." The old man leaned forward and looked over the top of his bifocals. "Like the rest of us, he's not getting any younger and, just between you and me, I think some of his screws are coming loose. No, the problem with your idea is proving it. If you think the ships work in groups, you'll have to get another ship down here to see if you're right."

"Oh, yeah."

"Unless…"

"Unless what?" Okun asked. Freiling had gone into a long blank stare. It was hard to tell if he was thinking something through or had fallen asleep with his eyes open. But suddenly, the old-timer snapped out of his trance and began explaining a complicated set of procedures for testing the multi-ship theory. Once he had explained the whole idea, Okun glanced at him sideways, and said, "Can you say that whole thing again?"

Half an hour later, Freiling had rustled up the other scientists and herded them into his room. They listened first to Okun explain his ideas, then Freiling told them the experiment he'd come up with. The others were not as convinced as Freiling, but liked it nonetheless. Besides, they were desperate to show Radecker some progress before he had a chance to start shipping them out. Once they had all signed on, they shuffled down the hall to see the boss.

They found Radecker still awake, and, once the ideas were explained to him, surprisingly cooperative. So cooperative, in fact, that he didn't even bother to think through the implications of what his science team was telling him. It was all mumbo jumbo to him. It didn't seem to bother him that the whole idea contradicted the one-ship-one-time theory he'd been so insistent about earlier that evening.

It was near midnight when Radecker picked up the phone and got through to a supply depot officer in Colorado Springs. It was a chance for him to flex his muscles and feel like he could actually get something done. By the time he'd finished the conversation, the supply sergeant on the other end had been sufficiently intimidated to promise the equipment would be flown to Nevada the very next morning.

Temporarily a functioning and coherent team, the men

of Area 51 said good night and went to bed.

It took two days to set the experiment up. The electromagnetic cannon was brought out of storage and given an overhaul while Okun, using mountain-climbing gear lent to him by Lieutenant Ellsworth, dangled from the sheer concrete cliffs of the bunker affixing dozens of sensors to the walls with duct tape. If his theory was correct, these sensors would give him valuable information about how the ships flew together—their positioning and distance. When everything was ready to go, the alien airship was hooked up to more machines than a patient about to undergo brain surgery.

Everyone had a job. Dworkin would monitor the input/output meters while Lenel operated the cannon. Freiling tracked the energy levels reaching the sensors, and Cibatutto stood ready to give the cutoff signal when the ship's temperature climbed past 140 degrees. That left Okun and Radecker with their hands free to watch the show. A mirror was positioned at an angle below the generator to let them see how it worked. Special prismatic crystal goggles were distributed. If everything worked like it was supposed to, they would allow the team to watch the energy surge spit out of the ship and travel through the room. When everything seemed to be in order, Okun gave the final go-ahead.

"Okey-dokey, boys, let's get it on."

Lenel was standing on the operator's platform of the cannon, a device that looked like a dentist's X-ray machine built to battleship-sized proportions. He adjusted his goggles, then threw the switch. Everything happened at once. The cannon sent a beam of arcing electrical power through the air, penetrating the walls of the ship and coursing into the generator. A tremendous crack ripped through the bunker, and the ship seemed to explode into flames of blue light. The glass on the instrument panel in front of Dworkin shattered, and Okun was sure he'd ruined the ship forever. But Lenel continued to fire. A firestorm of hazy blue light flared out of the ship in all directions, stabbing into the air in a zigzag dance of truly alarming speed, like a thousand ghosts looking for a way out of a pillowcase at the speed of light. When Cibatutto directed his attention to the generator at the bottom of the ship, Okun instantly knew why they called it the aqua-box: green light was spilling out of the opening and, on the surface of the mirror, Okun could see energy racing around the inside of the generator chamber like a waterspout, a cyclone of crystal green water. Then Cibatutto waved his arms, Lenel killed the power, and it all came to a dead stop. The room echoed with silence except for the frazzled sputter coming from one of the lighting fixtures, which popped and died. The whole thing had taken less than ten seconds.

The scientists all looked at Okun, who pulled off his goggles and stared wide-eyed at the ship. "That was pretty, trippy." It was a few moments before the young genius realized what had happened. He had been proved right. The energy wasn't simply leaching out of the ship; it was being forced out, purged, by the ship's design. And the aqua-box, as he had predicted, seemed to function as some sort of capacitor, a device which multiplied the energy before passing it back to the system. It had more than quadrupled the power input from the cannon, overwhelming the meters on Dworkin's output monitors and sending them into meltdown.

"Nicely done, young man, nicely done indeed! We haven't made this much progress in years." Dworkin and the others were jubilant. Even Lenel was smiling.

They began checking the registers on the meters wired to the sensors on the walls. Despite all the visual fireworks, Okun was surprised that they hadn't burned up along with

Dworkin's voltmeter. In fact, the numbers were rather low. Very little energy had reached the sensors up near the ceiling. That, he realized immediately, spelled trouble for his theory. The energy was dissipating much more quickly than he guessed it would. Then again, the violent, flailing, spasmodic way the energy had shot around the room could indicate a mistake in the way the scientists had put things back together.

Dworkin was already calling for a bottle of champagne. He was busy extolling this advance in their knowledge to Radecker when Okun called across the room, "Something's not right." He came and explained the sensor readouts to the others. "It means these alien ships would have to fly wingtip to wingtip in order to keep their communal energy supply alive."

"Still," Dworkin countered, "you have proved that the ship is designed to take energy in, magnify it, and pump it back out. Perhaps the presence of other ships would attract or draw the energy from this one."

Okun screwed up his face and shook his head no. "I don't buy it."

Lenel joined them and was characteristically blunt. "Of course this means we've spent twenty-five years screwing around down here for nothing. But at least now we know."

"Know what?" Radecker asked.

"The kid just proved this hunk of alien junk can't fly by itself. If we're ever gonna get it to fly, we'll need another ship just like it." When no one backed him up, Lenel asked, "Isn't that right, fellas?"

"That would seem to be the logical conclusion," Dworkin agreed. "Didn't we mention that part?"

"No! No one mentioned that," Radecker yelled. "Did I mention the fact that I can't leave until we get this thing to fly?" Radecker reached up and began massaging his temples. Obviously, he hadn't understood the full implications of the test until that moment. When he felt the impulse to grab the first seventy-year-old he could lay his hands on and begin choking him to death, he reminded himself to breathe deeply.

Okun wanted to run the test again at a slightly higher input level and see if he could get a different reading on the sensors. And an hour later, when the ship had cooled down, the scientists agreed. After carefully setting the levels on the energy input cannon, Okun asked the others to tell him if the flaring aura of light behaved any differently, then headed off toward the center of the ship.

"Where are you going?"

"Um, inside. I noticed last time that some of the gizmos inside the cockpit lit up, and I want to check out what's going on in there."

Dworkin chuckled. "Mr. Okun, I'm afraid that's impossible. I believe I've already mentioned to you that the energy levels we're using overheat the circuits and generate intolerably high temperatures."

Freiling concurred. "He's right, Breakfast."

"Brackish. My name is Brackish."

Freiling didn't seem to listen. "The inside of the cockpit gets hotter than a skillet. If you touch it, you'll get burned."

"Look, guys, I'm young, I'm nimble, I'm a natural athlete. Don't worry. When it starts getting hot, I'll get out quick."

"I won't allow it." Dworkin put his foot down. "Mr. Radecker, as director of the lab, would you please forbid this young man from going through with this foolish idea. The temperature inside the craft quickly rises to more than two hundred degrees. He'll roast. Dr. Lenel, come down off that gun. The experiment is canceled."

"Stay where you are, Doctor." Radecker thought about

it: *No more Okun, no more five-year contract.* Without their boy genius, Spelman would have to pull the plug on the project, or at least reorganize. "Mr. Okun, do you honestly think you can get out of there in time?"

Okun's mind made another odd connection. "Have any of you guys ever seen that show called *Thrillseekers*? Where these guys crash cars and jump motorcycles over things? Anyways, I saw this one where a guy, a stuntman, walks into a house, a little fake house they built for the stunt, dig? He's got his crash helmet and these fire-retarding overalls on. So, he waves to the crowd and goes inside. Then these other guys come and set fire to the shack and then throw this honkin' bundle of dynamite inside. A couple of seconds later, kablooey! The whole thing blows sky-high, and you see the stuntman come flying through the air—Aaaaagh!—in this perfect swan dive, and he lands on this big air mattress. For a minute he just lies there—*I might be dead*—but then he jumps up and takes a bow."

"I think I saw that one," Freiling shouted. "It was at a racetrack."

"If you have a point to make, why don't you get to it?" Radecker snapped.

"Are you dense?" Freiling demanded, wheeling around and looking at Radecker like he was the crazy one. "The boy is asking for some safety equipment. He needs a crash helmet and something to land on."

And fifteen minutes later, that is what he had. Cibatutto had taken a colander from the kitchen, lined the inside with foam padding, and attached a chin strap. By the time this makeshift headgear was ready, Okun and Radecker had created a landing pad by stacking mattresses under the hatchway of the alien ship. Okun strapped on the helmet, climbed the ladder, and practiced diving to safety. It was fun, it was simple, they were ready to go.

When he saw they meant to go through with it, Dworkin announced that he refused to participate and started to leave the hangar.

"Dr. Dworkin," Radecker called across the room. "I wouldn't do that if I were you. Have you already forgotten our deal?" The tall gaunt scientist stood there for a moment while his conscience wrestled with his sense of self-preservation. Finally, he turned around and returned a few steps closer to the ship. "How would the director like me to assist?"

"That's OK, you can just stand there and watch. Dr. Lenel, why don't you show me how to work this contraption. I'd like to operate it, if that's okay with our stuntman."

Okun realized Radecker was blackmailing the men, holding their embezzlement over their heads like a hatchet. And while it made him sad to see the regal old Dworkin having to kowtow to a man of half his years and a quarter of his IQ, he figured there was nothing he could do about it. Looking completely ridiculous standing next to the spaceship with the big stainless-steel strainer strapped to his head, he offered Radecker a manly thumbs-up, then, after a few deep breaths, climbed the ladder and disappeared into the dark mass of the alien vehicle.

Lenel turned the power dial a tad lower than Okun had requested, then showed Radecker how to activate the power by means of a simple switch. As he turned and stepped off the operator's platform, Radecker quickly reached down and cranked the power regulator up a full twist to the right. *That ought to do the job.*

Inside, Okun looked around uncertainly. This was starting to seem like a very bad idea. It wasn't the power surge that would rip through the ship in a moment; it was the dark interior. Being in there alone, he suddenly felt how foreign, how otherworldly this claustrophobic environment was. There was just enough light seeping through the cabin windows to cast dim shadows across the rounded walls, which were dripping with creepy, semiorganic technology. It felt more like a mausoleum than a flying machine. He was on the verge of chickening out, but instead he pulled on his goggles and yelled down through the hatch that he was ready.

As soon as the power switched on, the same loud crack ripped through the ship, knocking Okun slightly off-balance. He reached out to steady himself on the wall. All across the instrument panel lights snapped on, including the shell screen Cibatutto had shown him. He jerked his hand away from the wall when he felt it swell to life under his palm. Unfortunately, the momentum of his arm combined with the uncertainty of his feet to cause the natural athlete to trip once over his left foot, then immediately again over his right, all of it taking him farther away from the escape door. His stumbling landed him flat-ass on the floor directly in front of the shell screen, where he saw something that scared the bejesus out of him. A picture filled the vein-laced screen, a fuzzy, distorted image of a giant Y rising straight out of the ground. The alien technology gave this image a visual texture unlike any Okun had seen before. The picture spoke to him. Not with words, but in emotional terms. For reasons he would never fully understand, this simple image communicated a deep emotional sensation that hit him like a punch in the gut. It seemed like the loneliest, most desolate thing he'd ever seen in his life. He got the sense this great Y-shape was somehow an instrument of torture, an enemy. But at the same time, it was beckoning Okun, urgently calling for him to come. His plan to check the other instruments completely forgotten, Okun sat on the floor, mesmerized by the picture and his strong emotional response to it. Later he would be able to joke about the moment, likening it to reading a travel brochure for Hell written by Samuel Beckett, but at the moment he was in trouble. The temperature inside the ship was rising fast. Fortunately, something nearby started moving. The steering controls, that neatly folded stack of bones, opened itself and twitched to life like a pair of giant lobster legs. This distraction saved his life, occurring as it did just as a butt-bubbling wave of heat suddenly rose in the floor. In one giant stride, Okun crossed the cockpit and dived through the hatch, landing facefirst on the mattress.

Radecker switched off the power.

The scientists looked at the long-haired daredevil stuntman-cum-lab worker and waited for a sign that he would live. His exit from the ship could not fairly be called a swan dive, but it was pretty close, especially for a beginner, so the gentlemen were expecting him to leap up any moment and take a bow.

"Mr. Okun?... Mr. Okun?..."

5

INTO THE STACKS

Standing on a chair with his pants around his ankles and his ass toward the bathroom mirror, Okun examined his burns. The doctor who examined him upstairs in the hangar had assured him they weren't serious. But they were painful enough to keep him from sitting down for a few days. He gingerly pulled up his trousers, then examined his new piece of jewelry. He'd attached the ankh-shaped gizmo he'd found in the ship to a piece of leather string to make himself a necklace. He admired his new treasure in the mirror. "Groovy," he nodded. Then, feeling hungry, he went looking for food.

"Howdy, hot pants," Lenel barked out for the benefit of the other scientists when Okun wandered into the kitchen. The young men ignored the comment. He grabbed a box of cereal and lay down, belly first, on the daybed they'd brought in for him.

Cibatutto couldn't resist cracking a joke of his own. "We were going to have hot dogs for lunch," he sniggered, "but we can't seem to find any toasted buns!" The old men howled with laughter.

"Fortunately," Dworkin added, "it looks as though there's plenty of rump roast." This witticism brought on yet another round of guffaws.

When they were finished, Okun turned a jaundiced eye on them and tried out a one-liner of his own. "Hardy har har. You guys are so hilarious, you should work in Vegas.

Call yourselves 'Jerry's kids'—Jerry Atrics, that is." The scientists didn't get it. "As in Geriatrics? Oh, forget it." The men had been in the hole too long to know anything about the telethon.

For the next ten minutes, these distinguished gentlemen of science devoted their attention to the creation of one butt joke after another. The wisecracks were their way of welcoming Okun into their clique. He'd passed a major test the day before. Although he hadn't exactly spilled blood for the good of the project, he'd brought it to the surface of his skin, and that was close enough.

Freiling called for everyone's attention. "OK, Brecklish, I got one for you." He smiled devilishly. "I made it up myself."

"Brackish. The name is Brackish."

Freiling seemed to blank out for a moment. "Now I forgot the damn joke! No, wait, I got it. Why did the newspaper editor call the lobster?"

Brackish knew he was supposed to ask why. The Y! "Oh my God," he burst out, "I didn't tell you guys what I saw inside the ship!" He turned to Cibatutto. "You know that yellowy shell instrument deal with the all the little whatchamacallits running through it?"

Cibatutto nodded.

"When the energy came through the ship, it had a *picture* on it, and—I don't want you guys to think I'm a complete weirdo for telling you this, but—it was giving off feelings, emotions. Seriously, it was like the visual image was only one part of a larger message. There was another layer of communication going on, something meant to be *felt*—desperation, doom, abandonment, something like that. Now that I think about it, it might have been some kind of SOS, a distress call."

This announcement dramatically changed the mood in the kitchen. "That would fit nicely with your second-ship theory," Dworkin pointed out, skeptical.

"Did this image look like anything in particular?" Lenel inquired.

"You bet. It looked like a Y. Like a big old honkin' letter Y standing out in the middle of nowhere." His audience reacted strangely to this last bit of information, exchanging wide-eyed looks. "What's the matter? Did I say something wrong?"

Before anyone could answer, Radecker's footsteps came clacking down the hallway. Dworkin looked quickly across the table and put his index finger to his lips, telling Okun to keep this news quiet.

"It took all day, but I finally got Spelman on the phone," Radecker announced, marching straight to the fridge and fishing out a soda.

"And?"

"Well, I didn't explain all the particulars. I just told him we'd proved beyond any shadow of a doubt that the ship can't fly."

"And?"

"I don't think he believed me. He said, 'Your assignment is to get that ship to fly.' So I said, 'I'm telling you it cannot and will not fly.' 'Well, sir, I don't know what to tell you. You're assigned to the project for a five-year term or until such time as blah blah blah.' So I asked him what he would like for us to be doing out here. And you know what the son of a female dog says to me? He goes, 'You've got four years, eleven months, and twenty-six days to figure that one out for yourselves. Stay in touch.'" Radecker sat down with the others at the table and drowned his sorrows in a long slug of soda.

"Did you happen to mention the matter of our finances?" Dworkin inquired gingerly.

"Not yet," he said, with a look which suggested he still might. Glancing over his shoulder, he noticed Okun across the room, preoccupied with a reexamination of his burns

Radecker leaned in and whispered to the scientists, "I might be able to keep you guys off the hook. It didn't sound like Spelman plans to come out here for a visit anytime soon, so we might be able to just start killing off the other names on the payroll one by one. Every couple of months, we'll call the Treasury Department and say another one has died. By the way, I saw your life insurance policy. Cute trick naming one another beneficiaries. How did you ever get a policy like that?"

"Our banking friends in Las Vegas are very flexible."

"Also, it sounds like you guys can get everything you want in the way of materials and equipment—as long as Boy Wonder over there approves it."

"I don't understand," Dworkin whispered back. "Our appropriations have to be approved by Mr. Okun?"

Radecker rolled his eyes as if to agree that the idea was ludicrous. "Spelman was pretty clear. Whatever Okun needs in the way of research materials will be automatically OKed."

Lenel asked, "So why do you say *we* can get anything we want?"

"Oh, please," Radecker said dismissively. "Look at this punk. He'll do whatever I tell him to, and if he doesn't obey, I'll make his life miserable." An idea occurred to him. "Now, listen up. I respect you guys, and I think we can work together. I'll try to help you out with hiding the names of these dead guys. And I want just one thing in exchange." The CIA operative leaned in even closer and explained what he expected of the gray-haired men. When he was finished, he looked them in the eyes, one by one. "Are we all agreed on that?"

"What are you guys talking about?" Okun called from his daybed. No one answered, so he asked again. Finally Radecker turned around.

"We're discussing how we're going to get this ship to

fly. I just talked to my boss, and he's convinced you can do it."

"I can," Okun replied. "Just have your boss send us another ship exactly like the one we've got, and our problems will be solved."

"There aren't any other ships."

"Well"—Okun grimaced as he rolled onto his side—"there *are* other ships. We might not *have* any of them, but there must be other ships. Otherwise, the aliens couldn't have come to Earth."

"Sorry, pal. That's not the way it works. I can't tell you how I know, but I have it on very good authority that this ship came here alone."

Okun snorted. "Right. Who's your authority, some palm reader?"

"Military intelligence," Radecker fired back, not liking the younger man's tone.

"Military intelligence?" Okun asked. "Isn't that a contradiction in terms? Who are you going to believe, a bunch of Army dudes or what you saw with your own eyes? Our experiment showed the ship can't fly without other ships just like it. It's proved."

Radecker shrugged as he stood up. "All I know is what they tell me. And they tell me there was no second ship. From now on our official position is that there are no additional ships." With that he left the room.

Okun wasn't finished with the discussion. He threw his legs over the side of the bed and was about to follow Radecker down the hall when he realized he was sitting on his burns. His face contorted into a silent howl as he lifted his buns away from the blanket. When his posterior pain subsided, he appealed to his senior coworkers. "There's got to be a second ship, right? In fact, there must have been at least *three* ships at Roswell. If there were only two, both of them would have gone down. When this one crashed, it would have broken the power relay and knocked the other one down. Besides, what about all these people that say they've seen UFOs? Don't they all describe something that looks remarkably similar to the one we've got?"

Okun was angry and started pacing the kitchen as he talked. It was a side of himself he hadn't shown the others until that moment. It wasn't Radecker's ignorance of technical matters that bothered him. It was being told what he could and could not think. The idea that future research on the spacecraft would be limited by some anonymous panel of military experts really chapped his ass, so to speak. And then there was that phrase Radecker had used, *I can't tell you how I know.* "There's some kind of government conspiracy going on," he burst but. "It's the man, the establishment, the system. See what I'm saying?"

None of the scientists knew quite how to respond to their companion's ranting. "In fact," Dworkin said, "except for our latest experiment, there is little evidence to support your multi-ship theory."

"But that's all the evidence we need!... Isn't it?" He could see the scientists were avoiding making eye contact with him. "You said it yourself yesterday: this ship cannot fly without the presence of another."

Dworkin hesitated, then finally replied. "It's possible that we've misinterpreted the results."

"OK, what's going on here?" Okun stood over the elderly gentlemen like an impatient schoolmaster who'd caught them hiding something. "This is about those paychecks for the dead men, isn't it. Radecker's holding it over your heads." Of course, that was exactly what was happening. But none of them would admit it out loud.

Lenel was fed up with the whole idiotic situation. "You want to look for a second ship? Follow me." He marched out of the room, and, after a moment of hesitation, Okun followed him. The grizzled scientist led the way through the maze of halls toward the steel doors to the outside, muttering under his breath the whole while. Instead of turning toward the exit, however, Lenel stopped in the long hallway that the scientists used for storage and gestured toward the crates and filing cabinets pushed against the walls.

"We call this mess the stacks. In these boxes you'll find every government document associated with our research. You name it, it's in there. That means every scientific report, every position paper from DC, every memo, every police report on sightings, reported abductions, strange dreams, everything. Anything and everything that has to do with extraterrestrial life-forms."

Nodding, Okun surveyed the room. He did a quick calculation and guesstimated there were two hundred crates full of documents, each one holding about twenty reams of paper. At five hundred sheets per ream that meant there were about two million pieces of paper. Adding in the filing cabinets would bring that number closer to three million. "You might want to change the name from the stacks to something like *the piles*. Does anyone actually read this stuff?"

"Some of it. We get a hew shipment every first Monday of the month. We look through the box and pull out anything that looks interesting, but mostly it just gets dumped out here. Years ago, there was a fellow named Pike who had everything organized. If you needed to see a particular report, you'd go ask Pike. When the new reports came in, he'd make sure they got into the right hands. After he quit, I took over the job."

From the looks of things, Lenel hadn't been doing a very good job. Okun pulled open the top drawer of a file cabinet and looked inside. A few thousand pages of yellowing paper were strewn around in heaps. They had been stuffed carelessly into the drawer, with no regard for organization.

"What kind of filing system are you using here?"

"There is no system. The whole place is a damned mess now on account of Wells. That man was always in such a hurry. He'd come in here and take out a hundred files to find the one he was looking for. He never put anything back, and I got tired of doing his work for him. So I quit. I've had nothing to do with the stacks for the last ten years or so. Still, if there's anything in particular you need, I can probably help you find it."

Until then, Okun hadn't understood why he was being introduced to this ancient collection of worthless paper. He didn't know what was going on in Lenel's head, but apparently the old grump was expecting him to start reading this stuff.

"I should warn you," he went on, "that 99.9 percent of what's in these reports is a bunch of hooey. First you've got your crackpots who make up stories to get themselves noticed. Then you've got your little old ladies who see a spark on a telephone pole and wet their pants because they're sure it was men from Mars. But you've also got something that's harder to spot."

"What's that?"

"Reports started leaking out about what we had down here. Since there was no way to keep the files completely hidden, the geniuses at the CIA and the Pentagon started something they call disinformation. As if there weren't enough bogus reports of sightings and encounters already, they started making up new ones by the hundreds. Some of the most convincing stories were written by some hack sitting in an office making the whole thing up. They deliberately buried false leads, stories that seem like they'll lead somewhere, but then the trail goes cold, and you're back where you started from."

Finally, Okun had to ask. "Dr. Lenel, why are you showing me all this stuff?"

"If you're convinced there's a second alien ship, this is the best place to go looking for it."

It was three weeks before Okun made his first independent foray into the stacks. Life in the labs was beginning to settle into a comfortable routine. His elderly cohort continued with their repairs on the alien vehicle and, once his rear end had healed sufficiently, Okun joined them. Even though he was convinced they were wasting their time, they made pleasant company, and he assisted them as they puttered through repairs to the wiring system and damaged fuselage.

The atmosphere underground improved considerably once Radecker began spending his days at the Officers' Club. Groom Lake, the flat salt bed under which Area 51 was buried, was only a tiny fraction of the enormous Nellis Weapons Testing Range. At roughly five thousand square miles in area, the range was as large as a small European country. At its southern edge, near Frenchman Lake, was a cluster of buildings which, with their manicured lawns, swimming pool, and tennis courts could, from the air, easily be mistaken for a luxury hotel. It was a gathering spot for high-ranking officials from all areas of the base, a place to hold meetings or simply relax in the air-conditioned comfort of the bar. Radecker quickly discovered that a convoy of Jeeps traveled between Groom and Frenchman lakes twice a day, when a new group of soldiers came on duty. From six in the morning until six in the evening, his phone calls were rerouted to the lounge of the Officers' Club.

On one particular Friday, Okun was in the labs by himself. Dworkin and the others had left for their once-a-week excursion into Las Vegas. The previous two Fridays, the men had convinced Okun to join them. He was shocked by what he learned. After taking care of their banking business and other errands, the four old timers headed for the casinos, where they played high-stakes poker. They seemed to be on a first-name basis with nearly every dealer and pit boss they ran into. Apparently, they had been eighty-sixed from many of the major houses on the Strip because, although no one could prove it, they cheated at cards and always took home much more than they lost, often several hundred dollars between them. It was one more way they had found to end-run the funding restrictions imposed on them by the Pentagon.

It was spooky being down there by himself, so he didn't linger in the long dim hallway that housed the stacks. After a quick look around, he found the sloppiest box of all, the one that looked like it had been organized by a madman. He lifted out the first two hundred pages and took them back to his room, locking the door behind him—a habit he'd gotten himself into after the scientists showed him the corpses of the alien astronauts. Even though they were very very dead and floating in steel-reinforced tanks of formaldehyde, this extra precaution of locking his door provided the young man with the last little bit of psychological reassurance he needed to sleep peacefully. He put the documents on his desk and began to sort through them. He had intentionally selected the most disorganized set of files on the assumption that it would contain the last papers this mysterious Dr. Wells had been reading before they carried him away. He didn't expect these pages to lead him anywhere. But if they did turn out to be Wells's last readings, well, that would be pretty cool. Most of the pages were single-sheet memos concerning mundane topics like equipment orders, travel arrangements, and test results. He put these aside and turned his attention to one of the thicker documents. It was a report entitled "National Security Briefing Paper on Project Aquarius/B. Jones, Subject." At the bottom of the title page, there was a typed note:

WARNING! This is a TOP SECRET—EYES ONLY document containing compartmentalized information essential to the national security of the United States. EYES ONLY ACCESS to the material herein is strictly limited to those possessing Project Aquarius clearance level. Reproduction in any form or the taking of written or mechanically transcribed notes is strictly forbidden.

Bridget Jones was an unpopular, pudgy twelve-year-old from a well-to-do family living in a farming community about thirty minutes outside Cleveland, Ohio. She was a notorious liar, with a specialty for inserting herself into factual events. Whenever something newsworthy occurred, Bridget was there. When, for example, the Farlin brothers totaled their GTO into the front wall of the high school, Bridget told everyone she'd been riding in the backseat. When a half dozen sheep turned up missing from a farm a few miles down the road, Bridget filed a police report, complete with her own pencil sketches of the suspects. She claimed to have been out on a walk when she noticed four men loading the animals into the back of a Volkswagen. So when Bridget found a tiny artifact left behind after a close encounter with an alien spaceship, no one was prepared to believe her story.

About 9 P.M. on a Sunday evening she had been in the garage listening to her father's brand-new police scanner radio—just another one of dad's electronic toys—when she heard a voice she recognized and two words that caught her attention: flying saucer. The voice belonged to her neighbor, County Sheriff Jon Varner.

"Looks like we got a plane on fire out here, repeat, there's a plane coming in low, and it's on fire," she heard him yelling into his radio. "I'm on Brooderman Road, near the old Chalmers place. It seems to be flying level to the ground. My God! It's not a plane. It's a flying saucer!"

"Jon, what are you seeing out there?" the female dispatcher's voice broke in.

"About the size of a two-story house. Orange light, it's glowing, I guess it's red and gold, but it's hard to make out. Now it's halfway between the railroad tracks and Brooderman Road. It's getting closer."

"Jon, are you all right?"

"Jeannie, you should see this thing, it's unbelievable. It's going to fly right over me. It looks like there are some windows. I can see light coming from inside. I think it's—"

The patrol car's radio died. There was panic in the dispatcher's voice. "Jon? Officer Varner, are you all right? Can you hear me!"

Bridget switched off the radio, grabbed the flashlight off the shelf above the washing machine and jumped on her bike. The Chalmers place wasn't more than a mile and a half from her house. She tore down the driveway, then turned onto the main road. It was the fastest she'd ever gone on a bike, and she nearly lost control more than once as she scanned the sky for signs of the UFO. The warm breezy night and darkness of the road made her feel like she was racing through a dream. She turned onto Brooderman and saw the headlights of Varner's car far ahead. When she came within seventy-five feet, she got a bad feeling—like she was being watched—and slowed down, turning her head sideways to get the wind off her ears. She listened for footsteps, a murmur of conversation, anything that might signal this was a trap. But the only sound was the purr of the police car's idling motor, so she rode cautiously forward. The driver's door was open, and Varner was laid across the front seat flat on his back. Bridget pulled up, grabbed his foot, and gave it a shake.

"Mr. Varner, are you all right?" The officer stirred

slightly, so she gave him another shake, harder this time. "Mr. Varner, wake up."

She heard someone behind her and spun around. A tall stooped figure stepped onto the road. "Is that Jon Varner in that car?" he said, cinching up his housecoat. He was an older guy she'd seen in town before. "What's the matter with him?"

"I don't know," Bridget said. "I think a flying saucer got him. I heard it on my dad's radio."

The old man stepped past her and pulled the officer into a sitting position. Varner woke up but had no recollection of what had happened to him. The last thing he remembered was standing on the pavement watching the saucer moving overhead. "Didn't you see it?" Varner asked when he learned the man's house was close by. "It lit up the field like it was noon."

The man swore he hadn't seen or heard anything unusual. He'd been inside watching television when he got a call from Jeannie down at the station house asking him to come outside and check.

A few minutes later, two more police cars arrived with sirens wailing. The noise attracted more neighbors into the street. Passing motorists stopped to find out what was going on, and soon there were two dozen folks standing in the middle of the road listening to the officer tell and retell his story. Bridget joined a group of people who started searching the edges of the road for clues. She wandered several feet into the waist-high field of wheat and came across something strange, a depression in the grass. It looked like somebody had been lying in the spot only a few minutes before. She could see the tall grass untangling itself and trying to stand back up. Like a good detective, she made sure to check for footprints. There were none. There was no pathway leading to or from the place where the person had been lying. She turned and saw that her own path into the field was clearly marked by the trail of trampled grass.

"Hey, people, I found something! Come and look!"

Before anyone got there, she looked down and noticed something metal near the head of the body-shaped depression. She reached down and picked up the shiny object, which looked like a BB pellet.

"Honey, you shouldn't be knocking down that man's wheat," a woman's voice called out. "What did you find?"

"Mrs. Milch? It's me, Bridget. Come and look at this; I think it's important."

If the woman was reluctant to step onto the damp soil before, she was doubly so now that she knew who was asking her to come. Everyone knew about Bridget's little problem with telling the truth. But this was an urgent situation, so she followed Bridget's trail out to the spot. "OK, what is it?"

"Look, this is where the aliens probably held Mr. Varner down."

The woman didn't believe her. She said the depression in the grass was too small to have been made by a man. That it looked more like a little girl had made it. She asked why there wasn't another set of man-sized tracks between there and the road. When the girl protested that this time she was telling the truth, Mrs. Milch shook her head and pointed out the grass on the girl's knees. Bridget explained to the woman about having bent down to pick up the BB and tried to show it to her, but Mrs. Milch walked away.

Bridget had never felt so insulted in her entire life. She jammed the BB into her pocket, got on her bike, and rode away. When she got home and examined it under brighter light, she noticed that the object was covered with tiny bristles. Even with the help of a magnifying glass, these spiky projections were difficult to see. But she could feel them when she squeezed the object hard. The bristles felt like electricity under her fingertips.

* * *

News traveled fast. By the time she got to school the next morning, all the kids had heard there had been a UFO sighting the night before. Bridget made sure everyone in the school knew of the central role she had played in the drama. She stuck to the facts for the most part, but couldn't resist adding a few small wrinkles of her own. During the nutrition break, she told her classmates how she had driven the spaceship away by pulling the gun from the unconscious officer's holster and using some choice language to scare "the Martians" off. By lunch, she had made eye contact with one of the blobbish creatures through the spacecraft's windows and flipped him the bird. By the end of the day, no one believed a word. Just before the bell rang, Bridget raised, her hand and asked whether there could be show-and-tell the next day. She promised to bring in the "Martian BB" she'd found. Her classmates jeered their disbelief, but Ms. Sandoval, her favorite teacher of all time, said it was a good idea.

The next morning Bridget smelled another trap. A black-and-white was parked in front of the school next to another, suspiciously official-looking car. A policeman and a man in a dark suit were standing outside of her room talking to Ms. Sandoval. When she walked up, she knew from their smiles that they were not to be trusted. The man in the suit asked her about the BB. She admitted that she had it, and offered to let them see it, on one condition. She made both men promise they wouldn't take it away from her, that they wouldn't even touch it. The men agreed. Bridget opened up her lunch bag and started rummaging through it. Suddenly the policeman snatched the bag out of her hands. "Here, lemme help you look for it."

"You big liars!" she screamed in anger. "Taking advantage of a little kid! You're disgusting!" When the cop had emptied the sack out completely and determined there was nothing unusual inside, the men turned once more toward the girl. The chubby sixth-grader was smirking like a jack-o'-lantern, holding the BB between her fingers. "Ha-ha, I fooled you." Before either man could get to her, she popped the fuzzy little pill into her mouth and swallowed it.

She was rushed to Merciful Redeemer Hospital and admitted to the Intensive Care Unit. After vomiting several times, she'd gone into a sustained fit of dry heaves. Covered with sweat and moaning between gagging spells, she was like an overweight kitten trying to pass a large hair ball. In addition to her nausea, she complained of dizziness and a ringing in her ears. The doctors took X-rays but could find no sign of the foreign object. A toxicologist ran several blood tests but could find no poison. None of the experts could find anything physically wrong with her. Her mysterious illness became more mysterious still when it suddenly disappeared without a trace moments before her parents arrived. When her mother and father accused her of making the whole thing up, the man in the dark suit who'd driven her to the hospital stepped forward.

"Mr. and Mrs. Jones, my name is Bradley Kepnik. I'm with the Central Intelligence Agency." He flashed them his credentials. "I was there when the girl swallowed the object, and I'm positive she's not making this up. Could I have a word with the two of you in private?"

Bridget spent that night at home in her own bed. Agent Kepnik was there with her, sleeping on a cot in the hallway. He'd installed a lock on the outside of the bathroom door, which only he could open. They were going to wait this thing out. In the morning, the girl defecated into a shallow plastic tub which it was Kepnik's job to search. To her delight, Bridget learned she wouldn't be going to school for the next day or two. She spent the day raiding the icebox and watching soap operas. About three o'clock, under the watchful eye of her chaperone, she went outside to play handball against the garage door in the driveway. Despite her many invitations, Kepnik declined to join her, claiming old football injuries. Bridget stopped playing when a large passenger plane flew overhead. She watched it intently for a minute.

"What's the matter?" the fed asked.

"The guy who's driving that plane is named Cassella. He's the pilot. The copilot is named... I can't read it, Tenashi, Tanashawsee, something like that. They're eating potato chips. And there's another guy sitting behind them with headphones on."

"I see," Kepnik said smoothly. By now he knew all about the girl's mythomania. "And what's his name?"

"I don't know," she hissed back at him, annoyed. She knew when she was being treated as a child. "He doesn't have a jacket on, so there's no name tag. If you don't believe me call the airport. The company's name is Hartford Air. It's written on the backs of the seats."

Kepnik was beginning to get interested. By now the plane was nearly out of view. "Where's the plane going to land? And where's it coming from?"

"Well of course it's going to land in Cleveland, the airport's right over that way. But where are they coming from?" She closed her eyes and concentrated as if she were hunting around the cockpit. "Denver: And they took off at 11:45. This is neato. I can see inside the plane. Let's call the airport and find out if I'm right."

Kepnik phoned the Hartford Air arrivals desk and discovered there was indeed an 11:45 from Denver. He confirmed that the pilot's name was Mark Cassella and the copilot was Peter Tanashian. He didn't ask about the potato chips.

* * *

Accompanied by her mother and Agent Kepnik, Bridget was flown to Arlington, Virginia, and taken to the offices of Project Aquarius. Aquarius, its critics said, was proof that the Army had too much money and free time on its hands. It brought together psychics, astrologers, mediums, and other practitioners of the paranormal arts and tried to channel their talents toward military goals. Twelve-year-old Bridget was what the people in the office complex referred to as an RV. This was not a reference to her weight. RV stood for Remote Visualizer, and the Army had six people with this special talent under full-time contract.

The first step was to test her powers. She was introduced to one of the project's researchers, a forty-year-old woman with huge blue eyes, Dr. Joan Sachville-West, who did everything she could to put the girl at ease.

"We're going to try a simple experiment with these cards," she explained. "They're called Zener cards, and each one has a design on it. There are five different designs," she said, showing the icons to the girl, "and I would like for you to concentrate and try to guess which design is on the back of the card I hold up. Simple?"

"Wavy lines!" the girl shouted the second Sachville-West lifted the first card off the deck.

"Very good. You're right."

"Star."

"Right again."

"Circle."

"Excellent."

When Bridget had gone fifteen for fifteen, the woman took her hands away and asked what the next card was.

"I can't see it until you pick it up."

"Guess."

"That's not how it works," she whined. "I have to be able to see it."

"Give it a try. Just for fun."

Unhappily, Bridget guessed. "Another wavy lines card?"

Sachville-West turned it over: star.

"See! I told you!" Angry that the researcher's insistence had ruined her perfect streak, she retaliated by telling everyone what color underwear the scientist was wearing.

The woman only crossed her legs under the table and smiled. "You've got quite a gift."

The rest of the afternoon was devoted to giving the girl a crash course in geography. When her attention waned, and she refused to cooperate, her mother came to the rescue by opening her purse and pulling out a bag of candy bars. "My emergency kit," she explained with an embarrassed smile.

When Bridget had mastered the names of the seven continents and several bodies of water, the real work of Project Aquarius began. She was shown an aerial photograph of a Soviet Wolf-class submarine.

"Young lady," a man in an Army uniform began, "there are two submarines like this one in the water right now. Let's see if you can tell me where they are." The USSR had a total of four of these nuclear-powered subs. Two of them were in dry dock at that moment for repairs. One had been picked up on radar overnight off the Oregon coast and one was unaccounted for.

Bridget, working over a wad of chocolate, studied the globe sitting on the desk beside her. This whole thing was starting to bore her. She plunked one finger down in the Pacific Ocean near the Oregon coastline, then pointed to the waters off Cuba's southern shore. "Cienfuegos," she read the tiny print on the globe through a buildup of chocolate saliva.

"That's amazing," said the man in the uniform.

"Don't speak with your mouth full," said her mother.

* * *

For the next six days, Bridget Jones was the most powerful weapon in the United States military's arsenal. She located and described dozens of enemy positions around the world, many of them previously unknown. The girl loved being the center of attention, and she worked for peanuts—literally. Because of her penchant for prevaricating, each morning began with a series of new test questions. The researchers would ask her to remote-visualize locations they knew she had never visited, such as the Statue of Liberty, then ask her to count the windows in the observation deck. On the morning of her seventh day in Arlington, when asked about the leaning tower of Pisa, she answered that it was three stories tall. When asked what color socks the interviewer was wearing, she tried to sneak a look under the table. The experiment with the Zener cards was repeated. Her score was five out of twenty-five, the statistical average. Although she protested, it appeared that she had lost her powers. This seemed to be confirmed when Agent Kepnik came into the room holding a clear plastic evidence bag. A search of the young lady's morning stool had turned up a small metallic object.

Confronted with this evidence, Bridget told the truth. Her powers had deserted her. The BB, she said, looked different than it had when she swallowed it: it was half the size and was now completely bald, the fuzz of small bristles having apparently been eaten away by her digestive fluids. "So what happens to me now?"

There was a period of waiting while the proper officials reviewed the case. Eventually, they decided to follow a little-known government protocol, MJ—1949-04W/82. The family was relocated to an undisclosed location in France, where they were housed in a luxury villa owned by friends of the U.S. government and guaranteed an income of approximately $100,000 per year in exchange for their cooperation in keeping the matter silent.

Unfortunately, six months after moving to France, just as she was learning the language, Bridget and her family were killed when their car collided with a truck owned by the French postal authority.

Until he came to the ending, Okun found the story amusing. Remembering Dr. Lenel's warning, he wondered how much of it was true. But more interesting to him than the story of the girl, were the handwritten notes jotted in the margins of the report. They seemed to have been written at great speed and most of them were absolutely illegible. Only two were carefully printed, and both of them startled the young researcher. The first one read: "obj housed at AF Acad Colo Sprgs, evid #PE—8323-MJ—1949-acc21,21a." Evidence number? Okun wondered if there really were, somewhere in a warehouse at the Air Force Academy, a small plastic bag holding a metallic pea recovered from the excrement of a bratty twelve-year-old.

The other piece of noteworthy marginalia was a doodled picture. On the last page of the report, someone had drawn a three-dimensional figure of the letter Y.

6

ROSWELL

Every time Okun had tried to discuss the mysterious and troubling image of the Y, the scientists—normally so talkative, so eager to kick around ideas—would merely shrug their shoulders, agree it was very interesting, then go on to say they had no idea what to do with the information. After that, they changed the subject as quickly as possible. Up to that point, Okun had let them get away with it. But now that he'd seen the same image penciled into the margin of the Bridget Jones report, he was ready for a confrontation. His intuition told him the old men were hiding something, and he was determined to find out what it was.

The next morning, he came into the kitchen and found Freiling counting money. Vegas had been kind to them once more, this time to the tune of $675. Dworkin was studying a copy of the *Los Angeles Times* he'd picked up in town.

"Ahem." The young man cleared his throat. "Where's Radecker?"

"Working on his tennis game, I suspect. He didn't come back last night."

"Then we can talk."

Dworkin peered over the top of his newspaper. "Talk?"

"You guys are holding out on me. There's something you're not telling me."

Dworkin feigned indignation. He began to rattle on about the ethics men of ideas must adhere to, but Okun cut him short by tossing the Jones report onto the table.

"What's this?" Dworkin asked.

"Something I found in the stacks. It's about a girl who swallowed an object she found in the grass after a close encounter with a UFO." Dworkin thumbed through the pages. He seemed more interested in the handwritten notes than in the report itself. Noticing this, Okun asked if he recognized the handwriting. After a moment of beard-stroking indecision, the old man admitted that he did.

"This seems to be the chaotic penmanship of our dear friend Dr. Wells. Have I told you the interesting story of how he came to be named Director of Research for this project?"

Okun wasn't going to let himself be sidetracked again. "Check the last page."

Sensing he would find something unpleasant there, Dworkin reluctantly obliged. The sight of the block-perspective sketch of the Y seemed to startle him slightly. His mind scrambled to find a cover story. If only his long-haired coinvestigator had confronted him with this evidence during a poker game! In that situation, Dworkin was a different man, capable of saying whatever the situation required. He would have been able to make something up on the spot. But in matters of work, he was accustomed to always speaking the truth. He crumpled toward the tabletop like a house of cards under Okun's stern glare.

"Brickman, some stones are better left unturned," Freiling broke in. "None of us knows anything about that darn Y message."

But it was too late to back out now, and Dworkin knew it. He braced himself with a sip of tea, then explained. "Dr. Wells had a long obsession with this form, this shape. He claimed it was communicated to him by the alien shortly after the crash at Roswell. Like you, he said there was a feeling of urgent desperation associated with the transmission of the image. I believe you used the words 'doom' and 'abandoned' to describe it. In his last years he became more and more obsessed with deciphering the meaning of the symbol, until it got to the point of blocking out other thoughts. It drove him to insanity. As this mania progressed, he neglected more and more of his duties as director. We were able to mask the situation for several months, hoping he would make a recovery, but then he was called away to meetings in Washington. Apparently he behaved himself quite poorly and was not allowed to return to Area 51."

"Poor dude."

"Yes, indeed. The disintegration of his personality was a difficult thing to watch."

"Let's be honest," Freiling said. "The man was loopy to begin with. Slightly off-kilter."

"So what did he figure out about the Y?"

"Nothing."

"Nothing?" Okun asked, suspicious again. "He must have made *some* progress on it if he worked for years. Didn't he even have a theory?"

With a worried look on his face, the old man finally came completely clean. "Wells suspected a second ship. He believed that the Y was a signal, the alien equivalent of our SOS. There! Now you know."

Okun nodded with satisfaction. Once more, his gut instincts had proved to be correct—or, at least, he wasn't completely alone in having them. Someone else had arrived independently at the same conclusion, even if that someone was a mental case. There had to be a second ship.

"But Mr. Okun, I must ask you in the strongest possible terms to keep this information secret, especially from Mr. Radecker. As unsavory as this might sound, I promised him I wouldn't tell you."

"We all did," Freiling added. "If we didn't, he

threatened to tell his bosses about the extra paychecks we've been collecting. Next thing you know, we'd all be doing twenty years at Leavenworth."

Without endorsing that last comment, Dworkin admitted, "Mr. Radecker has found our soft spot. None of us wants to leave Area 51 at this late date. I hope you can understand that."

Again, Okun's head bobbed up and down. He knew how scared the old men were and realized he'd never be able to betray them. Still, thinking ahead to his next encounter with Radecker, he could feel the urge to lay the whole matter on the table. "Why doesn't Radecker want me to know about the stupid Y?"

"We made a deal with him. We're not to give you any information which might support your theory of a second ship. In fact, we're supposed to try and talk you out of it."

"But why?"

Freiling and Dworkin shrugged their shoulders simultaneously. "That's all the man wanted, so we agreed."

"It's especially curious," Dworkin added, "when you consider that there really *isn't* much evidence to support such a theory. It's rather far-fetched in light of the accumulated evidence."

Okun narrowed his eyes. "Are you trying to talk me out of it?"

"Don't take my word for it. Ask Dr. Wells."

"What the hell are you doing in here?" Radecker asked, poking his head into the vault.

Okun responded with his Bela Lugosi imitation. "I have come to the crypt to visit my long-lost friends." He had developed a morbid fascination with the alien bodies and came into the secured room every couple of days to watch them floating in their tanks. "It's like having an aquarium full of really strange dead fish."

"Well, I've got the information you wanted. If you want to hear it, come outside. This place gives me the creeps."

Okun stepped into the hallway and fastened the thick steel dead bolt, locking the bodies inside. He'd asked Radecker for help in finding the whereabouts of Dr. Wells. None of the scientists knew what had become of him after he failed to return from his trip to the capital. There had been a phone call from Dr. Insolo of the Science and Technology Directorate saying that Wells was being held for psychiatric observation and that Dr. Dworkin should take over his responsibilities as director during the interim. That had been four years ago.

"The good news is I found a copy of the report you asked for, the one Wells wrote in '47. That should be interesting. It's in Washington, but they're going to send us a copy. The bad news is he's dead." Radecker feigned disappointment. "The story I got from headquarters was he was in a meeting back in DC when he snapped. Just went berserk. Started shouting and throwing things at people. They took him to Seabury Psychiatric Hospital, where he was diagnosed as schizophrenic. Then about six months later, he was transferred to Glenhaven Home in Richmond. That's where he died about two and a half years ago."

Masking a wave of authentic disappointment, Okun shrugged. "No biggie. Thanks for checking it out."

"Just doing my job. I'll tell you when the report comes in."

Brackish smiled pleasantly until Radecker disappeared around the corner. Then he kicked the wall and used language his mother wouldn't have approved of. He was sure Wells, demented or not, could have given him information about other ships. He had already imagined the scene a dozen times: him walking down the deserted institutional corridors with all the windows heavily barred, a pair of bodybuilder orderlies unlocking a heavy steel door and pulling it open to reveal the insane scientist, hair standing on end as if he'd recently been struck by lightning, eyes bulging wide as he struggled to escape from his straitjacket. Oh, well. Lenel had warned him about promising trails suddenly going cold. After a moment of consideration, he realized he had no other choice: he headed back to the stacks.

This time, he was looking for something in particular. And even with Freiling's help, it took the next twenty-four hours to find it. Realizing it would take the rest of his life to read through the anarchic accumulation of archives in the stacks, Okun needed to limit the scope of his search. There had to be a way of separating the genuine reports from the rest. He had no idea how to do it, but reasoned that the logical place to begin would be with the one alien encounter he knew for sure had taken place: the one at Roswell.

The incident actually began two days before the crash. On July 2, 1947, radar screens scanning the skies above the White Sands Proving Grounds in New Mexico picked up an unsteady blip wandering back and forth. It appeared to pulse larger, then smaller, every few seconds, and the crew in the tracking room suspected an equipment malfunction. They called two other facilities, one in Albuquerque, the other in Roswell, and asked if they could confirm the sighting. Within hours, they had. There was no doubt that something was up there. All three tracking stations went on alert as Intelligence Officer Ian Leigh boarded a plane in Washington, DC. If the same phenomenon had occurred in another part of the state, there would have been less concern. But White Sands was a highly restricted area. Besides the secret rocket and missile tests being conducted there, White Sands had been the site, a couple of years before, of the world's first nuclear explosion. The Manhattan Project, led by Robert Oppenheimer, had caused a "controlled detonation" near Alamogordo in a quiet valley once called Jornada de los Muertos, or Trek of the Dead.

On the Fourth of July, the blip returned at approximately ten-thirty. This time it didn't wander across the radar screen; it tore across. According to those most familiar with the tracking technology, it reached speeds of better than a thousand miles per hour. What made these speeds all the more amazing was that the plane— or whatever it was—seemed to accelerate, then come to a dead stop, then accelerate again, racing helter-skelter over the southeastern part of the state. At 11:20, the blip flared into a wide splotch of light and vanished from the screens. After communication between the various tracking stations, they decided the ship had gone down somewhere north of Roswell. The search began at dawn.

Caesar "Corky" Riddle slammed the door of his pickup and started the engine. He was frustrated, more frustrated than his kids were, and now all of them were soaking wet. For a month, he'd been promising his three daughters a big fireworks show on the Fourth. He'd driven all the way to Albuquerque and spent a fortune at the Red Devil stand. Then he'd put up with the girls' impatience all day, telling them to wait until dark. But by the time evening began to fall over the desert, a storm had blown in. Thirty- and forty-mile-per-hour winds were gusting, pushing a thunderstorm up from the Gulf of Mexico. The Riddle family gathered on their front porch and watched the situation grow worse. Finally, about ten-thirty, the winds died down. The girls wanted to light the fireworks out on the road in front of the house, but Corky insisted on sticking to the original plan. So they piled into the truck and raced toward the park in downtown Roswell. As long as they had all that gunpowder, Corky figured, they ought to put on a show for the whole town. But at nearly 11 P.M. on a stormy night, the streets were deserted, and the park was empty. As soon as they were ready to start lighting fuses, the winds picked up again, knocking the blast cones on their sides. They kept at it anyhow, trying various ways of anchoring them to the ground. Then the rain came out of nowhere—it poured down in sheets—drenching the Riddles and their stockpile of fireworks.

They rode home in silence, driving north along 268. A bright flash behind the truck cast shadows of the family across the dashboard. Corky assumed it was another flash of lightning, but then a bright streak came over the top of the truck and shot away into the distance. A bright sizzle of white light, tearing through the night like a meteor. But it wasn't like any meteor they'd ever seen. For one thing, it wasn't falling. It was traveling parallel to the ground. And instead of a smooth stroke of light, this one was scattering blue-and-green energy. It reminded Corky of the shower of sparks created by a welder's torch. As it sank behind the hills and disappeared from view, he pulled onto the shoulder of the road and told the girls to stay inside. He got out and climbed onto the front bumper, expecting whatever it was to explode on impact. He cupped his hands behind his ears and waited. But everything stayed quiet.

He climbed back inside feeling a little better. His fireworks show had turned out to be a disaster, but at least they'd seen something unusual. The girls were excited again. They said it was God playing with a sparkler and talked about it all the way home.

Grant Weston had spent the afternoon hunting for fossils. He was the leader of a group of seven archaeologists, vertebrate paleontologists to be exact, who had hiked into the desert and set up camp for the three-day holiday weekend. The sudden rain had nearly extinguished their campfire, and he was adding dry kindling to it when the sky lit up above his head. He looked up and watched the hissing fireball flash past. A few seconds after it disappeared behind the trees, the group heard two crashing noises in quick succession. The first was a hollow thud, while the second was a sharp echoing crack.

"What the hell was that?" everyone wanted to know.

One of the graduate students initiated a brief panic by proclaiming they had just witnessed the crash of a flying saucer. But Weston proposed a more plausible theory. Familiar with that part of New Mexico, he explained that nearby Roswell Field was a testing site for the Army's new and experimental aircraft. Residents of the area, he said, had grown accustomed to seeing strange-looking planes in the sky. That calmed the nerves of his fellow campers. They discussed setting out immediately to look for the wreckage, but decided it was too dangerous. Judging from the trajectory of the streaking light and the sound of the crash, they estimated the craft had gone down about five miles north of their location. The moon was new, and the terrain could be treacherous even in daylight. There was nothing they could do until daybreak.

In all probability, Weston knew, there would be no survivors. But all night the possibility of a wounded survivor tangled in the wreckage haunted him. He couldn't sleep, and he wasn't the only one. Well before dawn, the archaeologists were sipping coffee, waiting for first light. They had packed up the first-aid kit and enough food and water for the day. As soon as they could see the edges of their campsite, they set out.

Progress was slow. The land was a mixture of rock, loose sand, and thorny scrub. Flash floods had cut steep ravines between the rolling hills, forcing the group to double back and find a new path every few minutes. About the time the sun began to rise, they noticed a spotter plane searching the area, a welcome sign. Within half an hour, the plane was circling over a spot about a mile east of them.

"They must have found the crash site," Weston reasoned. "Let's head in that direction."

A set of steep hills separated them from where the plane was circling. They followed a path between two peaks and came into an arroyo. A few hundred yards to their left, they noticed the tail of the craft. As they moved farther into the dry riverbed, the archaeologists, who had spent their lives studying earth's ancient past, stepped forward to meet its future.

"That doesn't look like an Army plane to me, experimental or not."

"It looks like a fat airplane without any wings."

Skilled in the reconstruction of events, Weston deduced what had happened the night before. "See those flattened bushes on the crest of that ridge? The plane must have bottomed out there—that was the thud we heard—and then bounced up and come down here." The black, roughly circular ship had plowed nose first into a sheer cliff. For the amount of rock it had shattered, Weston was surprised it wasn't in worse shape. He headed up the incline for a closer look.

When Betty Kagayama saw what he meant to do, she yelled after him. "Grant, what are you doing? Please don't go near it! Let's wait for help." She and Professor Weston had developed a relationship that was something more than platonic. "I don't care what you say; that thing isn't from earth."

"I've got to check to see if anyone's still alive. Here, take this." He handed her his field camera. "I'll climb up there and pose like a big-game hunter. We'll laugh about it later." Over Betty's protests, he jogged up the hill.

As he got closer, he knew she was right. The black ship hadn't been built by humans. He stopped a few feet from the tail section and examined the small markings cut into the surface. "Looks like hieroglyphics," he called down the slope. There was a hole torn open along the side of the ship. He squatted down and looked up into it. "Hello? Anybody in there?" He could see sunlight on the interior walls of the vessel. He considered squeezing through the gap, but the foul, acrid smell coming out of it drove him away. He walked around to the front of the ship and saw there were windows. To get to them, he began clambering up the pile of debris caused by the crash.

"Grant, someone's coming! Over there."

He looked in the direction Betty was pointing. Two black sedans followed by a dozen military trucks were cutting cross-country toward the site. He started to come back down the slope, but curiosity got the better of him. He knew how the military was. They'd shoo him away, and he'd never get to see what was inside. So he climbed high enough onto the slope so that he could step onto the edge of the disk-shaped craft, then carefully walked across the surface and peered in the windows. A pair of blunt, bony faces was staring back at him through the window. They looked like large death masks fashioned out of living tissue, gristle, and tendon. Horrified and repulsed, Weston fell backwards off the ship, then ran down the slope. Before he had rejoined the group, the first black sedan pulled up. The man who stepped out introduced himself as Special Agent Ian Leigh.

He talked with the archaeologists for a moment. He asked Professor Weston to sit in the sedan and directed the others to wait in a group off to the side. He then jogged back to the head of the military convoy and called a huddle with the commanding officers. One of them asked if he should take the civilians into custody.

"They seem like a cooperative group. We'll worry about them later. Right now our problem is these soldiers; they've already seen too much." The group turned and noticed six troop transport vehicles, each one loaded to the brim with gawking enlisted men. Like everyone else, they were transfixed by the sight of the wreckage. Leigh thought for a minute before coming up with a plan. "Here's what we'll do. We'll use these men to establish a cordon. Nobody comes in or out without my approval. Tell the men to walk back out of this ravine the same way we drove in. Put four or five guys up on the cliff above the ship and fan the rest of them out in a circle. Make sure they're far enough away to where they can't see what's going on."

"Why don't we just have them turn their backs?"

"Good idea. As soon as they're in position, you guys drive the trucks down close to the wreck, and we'll use them to create a screen. OK, get busy." Leigh moved around the crash site with impressive efficiency. It was as if he'd done all of this before. "Steiger, let's go; this is your big moment, kid. You're elected to be our welcoming committee," he called across the gravel to one of the men he'd brought in from DC. "Put on that protective gear. You're going in first." Steiger, a rail-thin man who stood well over six feet, popped open the trunk of the first sedan. A minute later, covered head to toe in a rubbery, lead-lined suit, he was moving toward the fallen spacecraft. He carried a Geiger counter. He moved around the outside of the ship for several minutes, sampling radiation levels, and found nothing abnormal. Very carefully, he approached the breach in the wall and reached in with the Geiger counter. Finding all levels normal again, he poked his head through the gap and cautiously climbed inside.

A few hours later, the work was finished. Every square inch of the impact area had been carefully photographed.

The three large bodies found inside had been sealed in lead-lined body bags, lowered through the opening, and piled into the back of an ambulance, which took them to the base hospital. After a loading crane had hoisted the ship onto the back of a flatbed truck, it was buried under a collection of tarps and poles meant to disguise the vehicle's shape. Before turning the archaeologists loose, Leigh had sworn them to secrecy. He reminded them that they were the only ones outside the military who knew about the ship, and he had cataloged a short list of accidents that might befall anyone who broke the silence. The next morning he would return to the site with a hundred soldiers, MPs with reputations for being able to keep their mouths shut gathered from six different bases across three states. After cleaning the area once by hand, they used industrial vacuum cleaners to remove every last shred of evidence. At that point, Leigh was convinced he had succeeded in making the whole situation disappear.

But that same morning, a man walked into the Chaves County Sheriff's Headquarters carrying a crate full of a strange, lightweight material he'd found scattered over a large area of his ranch. His name was Mac Brazel. He was one of those leather-skinned, scuffed-up cowboys who eked out a living by keeping cattle and sheep herds up in the hardscrabble mountains.

On the night of July 4, he'd heard a loud crashing sound, one that didn't sound like thunder. He'd forgotten about it completely until he found the field of shiny material. Initially he seemed angry. His sheep wouldn't go near the stuff and he wanted to know who was going to come out there and clean it up. But then he asked if his discovery might lead to him collecting some of the reward money that magazines had been offering to anyone who could prove the existence of flying saucers.

Until he arrived at the sheriff's office, he'd heard none of the rumors concerning the craft that had gone down north of town.

The sheriff, George Wilcox, came out of his office and examined the material. It was unlike anything he'd seen before. It seemed to be some kind of metal. Although it was as light as balsa wood, none of the men in the office could bend it. They tried hammering on it with a stapler and burning it with their lighters, all to no avail.

Wilcox was angry with the way the Army had pushed him out of the investigation of the crashed ship, refusing him access to the site. Nevertheless, he called Roswell Field to report Brazel's find. He spoke with Major Jesse Marcel, who said he'd come into town right away. Thinking the Army would shunt him aside once more, Wilcox dispatched two of his deputies to the Brazel ranch to look for the debris field. As soon as they left, the phone rang. It was Walt Wasserman, the owner of local radio station KGFL, calling to see if there had been any new developments in the investigation of the crash. Wilcox put Brazel on the phone and, after the two men talked for several minutes, Wasserman was given directions to the rancher's home.

Major Marcel arrived with a plainclothes counterintelligence officer, Sheridan Cavitt. After they had inspected the debris that Mac Brazel had brought to town, they instructed Sheriff Wilcox to lock it in a secure office, then made plans to follow Brazel out to his ranch. Moments after they left, the two deputies returned from the ranch. Instead of finding the field of debris, they'd come across a large circular burn mark in the grass. It was their opinion that something hot had landed in the spot, scorching the grass and baking the earth to a hard clay beneath it. They had come back to get a camera before it got dark.

Brazel led the two military officers, each of them driving

separate vehicles, across his rocky property to a wide-open Held of sand and knee-high dead grass. They were about twelve miles from the site of the downed saucer. Scattered over an area three-quarters of a mile long and two hundred feet wide, were thousands of pieces of the mysterious lightweight material. Most of them were very small, the size of a fingernail and just as thin; others were almost three feet long. After a short examination of the site, the officers agreed with Brazel that "something had exploded in the air while flying south by southeast." Brazel left when the sun began to set, telling the men that he had agreed to give an interview to KGFL. Cavitt and Marcel loaded their cars with as much of the debris as they could pack up before darkness fell. Cavitt drove straight back to the base, but Marcel was so impressed with the strange material, he stopped at his house to show it to his wife and son.

That night, station-owner Wasserman drove out to the Brazel property, picked him up, and drove him into town, where they made a recording of the rancher's story. By the time they were finished, the station was ready to sign off for the night. So they scheduled it for the next afternoon.

But the recording would never be aired. Much to Wasserman's surprise, he got an early-morning phone call from the Federal Communications Commission. He was ordered not to broadcast the interview. "If you do," the man warned, "you'd better start looking for another line of work because you'll be out of the radio business permanently within twenty-four hours."

Wasserman tried to get in touch with Brazel but learned a squad of soldiers had come to his house in the middle of the night and taken him somewhere.

Marcel spent about an hour at home. He brought in one of the boxes he'd filled that afternoon and spread the contents out on the kitchen floor. The family tried to fit the pieces together, but had no luck. They experimented with pliers, attempting to bend the paper-thin substance out of shape. They realized that there was more than one kind of material. While most of it was amazingly rigid, other pieces could be folded easily between their fingers. Whichever way this second material was folded or bent, it retained the shape.

"Look at this one, it has signs on it," Jesse, Jr., said.

His mother said the writing looked like hieroglyphics. The piece in question looked like a very small I-beam. It was about four inches long and appeared undamaged. The writing was a dull purple color etched onto the gray surface of the beam. Eleven-year-old Jesse, Jr., had seen hieroglyphs in schoolbooks, and knew these were different. They were geometric shapes, including circles and one pattern that looked like a leaf. The family couldn't tell if the images were meant to be read; they were evenly spaced up and down the flat surfaces of the beam.

The son asked the father if he could keep some of the pieces as souvenirs. Marcel said he would ask his commanding officer about it, but that night he made sure all the pieces were put back in the box, which he then delivered to the base.

The next morning, First Lieutenant Walter Haut, the information officer for the 509th Bomb Group, held a series of discussions with people who had information concerning the strange goings-on. He learned from Marcel about the debris scattered around Brazel's ranch and spoke with a few of the soldiers who had been out to the site of the crashed ship. Haut had received hundreds of telegrams and phone calls from all over the country asking him to confirm or deny the rumors coming out of the area. After gathering what he felt was a sufficient amount of information, he sat down at his typewriter and composed a brief, not very accurate press release. He then drove into town to deliver it. His first stop was KGFL. Not wanting to be hounded with a lot of questions he didn't have answers for, he handed a copy of the statement to the receptionist and slipped out the door while she was reading through it. He did the same thing at KSWS, the town's other radio station. Next, he drove to the newspaper offices of the *Roswell Daily Record*, stopping to chat with one of the reporters for a few minutes. By the time he came to his final stop, the *Roswell Morning Dispatch*, their phones had already started ringing off the hooks. As soon as the story had gone out on the wire, news editors from all forty-eight states had picked up their phones to confirm the story. While Haut was standing in the office, a call came in from Hong Kong. He didn't even know where Hong Kong was. There was certainly more interest in the story than he had anticipated. It was about noon, so he walked down the street to a hamburger stand and had lunch by himself, an extra copy of the press release sitting on the counter soaking up water and grease:

Roswell, N.M.—The many rumors regarding flying disks became a reality yesterday when the Intelligence Office of the 509th Bomb Group of the Eighth Air Force, Roswell Air Field, was fortunate enough to gain possession of a crashed flying object of extraterrestrial origin through the cooperation of one of the local ranchers and the sheriff's office of Chaves County.

Action was taken immediately and the disk was picked up at the rancher's home and taken to the Roswell Air Base. Following examination by Major Jesse A. Marcel of the 509th Intelligence Office, the disk was flown by intelligence officers in a B-29 superfortress to an undisclosed "Higher Headquarters."

Residents near the ranch on which the disk was found reported seeing a strange blue light several days ago about three o'clock in the morning.

J. Bond Johnson was a reporter and photographer for the *Fort Worth Star-Telegram*. At four o'clock, he was on the phone researching a local political story when his editor walked in, took the receiver away from him, and calmly put it in the cradle. He'd been on the phone himself and had arranged for Johnson to get in on something more interesting. "If it pans out," the editor said, "it'll be the story of the century." He told Johnson about the press release from Roswell, which had been dominating the wire services all afternoon. He'd been trying to get through to Roswell, but all the lines were jammed. Then, out of the blue, he'd gotten a call from General Ramey's office. They were bringing the saucer from New Mexico to the Fort Worth Army Air Field. He told Johnson to grab his camera and get over there before Ramey called anyone else.

Thirty minutes later, Johnson pulled up to the front gates, expecting to check in with the Public Affairs Liaison. To his surprise, the guard directed him straight to Ramey's office. He was shown in immediately. Laid out on the floor were big sheets of butcher paper upon which rested a gnarled combination of rubber, steel cable, balsa wood, and something that looked like dirty aluminum foil.

"This is what all the damn excitement's about," Ramey said, shaking his head. "There's nothing to it. It's a rawin high-altitude sounding device. I must have seen a dozen of these in the Pacific. The Japanese launched them all the time from Okinawa. My instructions were to examine it, then send it on to Wright Field. But the minute I laid eyes on it I knew what it was, and now I'm not going to bother." The general was, however, quite anxious to put a stop to the rumors about spaceships and men from the moon. He had Johnson snap a dozen photos of the balloon, then sent him speeding back to the office to develop them.

At one minute before midnight, one of Johnson's photos was sent out on the Associated Press news wire. The caption read: "Brigadier General Roger M. Ramey, Commanding General of the 8th Air Force, identifies metallic fragments found near Roswell N. Mex. as a rawin high-altitude sounding device used by air force and weather bureau to determine wind velocity and direction and not a flying disk. Photo by J. Bond Johnson."

The next morning, the story was dead. Newspapers across the country and many overseas ran tongue-in-cheek articles about Major Marcel, who had apparently leaped to cosmic conclusions. None of the writers bothered to learn that the major had previously been assigned to a meteorology station and had extensive familiarity with both weather balloons and high-atmosphere balloon bombs. Marcel was angry and humiliated.

But Ramey wasn't done with him yet. He ordered the major to fly to Fort Worth, which he did he following day. Before he came, he stopped by the sheriff's office and retrieved a few pieces of the debris still locked up there. Marcel brought the fragments into Ramey's office and demonstrated some of the material's exotic properties. The only logical conclusion, as far as Marcel was concerned, was that the stuff had not come from earth The men left the material behind as they went to a map room to try and pinpoint the exact location of the craft. When they returned, the material was gone. Instead, a ruined weather balloon had been brought in and laid out on the floor. On the general's orders, Marcel knelt beside the balloon to have his picture taken. Then, a few hours later, a dozen reporters were invited into the office for a good look at the "flying disk" Marcel had discovered. The newsmen wanted to ask the major questions, but Ramey had given him strict orders not to utter a single word. He was going to be the goat, the overexcitable idiot who had caused all this fuss, and Ramey was going to play the role of his benevolent commanding officer, speaking to the reporters on his behalf to spare him any further embarrassment.

Back in Roswell, Mac Brazel was also speaking to the press. A few of the local newspeople had gathered outside KGFL's audio room to watch Wasserman interview the craggy old rancher. An unmarked car with two intelligence officers inside had dropped him off and was waiting to take him away as soon as the interview was completed. Mac had spent the last two days in a guesthouse on the Army base. During that time, a large group of MPs had invaded his ranch, allowing no one to enter the property. Before they were ordered away at gunpoint, his neighbors had caught glimpses of soldiers working on hands and knees in the debris field.

Brazel told Wasserman a different story than he had during their first interview. He had been out inspecting his herds with his wife and son when he had come across the debris, he said. It was scattered over an area of about two hundred feet and seemed to be composed mainly of a rubbery gray material. Smaller pieces of heavy-duty tinfoil were strewn around the central hunk of the wreckage. He had noticed pieces of Scotch tape attached to it, as well as tape of another sort with little flowers on it.

He spoke softly the whole time and kept his eyes anchored to the ground. Before he was finished, Wasserman switched off the microphone. "This is all a load of bull, Mac, and you know it. These Army guys got you to change your story, didn't they?" Wasserman continued to pester Brazel for an explanation as he headed back outside. When they were out of earshot of the others, Brazel pleaded with the man, whispering, "Don't make me talk about it. It'll go hard on me and my family."

He got back in the car with the intelligence officers and drove away. He refused to speak of the matter ever again— not with Marcel, not with Wilcox, not even with his wife.

7

INTERVIEW WITH AN ALIEN

One morning about a week after starting his Roswell research, Okun stumbled out of bed at about eight o'clock. He was trying to remember his dream. It had something to do with him being a roadie for Frank Zappa and having to chase a grizzly bear away from the backstage area during a concert out in the forest. He had repeatedly yelled at the animal that it didn't have a pass. Without a pass it could not go backstage and would have to move away.

He put on the robe and slippers the other scientists had given him, unlocked the door, and started off toward the bathroom when he stepped on something lying outside his door. It was a thick yellow envelope which had been sealed with masking tape. He knew what it must be and tossed it on his bed. About twenty minutes later, he returned with a cup of coffee and tore the package open. He was right. It was the report Wells had written immediately after his so-called conversation with the creature from outer space.

On the night of July 5, 1947, Colonel William Blanchard phoned the Los Alamos Laboratories and asked to speak with Dr. Robert Oppenheimer, head of the Manhattan Project. He said it was an emergency situation with implications for the national security of the United States. Immanuel Wells, the midlevel scientist who had answered the phone, heard the urgency in the colonel's voice, but explained that all of the senior staff were traveling and could not be reached.

Blanchard was desperate to get some "scientific backup" and ended up telling Wells that three bodies had been recovered from a crashed airship. Wells asked what made that a special situation. After a moment of hesitation, Blanchard told him the ship was of extraterrestrial origin and the bodies were unlike anything his medical staff had ever seen. He and the examining doctors both wanted as much help as they could get without going outside New Mexico's large population of high-level security-cleared personnel. Wells left immediately, arriving at Roswell Field's small base hospital about nine in the evening, a few hours after the three bodies had been delivered from the crash site. Soldiers posted outside informed him the entire building was under a Stage Four Quarantine. If he chose to enter, he would not be allowed out until the base commander lifted the order. Wells didn't hesitate for a second. He knew he had been presented with a rare opportunity and was determined to get a look at these cadavers from outer space.

Inside, the lobby was deserted except for a handful of soldiers and a distraught nurse. When Wells walked up and put a hand on her shoulder, she jumped halfway out of her skin. Something had shaken her up pretty badly. She told him everyone had gone into the observation area because the doctors were just beginning the autopsy on the first "eebie." She had just come from another room, where she was helping prepare the other two bodies to be embalmed and airlifted away, but the sight of them had been too much for her, and she'd come into the lobby to get some air. When Wells asked what an "eebie" was, she explained it stood for EBE or Extraterrestrial Biological Entity.

The observation area was a darkened, L-shaped corridor with windows looking into the hospital's primary operating room. Wells could see the medical team hovering around a bulky shape lying on the table. At first glance, it looked like something dredged up from the depths of the ocean: an enormous clamshell surrounded by a mop of limp tentacles. Wells paced the length of the enclosure and studied the cadaver behind the glass partition. He soon became impressed with how similar, morphologically speaking, the creature was to humans. It was seven or eight feet tall and looked as if it might be capable of standing erect. The majority of its weight was contained in a very large head-chest region, which, even at close range, with its flared design and scalloped ridges, reminded him of a mollusk shell. This main shell was composed of two symmetrical halves which came together at the front, so that the seam between them created a long scar running from the crest of the head, down the center of the face, all the way to the pointed, coccyx-like projection at the bottom of the chest. The face itself was nothing more than a blunt slab of bone and ligament, with four short feeler-tentacles hanging off the sides. The eyes were hidden deep in narrow black sockets that looked like long gashes chopped into the surface of a rock. The creature could not be laid on its back owing to the presence of six rounded appendages, eight-foot-long tentacles, which sprouted from the back of the shell in the area of the shoulder blades. In contrast to the rigid exoskeleton, which protected the rest of the body, these long tentacles looked soft and pulpy, like thick ropes of flesh.

It was a menacing sight to behold. Apart from the obvious fact that it was unlike any creature found on earth, it appeared that it might also be *stronger* than any creature on earth. Though slender, its limbs showed a highly developed musculature. Even the muscles in its foot-long hands were visibly well defined. If the thing had lived and had proved to be hostile, Wells thought, it would have made a formidable opponent—especially in a forest or a jungle environment where its profusion of limbs would allow it to climb with ease.

The autopsy was conducted by Army surgeon Dr. Daniel Solomon and three assistants. His first step was to drag a large scalpel down the long seam connecting the halves of the skull, slicing into the cartilage tissue which filled the gap. When the incision was complete, efforts were made to pry open the large shell. This took some time and was finally accomplished by driving a large spike into the crevice. Piercing ammonium fumes poured into the air out of the head-chest cavity, forcing the medical team to back away from the body, their eyes watering. When the air cleared enough for work to resume, the four men positioned themselves on either side of the creature, twisted the snout toward the ceiling, then pulled hard in opposite directions. The shell cracked open, and Solomon's team made a gruesome discovery. Where they had expected to find the creature's entrails, they found instead another being, fully formed, tucked inside under a thick membrane of clear gel. The soldiers posted inside the operating room took aim at the ghoulish, glistening biomass. When it showed no signs of life, Solomon gathered his courage to come forward again. He reached in and prodded the figure with the blunt end of his scalpel several times. Eventually, he used a towel to wipe away some of the thick gelatin ooze and examined the thing more closely. He soon determined that it, too, was dead. Unclear whether this was a fully developed embryo or some sort of parasite, the medical technicians carefully lifted the smaller creature out from its hiding place, the gelatinous substance causing a loud slurping smack as it finally pulled free. Two puzzling discoveries were made. First, the smaller alien appeared to be of a completely different species than its host. Second, the larger animal appeared to have been gutted; there was a complete absence of anything the doctors recognized as internal organs.

While they were discussing these new revelations, someone standing near Wells in the observation hall called through the glass to Dr. Solomon, asking about the other two creatures. Immediately, the medical team went to the room where the other bodies were being prepared for shipment. Solomon put a stethoscope against the hard chest of the exoskeleton and, after listening for a moment, looked up and announced, "This one's still alive."

It was during the exhumation of the second alien that Wells became centrally involved. The second exoskeleton remained lifeless as it was lifted onto a gurney and wheeled into the operating room. But when Solomon inserted his scalpel into the seam and began slicing away the ligament holding the skull halves together, the tentacle-arms lifted weakly off the ground and tried to push the doctor away from the table. Suddenly Solomon understood the relationship between the two types of alien beings, explaining to his crew and the onlookers that the EBE inside seemed to be manipulating the larger body, which was being used as a biological suit of armor. Intent on reaching the hidden creature before it died, he called for help from the observation gallery. He wanted volunteers to restrain the extremities while he split open the torso. Wells was among the volunteers. He was given a pair of gloves and assigned the task of holding a tentacle against the tabletop. He grasped the serpentine appendage in two places, sinking his fingers deeply into its spongy flesh. As Solomon resumed work with his scalpel, Wells could feel the thing writhing weakly beneath his hands—a sensation which caused him to grow increasingly light-headed. He was on the verge of fainting when the ammonia vapors lifted into the room and momentarily cleared his head.

The creature inside began to struggle harder. There was a loud sound of cracking bone as the shell was fully retracted. Wells glanced at the tabletop and saw the goo-slathered alien wriggling around the chest cavity of its host animal. He felt his fingers losing their strength and his knees beginning to buckle. Fighting to maintain control, he focused his eyes on the edge of the table and began to hum the first melody that came into his head. Concentrating on his song, he kept himself conscious long enough for the medical crew to begin lifting the smaller body out of the larger one. Taking a deep breath, he raised his eyes to watch this part of the operation.

"Don't stop, keep on humming," Solomon commanded. "It's keeping it calm."

So, the physicist from the atom-bomb project continued to hum. When he heard the slurping noise that signaled the separation of the two animals, he looked up and found himself face-to-face with the goop-slathered body. The creature's enormous eyes, like reflecting pools of mercury, were open and looking straight at him. When a pair of heavy eyelids closed slowly over these quicksilver orbs, Wells felt as if a heavy curtain were being lowered over him as well. The room lost its shape, and he felt himself sinking toward the floor.

He came to the next morning, Dr. Solomon by his side.

"Welcome back. You got a little squeamish on us last night and passed out."

Wells sat up and accepted a cup of coffee, but as he brought it toward his lips, the smell of it struck him as repulsive, and he set it aside.

"I wanted to thank you," Solomon continued. "It was a brilliant idea you had, humming to the eebie like that. I guess music really is the universal language."

"I was just trying not to faint," Wells admitted, "but I'm

glad I could help. Is it still alive?" As quickly as he asked this question, Wells realized he already knew the answer.

"Yes it is, but I don't know how long that will last. We can't figure out how to help it. It's been dropping in and out of consciousness all night. We've offered it food and water, but it hasn't accepted anything yet. We aren't even sure how it eats yet. If it doesn't die from its internal injuries, it's going to starve to death."

"That would be good news, wouldn't it?" Wells asked.

"You're quick." Solomon smiled. Like Wells, he was in his early forties, but looked much older this morning after missing a night of sleep. "The military is overjoyed to hear it won't eat anything. They think it proves the alien can't survive here, but I'm not convinced of that. The thing is badly wounded—of course it has no appetite."

Although Solomon's idea had a great deal of common sense to it, Wells somehow got the idea that it was wrong. He sat staring into space wondering about this idea until Solomon spoke again.

"I'm off to try and get some sleep myself. They're in there questioning the eebie now. You might want to get some breakfast, then go in and watch." With that, he left the room.

Wells dressed himself and went into the lobby. A large buffet table had been set up with food passed through the quarantine perimeter. Although he had not eaten anything for well over twelve hours, he found he was not hungry. In fact, the food smelled rotten and repulsive to him, and he quickly made his way to the observation room in order to escape the odors.

The frail creature lying passively on the operating table was awake. Its eyes were open but turned blankly toward the ceiling. Standing at what they felt was a safe distance, a pair of agents from Army Intelligence were trying everything they could think of to initiate communication with the alien. Wells sat down and watched them work for the next six hours. They asked it questions in several languages, waved their hands, snapped, drew simple pictures on a tablet, then set the writing instruments beside the creature. They played music on a tape machine, then made a whole series of ridiculous noises with their mouths and hands, hoping something would catch the thing's attention and elicit a response. They showed it newly developed photographs of the crashed spaceship but got no reaction. When they had tried everything they could think of, they made way for another team. Wells, still sitting comfortably in the same spot, watched for another six hours as a second set of questioners went through a similar routine and achieved similar results. Eventually people began to notice this man who had not left his chair to use the bathroom, have a drink of water, or merely stretch his legs all day long.

The matter was mentioned to Dr. Solomon, who came into the observation room and took the chair, next to Wells, who barely noticed his arrival.

"Fascinating, isn't it?" Solomon said in reference to the alien. Wells knew why he had come, but said nothing, felt nothing. "Dr. Wells, you've been sitting here an awfully long time. Why don't you come out into the lobby and have something to eat?"

"Not hungry," Wells said matter-of-factly. It reminded the doctor that the EBE still had taken no food or drink. They had offered it lettuce, sugar, milk, bread, sliced peaches, and various meats, both raw and cooked. So far, these offerings had brought the only intelligible reaction from the patient— it had waved them away with a limp hand.

"It won't eat anything," Wells said. "It's made up its mind not to eat anything."

Solomon cast a long sideways glance at his companion. "What does that mean, *made up its mind*?"

"The injuries aren't enough to kill it. It's going to starve itself to death."

"What leads you to that conclusion?"

"I don't know. I just feel it. And the longer I sit here, the more convinced I am." For the first time in half a day, Wells broke his concentration on the alien to look Solomon in the eyes. "I can tell what it's thinking. It could eat the food if it wanted to, it's not a matter of it being poisonous. It wants to eat, but it is forbidden. And these interrogators aren't going to get anywhere. The thing communicates telepathically. You ought to try getting a psychic or a mind reader in here."

"Dr. Wells," Solomon whispered to avoid embarrassing his companion, "all of us are running on jangled nerves in here. Several people have noticed that you've been sitting here for—"

"Wait!" Wells's attention was once more riveted on the EBE. "It recognizes something." Solomon looked through the glass and saw the alien in the same position he'd been in for hours. A man inside the room was holding yet another piece of paper in its line of vision. He was about to go on to the next sheet when the creature lifted an arm and seemed to grasp at the image. The man walked the paper back and forth across the room and the creature turned its head, struggling to keep its eyes on the picture. There was an audible reaction in the observation area. Finally something had worked. The agent turned around and showed them what had caught the alien's attention: a block letter "Y."

Solomon looked toward Wells. "I think it's time we had a chat with Blanchard. Please follow me."

An hour later, Wells went inside the observation room a second time. His clothes were wrinkled, his eyes were red around the rims, and he needed a shave. Without hesitating, he quietly brought a chair across the floor and set it close to the alien's bedside. Unlike the interrogators before him, he took a seat, folded his hands in his lap, and merely sat there.

"Where are you from?" he whispered softly. He wasn't asking a question, just listening to the words. He knew he had to translate them into a language this creature from another galaxy could understand. *Where are you from?* he asked again, trying to push the idea out of his head and into the space separating their bodies. Where are you from? over and over, as if it were a matter of will, a matter of concentrating hard enough to find and flex those mental muscles mind readers must have. His instinct, or whatever was leading him, told him the creature communicated by ESP, which turned out to be pretty close, as close as his earthbound imagination could have taken him.

The creature rolled its head to look at him. Behind the almost-human face, the cranium was a thick, translucent plate extending straight back. Through the walls of the skull, Wells traced the lacy pattern of veins and watched small clots of tissue contract, then release. The way the eyelids closed over the surface of the moist mirror-black eyes, the way it had turned its head, and manipulated its fingers, everything indicated that this exotic creature possessed an intelligence similar to our own.

Wells decided on another approach: He tried sending eidetic imagery or mental pictures. But how to translate the question *Where are you from?* into images? He worked at it for a few minutes but found himself trying to mentally broadcast pictures of stick-figure bodies, simple houses, a question mark. He knew it was wrong, that his logic was too abstract, too human. Then, all at once, it hit him. He knew how to ask the question.

He thought of his own home, the two-story structure he shared with his wife in the hills outside of Santa Fe.

He meditated on this idea for some time, leading the alien on a tour of the house. He concentrated not only on what the place looked like, but also his feelings for it. Exploring his own heart, Wells lingered on the comfort he felt in this place and his strong sense of possession for it. He moved into the living room, empty now but still echoing with the warmth and laughter of visiting friends, and sat down in his favorite chair, remembering the feel of the upholstery under his hands. Without warning, this meditation was ended as his mind was abruptly plunged into a completely new reality. The frail creature on the table took the scientist on a tour of its own.

Even before he recognized that there was no light, he could feel the heat. Blast-furnace heat, the limit of what his body could withstand, came at him from all directions. And it was getting hotter the deeper he went. It was a cave, and he sensed the presence of other bodies moving around him, with him, hundreds of them. They were deep below the surface of a ruined planet, miles deep already, and following the sloped floor of the cave deeper still and closer to the center. This tunnel connected to others, which branched into others. The entire mantle of the planet was perforated by a great system of these caves, from ruined crust to molten core, and was home to billions like him. Long before, they had lived above ground in a lush infinite garden. Now everything was gone, dead, and they lived here. The rocky ground burned his feet, but instead of turning back, the pain only made him increase his speed. Running blind through the dark, he felt the space around him open up and knew they had come into a large cavern. He smelled the walls thick with food, lush carpets of a plant that felt like moss or lichen in his hands as he tore a heavy sheet of it free from the scalding rock wall, then immediately dragged it tugging and stumbling back into the passageway. Up one slope, then another, towing his heavy treasure closer to the surface. When the heat grew less intense, so did his urgency. The number of bodies around him grew, a dense crowd of them swarmed in like piranha from every direction and began ripping into the carpet of lichen. He stopped pulling and joined the fierce scramble, kicking and pushing his way deeper into the orgy until he found an open space and dived toward it, his mouth open wide, and sucked in a mouthful of the still-warm vegetation.

Wells found himself once more looking into the eyes of the visitor. He felt his scalp damp with sweat and his heart pounding. His first impulse was to recoil, to run from the troubling vision he'd been shown. But he fought it down. He could barely believe that the serene and noble creature before him could have come from such a repulsive place. Despite the troubling vision he had just seen, Wells smiled. He had broken through and established communication.

Later, his report to the military staff went poorly. The officers were only mildly interested in what Wells had learned and angry that he hadn't asked the questions they had previously agreed upon. Although the vision of the EBE's home planet might prove to be useful at some future date, it did not address the burning question of *why*. Why had these creatures come to earth and what did they want? To make matters worse, the scientist's behavior during the session was erratic. He rambled in his descriptions, became emotional, and frequently lost his train of thought. This led the soldiers to suspect his trance-vision was nothing more than his own hallucination.

Solomon intervened and explained his suspicion that Wells was suffering from dehydration. He had taken no food or water for almost forty-eight hours. Still, when someone brought him a glass of water, he adamantly refused it. By the end of the thirty-minute meeting, Wells had lost the confidence of those in charge. The decision was made to keep him away from the creature until his mental state improved. Others could use the same techniques to communicate with the EBE.

Others did try. They worked for days, without success.

On the afternoon of the fourth day, as Wells slept in one of the unused rooms, Solomon entered quietly, followed by a team of assistants. Wells bolted out of his sleep, knowing why they had come. Before he could get to his feet, the men grabbed him and pinned him down while Solomon used a hypodermic needle to inject a sedative into his arm. When he woke up twenty hours later, he was in a new room strapped down tight to the bed with a drip IV stuck into his forearm. When Dr. Solomon came in, he found Wells feeling rested and alert. Although he still refused to eat anything, the fluids in his system had brought him back to his senses.

"No one else has had any luck," the doctor told him. "And the creature seems to be getting weaker. If you're feeling up to it, the generals want you to go back inside."

As soon as he stepped inside the glass room, Wells could feel how close to death the alien was. He brought a glass of water to the creature's side and, still struggling to control his own hydrophobia, held it in front of the huge black eyes, mentally imploring the creature to drink.

He felt the thing's response: it was a command to take the liquid away. Wells complied, handing the glass to one of the soldiers behind him. Although he knew the frail body before him needed water, he empathized with its refusal. But the tone of the command was troubling. Wells got the sense of being "spoken to" as an underling, an inferior being, as if the scrawny half-dead form on the table were a delirious lord barking orders to a serf.

Following the script prepared for him, he got down to the business of asking the questions to which the Army needed to know the answers. He queried the creature about why it had come, about the chain of command among its species, about its military capabilities and whether other ships had entered earth's atmosphere. But the only answer Wells received was a vision of something that looked like an enormous Y. Perhaps owing to the visitor's weakened physical state, the vision had none of the power of its previous communication. It was a blurred mental image of a branching structure in the middle of a barren landscape. The blinding light of a sun washed the vision out, causing the scientist to squint. He assumed the place was somewhere on the ruined surface of the planet he had been shown before. He could feel the alien's desire to travel to this place, but that was all the information he could gather. And it wasn't what he was after.

He returned to the question of why the creature and its companions had come to earth. Having found the *window* or *channel* which allowed him to interact with the foreign being, he began to move more quickly, with more confidence. He sensed the alien understood his questions, but was too weak to answer. Wells sat back in his chair and contemplated the possibility that it was too late, that the creature had passed the point of being able to communicate. Although he was quickly learning how to share the creature's thoughts, he couldn't *feel* them with the same intensity he had previously. Then he had another idea, one he wasn't particularly anxious to try out. He looked at the hand resting on the table. It had two plump, opposable fingers, each about six inches in length. The hand was still covered with the piss-smelling goop that lined the chest cavity of the larger, tentacled, exoskeletal suit. Wells drew a deep breath, reached out, and laid his hand over one of the alien's fingers. He squeezed it gently, feeling the resinous substance squish into the gaps between his own fingers. A moment later, the second finger closed around Wells's hand, gripping it with the strength of a small child.

Why have you come here? Who are your leaders? What do you want? The questions traveled through one body and into the other. For two full hours, they sat motionless and in outward silence while the observers behind the glass looked on. Then the creature opened its hand and took it away. Wells whispered something to it, then came out of the room.

"Our friend," as Wells began calling the EBE, was a scientist-explorer, as were the other beings who had died in the crash. They had stumbled upon our planet during what seems to have been a random search through the universe. They somehow picked up energy, possibly radio waves, emanating from earth and came to investigate. One thing had been made perfectly clear—these aliens wished only to observe. They had taken great care to avoid being noticed and, although they did not seem to fear humans, wanted no interaction with them. They seemed to be just as interested in other animals and even plant life. "As a matter of fact," as Wells said, "I got the sense that our good friend found me physically repulsive. It was as strange for it to touch me as it was for me to touch it."

When he'd asked about the alien's social structure and chain of command, he was shown the image of a very tall alien, considerably larger than the others, which was some kind of leader or commander. There was a strong sense of benevolence associated with this tall creature. It was a protector of some sort, although it wasn't clear whom it was protecting. Wells had the most difficulty understanding the creature's reply to his questions about additional ships. He was shown a vision of the sixty-foot craft traveling through deep space. When Wells asked why there were no provisions on board and communicated the military's belief that the ship was only a short-range vehicle, the interview ended.

Hie scientist openly expressed his admiration for the space voyager, discussing the bravery it must have taken to embark upon a dangerous journey of the sort his friend had taken.

That evening Wells was standing in the hospital's lobby chatting with a group of officers. He was trying to describe the physical sensation involved in reading the alien's thoughts when he suddenly broke off in mid-sentence, complaining of dizziness. Reaching out, he grabbed one of the men by the arm, struggling to stay on his feet, then collapsed to the floor before anyone could catch him.

Both he and the alien had lapsed into a shared coma, one that would last for the next nine days. Solomon became convinced that the EBE and Wells had developed a sympathetic bond. It was, he argued, related to the phenomenon sometimes observed in human twins, where one can feel the pain of the other. He cited the Metcheck case, where a sister in Dallas called police in Connecticut to report a traffic accident. She claimed to have visualized her twin sister's car sliding off an icy road and plunging down an embankment. Although she had never visited Connecticut, she was able to describe several landmarks along the road and the exact place where the car had broken through a retaining wall. When the police investigated, they found the injured twin exactly where they had been told to look. Solomon feared the alien might be trying to take Wells with it, and won permission for the scientist to be moved away from the quarantine area. He was transported to Wright-Patterson Air Force

Base, where he remained until the EBE died.

When he woke up, he had permanently lost the use of both his legs, and movement in his upper body was impaired. After that, Dr. Wells no longer referred to the alien survivor as his friend.

8

THE BIKINI CONNECTION

After reading the Wells report, Okun opened his door and began wandering the hallways, lost in contemplation. He ended up pacing the corridor outside the vault room and decided to pay the dead aliens a visit.

The tanks lay side by side on the floor, a trio of steel-reinforced glass coffins filled with murky liquid. He squatted, put his nose inches from the glass, and sent a telepathic message to wake up. Each time he played this game, some part of him actually expected to see the twitch of a muscle, the blink of an eye, a sign of life that would send him racing through the halls hollering, "They're alive! They're alive!" But the pasty white corpses continued to float tranquilly in their formaldehyde graves. They looked as peaceful in death as the Wells report had described them in life. Their wide open eyes gave them a startled, innocent expression which almost made it possible to believe they had come here for the sake of pure science, that they had no ulterior motives.

But Okun wasn't convinced. Although he proudly considered himself a peacenik, he was also a realistic scientist. The creatures might be from a different galaxy, but they were still animals, with instincts and drives. If they were anything like humans, he doubted they could be as selfless as Wells made them out to be.

He thought back to a story he'd heard at Caltech about the emperor Napoleon Bonaparte. As he was preparing to invade Egypt, he was approached by a group of France's most famous philosophers and historians. Sensing this would be a historic moment, they wanted to witness and record the campaign firsthand. They appealed to Napoleon's ego, promising to write a book glorifying his exploits, one that would assure the general's place in history. He agreed, but only on the condition the academics stay to the rear of the march where they belonged, "with the whores and the cooking wagons." The professor who told Brackish this story said it illustrated the typical relationship between science and the military. "Where there is science," she said, "there is war. And the idea of pure science is nothing more than a myth. There is always another motive lurking beneath the surface."

At the time, Okun hadn't taken her too seriously, but here he was only a couple of years later working, basically, for the military. Sure, he had shoulder length hair, wore an ankh necklace, and had a "War is Unhealthy for Children and Other Living Creatures" poster taped to the wall in his room, but he, too, was marching at the rear of the caravan.

If he could have spoken with the dead aliens, he would have asked them about their biomechanical suits. The doctors present at the autopsy had concluded the two animals were of different species. Although the idea hadn't occurred to any of the medical examiners in '47, Okun wondered if perhaps the beings came from different *planets*. If so, it would indicate the creatures floating in the tank were members of a conquering race, one that had used the alien bodies in much the same way humans used, say, cattle. Either way, it made him want to become a vegetarian. The exoskeletal suits were, unfortunately, long gone. They were unintentionally destroyed when, to prevent the spread of otherworldly bacteria, they were sprayed with the insecticide DDT. The spray triggered a chemical reaction that reduced the shells to thick liquid paste.

Okun sat down on the nearest coffin, thinking about the question of a second ship. "Am I being paranoid," he asked the extraterrestrial life-form below him, "or does my government know about more of your guys' ships? Maybe there's even an Area 52 someplace. Otherwise, why would they be trying to discourage me from investigating that possibility?"

The aliens didn't say it was all part of a plan to keep the young genius motivated.

"Just the man I've been waiting to see."

"I don't like the sound of that. What's up?" Radecker, no longer trying to disguise the fact that he was on a five-year vacation, was dressed in tennis whites. A covered racket protruded from his small suitcase. He'd just returned from thirty-six hours of fun and sun on the shores of Frenchman Lake.

"Been playing tennis?"

"Yes, I have. You getting ready to head off to Woodstock?" the boss shot back defensively. Okun was wearing open-toed sandals and a grungy old T-shirt with Jimi Hendrix's silhouette on it.

"That Wells report was pretty interesting. Did you read any of it?"

"Glanced at it. Why? Is there something I should know?"

Okun scrutinized him for signs he was lying and thought he saw them. "It's just that the table of contents on the front page lists an addendum added a couple of years later, a section called 'Revision of Preliminary Conclusions.' But it's not there. Those pages are missing."

"And you think I took them?"

"I didn't say that." Okun tried to maintain a poker face, but failed. Radecker knew from the cocked head and the narrowed eyes that he was being accused.

"Look, you asked me for the report, and I got it for you. Why would I go to the trouble of having it sent here and then not show you the whole thing?"

Both of them knew the answer to that question. Because there might be information in those pages concerning additional ships. Brackish opened his mouth to say something, but stopped when he remembered the promise he'd made to Dworkin. He couldn't let Radecker know what the old men had told him.

"I'm not saying you removed the pages, but it looks like somebody did. Maybe somebody in DC wants to keep us in the dark about something."

"If that's true, there's really nothing we can do about it, is there?" He went off to his room to unpack.

Okun shook his head. He wondered if Colonel Spelman knew how Radecker was spending his time in Nevada. He knew from things the agent had said during their first days in the lab that he was ambitious, that he wanted to climb the career ladder at the CIA. But he appeared to possess only moderate intelligence and didn't seem to be a very diligent worker. For the first time, the idea occurred to Okun that perhaps Radecker wasn't a good CIA man. Maybe they'd chosen him because he was mediocre, expendable. But without a doubt, Radecker was right about one thing. If the Pentagon and the CIA didn't want them to know something, they had the power to keep the men of Area 51 in the dark.

Okun followed the labyrinth of hallways toward the exit doors and turned on the long row of lights that illuminated the stacks. Somewhere in that welter of printed material, he sensed, was the clue he needed. But where? Since his introduction to this wildly disorganized library, he had finished reading over forty reports. He pulled a pen out of his shirt pocket and used the palm of his hand as scratch paper. At his present rate of speed, he calculated it would take him 513 years to read every document in the room.

Suddenly dejected, he switched off the lights. It would be nearly a year before he turned them on again.

A month to the day after the arrival of the Wells report, Radecker came dancing into the kitchen waving a telegram in the air. "Pack your bags, gentlemen, we're taking this show out on the road! This just came in from Spelman," he announced, dropping the printout on the table in front of a gloomy Okun. "They've approved your proposal!"

"You must be kidding. I wasn't serious about that." After being depressed and listless for two weeks, Brackish had realized he had to do something, *anything*, to stay busy. With the help of his colleagues, he'd written a half-demented proposal to retrofit the alien spacecraft with human-built technology—half of which would need to be invented. The men had laughed at their ideas, realizing how ludicrous most of them were. For Okun, it had been just like sitting around brainstorming with the Mothers in his dorm room—except his new group would have been called the Grandpas of Invention.

One of the minor ideas called for in the proposal turned out to be astonishingly prophetic once the secrets of the alien technology were revealed years later. Although there was no particular need for it from an engineering standpoint, he decided to base the steering and velocity controls on telekinetic energy. Okun recalled Dr. Solomon's theory on how the aliens controlled their biomechanical suits through acts of will. Based on their fetuslike riding position inside the chest cavity and the fact that the visitors had no tentacles, Solomon had ruled out the possibility of the suits responding mimetically to the physical actions of the wearer. It must have been done through mental signals. Okun wanted to apply similar principles to the operation of the ship. Years before there was any such thing as Virtual Reality, he conceived of a "sensory suit" to be worn by pilots which would read their slightest physical impulses and translate them into a series of commands intelligible to the ship's control system. In his proposal, he'd called this function the "Look, Ma, No Hands Interface," explaining that it would "significantly reduce pilot reaction time."

Dworkin was struck dumb that the document had been taken seriously. He had urged his junior colleague not to submit it, warning that it would damage his credibility with the powers-that-be. After he read the telegram, he turned to Okun and raised his eyebrows. "Somebody up there likes you."

Spelman thought the plan was ridiculous. It showed how little serious work was being done at the secret labs. As soon as he was finished reading the document, he phoned CIA headquarters and asked to be put through to the Office of the Deputy Director. "Al, I'm worried about our boy. I think he may be losing his marbles. He just sent me this proposal to rebuild the blackbird with conventional technology. There are so many weird ideas in this thing my first thought was, 'uh-oh, we've got another Manny Wells on our hands.'"

"What does he want to do?" Nimziki sounded like he was busy doing something else, not really paying attention. Spelman ran through the basic outlines of the plan, making sure to mention some of its nuttier aspects.

"And get this," he quoted from the report. "'In order to accomplish these goals, we will need to spend time at the following research institutions: the Los Alamos National Labs, the Massachusetts Institute of Technology, the Lawrence Livermore Labs, the University of California at Berkeley, Oak Ridge'. There are about twenty-five places they want to go to."

"Let them go, it can't hurt."

The colonel couldn't believe what he was hearing. "In my opinion, it would be faster and easier simply to feed him some more clues. Radecker's obviously doing a better job than you'd anticipated."

"Not yet," Nimziki snapped. "I have my sources, and everything's going along fine out there. The kid needs a vacation is all. He's been down there long enough. Let's send them out. You take care of it."

Reluctantly, Spelman agreed, but not before chopping back the proposed itinerary to just a pair of sites: Los Alamos and JPL. He also arranged special security procedures. Dworkin and the others, he knew, could be trusted not to reveal any information about Area 51, but Okun was untested. Although Spelman had never met him face-to-face, everything he knew about the young man suggested he would be a major security risk. He assigned two of his craftiest agents the task of getting Okun to divulge sensitive information.

Radecker and his staff were away from their labs for ten months. Seven of them were spent at the prestigious Los Alamos National Laboratories, where the group enjoyed full access to the knowledgeable technical staff and the ultramodern equipment, before moving on to a shorter stay at the Jet Propulsion Labs in Pasadena, Okun's old stomping grounds. Twice a day, he glimpsed his alma mater from behind the tinted windows of the van that shuttled the crew between the labs and their hotel. Since they received the red carpet treatment everywhere they went, the trip turned out to be relaxing and enjoyable for everyone except Okun. Since he had never studied many of the subjects that the engineers around him—even Freiling—knew like the backs of their hands, he was forced to play catch-up. He spent most of the year with his nose buried in books about rocketry, aerodynamics, or the newly emerging field of computer science. It was his graduate school. Under the patient tutelage of his elderly companions, he crammed three years of study into ten months. Without revealing why they needed the information, the scientists were able to learn many things that would help them repair the ship once they returned—everything from advanced, solderless welding techniques to the design of microcircuitry. As for security concerns, Spelman's worries proved unnecessary. Okun was far too busy to sit around gabbing with strangers. Besides, both facilities were staffed by very normal, very responsible, people, who had reached their positions by following the rules. They dressed, spoke, and wore their hair in the manner they felt was expected of them. When these squares saw Okun trucking toward them in a hallway, they dipped into nearby doorways to avoid him. He caused a small panic among a group of secretaries one morning when he came in wearing his security clearance card pinned to a happy face T-shirt worn over a brand-new pair of plaid pants which revealed—and this was what horrified them—he wasn't wearing any socks under his EARTH SHOES. He had about as much chance of conversing about national security issues with these employees as if he had been a leader of the Black Panther Party. Spelman's spies never got close to him.

They began their trip "home" on a warm spring morning. Okun persuaded Radecker to let him pay his mother a quick surprise visit. But when the van pulled up in the driveway, a neighbor told Radecker that Saylene had gone shopping. On the long drive back to the desert, Okun found himself thinking about his mom and his friends. But then something triggered another memory. This one concerned a film he'd seen at Los Alamos months before. It was a dull old documentary about the work of the labs—the Manhattan Project, rocket experiments, and the history of the U.S. nuclear program. In one clip, Brackish got his first look at Dr. Wells. He appeared in the background of a scene at the laboratory. But the footage that kept replaying itself in his mind had been shot in the South Pacific. It was a bald and awkward moment of military propaganda that featured a Navy officer speaking to a group of coyly grinning native islanders. They were being moved off the Bikini atoll, part of the Marshall Islands Group, in preparation for a test of the newly built hydrogen bomb. The officer made it annoyingly clear these simple people were leaving of their own free will and had plenty of other islands to go to. A disturbing moment of history caught on film, but Okun couldn't figure out why he kept thinking about it. It seemed important somehow.

The moment he walked into his room and saw the Wells report sitting on his desk exactly where he'd left it, he knew. He stood stock-still staring at the pages, still holding his luggage. Very slowly he began to nod.

The next morning, after a phone call to Los Alamos, he gathered everyone for a meeting. "Remember that movie they showed us about Oppenheimer and von Braun? And there were all those scenes about the rocket tests they conducted around the time of the H-bomb?"

"Yes, what about it?"

"There was that one rocket that exploded, remember? It blew up after it left the atmosphere, and nobody could figure out why. This morning I called the labs and had them check the date of that footage for me. The explosion happened at 4:30 P.M. on July 5, 1947."

"So?"

"That means," Okun announced proudly, "it was 10:30 P.M. on July 4 in New Mexico. Which in turn means…"

"...it was just before our alien vehicle crashed," Cibatutto finished the sentence.

"Yup."

"And you think there's a connection between the two events?"

Freiling interjected. "That test was halfway around the world in the Southern Hemisphere. How would that affect something in the skies over New Mexico?"

"I have no idea," Okun lied, "but it's too much of a coincidence not to investigate."

Dworkin glanced at Lenel, and said, "I seem to recall seeing a report on that rocket's failure."

"Of course there's a report," Lenel groused. "Anytime you blow up several million dollars' worth of government equipment, you end up writing a report. Finding it is going to be a different matter."

Okun gestured grandly in the direction of the stacks. "After you, gentlemen." The old men let out a collective groan, realizing they would spend the rest of the day thumbing through old documents. Reluctantly, they allowed themselves to be herded toward the stacks.

A day and a half later, they found what they were looking for. The staff members opened a bag of pretzels and passed them around the kitchen table as Okun read from the report.

"We have returned to the Garden of Eden with the intention of blowing it up. The beauty of this tropical island is so astonishing one senses everywhere the hand of God in its creation. We can only pray He will forgive us." So wrote an English electrician of the Bikini atoll. He was one of over two hundred men employed by the Manhattan Project for a series of rocket and bomb tests to be conducted in the Marshall Islands. Although the tests were classified experiments conducted by the United

States, half of the conversations took place in German. A large contingent of technicians who had been working for the Nazis a year earlier now formed the backbone of the U.S. rocket program. In the closing days of the war, Wernher von Braun and his crew had been ordered to return from the northern island of Peenemünde to a country inn near Berlin. Hitler, determined to prevent them from joining the allies, sent a team of SS agents to execute them all. By sheer luck, a cousin of von Braun's learned of the assassination plot and led the engineers into American-held territory, where they surrendered. Within weeks, these talented scientists were reunited at the White Sands Proving Grounds in New Mexico.

"During the war, they had developed the deadly V-2 rocket, the world's first ballistic missile, which was capable of reaching altitudes of seventy-five miles. But the new rocket they were preparing to test at Bikini, the first of the Redstone weapons, would reach higher still. It would soar three hundred miles above the earth before making a controlled reentry and exploding a small bomb in its nose cone on the nearby island of Kwajelin. The film crews and reporters who had come to the island ignored the Germans, focusing instead on the upcoming test of the first hydrogen bomb. Nevertheless, these engineers felt their experiments were just as significant as those being conducted by Oppenheimer and company. If the launch was successful, it would mark the beginning of the space program.

"State-of-the-art equipment had been brought to Bikini in order to monitor the rocket's flight. High-speed cameras with newly improved telephoto capacity, ultrasensitive radar equipment along with infrared and radio tracking systems were set up under thatch huts not far from the launchpad. After a final check of all systems, the countdown began. Liftoff occurred without complications at 4:18 P.M. local time. With an earsplitting roar, the forty-ton assembly lifted into the cloudless sky, leaving the graceful arch of a contrail in its wake. The ground crew watched it rise until it disappeared from view, then gathered around the banks of monitors. Without warning, the rocket disintegrated at 185 miles. Until that moment, everything had gone exactly according to plan—a rarity in highly complex tests of this kind.

"Radar watchers reported seeing something in the rocket's vicinity flash across the screen a split second before the blast. The 'ghost' had appeared out of nowhere and vanished just as suddenly. The consensus among the technicians was that it had been a false reading caused by energy related to the explosion. There was just one troubling aspect to the way the shape had moved. It seemed to *accelerate*. As one of the observers put it: 'It was like a fish resting in the sand that darts away a moment before you step on it.'"

The report advanced several explanations for the cause of the explosion. One of these concerned "a layer of radiation in the atmosphere at an altitude of 185 miles." The authors of the report were puzzled and somewhat alarmed by the discovery of this layer. Okun would have read right past this section if Cibatutto hadn't interrupted him.

"The rocket ran into one of the Van Allen belts, that's what they're talking about."

Lenel grimaced. "Hogwash! The belts wouldn't cause a rocket to explode."

"Actually, since this rocket carried a signal bomb in its nose cone, the sudden shift in magnetism could have activated the detonator cap."

Lenel disagreed and began explaining why when Freiling interrupted with views of his own. Soon all the old men were talking at once, shouting to be heard over the others. Just as the argument began degenerating into finger-pointing and name-calling, Okun held his hand high in the air and screamed over the top of the noise.

"Excuse me! I have a question!" The room went suddenly quiet. "What is a Van Allen belt?"

Cibatutto recited from memory. "The Van Allen belts are two rings of high-energy-charged particles surrounding Earth, probably originating in the Sun and trapped by Earth's magnetic field. The lower, more energetic belt, is at an altitude of 185 miles from Earth's surface while the outer belt is at ten thousand miles. They were discovered by physicist James Van Allen. Their shape and intensity vary significantly with fluctuations in the solar wind."

The older scientists stroked their beards in contemplation. Okun, with no beard to stroke, came up with an idea. "These variations, do they follow any kind of a pattern?"

Again, Cibatutto had the answer. "Yes, they do. The belts experience seasonal fluctuations, but these do not correspond directly to Earth's seasons. The energy level of the inner belt remains low for several months, then erupts into short periods of intense activity."

"Hmmm, would it be possible to find out what season the belts were in on July 4, 1947, between the hours of 10 P.M. and midnight in New Mexico?"

"I don't see why not." Cibatutto brought a thick reference book into the kitchen and began working through a series of mathematical equations. Okun was too eager to let the man work in peace.

"How often does this inner belt thingie erupt?" Brackish asked.

"About five consecutive days each year, sometimes twice a year. You have to run each date through the equation." When he was finished crunching the numbers, Cibatutto stared down at the results, nodding in an unconscious imitation of one of his colleagues. "On the date in question, the energy was at its peak."

Okun grinned and turned to the others. "Anybody up for a wager?" The scientists, accustomed to taking money from men who asked them such questions, were all ears. "You guys choose whichever alien encounter you think is the most real, the one you think really happened, and I'll bet you a month of washing the dishes that it happened during one of these flare-ups."

"Eau Claire, Wisconsin," Lenel said without hesitation. The other men agreed. Next to Roswell, this was the case with the most convincing physical evidence.

In the Eau Claire case, a policeman claimed to have "surprised" an alien saucer hovering over a farmhouse. When the craft moved away, he pursued at high speed until it fired a blue ray, which struck his vehicle and knocked him unconscious. An examination of the car revealed it had undergone a massive failure of the electrical system. Everything from the ignition to the taillights was ruined. The spark plugs and points were melted. The officer involved lived through the experience, but died six months later of nervous depression. His vehicle was taken to the UFO evidence compound at the Air Force Academy.

Cibatutto worked the date of the Eau Claire event through the equation, then made an announcement. "The good news is we seem to have found a connection between the alien visitations and the activity of the Van Allen belts. The bad news is each of us has to do the dishes 1.55 extra times this month. I propose we go in reverse-alphabetical order." The old men cheered and slapped Okun on the back.

"Progress of this magnitude deserves more than dirty dishes," Dworkin declared. "It calls for champagne!"

If the group's new theory was correct, it would be the single most important discovery about the aliens since their ship had crash-landed twenty-six years before, more important than Okun's unproved discovery that the ships must fly in groups: If the visitors only penetrated earth's atmosphere during these short bursts of radioactivity, it would mean two things. First, researchers could weed out the many bogus sightings and reports of contact in order to concentrate their attention on the real McCoys. Second, it would give them the power to predict when the creatures would come again.

While the older men set to work finding all the files that fell into one of these windows, Okun checked the dates of the case studies he'd already looked at. To his surprise, only one of them turned out to be true—the Bridget Jones incident. The lying girl had been telling the truth after all.

It turned out to be a long day of pulling reports, but their enthusiasm was high. They brought a radio into the stacks and sang the songs they knew the words to. Even Lenel was cheery. As they searched, Okun had the bright idea of calling Radecker and telling him what they'd learned. Dworkin called him over and explained why that might not be such a good idea. "Yesterday in Los Angeles, as we were parked in front of your house, I watched your expression change when we learned your mother wasn't at home. It occurred to me then how much I'd like for you to be able to leave here when your contract is finished. I think that's what you want for yourself. So call Mr. Radecker if you like, but remember this: *the more you know, the deeper you're buried.*"

9

MRS. GLUCK AND HER DAUGHTER

Okun didn't understand the precise relationship between the Van Allen belts and the arrival of the spaceships. And he didn't much care. What was important to him was that the dates matched. Now he had a way of sifting through the rubbish and finding the gold. But he was dismayed by two discoveries. First; there were hardly any real reports. Lenel hadn't been exaggerating when he said 99.9 percent of everything in the stacks was a bunch of hooey of bullpucky or whatever he'd called it. After several days of combing through the files, they had found about four hundred case studies occurring during the specified five-day periods. Then came the long process of poring over them and throwing out the fakes that happened to have been reported during those times. The scientists ruled out all but sixty-two of the reported sightings and encounters. Only twenty of these had occurred later than 1960. And four of those were mere sightings. That left only sixteen good reports.

One of them was the Eau Claire, Wisconsin incident.

One was the Bridget Jones case, where the central witness was dead.

Then there were thirteen people who claimed they had been abducted. And that's where things got interesting. All told very similar stories. They had been driving along lonely roads or at home engaged in some quiet activity when they suddenly stopped whatever they were doing. The drivers pulled to the side of the road. The people taken from their homes sat down or stood still. All the abductees described being surrounded by short, quick-moving creatures with enlarged heads. Many claimed they had been flown to a spaceship, where various experiments were performed on their persons. Six of them described a leader who was much taller that the others. Okun knew from other reading he had done that mentions of a much taller leader were common.

But there was one report that stood out from the others. It was about a woman who claimed she had been interrogated about a Y-shape. Her file said she was a person in the public eye, and care was taken to expunge any clue to her identity. But Okun knew her name was Trina Gluck and she lived in Fresno. In fact, he knew her street and house number. Scrawled onto the front page of the document in a handwriting style he was learning to recognize was the woman's name and address.

Two weeks later, he rode into Las Vegas with the boys. As always, the van dropped them off in front of their bank, Parducci Savings. Nothing on the outside of the building let on that it was a bank. There was no logo, no place to park, no slot for night deposits. Inside, the lobby looked like someone's living room, with lots of family photos on the walls and too much furniture. There was a counter with two teller's windows and behind that a couple of doors leading to private offices. These doors were never open. Salvatore Parducci, a heavyset man with an appetite for fine suits and gold bracelets, was the manager. He spoke in a luxuriously soft voice punctuated by sudden bursts of loud, braying laughter.

Okun knew there was something unusual about the bank on his first visit. Moments after opening his new account, Salvatore came around the counter with his arms spread wide and embraced him. While he was being squeezed against the powerful man's girth, Salvatore looked down, and purred, "Welcome. My family thanks you for trusting us with your money." On another occasion, Okun watched a helicopter land beside the building. An old lady stepped out of it carrying a casserole dish and came inside. It turned out to be Signora Parducci, delivering lunch to her son. She flirted shamelessly with Cibatutto in Italian before disappearing into one of the back offices. Very shady.

This morning's transaction had been uneventful except for Okun withdrawing an unusually large amount of cash, three hundred dollars. "Feeling lucky," he explained with a grin.

It was a sunny morning, and the old fellows were in high spirits. They were marching down the boulevard toward a café that offered one-cent breakfasts. After that, it was onward to the casinos for a day of cards. Okun seemed preoccupied. He kept to the back of the pack, fingering the wad of cash in his pocket. "Hey, you guys," he called. The old men stopped walking and turned around. "Nothing personal, but I think I'll try my luck at one of the smaller casinos today. By myself." His friends were visibly disappointed.

"Hey, what happened to all for one and one for all?" Freiling asked. "We're supposed to play as a team." When that approach didn't work, he tried another. "We'll let you win a few."

"It's not the money. I just feel like being alone today."

"Completely understandable," Lenel declared. "I'm tired of looking at these ugly old coots myself. It wouldn't hurt to have a break."

"Dr. Freiling," Cibatutto cried. "This man called you an ugly coot!"

Freiling put up his dukes. "Who said so? I'll knock his block off."

As the two men began sparring, Dworkin came a step closer to his young friend, and silently pronounced the words, "Be careful." Okun wondered if he knew.

An hour later, he had rented a car and was heading west.

Brinelle Cluck was the girl he'd always wanted to meet—nerdy, artsy, and, in her own way, beautiful. It was love at first sight. She was a couple of years older and a couple of inches taller than him and as slender as a microscope. From her moccasins to her perfect miniature breasts to her long straight hair, she was, for him, a vision of loveliness. He immediately regretted having dressed like a total square.

"Do I know you?" she asked when she opened the door.

Hating to begin anything with the word "no," he answered, "Maybe in a past life. Were you ever a monkey in Tibet?"

Instead of slamming the door in his face, she actually thought about it for a second before she answered. "Yes, now that you mention it, I was."

They both laughed at her reply and spent the next thirty minutes rambling through one topic after another. After reincarnation, they talked about Brinelle's poetry and modem dance, the Beatles, Bangladesh, biointensive gardening, the world's scariest roller coasters, and the Carlos Castaneda books. Okun felt his heart racing with excitement when she reached out and briefly touched his chest. She fondled his ankh.

"I don't usually like jewelry, but that is the most outtasight piece. Where'd you get it?"

The question caught him off guard. "Um, I can't remember. I've had it for years."

When she asked him his name, he blurted, "Bob. Bob Robertson."

"I'm Brinelle Gluck. I wish I had a nice normal name like yours. You have no idea what it's like to get teased about your name all the time. So, Mr. Bob Robertson, what do you do? Got a job?"

"Yeah, I guess you could call it a job."

"What is it you do?" Okun was starting to get uncomfortable with this part of the conversation.

"I'm a scientist."

"Really? What branch of science?

"Boring stuff, planes, rockets, just a lot of technical stuff."

"I see. Where do you do all this boring stuff?

"Labs, mainly."

"No duh. I mean what's the name of the lab. My dad knows hundreds of people who work at Livermore and Stanford and UCLA."

He really liked this girl, and he wanted desperately to tell her the truth or at least to explain that he wasn't allowed to say. But he'd been coached a thousand times never ever to give that response. It aroused suspicion and curiosity, two things to which Area 51 was allergic. He had been told to turn and walk away or, if that wasn't possible, to lie.

"I work at JPL in the microcircuitry division. We do the circuit boards and harness wiring for the space program, mostly satellites."

Then she did something that broke his heart. She nodded. It was a big dopey nod with an expression on her face that showed how impressed she was. She had just gotten around to asking him why he'd knocked on the door when the phone rang.

"I gotta get that. Come in and sit down." Brinelle disappeared into another room.

Hie house was impressive. It was a small palace built in the Spanish style, with lots of exposed wood and high, whitewashed ceilings. He wandered into the sunken living room and examined a painting. It looked vaguely familiar, and he wondered if it might be the work of a famous artist. It was that kind of house.

He sat down on the sofa and let his life flash before his eyes. *This chick is mondo diggable,* he told himself *I haven't known her an hour, and I've already lied to her a couple of times. If I keep working at Area 51, I'll never be friends with her or anyone else. There are too many secrets to keep.* Suddenly, he pictured himself at forty, still with long hair, still puttering around with the spaceship, still single. When Dworkin and the others were gone would he continue to work down there alone?

Contemplating these matters, he reached into a bowl of nuts on the coffee table and was trying to open one with his teeth when another woman walked into the room. "And who might you be?" she asked.

"Um, hello. Is your name Gluck? Trina Gluck?"

"It might be. Who are you?"

"Hello, I'm Bob. Bob Robertson. I work at JPL in the microcircuitry division. We do a lot of the electronic work for the space program. I was just having a very pleasant conversation with your daughter."

The woman, elegant, in her late fifties, was obviously Brinelle's mom. From the way she was dressed, it looked like she'd just come back from a social function.

"Are you a friend of my daughter's?"

"Sort of. I mean, I hope so. But actually, I'm here to see you. I recently read the report on your abduction and wanted to ask you some questions about it."

Instantly, Okun knew he'd said the wrong thing. The woman's expression turned ugly. "Get out of this house before I call the police."

Okun tried to make her understand how important it was, but she wouldn't listen. Brinelle came back in and tried to take his side, but her mom was irate, screaming at the top of her lungs, tears on her face. When he stopped in the doorway, she began pushing the door closed. "Dr. Wells sent me," he blurted out, just as the door slammed in his face.

He stood on the doorstep, stunned. How could he have been so stupid? Up to that moment, he'd treated it all as a game, the Great American Flying Saucer Hunt. But obviously, it was a deep personal wound for this woman. The instant he'd mentioned the word abduction, a wave of pain had broken across her face. For Trina Gluck, it wasn't a game. Okun started off down the brick driveway when the door opened again.

Mrs. Gluck stepped onto the porch and waved him back inside. "If Dr. Wells sent you, you can come in."

The kidnapping, as she called it, had taken place about ten years earlier, shortly after her husband, a congressman, had declared his candidacy for one of California's Senate seats. It was Memorial Day weekend, and Brinelle was away at her first slumber party. Trina's husband was in bed reading. She was in the bathroom brushing her teeth when her arm suddenly relaxed to her side. A moment later, the toothbrush clattered into the sink. Although she'd never so much as imagined an encounter with aliens before, she somehow knew immediately what was happening. She was terrified and felt the impulse to scream, but couldn't. She still had control over her eyes and tried to turn toward the door, but her neck would not cooperate. She felt the first one come into the room a moment before she saw its reflection in the mirror. She described it as being about three or four feet tall with a large head and shiny silver eyes, but it moved about the room so quickly she couldn't get a good look at it. After the first one examined her hair and nightgown, others came through the doorway.

One of them stood directly behind her, hidden from view, and identified itself to her as "the friend." This creature spoke to her using her own voice for what seemed like a long time. The distinction between her own thoughts and those of the friend began to blur. She felt small hands touching her body in several places and heard them rummaging through the drawers and cabinets. She felt her shock settling into anger and struggled to regain control of herself. When the friend asked how they could help her relax and cooperate, she asked for her husband. Go get my husband out of bed. But a moment later she heard her own voice reply, "Your husband is asleep now."

She was taken outdoors and laid on her back in some of the bushes by the side of the house. The friend made her understand she had a skin disease, something contagious on her stomach and pelvis. Small hands lifted her nightgown while other hands lifted her head so she could watch the operation that would cure her. Silently begging them to stop, she watched a needlelike instrument slice into her skin. The blade opened a bloodless incision down the left side of her belly, from the rib cage down to the hip. A second instrument she couldn't see was inserted into the opening. As it slid between her skin and stomach, the friend congratulated her on being clean again. Still listening to her own voice being used by another being, she was given a brief lecture of some sort. It might have been on hygiene, but she couldn't be sure.

When the operation was finished she was put into a sitting position, then lifted up into the sky. It was the sensation of sitting in a strong net and being lifted by a very fast crane. She watched as the lights of the city receded between her knees.

Then she was in a gray room. She heard the soft rustling of their movements, like pieces of silk being rubbed together. She rolled her head to the side, and noticed she was lying on a platform or table a few feet above the floor. The room appeared to be circular, almost spherical in shape. A bank of windows was set low against the wall, almost part of the floor. Nearby she noticed a pile of clothing, old dirty clothes, and she had the sense that someone had been sleeping there. The friend came and repositioned her head so that all she could see was the blank gray ceiling. She was told that the examination would continue.

Then a new creature stepped into her peripheral vision and approached the table. It was much taller than the others, but she felt that it was different in other ways as well. It seemed to be a leader of some sort. It leaned in and brought its face closer until she could see her distorted reflection in the bulging eyes. They reminded her of insect eyes although the face around them was nearly human in shape. She closed her own eyes, hoping that if she ignored this tall creature, it would back away. But it continued hovering over the table, studying her.

Without using an audible voice, the leader began pronouncing a series of words or ideas, as if it were reading down a list. She knew she was being asked about each item, but did not understand her role in the exchange. The only one of these "words" she could recall later was the letter Y, and only because it had been asked of her repeatedly. Several times, the tall creature probed her thoughts for the meaning of this symbol. She tried to cooperate, thinking they might spare her life if she could give them the information they wanted. It was clear to her it didn't mean the letter Y in the alphabet. It occurred to her that it might be a place, a landmark in a city perhaps. She thought of the Space Needle in Seattle and the arch in St. Louis, but the creature seemed dissatisfied with these answers.

It stood up, and, as it moved away from her, she must have lost consciousness.

"My husband woke me up at two in the morning saying he'd had a dream someone was trying to break into the house. He went downstairs to look around and noticed the security alarm had been disarmed. It never worked properly after that, and we ended up having to have it replaced. I asked him for a glass of water because my throat felt dried out. When I sat up to take it, he noticed there were leaves and dirt all over my back and in my hair. We decided that I must have been sleepwalking and that I was the one who had turned off the alarm. We went down and checked the side of the house, because the leaves in bed matched the japonicas growing out there, but nothing looked unusual, no signs of struggle or anything like that. I told him about having this sensation that I'd gone somewhere, but at that point it was still buried at the back of my mind.

"We talked about it the next morning over breakfast, and I mentioned to him again about this sense of mine that I'd been carried off somewhere. He wanted to call the police, but I wouldn't let him. When he left for the office, I went up to the bathroom and took a shower. Then it all came back to me in a crash when I opened the medicine chest and saw my toothbrush hanging in the rack next to his. I never put it there. I was always very meticulous about standing it in the little ceramic cup. That little detail caused an avalanche. I remembered the whole thing at once. I didn't stand there remembering it piece by piece. It all came back to me in a single moment. I looked on my stomach and found a thin red mark, like a scratch, where I remembered them cutting me open. Later our doctor told me it was a scar. He said it was so thin that I must have had it since I was a child. But I know I didn't.

"We called the police, and that was a mistake. I felt utterly violated, like I'd been raped, and when I told everything to the police it was clear they didn't believe me! Then the FBI showed up and the CIA and the Army. I was going through a severe nervous breakdown, and they behaved as if I were making the whole thing up to get some attention. That's probably been the hardest part of this whole thing, being isolated and made to feel like I did something wrong. Dr. Wells was the first person who tried to understand what I was going through. He put me in touch with Dave Natchez and the survivors group, so I had some support, someone who believed me. Well, my husband believed me; without him I probably wouldn't have survived. Does that answer your questions?"

Okun felt a little overwhelmed by everything she'd told him. "Yeah, I think so."

"So how is Dr. Wells?" she asked, trying to lighten the mood. "Still crazy, I hope."

"Unfortunately, Dr. Wells passed away."

"How awful. I'm sorry to hear that. Were you close?" Not knowing how to answer the question, Okun merely shrugged. She went on. "I wish I'd written back sooner. I got a letter from him about six months ago, and I just haven't made time to answer it. Oh, I feel terrible."

"Six months ago?"

"Yes, I know. I have no excuse. I could have found the time."

"Could I see the letter?"

"Certainly." It bore a postmark six months earlier. The envelope was printed stationery from somewhere called Sunnyglen Villa in San Mateo, a town at the base of the San Francisco peninsula. The letter was only a couple of sentences long and revealed nothing.

"Do you have a phone I can borrow?"

He called Sunnyglen Villa and asked to speak with Dr. Immanuel Wells. The soft-spoken woman on the other end said Mr. Wells was ill and couldn't take any phone calls. She offered to take a message, asking if he was "with an agency." Okun said he was an old family friend and said he'd call back later. He stared down at the envelope, wondering what sort of mental institution would give itself a name like Sunnyglen.

It was the middle of the afternoon. If he was going to get back to Las Vegas before the van picked them up, he'd have to leave soon. After he thanked Mrs. Gluck for sharing her story, Brinelle walked him out to his car.

"Hey, what's your hurry? Why don't you stay for dinner?"

"Gotta get back to work."

"You're gonna drive to San Mateo right now, aren't you?"

Okun laughed. "I wish. No, seriously, I have to get back to Pasadena."

"I see. Paranormal investigator all day, jet propulsion engineer all night. Don't you hate it when people lie to you, Bob?"

"Yeah, as a matter of fact I do."

"Hey, I've got an idea," she said brightly. "Let's go visit Dr. Wells together. We can crash at my friend's place in Palo Alto."

Okun couldn't tell if she was being serious or not.

10

DISAPPEARING ACT

Yes, Okun hated it when people lied to him. He talked about the lies Radecker had told him as he drove toward San Francisco. And the more he talked, the angrier he got. "He told me my job was to make the spaceship fly. Fine. But when I tell him I need a second ship to make it happen, he tries to hide the information from me! What is that about? When I tell him I want to talk to Wells, he tells me the guy is dead! Screw you, Radecker!"

Later, he would claim that this tremendous sense of anger was what motivated him to drive north that afternoon instead of east like he was supposed to. But even in the middle of his yelling fit, Okun realized there was more to it than rage. He was curious. He wanted to meet this Wells character, see what he was all about. And there was something else, a need to assert himself—to take control of his research and stop putting himself at the mercy of Radecker.

Brinelle had talked Brackish into going to San Mateo, but not into taking her along. As groovy as the idea sounded, it wasn't worth the risk. He didn't want to read a newspaper article about her unfortunate collision with a postal truck. So he drove up the coast by himself, bought a map, and followed the address to an industrial area near the freeway.

Sunnyglen Villa turned out to be a slightly run-down Victorian mansion sandwiched between a bus yard on one side and a warehouse on the other. The property was surrounded by a tall chain-link fence with razor ribbon at the top. There were bars over all the windows, even on the top floor. When a security guard stepped onto the front porch and lit a cigarette, Okun put the car in gear and slunk away. It was a strange place for a mental institution. It looked more like a prison, and Okun had a feeling they weren't too keen on visitors.

He cruised around for a while until he found a suitable motel and checked in. It had been an unusually emotional day for him, and that night he did something he only did when he was feeling blue. He wrote lugubrious poems in the journal he reserved for the keeping of scientific notes.

The next morning he walked into a barbershop and told the man, "I've got a job interview today with an insurance company. Make me look like a square."

"Crew cut?" the barber asked.

Okun nodded—a pained nod. "A crew cut sounds perfect."

When he came out, his ears felt like twin jumbo radar dishes, and he felt the breeze on the back of his neck for the first time in years. His next stop was a department store, where he spent most of the money he had left on a business suit and a briefcase. He changed in the store's parking lot, getting help from a nice old lady who knew how to tie a tie. He was ready.

When he drove up, the front gate was open. He parked his car and walked up to the front door and tried the handle. It buzzed and clicked open. The inside of the place looked very different from the exterior. The entry had been converted into a waiting room like a doctor's office, with a few chairs and old magazines. A video camera in the corner slowly swept the room. There was a counter with a sliding glass partition behind which sat a willowy woman with a soft voice.

"Hi there. Can I help you?"

"I'm here to see Dr. Immanuel Wells."

"And your name, sir?"

"Radecker. Agent Lawrence Radecker, from Central Intelligence."

When the woman asked to see some identification, Okun glanced around to make sure no one was listening then whispered through the partition. "I'm on a special assignment, so I'm not carrying any ID. My instructions are to have you call headquarters, and they'll confirm. I was told you had the number."

"Oh, sure. Have it right here." She looked at him with big doe eyes. "If you'd like to have a seat, Agent Radecker, I'll call right away." She smiled and slid the glass door closed.

Okun tried to act casual. He picked up a magazine, but soon tossed it aside and began to pace. *CIA guys can pace if they want to*, he told himself, nothing suspicious about that. He glanced out the windows every few seconds to make sure no one was closing the front gate. He was already plotting a quick retreat if she asked him for the word of the day. Every morning, Radecker had a two-second conversation with someone calling from CIA headquarters. They would tell him the identification password for the next twenty-four hours, he would repeat it and hang up. The code words, of course, followed no pattern. Monday would be ZEBRA, Tuesday would be UNIQUE, and so on. He knew he'd never guess, so if she asked him, he was prepared to tell her he had it written down in the car.

"Thanks so much for waiting. If you'll follow me, I'll take you to Dr. Wells."

At the back of her tidy little office space was a thick glass door she unlocked with a key. They stepped through it into the home's dark central hallway and walked to the living room, where three men and one woman were gathered around a television watching a soap opera. All four of them were ancient, well into their eighties or nineties, and barely glanced up when the receptionist said good morning. The paint was peeling in places, and there was a slight reek of cleaning products in the air.

"Have you met Dr. Wells before?"

"Not face-to-face."

"But you know he doesn't talk anymore." She could see by his expression he didn't. "Maybe you'll have better luck with him. To tell you the truth," she said, opening a screen door, "it was a relief when he stopped. That man used to talk so darn much I had to wear earplugs."

They stepped outside onto the roomy back porch. A couple of deck chairs faced the backyard, which was a green riot of fruit trees, bushes, and weeds. A dilapidated gazebo was being strangled by heavy vines of wisteria. The lady walked up to a frail-looking man in a wheelchair and spoke as loud as her mousy voice would allow. "Dr. Wells, this is Agent Radecker. He's with the CIA, and he wants to ask you some questions." The old man didn't stir. She shrugged and smiled. "Well, good luck."

Okun pulled up a chair. He'd been expecting to meet a deranged and violent lunatic, but this guy, except for the wheelchair, looked like a member of the PGA's senior golf tour. He was clean-shaven, well groomed, and handsome in a balding, bulldoggish way. He wore pressed white slacks and a powder blue sweater that matched his piercing blue eyes.

"Dr. Wells? Dr. Wells? You can hear me, right? Look, if you can understand me, give me a sign. Make a movement or blink twice or something."

Without turning his head, the old man raised his right hand, then slowly lifted his middle finger.

"OK, that's a sign. Listen," he whispered, "I'm not

really from the CIA. I just said that to get in here. And my name's not Radecker. I work at Area 51, and I went AWOL so I could come and talk to you. I'm probably gonna be in VDJ, very deep Jell-o, when I get back, so help me out, man."

Wells turned and regarded his visitor, waiting for him to say more.

"Hey, can you write? If I ask you a question, can you write out the answers? I brought a pen."

"What's Area 51?" the old man asked in a raspy voice. "I've never heard of that."

So he *could* talk. Okun started nodding. "Are you testing me or don't you remember? You used to work there. You know, Groom Lake, underground labs, the crashed ship?"

"Go on, I still don't know what you're saying."

Derrr. It suddenly occurred to Okun what was happening. The old man was waiting to hear some proof that he wasn't some amateur UFO investigator. "OK, I got it. Dworkin. Lenel. Vegas every Friday. There's a long table in the kitchen with two picnic benches. The tiles on the bathroom floor are mostly white, but some of them are purple, and the handles on the middle sink don't match. Hey, what's the matter?" He noticed tears welling up in the old man's eyes. "Oh no, please don't do that." It was the second day in a row he'd made somebody cry.

"I knew you'd come. I've been waiting and waiting. Why did you make me wait so long?"

"I just found out where you were yesterday."

"Didn't Dworkin send you?" He turned suddenly paranoid. "Who sent you here?"

"Nobody sent me. Relax. Yesterday I talked to Mrs. Gluck, and she showed me a letter you wrote her. Dworkin and those guys all think you're dead. That's what we were told."

"So you came to break me out? You can't do it alone;

we'll need help. We'll go immediately into San Francisco. There are two television stations within a few blocks of one another. I've already written the press release, but it's in my room. Everything has been planned. I'll need one person to accompany me into the—"

"Whoa. Hold your horses there, *Kemo sabe*. You're losing me."

Wells started over and explained his plan. It was urgent, he said, that they alert the world of the impending alien invasion which, he said, could begin any minute. This was the same plan, presented to the members of Project Smudge five years earlier, which had led to his forced retirement and imprisonment. He pointed to the strings of barbed wire hidden in the foliage. He began explaining, in too much detail, the sequence of events leading to his ouster from Smudge, and expressed his deep loathing for the men who had opposed him.

Without stopping, he segued back to his moment-by-moment plan for breaking the story to the news media. Every movement had been scripted in his mind, every enemy reaction anticipated. It was a chess game pitting himself—and a few assistants—against the worldwide conspiracy to keep the matter quiet. As he spoke, Okun realized that Wells was, indeed, crazy. He wasn't the incoherent lunatic he had expected to meet, but he was obsessive-compulsive to the nth degree.

"It may already be too late, but we've got to try. Every man, woman, and child must devote himself to the salvation of the planet. Once they hear, once they understand that we face annihilation, they will make the necessary sacrifices. Everyone working together. It will require the transformation of the world into a single, tightly organized war machine. Politics, economy, society, all must change if we hope to survive." He said everyone who knew and didn't tell was a war criminal worse than

Hitler, the worst filth on the planet, and in the future he would call for their public executions. Okun himself was one of the conspirators, but wisely didn't point that out to the old doctor.

Obviously, once you were on this man's enemy list, there was no getting off it. So Okun, who'd spent the last couple of days acting, assumed yet another role. "I'm going to help you. I'll come back with reinforcements later, but right now let me ask you a couple of questions. The first thing is the addendum to your report. I read the part you wrote after the Roswell thing, but the part you attached later was missing. What was in it, your ideas about an invasion?"

"Don't belittle me, young man. These are not merely ideas. At the time of the encounter I believed I had been given a glimpse of the EBE's home planet. Later I came to believe I had been shown the planet which had once belonged to the host animals, the ones they had gutted and used like a suit of clothing. Have you seen the photographs of the larger bodies?"

"Yeah, they're horrible-looking."

"Before the planet I saw was ruined, it had been a jungle, a lavish hothouse of dense plant life. Endless, stretching to infinity. Even below the surface, it teemed with vegetation. Think of the differences in anatomy between the two creatures. Which one would be better adapted to this planet? The tentacles would allow the larger being to climb and reach and grasp. The other one was all wrong. Its body was too delicate for an environment like that. I'm sure the little fiend didn't show me his planet. I think he was explaining why he had come to ours. It's because they'd slowly ruined that place he showed me, consumed everything on the surface until they were reduced to tearing shreds of moss off the walls of caves. I think they're coming here to eat."

"Groady."

"Another thing. If this creature really was a scientist, then what was it doing hauling food around? That doesn't make sense to me. Because I had shared a personal memory with it, I assumed it had done the same. It certainly *felt* like a personal memory, so immediate, so real. But how could those two animals be the same? Then it occurred to me: they share thoughts, they share a mind, they must share a memory."

"Exactly. That's the same principle they used in developing their ships. They share an energy source just like they share mental activity."

"They're a hive, my friend, and that makes them dangerous. Individually, they may not be as intelligent as you or I. But collectively, they may be more powerful than we can imagine. Did Sam ever tell you about my experiments with the bees?"

Okun shook his head.

"I kept a hive for about six months out in the old shacks next to the main hangar. As an experiment, I began hiding their food source. But every day they'd find it within minutes. I expanded the radius to about two miles around the hive, moving the food to random locations at random times of the day. Then the scariest damn thing started happening. After about three months of this, I'd go to the place I had decided to put the food and they'd be waiting for me! After that I tried as many tricks as I could think of to fool them. And they'd work for a while, but they never worked twice. This went on until it occurred to me that they had learned to anticipate me. They'd learned my moves well enough to predict my behavior. In the end, I set the hive on fire. Now if bees can do that, imagine what these other monsters are capable of.

"And we're not even making it difficult for them. We bombard space with radio waves advertising our position.

That must stop at once. They're out there right now watching us, studying us, waiting for the moment to strike."

"You're absolutely right. So, you think there's more than one ship?"

"Are you stupid? Don't you understand what I'm telling you? There are *hundreds* of ships like the one we recovered, and they are nearby. They come every few months and snoop around our military installations or experiment on people and animals. Don't you know about all those bloodless cattle mutilations? Call the Pentagon and tell them to send you the files. Soon the time of study will be over, and they will attack. We don't know how powerful their weaponry is, but our Air Force won't stand a chance against the speed and maneuverability of their ships. In a few months all of our planes and missiles will be spent. Then they'll start picking off our ground forces. There won't be time to build the weapons we're going to need. We must sacrifice now to build a space defense network of our own. Satellite lasers, deep-space torpedoes, orbiting minefields of nuclear warheads. If we have time, we can put factories in space capable of building a fleet of warships, then launch an attack of our own. It may already be too late, but we've got to try. You have to get some good men and storm this place."

In a strange way, the more he talked, the more sense he seemed to make. Okun was tempted to ask about these other visits, but steered back to his original topic. "I'll look for the guys later. But right now I want to get my hands on a second alien ship." He explained the experiment which proved the captured saucer could only fly with a companion. "Do you know if the government has any more of them from another crash?"

"What about Chihuahua, Mexico?"

"What's that?"

"Have you seen the Majestic 12 documents?"

"The thing they wrote up for Eisenhower? Yeah, I saw them."

"It's in there." Okun had read the top-secret documents but had concluded that they were fakes, just more disinformation generated by the forces of darkness. It had a description of the "seized flying disk" that was full of inaccuracies. There had been one paragraph in the document that had been blacked out.

"So what's this Chihuahua thing about?"

"Simultaneous with the crash at Roswell, another streak of light had been observed moving due south. The Army collected scores of 'hard' sightings from people on the ground all the way from Roswell to Guerrero, a town in the mountains of Chihuahua State. A few days after the crash, we sent troops across the border. Just barged right in and surrounded the area where the local people said the thing went down. They searched for a long time, but didn't find anything."

"But you think there's one down there?"

"I don't know. I always meant to go down there and look around for myself, but I never did."

"And where was this exactly,?"

"Right outside of Guerrero." Once again, Wells began to explain why he had to get to the television station, but Okun interrupted him immediately.

"One last question. The Y. I saw it on one of the monitors inside the ship when we pumped some power into the system. I thought it was some kind of an SOS. Dworkin told me you had that same feeling."

This time Wells only shook his head. "I haven't figured it out. You say you spoke with Trina Gluck."

"Yes."

"Did you believe her?"

"I don't think she's lying. Yeah, I guess I believed her."

"If she's right, the aliens don't know any more than we do

what the Y is. For years I believed it was the alien equivalent of our SOS, but if so, why don't they recognize it?"

"Agent Radecker," the nurse called from the doorway. "You have a telephone call, sir."

"Our reinforcements?" the old man asked eagerly.

"Either that or VDJ." Okun extended his hand. "Thanks a lot for your help."

Wells looked at the hand, horrified. "You're leaving? You're going to leave me here? NO! You tricked me! You're with them, aren't you? You never had any intention of helping. Get away from me, you filthy murderer."

All the way through the house and back to the office, Okun could hear the old man howling curses at him. And it didn't look like life was going to get any better. He was fairly certain that once he picked up the phone he would be nailed by some internal security guy in DC.

He took a deep breath and picked up the receiver. "Radecker here."

"I thought your name was Bob Robertson."

"Brinelle?"

"Yeah. Listen, Secret Agent Whatever-Your-Name-Is, you are majorly busted. Two guys were just here from the FBI asking about you and, sorry, but we had to tell them where you were going. So you might want to get out of there."

"Thanks, Chief, I'll get on that right away."

"Are there people standing there listening to you?"

"Affirmative."

"And you want to sound like you're on official business?"

"Exactly."

"Cool. You better hit the road, but use that phone number I gave you, OK?"

"Will do. Over and out."

Okun started out the door, but thought better of it. Why should he run? What did it matter *how* he got back to

Nevada? It might be a more pleasant trip if he had some company. So he sat down in the waiting room and looked through some magazines until he heard a car skid to a stop in the parking lot.

11

A DEATH IN THE FAMILY

Brackish Okun spent the night behind bars. As he'd guessed, the FBI guys who took him into custody drove him all the way to Nevada, to the main entrance to the Nellis Weapons Testing Range. They were very polite with him the entire time, even friendly. He was never handcuffed or treated as a prisoner in any way—except for them following him into the rest room when they stopped for lunch. But it was a different story when they handed him over to the Military Police waiting for him at the front gates. He was searched, handcuffed, and tossed in the back of a Jeep. The MPs drove him to the Military Intelligence building and locked him in a windowless cell. He was woken up in the middle of the night and taken to an interrogation room, where he was questioned by a pair of officers. They demanded to know everywhere he'd gone and everyone he'd spoken with during his twenty-seven-hour absence. They warned him, however, not to tell the *whole* story. If he had divulged any compartmentalized information, anything about the work being done at Groom Lake, they wanted to know to whom he had done so, but reminded him they were not cleared to hear such information and telling them would constitute a violation of the law.

He told them the whole truth, but they acted as if they didn't believe a word of it. They grilled him for two hours, subtly leaning on him to change his story. When the session was over, he was taken back to the cell. At 7 A.M., he was awoken once again, this time by Radecker, who stood on the other side of the bars looking like a high-pressure radiator hose about to split open and spray the room with dirty boiling water. He screamed at Okun for a long time, telling him what a stupid and dangerous thing it had been to disappear like that. When the enraged CIA man stopped for breath, Okun tried to lighten the mood.

"Aren't you even gonna compliment my haircut?"

Radecker skewered him with a hard stare. "I trusted you," he hissed, "and you double-crossed me. You stabbed me in the back. Now you're going to pay the price. There's going to be a court-martial. A legal team is preparing charges against you right how. You're looking at some serious prison time."

"For what?"

"Let me see. Being absent without leave, impersonating a federal officer, trespassing, violating the Federal Espionage Act. All together you shouldn't get more than ninety-nine years. You'll be eligible for parole in about twenty."

"I didn't reveal anything," Okun assured him. "I swear. The only person I talked to was Wells."

Radecker flashed him a wicked smile. "Wells no longer has a security clearance. He doesn't have any official ties to this program. You blew it."

"You're kidding me, right? I didn't tell him anything he didn't already know."

"The guys outside don't know that. I guess I could talk to them for you, explain the situation, try to get the charges dismissed. But I'm not going to do that, and I'll tell you why. Because you intentionally embarrassed me. I get sent out here to baby-sit your hippie ass, and you pull this stunt. Where do you think that leaves me? I'm finished at the CIA, I'm a joke. Even the friggin' FBI is laughing at me."

* * *

But Okun was never charged with any crime. Apparently, he had unseen friends in higher places. A phone call from the Deputy Director's Office of the CIA instructed the base's legal affairs office to drop the case and overlook the entire incident. Radecker was told to restrict the young scientist to the labs and immediate environs, but to take no further disciplinary action. He was furious, but powerless to strike back.

When Okun returned to the underground labs, the mood was indeed somber. He wasn't the only one in the boss's doghouse. When Brackish had failed to rendezvous with them for the ride back from Vegas, the old men had tried one trick after another to stall the van's departure. First Freiling wandered off, pretending to have a senile episode, then Lenel complained of chest pains and was taken to a hospital. At dawn, when Okun still hadn't returned, they gave up and came home. Radecker was convinced they were in on the plot. The Vegas trips, he announced, were history. The old men would be allowed to drive into town only long enough to transact their banking business and fill their prescriptions at the pharmacy before returning to base. For Dworkin and company, being robbed of their only form of recreation was a crushing blow, and they couldn't help blaming Okun.

Spirits were low, and there was a poisonous atmosphere in the labs. Cracks began to appear in the block of solidarity shared by the older men. They began to quarrel with one another, and they made no secret of the fact that they were angry with Okun. Lenel confronted him one morning, asking if his "lark" had been worth it.

"What was so important that you had to go talk to him?" When Okun tried blaming the whole thing on Radecker and his lies, Lenel asked him again. "We told you Wells was crazy. Now I'm asking you if you learned anything by going to see him?"

Rather than answer, the young man with the crew cut retreated to his room. What *had* he gained by taking his trip up the coast? The onetime director of Area 51 had told him several interesting things, but nothing he could really use. The matter of the telepathic Y-message remained a mystery, and he had less freedom than ever to research the possibility of a second ship. Perhaps the only thing he'd really taken away from the meeting was the haunting vision of the earth being invaded by a conquering species from a distant galaxy. As preposterous as some of it had sounded at the time, Wells's words were taking root in Okun's imagination and growing stronger by the day. He tried to talk to the other men about them, but it was almost as if they were afraid of these ideas. Why else would they dismiss them so quickly when there was ample evidence to support them?

Radecker wasn't finished. He instituted an insidious new paperwork regime. Crate after crate of new equipment had begun to arrive for work on the retrofitting project. Under the new system, every piece of every shipment had to be cataloged in triplicate before it could be used. This meant separate forms to fill out for each bolt, each O-ring, each spool of wire. Then there was another piece of administrative sadism—the daily work proposal. The first hour of every morning was spent filling in these tedious forms.

Things improved slightly over the next two weeks. Cibatutto rigged up a discarded telex machine to help them get around some of the new paperwork, and Dworkin introduced a new card game—bridge— which the old men quickly mastered. One Friday night, Radecker came into the kitchen and found them playing a rowdy game of cards while Okun watched. Just when the wounds Okun had caused began to heal, Radecker tore them open again. He realized Okun had gotten away with humiliating him without suffering a scratch. Something must have snapped, because the next day he dug his claws into Okun the only way he knew how. If he couldn't punish the boy genius directly, he would hit below the belt. He had Freiling sent to a nearby Air Force base for psychological testing to determine if he was mentally fit to continue working at the highly classified labs. Freiling returned shaken and confused. The shrinks had ganged up on him, he said, deliberately done things to confuse him. The old man was terrified at the prospect of being sent to a retirement home-prison like the one Okun had described in San Mateo.

The whole group of them marched off immediately to Radecker's office, but he wouldn't talk to them. "I thought we had a deal, Mr. Radecker," Dworkin called as politely as he could through the closed door.

"Don't talk to me about it; go ask Okun. And think about this the next time one of you decides to cross me." They spent the rest of that Saturday taking care of Freiling, assuring him they wouldn't let him be sent away. When he finally relaxed and fell asleep, it was late at night.

Okun came into the kitchen and found Dworkin sitting there in the dark.

"What's goin' on, can't sleep?"

"A case of indigestion," Dworkin said. When Okun switched on a light, he saw a glass of water and a bottle of pills on the table. "It's probably just heartburn caused by a stressful day."

"You sure you're all right? Should we call somebody?"

The old man laughed. It wasn't that serious. He invited Okun to sit down, and asked him about his visit with Wells. He wanted to know all about the place he was being held and what he had said. After listening for a while, he asked Okun for his opinion. "Do you think he's right? Are we criminals for not telling the world?"

"Maybe. Especially when you look around here and consider the kind of manpower the government is devoting to this research. There ought to be hundreds of people down here, and what have we got? Four men over seventy years old and one doofus who doesn't even have a Ph.D. They aren't taking this project seriously at all. I think Wells is right about one thing. We need to get lots of people working on this. If word got out, people would have to take it seriously and band together to get ready."

"Possibly," Dworkin mused, "but I'm not convinced people would band together. I think it more likely that society would disintegrate. The way you reacted to learning about the ship and seeing the alien bodies was far from typical. When people really begin to believe we are facing annihilation, as Wells does, they tend to withdraw into themselves. I can imagine groups of frightened people abandoning their normal lives and retreating deeper into private misery, or forming private armies and taking to the hills. But that's all speculation," he said, finishing off his glass of water, "and it begs the question, because people are not going to be told. Even if one of us succeeded in putting ourselves on the evening news and telling the whole thing, no one would believe us. You know what happened at Roswell. They're quite skilled at making intelligent persons seem crazy."

"So what's the answer? Just continue going through the motions down here?"

Dworkin stared into his empty glass for a few moments. "I've spent most of my adult life in these rooms, and I'm not sure I have anything to show for it. I was married, you know."

"No, I didn't know that. Any kids?"

"No, thank heavens. But if there had been, I still would have left them. Dr. Wells and I had our differences over the years, but we always agreed the work being done here was important enough to justify our personal sacrifices. The work has been everything, and now I'm afraid it's over."

Okun knew what he must be talking about. "Because you're getting too old?"

"Precisely. It's been a few years since we've lost anyone, and I've allowed myself to forget what it feels like. If he sends Dr. Freiling away, we'll be reduced to four. Soon we'll all be gone, and I worry about what will happen then. I don't know if you are prepared to carry on here by yourself."

They let that idea hover in the air for a while. Brackish considered the possibility of following in Dworkin's footsteps, trading in all his possible futures for the lonely life of a lab rat. He thought briefly of Brinelle, her gangly limbs and wide smile. He knew he'd probably never see her again, but for the moment he let her represent everyone he might meet. Did keeping the labs open mean he would never again have a crush on a girl? Or decide at the last minute to go catch a movie with some friends?

"If these creatures ever did turn hostile," Dworkin pointed out, "you may be the only person in the world who could have us prepared. So far your sponsors in Washington, whoever they are, have denied you nothing. It might be time to petition them for some new personnel. I doubt whether we old fellows are going to be around here much longer."

Okun waved him off. "It's nothing we have to decide tonight. I've still got three years on my contract, and you four guys are going to outlive me by a decade. Now, come on, you should try to get some sleep."

"You're right." He sighed. "I'm feeling awfully tired."

In the morning, Dworkin didn't join them at breakfast. When they went in to check on him, they discovered he'd died in his sleep. One day after learning that Freiling's neck was on the chopping block, they had lost their leader. While Cibatutto got on the phone and began making burial arrangements, the others retreated to their rooms and their personal despair.

"Six down and three to go," Lenel whispered as the minister delivered a brief eulogy over the body. The ceremony was the same one given to the men who had died before Okun arrived. It was all part of a package plan offered to them through their bank. Parducci Mortuary offered embalming, makeup, coffin, a catered open-casket viewing period, transportation to the cemetery, flowers, and interment services all for one low price. The only thing not included was a police escort to the cemetery. The Parducci family, was not friendly with the police. When the minister was finished, he announced there would be a few minutes for those assembled to wish Dr. Dworkin their final farewells. There were more people in attendance than Okun had expected. Two of Dworkin's sisters were there and brought their families with them. There were four or five scientists who had worked with him earlier in his career, Ellsworth, accompanied by two other officers, and Dr. Insolo of the Science and Technology Directorate. Everyone formed a line and filed past the open casket, pausing to say a few words or lay a flower on Dworkin's chest. When Okun approached the pine box, he hardly recognized the figure inside. The cheeks were too rosy and the hair was fluffed up in a way Dworkin had never worn it. When someone behind him uttered the word "lifelike," Brackish felt his heart drop halfway to his knees and quickly headed outside to get some air.

He dumped himself onto a bench next to the chauffeur of the hearse, who was reading a newspaper. "How's it going in there?"

"Tough. Very tough." Okun's voice broke.

"Were you related?"

"Kinda."

The man nodded as if he knew what that meant. The two of them sat there for a few minutes watching the traffic on the street until the driver returned to his reading. Okun was thinking about what Dworkin had said about not knowing if he was prepared to continue the work. He felt a sudden urge to run away, to disappear into the city and hide, to start a normal life like the one the man next to him had. He turned to ask a question, but something caught his eye before he could. A headline on the newspaper read "Chihuahua Quake Darkens Parts of Texas" and then in smaller print, "Electromagnetic Mystery Hampers Construction Efforts." He leaned in closer and started reading the story off the back of the man's paper. The farther down the page he read, the more he nodded. At the end of the column, it said "continued on A6."

Under the watchful gaze of a security agent posted in the parking lot, Brackish went to the van and retrieved his journal notebook. He quickly looked over the notes he'd made after his conversation with Wells. "This is it, this is the real enchilada," he said to himself. He strode back to the ceremony. As he passed the chauffeur he snagged the paper out of the surprised man's hands and carried it inside.

The three older scientists were gathered around the open casket, solemnly conversing with their deceased friend. Okun joined them, thwacking down the newspaper on the coffin so he could straighten it out. "You guys," he said in an excited whisper, "I found it. It's in Mexico."

Bad manners were one thing, but this was flagrant boorishness.

"Brackish, this is neither the time nor the place," Freiling pointed out.

"He's right," Cibatutto growled. "For Sam's sake."

Okun looked them in the eyes. "Sam told me that he

always sacrificed his personal happiness for the sake of the work, and I'm sure he'd want me to read you what's in this article right this second."

Somewhat reluctantly, they made room for him and he stepped up to his place at the head of the coffin, where he kept the paper low and read in a whisper.

"'A massive earthquake measuring 8.2 on the Richter scale rumbled through the desert state of Chihuahua earlier this week, destroying villages, damaging highways, and toppling dozens of high-voltage power poles that bring electricity to the state as well as the Texas towns of Sierra Blanca and Van Horn.'"

"Get to the point."
He skipped down the column.

"'...but attempts to run power through the Nuevo Casas Grandes area have been delayed by severe damage to local roads and the inability to use radio or phones in the area. Indeed, nearly all electrical devices brought to the region known to locals as La Zona del Silencio, or the Silent Zone, experience some sort of disruption.

"'"It's been this way for a long time," said Octavio Juan Marquez, a spokesman for the power company. "Our radios don't work in some of the hills out there. We get a lot of static in some areas, and in others they die out completely. The local people say it's caused by the *chupacabras,* furry animals that hunt little children at night," he said with a laugh.

"'But for residents of the mud-and-thatch villages that surround the area, it is no laughing matter. Speaking through an interpreter, an Indian woman who lives in the area said, "What makes it so scary out there is how quiet it is. No plants grow out there anymore, and animals don't go there, not even insects. That's why people say the *chupacabra* live out there."

"'The untraceable atmospheric disturbances have baffled experts since they began in July of 1947.

U.S. troops stationed farther south in the town of Guerrero conducted an extensive geological survey of the area during the early 1950s, attributing the phenomenon to the huge amounts of iron ore found in the ground.'"

As Okun turned to page A6, he glanced up long enough to see that the scientists realized he was onto something. Any lingering doubts any of them might have had were erased forever when Okun turned the page. There was a small photo of construction crews working on the downed power lines. A long line of giant power poles stretched away into the distance, each one of them shaped like a giant Y.

As far as Okun was concerned, there was no need to read any further. He looked around at his fellow scientists with a look that said, *You know what we have to do now.*

The four men stepped outside and Okun ran through his theory on how the whole thing worked. "OK. We were right. There was another ship flying with the one at Roswell. They were scouting around or whatever when the missile was fired from Polynesia. The blur that moved across the radar screens before the rocket exploded must have been yet another ship. Maybe that ship was hit, or sent out a retreat signal or perhaps—I haven't figured that part out yet. But we do know the Roswell ship took off north and another ship flew south. The Army thought it crashed near Guerrero, and they invaded Mexico looking for it, but they were too far south. The Y must have been a signal from the downed ship."

"Then why didn't that third ship on the radar screen

come and pick them up?" Freiling asked, starting to get it.

"The wires overhead?" Lenel ventured. "Maybe the field of EM waves blocked their signal."

Four heads nodded.

"But that means," Cibatutto pointed out, "during their next visit, if the aliens visit again anytime soon, they will be able to receive the signal. It's probably still being sent if we picked it up last year."

"When's the next time we'll get a window of Van Allen activity?"

Cibatutto pulled out a pen and did a few calculations on the newspaper. "*Mamma mia. Dio de cane!*"

"Translation, please."

"Three days. The inner belt's energy peaks in three days."

Okun, unconsciously fingering the ankh-shaped figurine on his necklace, looked around the group. Trying his best to sound like Dworkin, he said, "Gentlemen, we find ourselves in a rather dramatic predicament. If we return to Area 51 after the funeral, we have little or no hope of finding the second ship before our alien visitors do."

With the ceremony over and Dworkin's coffin loaded in the hearse, people began getting into cars for the trip to the cemetery. Radecker walked to the front of the line of parked cars, expecting to ride in the hearse. "Have some decency, man," Lenel snarled at him when he touched the door handle. "You helped put the man in his grave. Let him take this final ride in dignity with his friends."

The two men traded icy stares until Radecker went farther back and climbed into the van. Lenel opened the passenger side door and wondered how he was going to get inside the vehicle. Okun, Freiling, and Cibatutto were already scrunched in tight next to the driver.

"No, absolutely not," the chauffeur said. "We can't have

anyone else ride in here. I'll get a ticket." But the scientists, some of the Strip's most experienced con men, could be very persuasive. The driver quickly changed his mind and signalled for Lenel to climb in. With some difficulty, he climbed onto Okun's lap, and the procession pulled out of the driveway and headed south along famous Las Vegas Boulevard. Before they'd gotten to the first stoplight, Freiling began chattering about the door.

"Did anybody check the back door? It wasn't closed all the way. When we get to the next light I'm going to get out and check it. The last thing we need is for poor old Sam Dworkin to roll out the back door and spill all over the Strip."

"Don't worry, sir, the door is closed."

"You're awfully kind to say so, and I know you mean well," Freiling doddered, "and I'm sure you're very good at your job, but at the next light, I'll just step out quickly and check."

It only took three stoplights for Freiling to annoy the man so thoroughly that he screamed, "All right already, I'll check the darn door." He got out and stormed to the rear of the hearse, opened the door, and yelled to the passengers in the front seat, "Like I said, the door was closed. Now I am going to close the door again and make sure it is securely sealed." But before he could execute his plan, Freiling had slid himself into the driver's seat and stomped down on the accelerator pedal. The tires screamed as the vehicle peeled out into the cross traffic moving through the intersection. The sudden momentum caused the coffin to slide out the back and crash, right side up, onto the roadway. Thanks to blind luck and the quick reactions of several drivers, the hearse bolted through the intersection untouched.

While his passengers held on tight, Freiling, who hadn't driven anything in over twenty years, pushed the Cadillac engine up to seventy miles per hour while Dworkin did his part by holding Radecker and the rest of the procession at bay.

Running over traffic islands, scattering pedestrians, and ignoring his passengers' pleas for him to slow down, Freiling pointed the nose of the machine at the center of the road and roared straight through town. They were headed for the Tropicana, but their driver was so focused on weaving through traffic he didn't see it until it was nearly too late. *What, here already?* he asked himself, and pulled the wheel hard to the right, steering toward what looked like a driveway. While several nearby cars swerved, skidded, and crashed into one another, Freiling ran the hearse onto a curb, blowing out the two front tires. Undaunted, he plowed through some of the landscaping, over another curb, and up to the Tropicana's front doors. While dumbfounded valets looked on, the three elderly fugitives, assisted by their younger accomplice, jogged through the front doors.

It wasn't long before Radecker pulled up, but long enough for the old cardsharps, who knew the building well, to make themselves hard to find. Half an hour after they'd disappeared through the front doors, he had forty men scouring the building in a door-to-door search. And just in case they'd somehow managed to slip out, he called in the sheriff's office and the Highway Patrol to set up a perimeter around the entire city. They were searching every car headed out of town. Radecker asked himself where the old men would go if they had already fled the building and, to his credit, he guessed right. He jumped in the van and tore down the street. A short distance later, he parked the car on the street outside Parducci Savings and ran inside.

Salvatore Parducci was in the middle of counting a stack of bills and didn't want to lose count. He ignored Radecker's questions about seeing three old men in suits until a hand swept across the counter and scattered the money on the floor. When Sal looked up, Radecker had a pistol pointed at his face. "Yes, sir, how can we help you today?"

"Where are they, damn it? They're hiding in here, aren't they?"

"The three old men? We got a lot of retired people as customers. Can you describe them for me?" In the background there was a sudden high whine that sounded like an electric motor.

"Lenel, Cibatutto, and Freiling," Radecker said, coming around the counter to search the office. "Recognize those names?"

"Very well. My family has been doing business with them for many years." Parducci held his hands away from his body. He remained perfectly still and perfectly relaxed, even when Radecker kicked open one of the locked office doors to look inside.

"When's the last time you saw them?"

"You're not with the IRS, are you?"

"What's that?" The whine of the motor had turned to a hollow slapping sound.

"What's what?"

"That noise?"

"Oh, the noise: That thupa-thupa-thupa sound? That would be Parducci Enterprises' helicopter."

Radecker rushed to the window and tore back the curtains in time to catch a glimpse of his employees lifting off. He turned back to the heavily bejeweled banker, who explained, "We're a full-service financial institution."

By the time Radecker's second APB in as many months went out to law-enforcement officials across the western U.S., the fugitive scientists were renting a car with cash at Ontario Airport in California.

12

CHIHUAHUA

With Okun at the helm, the crew headed south. The rental agency had put them into a brand-new Ford LTD station wagon, which bobbed and weaved down the freeway like a small yacht. Their plan was to slip across the border at Tijuana as quickly as possible. During Okun's last AWOL escapade, Radecker had mobilized a small army to find him. They could only imagine what kind of dragnet he'd set up this time.

Okun had never been to Mexico, so he didn't realize anything was strange when he pulled up to the San Diego side of the border and found himself in a long line of traffic waiting to go across.

"Something's not right here," Lenel said, leaning forward from the backseat. "There's supposed to be a line on the *other* side, not this one. Entering Mexico should be faster than this."

"Maybe things have changed since the last time you came down here." Okun shrugged.

"No. Turn around and get out of here," Lenel told him. But it was too late for that. They were in the middle of seven lanes of one-way traffic. So the older men quickly devised Plan B. One by one they slipped out of the station wagon and made their way to the footbridge. They would wait for one of the many tour groups crossing into Tijuana for a day of shopping and blend in with them. Okun thought they were being a little too careful at the time, but when he approached the gate he saw two men in suits and sunglasses walking back and forth, looking into every car. When one of them came close to him, Okun flashed him a peace sign and a smile. The man moved on without changing expression to continue his hunt. *Has Radecker figured out where we're headed?* Okun wondered. Then, he thought about the complicated path he'd taken to deduce the location of this second spacecraft. *Naw. Radecker won't figure it out.*

"Where are you headed?" the uniformed border guard asked when Okun pulled even with the booth.

"Ensenada."

"What's the purpose of your visit?"

"*Mucho* tequila."

The guy smiled, told him to drive safely, and waved him through.

He found the three old men waiting for him a hundred yards up the road. They climbed in, and off they went. Once they found their way to the road they wanted and were out of town, Okun drove twenty miles an hour faster than the rutted roads would allow.

That night, they pulled into the mountain town of Nuevo Casas Crandes about 10:30, expecting to find the place completely dead, out of commission until morning. All the way up the twisting road that took them into the foothills of the dry Sierra Madre mountains, they saw downed telephone poles and freshly broken cinder-block houses. But, in the "Grandes," there was little evidence of the huge earthquake that had rolled through the town a week before. The main street was lined with old wood-frame buildings. The brightest, loudest place on the block was the Taverna Terazas, which stood directly opposite the town's church. A jukebox inside filled the street with sound, adding to the noisy chug-a-lug of portable generators. A dozen men sat outside the bar, talking and laughing, chairs tipped back against the wall.

Lenel, Freiling, Cibatutto, and Okun, all of them still dressed in the suits they'd worn to Dworkin's funeral, parked the car and walked down the center of the street. Striding four abreast, they looked like a not-very-threatening group of gunslingers. The men outside the saloon were tough-looking dudes, vaqueros who looked like the real deal: dusty leather boots, dungarees, and Western shirts. They stopped laughing when the Norte Americanos walked up.

"*Hola, amigos,*" Okun called as he walked past them and through the front doors. The scientists followed him inside. The small bar was almost full. Okun came in and took a table near the jukebox, which was playing a rowdy ranchero song. Conversation lulled for a minute while the men at the bar turned around to have a look at these four dressed-up gringos, but then resumed. When a waitress walked past, Okun ordered them four beers, then leaned in over the table. "Once we find the Silent Zone, we'll drive down the line of power poles, and I'll find the point-of-view angle I got from the screen. I'll stand in the same relation to the power pole I saw in the image on the screen."

"You remember it well enough?"

"Trust me. It's Etch-A-Sketched across the inside of my brain."

"How are we going to find out where this place is?" Freiling asked.

Lenel motioned toward the bar. "Judging from the uniforms of those men at the bar, they work for the electric company. We could follow them out there in the morning."

"I have a better idea," Cibatutto announced. He paused to hand the waitress a twenty for the beers, and told her to keep the change. "We hire a guide."

"It better be somebody we don't like very much,"

Lenel warned darkly, "because if we actually discover an alien ship, he might not live very long."

Okun saw how it could work out. "Dr. C's right. It'll be faster if we have somebody who can take us out there. If we find a ship, we do our best to hide it from him. Two of us can stay out there while the two others ride back into town with the guy to call in our reinforcements. If he finds out about it, too bad for him. There's too much riding on this."

"Slow down, kid, you're starting to sound like Victor Frankenstein," Lenel said.

Freiling had been waiting for a lull in the conversation. He turned to Cibatutto. "I'm still wondering why you gave that waitress so dang much money?"

Hie answer walked up to the table. A skinny young mestizo kid, maybe seventeen, came over to their table, turned a chair around, and straddled it. "You wanna buy some pots?"

Okun did a double take. "Buy some huh?"

"Pots. Bowls. Ceramicas." He explained in plain English how Americans sometime came to Grandes wanting to buy pottery robbed from burial sites of the Mogollon Indians. He pronounced the word mo-go-YON. Others came to see the caves the Mogollon had once lived in.

"We're not here for pots. We want to go out to the Silent Zone." Okun pulled the rolled-up newspaper out of his pocket and showed it to the kid. "You know anybody who can take us to this place?"

"We will pay a hundred dollars," Cibatutto added.

"Me!" the kid yelled. "I'll take you. I'm not afraid of la Zona."

"Done. But only if we leave by dawn. *Temprano en el mañana*," Okun said, reaching across the table to seal the deal with a handshake. "What's your name?"

"Pedro." The cocky kid was grinning like he'd just swindled the gringos out of a million dollars. If he had known the risk he was taking, he would have asked for much more. Not only could he guide them to the Silent Zone, but he could lead them to the only hotel in town, and, for an extra few bucks, he would take care of getting the food and water stockpiled. He'd learned English living in Los Angeles for nine years, but his father decided it wasn't a good place for kids to be growing up and moved them back here to their hometown. Now Pedro was sitting around in bars offering strangers black-market artifacts robbed out of graves. The four men made a list of all the items they would need for the next day.

"Why do you wanna go out there?"

The four men looked at one another uncertainly.

"Can you keep a secret?" Okun asked.

"Yeah, of course."

"You really promise not to tell anyone?"

"Yeah, of course."

"We're treasure hunters," he whispered. "We work for a mining company, and we think these hills are loaded with treasure."

The kid came out of his slouch and sat straight up. "You mean gold and silver?"

"No. I'm talking about iron ore, millions of tons of it. We read about the Silent Zone and said to ourselves, there must be iron ore up there."

That sounded boring, and the kid lost interest immediately which was just what Okun intended.

Early the next morning, they met him outside their hotel. He'd found most of the supplies they'd ordered except the flashlights. He explained, however, that he'd gone into the church across the street and taken a bag full of candles. "I'll pay 'em back later." An hour before the first construction crews got rolling, the scientists followed their guide's directions to the edge of town, where they turned onto a dirt road. They headed out, driving the station wagon where it was never meant to go. They bounced along a badly rutted utility road, which carried them deeper into the hills. Eventually, they rounded a turn and found themselves in a huge flat valley at least ten miles wide. "This is the Valley of the Caves," Pedro told them. More than a valley, it was a huge open plain, largely barren. Towering in the distance were the Y-shaped power poles. Beyond them, sharp vertical cliffs led the way to endless hills climbing to distant peaks. Even from that distance, they could see that some of the tall poles were listing, damaged by the earthquake. As they approached the lines, they saw cranes, giant spools of wire, and other construction equipment. Some of the power lines had broken away from the poles.

They asked Pedro about the Mogollon Caves he had mentioned the night before. He told them what he'd learned from the black-market art buyers. The Mogollon Indians had built the caves and lived in them for centuries until they suddenly disappeared about five hundred years ago. He explained how the Mogollon, like other tribes in the region, had tied cradle-boards to the heads of infants, in order to cause deformations of the skull. They weren't natural, somehow, the kid said. Their heads were weirdly shaped, they made extraordinary pottery, and they built great cities like Paquime, then vanished suddenly without a trace. Their entire civilization abruptly ceased to exist, and no one knew why.

"Maybe the *chupacabras* ate them," Okun teased.

"You laugh now," Pedro said, "but just wait till you get out there. It's not natural. Nothing lives out there, not even flies." The word *chupacabra* was usually translated as "goat sucker." The legend of these feral four-legged creatures was the State of Chihuahua's answer to the

Loch Ness monster. "They live off the blood of other animals," Pedro went on. "That's why no animals will go into the Zone. Some people say they're like the pets of *los extranjeros*, the ones who came from outer space."

All heads turned toward the boy, who went on.

"A long time ago, they say a spaceship crashed down there by Guerrero, about a hundred miles south of here, and some of the Indians took care of the spacemen. They lived with the Indians for about ten years, and the *chupas* were their pets. But when the spacemen died, the *chupas* got lonely for their masters and ran away. Then they came to live in the Zone, and if any animals go in there, they kill them and suck their blood."

Okun's mind was already on other matters. "How much farther?"

"Keep going, it's still far." A few minutes later, Pedro was leaning forward, looking for something in the cliffs. "There's one." He pointed. "That's one of the caves."

When the scientists saw what the kid was pointing at, their jaws dropped. Each time Pedro had mentioned caves, they had pictured tunnels leading into the ground. But now they saw what he was talking about. High above the ground they saw a gigantic recess scooped out of the face of the cliff, two hundred feet across and fifty feet tall. Small adobe houses were built inside, some of them perched at the very edge. It was a very small town constructed inside the giant cubbyhole three stories above the ground. Without a word, they all piled out of the car for a closer look. Even though they were racing against time, this place deserved a quick tour. They had all arrived at the obvious conclusion: *This cliff dwelling is large enough to hold one of the alien ships.*

Getting up to the cave involved negotiating a series of stone stairs and rickety wooden ladders, which the older men did surprisingly well. They wandered deeper under the stone ceiling toward the nether reaches of the cave. It was deep enough to hold two vehicles like the one at Area 51. Crumbling mud-and-stone walls that showed a string of single-room apartments had been built against the interior walls. Several of the walls at the back still retained their curiously shaped, windowlike doorways. The ceilings were blackened in several places with the soot of ancient fires. Broken bottles and crushed beer cans had been scattered around by the local kids, who used the prehistoric cliff dwelling as a modern party spot.

Pedro led the men toward the edge and pointed out a narrow stone trail cut into the cliff. He called it the back door, and explained that most of the caves had such entrances. "If somebody tried to attack them, the Mogollon pulled up the ladders. If somebody tried to come in on one of these trails, you could knock them off with a big stick."

Before climbing down, the men stood at the edge of the cliff, feeling the warm wind blowing straight up its face, and admired the spectacular view. The open sweep of the land gave way to the infinite desert stretching out to the curve of the earth. It was a beautiful morning, shirtsleeve weather and cloudless electric blue sky.

"I can't think of a better place to hide a ship," Freiling commented when the boy was out of earshot.

Back in the car, they followed the line of power poles, moving over the rough earth at speeds which threatened to snap the suspension of the heavily loaded station wagon. Pedro said they were getting close and turned on the radio, telling them, "When it goes out, you know you're in la Zona." When the radio suddenly developed static, everyone looked at one another. When it died completely, they kept their eyes straight ahead, scanning the hills for anything unusual.

"How big is this area? Where the radios won't work," Okun asked.

"Big, I don't know."

"Have you been to the other side, where the radios work again?"

"Yeah, it's over there near Galeana. I don't know how far it is."

The men in the backseat unfolded a map of the area and asked him questions, trying to determine the size of the Silent Zone. Eventually they decided the center of it was about five miles ahead. After three miles, Okun slowed down and took a long look at one of the huge steel power poles. He switched off the car and got out, still focused on the Y-shaped tower. But something else caught his attention.

"Wow. Listen to that." They were surrounded by an ocean of soundlessness. Except for the occasional puff of a breeze rustling through the weeds, there was absolute stillness. Until that moment, Okun and the others hadn't realized how much background sound they'd been listening to all day: the flapping wings of birds, things crawling through the bushes, the buzzing of small insects. Suddenly, each man could hear how loud his own breathing was.

"You see?" Pedro asked. "That's why they call it the Silent Zone."

Okun took out his notebook and examined a sketch he'd made of the Y a few days after he'd first seen it. Then he climbed on top of some nearby rocks. He moved left, then right, then forward, until what was in front of his eyes matched what he'd seen on the screen. If the pole in front of him was the one in the alien transmission, the ship must be somewhere very near where he was standing. He disappeared into some bushes growing at the base of a cliff, reemerging a few moments later and shaking his head.

"Let's try the next pole."

They drove a few hundred feet past the next pole and

went through the same routine. This time, everyone helped scour the rocks and bushes along the base of the cliffs. But this proved to be impractical because it took the old men so long to get back to the car. It was already early afternoon, and, although no one said anything out loud, they all knew time was running out. Even Pedro started to pick up the pace. He and Okun working together could investigate one of the spots in five minutes. Each time they climbed back in the car, Okun stared down the long row of power lines, stretching off toward the vanishing point, and reminded himself, *We have all night and tomorrow morning—be methodical, be patient.*

They came to another set of cliffs and found two cliff dwellings in roughly the right relationship to the nearest power poles. The group spent a precious hour exploring these two caves and the area around them. As they drove toward the next pole, Lenel brought up the subject of contacting Spelman.

"It's getting late. We should call Spelman tomorrow morning whether we find it or not. If we're right about all of this, there's a good possibility there will be air traffic in this area tomorrow night. We'll explain the whole theory and maybe convince him we're not crazy."

"All the phones are dead in town. We'll have to drive clear down to the main highway again."

"And we're already down to half a tank of gas."

"Maybe we should go back into town and figure out our next move."

Okun kicked the dirt. He wasn't ready to give up, but knew the men were right.

"Hey, look up there," Freiling interrupted. "Look at that cactus and all the plants around it. Isn't that kinda fishy? All these cliffs around here are bare rock, but there's a bunch of plants all growing in one little area up there."

The crew walked to the base of the cliffs and looked

up. They were standing near a twenty-foot rock wall, which led to a steep, forty-five-degree slope, which led in turn to a second set of much taller vertical walls. There was something odd about the patch of rock Freiling had pointed out. All day, they'd been noticing agave plants and cacti clinging to the rocks. After establishing toeholds on the cliffs, the plants spread their roots over the exposed surface of the rock. No roots were visible on this cliff despite the number of plants. Could there be a hidden cave up there?

Pedro climbed up the wall in front of them, then walked carefully up the slope until he came to the top. The cliffs surrounding him formed an eerie tower of ribbed rock bleached pale yellow by the elements. Great black streaks ran down them, as if someone had poured buckets of tar over the sides.

Okun went back to the car, retrieved a tire iron and a candle, then scrambled up the hill himself. When he reached the narrow shelf of flat rock at the base of the upper cliffs, he noticed a couple of strange things. The area Freiling had pointed to was smooth. It didn't match the wavy rocks of the neighboring cliffs. Also, there were long, thin cracks running through it. They looked like the ones he'd seen in plaster walls after quakes in Los Angeles.

He stepped back, spotted a squarish hole near his feet, and poked the tire iron into it. He couldn't find the back of the opening. He lay down and put his face up to the hole, but could see nothing. Running his hands over the surface of the cliff, he became convinced it was a wall built to conceal one of the caves. He picked up the tire iron and used the wedge end to begin chipping away at the face of the hillside.

The surface was hard, but it wasn't the solid boulder it appeared to be. Handfuls of sand and small stones rolled away down the slope behind him. When one of his strokes caused a dull sound, he brushed away the last pieces of debris. Something in the hole was made of a soft, patterned material. On closer inspection, it turned out to be dried grass woven to form a kind of mat. He pushed on it and felt it give. *Strange.* He slashed at the matting with his tire iron and succeeded in breaking through it. He started fumbling with one of the candles to look inside, but before he could light it, he knew he had found what he was looking for. Wafting out of the hole came a distinctive aroma, something like ammonia.

"We got it. It's here!" he yelled down the cliff. "I can smell the pod chairs from here." He lit a candle and inserted it through the hole. The cave inside was huge, narrower than the first cave but much deeper. And sitting in the middle of the space, about twenty paces from him, was a dusty alien spacecraft. "Gotcha, baby," he told the ship. "I can't believe I finally found you!" He backed out of the hole and started jumping around, waving his arms in the air screaming, "It's here. It's here. I can see it. We did it!" In his excitement, he jumped too high and the gravel underfoot gave way. He crashed to his back, then started sliding down the slope. He was headed for a two-story plunge to the rocks below, but reached out at the last second and latched on to one of the bushes, his body doing a 180-degree flip. Head dangling over the edge, he smiled at the upside-down scientists. "There's a ship in there. Identical to the one we've got. I think it's time to call in the Marines."

"Young man, get away from that opening," Cibatutto cried jut. Pedro had come back across the huge stone shelf to see what all the excitement was about. Noticing the hole Okun had shipped into the wall, he started poking around it, curious.

"Hey, Pedro, get away from there."

"What's in there?"

"Nothing, please don't go near it."

"Why not? I wanna see it."

Okun was too far down the slippery slope to get there in time. He knew if Pedro saw the spaceship, it would go hard on him. Desperate, Okun yelled as loud as he could. *"Chupacabra!"* The kid froze in his tracks. "We're not really looking for iron. We're looking for the goat sucker, and this is his home. Don't let him pull you inside!" Suddenly the boy wouldn't be far enough away from the hole. He retreated along the narrow shelf at the base of the upper cliffs until he was around a corner.

Thirty minutes later, the five of them were standing around he car again. Pedro had found two trails running along the edge of the cliff. One of them was a switchback leading up to the top of the bluffs, while the other one came out of the hills not far from where the car was parked.

It was time to split up. Okun and Lenel would stay and investigate the ship while Cibatutto and Freiling took the kid to find the nearest phone.

"Time is of the essence," Cibatutto observed. "We've only got about twenty-four hours until our friends show up." So off they sped to find the nearest phone.

"Let's hurry up and get inside before dark."

Okun helped Lenel, unsteady, climb the narrow trail. They came out onto the great stone shelf outside of the hidden cave. Lenel sat down and watched the sun sink toward the horizon as Okun used the tire iron and his bare hands to cut a doorway into the cave.

13

THE MOGOLLON CAVE

Radecker had been so busy setting up his dragnet And feeling sorry for himself, he didn't get around to questioning the chauffeur until the next morning. The man had spent the night sleeping on a bench at the police station. He repeated everything that had been said in the car, including a verbatim account of Freiling's infernal jabbering.

"In my opinion, it's something the young guy saw in the newspaper." He described how Okun had snatched the paper but of his hands and was still holding it as they began the drive toward the cemetery. "If these guys were dangerous criminals, why wasn't I warned? And who's gonna pay for fixing up the hearse?"

When one of the cops handed Radecker a copy of Saturday's paper, it didn't take him long to figure out which story had caught Okun's eye. Now it was his turn to nod. By he time he was finished reading the story, he knew exactly where they were headed. He grinned at the chauffeur and wrote a phone number on the back of his business card. "You've been very helpful. Call this number. They'll fix your car." Then he turned, to one of the cops. "I need to use a phone for a private call."

He was shown into a small office and dialed Spelman's direct line. "I think I've figured out where they're headed."

Spelman told him to hold the line, then passed the receiver to someone else. "Is this Radecker?"

"Yes, sir. Who's this?"

The man ignored him. "We found out your boys rented a car at Ontario Airport yesterday. The vehicle is a gold Ford LTD station wagon with wood-trim panels, California plates CYS 385. You got that?"

"Yes, sir."

"You say you know where they're headed?"

"I believe so, sir. But before I say anything, I'll need to know who I'm talking to and if you have proper clearance."

"This is Deputy Director Nimziki. Now where are they?"

"Mexico, sir. Somewhere in the State of Chihuahua, probably in the town of Guerrero." He went on to explain Okun's sudden interest in the newspaper and the likely connection to a paragraph in the Majestic 12 documents he had personally inked out before handing the document over to Okun. "He must have learned about it from Wells."

"You think they're down there looking for an alien vehicle?"

"Yes, sir," Radecker said almost apologetically. He'd been given very few specific instructions on how to do his job, but one thing had been made crystal clear: deny Okun access to information concerning other spacecraft. It seemed simple enough, but he had failed miserably. Okun had learned everything, despite his efforts. "With your permission, Mr. Nimziki, I'll fly down there immediately and round them up."

There was a pause while the man on the other end thought it over. "No, that won't be necessary. You've served your purpose. Collect your things and report back to Company Headquarters for reassignment."

"Yes, sir. Thank you, sir." He hung up the phone, confused. Until that moment he had no idea who'd been pulling the strings on the project, and he was surprised it went right to the top, Nimziki's office. Everyone in the company knew the presidential appointee wasn't the real power at the CIA. Day-to-day operations and who-knew-how-many covert operations were increasingly run out of the Deputy Director's Office. It was only a matter of time until he was named to head the Agency. But what had he meant by *You've served your purpose*? That sounded ominous. At least he'd mentioned reassignment. Radecker allowed himself to be optimistic in spite of the mess he'd allowed to happen. Perhaps he was going to be promoted after all. At least he knew that wherever they sent him, it couldn't be any worse than being trapped in Area 51.

The front wall of the cave was an ingenious construction of meticulously stacked stone, woven grass, and mud. After baking in the desert sun for twenty-five years, it was almost as hard as solid stone. When Okun hesitantly stepped through the opening, he noticed another curious piece of construction material: a large section of shell armor. He recognized it as the circular door of the alien ship. The last light of day was coming through the squarish hole Okun had found earlier. When he lit one of the candles and approached the hole, he made a rather gruesome discovery. Something was lying in front of it. The thing looked like a degraded plastic bag with hands and feet. He moved closer and discovered it was the decomposed body of an alien. The hands and feet, made of a thicker, tougher material than the rest of the body, were decaying more slowly. Lenel came up behind him, holding a candle of his own.

"He must have been looking out his little window waiting to be rescued when he died. The electromagnetic field generated by the power lines must have created a ceiling which allowed the signal to travel laterally, but not upward. That must be why the aliens never located the distress signal."

Okun lowered himself toward the body until his face

was only inches above the decomposed corpse and looked through the opening. "Guess what the last thing he was looking at when he died?"

"A large Y standing in a desolate landscape?"

"Bingo."

"It looks like this one has been dead for years. But we picked up his visual signal less than two years ago. Does it mean there's a telepathic interface between the creatures and their ship?"

"Makes sense. And this little guy must have programmed the ship's sending unit to repeat the message endlessly." He looked over his shoulder at Lenel. "Now I know why the image felt so lonely. This would be a crummy way to die, marooned in a cave on some foreign planet."

Lenel grunted. He wasn't about to start feeling sorry for the extraterrestrials. He walked deeper into the darkness to take a look at the ship. They lit a dozen candles, which cast an eerie, dancing glow around the ceiling. Like the first cave they'd explored, this one had mud-brick apartments standing side by side around the perimeter of the space. Staying close to one another, the two men began walking around the ship. "This one didn't crash," Lenel observed. "There's no sign of damage anywhere. The shell armor seems to be in perfect condition. I don't even see scrape marks."

Okun squatted down. "One problem. Where are the thrusters? This baby's lying flat on its belly. Shouldn't it be raised up off the floor?"

Lenel shrugged and moved on. They walked all the way around the exterior of the ship, pausing to make an investigation of the small rooms farthest from the mouth of the cave. They found several Mogollon artifacts, including what seemed to be a grinding stone, but no evidence at all that the alien had used the rooms. As they returned to the ship and came around toward its nose,

Okun's attention was drawn to something happening behind the windows. He was about to say something when he took another step and fell into a hole. The sudden scream and downward flicker of candlelight scared Lenel half to death. "Okun? What happened?"

"I'm OK," he said, "but be careful. There's a hole over here." When he struck a match and relit his candle, Lenel came to the edge of the three-foot-deep pit. He reached a hand down to help Okun climb out, but Okun didn't take it. He was sniffing. "The ammonia smell is stronger down here." He turned around and noticed he was in a trench that led in he direction of the ship's door. "It looks like this tunnel leads inside the ship. Should we go in?"

"What if I said no, that we should wait for the help to get here?"

Okun admitted, "I'd probably go in anyway."

"So why are you even asking?" the habitual sourpuss mapped. "Help me down into this hole."

They crawled the thirty feet to the center of the ship on heir hands and knees, the ammonia smell growing stronger. When they were under the open hatch, Okun saw the light of his candle flickering across the dark interior of the ship. Something suddenly struck him as terribly wrong. As Lenel caught up with him, muttering something under his breath, Okun reached out and arrested the old man's progress with a hand clamped onto his shoulder. He was looking up into the ship in a way that made Lenel very uneasy.

"Now what?" he whispered.

"Listen. You hear that?" Okun was moving his index finger around in a very slow loop to show how the sound was repeating itself. After watching him do this for a minute and not hearing anything, Lenel spoke a few decibels louder than he needed to.

"My ears are shot. I can't hear anything."

Cautiously, Okun stood up, not sure he was going to like what he saw inside. Was it possible there were survivors after all these years? He thought of Trina Gluck's story, and how she'd been nose to nose with the Tall One. Although there was no one moving inside the ship, he was amazed when he located the source of the repetitive noise: the instrument panel at the front of the ship was surging to glowing life every few seconds. He climbed inside and walked to the front of the ship. He knelt and timed the surges against his wristwatch. To find part of the ship working didn't amaze him. He'd expected to discover the signaling system still carrying the message with the Y. But what he saw happening around him made no sense. *All* the systems were pulsing to a very slow heartbeat. "This is impossible," he yelled. "This thing is using way way way too much energy. Why does it have so much juice left?" He turned and went to confront Lenel with these questions but suddenly leaped backwards, sprawling against the dashboard, his heart suddenly pounding like a fire bell.

"What's the matter with you now?" Lenel demanded, crawling into the cabin.

A speechless Brackish could only point to something on the floor. Lenel walked over and found three more decomposed bodies in the corner. They had been left in sitting positions, but, over the years, the heads and chests had collapsed in on themselves, sinking to the floor. Three sets of legs pointed toward the front of the ship. Okun had been so intent on checking the instrument panel, he'd literally walked right over them without noticing. The papery remains of a leg had been packed down under his shoe.

"Don't worry. They're just as dead as the one outside, and you didn't seem scared of him."

Okun looked at the cadavers like he'd just swallowed a mouthful of chunky milk. "But the way they're sitting there. Creep-o-rama extraordinaire."

"What's this power issue you were hollering about?"

Brackish got back to business. "Look at these instruments!" The two of them watched the instruments run through their four-second cycles. The yellow shell glowed dimly, the bony arms of the steering mechanism twitched, the set of tubes under the pod chairs expanded. "Where is all this energy coming from?"

"Beats me." The old man shrugged. He started to say something else, then stopped.

"What? What were you going to say?"

"Based on what we know about these ships, what's the most logical energizing source?"

Okun's mind toiled in darkness for a few moments until a lightbulb popped on. "You're suggesting these power surges are coming from another ship? Which must mean there's another alien vehicle within transmission range. Which means..."

"Exactly. They could be on their way down here right now."

This theory did not brighten the mood of any of the life-forms inside the cabin, living or dead.

"Wait a sec," Okun complained. "We worked out the Van Allen connection a couple of times. We're supposed to have until tomorrow!"

"Don't get your knickers all twisted up, son. It's only an idea. Who knows where this power is coming from. Maybe this ship is using the earth's natural electromagnetism as a battery, or maybe this is what happens every time the belts show increased radioactivity."

But half an hour later, the instruments were pulsing in three-second cycles. Both Okun and Lenel were convinced an alien ship, perhaps even a small armada of them, was approaching Chihuahua.

"I figure we've got an hour, maybe two if we're lucky,"

Lenel said. "This ship is in perfect shape. We've got to learn as much as we can before they get here. I'll go below and try to get a look at the aqua-box. You stay here and learn what you can about the control mechanisms." Okun, mind racing in a thousand directions at once, vaguely agreed. "And because this is an emergency, I'm going to lend you my secret weapon." Lenel reached into his breast pocket and pulled out a three-inch-long screwdriver. "Pull that panel apart and make us some schematics drawings we can use on the ship back home."

As Lenel trudged off, Okun absentmindedly set to work prying the control system components out of their fittings. When he began to sketch, his mind began to wander. He'd poured his heart into finding this ship, and now it looked like he was going to lose it again. He wondered how tough the aliens really were. Could he and Lenel, like the ancient Mogollon Indians, defend their cave? He imagined pelting the unwelcome visitors with rocks as they tried to climb the hillside. If that failed, there was always the tire iron.

When they saw Mad Dog Okun at the top of the slope wearing a menacing sneer, would they turn and run? Would they fight? Or would he feel his body go numb and the weapon drop from his hands like Trina Gluck's toothbrush had dropped into the sink?

Then there was another possibility. When the approaching aliens were close enough, the craft he was sitting in would most likely be able to fly. He pictured himself glued into the pilot's pod chair. When the first eebie showed itself in the freshly cut doorway, he would slam the ship in gear, blast through the wall, and fly north to Groom Lake before the aliens knew what hit them. Two drawbacks of this plan were that Okun had never flown any type of aircraft in his life, and he didn't have the foggiest notion of how the ship's controls worked.

He went back to the tire-iron scenario.

He had finished sketching the major components of the control systems into his notebook when he heard Lenel cursing and grumbling below the hatchway. He checked he cycles again. The power throbs were coming every second and a half now and appeared to be growing stronger. *Very* soon, the ship would be receiving a continuous flow of energy. Staying as far as possible from the straight-legged remains of the three bodies, he went to see what all he noise was about.

"I can't dig this out. I'm too damn old." Okun stepped down into the tunnel and checked Lenel's progress. He'd managed to dig about a foot and a half back toward the aqua-box. That left three and a half feet to go. Okun took the tire iron and began working furiously, driving it into the earth walls and breaking off handfuls of dirt with each thrust. He should have been doing this job all along. None of the schematics he'd made would be worth anything if they couldn't figure out the power-generating system. But the floor of the cave was packed hard, and it quickly became clear he wouldn't reach the door to the aqua-box in time.

He and Lenel both froze when they heard an unfamiliar sound. It was coming from inside the ship. When they looked inside, they saw that the lights on the instrument panel were no longer strobing. The ship was up and running.

"It's time to get out of here."

"Not yet," Okun said. "We've got to get a look at the power system." He proposed the idea of defending the cave to Lenel, who looked at him like he was crazy, then got down on all fours and started crawling out from under the ship.

"You stay here if you want to. That's not the way I want to die."

Out of frustration, Okun stabbed the earth several

more times with his tire iron. But then, realizing it was too late, he collapsed against one of the walls, sweating profusely. As he was considering his next move the whole ship seemed to let out a shuddering moan. There was a loud cracking noise as it began to lift off the ground. It rose slowly, an inch at a time.

Lenel, candle near his face, seemed to rise with it. Standing on his knees, he straightened up as far as the rising ship would allow. He had a wide-open expression of wonder on his face, like a kid watching a magic show. He let out a giddy laugh, looking back toward Okun. "Will ya look at that! It's the most beautiful thing I've ever seen." The ship continued lifting until it cracked hard against the stone ceiling, sending a few chips of rock skittering down its sloped sides.

"The thruster rockets seem to be in good shape. Looks like they dug holes for them to sit in."

The black alien ship, a perfect twin of the one at Area 51, floated three feet above the ground, as mute and mysterious as a sphinx. Okun, oedipal, wanted to solve one more of its riddles before he left the cave. Ignoring Lenel's protests, he wriggled himself into the freshly created gap between the hull of the ship and the floor of the cave. He began pulling at the cover door of the aqua-box.

"Uh-oh," Lenel said. "What's that?"

"What's what?" Okun grunted between tugs.

Lenel shuffled toward the door to the cave, leaned outside, and searched the sky. Many miles from the nearest city lights, the stars shone down unobstructed and seemed to form a plush and twinkling blanket in the sky. While he was watching, one of these stars seemed to split in two. Part of it remained high in the atmosphere while another one moved closer.

"We've got company! They're here." Lenel turned around and shouted. "It's time to go."

"Almost. I've almost got it." With a final yank, Okun liberated the door from its slot. It came free of the ship and landed heavily on top of him. When Lenel heard the ooof! sound, he repeated his warning that it was time to leave.

"Start without me," Okun called from beneath the door. "I'll catch up."

Lenel poked his head out the door indecisively and looked at the stone shelf leading to the trail. "All right. I'll take the same path we came up on. Meet me at the bottom of the hill. How much longer are, you going to be?"

If Okun couldn't find a way to get his head and chest out from under the heavy section of shell armor, he was going to be there permanently. "A minute or two," his muffled voice answered.

"OK, two minutes. No longer!" Lenel warned. He could see the swirl of green light coming from beneath the ship and knew Okun had gotten the door off. He stepped through the opening and began edging along the top of the slope.

Okun concentrated on making himself very skinny and eventually succeeded in worming out from under the door. Then he looked up and beheld the spectacular play of light caused by the aqua-box, its energy racing around the inside of the chamber like a transparent cyclone of crystal green water. An exact clone of the one at Area 51, it exhibited the same paper-thin walls of rock, the same hairwidth filaments arranged in a complex geometrical pattern. But there was one important exception: floating in the center of the hexagonal chamber, suspended in midair, was a small piece of metal shaped like an ankh. Like a gyroscope, it was spinning and rolling while remaining in one spot. It seemed to be gathering the energy off the sides of the hexagon and sending it out in a controlled manner. Each of the ankh's four arms sent out a razor-thin beam.

He remembered the chaotic way the other ship's box had purged the system of energy and how the ships would have had to fly improbably close to one another. This was the answer, and it had been hanging around his neck the whole time. Incredible!

When something moved across the doorway, Okun reached out and grabbed the tire iron. But it was only Lenel, who immediately concealed himself behind the rock wall. "Too late. They're here." He pointed up through the ceiling. "They've found us, and it's too dark out there for me to see where I'm going."

Okun gathered up his possessions. He'd seen how the aqua-box worked. He was ready to help Lenel make his escape. But as he made to leave, he decided he needed to try one last experiment. He slipped his necklace off and tried to undo the knot, but couldn't. "Might work anyhow," he muttered. He wanted to switch the two ankhs, to make absolutely sure they were interchangeable. He reached up and pulled the spinning piece out, preparing to switch them. Immediately the ship lost power and began settling toward the floor. Okun hadn't counted on that. He shoved the new piece into the chamber and closed his eyes tight, expecting to feel the weight of the ship crush down on his chest. Luckily, it accepted the second ankh, leather string and all.

If I take both ankhs, they won't be able to fly this ship out of here! He decided to go for broke.

"What in Hades are you doing over there? They'll be coming through the door any second. Let's get—" Lenel, glancing outside, saw something that stopped him in midsentence. Hovering directly overhead was the nose of an alien saucer. It crawled forward until it was away from the cliffs, then turned itself around and crept closer. Peeking around the corner of the doorway, Lenel had a clear view through the windows into the interior of the craft. A handful of the large-headed creatures were gathered at the windows, inspecting the cliff.

"How we doin' over there?" Okun called over his shoulder. He was too focused on his task to notice that Lenel's answer was an unintelligible stammer. He was trying to get his ankh out of the aqua-box without having the ship squash him. He had crawled back into the trench and was reaching with the tire iron, trying to snag the loop of leather string. But this was as difficult as a carnival game owing to the fact that the spinning ankh was moving the string in all directions.

The hovering saucer pressed in closer. Lenel picked up a large rock and stood with his back pressed to the wall, his eyes glued to the doorway. He planned to clobber anything that stepped inside. He felt the nose of the spacecraft bump against the wall and wondered if they were going to use the ship as a battering ram to open the cave. He found his voice long enough to whisper hoarsely across the darkness of the cave: "They're right outside."

One last try, Okun told himself. *I know I can get it.* But before he could take a final stab at the dancing leather string, a powerful blast of white light entered the cave from outside. It was sweeping across the floor and heading his way. Faster than he knew he could move, he rolled into the trench, hiding himself a split second before he was seen. The search beam scanned the cave's interior for several seconds before abruptly shutting off.

"Now do you believe me?" Lenel's voice was trembling. "Please, Brackish, let's go."

Cowering in the trench, Okun asked if the ship had moved away. Suddenly his idea about challenging the aliens had vanished. When Lenel reported that it had flown a little way off, Okun leaped out of the trench and ran for the door. Without a word, he helped his old friend step through the hole and out onto the ledge. The spacecraft was hovering near the bottom of the cliffs, not far from where the station wagon had been parked a few hours before. Okun was more terrified than he'd ever been. He felt the strong urge to sprint away down the cliff and be well hidden by the time the aliens came out of their ship. But he couldn't abandon Lenel, especially after making him wait so long to escape. He tried to pull the man along gently, but was afraid of knocking him off-balance. When they came to a flat section of the stone ledge, he left Lenel for just a moment to run ahead and check the switchback trail Pedro had shown him that afternoon. It looked too treacherous for the old man. As Lenel took the last few steps toward Okun, he lost his way and walked off the narrow trail. He landed on the gravel slope and crashed hard against the rocks. By the time Okun got to him, he had slid ten feet down the hill and was clutching a handful of shrubs. Desperately searching for a way to reach his friend, he heard the old man whimpering in pain. Even the quietest sound was a roar of noise in the Silent Zone.

"Lenel," he rasped, "reach up here and grab my hand. I'll pull you up."

The old man shook his head. "I think I broke something. You get out of here. Get back to Area 51."

"Not without you I'm not." Okun wedged the toe of his shoe into a fissure in the rock and started lowering himself headfirst down the slope. Before he could grasp the old man's wrist, the root of the bush Lenel was holding gave way, and Lenel began sliding down the rocky slope. Horrified, Okun made a last desperate lunge, but couldn't reach him. The old man slid away until he plunged over the side of the lower cliffs and landed a second later with a sickening thud.

"Lenel, are you all right?" he whispered, knowing his voice would carry to the bottom of the cliffs.

No answer. He was about to start down the hillside

to find his friend when he heard a metallic click echo through the valley. Then he watched a circular pool of light form on the ground below the ship. The hatch door had been opened. Adrenaline pumping, he ran a few more strides along the trail before diving into a shallow foxhole near the base of the trail leading to the top of the cliffs. Climbing the trail now would definitely expose him.

He looked down on the ship until he saw the little beings step onto the ground and begin wandering around the area. They moved toward the base of the hill, to the place where Lenel's body must have fallen. Although he couldn't see Lenel, he could see the creatures standing around him. He wanted to shout at them to get away from his friend, but was too terrified even to move. Suddenly, they abandoned Lenel and began climbing the hillside. Okun knew that probably meant the old man was dead.

Peeking and ducking, he watched the aliens trying to climb the first steep wall toward the cave. From everything he'd learned about them, he expected them to be much more nimble. But they were having just as much trouble as he had had with the rocky terrain.

It occurred to him he could probably make a run for it. In fact, he probably *should* because his foxhole was only seventy-five feet from the opening. When they realized someone had been messing around with their ship, wouldn't they come out and search the area? *Maybe they'll think Lenel was in there by himself.* No, he had to get out of there immediately. He reached down to grab his notebook and his ankh and realized he'd left them inside! He slapped himself in the forehead. The searchlight scanning the cave had scared him so badly, he'd forgotten to pick up his things. He'd come all this way only to blow it at the very end. He briefly considered making a mad dash back to the door, ducking inside to grab his possessions and racing out again. But, like the other heroic plans he'd made that evening, he thought about it too long. Soon six of the awkward little creatures were approaching the mouth of the cave. At the bottom of the slope, he spotted a taller creature, climbing the hillside even more awkwardly than the others. *That must be the Tall One.*

The smaller aliens had already been inside for a couple of minutes when the Tall One reached the top of the slope. They came outside and flitted around the taller creature, seemingly agitated. As Okun watched this scene unfold, the Tall One turned its head in a very deliberate way and seemed to look directly at Okun across the darkness. Okun ducked out of sight, fighting to control his fear. It was dark; maybe he hadn't been seen. His heart racing like it was going to explode, he quietly turned on his back and tried to clear his mind. He knew he had to stay hidden, but he also knew he had to run. He heard the sound of their feet moving across the gravel again. Were they moving in to surround him? He flipped back over and glanced up at the switchback trail. It was time to find out who could run faster, a terrified earthling or these creatures from who-knew-where. But when he peeked once more over the edge of his hiding place, the creatures were in retreat. The six smaller ones were marching away down the hillside and the Tall One was disappearing alone into the cave.

They climbed down the lower cliff and didn't walk over to Lenel's body. They went straight to their ship and climbed in. Okun counted them again to make sure none of them were sneaking around to ambush him. A moment after the circular door snapped closed, there was a whirring hum and the sixty-foot craft zipped straight up into the air, disappearing into the canopy of stars at a fantastic rate of speed. When the ship was gone, the zone of silence swallowed him once more. He heard the Tall

One moving around inside the cave. Somehow, being left alone near this most terrifying of the aliens was worse than being near all six of the others. *Is the Tall One reading my mind right now? Does he know I'm out here?*

No longer indecisive, Okun began his escape. He pushed himself quietly away from the gravel of his hiding place and I stepped back onto the trail. He began climbing the narrow trail to the top of the cliffs, which was littered with pebbles and sand. Each footstep became a matter of life and death. To help him find the Zen of the moment, he imagined himself as Grasshopper, the young Shao-Lin priest from the *Kung Fu* television series. Hands gliding through the air, knees bent, Okun climbed the treacherous slope as delicately as if it were a rice-paper carpet he could not afford to tear. When he reached the top of the bluff, he found himself on a large mesa. After a final glance over the side to make sure he wasn't being followed, he tore away at a dead run. He ran as fast as he could in a straight line across the open plain, looking over his shoulder every few seconds. When he got to the far side of the plateau, he wasted no time. He ran down this new set of slopes which were every bit as treacherous as the ones outside the cave, something he could never have done if his system weren't overloaded with adrenaline. It didn't matter to him that he was running ever deeper into a waterless no-man's-land where he might die of thirst or starvation. His immediate problem was getting as far away from the cave as humanly possible. He wanted to be miles away when the Tall One came out of the cave to look for him. After twenty minutes of sprinting, a stabbing pain in his side forced him to stop. He limped to a place between two boulders and collapsed in the sand, gasping for air and dripping with sweat. He was sure they wouldn't find him here, even if they came looking.

When he'd been lying there long enough for his

breathing to return to normal, he heard a droning sound in the distance. He listened to the sound for a long while until he recognized what it was—an airplane engine. It was coming from the direction of the power lines. Cibatutto and Freiling must have reached a phone and called in the Marines. He wanted to run back the way he'd come and help them locate the cave, but he was beyond exhaustion. All he could do was hope the military found the spot before the Tall One escaped with the ship. Struggling to keep his eyes open, he listened to the plane's engine purring in the distance.

1 4

THE OKUN ERA BEGINS

Even before he opened his eyes, he felt the presence standing over him. He was lying on his stomach and felt every nerve ending in his body tingle to full alertness. His deepest instincts told him not to move, not to change his breathing. He was certain he was being watched.

A voice asked, "Mr. Okun?"

Brackish deftly flipped himself onto, his side and cocked his leg back, ready to mule-kick his attacker, when he noticed he was in a hospital. The doctor at his bedside, who had almost taken a face full of foot, was a young man with a goatee, a buzz cut, and a very intense look on his face. He hadn't flinched.

"Feeling better this morning?"

"Dude, I was just about to kick your teeth out. You're supposed to get out of the way when that happens."

"Much better than yesterday, I see."

Okun looked him over. "What do you mean? How long have I been here? Where am I? What's wrong with me?"

The man arched an eyebrow. "Much much better." He introduced himself as Dr. Issacs and explained they were at Fort Irwin, California. Okun had been there for a week, and although there was nothing physically wrong with him, he was suffering from an extremely unusual form of memory loss. Although Okun could remember everything that had gone on in Mexico, he could recall none of his stay in the hospital. Each morning for the past week, he had woken up anxious to tell about the alien ship he'd found. Although he was only half conscious, he managed to relate the story accurately and in some detail. When Issacs and the other doctors explained to him that he'd already told them about the trip south of the border, he became quarrelsome, refusing to believe them. Each morning he asked if the ship had been recovered, if Lenel was dead, and whether his ankh necklace had been found. He remembered the answers he received until he slept again—whereupon he forgot everything. Even when he drifted off for a ten-minute nap, he woke up surprised not to find himself in the desert. Dizzy and confused, he began asking the doctors where he was, how long he'd been there, whether the ship had been recovered, and if Lenel was still alive. Issacs, who was not a psychiatrist, said it was a case of amnesia unlike any he could find described in the medical literature and had no idea of how to go about treating the condition. Gazing steadily, almost menacingly, down at his patient, he expressed a guarded optimism. "You've seemed groggy all week, but today you appear to be quite alert. I take it as a good sign."

Okun looked confused and opened his mouth to speak.

"Before it occurs to you to ask," Issacs cut him off, "let me assure you that Dr. Lenel is alive and well. He broke two ribs and fractured some bones in his left hip, but his doctors expect him to recover nicely. Your story matches his in every detail up to the point where he fell down the hill, and we have no reason to suspect your account of the facts after that point."

"So, what you're telling me is"—Okun wanted to get this straight—"I keep not remembering yesterday."

"Precisely. Or you might say you keep on un-remembering it in your sleep, and I don't mind telling you that the whole thing has begun to get on my nerves. We've had the same conversation every day this week." He explained that the two of them had spent hour after hour arguing because Okun refused to believe Issacs when he said Okun had told him the same exact story the previous day. "Frankly," the stolid young doctor said, "it's become incredibly tedious."

Okun was beginning to wish he'd kicked this guy when he had the chance. He tried to remember yesterday. The last thing he could recall was finding the spot between the boulders and listening to the plane's engine. He started to ask Issacs something, but the doctor held up his hands.

"Before you begin asking your usual questions"—he rolled his eyes wearily—"perhaps you'd allow me to answer them for you. First: the search planes located the cave shortly after dawn on Monday morning. The exterior wall had been destroyed, very possibly broken from the inside out, but there was no other evidence of the ship you and Dr. Lenel have described. Second: *no*, your necklace was not in the cave. Third: *no*, the other ankh was not in the cave either. Fourth: *yes*, the recovery team headed by Mr. Jenkins searched in the loose earth where you had been digging. Fifth: you were found by two members of the search party, a pair of agents from the CIA's Domestic Collections Division. Am I going too fast for you?"

"No one even saw the ship leaving the cave?"

"Radar abnormalities were observed in the region, but no definitive sighting was made."

"So, basically, we came away empty-handed?"

"Yes, it seems so."

Okun buried his face under his pillow and briefly considered smothering himself. Issacs, who briefly considered helping him, went on. "I'm very encouraged by the fact that you appear to believe what I'm telling you this morning. It may mean you're cured. Today is different for another reason as well. Colonel Spelman is visiting from Washington and is waiting to see you. I'll show him in."

A groan came through the pillow when Okun heard he would have to face Spelman. He was positive he was about to be bawled out by an irate soldier for all the rules he'd broken and all the damage he'd caused. But when the barrel-chested officer came into the room, he was all handshakes and smiles. He didn't seem angry at all.

"Nonsense," Spelman said, when Okun began apologizing for the way he'd chased after the second ship. "You did your best. If we had trusted you a little more, and sent you down there with some military backup, we would have captured the thing and maybe even taken some prisoners. But we were a little nervous after your visit with Dr. Wells. You couldn't have played it any better than you did."

"I need to get back there, Colonel. I need to search the cave for something. See, I had this necklace with a little piece from the ship shaped like an ankh—that's the ancient Egyptian symbol for life. Anyhow, I—"

Spelman turned away, and said, "Dr. Issacs, would you mind stepping outside for a moment and keeping the hallway clear. Mr. Okun and I have some issues to discuss." When the doctor had gone, the colonel reached into his breast pocket and pulled out Okun's leather necklace with the ankh still attached. "When the DCD found you sleeping between those rocks, this was lying at your feet. They brought it directly to me."

"Impossible!" Okun gasped. "I left the necklace inside the cave. I'm positive about that."

"That's what I heard."

"Then how did they find it next to me?"

"I was going to ask you the same question."

Okun shuddered at the idea of the Tall One stealing up and examining him while he slept. *Was that all he had done?* The two men talked for a long time before agreeing the facts seemed to indicate that the Tall One had wanted

Okun to have the ankh-like instrument. *Why* he would want this was another question altogether. Spelman had a theory about it. He began by asking if Okun was familiar with the Bridget Jones incident. Okun said he was. "Then you know these creatures possess implant devices our technology is unable to detect. As soon as you were brought here, we ran a number of X-rays and other tests, and while we were unable to find anything unusual, we can't rule out the possibility that you've been tagged somehow."

"Come again?"

"When the Jones girl found the object, she described a depression in the grass shaped like a man. I've always felt the eebies must have been on the verge of implanting the BB-sized device into the police officer when they were interrupted, probably by the girl's arrival on the scene. We have every reason to believe your encounter with these creatures was more than one of physical proximity. Ask yourself why you were still asleep so late in the afternoon when they found you? Where did this strange thing about forgetting the previous day come from? And I don't need to tell you how often abductees tell us about experiencing false memories or how they lost track of themselves for a day. Maybe your encounter was more involved that you can recall."

Okun considered this possibility. "Have I developed any strange powers like she did?"

Spelman shook his head. "Except for being groggy and argumentative all week, Issacs tells me you're normal. Keep in mind this implanted device business is only a theory, a worst-case scenario. But it's at least possible they gave you back the necklace hoping you'd carry it to another one of their ships. If they've marked you in some way that allows them to track your whereabouts, you could lead them to Area 51. It might all be a ruse to hunt down their missing ship."

"I see. So I'm probably banished for life from going back there."

"Actually"—Spelman smiled—"that's another thing I wanted to talk with you about. We are prepared to offer you the position of Director of Research at the facility. It would always be a risk moving you in and out. But if we took certain precautions, we feel confident you and the ship would be safe."

"What kind of precautions?"

"You told Dr. Issacs the downed vehicle was emitting a beacon signal."

"Right. The image of the Y. You already know about that, too?"

"Yes, you told us on Tuesday. You said the electromagnetic field generated by the power poles must have created a roof which prevented the space-based aliens from receiving the distress signal."

"So you're saying we could rig up some mobile unit to generate EMF waves, and I'd travel to the labs under it? *Très* cool. But wouldn't it just be easier to hire somebody else?"

The two men looked at one another for a long beat. "At this point," the colonel said, "we don't feel anyone could replace you. You know so much. It would take many months, perhaps years, for someone to learn what you already know."

Okun heard Dworkin's voice ringing in his ears, *The more you know, the deeper you're buried.*

Spelman stood up, preparing to leave. "You're the only one we're considering at the moment. It's the job we had in mind for you when you were recruited. Take some time to think it over. We know from Agent Radecker there are many changes you'd like to make at the labs. As Director of Research, you would have the power to make them. But once you're in the door, you'll have to stay down there.

You won't be able to sit outside and do your watercolor painting anymore, and there won't be any weekend trips to Las Vegas." Before he turned to go, he added, "As much as I'd like to see you accept this assignment, I have to admit I don't know how I'd choose. Here, hold on to this while you make up your mind." He landed over the ankh and leather necklace.

Before Spelman was quite out the door, Okun asked one last question. "I take it Radecker's no longer the director. He's not here at the hospital, is he?" Okun didn't need any more grief this morning.

Spelman suppressed a smile. "Agent Radecker has been promoted. He's now the Chief of Intelligence at the CIA office in Barrow, Alaska. Just above the Arctic Circle."

The next day, Okun remembered yesterday.

Soon afterward, he was discharged from the hospital. But not before he'd developed a grudging admiration and bickering friendship with the multitalented Dr. Issacs. No older than Okun, he was a pathology intern at Bethesda Naval Hospital in D.C. He held a B.S. from Cornell in astrophysics and claimed to be an expert in ancient mythology. Since his first days at Area 51, Okun had seen the need for medical expertise in the labs. Further autopsies needed to be performed on the recovered aliens, tissue samples needed to be analyzed, and the ship itself was largely composed of living tissue. If he accepted the position and became director, Issacs was exactly the sort of man he'd seek to hire.

When he was discharged from the hospital, Okun went home to see his mother. He arrived unannounced early one morning and walked into the house. He found Saylene reading the paper and sipping coffee. She jumped into his arms, and while they were hugging, a man walked out of the bedroom to see what was going on. His name was Peter, and he seemed to have spent the night. Okun looked at his mom and knew by her expression that things had changed around the house. She called in sick and they went out for an all-day lunch. She told him everything that had happened while he was away, how much she liked his haircut, and all about her relationship with her new man. She knew enough not to ask what he'd been up to during the same time, but it was uncomfortable how lopsided the conversation became. It didn't help that Brackish was distracted. He glanced around the restaurant every few minutes like he was expecting someone. The two of them made a plan that Saylene would take a few days off at the end of the month and they'd take a trip together—just the two of them. But it was a journey they would never take.

Every day that Okun was home, he was sure they would be watching him. He developed a habit of glancing over his shoulders when he walked down a street. When he borrowed the car, he spent more time watching the rearview mirror than the road. He was positive the phone was tapped and the house was bugged. He walked around the neighborhood looking for a van with tinted windows and extra radio antennas. But search as he might, he could find no shred of evidence he was under surveillance.

One day he received a piece of mail. Inside there was a note: "Thought you'd find this amusing. Hope all is well. Spelman." Enclosed was a newspaper article from an El Paso newspaper with a headline that read:

Mythical Monsters of Mexico, number of chupacabra sightings rise after youth tells story.

There was a photograph of Pedro standing in front of the cliffs where they'd discovered the hidden ship. Okun got a kick out of the article, but didn't believe the implication of Spelman's note. *Hope all is well. As if he doesn't know exactly how I'm spending every minute.*

The attempts he made to reenter his old life proved futile. He called friends and visited a few of his old professors at Caltech, but their conversations were strained. He found himself growing more adept at steering the conversation away from himself, but as he listened to these people talk about their lives and concerns, something kept him from nodding. For some reason, he couldn't enjoy normal people as he once had. He told himself his distraction was due to being followed around all day. So he devised a plan to flush the spies around him out of their hiding places.

One afternoon he phoned a television station and asked to speak with a reporter. He said he had a major news story concerning extraterrestrial visitors. Of course, the journalist didn't believe him, so he told her enough to show her he was serious. And enough to make whoever was listening in on the conversation very nervous. They made an appointment for the next morning. Okun hung up the phone and waited on the front porch for the unmarked sedans to start arriving. But no one came. The next morning, he dressed in a suit and drove to the station. When he came through the front doors, there were no federal agents waiting there to arrest him. *I guess they're not watching.* He sat down in the lobby and considered what to do next.

Although he had not gone to the station intending to talk with anyone, he considered going ahead and breaking the story. He could imagine Wells's reaction if he saw the announcement on television. He'd immediately demand that the nurse release him so he could assume the role of Earthling Dictator. He was crazy, but he had a point: didn't the people of earth deserve to know about the visitors? Wasn't it somehow the birthright of every human to know the truth? That's what he'd always been taught. He, Brackish Okun, could end a quarter-century-old conspiracy simply by keeping this appointment he'd made. He could give them names, technical sketches, report numbers, and he could explain the significance of the trinket he was wearing around his neck. The government's public relations teams and CIA disinformation specialists would have a hard time discrediting his story.

But now that it was in his power to do this, he wasn't sure it was the wisest path. Dworkin hadn't thought so. He remembered quite clearly Sam's warning about society disintegrating under the strains of uncertainty and fear. He'd felt the effects himself, having trouble sleeping at night wondering if he really had been *marked* by the Tall One. Breaking the story would certainly cause a panic, and there was no guarantee it would produce any benefits. Politically, it would play right into the hands of those ugly, fascist men who wanted to turn America and the world into an armed camp.

In the end, the question of whether to tell what he knew came down to a decision between two very different approaches to the world. In Okun's mind, it became a choice between Dworkin and Wells.

He stood up, walked out of the lobby, and climbed back into his car. Out of habit, he found himself glancing too often into the mirror. Every time he did this it reminded him that he was free. No one was looking over his shoulder anymore. He was surprised when this didn't make him feel any more at ease than he had since he'd returned home. It just made him feel disconnected. He realized why he had been go distracted, so unable to nod, when he was with his old friends. It wasn't lurking spies. It was that their hopes and dreams and daily problems, everything that was important to them, seemed trivial compared to the task of learning about the alien visitors. The whole time his mother had been describing how she met her boyfriend, Brackish's mind was 185 miles from earth, contemplating the next period of increased radioactivity of the inner Van Allen belt. As he drove home, he told himself, *I know too much to lead a normal life,* and realized how true Dworkin's words about knowing too much had been. He didn't need any CIA spooks to bury him; the knowledge he was carrying around in his head did that on its own. By the time he pulled into the driveway, he'd decided he was going back. He would have gone back even if they weren't offering to make him director. Like his older colleagues, he felt the work in the labs was more important than his personal destiny.

He called Spelman, and said, "I'm ready to come back, but I have a couple of conditions."

"Go ahead, I'm listening."

He spent a month at Edwards Air Force Base working with NASA engineers on the vehicle that would carry him back to the facility beneath Groom Lake. The result was a heavily modified VW van completely covered with a gray material derived from Teflon. A portable power station in the rear cargo area generated a force field of electromagnetic energy strong enough to disrupt the radio reception of the cars he passed on the drive out to the desert. The engineers who helped him build it nicknamed the vehicle the Stealth Wagon and thought the military might be able to apply the radar-deflecting material they'd designed to the construction of new aircraft.

When he motored up to the X-shaped landing strip outside of Area 51, he could see evidence of new construction. The shantytown of wooden houses which had once housed the lab's staff had been torn down to make way for the construction of a giant sliding door, one that would allow the spaceship below to make a quick exit if the need ever presented itself. He drove the Stealth Wagon into the hangar and rode the new freight elevator down the six flights to the floor of the lab. Everything looked different. When he came into the long narrow hallway which had, for years, housed the chaos of the stacks, he found it freshly painted and brilliantly lit. A small work crew was busy organizing the files and entering their catalogue numbers on the lab's new computer system. An elevated walkway had been installed down the center of the long room, which Okun planned to make a dust-free research area. As he walked farther along, he found a crew of hard hats excavating space for the new electrochemical research unit. He came to the huge concrete bunker that was home to the captured alien spaceship. The room was empty except for a giant crate seventy-by-seventy and twenty feet tall. Stenciled on the outside of this oversized wooden box were the words CHEMICAL EXPLOSIVES—NO SMOKING. He toured once around the box to make sure the ship within could not be seen. On his way out of the bunker, he noticed a doorway that hadn't been there before and went inside. It was the new medical facility, complete with a glass-enclosed operating room. Although the workmanship was marvelous, something about the room gave him the creeps.

The door to the kitchen was locked. After pounding on it to make himself heard over the noise of the construction crew, the door was opened by a young man who stared at him in a slightly demented way. Dr. Issacs, his first hire.

Even before he stepped inside the familiar room, he was getting an earful from Lenel. "What kind of boss are you, anyhow? Ever since you took over it's been so dam noisy down here we can't get any work done." The old man was in a body cast that went from his underarms to his kneecaps.

"You look like a mummy in a swimsuit," Okun opined.

While Freiling and Cibatutto stepped forward to welcome Brackish back, Lenel tried to sustain his grouchy demeanor. "If I do," he snapped, "I've got you to thank for it."

"That's right," Freiling came to Lenel's aid. "We've heard all about how Dr. Lenel saved you from falling off that cliff."

"Saved me?" Okun asked, flabbergasted. He turned to Lenel, who was shooting him a look that said *don't you dare tell*. "Oh right, saved me." He grinned. "By the way, Dr. Lenel, I haven't had a chance to thank you for that."

"All part of the job," Lenel grumbled.

Owing to the presence of the construction crews, the staff was prevented from working on the ship for nearly three full months. During this time, they kept themselves busy with whatever small projects could be brought into their sleeping quarters or the kitchen. To everyone's dismay, Issacs turned out to be a neat freak and was continually chiding his coworkers to keep the place organized. "You can't teach an old dog new tricks," was the stock reply he received from the trio of senior citizens. But he kept after them, and slowly they began to see his point.

When the last new rooms had been finished and the last unauthorized personnel left the labs, the men descended on the alien spaceship like a pack of starved dogs. They were eager to apply all they had learned from the undamaged craft they'd found in Mexico. For six full months, they rewelded, rewired, rethought, and rebuilt every inch of the ship. After a series of preliminary tests they felt it was time to invite Spelman to Area 51 for a demonstration.

He arrived on a cloudy morning in early July and brought some guests, all of them former members of the now-defunct Project Smudge: Jim "the Bishop" Ostrom, Jenkins, the new chief of Domestic Collections Department, whose men had found Okun sleeping in the desert, and Dr. Insolo from the Science and Technology

Directorate. Okun recognized him from Sam's funeral. After a quick lunch, the guests were invited into the concrete bunker to witness an experiment. They gathered on a newly built observation platform while the scientists readied their monitoring equipment. When everything was ready, Okun addressed his visitors.

"Several years ago, my predecessor, Dr. Wells, developed a technique of feeding high-voltage power into the ship's energy system and found he could achieve low levels of performance from the instrumentation within. Partially because the design function which expels energy from this system was incomplete, excess or clogged power generated high temperature levels." He was only at the beginning of his speech, but saw from the blank looks on the faces of his audience there was no point in continuing with the lecture. Instead, he simply said, "Watch this."

He passed out pairs of prismatic goggles, then gave a signal to Freiling, who was standing on the operator's platform of the energy cannon. The old man threw a switch, and the room filled with a shrill buzzing sound as the gun began bombarding the alien ship with power. A loud crack ripped through the vessel and bounced off the concrete walls. Lenel gave an OK sign from the output meter he was watching. Cibatutto directed the visitors' attention to the mirror at the bottom of the ship, where they watched the swirling green cyclone being created by the aqua-box. And, through the special filters of the goggles, they were able to watch the energy being purged from the ship's system. Instead of the spasmodic and undirected waves they had seen before, the energy was now channeled through the arms of the whirling ankh. Four pinpoint beams traveled around the walls of the bunker, searching for another ship to power.

A moment later, the wooden trestles holding the ship off the floor groaned as the weight bearing down on them began to ease. Slowly, like an ancient pterodactyl riding an updraft, the ship lifted into the air. The moment it did so, the scientists abandoned the monitors they were watching and threw their arms in the air, cheering.

"Holy guacamole!" Okun gasped. When a nod wasn't enough to express his excitement, he began bouncing up and down, then turned and grabbed the first body he could find— it happened to be Spelman's—and bounced around with the colonel wrapped in his arms. He leaped from the platform to the floor of the bunker, still bouncing. The ship had lifted two feet above the trestles. He gave Cibatutto five, then bounced over and kissed Lenel on the forehead before the old man could swat him away. When he came to Dr. Issacs, a little of the air went out of his tires.

As calm, cool, and collected as ever, Issacs indicated the heat gauge. "The temperature inside the ship is 160 and climbing," he called out over the screech of the electrocannon. "It's time to shut down."

Okun turned and waved the cutoff signal. But Freiling remained oblivious, hypnotized by the dark bird floating before him, until Okun ran up next to him, and yelled, "TURN IT OFF!" The old man flipped the kill switch, abruptly bringing the power level down to zero. The saucer crashed down onto the trestles, which cracked and teetered, but, fortunately, did not collapse.

"Gotta work on the landing," Freiling observed, pulling off his goggles, "but I'll be damned if we didn't get her to fly."

"We sure did, Daddy-o!"

"I only wish Sam could've seen this."

Okun smiled sadly. "Me too."

The scientists rejoined their visitors on the observation platform, then repaired immediately to the kitchen. According to the long-established rules of procedure at the top-secret facility, champagne was served.

Somewhere between the uncorking of the bottles and the departure of the visiting dignitaries late that afternoon, there was an important exchange of documents. Okun went first.

As Spelman had requested, he'd prepared a report detailing everything he knew about the aliens up to that point. It ran to over two hundred pages. At the end of it, he tried to answer the question of how great a threat the aliens posed to the world in general and the United States in particular. He found the question nearly impossible to answer. Despite all that had been learned about them, the most basic question of all remained a mystery: What did they want? The possibilities ranged all the way from the hope they were beneficent beings bearing gifts to the fear they had come to invade the planet and take it away from us. Okun took both possibilities seriously. But his gut told him it was bad news, VDJ. They were dealing with an intelligent race with advanced technologies. Their ships were armed, they used other beings as armor, and they had offered no sign of friendship. If Wells had interpreted the vision of the alien planet correctly, they were also dealing with a catastrophic food shortage. Perhaps the encounters were few because these were only scout ships. On the other hand, they had made no sign of being hostile either. Never once had they demonstrated a clearly malicious intent to humans, with the possible exception of the Eau Claire case. They had ample opportunity to torture, maim, or kill any of the people they'd captured. Instead they had been released unharmed, and although many of these people came away from the experience traumatized, an equal number longed for it to happen again.

Then there was Okun's own experience. He recalled how wildly terrified he'd been of being detected by the aliens outside the cave. But looking back on it, they must have known he was there all along. Instead of harming him, the Tall One had given him the ankh, allowing research to continue. It might even turn out they were shy tourists ferried through a time warp in the Van Allen belts for five-day vacations, observing earth from the safety and comfort of their flying fortresses—their version of visiting a safari park. Who knew? he concluded that it was too early for conclusions and called upon the military and intelligence branches of the goverment to aid in the recovery of more evidence. To this end, he proposed a handful of clever stratagems designed to lure the creatures into traps.

Spelman accepted the report with the promise that it would circulate through the highest levels of the government.

"Including the president?"

"Especially the president."

Okun actually breathed a sigh of relief when he learned that soon this important information would be in the right hands. It was too heavy a responsibility for him to carry around, and he didn't feel right about the CIA and the Army being the only ones to know about it.

"Now we've got something for you."

Dr. Insolo snapped open the locks on an attaché case and pulled out some pieces of paper. "The only reservation any of us had about appointing you director concerned your educational qualifications. Something isn't quite right when the leader of one of the nation's top laboratories doesn't hold a Ph.D. But given the restrictions on your travel, we knew you wouldn't be able to attend classes. So, we took the liberty of transferring your credits from Caltech to the United States Naval Postgraduate School, where I'm a member of the faculty. Hope you don't mind." He held up what looked to Okun like a diploma and read what was printed on it. "Whereas the candidate, Brackish Okun, has exhibited full mastery of the body of knowledge and technologies associated with his field of study, and whereas he has made a unique and original contribution to this field, he is hereby awarded a doctorate of philosophy in Xenoaeronautics."

Spelman was the first to extend his hand. "Congratulations, *Doctor* Okun."

"How utterly cool," Okun enthused, reading over the diploma. When he looked up he was surrounded by the smiling faces of his friends and guests. Without realizing it, they had all begun mirroring the minuscule cranial motion so characteristic of the lab's director. The entire room was nodding.

"The end." Nimziki smirked when he saw those words on the last page of Okun's report. "What does he think this is, a bedtime story?"

"Sometimes he's a little weird." Spelman chuckled.

"What did you think of it?" Nimziki asked, tossing the report onto his desk.

"It's wordy, and parts of it don't make much sense, but the ideas are strong. Overall, I'd say it's a balanced presentation of the evidence. I'm anxious to hear what the president has to say about it."

"Yeah, me too," Nimziki said absently. He wasn't any great fan of President Ford's. When it had been time to appoint a new director of the CIA, Ford had ignored the unanimous recommendation of the intelligence community that Nimziki get the job. He had named one of his longtime political allies to the post instead.

"I especially liked his ideas about how to capture another ship."

"Yeah, I'll have to reread those. Smart."

"And what about his ideas for slowly introducing the truth about the aliens to the public?"

"The stuff about saturating the media with alien stories before breaking the true story. Interesting. I'll have to give it some more thought." Spelman could see Nimziki was tired and distracted by other thoughts. That was understandable. It was almost eleven o'clock at night, and they'd both been at work since early that morning. "I think I'll get out of here and let you go home." Spelman walked to the door, then turned, and said, "Please let me know as soon as you get any reaction from the White House so I can pass it along to our team out at Groom Lake. I'm as anxious as they are. And, Al—" he waited for Nimziki to glance up—"we all did a hell of a good job on this one, didn't we?"

"Yeah, we sure did, Bud. But listen, don't expect an immediate response from the president. You know how they are over there. They want to preserve their plausible deniability option. But the moment I hear anything, on or off the record, I'll let you know."

When Spelman was gone, Nimziki thumbed through the report once more, then walked into the next room and fed it into a paper shredder. He turned out the lights and went home.

INDEPENDENCE DAY

WAR IN THE DESERT

CREATED BY DEAN DEVLIN &
ROLAND EMMERICH
NOVEL BY STEPHEN MOLSTAD

I'd like to thank Michael Hawley, Christopher Rowe, Paul Zahn, John Storey, Lisa DiSanto, Will Plyler, Dionne McNeff, and everyone who offered me help while I was writing this book. I apologize for taking so few of your excellent suggestions, but I'm a mule at heart. Finally, I need to thank John Douglas and my dear wife Elizabeth for putting up with me all the way to the end.

1

THE ATTACK BEGINS

The original city on a hill, Jerusalem, was a symbol of all that was best and worst about human beings. It had stood for millennia above the Judean plane, protected by sturdy stone walls that had glinted gold in the sun since the time of Christ and, seven centuries later, the time of Mohammed. Those walls had held back large armies and entire nations of crusaders clamoring at its gates, desperate to enter, certain that being inside would bring them closer to the paradise of heaven. It had been conquered eighteen different times.

Over the years, the city's walls had borne witness to some of humanity's deepest and most uplifting meditations on the question of what it meant to be alive. But they'd also seen their share of needlessly spilled blood. There had been countless acts of pettiness, backstabbing and sadism—all committed in the name of a merciful God. A tenth century poet described Jerusalem as "a golden basin filled with scorpions." It was sacred ground to all three of the West's major religions: the place where King David's temple had housed the Ark of the Covenant, where Christ was crucified and resurrected, and where the prophet Mohammed stretched open his arms and ascended to heaven. It was said that you could choke to death in Jerusalem, the air was so thick with prayer.

Reg Cummins had first encountered the city as a grungy twenty-year-old backpacker. He'd enlisted with the Royal

Air Force but had three months until he was scheduled to report. In the meantime, he was determined to see some of the continent. From his home in Kew in London, he traveled down through Italy and hopped a boat to Greece. After a month on the beach, he decided he was looking for something more, something further from his experience, something more exotic and challenging. So he went to Jerusalem. He slept where he could and spent his days exploring the covered markets, tunnels, and religious shrines. He drank tea and bargained in the souks, got himself invited to shabbat dinners then sang and danced with his hosts. He wandered the cobblestone streets, argued over the price of onions and the nature of sin, and spent a couple of nights camped out in a courtyard of African mud huts with the Ethiopian Coptic priests in their compound. Jerusalem had always made him feel vital and completely alive. That seemed like a very long time ago.

Now, several years later and hundreds of miles away, as he watched images of the city on television, Squadron Leader Reginald M. Cummins, an instructor with the Queen's Flight and Training Group, Mideast section, felt dead inside. It was noon on July 3rd, and outside the sun burned hot white in the sky. He was in the Foreign Officers' Lounge at the Khamis Moushalt Airfield in Saudi Arabia, along with every active-duty RAF airman stationed in that country except the Commandant—all six of them—staring in grim disbelief at the CNN report unfolding on the screen.

An alien aircraft of staggering size had arrived the night before and parked itself directly over the ancient city. The hovering gray disk stretched out for miles in every direction, leaving only a ring of blue sky low on the horizon. When it arrived, the ground shook with its massive rumbling. It had moved at a constant speed and elevation, closing over the top of the city like the thick stone lid of a sarcophagus. The moment the ship stopped moving, everything had fallen deathly quiet.

The vessel looked like the very embodiment of evil. It was dark, hard and strictly utilitarian in design. It was gruesomely industrial and, at the same time, somehow alive. The whole dark mass looked biological, like an exoskeleton of some sort.

The sight of the gigantic airship triggered a wild, violent exodus. People gathered up whatever they could carry with them and ran. Over a million refugees were scrambling toward the hope of safety, some of them on the roads leading to Tel Aviv or Amman, others hurrying on foot through the hills. In most people's minds, it was the end of the world. For others, it was the armies of the Lord announcing the moment of redemption. By noon, Jerusalem was empty except for military personnel, New Age types who had come to welcome the ETs, and stern religious zealots wielding bats and bricks, determined to protect their sacred buildings.

Variations of this scene were occurring all over the planet.

Less than twenty-four hours before, thirty-six of these enormous ships—soon to be known as city destroyers—had disengaged themselves from an even larger spacecraft, the "mother ship," which was one fourth the size of Earth's moon. Very quickly, they began their simultaneous, free-fall entry into Earth's atmosphere. They descended in huge billowing clouds of flame and smoke as the friction they generated combusted the oxygen around them. Upon reaching their target elevations, they came to a sudden and inexplicable halt. Completely unscathed, they drove out of the smoke clouds and moved into position over thirty-six of Earth's most populous and strategically important cities. None of them had made any discernible attempt to communicate.

Reg Cummins drew in a deep breath and turned away from the hypnotic images on the television set. Wanting to clear his mind, he walked to the bar at the far side of the room and poured himself the stiffest drink in the house: a glass of lukewarm soda water. The initial shock of the invasion was beginning to wear off and, in its place, a grim sense of helplessness was spreading around the globe. It was evident in the comments made by the CNN reporters, in the communiqués issued by the world's governments, and, as Reg could see with his own eyes, in the attitudes of his fellow pilots. Normally, they were an obnoxiously loud and boisterous group, always laughing, roughhousing and complaining bitterly about the hardships of life in this remote desert locale. Now they looked like a group of defeated men. They slumped in their chairs, as still as statues, and their heads hung in worry.

If the aliens decided to pick a fight, they wouldn't get much resistance from a group like this. Reg knew he had to do something to change the atmosphere. When his eyes fell on the billiards table in the center of the room, he knew what he had to do.

"All this alien nonsense is starting to bore me silly," he called across the room. "And you blokes are going to ruin your eyes watching that rot all day. Anyone interested in a game of billiards?" Immediately, everyone's attention was sucked away from the news program. The men looked positively alarmed.

"Anyone interested?" Reg asked, nonchalantly selecting a cue from the rack on the wall.

"Impossible!" said one of the pilots.

"You? Play a game of pool?" said another in disbelief. "You're finally going to do something more than talk?"

"That is correct," Reg said, chalking the tip of his cue. "This time I'm really going to play. Anyone here think they're good enough to take me?"

The six pilots, wearing their flight suits in case they were ordered into the air on short notice, came toward the table. All of them had heard Reg talk about his days as a championship level player, but this was the first time any of them had seen him actually holding a cue.

"Who's the best player?" Reg asked, as if he didn't already know.

A tall, beefy man named Sinclair stepped up to the table chewing on the stub of a cigar. "That would be me, Teacher," he said. "You're serious, then? You want a game?"

"Oh, yes. I'm serious, quite serious."

Major Cummins (aka the Teacher, an affectionate nickname given to him by the Saudi pilots who were his students) was famous for three things: for being widely considered the best pilot in the Middle East; for having suffered a very painful and career-threatening lapse of judgment during the Gulf War; and for bragging about his days as a pool player before joining Her Majesty's Air Force.

'This is turning out to be a day full of surprises," said a man named Townsend. "First, a bunch of aliens arrive from outer space and now something truly shocking. I hope I'm dreaming."

"What's this all about?" Sinclair asked, snapping open the leather case that held his personal cue. "You trying to distract us from our troubles?" When Reg shrugged without answering, Sinclair invited him to lag for break.

Reg looked confused. He didn't appear to understand the question. "Why don't you go ahead and show me how it's done?"

"Gladly," Sinclair said with a smirk. He leaned over the table and stroked the cue ball to the far side of the table. It bounced off and rolled back to within an inch of the near rail. It was a nice shot, the onlookers agreed, one that would be nearly impossible to beat. Sinclair marked the position with a chalk cube, satisfied that he'd already won. "Your turn, Teacher."

Reg studied the table. "Now what's the idea here? I have to get the ball closer than yours without touching the cushion, is that it?"

"That's it exactly." Sinclair grinned wickedly. "Best of luck to you."

Reg cleared his throat. "Well, here goes then," he said, lining up his shot. The awkward way he held the cue in his hands made it clear he didn't know what he was doing. He was on the verge of shooting when he suddenly backed away. "Wait, I just thought of something."

The men all moaned loudly, believing Reg was going to back out of it, but he surprised them again.

"We haven't made a bet. Shouldn't we make a wager of some kind?"

"What can you afford to lose?" someone laughed.

Reg looked at the man curiously. "Lose? What makes you think I'm going to lose?"

"Fifty quid then?" Sinclair asked, doubting Reg would want to risk that much.

"Make it one hundred."

The men roared with laughter at his misguided bravado. Despite his obvious lack of skill, he actually seemed to believe he stood a chance against the mighty Sinclair. He leaned over the table again and quickly stroked his shot. The white ball sailed across the green felt.

'Too hard," Sinclair announced as soon as the ball rebounded off the far cushion.

"I don't think so," said his challenger. "I'd say that's just about perfect." A moment later, the ball stopped rolling a mere fingernail short of the near rail. Reg looked Sinclair in the eyes. "Does this mean I get to break?"

The big man squinted back at him and nodded, beginning to realize that he'd been had.

Reg's break shot was a thing of beauty. The cue ball fired across the table with surprising power and scattered the colorful spheres in every direction. There were three soft thunks as two solids and a stripe fell into three separate pockets.

"Listen to the Teacher, friends," Reg said, circling the table like a jungle cat. 'Today's lesson is about making assumptions and how much trouble that can get you into." He paused long enough to hammer the twelve ball into a side pocket and the nine into a corner. "I'm certain you've all seen that diagram about the word assume. You know, the one that says: when you assume, you make and ASS out of U and ME." He tapped the orange five ball in the corner. "Well, there's been too damn much assuming going on around here this morning and I'll give you an example. You all assumed that just because you'd never seen me play, that I couldn't find my way around a table." He glanced up at Sinclair and smiled. "Combination bank shot. Three ball in the far corner." A moment later, it fell in.

"The same thing is happening with these spaceships. Everybody's making assumptions." He sunk the two ball then broke into the exaggerated accent of a terrified Scotsman. "Oh, fer crackin' ice! These huge fookin saucers are parked all over the fookin warld. It can mean one thing and one thing only: total fookin annihilation fer the yewmin race." The men chuckled at his imitation, but they also got the message. In quick succession, Reg sank every ball left on the table then tossed his cue on the table. "The truth of the matter is, you just can't tell what sort of a player a bloke is until he makes a few shots. So let's wait to see what kind of players these aliens are before we quit and hang up our cues, okay?"

"And if they turn out to be sharks like you?" Sinclair asked with a laugh.

"In that case, we'll show them what kind of shooting good English lads can do, right?"

"Right!" the men answered in one voice. With the fire back in their eyes, the men began a raucous discussion of the punishment they would mete out if the aliens started any trouble. They were laughing and arguing when a blast of heat and bright light swept into the room.

The door of the darkened lounge had pulled open and Group Captain Whitley, a man with the long neck and stooped posture of a vulture, stepped inside. He was the highest ranking RAF officer at Khamis Moushalt but had been in the Middle East only a few weeks. He carried a map of the region that he'd ripped from the wall of his office. He was sweating from his short walk across the base. It was already ninety-six degrees Fahrenheit outside and it was only going to get hotter.

"I'm going to need a volunteer," Whitley announced, knocking glasses and ashtrays off the bar so he could flatten out the map. "Here's the situation. Forty of our birds, Tornadoes, are trapped over the Mediterranean. They've been in a holding pattern for the last half-hour near Haifa. Somebody's got to go get them."

"Why?" asked one of the men. "What's the matter?"

Whitley grimaced in disgust. "Every nation in the region is closing down its airspace. Israel was the first. About an hour ago, they started chasing out all foreign planes, allies included. Five minutes later, Egypt and Syria started doing the same damn thing, so our boys can't just detour around. Besides, they're not fully trained pilots. They're just a bunch of warm bodies acting as chauffeurs. It's a hideous mess out there, hideous."

"What the hell is Israel's problem?" Sinclair asked. "Last night they agreed to allow foreign planes."

Reg took an educated guess. "There must have been a skirmish. If I know the Israelis, they've been shadowing every group of Arab planes that comes in for a look at that alien craft. Somebody started playing chicken— probably some Iraqis—and before they knew it, they were in a dogfight."

Whitley's dark eyes opened wide in surprise. He didn't know Reg well and, after reading his personnel file, regarded him with caution. "The major is correct," he told the men. 'Two Iraqi planes were shot down. In retaliation, missiles were fired onto the road leading to Tel Aviv resulting in civilian casualties. Then, of course, all hell broke loose."

"Oh, that's bloody lovely," said one of the pilots in disgust, "that's just beautiful. The aliens must be laughing their little green arses off right now. They won't have to waste any ammunition in this part of the world. We'll kill ourselves off before the bastards have the chance to do it themselves."

"Enough talk," Whitley snapped. "Who's going?"

Six pilots loudly volunteered, but Reg quieted them with a look. "Sorry lads, winner breaks!" Then he turned to the Colonel. "I'm your man, sir. Where do those planes have to go?"

A bead of sweat rolled off the tip of Whitley's beak-like nose. "They're headed to Kuwait. But, look, Cummins," he said tensely, "maybe someone else would be better for this mission. It's not that I doubt your skills, but there are hundreds of warplanes out there from a dozen different nations. And as I say, these boys flying the Tornadoes don't know what they're doing. This is a live-fire situation and it's going to be, well, confusing." The men fell into an awkward silence. They knew that the colonel's reluctance to give Reg the mission was based on something that had happened many years before, something none of them ever mentioned in front of the Teacher. Whitley, a newcomer to the base, didn't understand that his fears were groundless and that Reg was, by far, the best man for the job. He was the only one who had never flown alongside the Teacher and seen the impossible things he could do in a jet. Besides, Reg knew the region well enough to fly without navigation systems, and he understood the tactics of the Middle East's diverse air forces better than anyone.

Whitley's lack of confidence stung Reg like a hard punch to the heart, but he didn't let it show. "I'm your man, colonel," he repeated firmly. "I'll find those planes. I'll bring them to their destination safely."

Whitley shook his head. "I've read your file, Cummins. We can't afford any... lapses. Now, who else volunteers?"

The other pilots looked at the ceiling, at the television, anywhere but at the Colonel. It only took a second of being ignored for Whitley to realize that the decision had been made for him.

"So that's how it's going to be. Very well then, Major, the mission is yours. Good luck. Your take off has already been cleared with the tower."

"I'll see you gentlemen this afternoon," Reg said over his shoulder as he pushed open the door and headed away across the blistering hot tarmac. The others moved to the windows and watched him go.

Whitley crossed his long arms over his chest. "There goes a man looking for trouble."

"Not at all," said Sinclair. "There goes a man looking for redemption."

As his British Aerospace Hawk thundered over the razor-wire perimeter fence of the Khamis Moushalt facility, Reg looked down at the base that had been his home for the last few years, a nine-square-mile patch of pavement in the middle of a desert. It was a horrible place to live and was considered the worst assignment an RAF man could draw. No one except Reg had ever volunteered to be there. Saudi Arabia could be a strange, hostile, and cruel place, ruled by restrictive Islamic social codes. But Reg had found the Saudis to be an honorable people and had made many genuine friends among them. He had trained many of the Royal Saudi Air Force's best pilots during his years in the country since Desert Storm.

There was plenty to think about during his flight north. His cockpit instrumentation was showing a contradictory jumble of digits and flashing zeroes. All satellite-dependent systems were unreliable. But he'd made the flight to Jerusalem many times and knew the way by heart. He tried to keep his mind clear, but couldn't help thinking about what Whitley had said about lapses. Could it be that the man had a point? After all, even though he'd engaged in hundreds of mock battles during the last several years, this was the first time he would be facing a live fire situation since his last, ill-fated sortie over Iraq.

As he flew past the ancient ruins of Petra, he got his first glimpse of the alien ship. It was only a gray blot on the horizon but Reg felt the hackles raise on the back of his neck. His warrior instincts told him to attack the thing at once, but as he came closer, it grew to an impossible, intimidating size and his passion cooled. Dominating the sky, it seemed to cover half of Israel. The astounding thing was that something so vast and heavy could float. It was an egregious violation of the laws of physics and the closer Reg flew to the city-sized airship, the more it dawned on him that he was in the presence of a powerful civilization far in advance of his own. He felt a sudden chill and began to grasp why not a single government around the world had decided to declare war on the uninvited guests.

At the same time, it produced a dark attraction. There was a certain sort of ominous, magnetic, unholy beauty to the craft. Its sleek gray dome, glinting in the midday sun, was made of an exotic material he'd never seen before. It was something out of a beautiful nightmare, like a medieval fortress from the twenty-fourth century built in the clouds.

Mesmerized, Reg flew closer until he became distracted by a stinging in his eyes. It took him a moment to realize that sweat was pouring down his face and blurring his vision. When he wiped his forehead clean, he noticed his hand was trembling. It had been so long since he'd felt anything resembling fear at the controls of a plane that he didn't recognize it for a moment. In a sudden rush of self-doubt, Whitley's words echoed through his head. Maybe he wasn't ready for the real thing.

Distracted, he didn't notice a pair of Syrian MiG Fulcrums moving up behind him at top speed. They passed above him by a scant few hundred feet, then deliberately cut across his path. When Reg hit the turbulence of their jet wash, his Hawk shook as though the wings would snap off. Regaining control, he rose a thousand feet in altitude and flipped his radio to the general frequency.

"Thank you, friends, for that warm welcome," he said to the Syrians, figuring that having had their fun, they would leave him alone. But his heads-up display showed them arcing around for another pass. Realizing he was under direct attack had a curious effect on Reg. His hands stopped shaking, his heart rate slowed and something like a smile crossed his lips. "If you boys want to dance," he said into his radio, "let's have a go."

Far below, he saw the brilliant blue of the Dead Sea on Israel's eastern border. He cut his speed to let the Syrian planes catch up. The Hawk's automated systems honked a warning alarm as the MiGs came within firing range behind him. When they were almost upon him, Reg snapped back hard on the controls and sent the Hawk into a sudden vertical climb. As he guessed, the faster, more maneuverable MiGs stayed on his tail, following him upward and closing the distance. He looped over backwards, pointed the nose of his plane to earth and plunged full-throttle toward the Dead Sea. The Syrians continued the pursuit.

The three planes plummeted toward the blue surface of the water at hypersonic speed. Reg gave no indication of pulling up. He increased his speed. In his earphones, he could hear his pursuers talking nervously in Arabic. Soon, they were screaming at one another to level off as their altimeter readings approached zero. They broke out of their dive, watching in amazement as the English plane continued to head straight down.

A big grin spread across Reg's face as he calmly brought his plane parallel to the water with plenty of room to spare. Just as he'd expected, the Syrians had pulled up in a panic, forgetting that zero on an altimeter indicated sea level. But the Dead Sea, the lowest point in Asia, was more than nine hundred meters below sea level.

With his confidence restored, Reg ignored the flashing lights on his display panel and crossed into Israeli airspace with an airspeed of 1,000 KPH and an altitude reading of minus 700 meters.

Outwardly at least, the gigantic alien ship over Jerusalem was an exact replica of the thirty-five others. The front of it was marked by a slender black tower, three-quarters of a mile tall, set into a crater-shaped depression in the dome. Soon after it had parked itself over the ancient capital, it began to spin slowly like a wheel, completing a revolution every seventy-two minutes.

Reg was approaching from the southeast but knew that the Tornadoes were on the opposite side, the northwest. He scanned the skies searching for the safest way around the fifteen-mile-wide obstacle, but everywhere he looked, Israeli jets were patrolling in clusters. Hundreds of other planes were prowling just beyond the border. Only the murky area directly below the alien megaship was deserted. Quickly deciding that would be the path of least resistance, he darted into the deep shadows cast by the floating behemoth.

The bottom of the ship was not the smooth surface it appeared to be on television. Instead, it was studded with endless rectangular structures the size of warehouses. They were arranged in precise rows and the spaces between them formed broad boulevards that ran to the center of the vessel. Subtle color differentiations on the surface created a pattern that looked like a vast daisy, the petals of which stretched several miles to the ship's perimeter. As he approached the eye of the flower, he glanced down at Jerusalem. The exact center of the giant ship was directly above the city's most distinctive landmark, the Cubbat As-Sakhrah mosque, the famous Dome of the Rock.

It occurred to Reg that the mazelike underbelly of the ship was a twisted mirror image of the beautiful city below. Jerusalem, one of the most revered cities on the planet, was staring up at a dark reflection of itself. He glanced down as he tore past the walled Old City.

Continuing on his way, he steered toward the horizon, a low, blue ribbon of open sky. When he emerged from beneath the ship, he flew unopposed to the Mediterranean coast and slipped out of Israeli airspace. It didn't take him long to locate the forty British planes. They were in a disorganized holding pattern, flying long slow loops about five miles from shore. He established radio contact with the group's commanding officer.

"Lost Sheep, Lost Sheep, this is Guide Dog. Do you read?"

A sputtering, panic-stricken voice roared back. "It's about bloody well time somebody showed up! Is that you in the Hawk, Guide Dog?"

"Affirmative. This is Major Reg Cummins out of Khamis Moushalt. I'm given to understand that you're in need of my services."

"This is Wing Commander Colonel Thomson. What we need is to get to a friendly airfield and land these planes!" the officer shouted. "We're not pilots, man. We've got no business flying these planes, especially in these circumstances. The blasted Israelis have been threatening to shoot us down. Now I'm ordering you to get us the hell out of here at once."

Although Reg had been warned that the men piloting these sophisticated warplanes were not the best pilots, he was surprised at the man's hysterical tone. "Colonel," Reg said calmly, "you and your men are in good hands. I intend to deliver all of you safely to our base in Kuwait. Now if you gentlemen will kindly follow me to the south along the coast…"

A new voice, much younger than Thomson's and speaking in a working-class London accent interrupted. "Pardon me, Major Cummins. No disrespect intended, but heading south takes us closer to that big ugly wanker sitting over Jerusalem. I, for one, would prefer to stay as far away from that monster as possible."

"That's quite enough, Aircraftman Tye," Colonel Thomson said sternly. "Let the man lead."

"Airman? Did someone just say 'airman'?" Reg said incredulously. "What the hell is an airman doing flying a Tornado?" Like most militaries around the world, the RAF only gave wings to officers. "What's going on here, Thomson? You've got cadets flying these planes?"

Before Thomson could answer, Tye spoke up again. "It's worse than you think, Major Cummins. I'm not even a cadet. Just a lowly mechanic, but don't you worry about me. I've got it under control." Reg had to admit that the kid had a point. It was hard to tell from a distance but Tye seemed to be handling his plane better than most of the others. Certainly much better than his commanding officer, Thomson. He wondered how it was that a mechanic had learned to fly one of Britain's newest and most lethal jet fighters, but decided not to ask.

"Hold on," demanded a new voice. "Why south? Last time I checked, Kuwait was east of here."

"Quite right. We could go that way," Reg said. "In fact, that's a brilliant plan if you chaps think you're ready to square off against the Israelis, the Syrians, the Jordanians, and the Iraqis. How does that sound?"

"Never mind," replied the voice. "I humbly withdraw the suggestion."

The young Londoner, Tye, spoke again. "Yes, when you put it that way, Major, heading south sounds lovely. Suddenly, I'd love to get a better look at that spaceship."

The group formed up behind Reg and flew along the coast keeping to an elevation only slightly lower than the edge of the alien ship. The closer they came, the larger grew the lump in Reg's throat. Guessing that the others must be feeling the same way, he choked down his fear and got on the radio playing the role of friendly tour guide.

"Coming up on your left, gentlemen, you might notice a very large, dark gray aircraft from outer space hovering just a few thousand feet above the ground. We ask that you kindly refrain from feeding the aliens and please remember to keep all arms and legs inside your cockpits at all times."

Nervous laughter came back over the radio and several men made jokes of their own. But just as they approached the nearest edge of the disk, shouting erupted. Movement was detected along the bottom of the craft. Reg immediately shed a thousand feet of altitude. When the Tornadoes followed him, they had a clear view of what was happening.

Mammoth hatch doors were lowering to create a mile-wide opening at the eye of the daisy design. A sparkling jade-green light spilled from the interior of the ship and washed over Jerusalem, illuminating the city as if it were some kind of magical kingdom. It was such a beautiful sight that, for a moment, it was possible to believe the aliens had benign intentions after all. But soon, the tip of a massive cone-shaped mechanism lowered through the opening.

"What in the world is that?" gasped Thomson.

Reg thought he knew. He clenched his teeth and fought against the impulse to abandon the novice pilots to make a run at the jewel-like cone. His fingers itched to unleash his Sidewinders at what he feared was some sort of weapon. But he remained on course, even as a tightly focused beam of white light stabbed downward from the tip of the cone and touched the golden cupola of the Dome of the Rock.

"Communications beam?" someone asked with withering hope.

Reg shook his head sadly. He did not say the words aloud, but mouthed them behind his oxygen mask: targeting laser. A moment later, to his horror, Reg saw that his instinct was right.

A blinding blast of light ripped out of the cone and smashed down on the golden domed mosque, shattering the building into a billion pieces from the inside out. A dense pillar of fire began to build up over the blast site as the weapon continued to fire, adding more and more energy. Then, all at once it exploded outward and began to rip through the city, a tidal wave of flame rolling across the ground, utterly destroying everything in its path. It only seemed to gather momentum as it moved. Spreading relentlessly from the epicenter, a fiery wall of destruction several hundred feet high moved beyond the walls of the city and into the surrounding hills and suburbs. With the speed and force of an atomic explosion, it scoured Jerusalem from the face of the Earth, vaporizing in a handful of seconds what it had taken humans two thousand years to build.

At length, the bright beam coming from the firing cone

shut off. But still the explosion rolled outward. With a momentum of its own, the blast shot beyond the city limits, breaking apart the surrounding towns and villages. It threw automobiles, buildings and bridges hundreds of feet into the air before burying them under a molten sea of flames.

Even after the flames themselves stopped moving outward, the residual heat continued for another mile, killing everything it touched. Where one of the most beloved cities of the world had stood scant seconds before, there was now only a twenty-mile circle of scarred, scorched earth. Half a million human lives had been extinguished.

None of the English pilots had spoken a word since the blast began. Reg broke the silence with a terse command. "You men continue south." Then he broke abruptly out of formation, turning to port for an attack run against the giant city destroyer.

He was not alone. From every corner of the sky, pilots from every nation in the Middle East temporarily forgot their longstanding rivalries to attack their common enemy. Without a word passing between them, Reg joined a group of eight Iranian jets which adjusted their positions to make room for him in their formation. He had only a few missiles loaded aboard his Hawk, but when the Iranian flight leader shouted the signal, he fired two of them. His AIM-9 Sidewinders kicked forward and joined the barrage of Iranian weapons. They all exploded at the same time, a full quarter mile before reaching the polished surface of the alien craft.

"What the hell was that?"

As the missiles detonated, they produced an odd atmospheric disturbance. The air surrounding the city destroyer rippled visibly like the surface of a pond disturbed by a handful of pebbles.

"Pull up!" Reg shouted to the Iranians. "They've got some kind of energy shield!"

The stunned pilots saw that he was right and yanked back hard on their yokes in a desperate bid to avoid the invisible barrier. For some, the warning came too late. Four of the eight splattered themselves against the shield and burst into flames without penetrating to the other side. As Reg and the others leveled off, they could see the same thing was happening all around them. Missiles and jets were exploding against the invisible wall protecting the dark ship.

In his headphones, Reg could hear Colonel Thomson screaming, cursing and demanding that he finish the job of escorting the squad out of the area. After studying the melee unfolding around him for another minute, Reg saw that there was little hope of damaging the ship. Reluctantly, he turned south to rejoin the Tornadoes.

Only a moment after he spotted the Tornadoes, the already-disastrous situation got worse, much worse. A fresh round of shouting erupted over the radio. Reg looked over his shoulder at the black tower that marked the prow of the city destroyer. Near the top of it, a portal had appeared. What had seemed like a solid surface only moments before now bore a wide opening from which hundreds of small craft were emerging. They ducked and turned with incredible aerodynamic agility, like an angry swarm of bees boiling out of a disturbed hive. They quickly split into packs and moved to confront the human jets.

"Finally," Reg said to himself, "someone our own size to pick on."

"What now?" Thomson shouted. "What do we do, Cummins?"

"There's only thing you can do in a situation like this, Colonel. Run like hell. Get out of here as fast as you can. I'll try to buy you some time."

Reg wheeled around to face the oncoming enemy and spotted a gang of ten or twelve of them headed his way. They were sleek, lethal-looking machines with large reflective windows and curved rods extending from their noses like sets of pincers. Instead of a stable formation, they darted over and under one another in a continuous shuffle. As they streaked closer, white-hot energy pulses formed between the pincers before firing through the air. They look like the scarabs in the Egyptian Museum of Cairo, thought Reg, but they fly like bats.

Before Reg came within range, the alien detachment came under attack. Arabs, Israelis, Turks, Greeks and Africans closed in on them and filled the air with missiles and large-caliber gunfire. Reg flew toward the melee, bobbing and weaving to avoid the stray blasts from the alien pulse weapons that were streaking through the air. A moment after he joined forces with a Sudanese pilot, the man's MiG burst into flames and disintegrated. The scarab that had fired the deadly shot buzzed over the top of Reg's Hawk. In a heartbeat, Reg banked hard and fell in behind him. The alien pilot seemed not to realize he was being followed. Or perhaps he didn't care. He swooped to attack another jet, an American F-15, but before he could fire another pulse blast, Reg locked on with his targeting system and sent a Sidewinder flashing through the air. It scored a solid hit, exploding with devastating power against the rear of the attacker.

"One confirmed kill!" he reported, keying his radio to the common band. But as the smoke cleared, he realized that he had spoken too soon. The attacker was still in one piece. It wobbled through the air for a moment, reeling from the force of the blast, before righting itself and moving on as if nothing had happened. "Bad news," he shouted. "These little buggers have shields, too! Break off the engagement."

That was easier said than done. The nimble alien

attackers were destroying jets almost as fast as Reg could count them. It wasn't a dogfight, but a one-sided aerial slaughter. Reg turned south again and tried to find a way through the mayhem. More than one of the aliens sighted on him and came in firing pulse blasts, forcing him to use every trick in his considerable repertoire to avoid being shot down. Reg managed to stay alive, but the less-skillful pilots around him were not so lucky. Shaking off the last of his alien pursuers, he leveled out at five thousand feet, pushed his twin turbo fan engines to their maximum speed and tore south along the coastline. He saw no sign of Thomson or the others, and was thankful that they appeared to be safely out of the area. Then, a lone Tornado came roaring up behind him and stationed itself off his starboard wing.

"Who the hell is piloting that Tornado! You lot are supposed to be long gone!"

"It's Airman Tye, sir. I'm your new wingman."

A fast-moving pair of blips on Reg's radar screen told him danger was approaching. Two of the scarab attackers were giving chase and they were gaining fast. He might be able to save himself with clever maneuvering, at least for a while, but now he had to worry about the young fool of a mechanic who had come to help. Burning with anger, he looked to his right and leveled an icy stare at the man in the Tornado's cockpit.

Tye responded with an enthusiastic salute and a nod of the head.

"Listen to me," Reg called. "Do you know if that plane has had its avionics update yet?"

"Installed it myself, Major," Tye responded proudly a moment before a pulse blast sailed between their two planes.

"Major," the young man shouted, "we've got aliens right behind us!"

"I see them," said the Teacher as calmly as if he were

conducting a routine training mission. "Now, here's what I'd like you to do. Come up about twenty meters and fire off the portchaff."

To Reg's surprise, Tye executed the order quickly and with great precision. As the enemy closed in behind them, a cloud of aluminum slivers exploded into the air. Designed to confuse the homing systems of enemy air-to-air missiles, the tiny magnetically-charged bits of metal adhered to the attackers. Blinded and confused, they broke off the pursuit.

"Excellent work, lad!" roared Reg. "Where did you learn to fly like that?" Then, before Tye could answer, Reg laughed and said, "Forget I asked. I'm sure I don't want to know."

"Cummins! Where are you? Cummins, is that you?" The desperate voice on the radio belonged to Colonel Thomson. "For the love of God, man, where are you? Help us."

"I'm here, Colonel. What is your position?"

"I don't know. I think we're... everyone's dead, everyone's been shot down. We tried to fight them off, but they have shields and they were everywhere. Everyone's gone."

Another Englishman shouted over the airwaves. "Guide Dog, this is Sutton. Colonel Thomson and I are circling just north of the Red Sea, over the town of Eilat."

Within minutes, Reg and Tye spotted their companions and flew to meet them. Of the thirty-eight Tornadoes that had gone ahead, only two remained. Thomson had calmed down considerably by the time they arrived.

"We're all that's left," he reported.

"What happened," Reg demanded. "You should've been out of the area long ago."

"We ran into the whole goddamn Egyptian Air Force," Sutton snarled. "They came roaring north, headed straight at us, and it was all we could do to get out of their way. We were in the process of regrouping when those little alien bastards came out of nowhere and chewed us to pieces."

"What do we do now?"

"I'm afraid escorting you to Kuwait is out of the question. Not enough fuel. Looks like I'll have to bring you boys home with me to Khamis Moushalt."

"Where the hell is that?" demanded Sutton.

"Just follow me," Reg answered. Continuing south from Eilat and hugging the edge of the Red Sea, the quartet soon crossed into Saudi Arabia. Partly out of habit and partly to restore a sense of purpose, Reg formed them into a staggered diamond formation. This lone sense of order in the aftermath of the devastating air battle attracted every lost pilot for miles around. One by one, they joined Reg's armada until they were nearly fifty strong. Soon, the group was flying over the dramatically contrasting Asir mountain chain. The green western slopes ran down to the Red Sea and were lush with vegetation, while the eastern slopes were devoid of life and marked the edge of a vast, inhospitable desert.

A few of the pilots had come mentally unglued. Through his radio, Reg could hear them sobbing like small children and jabbering uncontrollably in languages he didn't understand. Trying to think, he blocked out the noise and almost missed the message coming from his home base. The voice was barely audible above the din. "Khamis Moushalt Airfield to southbound flight. Do you read?"

"Affirmative, Khamis Moushalt. This is RAF Major Cummins."

"Major," said the flight controller, "please instruct any RAF pilots in your group to switch to the private band. Over." Reg and the other Brits quickly complied.

"Hello, Major," Colonel Whitley said. "You're still alive!"

"Yes, a few of us survived. But only by the skin of our teeth. They destroyed Jerusalem. Wiped it off the map."

"Yes, I know. The attack was simultaneous and worldwide. All thirty-six of their ships fired at once.

London, Paris, New York, Moscow, all of them. They're all gone."

"London," Tye repeated softly, expressing a huge amount of grief with a single word.

"Listen," Whitley went on, "I've been talking with the American commander. He's got thirty F-16s ready to escort you in. Add our six instructors, and you've got thirty-six. Will that be enough to hold off those aliens?"

"Don't bother," Reg shot back. "If the aliens come after us, more planes won't make any difference." He began explaining the shields they'd encountered on both the city destroyer and the scarab attack craft, but Whitley cut him off.

"What do you mean if they come after you?" Whitley asked. "You'd better have a look at your long-range radar."

Reg studied his screens and saw that they were clear. For a moment he hoped that the colonel was mistaken, but his heart sank into the pit of his stomach when he noticed a cluster of blips creeping into view at the top of the screen. It was a squadron of at least two dozen alien attackers.

"We are officially dead meat," Sutton groaned. "It's over."

"Our intel officer here in the tower has been monitoring your situation for several minutes. He's convinced the enemy is following you." Whitley paused to let the pilots draw their own conclusions. "Change your mind about that escort?"

"Negative!" Reg shouted. "I'm telling you that won't do any good."

"Then we've got a major problem," Whitley said, "because there's no way the Yanks can get all their planes off the ground before you get here. They've got over two hundred birds parked on the tarmac and if you bring—"

"I understand," Reg interrupted. "We'll turn to the east and lead them away from you."

"Very well," Whitley said after a brief pause. "Good

luck, Cummins, and good luck to the rest of you men." Then he was gone.

Reg switched back to the common frequency and issued the new orders. "Turn away from the coast and proceed due east. We have a large force of alien attack craft closing to our rear. Turn east immediately." Most of the pilots were still too shocked and confused to oppose the order, despite the fact that there was nothing but empty desert in that direction. The entire group turned away from the water. All except for three planes. Reg ordered them to rejoin the formation several times before deciding to chase after them. He called for Tye and Sutton, both of them decent pilots despite their lack of training, to form up on his wings.

Two of the renegade jets were Iraqis, the last people on Earth Reg wanted to shoot down. "Iraqi pilots, you are headed in the wrong direction. Our flight is heading east."

One of them shouted back that Reg could go to hell. He said that he and his partner were low on fuel and that there was nowhere to land in the desert.

Reg considered explaining the situation to them, hoping he could persuade them to cooperate. But there wasn't enough time so he adopted a more efficient approach. "British Tornadoes," he said, "you are red and clear. Lock on and fire at will."

"No! Wait!" cried the Iraqis. "We agree to follow you. We are turning!" Cursing energetically in Arabic, the two men reluctantly set off to the east. Reg sent Tye and Sutton with them to make sure they rejoined the rest of the group. Then he closed quickly on the last southbound plane, a twenty-year-old Chinese J-7 with Egyptian markings. The pilot was muttering unintelligibly into his radio mouthpiece and didn't respond to Reg's repeated warnings.

Hoping to snap the Egyptian out of his stupor, Reg flipped his Hawk over and moved up until he was right on top of the J-7. The canopies of the two planes were separated by only a few feet. The Egyptian looked up and saw the Englishman hanging upside down above him pointing to the east, but the strange sight failed to register in his grief-stricken mind. He continued along the same path, muttering the whole while.

Reg saw no harm in letting the man go his own way. In his present condition, there was little chance of him leading the aliens to Khamis Moushalt or any other airfield. But Reg felt badly about leaving him, so he shot ahead and attempted to take the Egyptian "by the hand." He maneuvered himself directly in front of the other plane and began a gradual turn to port, hoping the disoriented pilot would unthinkingly follow him. But something went horribly wrong. A warning buzzer sounded, and when Reg twisted around, he saw an R.550 Magic missile streaking toward him, homing in on his heat exhaust. Reg screamed and jerked the controls hard to port, lifting as he went. The missile chased after him, quickly closing the distance.

"Damn it! Somebody finally caught me with my guard down." Although he'd been "fired" at hundreds of time in training exercises, he'd never been "killed." Then again, he'd never made himself into a sitting duck the way he had for this demented Egyptian.

Reg continued to turn as tightly as his Hawk would allow, the G force crashing him against the right-hand wall of the cockpit until he was headed back toward the J-7. Although he hadn't planned it, he realized that looping around had provided him with one last card to play, one last slim hope of avoiding being blown apart. He steered himself onto a collision course with the Egyptian, speeding toward him almost head-on, as the missile continued to hunt him down. He bore down on the plane until he was close enough to see the man's eyes looking back at him blankly. Then, at the last possible moment, he swerved and felt the concussion behind him as the Magic missile destroyed the plane that had fired it.

Without celebrating his narrow escape, without even glancing back at the falling debris, Reg sped east to catch up to the others. Of course, he was glad to have survived the encounter. But as he looked north and saw the squadron of alien attackers becoming visible in the distance, he realized that his being alive was probably only a very temporary state of affairs. Only a moment after struggling to save himself, he found himself hoping the aliens would chase him out into the desert and hunt him down.

But that didn't happen. The scarab planes resisted the temptation to snack on Reg's small band of refugee pilots and instead continued south toward the feast awaiting them at Khamis Moushalt. As he headed deeper into the desert, Reg switched over to the private frequency and heard the tower operator desperately calling out the alert. "Incoming! Incoming!"

2

RETREAT

Leaving the Red Sea behind them, Reg and his motley crew of survivors headed out across one of the most inhospitable environments on the face of the Earth, the great sand desert of the Arabian peninsula. Stretching out to the horizon in all directions, it was an ocean of gently undulating sand dunes, some of them a hundred meters tall. Shaped by the wind, they looked like the cresting waves of the ocean that had once covered the land. The Arabs called it Rub al-Khali, the Empty Quarter. It was a place the fiercest Bedouin tribes feared to cross, even in the ubiquitous Toyota trucks that had long since replaced camels. The international borders running through the area had never been precisely defined. No war had ever been fought for its control. It was one of the only places on the face of the planet that no one wanted.

The shouting, arguing and whimpering that had filled the radio waves subsided as the pilots headed deeper into this awesome and pitiless landscape. Fuel levels were running dangerously low and the warning systems aboard the planes began to sound. It appeared as though they had eluded one enemy only to run headlong into the arms of another. Instead of a swift, explosive death from an alien energy pulse, they now faced a slow, painful one in the desert. Their only hope was to find one of the tiny oases that dotted the desert. But the Empty Quarter was roughly the size of Texas, which meant they were looking for a needle in a field full of haystacks.

Reg had visited a few oases. They were not grass green patches of land full of swaying palm trees that most Westerners imagined. Instead, they typically consisted of a few tiny buildings and an oil derrick or two. A few of the places were marked on Reg's onboard maps, but without satellite navigation systems the maps were useless. The Empty Quarter offered no permanent landmarks by which to navigate. It was a place that gave up no secrets.

One by one, the jets began to run out of fuel and fall from the sky. The first to go down was a Jordanian. Before he ditched his plane, the terrified pilot begged his countrymen to remember the coordinates and send rescuers for him as soon as they could. They promised they would, but everyone knew it wasn't going to happen. Moving deeper into the desert with each passing minute, the pilots scoured the landscape with their eyes and called for help over their radios. Four more pilots were lost to lack of fuel, and Reg began to feel the panic level rising in his chest like the waterline in a sinking ship. The red warning light on his own fuel meter began to blink. It was only a matter of time.

Just when all seemed lost, a Libyan pilot spotted what looked like a column of smoke rising on the horizon.

"That looks like an oil fire," said Tye.

As the group turned and raced in that direction, one of the Israelis, a man with a froggy voice, quoted from the Bible. "And the Lord went before them by day in a pillar of cloud." Then he asked, "Are you a believer, Major Cummins?"

"Let's just say I believe we're going to need all the help we can get," Reg replied.

The source of the smoke came into view. A crashed tanker plane was burning out of control. The jet fuel it had been carrying had spilled over a wide area and was belching a mushroom cloud of black smoke high into the hot, motionless air.

It took Reg a moment to recognize the place, though he'd flown past it with his students more than once. It was an oil-drilling station set atop a barren, rocky plateau. It was surrounded by a ring of stony hills that kept the ever-shifting dunes from burying the plateau in sand. Since Reg had seen it last, the site had been transformed. It was now a small military airfield. Over a hundred Saudi combat planes were parked alongside a freshly repaved landing strip.

"I don't believe my eyes!" Tye shouted. "We're saved."

"It must be a mirage," Sutton said. "What is this place?"

"My guess is that this must have been a designated fallback position for the Saudi military," Reg said. Then he added, "Would've been nice of them to let us know about it."

"Why haven't the bastards answered our distress calls?" Thomson fumed.

"I suggest we go down there and ask them."

None of the pilots bothered to request permission to land. Jostling for position, they lined up nearly nose cone to tail fin and descended toward the runway at the same time.

When Colonel Thomson saw the situation he was in, he shrieked and rolled out of formation. His fuel gauge had long since run to zero, but he decided it would be safer to risk another loop around. He hadn't flown a fighter jet for more than a decade and was more than a little rusty.

Earlier that morning, before dawn, he'd been in his office on the island of Cyprus, packing his personal effects neatly into cardboard boxes. The entire base was closing and he was preparing to be transferred to an aircraft carrier in the Mediterranean. Then the surprising news arrived that the colonel would instead be flying a Tornado jet fighter to Kuwait. He was given ten minutes to report He poured himself a capful of whiskey and looked around the office, deciding what to bring. The first thing he picked up was the photograph of him standing between a pair of much taller men, President Whitmore and the Italian prime minister, but he quickly tossed it aside. He ended up taking just three things: a recent picture of his wife and three daughters, which he creased and slipped into his wallet; a red, dog-eared copy of *The Traveler's Guide to Handy Phrases in Arabic*; and a pearl-handled revolver his father had given him years before. He loaded the pistol, tucked it inside his jacket and left without closing the door behind him.

"Thomson, you were on a good approach," Reg said. "Why'd you pull up?"

"A man needs room to land a plane!" the colonel yelled back. "I'm not a damned stunt pilot!"

Resisting the urge to ask the colonel exactly what kind of pilot he *was*, Reg coached him into a passable landing. Tye and Sutton, on the other hand, handled themselves like seasoned veterans, landing their Tornadoes almost flawlessly.

When he lined up for his own landing, however, Reg's luck finally deserted him. His Hawk sputtered and flamed out as the final dregs of jet fuel were consumed. Quickly sizing up the situation, he saw there was no way to make an unpowered landing. Too many jets were still on approach and he was losing altitude fast. But there was an even more pressing problem. He was heading toward a row of gleaming Saudi F-15 Eagles parked near the foot of the runway and was going to demolish them if he didn't do something. Acting on instinct, Reg jammed his yoke all the way forward, tilting the nose of his plane straight down. The Hawk plummeted toward the ground like a heavy stone. A moment before he crashed into the plateau wall, he hugged his arms and legs close to his body and activated the explosive bolts of his ejection seat.

The clear canopy ripped away, and Reg hurtled out

of the doomed jet fighter, flying *parallel* to the ground at a sickening rate of speed. The silk canopy attached to his harness acted as much as a drag chute as it did a parachute. As he shot through the air like a human cannonball, Reg caught a momentary glimpse of the dumbfounded expression on the face of a Syrian pilot who was flying in the same direction.

As his Hawk piled into the ground and exploded in a huge fire ball, Reg drifted down to the tarmac and hit the ground running, following the jets down the runway. Skidding to a halt, he hustled to flatten his chute and pull it to one side, where it wouldn't hamper the few planes left to land.

He marched down the runway until he noticed three British pilots staring at him in disbelief. By the time he walked up to where they were standing in the shade of a freshly parked Tornado, he was drenched in sweat. It was well over 110 degrees Fahrenheit. One of the Brits was a gangly red-haired lad who was shaking his head in stupefied amazement. Reg didn't need to see a name tag to guess who he was.

"Better close your mouth there, Airman Tye. It's wicked dry out here in the desert."

Things in the camp did not get off to an auspicious beginning. The Saudis insisted on keeping the new arrivals away from their planes and tents. The contingent of international pilots was kept segregated on one side of the plateau, well away from the landing strip. The armed soldiers the Saudis posted along their *border* refused to answer questions, even from pilots who came from countries allied with Saudi Arabia.

To make matters worse, the pilots quickly balkanized themselves into national groupings and kept well away from their traditional enemies. Everyone in the international part of the camp, it seemed, was angry with the Saudis and deeply suspicious of one another. Even Reg Cummins was having trouble cracking the code of silence among the Saudi guards and wringing information from them. As he was trying, screaming erupted from the Israeli group.

The Israelis had been the first to isolate themselves from the others, most of whom were Arabs. There had been a great deal of shouting in Hebrew since they had withdrawn to the shade of their planes, but it seemed directed toward one of their own. After a shrill, piercing cry rang through the air, the man who seemed to be causing most of the disturbance broke free of the group and came sprinting wildly across the dusty earth toward Reg. Both Sutton and Tye, lounging in the nearby shade, stood to meet the challenge but Reg motioned them back.

"What are you?" demanded the crazed Israeli. He had a haunted, terrified look on his face and was dripping with sweat.

"Easy there, pilot," Reg said. "I'm an English officer. We're allies."

"English? What is English?" he screamed. Two of his countrymen ran up behind the man, whose name tag identified him as GREENBERG and took hold of his arms, but he continued to rage. "That means nothing now. I want to know if you are human? Are you a human or one of them?"

"Human," Reg assured him, "one hundred percent human."

The answer seemed to calm the man down, but only for a moment. With the strength that only the demented possess, he threw both the men restraining him to the ground and ran to the next group, the Iranians.

"What are you? Are you human?" he screamed at a muscular pilot who had stripped to the waist. The man didn't answer, but scoffed and turned away. When Greenberg took another step toward him, the Iranian threw a sudden, vicious elbow to the middle of the Israeli's face. A fountain of bright red blood flew through the air as Greenberg crumpled to the ground. One of the men chasing Greenberg started a shoving match with the Iranian and soon the entire Israeli contingent was converging on the site.

Reg groaned a little. "Let the games begin," he said, half in disgust before he, too, started hurrying toward the trouble. Before he got there, however, an unlikely figure appeared in the center of the impending storm, shouting for order in atrocious Arabic. The man waved a well-thumbed red phrase book in the air with imperious authority. Reg blinked. It was Thomson.

The gathering mob, which had been on the verge of embarking on a full-fledged rumble, came to a dead stop, startled by the force of the colonel's command, even though none of them had understood a word he had said. Thomson did not cut an impressive figure. He was an average-looking man, well under six feet tall, and a bit thick around the middle. He sported a pencil-thin mustache and, like many balding men, let what little hair was still left to him grow long enough to comb over the top of his shiny scalp. Curiously, despite being overweight, he hardly perspired at all.

"Now then," the little colonel roared, "what's all this nonsense about?" When the two sides recovered from their shock and again began to shout at one another, Thomson leapt between them, drawing their anger to himself like a lightning rod and diffusing it. As the dispute raged on, he continued to consult his phrase book and shout appropriate phrases over the noise of the assembly. In this manner, he staved off an all-out brawl long enough for Greenberg to be led away. The Israeli was covered in his own blood, and his nose was obviously broken.

Reg was feeling somewhat broken himself. He thought

of Jerusalem, obliterated, and sympathized with the jabbering Israeli. After everything that had happened— the city leveled by an unfightable foe, the destruction of his home base, the loss of those pilots over the desert— Reg could understand why madness might be an attractive alternative. Giving in to fear and paranoia seemed, under the circumstances, perfectly natural. It relieved a man like Greenberg of the responsibility of figuring out what to do next.

Even as tensions between the Iranians and Israelis began to dissipate, Thomson continued to quote the scripture he found in his copy of *The Traveler's Guide to Handy Phrases in Arabic*. It wasn't clear whether he realized what an ass he was making of himself.

Finally, one of the Iranians who was laughing at him filled him in on a little secret. "Colonel, perhaps you are unaware of the fact that none of us standing here are speakers of Arabic, not native speakers at any rate."

Thomson, befuddled, looked at the man and then at his trusty handbook. "How do you mean?"

The Iranian laughed again. "We speak Farsi, and the Jews speak Hebrew. Actually, I have picked up a bit of Arabic, enough to know your accent is absolutely abominable!"

With tensions temporarily abated, the two groups returned to their respective enclaves. Reg, braving the heat, walked to the edge of the plateau and looked over the lip of the crumbling sandstone abutment. Below him, he watched a handful of Saudi soldiers trying to extinguish the still-burning remains of his Hawk and the crashed fuel tanker. The soldiers, wearing traditional red headdresses, and armed only with shovels and small fire extinguishers, did the best they could to suppress the flames. Great clouds of black smoke continued to billow into the windless blue sky. The smoke announced their location for many miles around, a beacon to wandering pilots. Indeed, more planes were arriving all the time, most of them straggling in from the north. But if human pilots could use the fires to find the camp, the aliens surely could as well.

When he rejoined the other pilots, Reg found a large number of them haranguing the guards. They were demanding to know the news from their home countries, if the aliens had landed, and whether or not their planes would be refueled. The more the guards refused to speak, the angrier and more insistent the pilots became. Reg noticed a couple of the Saudis slip away from the confrontation and hurry into the tent town they had erected among the planes on the far side of the runway. In addition to the tactical fighters, there were a number of transport and cargo planes. There was a fuel tanker identical to the one that had crashed and a score of private luxury jets, undoubtedly the property of wealthy families. Reg wasn't surprised to see the civilian aircraft because he was familiar with the way rich Saudis, especially members of the royal family, considered the armed forces almost as personal bodyguards.

Soon the two men who had slipped away returned, leading a small army of machine-gun-toting reinforcements. They fanned out and crouched along the runway as if they expected a battle.

Their commanding officer was a huge, powerfully built captain with severe eyes and a hooked nose. Like the other Saudis, he wore a *keffiyeh,* the checkered red-and-white headcloth held in place by black cords. Despite the oppressive heat, he was dressed in an olive drab uniform made of wool. All business, he marched toward the refugee pilots, shouting orders in Arabic. When he noticed the Israelis, however, he stopped in his tracks. For a moment, he seemed to be at a loss. Then he cleared his throat and made an announcement in English.

"Jews are not allowed in the Kingdom of Saudi

Arabia. This is Islamic holy land."

Pilots from several nations were shouting, trying to get his attention, but all fell silent when the senior officer among the Israelis, who happened to be a woman, bulled her way to the front of the crowd. When he saw her, the Saudi captain backpedaled. He had just gotten used to the idea of dealing with Jews, but now a *female Jewish fighter pilot* who shared his rank? This seemed as impossible to comprehend to the Saudi as the sudden arrival of aliens from outer space.

"You don't want us here? We'd be happy to leave. Just give us enough fuel to get the hell out of here."

In rough English, the Saudi announced that the airfield was in a state of heightened alert until the fires burned themselves out. The pilots were to remain with their planes. Water and food would be brought to them, along with shovels so they could dig their own latrines. They were not, under any circumstances, allowed to leave the area that had been set aside for them until the commander of the base gave the go-ahead.

"And when might that be?" inquired Thomson.

"Commander Faisal is still studying the situation," came the reply.

"Well, what about an update on what's going on out there?" Everyone understood Thomson's vague wave to the north to mean the entire world.

"You must be patient, Colonel," said the hook-nosed man. With a last, hate-filled glare at the Israeli woman, he turned on his heels and walked away.

"Arrogant son of a bitch, isn't he?" asked Sutton. He was about Reg's age, somewhere in his mid-thirties, with a flattop haircut and a sharp cast to his features. He shook his head in disgust. "I don't know who's worse," he continued, "the aliens or these self-righteous bastards."

"The Saudis are all right," Reg said. "A bit high-handed

sometimes, but they usually end up doing the right thing."

Sutton wasn't convinced. He lit a cigarette and squinted into the harsh afternoon sunlight. "We haven't been here an hour yet and already there have been a dozen arguments, one fistfight, and now we're being treated like bloody prisoners of war! I wouldn't say they're doing the right thing at all. No, things are not going well."

Reg didn't answer, just watched as the man inhaled deeply on his cigarette.

"Things are probably a bit more comfortable for whites up there in Kuwait," Sutton said. "Too bad you weren't able to follow your orders and get us through." With that, the lieutenant turned and walked back to the shade of his plane.

The blazing sun had one beneficial consequence. It made arguing while standing out in the open an impossibility. Soon, the pilots had retreated to their own mini-enclaves based on nation, still mistrustful of one another. They stretched out on the sand beneath their planes, fitfully trying to rest.

Reg saw soldiers of the Saudi army taking up positions all around the plateau. They were armed with "handheld" SAM launchers, bulky bazooka like weapons. He could see them on the high dunes in the distance. Ready to defend against incoming alien ships. *Futile,* he thought.

At one point, midway through the afternoon, a Jordanian pilot was called to the main camp. When he returned, word spread among the international pilots that the Saudis had asked him a few questions about the capabilities of the alien attack craft. The man had told them that others had been more involved in the fighting than he, particularly the British officer called Cummins, but they hadn't seemed interested. Sometime after that, the Saudis finally brought buckets of water and boxes of crackers and distributed them.

What news was passed among the pilots took a circuitous route. The Iraqis had made sure they were as far as possible from their sworn enemies, the Iranians. The Israelis stayed as far as possible from everyone.

It was Thomson more than anyone who facilitated communication. He spent most of the afternoon shuffling from one encampment to the next, bringing his own fussy brand of diplomacy to the situation. No one was convinced by anything he said, but on the few occasions he stepped between arguing parties—once there were even knives drawn—he gave the frustrated pilots a way to back down without losing face.

Unwittingly, he also provided comic relief. Most of the pilots were fluent in English, the international language of aviation, but Thomson persisted in dragging out his phrase book and tripping over elementary Arabic phrases at every opportunity. He would deliver his mispronunciations with great authority, then move on to the next group.

Eventually, he returned to the three British planes, where Tye and Sutton lay sprawled in the sand. Reg was leaning against a Tornado's landing gear, half-dozing.

"Keeping eyes open and ears alert, I see," Thomson said. He was covered in dust from head to toe.

The two men on the ground just muttered and ignored the colonel, but Reg asked, "Any news?"

Thomson looked over his shoulder at the various groups of pilots. "It's shocking. Intellectually, I knew these people hated one another, of course. It's all over the telly and the newspapers. But to witness it up close like this, it's enough to turn your stomach."

Reg was no stranger to the strife of the Middle East, but this was Thomson's first visit to the region. The colonel continued, "I was talking to those blokes from Syria, for example. Educated fellows, polite. Worried about their families, of course. But when the subject of the Israelis came up it was like I'd thrown a switch and turned them into demons or some such. They started going on about how when night comes, they were going to sneak over there with knives and sever a few heads. Quite disturbing really." Thomson shivered in the heat. "Do you suppose we should go over and warn them?"

Reg looked over at the large Israeli contingent and noticed they'd posted guards of their own. "I wouldn't worry about them, Colonel. They're used to being surrounded by unfriendly nations."

Thomson studied the Israelis himself. "Humph," he said. "Looks like somebody has already warned them. Still, if I was a wagering man, I'd bet someone dies before the night is out."

Sutton stood, stretching. "I'd say chances are good that we'll *all* be dead before the night is out."

Thomson ignored the remark. The portly officer ran his fingers through his thinning hair before lying down on his back in the shade. He laced his fingers over the bulge of his stomach and fell instantly asleep. The roar of a Saudi jet lifting off did not drown out his snores.

Time passed, and the British pilots became lost in their own thoughts, speaking to one another very little. Reg scanned the airfield, hoping to catch sight of any of his former students, but saw no one he recognized. He was mystified by the behavior of their supposed Saudi allies, but was willing to wait at least a little while for more information.

The wait ended when the burly Saudi captain returned to "Embassy Row"—as Tye had taken to calling the international part of the airfield—and sent his soldiers to each contingent of pilots with a message. They asked each group to select a representative to meet with the camp's commander.

"I'll pass," Sutton said immediately. "There's no telling what mischief these blokes are up to."

"If they're serving food, sign me up," Tye chimed in. "I'm half-starved."

Sutton gestured toward the sleeping figure of Thomson. "Mr. Phrase Book over there is our ranking officer. Maybe we should wake him up."

Reg was a more logical choice to act as representative because of his years of working with the Saudi military. He was the only one of the Brits with the first clue about the political dynamics of the region, but he felt certain the Saudis weren't ready to hold a serious meeting so he leaned back against the landing gear. "I don't know what's worse," he said, "the colonel's snoring or the growls coming out of Tye's stomach. You go on ahead, lad, and if they're serving bangers and mash, bring us back a doggy bag."

Without waiting to hear Sutton's response, the gangly mechanic left to join the other representatives. Sutton turned away with a petulant shrug and returned to his spot in the shade. "Fine," he said.

Reg lay down on his back and closed his eyes. But before he could drift off to sleep, a harsh Saudi voice startled him. "Englishman, wake up." The burly captain was looming over him. "Is your name Cummins?"

After a glance down at his name tag, Reg smiled up at the soldier. "Yes, I suppose I am."

"You will come with me," he said impatiently, and when Reg didn't leap to his feet, he added, "Immediately!"

The two Brits exchanged a look. Sutton was alarmed. "I'm thinking it cannot be a good thing that he knows your name. I wouldn't go if I were you. Could be trouble."

As Reg stood and brushed the sand from his uniform, the Saudi repeated, "Immediately!"

Sutton scrambled to his feet. "You don't have to go

anywhere with this damn towel-head, Major. He's got no authority over you."

Reg grimaced at his compatriot's ugly remark. "Sutton, don't worry. I'll go."

When the captain turned and began leading the way, Sutton caught Reg by the arm. 'Take this," he said, showing him the pistol concealed in his waistband.

"Thanks just the same," Reg said with a glance toward the dozens of heavily armed Saudi soldiers around the airfield. "I doubt I'd have the chance to use it, even if I wanted to." With that, he moved off to join the representatives moving toward the Saudi camp.

As the group made its way between the white tents that served the base as barracks, Reg took special note of the civilians milling about, women and even a few children. The women were covered from head to toe in long skeins of black fabric, the *abayas* dictated by Muslim custom. Regardless of the temperature, Saudi women were bound by law to cover themselves like furniture in an abandoned house. It was a custom Reg found personally distasteful, but one he'd come to ignore.

The representatives were marched past an open-sided tent crammed full of radio equipment. About a dozen technicians sat at their stations under a low roof of camouflage netting. They all turned and stared inquisitively at the foreign pilots.

A Jordanian pilot walking just ahead of Reg and Tye gestured toward the radio tent. "We should make friends with those men over there. Maybe they can tell us what's happening out in the world."

Tye took this immediately to heart. "Hello, gents," he called to radio operators with wave and a smile. "Any word from England?" The Saudis merely stared back at him. In the time-honored tradition of English speakers everywhere, Tye tried again, speaking slowly and in a louder voice. "WHAT... IS HAPPENING... IN ENGLAND?"

The only result of this was that the other dozen pilots walking with him began shouting questions of their own, mostly in Arabic. The Saudi captain barked an order, and the group moved on.

"That's *not* exactly what I had I mind," said the Jordanian.

"They weren't picking up anything, anyway," said Reg. "Otherwise, they would have been too busy to stare at us."

There were several small cargo planes scattered about the center of the camp, but by far the largest object in sight was an American-built C-130A cargo plane. It towered above the others, its great bulk providing shade for a dozen or so tents pitched beneath its one-hundred-foot height. The tail section had been raised on its hinges, allowing direct access to the belly of the plane. A squad of soldiers casually guarded the interior, sitting around the top of the landing ramp. They, too, stared at the bedraggled group of pilots, while tightening their grips on their AK-47s.

Finally the pilots came to a large tent at the very center of the Saudi camp. A noisy gas-driven generator provided power to the air-conditioning system cooling the tent's interior. A soldier stationed at the entrance seemed to have as his sole responsibility ensuring that the flap stayed closed. The tent had originally been white, but, like the others, was now coated with the tan brown dust of the surrounding desert. The hook-nosed captain roughly ordered the pilots to halt.

"That bloke's got a red-hot poker jammed up his rear, doesn't he?" asked Tye, eliciting a few chuckles. "Where exactly does he think we'd be wandering off to?"

"They are trying to show us how strong they are," answered the Jordanian, without emotion.

"Well, I wish he'd just lift something heavy above his

head and have done with it," Tye replied. "It's too bloody hot to stand around in the sun. I feel like a slab of bacon that's been left in the skillet too long."

He looks it, too, thought Reg. The pale mechanic's skin was beginning to turn the same shade as his flaming red hair, and his shoulders were slouched. The sun was literally shrinking him.

Tye glanced around with half-closed eyes. The shade on the eastern side of the tent attracted his attention. "Why can't we wait over there?" he asked loudly.

Reg smiled. "I suppose you could try to walk over there and find out."

Tye considered the idea. "Say," he asked hesitantly, "don't they still stone people in this country? Cut off their hands and all that business?"

Reg shrugged. "It's a harsh place."

"Actually," said the Jordanian, eyeing the shade, "that's not a bad idea. Let's go and wait in the shade. We're all brothers here. No one is going to shoot us." He stepped out of line and began walking slowly toward the spot. The Saudi guards lowered their rifles at him, ordering him back. But he continued moving, hands in the air, speaking in a friendly tone. "The sun is making us ill," he explained.

They tried to block his path and push him back toward the others, but the Jordanian bulled ahead, eventually pushing his way past the last guard and sitting down in the shade. The other pilots followed his example, ignoring the threats and warnings from the soldiers. Once they had all seated themselves along the side of the tent, the corporal who had been left in charge of the situation tried to save face by yelling, "No more moving! I order you to sit down and stay where you are!"

The pilots looked up and down the line at one another and, for the first time, shared a smile. It was a small victory, but it was something. Tye stretched out his long, tired legs and turned to the Jordanian. "This is much better. Cheers!"

"Yeah, that was a pretty good move," said the Israeli representative, adjusting his thick eyeglasses. "Now ask them to bring us some Cokes, and maybe some sandwiches."

The Jordanian and the Israeli introduced themselves to the Brits. The Israeli's name was Yossi. His voice sounded like gravel and he had a shock of short black hair. The black-plastic frames of his glasses dominated his face. He seemed about Tye's age and Reg thought he looked more like a math student than a fighter pilot. Although Yossi had a friendly demeanor and even cracked a few jokes, he never smiled.

The Jordanian, Edward, was closer to Reg in both age and height. He, too, was friendly with the Brits who sat between him and the Israeli pilot. Except for Yossi's initial comment, the two of them studiously avoided speaking to one another.

Tye pointed to the small green, white, and yellow patch sewn on to Edward's flight suit below the Jordanian flag. "What's that insignia?" he asked.

Edward glanced over at Yossi. "Ask your Jewish friend over there," he said. "He knows what it is."

Yossi looked at the patch. "It means he's a Palestinian. Half the Arabs in Jordan are Palestinians and the king lets a few of them join the armed forces so the others can feel better about themselves."

Tye, always more interested in machines than politics, turned to Reg for clarification. "Palestinians and Israelis don't get on very well, do they?"

Yossi answered instead of Reg. "Arabs are like Gentiles," he said. "You've got bad ones and you've got good ones."

Edward snorted. "And the only good Arabs are the dead ones, right?"

"Hey, look, I got no problem with you," Yossi shot back, pointing a finger. "Israel, Jordan, whatever. We don't even know if they exist anymore, but if you want to carry on old fights, I'm ready."

Edward laughed again. 'Take a look around you. You're not in Tel Aviv, my friend. You should watch your tongue out here." He gestured broadly at their surroundings. "These Bedouins have a saying: *A night in the desert is long and full of scorpions for the man who does not belong there.*" He flashed Yossi a smile that managed to be simultaneously cheerful and threatening.

The large Saudi captain emerged from the tent with someone Reg guessed must be Faisal. He was a dark-skinned man in his late forties and had flecks of gray running through his carefully trimmed beard. The long, cream-colored robe he wore loosely over his military uniform made him look like a sheik. He seemed completely relaxed, even jovial, as he strolled away from his tent, speaking in a low voice to the captain, but Reg sensed that he could be a dangerous man.

The two men ambled to an open spot in the sand where they were met by a soldier who handed them a pair of rolled up mats. At the same time, one of the radiomen approached from the communications tent carrying a portable Sony stereo.

A different soldier threw a bundle of mats toward the pilots, and several of the men casually stood up to take one. "What's going on?" Tye wondered aloud.

On all sides, men began to spread the mats on the ground. The soldiers guarding the pilots laid their weapons aside and knelt in the sand. The radioman pushed a button on the stereo and the musical voice of a prayer leader, a *muezzin*, filled the air. All of the Saudis and most of the international pilots prostrated themselves on their mats, bowing their heads to the north.

"Oh, now I remember," whispered Tye, "Islamic people have to pray five or six times a day, don't they? And they all face that same city, what's the name of that place?

Mazatlan! That's it, they all pray towards Mazatlan."

"Mecca," Reg corrected him. "They face Mecca, the Holy City."

The muezzin's song, rich and clear, rang through the camp and echoed off the surrounding hills. All of the Muslims in the camp, soldiers and civilians, prayed together, and a feeling of tranquility fell across the plateau, stilling the most warlike of hearts.

Tye rocked back and forth as he listened to the singing, then leaned toward Edward. "That's actually quite beautiful," he said before narrowing his eyes and giving the Palestinian the once-over. "Hey, why aren't you praying with them?"

"Because I'm a Christian," Edward replied. "Why aren't you?"

When the prayers were over, the hook-nosed captain and the man in the cream-colored robes stood and continued speaking quietly to one another. From their gestures and glances, it was clear they were discussing what to do with their unexpected guests. They appeared to take special note of Reg and the Israeli representative, Yossi. After a few moments, they walked toward the strip of shade where the pilots had planted themselves. Reg and the others labored to their feet and dusted themselves off in preparation for the meeting.

"Welcome!" shouted the burly captain sternly. "Our most respected leader, Commander Ghalil Faisal, welcomes you. But he warns you that this place is a military facility of the Kingdom of Saudi Arabia, governed by the laws of the Holy Koran." As the captain spoke, Reg and Faisal stared at one another, sizing each other up. "The Saudi people are famous for their generosity," barked the captain. "Our supplies will be shared with all of you. Our bread will be your bread. You will receive tents, food, and water."

"All of us?" asked Yossi in his raspy voice.

The captain gritted his teeth and looked away from the Jewish pilot, offended by his very presence. He glanced toward Faisal, who returned a barely perceptible nod.

"Our commander has declared that the old battles are over. The hospitality we show to our Muslim brothers and our friends from the West will also be offered to the Zionists during their temporary stay in our country."

Faisal then offered the pilots a perfunctory salute and withdrew to the air-conditioned comfort of his tent, adjourning the meeting without having spoken a single word.

"You will follow me to the supplies," shouted the captain, turning on his heels and marching away. The pilots looked at one another in confusion before following. *Was that it?* Between them, they had a thousand urgent questions about the situation in the rest of the world and what the Saudis planned to do. The captain heard their grumbling. When they returned to the C-230 cargo plane, he paused at the foot of the access ramp. "There will be another meeting tonight. You may discuss your questions with Faisal at that time."

The huge plane was the supply depot for the camp. The crates and storage tanks stacked inside held enough provisions to sustain the troops for several weeks. Tye was the first one inside the plane. Rubbing his hands together eagerly, he faced a gray-haired supply officer across a small table.

"I'd like a big juicy cheeseburger, please, no pickles. And a side of chips."

The supply officer blinked in confusion before handing Tye a large bundle that included a four-man tent, a plastic water bucket, blankets, a first-aid kit, and a copy of the Koran. Heading back down the ramp, Tye thumbed through the book, disappointed. "This is all in Arabic," he complained to Reg, "and there's no pictures."

Reg looked around and noticed a group of soldiers lounging in the shade beneath the cargo plane. One of them stood up and came trotting into the sunlight.

'Teacher!" he shouted. "I can't believe it. Major Cummins, how are you? How did you find us here?"

"We were in the neighborhood and thought we'd stop by to say hello." Reg smiled.

The Saudi officer was in his late twenties, light on his feet, and wore a flashy gold chain around his neck. His striking green eyes and dashing good looks gave him the appearance of a young movie star. His lips curled into a mischievous grin below his light mustache. The two men shook hands then kissed on each cheek, in the Arab style.

"Well, I'll be damned," Reg said, shaking his head in disbelief. "Khalid Yamani is here." Of all the Saudi pilots Reg Cummins had trained, of course it would be this one who found him here. "I see you're loafing in the shade, as usual."

"No, no, Teacher," Yamani protested good-naturedly. "As always, I am working very hard. I wanted to keep working but these men," he said, gesturing to his friends, "they are soft. They begged me to give them a short break because they could not keep up with me. What could I do?"

The other soldiers heard him lying and shouted a few comments of their own. Khalid waved them off and flashed Reg a disarming, high-wattage smile.

Khalid Yamani was probably the worst student Reg had ever tried to teach, but also one of his favorites. He was an easily distracted, sometimes reckless pilot and at first Reg had been mystified over why he had been promoted to the advanced tactical fighter school. Only when he tried to have the young man sent down—for his own safety—did he learn that Khalid's father was one of the richest and most influential men in Saudi society, an oil baron with vast, worldwide holdings who kept close personal counsel with the king.

Reg was a respected and well-liked teacher but he was also very demanding. He had absolutely no tolerance for sloppiness and lack of concentration. At first, his students didn't understand the ferocious anger he turned on them when they made lazy errors, but eventually someone would tell them, explaining in whispers or waiting until Reg wasn't around to hear.

Khalid had driven him crazy on several occasions, but the young man had such a charming, good-natured way about him that Reg could never stay angry for very long. Khalid's love of life was so infectious that he'd occasionally managed to drag Reg with him to off-base parties, swanky, secretive affairs held in private homes where upper-class Saudis dressed in Western-style clothing and sipped alcohol. The parties were an open secret and were rarely disturbed by the religious police, as long as they remained behind closed doors. Khalid, a handsome fighter pilot and eligible bachelor from a wealthy family, was invited to many such gatherings and never missed the opportunity to attend. He reveled in Western habits, being largely westernized himself. He'd spent his high school years in Houston, Texas, while his father bought and reorganized an oil company there.

"As a matter of fact, Teacher, I've been expecting to see you. The men have been talking about a trick someone used against the aliens—using chaff to blind them. I said to myself, 'Self, that sounds like Reg Cummins.'"

"You heard about that?" Tye asked, impressed.

"It wasn't me," Reg said quickly. "It was this beanpole of a mechanic here. He flew a very respectable flight." He introduced the two men, who shook hands warmly.

"The major is just being modest," Tye said. "I fired off the chaff, but he was the one who came up with the idea. I was too busy wetting myself to come up with anything that clever."

The three of them continued talking until all of the representatives had received their supply packages. As they started back, Khalid took Reg by the arm and led him in a different direction. "Stay a while, Teacher, there's someone I'd like you to meet. But first I have a question: *Can we win?*"

"That's the question of the hour isn't it?" Reg thought for a minute before answering. "I'd say we've got a snowball's chance in hell."

"Ah," grinned Khalid, "excellent! Then there *is* a chance." He gestured toward a row of private jets. 'Teacher, my father is here. He is not well, and I know it would ease his pain to meet you. Would you mind?"

It wasn't an offer Reg could very well refuse. "I'd be honored."

The two of them moved along the perimeter of the Saudi tent town, maintaining a low profile, until they reached a luxury Learjet tied down near the lip of the plateau. The sun was low on the horizon and the heat was lifting. Reg noticed a large tent standing by itself quite some distance from the rest of the camp.

"What's going on out there?" he asked.

Khalid shook his head sadly. "They are calling it the Tent of the Fearful. Since the demons began to arrive, many people are losing their minds. Last night, they screamed and screamed. No one could sleep."

"I don't hear anything now."

"Morphine," Khalid explained before climbing a set of steps. The Yamani family crest was painted prominently on the exterior of the plane. Khalid paused on the top step and turned to Reg. "When I told you my father was not well..." He didn't finish the thought, but gestured meaningfully toward the Tent of the Fearful before heading inside.

The interior of the plane was a different world. It was

a soothing, air-conditioned place with art on the walls and plush carpeting. There was a kitchenette/dining area with marble countertops and leather upholstery.

Khalid stepped through an interior doorway into his father's room and turned down the volume on a wall-mounted television set. Karmal Yamani was a frightened, unshaven, elderly man with bloodshot eyes. He lay on a narrow bed, his head propped up by a spray of golden pillows. While vice minister of petroleum exports, he and his brother had been the chief architects of the 1973 oil embargo, an exercise in economic brinksmanship that had quadrupled his nation's wealth almost overnight. He was known as one of the most shrewd and powerful men in the Middle East, but none of that was evident at the moment.

"Father! I have excellent news," Khalid said very loudly. "Here is a great friend of mine, Major Reg Cummins. He was over Jerusalem when the attack began. He tells me that the aliens are very strong, but he is confident that we can beat them. He believes we can win the war!"

The old man pushed himself up into a sitting position and a looked at Reg hopefully. "How? How can we defeat them?"

Reg silently cursed Khalid for putting him on the spot. He didn't want to lie, but telling the truth threatened to crush the old man's fragile spirit.

He hesitated, choosing his words carefully. "Well, for one thing, we've discovered we can blind them temporarily. We're studying how to use that to our advantage," Reg said. "Besides, sir, human beings are a tough lot. We always seem to find a way."

"Blind them, you say?" The elder Yamani's self-control was returning. He straightened his clothes and apologized for his appearance. "It is embarrassing for me to receive you like this, major, but since the spaceships arrived I have not been a well man."

"We're all in a state of shock," Reg said. "It's very understandable."

"Yes, my condition is not uncommon during wartime"— Yamani nodded—"but it is a very dangerous one. Great fear can be contagious, spreading from man to man until an entire army can no longer fight. We must quarantine those whose knees have turned to water, as mine have. This is the same advice I gave to Ghalil Faisal. Are there any such men among the foreign pilots?"

"One or two," Reg answered.

"You must isolate them immediately! Move them to the tent in the desert with the others! Khalid, arrange this with Faisal."

Each time Khalid heard his father mention Faisal's name, he made a sour face and pretended to spit on the floor. "The man is a swine," he said with a vehemence Reg didn't understand.

Just then, a jet fighter screamed overhead and Mr. Yamani's composure collapsed completely. He rolled away from the window near his bed, shielding himself with the blanket. Khalid went to his side and tried to comfort him as Reg stood by awkwardly. Although the old man could diagnose his condition, he was obviously helpless to control it. Eventually, Khalid led Reg out of the room and back to the kitchen area.

"Thank you, Teacher," he said, pulling bottles of French mineral water from a refrigerator and sliding into one of the seats at the table. "He is more at ease now." Reg took a couple of dates from a bowl and popped them in his mouth as Khalid poured. "Now, tell me what happened over Jerusalem, Teacher, every detail. Together we will discover a weakness, a way to fight them."

Reg swirled the water in his glass. "I could use something stronger if you've got it," he said.

Khalid started to get up, but quickly changed his

mind. "It would be unwise of me to offer you alcohol on my father's plane, but I will try to send a package to your tent this evening." He pointed forward and aft, indicating there were others aboard the jet.

After much prodding, Reg began to recount the one-sided battle he'd fought that day. Up to that moment, he'd been doing his best to keep the memory of it buried, but now he let the scene flood back to him. He talked about the enormous firing cone and the circular wall of destruction it had unleashed. He described the missiles exploding against the giant ship's shields, the ill-fated dogfight with the scarab attack ships. In a very real sense, the memory of the massacre was more devastating than the event itself. Several times during the retelling, Reg had to stop and gather himself before going on. And each time he did so, he would glance out the portal and see the Tent of the Fearful in the deepening twilight.

During one of these pauses, a door opened and a beautiful young woman in her early twenties stepped into the dining area. Tall and slender, she wore her lustrous mane of coal black hair pulled back into a thick ponytail. She was dressed in blue jeans and a T-shirt bearing the logo of Stanford University. Reg's eyes couldn't help lingering over the curves of her body. It had been a long time since he'd seen a Saudi woman in anything except a black shroud, and longer still since he'd seen a woman as beautiful as the one that stood before him. One look into her bright green eyes told him she had to be Khalid's sister.

Khalid was not happy to see her. The moment she showed herself, he began shouting in Arabic and waving her out of the room. She studiously ignored him, casually moving to a set of cabinets above the sink. When she stood on her toes and reached for the handles on the high doors, the T-shirt climbed her torso revealing the clear dark skin on her stomach and the small of her back. Reg reached nervously for his water glass without looking away, without even blinking.

Khalid sprang to his feet, showering her in curses and demanding that she return to her quarters. He pounded his fist on the table, spilling his water. This finally cracked the young woman's cool demeanor. She turned away from the cabinets and shouted back venomously at her brother before approaching the table.

"This must be the English pilot you've spoken of so often," she said to her brother in a flawless American accent. "You never mentioned that he was so handsome." If the comment was designed to get under Khalid's skin, it worked. He erupted into a fresh round of shouting. She ignored him and locked eyes with Reg. "Forgive my brother's idiotic behavior. He pretends to be progressive but he's a very typical Saudi male chauvinist pig." With that, she left the room leaving the two men in silence.

"Well, that was interesting," Reg said, pouring Khalid a fresh glass of water. "I've never seen you react like that to a Saudi woman in Western clothes."

"My sister!" Khalid said, scowling at the closed door. "She has always been defiant, but now it is worse, much worse. Since she returned from America, she does nothing but make trouble. I apologize that you had to see her like that."

Reg hadn't exactly minded. In fact, he thought of asking Khalid to invite her back in, but decided to say nothing.

"We are seeing this problem more and more in Saudi Arabia," Khalid told him.

"What problem is that?"

"These girls," he said with a dismissive wave. "They return from university in Europe or America with the idea of challenging the man's authority. They rebel against everything, mindlessly. It lasts until they marry and begin to bear children."

Reg bit into another date. From an Englishman's

perspective, the way Saudi women were treated amounted to legalized slavery. They were kept virtual prisoners in their own homes and had few legal rights to protect them from the whims of their husbands, fathers and brothers. Some years earlier, the entire English military presence had withdrawn from the country in protest when a Saudi father legally executed one of his daughters by drowning her in the family swimming pool after finding her alone with an unmarried man. The man was not charged.

Khalid sat down and sipped his water, then whispered across the table. "Fadeela is an especially unhappy and willful girl. I am sad to say that the blame for this must rest largely with my father. He has allowed her to develop unrealistic expectations about her future."

"Such as?"

"It is not important," Khalid said with a sudden, broad smile. "But I pity the man who takes her one day to be his wife. He will be buying himself a lifetime of headaches. But enough! We have more important matters to discuss."

Still convinced he could discover a chink in the alien armor by listening to Reg's account, Khalid began quizzing him on every aspect of their technology. But they were soon interrupted again, this time by a knock on the outer hatch. A soldier had arrived with an important message. Khalid excused himself and spoke to the man outside.

Reg hungrily filled his mouth with dates and studied the richly appointed interior of the jet. He was still chewing when a door opened and Fadeela returned. He watched her reach into the cabinet above the sink and retrieve a bottle of brandy then slide into the seat across from him. She poured drinks into a pair of fresh glasses and leaned toward him intensely.

"I've been listening to you talk to my fool brother. Before he comes back, I want you to tell me your plan for defeating the invaders."

Reg's eyes opened wide. *Plan? He didn't have so much as a single solid idea, much less anything that could be called a plan.* But his mouth was too full of sweet, sticky fruit to say any of this to the woman staring at him across the table. He held up a finger and chewed rapidly. Hoping to clear his mouth, he took a swig of the drink she'd poured him. While it was an excellent brandy, it was also the first alcohol to pass his lips for many months. He shuddered and coughed as it crashed through his system. It was some moments before he was able to speak.

"Here's the thing, Miss Yamani, I don't have a plan. I don't think anyone does. We've never seen anything like this before, and at the moment, my only plan is to stay alive long enough to make a plan."

"Unacceptable," she said, shaking her head in disappointment. "We cannot simply wait here, huddled in the desert, while the world goes up in flames. They're moving, you know. They're moving toward a fresh set of targets. While you sit here chattering with Khalid and eating dates, we're being systematically exterminated."

Systematically exterminated. The ugly phrase put a knot in Reg's stomach and he reached for the bottle. "What about you?" he asked, pouring. "Do you have any ideas?"

For the first time, Fadeela's expression softened. She seemed surprised to be asked for her opinion. "Of course I have ideas. But this is Saudi Arabia and none of the men in charge is interested in what a woman might have to say."

"I'm listening," Reg said evenly.

"We need to find a way to penetrate their shields. How can we circumvent them? Are they vulnerable to electricity? To chemicals? Maybe to something as simple as water? We must try everything. What about nuclear weapons? We should be laying plans to attack their mother ship which is out in space. Perhaps that one does not have shields. There are still a thousand options."

Reg nodded seriously, as if he were considering her ideas despite their obvious impracticality. It didn't take Fadeela long to realize what he was doing.

"Don't patronize me, Major Cummins," she hissed. "It is true that I have no military training, but at least I realize the need to find a solution as quickly as possible. And the first thing I would change is that you foreigners should not be kept in isolation. We should all be talking to one another, searching for a strategy. We need more communication, not less. But that idiot Faisal does everything he can to keep you divided. It is easier to control you that way."

"In all fairness, Miss Yamani, the foreign pilots were divided long before we arrived here."

"Stop calling me Miss Yamani. My name is Fadeela," she said. "The point is that we can no longer afford to act like Saudis, or Iraqis, or Egyptians, or whoever. We must begin to think and act together, as humans!" She paused long enough to take a sip of her drink.

"I notice you and your brother have at least one thing in common. You both seem to dislike this Faisal character."

Fadeela's lips curled when she heard the name. "Ghalil Faisal makes all of his decisions based on his own interests. He is a snake."

"I'll keep that in mind."

There was an awkward silence during which Fadeela continued to stare across the table as if she were waiting for him to say something brilliant, something that would lead to the swift and sure destruction of the invaders. Reg tried to avoid making eye contact. Each time he looked at her, he felt thrown off-balance by her disconcerting green eyes and the beauty of her face—inappropriate thoughts during a military strategy session. He glanced out the window and saw that Khalid was still talking to the soldier.

"Major, I must ask you another question."

"Stop calling me 'Major,' he said, imitating her. "My

name is Reg."

She didn't react. "I am wondering, Reg, what is it that you fight for?"

The question took him by surprise. "I'm not sure what you mean. Are you asking what *cause* I'm fighting for?"

"Precisely. Do you fight for the love of your country?"

"I *serve* my country," he told her, "but I'm not one of these rah-rah, Rule-Britannia types."

"For a wife and children then?"

"Haven' t got any of those. Why are you asking?"

Fadeela studied him sadly. "Because I don't see the man my brother has described to me."

"I'm afraid Khalid has a tendency—"

"His tendency," she interrupted, "has been to describe you as an intelligent and resourceful warrior. But you don't look that way to me."

Reg's anger flared suddenly to the surface. "Look here, princess, I'm awfully sorry I can't whip up a quick fix to your pesky alien problem, but I've trained half the men in your bloody air force. I'm a pilot and a teacher, and a damned good one. I don't need to apologize to you for not being something else!"

Fadeela leaned toward him, matching his anger. "The time for teaching is past us. Now is the time for action, for warriors. But you have nothing to fight for."

They stared murderously at one another until Reg sniffed and turned away. "It's been a long, hot day and I'm completely knackered. Maybe—"

"And don't call me princess," she interrupted again. "I hate that. I am *not* a princess." She stuffed the cork back into the bottle, put it back in its place then headed toward her room. She stopped and turned, wanting to say something before she left. All the harshness left her face as she struggled to find the words she wanted, but after a moment of trying, she gave up and closed the door.

3

MEETINGS

By the time Reg made his way back to the international side of the runway, darkness had fallen. He found that a small forest of tents had sprouted beneath the wings of the jet fighters. Reg had thought that the tents, a goodwill gesture from Faisal, might have fostered a spirit of cooperation among the different groups of pilots. Instead, they had only encouraged the contingents to move farther apart. The Iraqi tents were pitched as far as possible from the Iranians, Reg noted, and the Israelis appeared to have negotiated with the Jordanians so that Edward and his friends formed a buffer zone between Muslim and Jewish camps. A diagram of the camp would have nicely illustrated the geopolitics of the region.

Reg made his way toward the British tents, pitched directly beneath the wings of the Tornadoes. As he passed behind the one enclave, laughter rang out. Looking over, he saw that Thomson was sitting cross-legged among a group of Syrian pilots. As he thumbed through his phrase book, straining to read in the dim light cast by the small dung fire, one of the pilots threw some dried branches across the flames. The smell of sandalwood floated through the chill night air.

It's good he survived, thought Reg of the lieutenant colonel. *He may be setting himself up as a laughingstock, but he's doing a good job as ambassador-at-large, too.*

There was no movement at the British camp. A neat

stack of dung briquettes sat next to a basket of scented kindling, but neither had been disturbed. Reg assumed the other two Brits were talking with some of the internationals. He'd not been lying to Fadeela when he told her he was tired, so he chose a tent at random and lifted the flap, intending to crawl inside and go to sleep.

There was a sudden movement inside the tent, followed immediately by the unmistakable metallic click of a pistol being cocked. Reg stumbled backward as Sutton emerged from the tent, looking around wildly, obviously just awakened.

Seeing Reg sprawled on the ground, Sutton put the gun on safety, and growled, "Damn it, Cummins! What the hell are you doing sneaking about?"

Sitting up and dusting sand off of his flight suit, Reg said, "Tad jumpy, aren't we?"

Tye crawled out of another of the tents, as Sutton replied, "You scared the piss out of me. In case you haven't noticed, there's an alien invasion going on. Call your name out next time." Sutton reached back into the tent for his boots, pulling out a pack of cigarettes as he did so.

Tye said, "So, Major, I guess you're pretty tight with the Saudis."

"What are you going on about now, Tye?" asked Reg.

"Well," said the young man, "that big captain knew your name. So did that Saudi pilot at the supply plane. Then you went off to the private planes while the rest of sat out here freezing our arses off. What kind of crazy place is this, anyway? Hot as the devil during the day, then cold as a Shetland Islands winter at night."

"That's the desert for you," said Reg. "As to being 'in tight,' that's probably an exaggeration. I have a few friends in the Saudi military establishment. Quite a few of these fellows went through the Flight and Training program at Khamis Moushayt."

"One of the Saudis at the supply plane told Yossi and me that you're a top gun, that you kicked some serious butt in Desert Storm."

"You heard wrong," said Reg a little too harshly. He didn't want to discuss his performance during the conflict with Iraq.

Sutton had his cigarette lit and was looking doubtfully at the fuel they'd been provided for a campfire. "This grease monkey is convinced you're going to save us." He picked up a briquette and sniffed it. "What is this shit, some kind of charcoal?"

"You've got it backward. It's charcoal made out of shit," said Reg. "That's dried camel dung, Sutton." As the lieutenant cursed and began scouring his hands with sand, Reg turned to Tye.

"Look, lad," he said, "I can fly a plane, sure. But no amount of fancy flying is going to do us any good against these aliens. You saw their shields. You saw the maneuverability those fighters of theirs possess. If we're going to beat these bastards, it's not going to be through head-to-head aerial combat."

"Especially since there probably aren't that many combat aircraft left to send against them," said Sutton. "Rumors are going around, pretty much confirming what we heard from Khamis Moushayt before they went off the air. Thirty-six cities destroyed, and now the blighters have moved on to have a go at another thirty-six. A radio message came in from some Druse militiamen holed up in the mountains of Lebanon. They reported that the Jerusalem ship was moving into Jordan."

"What about the one over Turkey?" asked Reg, worried that they might have two ships to worry about in their neighborhood instead of just one.

"We've not heard anything at all from farther north,"

said Tye. "Which is just as well, I suppose, given what these Saudis are planning."

"And what's that?" asked Reg.

"That tall Ethiopian, Remi, told us that the Israelis told him the Saudis had been talking to the Egyptians. Apparently, they plan to go in with guns blazing if the local ship moves toward Mecca. They told the Egyptians the only way to get their planes refueled was to help defend the city."

Reg nodded meditatively. "Makes sense," he said. "From a Muslim's point of view at any rate."

"It doesn't make any kind of sense at all!" Sutton said. "This Faisal is apparently some kind of religious fanatic!"

"Oh, come off it, Sutton," Reg said. "Mecca is one of the high holy sites of Islam. They've already seen Jerusalem destroyed, and the bulk of Saudi Arabia's domestic military doctrine is built around defense of Mecca. A lot of these pilots would consider it their sacred duty." Reg paused. "I hadn't thought of it; Jerusalem, Rome. I wonder if the aliens are intentionally targeting religious sites."

Tye pursed his lips. "Wasn't there one over Los Angeles?"

"Good point," conceded Reg. "It was just a theory."

Sutton angrily flicked his cigarette butt into the sand. "Don't give me that rot about 'sacred duty,'" he said. "These foreign pilots will take the Saudis' fuel and *say* they'll defend the city, all right. And then as soon as they're in the air they'll head off in whatever direction they please."

Tye chimed in, "That's what Lieutenant Sutton says we should do, too."

Sutton crouched in the sand between Reg and Tye. He handed his lighter to Tye and indicated that he should hold it to light the map he sketched in the sand.

"Look here," he said. "If these holy warriors will top off the tanks in our Tornadoes, we might be able to make it to Diego Garcia." He sketched a long line to the British possession in the Indian Ocean, site of a major British air base.

Reg shook his head. "We don't even know if the facilities there still exist. The aliens could have been there by now."

"That's a risk I'm willing to take," replied Sutton. "At least there's a chance we could be back among our own kind."

Reg sighed and crawled into one of the tents. "You're even less bright than I'd thought, Sutton," he called through the canvas. "Think about it. If we hadn't spotted the smoke from that crashed tanker today, we'd be dying of thirst in the deep desert, assuming we survived bailing out of our planes. And now you want to fly over open ocean with no satellite navigation aids and intermittent radio communications, hoping that you'll find the island before your fuel gives out."

"I'd risk it to get out of here," came Sutton's reply. "Look, Cummins, I think it's great that you're having a love-in with your Arab pals, but we've got to launch a counterattack against these damned aliens before it's too late. Sitting out here in the desert is a waste of everybody's time. We should *all* get back to our own armies. That's the only way we have a chance of making a difference; it's the only way to make sure we have a planet left to fight for."

Reg lay on his back in his tent. He had to admit that Sutton did have a point. There were too many factions in the desert camp, all working at cross-purposes. It would be impossible to plan an effective assault on the aliens.

He closed his eyes. It had been a terribly long day, the longest day of his life, and he desperately needed rest. But as he lay there, he couldn't stop his mind from churning. Sutton's last remark had been too close to the question Fadeela had asked him: What do you have worth fighting for?

* * *

When the moon had climbed above the dunes towering on the horizon, the representatives from each country present were again called to Faisal's tent. The British decided to try to get away with sending three representatives. Reg, Thomson, and Tye left Sutton to hold down the fort.

As they approached the runway, they were met by a pair of Israelis: the thin, bespectacled Yossi and his female commander. From the moment the Brits saw her, they could tell the Israeli pilot was wound tight. She had a trapped look. The name on her flight suit was Marx, but she introduced herself simply as Miriyam. She was short, solid, and strong. The dark circles under her eyes were visible even by moonlight, and her mass of coiled auburn hair bounced with an anxiety of its own.

"I can't believe that they've kept us out here all day," she said. "We need just two things from these Arabs: jet fuel and access to their radios. We have to insist on this, as a group. If they won't give us what we need, we'll have to take it."

Reg looked at Yossi, who merely shrugged. Neither the two of them nor Tye wanted to attempt calming Miriyam down. But then Thomson stepped into the breach.

"Captain, you might want to exercise some restraint in this meeting, as a woman. These Arab men are extremely old-fashioned, you know, not exactly a bunch of women's libbers."

Miriyam stepped up and grabbed Thomson by the lapels. The two of them were approximately the same height, but Thomson easily outweighed her. She took no notice of that as she lifted the colonel off his feet and spoke through clenched teeth. "I can handle myself."

As she eased Thomson to the ground, however, some of the anger seemed to go out of her. "I apologize," she said. "Of course you are right. I will try."

As they approached the command tent, they could see

that it was already crowded. The flaps had been tied back, and several Saudi soldiers stood guard. The five of them stepped up to the entrance and peered inside. The tent was crowded with forty or fifty people, a mixture of Saudi officers and foreign pilots. They stood in small groups, speaking in hushed tones. Low-ranking officers moved through this edgy crowd, offering steaming tea in plastic cups. It had the appearance of a grim cocktail party.

As the five new arrivals hesitated at the entrance, a handsome Saudi officer made his way through the crowd, opening his arms to greet them.

"*Salaam alechem,* my brothers. I am Ghalil Rumallah Ibn-Faisal. It is the will of God that we meet here this evening. He has brought you here to support us in our fight against this most terrible enemy."

Reg hadn't recognized the camp's commander without his robes, but he saw now that this was the man who had spoken with the Saudi captain at the prayer session earlier in the day. Now he was dressed in a sharply tailored khaki dress uniform. Numerous military decorations were plastered across his chest.

Thomson greeted the man warmly. *The man's only been in Saudi Arabia for a day,* thought Reg, *but he already knows that flattery is the grease that turns the wheel here.*

"You Saudi chaps deserve three cheers from all of us," said Thomson. "It took crack judgment and foresight to organize this camp as quickly as you've done. Without this base we'd all be lost, completely lost."

That's true enough, thought Reg, as a big smile spread across Faisal's face.

"How did your lot pull this all together so quickly?" Thomson asked.

Faisal joined them outside the tent and spoke. "I tell you, when I first saw the fires in the sky I trembled like a woman, but then I sank to my knees and prayed for direction. And Allah, in his wisdom, showed me what I should do. He told me to build an army in the farthest desert, where my people could gather themselves until the chosen moment. From this place, it was revealed to me, we will join the battle and win a glorious victory."

Reg kept his features schooled in a neutral expression, as did all of the others except for Miriyam, who scowled. And Thomson, of course, who nodded and grinned broadly.

"Sounds marvelous," said the colonel. "If this vision of yours is correct, it sounds like we can't lose."

Miriyam suddenly let out a sharp cry of disgust. "This is not a time for children's stories," she hissed. "God did not bring me here to fight under Arabs! We demand that you give us fuel at once so that we can return to Israel."

Yossi put his hand on her shoulder in an effort to calm her outburst. That only succeeded in making her angrier and louder. She pushed his hand away and stepped closer to Faisal.

"You can all stay out here in the middle of nowhere and talk to one another as long as you please!" she shouted. "Just give us our fuel!" The sound of her voice made several people in the tent turn to see what was happening.

Faisal's reaction surprised Reg. He expected the commander to react to Miriyam much as Khalid had to Fadeelah that afternoon. Instead, Faisal only seemed amused. In a voice loud enough to be heard throughout the tent, he addressed Yossi.

"Mr. Israeli," he said, "your superior officer, he is acting like a woman." Then, pretending to see her for the first time, he gasped, and said, "Allah be praised! He *is* a woman!" A wave of nervous laughter swept through the tent, but Faisal's smile melted as he took in the group of Brits and Israelis. He spoke again, this time much lower, and in a menacing tone.

"I am bound by a very old Bedouin custom," he told them. "I must welcome all who reach my tent. Even if he is my worst enemy, even if he is a jackal who murdered my only son, I must welcome him for a period of three days."

"What happens after three days?" asked Tye.

"The wise guest," answered Faisal, "doesn't stay to find out." He motioned for a pair of guards, who stepped between the Israelis and the entrance of the tent. Then he turned and looked directly at Reg.

"I think it would be best if these people waited outside. Englishmen are well-known for their fondness for Jews, so we will trust you to represent their interests at our planning conference." With that, he clapped a friendly hand against the back of Tye's neck, causing the sunburned mechanic to wince, and led the British pilots into the tent.

Thomson worked fast, attempting to smooth over the incident at the entrance. He introduced himself and his comrades. "We're beginning to add up to quite a force," he said to Faisal.

"Yes, Colonel," came the reply, "and we expect more pilots to join us soon. Small groups of planes have hidden themselves throughout the Empty Quarter. We are finding more of them with each passing hour through our radios."

Reg spoke for the first time. "There's a difference between gathering firepower and building an army, Commander. Without a common purpose, this is just a collection of men and machines." Thinking of Fadeelah, he continued, "There are some who might say that you've been hampering any chance for unity."

Again, Faisal looked amused. "Quite the opposite," he said. "In fact, I am confident that this meeting tonight will bring us together." With that, he walked away.

When he'd reached the lectern set up at one end of the tent, the Saudi commander addressed the crowd. 'Take your seats, gentlemen," he called. The men arranged themselves on the carpets in a rough circle, with Faisal at the head. A dozen or so Saudi pilots, including, Reg noted, Khalid Yamani, sat in a row behind Faisal. Reg noticed for the first time that the coffee and tea services along one wall were being attended by a group of Saudi women, a flock of crows in their veils. Reg searched for a sign that Fadeela might be among them, but there was no way to penetrate the disguising *abayas*.

"This morning," Faisal began, "thirty-six of the planet Earth's largest cities were reduced to ash by the alien devils. The large ships, those of you who fought at Jerusalem called them city destroyers, then proceeded toward a second round of cities. Flights of the smaller ships have destroyed many secondary targets along the way, concentrating on military bases." There was an easy murmur in the crowd.

"Some of the second-wave cities have already been destroyed," Faisal continued. "Others face certain destruction within a short time. The situation is dire. But I do not believe that it is hopeless!" The commander pounded on his podium to emphasize this last point.

"The question before us now," Faisal said, "is a simple one. What course of action shall we follow? I seek your counsel. Who among you will speak first?"

The leader of the Iranians sprang to his feet. "We must attack them immediately!" he shouted. "Every pilot we have should be in the air." A handful of the men and even a few of the women shouted their approval, but one of the Syrians quickly rose to his feet, quieting the crowd.

"I agree with my Iranian brother that we must strike back as soon as possible," he said. "But we have seen their power. They are demons, yes, but demons possessed of incredible strength. Our normal tactics are useless against this enemy."

Another Syrian rose and picked up where the first had left off. "Therefore," he said, "we have developed a plan.

A way to use the enemy's own tactics against them."

"Rather than attacking from many directions," continued the first, "we will fly in a single column as we saw them do in the attack at Khamis Moushayt." Reg was startled at this revelation. He hadn't been aware that any intelligence on the Khamis Moushayt attack had been gathered.

"Using such a maneuver," the Syrian went on, "we can combine all of our firepower, bringing it to bear on a single concentrated point."

Anticipating the obvious argument, the second man spoke again. "This will, of course, leave our flanks exposed. We will surely lose many planes. But we believe that, in this way, we can break through the unseen shell that protects them."

Conversations erupted all over the room, points and counterpoints relative to the Syrian proposal being argued with ferocity. Just as Faisal was about to bring the group back to order, the voice of the Jordanian delegate, Edward, rang across the tent.

"These are the most powerful enemies humanity has ever known," he said. "We must use the most powerful weapons humanity has ever developed against them."

The room quieted instantly. Edward continued to speak into the stillness. "The Jews have nuclear weapons. But where are the Jews?" He looked around the room. "For the first time in my life, I want to see Jewish people, and now they have all disappeared."

Faisal spoke. "In fact," he said, "the Zionists are delaying the use of nuclear force only at the request of the United States. The American president has convinced the international community to delay their use until we can be sure that the aliens are vulnerable to them. They are preparing to launch a nuclear strike against the city destroyer approaching their city of Houston even as we speak!"

A cocky young Iraqi pilot stood. "Chemical weapons,

then. They might eat through those shields." The room exploded into debate once more, with the Iranians hurling invective against the oblivious young Iraqi. The Iranians well remembered the hundred thousand of their countrymen who had died when Iraq violated international law and used poison gases and biological agents in the Iran-Iraq conflict.

Faisal quickly brought their debate to a close, however. "This is not an option," he said flatly. "The Kingdom of Saudi Arabia does not own these ghastly weapons, and we will not permit their use within our borders."

With weapons of mass destruction at least temporarily ruled out, more and more of the pilots began speaking in favor of the Syrian plan. The feeling that some sort of immediate action was called for ran high in the tent.

Thomson, surprisingly, had remained quiet throughout the discussions, choosing instead to watch the interactions with great care. At length, he leaned over and spoke to Reg and Tye. "Look at these international pilots, will you? I don't believe they give a flying fig what we decide to do here. I suspect that as soon as they're fueled up and in the air, they'll be heading for home."

"I'm sure Faisal has given that possibility some consideration," Reg said dryly, still looking at the gallery of women. If Fadeela was among them, she made no sign.

"Major!" hissed Tye, drawing his attention back to the front of the tent. Faisal was pointing directly at him.

"For those of you who do not him," said the Saudi commander, "this is Major Reginald Cummins. He has lived among us for a long while, teaching our most advanced pilots. They tell me that he is the finest pilot in the Middle East." Reg saw Khalid nodding enthusiastically behind Faisal.

"Teacher," said Faisal, in an almost imploring tone, "tell us what we must do to defeat this enemy."

Placed firmly on the spot, Reg had no choice but to

stand and address the crowd. He was sure they did not want to hear what he had to tell them.

"I know many of you were not involved in the fighting this morning," he said. "And I can understand your impulse to attack. But I know that many of you *were* there"—Reg glared at the Syrians as he said this—"and I can't believe that you're proposing a direct assault."

Some of the pilots who had remained silent until now nodded agreement. Reg continued, "The aliens are capable of putting five hundred of those attacker craft into the air within a matter of seconds. And when we fought them toe-to-toe this morning they went through us like we weren't even there. Even if we assume that a combined arms attack against the city destroyer's shield will bring it down—and I have my doubts about that—we'd be sitting ducks for half a thousand screaming fighters that carry their own shields! They'd take out every plane in your 'column' in a heartbeat. Why start a fight if we don't have the slightest chance of winning it?"

Pilots from more than one country shouted to be heard at once. The gist of what they were saying was that every hour of delay meant more devastation.

"Until something changes," Reg continued over the protests, "it would be suicide to confront them. As long as those shields are in place, there's nothing we can do."

"I think," said Faisal, "I think that our friend would not be so ready to make sacrifices if we were discussing English cities."

"At least one English city *has* been destroyed, Commander," Reg said. "As a matter of fact, except for the Israelis, we're the only people here who have lost a city to these attackers."

Thomson stood, joining Reg. He said, "We're looking at the bigger picture. This battle can't be about individual cities or countries. Not Birmingham or Cairo or Timbuktu.

We are discussing how we can save the *world*."

Edward spoke again, tears in his eyes. "As we speak, one of the city destroyers is approaching my capital. That is my home. It is where I left my family. I don't know if my children are safe." He made no move to wipe away the moisture from his cheeks. "Amman will be destroyed in fire, and there is nothing I can do to prevent it. But I agree with these Englishmen. We must hold back and wait for the right moment to strike.

"It is logical that if they have come here to invade the Earth," Edward went on, "eventually their ships will land. Perhaps when they do, their shields will come down. And when that happens, we will be there to destroy them. But only if we are still alive. For the time being, we should wait."

Once more, discussions broke out around the room. As he seated himself again, Reg felt a hand on his shoulder. Tye leaned over and whispered to him, "Have you forgotten about Lieutenant Sutton's plan, sir? We're supposed to convince them to get up into the air so we can head away."

Hearing him, Thomson leaned over to answer. "Odds are, that's what half the people in this tent are discussing right now."

Faisal allowed the debates to simmer for a few moments before he called for order.

"There are two plans before us," he said. "Some of you believe that we should strike immediately with all of our forces. Others counsel patience, advising that we wait for a surer opportunity for victory. I believe that the correct path lies between these two options. The orders I was given state that I am to continue standing Saudi policy and protect all parts of the kingdom. But after hearing your wisdom, I realize that these dark times call for compromise.

"For now, we will follow this good Jordanian's advice and bend our efforts to learning more about these villains. However, on one thing we must remain firm. If the aliens should send a ship against Mecca, the Holy City of our Prophet, then we shall attack no matter the cost. No matter the cost."

Tye whispered to Reg, "I told you that's what we heard."

"Because of the constraints on our supplies, I can only offer Saudi jet fuel to those pilots who will join us in this glorious task."

Exasperated, Thomson stood again. "We just went over this. Whether it's Mecca or any other city, the fact remains that a premature attack would be suicide. If we learn that a city destroyer is moving south, then we should, of course, evacuate the city, but there's no reason to send good men to their deaths."

Faisal spread his arms, holding palms upward. "All things are in the hands of Allah," he said. "A man who martyrs himself in the defense of Islam we call a *shaheed*, a witness. Those who join Faisal's *jihad* to defend Mecca will all bear this most honorable title."

Reg remembered what Fadeela had told him about Faisal's thirst for glory. *And now he's running his own private* jihad, he thought.

Thomson was flustered. "Wouldn't it please Allah all the more for you to show patience and wait for a real chance to beat these monsters?" he asked.

"Allah rewards no one more richly than the *shaheeds*," Faisal countered. "A man who dies in the name of God while defending Islam ensures a place for himself and his family in Paradise, where he will be rewarded with seventy-two virgins."

"Virgins? What have virgins got to do with this?" asked Thomson, incredulous.

"Sounds lovely to me," said Tye.

Reg took advantage of the rough laughter that followed Tye's wistful comment to whisper to Thomson, "Don't try to argue the Koran with a Muslim, Colonel."

"Colonel Thomson," Faisal said, "perhaps it is impossible for you, a Christian man, to appreciate how important Mecca is to Muslims. We face it five times each day during our prayers. It is never far from our thoughts. It is literally the center of our world. It would be a form of suicide for us *not* to defend the city." He looked around the room. "How many of you Muslim soldiers are prepared to do nothing while Mecca is destroyed by fire?" Faisal's gaze slowly swept the room his expression stem. Naturally, no one raised his hand. The commonality of purpose that appeared to pervade the room seemed, for the moment, quite genuine. But Reg's gut told him that the enthusiasm for Faisal's plan was manufactured, a smoke screen designed to give the pilots the opportunity to fuel up their jets and return to their home countries. Reg sighed, and stood once more.

"It's a bad plan, and I won't participate in it," he said. "Until the situation changes, it doesn't matter what city we're defending. And as to the holy purpose of this mission," Reg paused, not at all relishing what he was about to do, "as to the holy purpose, well, I hope none of you have it in the back of your minds to take advantage of Faisal's plan to fuel up and return to your homelands. It would be a simple matter, after all, for Faisal to keep a couple of chase squadron planes in flanking positions with orders to shoot down any deserters."

Many in the tent stared at Reg in angry silence, stunned that he was ruining their plan for escape. Faisal broke the silence.

"Major Cummins, your points are well made, and you are quite correct. I have anticipated that there might be some small number of false hearts and anticipated as well the necessity and the *means* to punish traitors and deserters."

His point to the other pilots made, Faisal turned a venomous grin on Reg. "I am not surprised that you cannot feel sympathy for a Muslim cause despite the friendship and admiration your Saudi students feel for you. I understand that you shot down a young Egyptian pilot this morning." He paused to let the accusation linger in the air for a moment. "Shot him down like a dog, though you had no authority over him, because he refused to obey your orders."

"That's a bloody lie, and you know it, Faisal!" shouted Tye, leaping to his feet for the first time.

Reg gestured for the mechanic to be seated, taking the opportunity to calm his own seething anger. "I didn't fire on the Egyptian, Faisal. I did what I had to do to save myself, and I did so in an attempt to lead the aliens away from Khamis Moushayt."

"And Khamis Moushayt is now in ruins, yes? And so the Egyptian boy is dead for no reason, as dead as all of the British and American pilots whom you failed to save when you fled into the desert."

Many of the Saudis and those international pilots who had not been part of Reg's group were now whispering to one another in angry tones, gesturing at him with thinly veiled contempt.

"Major Cummins," Faisal continued, "if you choose not to fight, so be it. May Allah forgive you." He turned to address the entire group. "And may Allah forgive all of you who will not join me in pledging to defend Mecca.

"Those of you who do not wish to join the *shaheeds* may leave us now. Your input is no longer needed."

During the first tense moments before anyone stood to leave, Reg tried unsuccessfully to make eye contact with Khalid, but the usually cheerful young man was staring somberly at his feet. Edward was the first to stand and leave. Much to everyone's surprise, all three Syrians followed immediately behind the Jordanian. Then Remi, the lone Ethiopian, left. With a disappointed sigh, Tye stood, his head reaching almost to the roof of the tent.

"Well, I'd say that was a smashing failure. We might as well get out of here." One by one, exactly half of the international pilots filtered out of the tent. Reg was among the last to leave.

Before he turned, Faisal smiled at him once more, and said, "Who's standing in the way of unity now?"

That bastard planned every bit of this meeting, start to finish, thought Reg.

Outside, Thomson and Tye stood waiting for him.

"You didn't win us any friends with your last speech, Major," Thomson said.

"I'm not running for Most Popular Fighter Pilot, Colonel," Reg said, voice clipped. "Believe it or not, I'm trying to keep us all together."

Tye wasn't convinced. "Lieutenant Sutton's going to go ballistic," he said. "Now there's no chance for Diego Garcia." He glanced back into the tent. "No chance for virgins either, I'll warrant."

The Saudi guards posted outside the meeting didn't order the pilots back across the runway, so they stayed, waiting for the meeting to break up. None of the international pilots would even glance in Reg's direction.

The various factions whispered ominously to one another, glancing over their shoulders to make sure none of the Saudis was within earshot. It was a novel sight to see Miriyam, the Israeli firebrand, in hushed conversations with pilots from Iraq, Iran, and even Syria. Reg was certain they were hatching some scheme for seizing control of the fuel tanker; but as he was being shut out, it was only a guess.

Thirty minutes later, the meeting inside the tent was over, and the participants began to stream out into the cool midnight air. They seemed to be in high spirits, confident that they would either turn back the invasion or earn Paradise trying.

Reg kept an eye out for Khalid. He wanted to speak to the young pilot and his father. It was Reg's hope that the elder Yamani held enough influence—and still had enough of his wits about him—to steer Faisal away from his plan. But when his former student emerged from the tent, Faisal himself his escort, arm draped over the younger man as if the two were long-lost brothers, Reg could only watch as they wandered away between the tents, locked in discussion.

"The meeting is now finished. You will return to your encampments!" It was the burly Saudi captain again, looking menacingly strong as he herded the international pilots across the runway.

Reg hung back in the shadow of an F-15 and managed to escape the notice of the Saudi guards. Once he was sure he was unobserved, he trotted quietly through the camp, making his way to the line of Learjets. Moving surreptitiously from plane to plane, he eventually came to the Yamani jet, light streaming from its portals. With a last glance around, he climbed the stairs and raised his hand to knock on the hatch.

"There is no one inside who wishes to speak to you, Major Cummins," came a soft voice from beneath the plane's fuselage.

Reg was startled, but he maintained an even demeanor as he leaned over and peered into the darkness beneath the jet. In her black *abaya,* Fadeela Yamani was an invisible specter. Only when her green eyes caught a flash of light from across the camp could Reg make out her location.

"I need to speak to your father and brother, Miss Yamani," Reg said formally. "Your Commander Faisal is determined to kill every man in this camp in his quest for personal glory."

"I am sure that is true, Major Cummins," she replied,

stepping out of the shadows and motioning for him to join her on the ground. "But Ghalil ibn-Faisal is in that plane right now with my brother, seeking my father's blessing."

Reg glanced up at the portal nearest to him. Sure enough, just then Faisal's bulk passed the window as he paced, arms waving, obviously exhorting the Yamani men to throw their support to him.

"Guess I'll have to talk to them some other time," Reg said. He considered his best route back to the British tents, but then decided he wasn't quite ready to face Sutton's inevitable tirade. There was a break in the plateau lip near the Yamani jet, a draw filled with sand forming a rampway out into the dune sea.

"Think I'll just take a walk then, if you'll excuse me. Good evening, Miss Yamani."

He turned to go, but she caught his arm. "Major, wait. I'll join you."

Reg guessed that Fadeela was waiting outside of the plane on the orders of her father or brother, so that she would not disturb their meeting. He knew that her suggestion that she join him could land her in quite a bit of hot water if they were caught.

"Miss Yamani, the risk—"

"The risk, Major Cummins," she interrupted, "is mine to take." With that, she took his arm, and they walked quietly out into the dunes.

Once they were away from the camp and hidden from view in a depression between dunes, they sat on the slip face of one of the hills of sand and looked up at the stars.

"I'm surprised that you have any desire to be around me after our last conversation," Reg said.

"I was at the meeting tonight," she said. "And yes, I could tell you were trying to pick me out. I can play the anonymous role Islam demands of me when it suits my purposes, Reg."

Noting that they were on a first-name basis again, Reg

asked, "What about the meeting made you decide that I was worth a stroll in the desert?"

Fadeela reached up and took off her headdress, shaking her hair loose and breathing the night air. "I decided that I was wrong about you, somewhat," she said.

"Somewhat?"

"Yes. You are a sensible man to oppose Faisal's plan, but you do not dismiss him or the others as fanatics as some among the Christians and Jews surely have."

"I've been knocking around the Islamic world for a long time, Fadeela. I know what Mecca means to you."

"No," she said. "Not to me. I am not Muslim, Reg, not in a way that the *imams* would acknowledge. I believe in a motivating force in the universe, but I do not believe that its only aspect is the God of the Prophet. There is much wisdom in the Holy Koran, and I pray dutifully. But when I open my heart in prayer, the God I feel is a nurturing force, feminine... and empowering."

Reg considered this. "I think you're right about the *imams,* there, Fadeela. Sounds a bit California."

"I asked you before what you had to fight for, Reg. You couldn't answer. In the meeting, though, I saw a spark of something in you. Maybe I should rephrase the question. Tell me, Reg, what do you believe in?"

"Well," Reg answered, "my mum raised me as a devout Apathetic, but as the years have passed I've found I just don't care that much about it anymore."

She chuckled, but didn't let him off the hook. "Always the glib comment," she said. "At least when you're not facing down enemy fighters."

"No," said Reg, "I'm at my glibbest in those situations."

"Warrior and clown, then," she said. "And neither mask is enough to hide the pain beneath."

Reg sat stock-still. How could she know?

"Do you know what I want, Reg Cummins?" she

asked. "I want to drive a car. Isn't that funny? With all of the restrictions placed on women in Saudi Arabia, these clothes, our subservience to our husbands, with everything else, what I miss most about Stanford is driving. I suppose if I ever want to drive again, I'll have to go back there."

Relieved that she seemed to be changing topics, Reg replied, "Khalid said that your father was comparatively liberal with your upbringing."

"He was," she said. "He gave me enough freedom to want more. That's another reason I can't say I'm really Muslim any longer. My cousins and aunts, they're all capable and intelligent women. Many of them chafe against the system, sure, but eventually they capitulate. Well, that's my word. They would probably say they grow up."

"It's a harsh system," Reg said.

She indicated the desert with a graceful sweep of her arm. "It was designed for a harsh people, Reg, a harsh people living in a harsh place. I can't live in it and be true to myself, but I can't condemn it outright either. Oh, I fight with Khalid to be sure. He really is a pig. But I don't want to cause him pain, any more than I want to cause my beloved father pain. But for me, pain is something to be healed"—she raised the scarf in her hand—"not hidden."

Hook, line and sinker, thought Reg, realizing that she'd caught him. *And I can't believe this, but I think I'm glad she did.*

Reg brought his hands together and thought, trying to find words. Finally, he said, "I flew bombers before I switched to fighters, in the war, I mean."

Before he could go on, a shout rang across the desert. "Miss Yamani? Are you out there?" It was Faisal.

"Damn the man!" she hissed. "He finished meeting with my father and brother earlier than I expected."

Other voices called her name, the sounds drifting across the dunes.

"You have to hide, Reg," she told him. "I will let them find me, but it is death for you if they find us together! Faisal will have you shot on sight!"

With that, she stood and headed back for camp. "Fadeela, wait!" Reg called softly, but just as she reached the crest of the dune, a flashlight beam played across her, illuminating her face as she hastily knotted the head scarf into place.

A gravelly voice shouted in Arabic, and Reg could hear more men converging on the opposite side of the dune. He crawled stealthily to the lip and looked down to see Faisal confronting Fadeela. A half dozen soldiers stood around him and a small, wrinkled man with a full turban and a long gray beard. Reg recognized the man as a *mutawa*, sort of a religious policeman.

The man was soundly berating Fadeelah, raising a hand as if to strike her, but instead stripping her hastily tied scarf from her head. Several of the soldiers laughed coarsely.

Eventually, Faisal stepped in front of the religious man and waved him off. He stepped closer to Fadeela and spoke to her gently. To Reg's shock, he reached out and gently stroked her face with the back of his hand. This sort of thing was expressly forbidden, Reg knew, but the *mutawa* just stood by, grinning. *Must be in Faisal's pocket*, thought Reg.

Fadeela stood her ground, straight as an arrow. Only when Faisal leaned in and made as if to kiss her did she break away, running for the ramp of sand that led to her father's plane. A pair of the soldiers moved to intercept her, but Faisal called them off. He said something to the *mutawa*, and they both laughed.

When the Saudis had gone, Reg crept away, making for the British tents.

4

A MUCH TOO CRAZY PLAN

The second day of the end of the world began in silence. There were no sobs from those who had cracked under pressure. The foreign pilots who were unable to maintain at least a veneer of self-control, such as the Israeli Greenberg, had been removed in the night to the Tent of the Fearful, where they were injected with morphine.

Reg lay in his tent as the sun began to climb. The sounds of the camp slowly coming to life around him drifted through the canvas, but having made enemies of almost everyone in the camp the previous evening, Reg felt no great need to venture forth just yet.

Even as the morning wore on, the level of activity did not begin to approach the breakneck pace of the day before. It was as if everyone in the camp had taken time to ponder the tremendous gravity of the situation before them. Millions of people all around the world were dead, and more were no doubt dying with each passing moment, victims of a merciless enemy of seemingly limitless power. An enemy that Ghalil ibn-Faisal would soon be leading many of them against, no matter the odds.

Reg had no doubt that Faisal would lead his men against whatever city destroyer was nearest, whether it was actually headed toward Mecca or not. It was clear to him that Faisal intended to turn the desperate situation to his own advantage, no matter who suffered in the process. He would gladly pervert his pilots' genuine religious fervor to his own ends and force the less devout among them along by whatever means he had at his disposal.

The presence of the foreign pilots had no doubt complicated Faisal's plans considerably, but the man had proven to be a fast thinker, rapidly turning any situation to his own advantage. Reg thought of all of these things, and of Fadeela, until the heat of the day eventually forced him to leave the tent.

It was around ten in the morning and the sun had only just begun its daily assault, already pushing the mercury past a hundred degrees Fahrenheit The other British pilots were just returning to their area, pink-faced and soaked with sweat. Thomson had brought Reg some breakfast, a paper cup filled with cold yellow beans in a spicy red sauce. Tye contributed some broken crackers from one of his many pockets to round out the meal.

None of the three had done much more than mutter a greeting before Reg dipped his cup in the communal water bucket and sat back on his haunches in the fractionally cooler shade of a Tornado.

Thomson, looking as if he were finally running out of hope, spoke to Reg. "Guess you haven't heard about Houston, then," he said.

Reg remembered Faisal's news of the Americans' planned nuclear assault from the night before. A single glance at the faces of the other three RAF men was enough to tell him that the attack had met with failure.

"We're screwed backwards and sideways," said Sutton. "What else can we throw at those bastards?"

"Edward talked to one of the radiomen. They said the Americans reported that the destroyer didn't even move when the bomb went off. Those shields must be impenetrable."

Reg took a drink of water. "I wonder if this changes Faisal's thinking at all," he said.

"I hope not," muttered Sutton darkly.

Reg looked around at the other three men, noticed how none of them would meet his eye.

He sighed, and chose Tye. "Okay, what is it?" he asked the tall youth.

"What's what?" Tye asked in turn.

"What is it you're not telling me?"

"I don't know what you're talking about," Tye answered. Reg hadn't thought it possible for the mechanic to turn any redder, but as he lied, Tye's face glowed a fraction more crimson.

Thomson shifted uncomfortably, then threw his hands up in the air. "It's vile," he said, "but we can't just sit out here forever."

"Did we not agree just five minutes ago not to tell him until after the Saudis took off?" snarled Sutton.

Reg held up his hand. "No, no," he said to Thomson. "Don't go against the plan. What if I'm captured, and Faisal turns his knife boys loose on me to find out what I know, eh?"

He stood and stretched, looking around at the other international contingents. He saw that the Israelis had removed the access panels from their fighters and were tinkering in the electronics compartments.

"As long as I don't know what you lot are up to, I can't give away the plan," he said, turning back to the others. He walked over and crouched next to Sutton.

"As it is, I'll have to tell them something to save my own skin, of course. Just make up something nonsensical. What should I tell them?"

The surly lieutenant scooted away from Reg. "I don't care what you tell the buggers," he said.

"How about this, then?" Reg asked. "How about I tell them that we've estimated that the Saudis have about two hundred men in this camp all told, and that we figure they've got about a hundred and twenty operational planes." Tye looked up at Reg, eyes wide.

"Once they fly off to bring everlasting glory to Ghalil Ibn-Faisal," Reg continued, "that leaves just eighty or so soldiers guarding the camp—and the fuel dump. And, of course, the fifty or so international pilots who haven't signed on with Faisal's *jihad*, I suppose they'll still be here. Playing cards, probably."

Thomson looked vaguely embarrassed, but said nothing. "Next," said Reg, "I'll get really creative. I'll tell them that the Israelis almost always stockpile small arms and the odd submachine gun on their planes in case they go down in hostile territory. These Arabs will believe any crazy thing about the Jews, won't they, Sutton?"

"Who told you?" the lieutenant muttered under his breath.

But Reg wasn't finished. "Now, by that point, Faisal's men will probably be really angry with me. They'll ask me what kind of fools I take them for. *'The foreign pilots conspiring to take over the camp once the bulk of our forces are away?'* they'll say. *'That crazy Miriyam distributing guns?'*"

"You've made your point, Major," said Sutton.

"*'Do you think we're children, Englishman?'* I hope there's no kicking. I can't bear to be kicked. *'What makes you think we'd believe the foreigners would come up with such a STUPID, BLOODY OBVIOUS PLAN?'*"

"Sutton here was pretty sure it would work," said Tye.

"Shut up, Tye," said Sutton.

Reg turned to the colonel. "You realize there are civilians over there," he said.

"I told you he'd be a problem," Sutton fumed to the others. "Look here, Cummins, that Miriyam has got it all figured out. You can sit here and take shit from Faisal all you want, but the rest of us have better things to do. The only thing we need from you is that you keep your mouth shut, understood?"

"Lieutenant Sutton," said Reg, "if I didn't know any better, I'd think that you just addressed a superior officer in a disrespectful tone. Shame, shame, Sutton. Shame, shame."

Before the lieutenant could reply, there was a commotion on the opposite side of the runway. One of the radiomen, still wearing his headphones, was trotting toward the British planes. He was clutching a piece of paper in his hand and shouting in Arabic. One of the guards along the perimeter of the foreign enclave waved him through.

The man stood before them, then, still shouting, obviously repeating himself and stumbling over words in his haste.

"What the devil is he saying?" asked Thomson, frantically thumbing this pages of his phrase book once more.

Reg had been listening to the man closely. Finally, he raised his hands, indicating that radio operator should calm down. "*Feh hemt, feh hemt,*" said Reg. *I understand, I understand.*

The radio operator nodded, then ran to the next encampment, where he spoke just as swiftly to the Egyptians.

Reg spoke to his companions. "He says they're picking up some kind of message in English, along with some Morse code. They can't understand all of it. Let's go have a look."

"Wait," Sutton said. "That doesn't make any sense. They've got plenty of men over there who speak English. They don't need us. Sounds like an ambush."

Reg looked at Sutton gravely and nodded. "You may be right. They'd obviously want us to be standing next to *their* airplanes instead of *our* airplanes when they open fire. I'll give you a detailed report if I make it back alive."

When Reg began running toward the radio tent, he found that Thomson was right on his heels.

"Slow down, Cummins," puffed the colonel. "I'm coming along."

"What about Sutton's ambush?" Reg asked.

"To hell with Sutton." The portly colonel waved his arms. "I'm going to ambush *him* if I have to stay around him much longer."

Members of almost all of the other international contingents were converging on the radio tent. Reg was startled to see that many of them were now openly carrying weapons. Sensing one such armed man beside him, Reg turned to see Yossi, trotting along and carrying an Uzi.

When he saw Reg looking at him incredulously, Yossi shrugged, and said, "Miriyam said I should invite myself along. I thought I'd stick close to you Englishmen, since 'your fondness for Jews is well-known.'" His imitation of Faisal was surprisingly good, but Reg doubted that it would come in handy if any of the Arabs were unhappy with a gun-toting Israeli showing up at the radio tent.

There was a crowd around the radios. The shaded area beneath the open-sided camouflage tent looked like an electronics bazaar. Much of the equipment Faisal's team had gathered up was surplus, some of it older than the soldiers themselves. The tent resembled an Arab market, with fifty different conversations going on at once. But the noise and activity quickly melted away as the foreign visitors stepped beneath the canopy inside. As Reg had feared, the Arabs interpreted Yossi's presence as a taunt.

Khalid hurried toward Reg and pulled him to one side. "They have destroyed Amman, and now they are moving south. I spoke with Faisal and tried to convince him we should follow your advice, but he is committed. Unless the ship changes course, he will order an attack within the next two hours."

As Reg listened, he watched over Khalid's shoulder, keeping an eye on the other Saudis. Some of them were demanding that Yossi state his business, meaningfully grasping the handles of their pistols. Finally, one of them thumped the Israeli in the chest, and shouted, *"Imshi!" Scram!*

Reg interrupted Khalid. "How do you say 'lawyer' in Arabic?" Khalid blinked, confused by the question. But he answered. "*Advocat.* Why?"

"Going to use some Thomson school diplomacy," Reg said before he joined the knot of Saudis surrounding Yossi. Once among them, he shook his finger at the largest man, loudly proclaiming something in halting Arabic. There was a brief silence, then all of the Arab speakers in the area began laughing.

Remarkably, Thomson had left his phrase book at the camp. "What did you say?" he asked.

"I said not to worry about Yossi. He's our lawyer."

One of the radio operators pointed at the machine gun the Israeli soldier held and cracked a joke of his own, which Khalid translated: *"Yes, and I see he remembered to bring his fountain pen!"* When the men had had their laugh, they began turning back to their workstations.

"Now," Reg asked, "where's this Morse code?"

Khalid led the way to the center of the tent, where the camp's best radio was being monitored by a trio of technicians. They were all listening intently, scratching out notes on pads of paper. By their expressions, Reg could tell they were frustrated. One of them slipped off his headphones and handed them over to Reg.

He put them on, expecting to hear a sequence of dots and dashes. Instead, there was a roar of static. It seemed to be nothing but a storm of interference noise, but then he heard it: a faint voice shouting through the blizzard. Reg closed his eyes and tried to make out what the voice was saying... *States government has captured... shield we will... alien mother ship outside... do not engage... forces happy...* The voice belonged to an American man who was speaking in an urgent but controlled tone. It seemed impossible to piece together the fragments of what he was saying.

If this broadcast is coming from America, thought

Reg, *there's no telling how many times it's been relayed, boosted, and amplified before it reached the Empty Quarter.* "Can't make it out," Reg said to the operator sitting next to him. "It's just so much sonic mush." He began to remove his headphones, but the Saudi motioned for him to keep listening.

"Wait," said the man. "You will hear."

He was right. A few seconds after the voice transmission was finished, a Morse sequence began. This, too, was faint, frequently interrupted, and barely audible. Reg quickly realized the spoken message was being repeated in this different form. He grabbed a pad and pencil and began writing, decoding as he went. The brief message was continuously recycling itself, and, after ten minutes, Reg had as much of it as he thought he could gather.

Everyone in the tent waited anxiously as Reg compared his own notes to those taken by the other men. Like a person solving a crossword puzzle, he fit the pieces together fragment by fragment. When he was finished, he read it over a couple of times and couldn't help but smile. When he stood up from the table, every pilot in the immediate vicinity rushed up to hear the news.

"It's from the Americans," he announced. "They want to organize a counteroffensive." A guarded cheer went through the crowd.

"It's about bloody time," Thomson harrumphed. "What's their plan?"

"It's… well, it's damn creative."

"Read it!" several men demanded. Soldiers and civilians were streaming in from all directions.

Reg cleared his throat. "It says: 'To any and all remaining armies of the world. The U.S. military has captured one of the alien attack ships, has learned to circumvent and disable its protective shield. We will attempt to disable all shields worldwide. Preparing now to infiltrate alien mother ship outside Earth's atmosphere and use computer interface to temporarily disable source of shields. If successful, we anticipate only a small window of opportunity. Please commit all possible military resources to worldwide synchronized attack to begin at approximately 03:15 GMT. We will announce success or failure of our mission at that time. Conserve your weaponry. Do not engage enemy. Accept civilian losses. This action authorized by U.S. President Thomas Whitmore. Continue to monitor this frequency. Relay message to other forces in your area. Happy Independence Day."

As one of the radio operators repeated the message in Arabic, the tent and surrounding area filled with murmured discussions. Reg looked down at the paper in his own hand. The word *harebrained* went through his head, followed closely by *impossible*.

But then again, at least it's a plan, he thought. *And who knows? The Americans have surprised me before.*

After the initial flush of enthusiasm, questions and reservations about the plan started to crop up. How were the Americans going to get into the mother ship? How were our computers going to interface with the alien technology? How would anyone know when the shields were down, assuming they ever came down at all? "No, no!" protested one of Khalid's men. "This is a bad plan, too much crazy."

But this man was in the minority. More and more of the pilots, both Saudi and international, began discussing how the group might work together to fulfill their role in it.

Then, from the edge of the tent, a booming voice interrupted the gathering. "We Arabs are a proud people until our foreign masters tug on the leash," said Commander Faisal, striding to the center of the group. "Then we forget our own obligations in an instant." He was obviously displeased with the way some of his men were embracing the new plan. He shook an admonishing finger at them. "As soon as the Americans, the *infidel* Americans, speak, you turn into lapdogs! A few words over a radio, and you forget the Holy City!"

Reg felt the energy and enthusiasm begin to drain from the group. The influence that Faisal had over his men could not be underestimated. He was a charismatic man, capable of rousing hearts and raising morale with a few well-chosen words.

Somebody needs to choose the right words to turn this thing around, Reg thought. *This American plan is madness, but it's the only chance we've got.* Reg looked at Thomson, considering whether the colonel would be able to turn the tide of opinion against Faisal.

"I think someone's trying to get your attention, Major," Thomson said. Reg looked to where the colonel was pointing and saw a handful of Saudi woman. Piercing green eyes stared at him from behind the shrouding *abaya* of the tallest. It could only be Fadeela.

Knowing that there was no way, in this public forum, that she would be able to speak to him, Reg watched as she slowly raised her arm and pointed directly at him.

She's thinking the same thing I am, Reg thought, *and she wants me to talk to these men. But they despise me after last night!*

Fadeela lowered her arm, but continued to hold him in her gaze. He could see the questions in her eyes. *What do you have worth fighting for? What do you believe in?*

Reg considered then that Fadeela Yamani might be the bravest person he had ever known. She lived her life as if walking a treacherous path, fraught with danger. Holding to the strictures of her society on the outside, internally she longed for a life of independence, of freedom of a sort no one in her position should ever hope to obtain. But she did not give up hope; she did not give up the fight.

It's her, Reg thought, simply. *She's worth fighting for. I believe in her.*

Reg saw a half-full water barrel immediately behind the spot where Faisal still stood, haranguing his men. He walked over to it and did something guaranteed to draw the rapt attention of every one of these desert-bred men. He turned it over.

Faisal cursed and leapt away, narrowly avoiding muddying his highly polished boots. When he turned, Reg had already overturned the barrel and climbed atop it.

Reg clutched the American message in his hand and held it above his head. "This plan," he said in a loud voice, "may be the most foolhardy damned plan I've ever heard of. There's no logic to it! It depends on a thousand variables and perfect timing among hundreds of units spread across the globe." One of the Saudi soldiers started to approach, but Reg saw Faisal wave him off. *He thinks I'm going to argue for doing nothing,* thought Reg. *Good.*

Reg caught the eye of the pilot who had disparaged the plan earlier. "'Too much crazy,' right? Risking all on a one-in-a-million chance that the Americans will accomplish what? That they'll shut down the shields for a few moments at best! Their President Whitmore must think we're crazy!" A few of the Saudis were nodding, but Reg saw that more of them were disappointed that he wasn't arguing for the plan. *I don't want to be a disappointment,* he thought, and continued speaking.

"Or maybe I should say that Whitmore must *hope* we're crazy. The Americans must *hope* that we'll join them. That is, after all, what they're offering us. Hope. The first glimmer of hope we've had since the aliens destroyed Jerusalem."

"Hear, hear!" shouted Thomson. Several of the other pilots joined him in shouting encouragement.

"We're from different countries," Reg continued. "We speak different languages. Two days ago some of our countries were openly hostile to one another. Do you remember? Do you remember two days ago? It seems like ten years, doesn't it? Those old conflicts, those hostilities, they're meaningless now. What's important is what we have in common. What we have in common is the greatest enemy mankind has ever known. And now we have hope!" More of the men shouted approval, and Reg kept on.

"We have hope that we can knock the invaders from the skies! We have hope that we can take back what is ours! We have hope, a *real* hope, of fighting a battle we can win!" They were his now, Reg saw. Every pilot within earshot was clapping and shouting, banging their hands against barrels like impromptu percussionists or simply jumping up and down. Every pilot except one.

It's one thing to convince them, thought Reg, staring at the grim visage of Ghalil ibn-Faisal, *but another thing altogether to convince the man with the power.* Again, Reg remembered what Fadeela had told him, that here was a man motivated solely by personal glory.

"Or maybe," Reg said, holding his hands up for silence, "maybe we should act prematurely. Maybe we should throw ourselves against the aliens *before* their shields are knocked down, *guaranteeing* that they will destroy us, and survive us. Maybe we should make a futile gesture instead of a genuine attack, and *ensure* the destruction of Mecca. And Riyadh. And Baghdad, and Addis Ababa, and every other place any of us hold dear.

"Maybe it won't come to that, though. Maybe some pilots from somewhere else in the world will be able to take out our assigned city destroyer after they've saved their own people. After all, just because we don't fulfill our part of the bargain doesn't mean that the other thirty-five ships won't go down. Just the ship in the Middle East left. And why? Because when it finally counted the most, the people of the region couldn't act together for the common good. When it finally mattered the most, the chance at the glory of victory wasn't enough to make them see something bigger than their own problems."

"No!" shouted a voice from the crowd, and Reg saw that it was Yossi.

"We *can* work together," said another voice, a Syrian.

"Can you?" asked Reg. "Can Muslims and Christians and Jews fight side by side?" The crowd roared, *"Yes!"*

"Can Persians and Arabs and Europeans and Africans unite to rid the world of this horrible scourge?" And again they roared, *"Yes!"*

Then Reg threw his own arms into the air, and shouted, "Victory!"

The cheer spread through the whole camp in a heartbeat. *"Victory! Victory! Victory!"* The desert rang with the international chorus.

Climbing down from his makeshift pulpit, Reg caught sight of Fadeela once again. Was it possible to notice a grin from behind an *abaya*? He thought so.

"You are quite a speech maker, Major Cummins," someone behind him said. It was Faisal, of course. "I can raise no objection to the American plan now. But it will have to be incorporated into my own, of course." The Saudi commander held up a dispatch.

"The alien ship has turned south, toward Mecca. We will fly to defend the Holy City, as planned. If the Americans have brought the shields down by the time we arrive, so much the better." Faisal wadded up the paper and threw it in the sand at Reg's feet.

"In *either* case," he continued, "once they pass the city of Usfan we will attack."

5

COUNTERATTACK

The main battle in the camp that afternoon was between debilitating heat and the determination of the pilots to prepare their planes for the showdown. The work required them to spend long stretches of time exposed to the punishing sun. They stripped parts off of the damaged jets in order to repair others, replenished their fuel tanks one bucket at a time, and jury-rigged missile firing systems to accommodate unfamiliar weaponry. There was little time to discuss strategy and tactics. As the sun leaned to the west and the men in the radio tent continued to track the city destroyer's progress toward Mecca, the pilots went through their final checklists.

At five-thirty the planes were lined up on the runway, ready to go. Nearly two hundred pilots climbed into their cockpits and fired up their engines. But Reg was still on the ground inspecting the Tornado that had been Thomson's plane and stealing occasional glances toward the Saudi camp. Since Thomson was the least accomplished pilot among the Brits, he had volunteered to sit with the Saudi radio technicians to help decode the next message from the Americans. Sutton and Tye, already strapped in, were watching Reg, wondering what was taking him so long. A moment later they had their answer. From between the Saudi tents, a veiled woman emerged and marched purposefully onto the runway. Her black, ankle-length *abaya* moved in time with her long, athletic stride, and she carried something in her hand.

Reg knew who it was. Like a smitten teenager, he'd delayed getting into his plane for as long as he could, hoping that she would find some way to see him off. He'd hoped that she would wave to him from between the tents, or send word through a messenger. But Fadeela was bolder than that. She walked directly up to him, ignoring the hundreds of people who were watching, and handed him a photograph. Reg caught a quick glimpse of her bright green eyes before she turned on her heels and walked away without a word.

He looked down at the photograph. It showed a young girl—too young to wear a veil—riding a camel toward the finish line of a race. Her green eyes were turned toward the camera, and she was laughing triumphantly. He turned it over and read the words written on the back: "A kiss for luck."

A smile spread across Reg's face as he tucked the photograph into his breast pocket. *It's almost as if she can read my mind,* he said to himself as he climbed into the jet. *It's exactly what I needed. Something to remind me what I'm fighting for.*

They flew west, nearly two hundred strong, to the edge of the desert before turning due north. Eighty of the Saudi planes took the lead, flying in crisply formed wedges. They were followed by the international pilots, seventy-three of them, straggling along in ragtag fashion. Another Saudi squadron brought up the rear, prepared to hunt down any pilot who tried to run. They followed the Asir mountain chain up the country's west coast. The terrain on the two sides of the mountains was starkly different. To the left, the hills were covered with trees all the way down to the lush coast of the Red Sea. To the right, rocky cliffs and canyons ran down to the lifeless floor of the

Empty Quarter's great sand desert. There was no sign of the enemy, but for the first time in years, Reg felt nervous being up in the air.

As they approached Mecca, they looked down at an awesome spectacle. From all directions, the Islamic faithful were converging on the Holy City. For mile after mile, the highways were choked with traffic. Brightly painted buses, private cars, and rivers of people on foot were all surging toward the famous mosque.

"Major Cummins," Faisal's voice came over the radio, "ahead you can see our Holy City. I think you are very fortunate to see this sight. Under normal circumstances, of course, only believers are allowed here. So today, I declare you and the others to be honorary Muslim pilgrims—*hajjis*."

"*Allah inshallah*, old bean," Reg said, smiling.

As they caught sight of Mecca's great mosque, they saw that there was a sea of believers crushed into the immense courtyard. They were moving in slow circles around the cube-shaped Kaaba, the shrine that stood at the center of the open space. According to Muslim belief, this stone structure was originally build by the first man, Adam. As the planes roared past, many of the Arab and African pilots broke into the same ritual prayers being chanted by the faithful below: Lord God, from such a distant land I have come unto Thee… grant me shelter under Thy throne.

Several minutes north of Mecca, Faisal's voice returned to the airwaves and called everyone's attention to a small city nestled in the hills. It was Usfan, the place he had chosen as his line in the sand, the point beyond which he would not allow the aliens to pass.

Directly ahead, the monstrous bulk of the city destroyer hovered like an airborne cancer between the blue sky and the dun brown earth. The radios erupted with nervous chatter as the pilots called out the sighting. A moment later, Thomson's voice came from the radio tent back in the Empty Quarter.

"Sounds as if you've made visual contact. Is that right?"

He was answered simultaneously in half a dozen languages. Everyone monitoring the frequency confirmed that the destroyer was in sight, then began asking the colonel for information on its airspeed, elevation, and distance.

"Pilots, pilots," Thomson broke in, "these transmissions are being recorded. Please try to speak one at a time, and identify yourselves when you do."

"What the hell is the point?" asked Sutton, his voice dripping with disgust.

"The point, Lieutenant Sutton, is that you never know. If you chaps pull off a miracle and beat these sons of bitches, it'll be one for the history books. This audiotape we're making might show up on the BBC someday, and you'll be famous."

Sutton scoffed. "Thomson, I wish you were up here to see this thing we're facing. Then you wouldn't sound so damn chipper. In a day or two, there's going to be no one left to read any history books. But go ahead and make your tape. Maybe the aliens will find it someday and get a good laugh out of it."

Tye came on the radio. After stating his name as the colonel had asked, he said, "The thing I would like to add to the historical record is that I wish Sutton would keep his bleeding pie hole closed until he has something useful to say for himself."

Several other pilots laughed and seconded Tye's motion.

At a distance of fifty miles, the dome-shaped saucer began to dominate the skyline. It was plowing inexorably forward at approximately two hundred miles an hour, the embodiment of certain doom.

Faisal continued to lead them straight toward the obsidian tower that marked the prow of the destroyer until, at a distance of twenty-five miles, he banked away to the right. Group by group, the rest of the jets followed suit.

"Ten more minutes, Teacher," Khalid radioed to Reg. "In ten minutes we find out if the Americans were successful. I don't think the alien ship will reach Usfan before then."

"I agree," Reg said, "but that's not going to leave us much of a cushion."

"Not to worry," Miriyam said. "I already did the math. We have twenty minutes until they get to Usfan."

"Which means we have a little more than ten minutes to bring down the destroyer before it reaches Mecca," Reg pointed out. He studied the massive alien ship before adding another thought. "Even with their shields down, our missiles might not be enough."

"Luckily we are not the only ones here," said Remi, the Ethiopian pilot they'd met the previous afternoon. "More and more jets are coming every minute." It was true. There were at least a dozen groups of fighters in the area, but they looked pathetically small compared to the advancing city destroyer.

"There is no reason to worry," Edward said, trying without success to mask the fear in his voice. "Today will be like the story of David and Goliath. We'll find a way to knock down this giant with our small weapons."

Yossi couldn't let the opportunity to needle Edward slip past. "David was a Jewish hero, you realize."

Edward laughed. "Yes, I know. But he's like the Palestinians. We used to fight your Israeli armored jeeps with only bricks and stones."

"And look how successful you were," said one of the Iraqis. "You had to run away and live in Jordan."

After a long pause, Edward spoke again. "You're right. But today will be different. Today, the little guys are going to win."

Pondering Edward's prediction, the pilots maintained

a tense radio silence for the next few minutes, hoping to hear from the Americans. At exactly 6:15, the moment the message was scheduled to arrive, the radio erupted with shouting. It was not the Americans; it was Faisal. He began issuing a long string of orders, speaking only in Arabic. The Saudi jets that had been flying at the rear of the formation accelerated past the international contingent to join the rest of their countrymen.

"Would someone care to translate?" Tye asked. "What's going on?"

"It's obvious, isn't it?" Sutton grumbled. "They're preparing to attack."

Reg could see that Sutton was right. Faisal wasn't going to allow the Americans any extra time, even though the destroyer was still miles from Usfan. As the Saudi F-15s positioned themselves, Faisal monopolized the airwaves, calling to his men in an urgent but controlled voice.

Reg thought a premature strike would be disastrous on two counts. Not only would it be a waste of scarce firepower; it might also draw the scarablike attacker ships into the air. If their shields were still operational, they would make short work of the few hundred jets that had massed for the counterattack. He shouted into his radio, trying to get the Saudi commander's attention and urging him not to jeopardize this last, slim hope of bringing down the enemy ship.

Faisal ignored the warning and continued speaking to his men in the rhythmic, hypnotizing voice of a fire-and-brimstone preacher. Although Reg couldn't understand the individual words, he knew Faisal was exhorting his pilots to bravery and self-sacrifice, preparing them for martyrdom.

"I'd just like to point out," Sutton said quietly, "that now would be an excellent time for us to get the hell out of here." Ever since the Saudi watchdog planes had moved forward to join the attack formation, members of the international squadron had been quietly peeling away and flying toward their home countries. Nearly a third of them were gone. "Anyone out there interested in heading for Kuwait?"

No one answered. Everyone who was going to run had already done so. As Faisal's speech built in intensity, Reg and the others kept their ears open, hoping to receive word from the Americans before the Saudis launched their attack.

"Khalid Yamani, can you hear me?" Reg called. "You've got to convince him to wait. Tell Faisal to give it five more minutes."

There was no reply.

As Faisal's speech reached a crescendo, he shouted a question to his men, and they responded with a roaring war cry. Then the entire squadron turned as one and broke into an attack run. They dived at a steep angle, picking up speed as they streaked toward the their target, the destroyer's obsidian tower. To Reg, it was a horrible, incomprehensible sight. He sensed that a hundred men were about to give up their lives in exchange for nothing.

"Khalid, if you can hear me, break off," Reg said desperately. "Get out of there before they launch their attack ships. Save yourself for the real battle." To Reg's surprise, Khalid answered.

"Too late, Teacher," he said in a calm but tremulous voice. "Together, we will either shoot these infidels down, or we will die in glory. All things are in the hands of Allah."

"The words of a doomed man," said Miriyam.

Reluctantly, Reg admitted to himself that she was right. There was nothing more he could do for Khalid. "Let's start climbing," he told the others as he pulled back on his controls. "As soon as they launch, we're going to have company up here."

"Alien fighters?" Edward asked.

"And plenty of them."

As Reg turned, he couldn't resist taking one last glance

back at the diving squadron. When he did, he noticed something out of place. One of the Saudi jets lagged behind the others before turning sharply in a new direction. Reg thought he could guess who was piloting the rogue jet.

"Commander Faisal," he said, "it looks as if you have broken formation. Where are you headed?"

There was no answer. The squadron continued to plunge toward the mammoth alien airship.

Reg shouted, "I repeat: Saudi commander, you have broken formation. You are currently running in the wrong direction."

This time Faisal answered. "Do not interfere!" he screamed. A moment later, he had gathered himself and continued in a calm voice. "I'm afraid you are mistaken, major. You must be watching the wrong plane."

Reg stared down at the tiny shape of the wayward F-15 and decided to bluff. "Negative, Faisal. I'm directly above you. Close enough to read your wing markings. You are running away from the engagement."

After a moment of hesitation, Faisal answered. "Stay out of this, Cummins! I am not running. I am... I am positioning myself to observe the attack."

"Admit it, Faisal!" Reg shouted. "You're saving yourself because you know what's going to happen to those men. Order them to it break off."

"Damn you, Cummins, stay quiet! Cooperate with me and you will be rewarded."

"And if I don't?"

"Then I will personally shoot you out of the sky."

Reg, boiling with anger, resisted the impulse to swoop down on Faisal and unload every piece of ammunition he had aboard his aircraft. Instead, he sucked in a deep breath then growled into his headset. "I wouldn't advise it. You'd only be wasting another one of your king's planes."

Faisal scoffed. "King Ibrahim is no longer a factor. The

Saudi Air Force is now completely under my command and it is my will that—"

Reg cut him off and switched back to the previous frequency. "Khalid, look around. Faisal's gone. He knows you're doomed and he's saving himself. Get out of there now!"

Khalid and several of his fellow pilots began speaking to one another and quickly realized that Reg was right—Faisal had deserted them. Khalid swung into a turn, shouting instructions in Arabic.

"What's he saying?" Reg demanded.

Edward translated. "He's calling on the other pilots to follow him."

Only twenty of them did. They wheeled out of the attack formation and began looping around to rejoin Reg's squadron just as the Saudis fired on the destroyer. They unloosed a huge barrage of Sidewinders and Sparrows, which sliced through the late-afternoon sky, all headed for the same target area. Taken together, the missiles carried enough explosive charge to flatten a medium-sized city, but when they came to within a quarter mile of the destroyer, they all detonated harmlessly in midair. The protective shield was still in place. It became visible momentarily as it rippled gently under the impact. Shouting and cursing, the Saudi pilots fought to turn their planes in time to avoid crashing into it.

A moment later, Reg's fear became an ugly reality. A large portal suddenly appeared near the top of the gleaming black tower. Where a moment before there had been only a smooth, polished surface, there was now a gaping orifice leading onto a wide tunnel. Within seconds, hundreds of alien attacker ships darted into the open air like hornets spewing from a disturbed nest. They scattered in every direction, but the main force shot down the face of the tower to engage the Saudi squadron. In the dogfight at the base of the tower, the Saudi jets were outnumbered five to one by their shielded enemies. The slaughter was under way.

"Where are those damned Americans?" Reg growled as he watched the scarab fighters annihilate the Saudi forces.

Khalid and his small band of renegades were racing toward the international pilots' position. A group of perhaps fifty aliens fell in behind them, knitting through the air fluidly in their distinctive over-and-under formation.

"Should've headed for Kuwait when I had the chance," Sutton said when he saw them coming.

"Let's get the hell out of here," Reg shouted. "Head west, directly into the sun. Now!"

"What about Khalid? Shouldn't we help them?"

"No. There's nothing we can do. Follow me!"

The sun was just above the horizon but still blindingly bright. As Reg flew toward it, a strange clicking disturbance sounded in his earphones. Fearing that it was the sound of alien homing devices, he ordered his fellow pilots to shed altitude and pick up speed. Then, like a trumpet blast, Thomson's voice burst onto the airwaves.

"They're down!" he bellowed. "The shields are down! The Americans are telling everyone to attack immediately, before they go back up!" All at once, Reg recognized that the clicking sounds were Morse code.

"Thomson, are you sure the message is accurate?"

"Yes, yes! We're getting reports of damage to the alien destroyers. It's not just the Americans. Everybody's hitting them."

A lethal smile crossed Reg's lips, and his fear evaporated. His hands, which had been shaking, steadied themselves. He knew that the absence of the shields was no guarantee of victory, but he relished the idea of meeting the aliens in a fair fight. A moment before he whipped his Tornado into a sharp turn, he spoke calmly to the others. "You heard the man, ladies and gentlemen. It's party time."

As the international pilots hurried to defend Khalid and his besieged cohort, there was a flash of green light in the distance and cheering on the airwaves. One of the jets had scored the first kill against an alien attacker.

"Bloody amazing!" said Tye. Hearing that the shields were down was one thing, but actually seeing one of the invincible aliens bite the dust was quite another. Suddenly the pilots were like a pack of wolves with the taste of blood in their mouths. They jammed their controls forward and rocketed toward the conflict.

"They're on our tails," Khalid yelled. "Help us!"

"Fly directly into the sun!" Reg shouted. "We're headed straight toward you."

"Where are you? I can't see you!"

"That's the point, Khalid. You can't see us, and, hopefully, neither can they. When I give the order, I want you and your boys to break into a vertical climb. Straight up, you got that?"

The F-15 Eagle flying just behind Khalid's was vaporized by one of the alien pulse blasts. "Yes, yes, I understand. But hurry!" Khalid's group continued to fly blind, weaving and jigging, as the alien contingent behind picked off one after another of them.

"Almost... almost," Reg repeated calmly. Then, when the nose of his plane was less than a mile from Khalid's, he gave the order.

"STRAIGHT UP! NOW!"

Dogged pursuers, the alien ships followed the Saudis upward, losing speed and exposing their undersides as they did so. Without realizing it, they'd lined themselves up like ducks at a shooting gallery. They never saw the international pilots coming. In a matter of seconds, more than half of the alien column was destroyed. A flash of jade green light accompanied each kill.

"Go in groups," Miriyam shouted. "Hunt them down."

It was good advice, but Reg knew he was good enough to be a group of one. After assigning Tye and Sutton to chase down one of the nearest alien craft, he set his sights on another. He quickly tucked himself behind the targeted ship and began angling for a proper shot. The alien pilot ignored him, turning to attack a pair of Iraqis. It was obvious to Reg that whoever—or whatever—was flying the attacker, no adjustments in tactics were being made to compensate for the loss of the shields.

"Not much of a thinker, I see," said Reg, launching a Skyflash missile. It struck the alien ship squarely, blowing it to jade-green smithereens. It was the precise shade of green that Reg had seen cast on Jerusalem moments before the city was destroyed. Must have something to do with their energy source, he noted.

All around him, other pilots were bringing down alien ships. He heard the Ethiopian, Remi, shout, "Now go back to hell where you came from," a second before he destroyed the alien he was chasing. When Miriyam and Yossi fired simultaneously at the ships they were following, two more green flashes lit up the sky.

"And Israel scores two!" Yossi shouted like the announcer at a soccer game.

"Saudi pilot," Edward warned, "you have an enemy to port."

Reg looked above him and saw that Khalid was in trouble again. He responded at once, climbing to put himself in position. But before he arrived, Khalid had executed a wing-over roll, doubled back on his enemy, and destroyed him.

In his steady, workhorse way, Sutton was destroying alien ships and keeping Tye out of harm's way. There was nothing spectacular or daring in the way he operated his plane, but his pursuits were patient and relentless. Rather than use up his supply of missiles, he was doing all his damage with the Tornado's 27mm cannons. He didn't call out his kills as many of the others were doing, choosing instead to go quietly about his business.

Tye, on the other hand, a mechanic who had never fired a missile before, began celebrating loudly after one of his missiles connected with an enemy target. It didn't matter to him that he'd used up nearly all his ammunition, or that the attacker he'd destroyed wasn't the one he'd been aiming at. Just killing one of the bastards was enough. He went on whooping and cheering until Reg reminded him that the battle was only beginning.

In Hebrew, Farsi, Turkish, English, Amharic, Yoruba, and several dialects of Arabic, the pilots cursed and taunted their nonhuman enemies. As the last few alien ships were being hunted down, Reg took a moment to watch the other pilots at work. One of the Iraqi pilots, he noticed, was especially effective, gunning down one attacker after another.

"This one is the bread!" the Iraqi yelled as he dropped his MiG-29 behind his next target.

"I think you mean toast," Tye corrected him.

"Yes, the toast!" the boyish-sounding Iraqi agreed as he unleashed a volley of armor-piercing shells. "This one is the TOAST!" The large-caliber bullets ate away at the attacker's shell until it exploded into a messy green blur of debris.

Once the last attacker had been shot down, the group turned its attention back to the city destroyer, which was moving inexorably forward, undeterred by the loss of its shields. It had already swallowed Usfan in its shadow and was closing in on Mecca. If the ship could not be shot down, or driven away from the city very quickly, hundreds of thousands of lives would be lost, and one of the earth's most important cities would be obliterated.

As Reg led the way toward the front end of the city-sized craft, he watched the bombing attacks already under way.

A group of MiGs was circling the crown of the destroyer's domed roof completely unopposed, strafing and bombing at will. Their missiles gouged deep craters into the armored surface, but it was not nearly enough. The ship was so large that the damage was inconsequential.

As Reg studied the problem, some of the pilots in his group raced ahead and fired a salvo of missiles. They struck squarely and caused spectacular explosions, but the problem was the same. The exterior shell was not penetrated, and the destroyer continued to move calmly forward as placidly as a bull moves through a swarm of flies. It only decelerated when its prow approached the northern outskirts of Mecca and began to seal off the sky over the crowded city.

"It's impossible," Sutton announced with characteristic pessimism. "We just don't have the firepower."

"He's right. At this rate, it'll take us a week to knock this thing down."

"Only a few minutes until it fires on the city. We've got to do something quickly."

"Let's use everything we've got, then go and find some more weapons."

"Where are we going to find them?" Miriyam asked. "All the bases are destroyed. I've only got two Sidewinders and a Python left."

Remi, the Ethiopian pilot, suggested using the last of their armaments against the skyscraper-like tower. "It looks like a control tower," he pointed out. "If we can damage it, they won't be able to steer. Even if they fire on Mecca, maybe they won't be able to go on to the next city."

Behind Reg, the team raced toward the leading edge of the megasaucer and watched its seventeen-mile-wide shadow darken the city below. There was bad news waiting for them when they arrived. Remi's idea, although logical, wasn't working. A group of Egyptian and Sudanese jets were skirmishing with a swarm of the scarablike attackers, and firing on the tower without effect. The structure, anchored into a wide dimple in the ship's surface, was made of a material that absorbed the missiles' impact without breaking apart.

"Scratch that bright idea off the list," Sutton droned. "Now what are we supposed to do?"

No one answered. The group seemed to be at a loss.

But Reg had an idea, one that had been brewing ever since the battle above Jerusalem. He craned his neck back and studied the polished face of the jet-black tower. He noted that the large portal that allowed the alien attackers to pass in and out of the ship was still open. *What would happen*, he wondered, *if I ducked inside?* Since his Tornado obeyed a different set of aerodynamic principles than the attackers, which could come to a dead stop and still remain airborne, he could guess the most likely outcome: He would merely splatter himself against an internal wall or other immovable object. But the destroyer was now completely covering the city below, and unless something was done quickly to disrupt the alien attack, hundreds of thousands of lives would be lost.

As the other pilots in his group discussed their next move, Reg tuned them out and kept his eyes on the portal, wondering if he should take the risk of flying into the alien ship. The question wasn't whether he would survive— that seemed unlikely—but whether he'd accomplish anything. In a way, it was the same question he'd been asking himself ever since the Gulf War. He'd spent the last several years in Saudi Arabia trying to work off the insurmountable debt he owed to the people of the area. Was the kamikaze mission he was contemplating a way of settling the score?

Shouting from the other pilots snapped him back into the present. The clicking noise had returned to the radio.

"We're getting another message from the Americans," Thomson told them. "It's brief. Hold on a moment while we decode it." Thirty seconds later, Thomson came back onto the airwaves. By that time, the destroyer had come to a dead stop above the city, centered over the Great Mosque. "Good news, excellent news. Finally, we have—"

"WHAT DOES IT SAY?"

"Right. Sorry about that. It says: Small missile strike against firing cone at center bottom causes chain-reaction explosion. Guarantees total kill."

"A total kill, you say?"

"That's what it says here," Thomson assured them. "'Guarantees total kill.'"

Yossi cracked a joke. "And we get our money back if we're not one-hundred-percent completely satisfied, right?"

After a last glance at the open portal, Reg pointed the nose of his jet at the ground. "Follow me," he called to the others. "Let's go find that firing cone."

As the group shed altitude and took a look at the underside of the destroyer, they realized that reaching the center would be no easy task. More than a hundred of the surviving alien fighters had massed themselves in the deep shadows and were flying in agitated circles, firing their pulse cannons down at the city. At the same time, the people of Mecca had no intention of going down without a fight. They'd installed dozens of surface-to-air missile stations and were using them with impunity. Their rockets flew straight up and smashed into the ship's hard underbelly.

As they patrolled the perimeter of the gigantic ship and surveyed the scene, a set of enormous doors at the center of the ship began to retract. Soon, all of Mecca was bathed in the resplendent green light that spilled out of the destroyer's interior.

"Listen up," Reg said. "We've going to play follow the leader, and we've only got one chance to do it right. We'll go in single file, fast and tight, nose to tail. I'll take the point and keep the path clear until I'm out of ammunition. After that, Miriyam moves to the front. When she's empty, you back there in the second Iraqi plane, what's your name?"

"Mohammed."

"I've been watching you. Nice shooting back there. Do you have any missiles left?"

"Yes, of course. I hate to waste them."

"Excellent. You're up third. The rest of you save your missiles for the target."

"And then?" someone asked.

"If we're not dead by then, we'll think of something. Now fall in behind me," he called, before leading them under the edge of the destroyer.

Even though the sun was beginning to set, the sudden transition from the light of the open sky to the oppressive gloom below the ship meant the pilots had to fly blind until their eyes adjusted. Maintaining his speed, Reg focused on the lowering hatch doors and the green light that showed between them. Entering the airspace under the destroyer was like flying into an enormous round room with no walls to hold up the ceiling. Reg stayed as high as he dared, only two hundred feet below the underside of the ship, which was studded with rectangular structures that looked like hanging storage containers. These large, boxlike structures were arranged in precise rows, and the gaps between them created a dizzying optical illusion of slow-motion movement as the jets raced past. Adding to the disorientation was the fact that the main source of light was the reflected green glare coming from the city below. This created the sensation of flying upside down over a dark industrial landscape.

Fighting through his own confusion, Reg steered his group gently away from oncoming bands of attackers, doing his best to conserve his weaponry. After destroying a handful of the attackers, he shouted, "I'm out! Miriyam, take over."

The Israeli captain took a different approach. Instead of avoiding confrontations with the enemy planes, she steamrollered straight ahead and blasted everything that stood in her path. Very soon, the last of her missiles was spent, and she called for Mohammed to take over.

Just then, a surface-to-air missile streaked upward and demolished the Iraqi MiG carrying the last of Mohammed's fellow countrymen. The young pilot took over the point position, but was clearly unnerved. He began veering off course, leading the team off course.

"Follow the street!" Reg coached, and it was obvious to everyone what he meant. The wide paths between the outcropping buildings above them formed wide, straight "boulevards" that ran from the edges of the ship to its center. Although the firing cone and the hanging doors were still miles away, the "street" was directly above and provided a clearly marked path to their destination.

Just as Mohammed regained his bearings, trouble came streaking toward him in the form of an alien attack squadron. A tightly clustered group of at least forty fighters was headed directly toward them. Mohammed hesitated for a moment, stricken with indecision. By the time he activated his missiles and sent them flying, he knew it was too late for the pilots behind him to fan out and try to slip past the onrushing enemy squadron. All nine of the missiles he'd fired connected with their targets, but the rest of the alien force continued toward him, firing their pulse cannons as they came. The balls of condensed energy sliced wildly through the air, narrowly missing Mohammed's MiG. Acting on instinct, the young Iraqi shouted out an order to the rest of the crew.

"UP! UP! Pull up!"

Since they were already skimming the underside of the

city destroyer, the other pilots couldn't believe what they were hearing.

"There's no more room," yelled Sutton, who was flying in the second slot. "We're up as far as we can go."

But when Mohammed lifted away, giving him a clear look at the aliens bearing down on them, Sutton jerked back on his controls and followed the Iraqi pilot upward. One by one, the rest of the team quickly followed suit.

Besieged by a hailstorm of pulse blasts, and moving at close to Mach speed, Mohammed led them higher and higher until they were flying down the center of one of the so-called streets, which was barely wide enough to accommodate their wingspans. The hanging buildings on either side of them rushed past in a blur, the ceiling was only a few feet from the tops of their cockpit canopies, and more than one pilot was screaming at the top of his lungs. With a razor-thin margin of error, they held their collective breath and concentrated on steering straight down the narrow pathway until the attackers shot past them below.

When they ducked back into the open air, the alien squadron was well out of range, and they appeared to have an unobstructed path to the center of the ship. As the pilots cursed and panted and wiped the sweat from their brows, Reg congratulated Mohammed. "That was a nifty bit of work, lad."

"Nifty?" Tye asked, incredulous. "It was like flying through a shoe box. Remind me never to get into a coach with either one of you two maniacs."

Mohammed stayed in the lead position, steering toward the gap between two of the giant hatch doors. The firing cone, visible beyond them, was now fully extended. In a matter of moments, its destructive power would pulverize Mecca.

"More bad news," Sutton reported. "We've got a bogey ahead and to the left."

Reg peered down and saw that, indeed, an aircraft was streaking upward at a steep angle into their path. But it wasn't an alien attacker. It was a Saudi F-15.

Reg keyed his radio. "Commander Faisal, I thought you'd be halfway to Riyadh by now. Decided to come back and join us?"

"I have come to save my people!" he shouted back. Unfortunately, Faisal wasn't traveling alone. He had picked up one of the alien attackers, and it was closing behind him.

"You've got company," Reg told him. "There's an attacker below and behind. Don't bring him up here, we're in position."

"There is no time!" Faisal screamed back. An intense beam of white light was shooting from the tip of the firing cone, fixing itself on one of the tall minarets of the Great Mosque. "They are going to fire!"

Faisal continued on his course, oblivious to both the alien behind him and the fact that his trajectory conflicted with Reg's squadron's. When the other pilots recognized the danger he was putting them into, they shouted at him to lead the attacker away. Faisal jigged and juked as the attacker began to fire its pulse weapon, but maintained his bearing.

"He wants the first shot," Khalid said. "He's going to cut us off."

"I'll take care of this," Reg said, diving out of line. He jammed the controls forward, milking every kilonewton of power from his twin turbofans. When he leveled off, he was right behind Faisal. "Turn off, Faisal!" Reg threatened.

"Shoot him down," one of the pilots urged.

Reg was sorely tempted. He wasn't actually out of missiles. He was still holding a Skyflash under his left wing, just in case. He sighted on Faisal's F-15 and wrapped his hand tight around the grip trigger. But instead of downing the treacherous Saudi commander, he abruptly cut the fuel supply to his engines. Then he accelerated again as the alien fighter moved ahead of him. In a few seconds, he had positioned himself, locked on, and fired. The alien ship blew apart in a bright green flash.

Faisal jostled his way to the front of the line. To avoid a collision, Mohammed was forced to swing away only seconds before reaching the giant hatch doors. In order to shoot the gap and save himself, Mohammed swerved back toward the group, forcing everyone to decelerate. By the time they came into the clearing around the firing cone, Faisal's missiles were already streaking away.

"Fire! Fire everything!" Reg yelled.

Scores of missiles shot toward the glittering weapon. Faisal's AMRAAMs got there first and blew two large holes into the massive green structure. Debris rained into the sky. A moment later, when the other missiles struck, a chain reaction began to travel up the firing cone and into the body of the destroyer, just as the American communiqué had promised.

Reg looked up into the glowing recess of the ship. A massive open chamber surrounded the dangling gun tower. And through the blaze of the explosions, he caught a momentary glimpse of the destroyer's interior: The central chamber was a single room approximately three miles across, with towering vertical walls. Hundreds more of the attacker ships were moored in clusters around the periphery. It looked like the inside of a high-tech beehive.

"It's starting to blow; let's get out of here!"

The quick series of muffled explosions that traveled up the pylon-shaped firing cone were giving way to stronger and stronger blasts. Shrapnel and smoke filled the air.

As the pilots turned and raced to get out from under the destroyer, there was a brief, dizzying moment when their planes appeared to lose speed and come to a dead stop. But it was only another optical illusion, caused when the destroyer above them began to move. With astonishing power, the megaship accelerated to high speed in only a matter of seconds. It quickly outpaced the jets, leaving them behind as it streaked away to the southeast. Just as it began to lift away, a massive explosion ripped through the top of the dome like a shotgun blast blowing through the top of a skull. It hobbled forward at reduced speed until an even larger explosion tore away its entire left side. Still moving, it began to list and sink toward the desert floor.

Cheering and screaming, the surviving pilots chased it out over the desert, emptying their guns and using the last of their missiles against the dying giant. Exploding from within, it lost momentum and finally plunged toward the earth. It bellied out on a rocky plateau, bounced once into the air, then slid for several miles before coming to rest in a huge cloud of dust.

Through it all, Reg maintained his calm, professional demeanor. As a wild celebration broke out in the air around him, he climbed to a higher altitude and scanned the darkening horizon. He checked his gauges and flipped through the various radio frequencies as if he were just finishing up another, day at the office. He couldn't help taking a dim view of the disorderly air show going on below him. It went against every habit he had developed during his years as a teacher. Every channel was filled with deafening, whooping cries of victory. Ecstatic pilots flew barrel rolls and loop-the-loops over the burning wreckage, firing their guns recklessly as they went. Clenched fists pounded out their excitement on the walls and canopies of a hundred cockpits.

Reg tried to ignore them. He tried to remain calm. He fought against the urge to join the celebration for as long as he possibly could. But the revelry was infectious, and soon he was grinning from ear to ear. Then he found himself pumping his fist in the air.

"We did it!" he shouted. "I can't believe it. We beat the bloody bastards!"

The giddy realization that they'd done the impossible, that they'd saved the planet from these seemingly invincible foes, surged through him all at once, and he found himself shouting and laughing along with the others. He got on the radio and added his voice to the sea of noise. He roared and laughed. He shouted until his throat was hoarse and his eyes were filled with tears, ecstatic that he was victorious and alive.

Order began to restore itself when Faisal began calling out a message in an enthusiastic tone of voice. He shouted happily back and forth in Arabic with some of the other pilots. Reg could tell he was delivering instructions of some sort, but the only thing he could understand was the name of a city—At-Ta'if. By the time he found Khalid on the radio, Faisal was long gone.

"He says he's already spoken to the king," Khalid translated over the noise of the celebration. "We're directed to land at At-Ta'if because the king wants to congratulate all of us personally. There's going to be a party."

"I should bloody well hope so," said someone with a Londoner's accent.

"Is that you, Tye?" Reg asked. "I thought you'd be in Paradise with those seventy virgins by now."

"Seventy-two, actually. No, not yet, Major. Maybe I've got nine lives. What say we get out of here and go see about this party with the king?"

"You go ahead. I'm going to wait for the smoke to clear so I can take another look at the ship, just to make sure. Did Sutton make it?"

"Hate to disappoint you, Major, but yes, I did," Sutton said.

"Glad to hear it. You two follow the others to At-Ta'if and warm things up for me."

They pulled away, and Reg patrolled the sky, waiting for the evening winds to clear the dust and smoke away from the downed destroyer: He wasn't alone. Twenty or thirty other pilots were also biding their time, flying laps around the crash site until they could inspect the kill. Khalid was one of them. He sounded hesitant and distracted over the radio, not like he'd just helped win a stunning victory.

"Khalid," Reg said, "I thought you'd be off meeting the king by now. What's the matter?"

"I'm worried about Faisal," he explained. He reminded Reg that an hour before he'd disobeyed orders and deserted his squad during an attack. Even though it proved to be the right move, he didn't know how Faisal would react.

"If Faisal's as shrewd as I think he is," Reg said, "he won't want an investigation. He wasted the lives of a whole squadron. Besides, he got what he wanted. Mecca wasn't destroyed, and now he'll probably run around telling everyone that he's personally responsible for saving it." Reg chuckled at the idea. Khalid, who knew Faisal better, didn't.

Reg thought about it for a minute and came up with an idea. He radioed Thomson, still at the tent in the Empty Quarter. Earlier, the colonel had mentioned that he was tape-recording their transmissions. "Thomson, do you think you can get me a copy of that tape?"

"I'm not sure," he answered. "The tape doesn't belong to me, and the equipment out here isn't exactly state-of-the-art, but I can try. Any particular part of it?"

"The whole thing. And, Colonel, it's important. See what you can do."

"No promises, Cummins. I'll see you at At-Ta'if in a couple of hours. Word is that the Saudis have some planes coming to pick us up. We're all a bunch of bloody heroes, mate."

"Roger. See you there."

The air over the destroyer began to clear. The sun had already extinguished itself in the Red Sea, but in the last lingering light of day, Reg and the others saw what was left of the ship. To their dismay, they noticed that roughly a quarter of it was still intact. When it hit the ground, the whole vehicle had splintered, cracked into millions of pieces the same way a car's windshield breaks during a collision. Like tempered glass, it sagged in places but still retained some structural integrity.

Yossi was among the circling pilots. "Hey, I might want my money back on that guarantee," he said in his thick accent. "Does that look like a total kill to you?"

"It looks fairly dead from my angle," Reg countered, "and it looks like it's burning inside. I wouldn't worry about it. The impact of the crash probably killed anything that wasn't nailed to the walls."

"Probably you're right."

Both of them were thinking the same thing: Probably wasn't good enough. They made a couple of additional passes, scanning for signs of movement, until it was too dark to see much of anything. Then they flew off to join the rest of the pilots at At-Ta'if.

Inside the ship, large doors were rolling closed to contain the spread of what the aliens hated most: fire.

6

VICTORY PARTY

The airfield at At-Ta'if served both civilian and military purposes. The swarm of alien attack planes that had pounded the place with bursts from their energy cannons didn't discriminate between the two. Nearly every building at the facility had been destroyed. In the absence of electrical power, ground crews had lined the only undamaged runway with pots of kerosene and set them ablaze to guide the victorious pilots to the ground.

Reg, Yossi, and Khalid were among the last to land. When they taxied up to the damaged main hangars, there was a cheering crowd waiting to greet them. Their nationality made no difference to these people. The only thing that mattered was that the pilots had saved them from the horrible, ghastly invaders. The civilians rushed in to surround the planes, cheering and shaking their fists in victory. A contingent of Saudi soldiers pushed their way through the crowd and led the pilots to a fleet of waiting limousines.

"Welcome to being heroes, gents." Tye was standing in one of the limos, his head and torso poking through the sunroof. He towered above the roof of the car like a sunburned giraffe. "There's a party in our honor at the royal family's compound. Hop in."

They left the airfield and sped east through one of the finest suburbs of At-Ta'if, Tye still hanging out the sunroof. But the trip wasn't all cheering and smiles. Parts of the city had been hit hard by pulse blasts. They drove past working-class Saudis who were retrieving their possessions from smoldering buildings. In one spot, bodies were laid out on a sidewalk, surrounded by mourners. When the drivers slowed to steer around the pedestrians, Reg looked out his window and made eye contact with an older, unveiled woman. She was cradling a dead boy in her arms and wailing with grief. But as the limousine passed, she did a remarkable thing: She pumped her fist in the air and let out a ululating war cry in honor of the victorious pilots. Beneath the surface of their new riches and creature comforts, Reg realized that Fadeela had been right: The Saudis were still a fierce, desert people.

A short time later, they arrived at their destination, the royal family's summer palace, and entered a world of nearly unimaginable opulence. Behind the heavily guarded gates, a broad swath of manicured lawn rolled up a gentle slope toward a magnificent white mansion. It was an architectural fantasy, part storybook European castle, part Arabian palace. A pair of domed minarets stood on either side of the ornately tiled building. The winding driveway led them beneath canopies of palm trees and ferns. All the doors and windows of the great house had been thrown open, revealing that a lavish party was under way inside. Guests spilled out onto the tiled verandas and balconies overlooking the gardens.

Their limousine driver steered away from the main house and took the sweaty pilots to the compound's Olympic-sized swimming pool. They showered in the cabanas and changed into the Arab-style clothing provided for them. The ankle-length shirts, called *thobes,* fit Yossi and Reg comfortably, but Tye's was a full six inches too short. They marched up the hill to join the gathering.

"I feel like I'm wearing a dress," Reg complained.

"How do you think I feel," Tye said, his hairy, freckled shins poking out below his hemline.

"Don't worry. Both of you look very beautiful and

sexy," Yossi joked without smiling. Then, looking around him, he said, "To have a garden like this is every Arab's dream."

The grounds were lush beyond reason. There was a greenhouse full of orchids. Pomegranate and citrus trees grew beside birds-of-paradise, date palms, and many other exotic plants. There were peacock blue tiles lining a circular fountain and actual peacocks wandering the lawn. Mercedes-Benzes and Rolls-Royces were parked along the driveway, and a group of well-heeled Saudis stood admiring an elaborate, man-made waterfall. Off in the distance was another building that looked like a French château. As the three men began climbing the steps to the party, waiters rushed toward them to offer golden caviar and sweet tea.

"I can't believe this place," Reg remarked, as they crossed the patio.

"What's the good of owning a country if you don't have a nice house or two," deadpanned Yossi.

The elaborate main doors of the house opened onto a ballroom. Well-dressed men, and Saudi women with sheer veils concealing their diamond necklaces mixed with soldiers and pilots in loud conversation. There were more than two hundred people inside, but the room was large enough to accommodate twice that number.

When they saw Reg enter, many of the pilots broke off their conversations and came over to greet him. They were all heroes to the world, and Reg was a hero to them. One by one, they embraced him, some of them with tears in their eyes. Khalid was among them.

With a big grin on his face, Reg put an arm around his old friend.

"We made it. We actually did it."

"It was a piece of pie. I mean *cake*. It was a piece of cake."

The two of them laughed. Khalid stepped back and

admired his friend's new wardrobe. "You look good in Saudi fashion, Teacher. It suits you. But on you," he said, turning to Tye, "it looks like a dress."

A hyperkinetic American woman, wearing a wireless headset, introduced herself to Reg as Mrs. Roeder. Blinking rapidly, she explained that she and her husband were "event coordinators for the House of Saud." She pointed out Mr. Roeder, a man in a suit and tie, who was standing halfway up a staircase on the far side of the room. He nodded back. She took Reg by the arm and began leading him across the room. "The scuttlebutt is that you sort of took charge of the non-Saudi forces during the air battle today and helped Commander Faisal out," she said.

"Helped him out?" Reg asked with an incredulous glance. "I suppose that's one way of putting it."

"Well, the king heard about it, and he's very anxious to meet you." She glanced up at the balcony overlooking the party. A grinning elderly man in a white robe leaned over the balustrade and beckoned them upstairs. Reg recognized him immediately, having seen his photograph hundreds of times. It was Ibrahim al-Saud, the king of Saudi Arabia. Faisal was standing right behind him.

As Mrs. Roeder led them up the stairs, Khalid put a hand on Reg's shoulder.

"Have you heard from Thomson? Did he get the tape recording?"

"He'll be here soon," Reg assured him, as Mrs. Roeder tugged at his arm. "Nothing to worry about."

"I suppose I should say thank you," the American woman said, speaking a mile a minute. "We all should. You guys were incredibly brave up there today."

"All in a day's work," Reg joked.

"I mean, what do you say to a bunch of guys who just saved your life? Thanks, right?" Just as quickly, she was on to another subject. "Let me tell you something.

It wasn't easy pulling this party together. Everything is such a mess out there. It's absolutely crazy. *You* try getting fresh lettuce in the middle of an alien attack. But the king really wanted to express his appreciation so we're doing the best we can." She was distracted by a message coming through her earpiece and stopped to listen.

"This one?" she asked, pointing toward Khalid. "Got it." With a professionally ingratiating smile, she put her hand on Khalid's shoulder.

"Sir, they're asking that you not come upstairs. They'll talk to you later. Would you mind?"

It looked like Faisal might make trouble for Khalid after all. Maybe for Reg as well, since he'd loudly urged Khalid to disobey the orders to attack. The two men exchanged a tense look before Reg continued up the stairs.

"I'll put in a good word for you," he said.

Once he was above the crowd, Reg scanned the partygoers, looking for Thomson. The colonel's diplomatic skills would've come in very handy right about then, but he was nowhere to be seen. Instead, Reg's eyes fell on a tall, veiled woman standing near the doors. Despite her coverings, he knew instantly that it was Fadeela. Standing with a group of women, she raised her glass ever so slightly in a clandestine toast. Reg smiled conspiratorially as he reached the top of the stairs.

"Your Majesty, may I present Major Cummins of the British Royal Air Force."

Reg had never met a king before and didn't know what he was supposed to do. After running his fingers through his hair, he did the same thing he would have done upon meeting the queen of England. He knelt down and bowed his head.

The king's broad grin erupted into a belly laugh. When Reg looked up, everyone around him was laughing, too. Mrs. Roeder joined Reg at floor level and blinked.

"There's really no need for that, Major. In this country, people consider the king their equal. A simple handshake would be appropriate."

Chagrined, Reg got to his feet. Obviously there was no harm done because the king put his arm around Reg like he was part of the family and introduced him to eight or ten of his brothers, nephews, and advisors. The patriarch of the al-Saud clan was well into his seventies, a tall thin man who was a little unsteady on his feet but mentally very sharp. He offered Reg a chair.

"Commander Faisal informs me," the king began with a twinkle in his eye, "that you were a great hero today. That you rallied the foreign forces on our soil and led them capably in the battle."

"I did what I could," Reg replied, shooting a glance at Faisal.

"No, no. It is not a time for false modesty. If Faisal tells me it is so, it is so. And he tells me that without you, our Holy City would have come to ruin. For this we can never thank you properly. We al-Sauds are the custodians of Mecca, and it is a responsibility we take very seriously. You have given us a very great gift in helping to save Mecca from these godless invaders, and it is my plan to reward you handsomely."

Reg's ears perked up. When the king of Saudi Arabia, one of the wealthiest men in the world, used the words "reward you handsomely," he wasn't talking about a gold watch and a weekend in Bahrain.

"There is no need to decide now. Think about it for a day or two and decide what you would like to have. If it is within our power, it shall be done."

Reg surprised himself by immediately glancing toward Fadeela. "That's very generous. I'll give it some thought," he said. "Can I ask why you didn't want to see Khalid Yamani? He deserves as much thanks as I do."

The expression on the old man's face instantly soured. "Kamak Yamani has long been a valuable and beloved servant of ours. He has done much to enrich the people of our country, but his son, Khalid, has brought him nothing but shame and grief. Faisal has told me Khalid was a student of yours."

"That's right," Reg said. "He's also a friend."

"I see," said King Ibrahim, with obvious displeasure. But my offer to you is still good. You will be rewarded for your bravery just as Khalid Yamani will be punished for his cowardice."

"Cowardice?" Without meaning to, Reg scoffed at the king's words. "Without Khalid we might not have succeeded today. He should get as much credit as anyone. He showed more courage than some of your other pilots." Again, Reg glanced pointedly at Faisal.

The king's eyebrows arched, and his face iced over. He exchanged a few words with Faisal before turning back to Reg, explaining a little history to him in a chilly tone.

"I am told you were a pilot during the Gulf War and that you made a rather serious and costly mistake, is this right?"

"Yes, sir," Reg admitted, suddenly quieter. Every high-ranking Saudi knew about Reg's "mistake."

"In that same war, your friend Khalid Yamani also made a very grave mistake. Yours was an error of judgment made under the stress of battle. And I understand your superiors have forgiven you." That was partially true. "But Lieutenant Yamani's error was made in calmness. His heart, I am afraid, is corrupted with the poison of"—he turned to one of his assistants for a translation—"poisoned with malice and jealousy."

Faisal leaned forward and explained. "He accused me of lying and of cowardice. He said I was not the one who repulsed the attack of the Iraqi national guard. It was a serious matter to do so," he said in a threatening way that implied Reg would be wise not to make the same mistake. "But, because of the great standing and reputation of his father, he was spared from the punishment he deserved. Today he ran from the battle and disobeyed my orders. This time there can be no mercy."

"Mercy? Mercy?" Reg asked, getting visibly angry. "Why should he need your mercy?" Mrs. Roeder quickly put a firm hand on Reg's shoulder to remind him where he was, but it didn't do much good. He yelled past the king at Faisal. "You ordered those men to their deaths when you could have waited. Khalid was right to disobey that order. I would have done the same thing."

Faisal turned to the king. "You see, even the foreign pilots clearly understood my orders."

Without meaning to, Reg had further incriminated Khalid.

The king stood up to show that the interview was over.

"Tonight is a time for celebrating. We are here to rejoice in our victory. We will handle this unpleasant business at a future time. I am sorry to have detained you for such a long while, I'm certain you have friends and comrades you wish to greet more than a tiresome old man. Mr. and Mrs. Roeder, please invite Major Cummins to the events tomorrow and make sure he has everything he needs." He smiled warmly and clasped Reg's hands in his own. "Once again, we thank you most humbly."

Reg stood up, but wasn't quite ready for this royal audience to end. He already knew what he wanted as his handsome reward: He wanted Khalid to be fully exonerated. But the Roeders each took one of his elbows and firmly guided him toward the stairs.

"Take a tip?" Mr. Roeder asked. "Don't raise your voice to anyone in the royal family. Doesn't usually work out in your favor."

"Major, if you don't have any plans for tomorrow,

please come out to the spaceship with us," Mrs. Roeder said in one ear.

"The king is heading out there in the morning with a huge entourage," her husband said in the other.

Reg looked surprised. "The spaceship? Aren't you worried about survivors?"

"We're *hoping* for survivors." Mrs. Roeder blinked. "The king wants his picture taken with some of them. You know, standing there with his boot on their necks and his sword raised in the air. Something to boost morale while the country's getting back on its feet."

"But more importantly," Mr. Roeder went on, "how are we going to learn about them if there aren't any survivors. We've *got to* make these suckers talk. Find out where they came from and why they did this to us."

"Exactly. The king has already called some translation experts in from Switzerland."

"They're mathematicians and biologists mainly," Mr. Roeder said, glancing at his watch. "People who might be able to figure out how to communicate with the aliens."

"Not that the Saudis don't know how to interrogate a prisoner, you understand, but this is a unique situation. They're arriving tonight."

"I hope you'll come tomorrow. There's going to be film crews, foreign ambassadors, and lots of the royals. It should be interesting. A real historic-moment type of situation."

"Also, that would be the perfect time to ask for your reward from the king, so we could get pictures of the whole thing. It'd save us from having to set up a separate ceremony."

"Well, it was sure nice to meet you. All you pilots are being housed in the guest quarters on the far side of the pool. Looks like a French château, you can't miss it. Very luxurious. You'll love it." Then they hurried away to take care of other business.

Reg searched the party, looking for Khalid and

Thomson. If the colonel had the tape, it would be enough to make Faisal back off. It contained the proof of his cowardice during the dogfight.

Reg found Tye instead and enlisted his help. The two of them searched the extensive grounds of the royal compound. As they hunted through the gardens, checking the various gazebos and greenhouses, they passed a large gaggle of strolling Saudi women.

"Babe alert," Tye said out of the side of his mouth. "Check out those sexy veils!" But as they passed by, it was the women who did the checking out. The black-gowned figures surrounded the men, sizing them up, and offering opinions on their manly attributes.

"How handsome this one is."

"I like the other one. Cute, la?"

"Not enough muscle. I think he will blow away in a strong breeze."

One of them stepped forward and, although it was dark, Reg knew who it was beneath the dark headcloth. She complimented him.

"He is handsome, brave, and unafraid of women. Why don't we have more Saudi men like this one?"

When Reg took her by the arm and pulled her aside, the other women gasped at his forwardness.

"Major Cummins," Fadeela protested, "every garden has a thousand eyes. This is not a safe place for us to talk."

"Listen, Fadeela, I've got something important to tell you." He paused to consider how he should break the news. It was just long enough to give her the wrong idea.

"There is a rumor," she said, "that the king will reward you with whatever your heart desires. If you are going to ask my advice about choosing a Saudi bride, I can recommend a very lovely and talented young woman."

"That's not it," he broke in. "Khalid's in trouble. Serious trouble, I think."

"What has he done now?" she asked, suddenly serious.

"Today, in the air, Faisal ordered his men to attack the destroyer before the shields came down. It was a stupid order, and all the men who obeyed it are dead now. Your brother broke away with a few others. I think it was common sense, but the king is calling it treason. He also mentioned that Khalid did something like this before, that he crossed Faisal during the Gulf War."

"Where is my brother now?"

"We've looked everywhere for him. I think he might have run off somewhere."

"Faisal will be the ruin of my family yet! He is more treacherous than the aliens who tried to destroy us!" She sat down on a garden bench and put her head in her hands.

"What happened before?"

"According to my brother, Faisal ordered an attack on a few Iraqi jets flying inside their own borders. They shot the planes down and then flew home, where Faisal created an elaborate story about facing down a large group of bombers. It was all designed to turn him into a hero. When Khalid went to his superiors, he was told to keep his mouth shut so he wouldn't embarrass the Saudi army. It was my brother's word against Faisal's and that of his henchmen. I must go and find my father. He will be forced to bargain with this evil man for my brother's amnesty."

"I may be able to help," Reg said.

"This is a Saudi matter now," Fadeela said. "No outsiders will be allowed to speak at the trial."

"I won't need to speak. I can give Khalid something to use against Faisal." Then he told her about the recording.

"Not only is he handsome and brave and unafraid of women, he is very clever as well."

Just then, a messenger arrived. He was one of Fadeela's nephews, who spoke to her urgently in Arabic.

"They've arrested Khalid at the airport," she told Reg.

"He was trying to escape in his plane. They're bringing him back to stand trial tonight. The king is very angry." As she and her friends hurried away toward the palace, she turned and called back to Reg. "Please bring us the recording. My brother's life may depend on it."

"Did you see that?" Tye asked when the women had gone. "I was only about sixty-five virgins short of paradise."

"Let's go."

"Go where?"

"Back to the airfield. We've got to find Thomson."

Standing at the edge of the runway, they watched as the two C-130s landed, then kept careful eyes on the gangplanks as the passengers disembarked to the cheers of the crowd. It was past midnight, and the crowds were thinning, but there were still a lot of people out there. Thomson was nowhere to be seen. Reg approached a man with a familiar face, the burly Saudi captain who had treated them so roughly the day before. Reg was a little apprehensive about talking to him again, and was surprised when the big man turned to him with a smile and lifted him off the ground in a bear hug. When asked if he'd seen Thomson, the captain looked around him, surprised that the British lieutenant colonel wasn't among the disembarking passengers.

"Everyone wants to find this little man," he said.

"Who else?" Reg asked.

"I don't know. Some soldiers who arrived with the transport planes," he said. "They were looking everywhere for him."

"Some of Faisal's men?"

The captain didn't know.

"Are you thinking what I'm thinking?" Tye asked. "That Faisal's covering his trail?" Reg didn't answer, but it certainly looked that way.

By the time they drove back to the palace, Khalid's trial

was almost over. It was being held in the king's quarters on the second floor of the palace. Guards had been posted at the bottom of the main stairway to ensure privacy. Nevertheless, a steady stream of soldiers and members of the royal family passed back and forth through the cordon, delivering news to those waiting on the main floor. Most of the guests, including the pilots, had gone off to bed or to more private parties. A somber mood had settled over the fifty or so people who were still there.

One of the Saudi royal princes approached Tye and Reg, eager to share what he knew.

"That fool Khalid Yamani told them everything. He should have remained, humble and silent and begged for mercy. But instead he became angry and accused Faisal of stupidity and cowardice. Now they will be harder on him."

"How hard?"

"Usually these things are settled with money, and the Yamanis are rich," the prince said, "but they were lenient with Khalid the last time. This time the penalty will almost certainly be death."

Reg tried to persuade the guards at the base of the stairs that he had important evidence to present at the trial, but they wouldn't allow him to pass. Frustrated with his helplessness, he spotted Mrs. Roeder pacing the balcony, talking into her headset. He caught her attention, and she signaled she'd be right there. In the meantime, Fadeela arrived, escorted by her nephew and a few of her veiled friends.

"Major Cummins, you are just in time, thanks be to Allah. Where is the tape?"

"The man who made the tape wasn't on the plane back from the Empty Quarter. I'm still looking for him. I'm sorry."

Fadeela made a sound as if she'd been wounded.

"What can I do for you, Major?" asked Mrs. Roeder, coming down the stairs.

He asked her to speak with the king and try to persuade him to delay the sentencing until Thomson could be found. She blinked back at him.

"I'll see what I can do," she said in that breezy, American way that meant he was asking for the impossible.

Fadeela walked past Reg and took hold of Mrs. Roeder's arm, pulling her closer and whispering something to her. Then she removed one of the ruby rings from her finger and pressed it into the American woman's palm. Mrs. Roeder hurried up the stairs into the room where the trial was being held.

"If only we could find Thomson," Reg said to Fadeela with a worried look. "I'm afraid something might have happened to him. Faisal has every reason to want that tape as badly as we do." One of the guards barked a warning, reminding them it was forbidden for them to speak to one another. Reg fixed him with a stare, daring him to enforce the rule. The soldier backed off.

"Major Cummins," Fadeela began quietly, "you have been of great service to my family, and I appreciate everything you have done. I believe you tried your best, and I wish things had turned out differently. Good-bye, and thank you again."

She turned away from him and surrounded herself with her friends. Reg didn't know what she was talking about, but it didn't take long for him to find out. Faisal came striding out of the king's quarters and hurried down the stairs. In spite of their previous encounter, he greeted Reg warmly. He looked relaxed and, as usual, supremely confident.

"What do you know about Thomson?" Reg said in a not-so-friendly tone. "He wasn't on either one of the planes coming back from the camp, and he was seen talking to some of your men before he disappeared."

A look of concern spread across Faisal's face. "Yes, I learned a few moments ago that he was not aboard the evacuation flight. I have been waiting to see him myself. I believe he made an audio record of today's battle, which I would like very much to play for the king. It confirms Khalid Yamani's guilt. I hope nothing has happened to Colonel Thomson. He is an excellent man."

"You know as well as I do that tape would ruin you. How convenient that it didn't show up."

"I'm confident that it will, eventually."

Fadeela came to the stairs and spoke to Faisal in Arabic. Whatever she said put a smile on his face. They said a few things back and forth, none of which Reg could understand, before she lifted her veil away from her face. This shocked the people around them but delighted Faisal, who laughed in recognition. For the second time in as many days, he had seen this beautiful woman's naked face. An elderly man standing nearby was not amused. When he saw the maiden exposing herself in the company of men, he used his walking stick to strike her hard across the back of her legs and yelled at her. Reg grabbed the old man and pulled him roughly away from Fadeela.

"It looks to me like you care too much about this girl, Major," Faisal said.

"I'm a friend of the family," Reg said.

"And soon, a friend of her husband as well," he laughed. "We've just now made an interesting arrangement. If her father agrees, which I believe he will, Fadeela and I will be married tomorrow." Faisal headed back up the stairs, chuckling to himself.

"*Married?* What did you say to him?" Reg demanded.

Fadeela didn't answer him. Instead, she and her friends hurried away.

Down the slope from the royal mansion, past the swimming pool, was a large château, a gaudy replica of a famous French castle in the Dordogne Valley. The sounds of laughter, conversation, and music drifted out its windows and into the warm night air as Reg and Tye came walking somberly down the hill. The news that Fadeela was going to marry Faisal had hit Reg hard, and he was in a mild state of shock.

"That poor girl," Tye said, "trading herself away to save her brother. She must love him. I don't know if my sister would do the same for me."

Reg was hardly listening. In the short time he'd known Fadeela, he'd come to admire her spirit, the way she refused to be dominated. She was tough, beautiful, and ruthlessly honest. The more he learned about her, the more he felt himself drawn to her. It was for her sake that he had found the courage to stand atop a water barrel and convince a hostile group of soldiers they should support the American plan to defeat the city destroyer. But now, only a few hours after deciding that Fadeela's freedom was something worth fighting and dying for, it had been ransomed away.

When they entered through the arched stone doorway of the château, they were greeted by a butler, who returned their military uniforms, laundered and ironed. The man led them down the richly appointed hallways, carrying a lantern to light the way since the electricity was not working. Reg would have been happy to call it a night, but Tye came into his room after getting changed.

"Time to join the party, sir. Throw that uniform on and let's go."

"Not tonight," Reg said. 'Too much on my mind. Besides, I feel like I could sleep for a month."

Tye did not find that answer acceptable. "Listen to yourself. A few hours after you save planet Earth from certain doom, and you're ready to mope around your room and turn in early." Reg looked at his watch. It was past midnight, but Tye wasn't finished. "I know you're unhappy about this business with Fadeela, but that's exactly why I'm not going to let you sit in here by yourself. Let's go. You can sleep when you're dead."

Two minutes later, they were walking down the hallway with candles, poking their heads through open doorways to inspect the parties going on inside the rooms. Behind one of the closed doors, they heard Miriyam's voice. It sounded like there was a party going on inside, so they knocked.

"We are nobody inside of here," laughed a man with an Arab accent.

"Go away," yelled another. "We gave at the office."

"Only pilots allowed inside!"

Tye banged hard on the door. "It's the police. What are you doing in there?" A moment later the door opened a crack and Yossi's face, framed by his thick glasses, poked outside. When he saw who it was, he pulled the door open wide and offered a crisp salute.

"Major Cummins, nice to see you. Come in."

A dozen people were crowded into the candlelit room, laughing and talking. It was a scene that would have been impossible before the invasion. Miriyam, an Israeli, sat on a sofa squashed between Edward, the Palestinian from Jordan, and a gray-haired Syrian pilot with his arm in a sling. Yossi, the Ethiopian Remi, and one of the Iranian pilots crowded around Reg, welcoming him to the party. Everyone was relaxed and in high spirits.

They laughed and talked about what it had been like facing the aliens that afternoon until there was another knock at the door. It was Sutton, returning with a case of warm beer. He was followed inside by Mohammed, the crack Iraqi pilot who had flown so brilliantly. He looked different than Reg expected him to. He was in his early twenties, with a gap-toothed smile and a peach-fuzz mustache.

"Good flying out there today," Reg said when they were introduced. "Where'd you learn to handle a plane like that?"

"Naturally I am a very great pilot," he announced with a big grin. "I am an Iraqi." The other pilots moaned when they heard him bragging and pelted him with pillows from all directions. Mohammed ducked and moved for cover.

"I heard a nasty rumor down in the service kitchen," Sutton said, offering Reg a beer. "Khalid's sister is going to marry that bloody Faisal. If she doesn't, he's going to have Khalid's head lopped off. It's all anyone's talking about. And get this: They're going to have the ceremony out at the crash site tomorrow while the king's having his photo taken with a bunch of dead aliens."

"Let's *hope* they're dead."

"Of course they are. Nothing could have survived that crash."

"It's disgusting," said Miriyam. "The way they treat the women in this country is disgusting. The men take many wives and keep them like prisoners and slaves."

"That is the old way," a Saudi pilot said from across the room. "We young Saudi guys, we only have one wife. It's better than it was." He was trying to be conciliatory, but it didn't stop an argument from starting to boil. Miriyam, the only woman in the room, tried to show the Arab men in the room that they were all sexist pigs. Predictably, they took offense, and the shouting match was on. It was still raging ten minutes later when Reg slipped out the door and returned to his room.

He lay in bed for a while listening to the sounds of the celebration before drifting off into unconsciousness. Less than two hours later, he woke out of nightmare and sat bolt upright in bed. Realizing he wouldn't be able to get back to sleep, he put on his freshly laundered uniform and went downstairs.

The royal servants were busy preparing a lavish breakfast for the pilots in the château's lobby. Buffet tables were piled high with food, but the only thing Reg wanted was black coffee. While he was drinking it, two more pilots came downstairs and joined him: Mohammed—the young Iraqi—and the captain of the Israeli pilots, Miriyam. The three of them sat down on plush couches beneath an original oil painting Reg recognized as the work of the French post-impressionist Bonnard. While the other two chatted groggily, Reg stared out the darkened windows toying to answer a question: The night before, he'd helped win the most important battle humanity had ever fought. So why did he feel so dead inside the next morning?

He stood up, and said, "I'm not waiting any longer. I'm heading out to the ship."

Miriyam and Mohammed looked at one another in surprise, then followed him out the door.

7

"INTO THE SHIP"

Reg, Miriyam, and Mohammed were taken to the At-Ta'if airfield by one of the army of limousine drivers who would transport the royal entourage out to the crash site later that morning. The first people they met upon arriving there were a squad of United Nations Peacekeepers. They were Frenchmen who had come from Somalia to help the Saudis in their "mop-up operation." Their commanding officer, a man named Guillaume, was frustrated with the Saudi ground crews. They said the earliest the Frenchmen could be airlifted out to the downed alien ship would be that afternoon.

"You have many helicopters empty," Guillaume shouted angrily, pointing to a group of H-110s sitting idle near a ruined hangar.

"It cannot be helped," one of the Saudis told him, glancing toward the heavens.

Reg received a very different reception. A handful of the Saudis knew him from Khamis Moushayt, while many others recognized him as one of the pilots who had saved Mecca. They crowded around him, Miriyam, and Mohammed, smiling and shaking hands. There would be no problem arranging a trip out to the ship. Arrangements were made immediately.

When Guillaume and the other Peacekeepers saw what was happening, they were incensed. "You can find a way to bring these tourists, but not for us?"

Reg pulled Guillaume aside and offered him a deal. In exchange for the privilege of flying out to the ship aboard "Reg's" helicopter, the Frenchmen promised to allow Reg and his two partners to accompany them on their trip inside the ruined city destroyer. Guillaume was a stocky, rough-looking character with a bushy blond mustache and piercing blue eyes that matched the blue U.N. beret he wore on his head. His face was full of small scars that looked like the results of a grenade explosion. He didn't like having to strike deals in order to do his job, but he accepted, and within a few minutes, his squad of eighteen lifted off in one of the H-110 helicopters.

A pink glow, the first light of the new day, filtered through the smoke and grit hanging over the eastern horizon. What was left of the ruined alien ship was still smoldering. It had come to rest in a hard, stony part of the desert, seventy-five miles southeast of At-Ta'if. In the murky light, it looked like a strange, archaeological wonder, a ruined city from some long-lost civilization. The desert was alive with hundreds of trucks and tanks stationed around the perimeter of the felled giant. They looked pathetically small, like Lilliputians surrounding a sleeping Gulliver. The greater part of the destroyer had been flattened or torn away completely by the chain-reaction explosions. What remained was nothing more than a steaming jungle of carbon black debris.

Reg ordered the pilot of his chopper toward the front of the destroyer, the only part that was still largely intact. This wedge-shaped remnant towered above the rest. There was a four-mile curve at the nose of the destroyer, and it was two miles deep. The roof over this fragment maintained its convex shape, but in some places had lost its structural integrity and hung like a heavy sheet of shattered glass on the supporting structures hidden beneath it. The whole thing looked unstable. Although it was only a fraction of what it had been, it was terrifyingly large.

There are going to be survivors, Reg thought.

"Fly inside," he told the pilot. He pointed toward one of the large breaks in the dome. The pilot thought he was kidding. He wasn't. The hole in the roof was the size of a small lake. After hovering over it uncertainly for a moment, and looking nervously again at Reg, the pilot let his craft sink into the opening. They dropped fifty feet and noticed something climbing the walls around them. The soldiers nearest the open door switched on the flashlights attached to the barrels of their assault rifles and took aim. They were surrounded by vines as thick around as a man's waist, which was extremely thin given their incredible length. They appeared to be made of stone.

The shaft they had flown into was seemingly without bottom. Even under the glare of the flashlights, they couldn't see the floor of the room. Since the roof had been blown out, it seemed that a powerful explosion must have traveled upward through the shaft. There was no way to tell whether the vines showed signs of damage. A hundred feet separated them from the nearest wall, but the sense of claustrophobia was strong. Guillaume yelled at the pilot to take them back toward the open air. The pilot glanced at Reg, who nodded his agreement.

It was hard to say whether the vine-structures were grown or manufactured. There was a regularity to the way they snaked up the walls that didn't look quite natural. Reg hardly thought about it. He sat in the copilot's chair feeling numb and heartbroken. The only thing he was anxious to do was verify that there were no survivors. When that was done, he would leave Saudi Arabia the fastest way he could.

Outside, they followed the slope of the ship down to the main concentration of Saudi forces. Their path brought them to within a mile of the huge black pillar that stood like a monumental skyscraper at the nose of the destroyer. It was leaning now, held up by a section of the dome that had deep fissures running through it. But the gleaming structure itself showed no signs of damage.

"That's where we're going to find them," Guillaume said, sitting next to Reg. "It's probably their control tower."

"Looks like the tower is about to tip over backwards. I'd hate to be inside when that happens."

"I hope they are still alive," Mohammed said, hungry for a fight. Instead of answering him, everyone turned away to look at the impossibly large scale of the craft.

As the sky brightened, Reg could see the terrain surrounding the ship more clearly. They were far from the nearest village, and farther still from At-Ta'if. The terrain was uneven. Acacia and other scrub brush clung to the walls of the wadis, shallow canyons formed by rainwater. The rest was low rocky hills all the way to the horizon.

Ground troops had already penetrated into the ship. A spectacular triangular breach had opened at the edge of the craft, a mile from the base of the black tower. Trucks were driving up into the gap and disappearing into the darkness of the interior.

Before the helicopters touched down, a jeep came speeding toward them from a headquarters tent. The man in the passenger seat was an older, rail-thin Saudi who stood straight up and held on to the windshield for balance as the vehicle swayed and jolted beneath him. He didn't look like a soldier. He was unarmed and wore an ankle-length *thobe*. But his businesslike demeanor made it clear that he was an officer with a lot of work to get done. Before the jeep had come to a complete stop, he jumped into the sand and marched closer to the helicopter, keeping one hand on his *keffiyeh* to keep it from blowing off his head. Guillaume and Reg met him under the whirling blades, where the three of them shouted to one another over the noise until the Frenchman waved his troops onto the ground.

When the helicopter lifted away, the Saudi addressed the soldiers in fluent French. He identified himself as Lieutenant Rahim, briefed them on the situation inside the destroyer, and said that he would personally lead them inside for a look around. He made it clear that the Peacekeepers would be asked to leave once they had determined there were no survivors, because the king had declared the crash site a national military facility. When he was finished speaking, he turned to Reg and asked, in English, if there were any questions. Reg shook his head no.

"What did he say?" Miriyam asked one of the Peacekeepers.

"He said the aliens are all dead."

A troop truck lumbered forward, and the men piled in, taking positions on facing benches. There were no seats left by the time Reg and Miriyam followed Mohammed up the steps, so they decided to stand. They quickly thought better of it once the big truck began lurching over the bumpy earth. They immediately sat down on the floor of the truck and ended up clutching the legs of the soldiers to keep from being thrown around. Lieutenant Rahim was a man in a hurry to overcome some serious obstacles, at least that's how he drove. He smashed into potholes and ran down the banks of ten-foot-deep wadis while turned halfway around in his seat briefing the soldiers on the situation. The U.N. squad held on tightly and listened to him yell over the grind of the engine, their powder blue jumpsuits matching the early sky lightening above them. They were a seasoned group of professional soldiers who worked so well together they hardly had to speak. Reg felt like they would be able to take care of business if it came to that.

When the truck arrived on flatter ground, the baby-faced soldier whose leg Reg was holding, bent forward and asked a question. "Does this mean we are in love?" His comrades all burst out laughing. His name was Richaud, the joker of the squad. Reg sat back, a little embarrassed. Another man nudged him with a boot, the squad's medical officer. He looked down at Reg and shook his head.

"Your skin is very red, too much sun. Put your hand out." He uncapped a tube of ointment and squeezed some out. Reg thanked him and put it on. "You three look pretty funny down there. How did you come together?"

"It's a long story."

The man's name was LeBlanc. He had a stray eye, said he was a medical doctor, and had the curiosity of a ferret. He kept glancing ahead, anxious for the encounter to begin.

As they approached the giant triangular break in the wall of the destroyer, the huge bulk of it hung over them, hundreds of times the size of Saudi Arabia's largest supertanker. The way up into the ship was via a steep, uneven pile of rubble. Debris had spilled out of the opening, creating a natural ramp. A man directing traffic at the foot of the slope raised a red flag and brought Rahim's wild ride to a temporary halt. The path up the ramp could only accommodate one-way traffic, and a convoy was coming down at that moment. Two pickup trucks and a jeep were moving slowly and carefully along the treacherous path. As they sat there idling, Reg was sure Rahim wasn't going to be as cautious. As the vehicles got to the end of the ramp, Rahim released the emergency brake and lurched forward. But when he saw what was tied to the front of the jeep, he hit the brakes again.

The next moment, everyone was craning their necks to see. The men in the jeep had a carcass tied across the hood, like deer hunters returning home successful. It was a gray bulky mass that looked like a giant crustacean shell, except that it had a stump of a face. Long bony arms and legs mingled with the ropes, as well as a profusion of thick tentacles, some of which had worked their way free and were dragging along behind the wheels. The body seemed too thin to support the heavy, scalloped shell of its head and thorax, but the limbs looked strong. They were muscular and covered by an exoskeleton. Stretched over the engine of the jeep, the alien's body was nearly ten feet long and the color of a freshly unearthed grub. Guillaume yelled at his troops to stay where they were as he and Rahim jumped out to have a look. After a moment, the jeep took off to the north. Reg could see that it was headed toward the area a couple of miles away that was being prepared for the royal photo op. It didn't surprise him when Guillaume returned and explained that since the corpse was in good shape compared to most the Saudis were finding, it was going to be used in the ceremony.

Instead of driving up the ramp and into the ship, Rahim ground his engine into gear and turned south, following the two trucks. A few hundred yards later, they came to the place where the Saudi army was dumping the alien bodies. It was a quarantine area, and a stench like ammonia was thick in the air. Everyone got out of the truck and walked up to a roadblock that was guarded by a pair of Pakistani men in turbans.

The two trucks they had followed stopped next to a long pile of slick gray body parts and immediately began to unload more of the same. The flatbeds were piled high with the wreckage of alien bodies. Arms and legs and skull fragments were dragged off the trucks and tossed onto the five-foot-high pile that was already forty feet long. Reg and Guillaume said they wanted a closer look, so Rahim led them past the armed guards. Guillaume stopped and called back to LeBlanc, the medical officer, waving him forward. The biting, acrid smell in the air became stronger the closer they got to the meat pile.

"This is a very bad job to have," LeBlanc said to Reg as they watched the men off-loading the stinking cargo. The dead bodies were a potential biohazard, and no self-respecting Saudi was going to sully himself with that sort of work. Instead it was done by Filipino and Indian men who wore only gardening gloves. In lieu of gas masks, they'd tied shirts around their heads to cover their noses. At least there wasn't a lot of blood. In fact, there wasn't any. LeBlanc pulled on a pair of surgical gloves and moved up to the small mountain of carnage. He yanked a section of tentacle away from the pile. Reg looked over the man's shoulder as he examined it.

"Is this air safe to breathe?" he asked the doctor. "Aren't foreign microbes a danger? Things we have no immunities to?"

LeBlanc sniffed at the air. "It's nothing. A little ammonia, it keeps you awake." He lifted the severed end of the thick tentacle to his nose with both hands and smelled it carefully. "This is not the source of the odor. It makes no smell. It is strange," he said, examining the eight-inch-thick tube of flesh. "No bones, no shell, no blood vessels."

He used a pocketknife to scrape away the sand clinging to the moisture and dig out a square of white flesh. After sniffing at it and running it between his fingers, he shrugged and tossed it aside. "Like a lobster," he said, looking up at Reg with his wandering eye. He was a strange man.

The tentacle was covered with a tough, gray skin that had striated markings like those found on the body of an earthworm. At its tip was a tough, two-fingered pincer claw. When each half closed, they formed a spearhead. After playing with it for a moment or two longer, LeBlanc returned to the pile and retrieved a three-foot-long slab of shell and carried it back to Reg. The inside was covered in some kind of sticky gelatin or fat. LeBlanc gathered up a glob of it, then watched it slowly plop off the end of his knife blade.

"This is the substance that is making the smell," he announced, his eyes watering slightly from the fumes. When he flipped the twenty-pound fragment over, the left half of a bony face was staring back up at him. A smooth, rounded forehead bulged above a deep black eye socket. There was no eye. The lower half of the face, where the mouth would be on a human, was a confused mass of cartilage tissue full of crisscrossing channels, as if it had been hacked at with a machete. It was part of the creature's exoskeleton.

"That's the ugliest damn thing I've ever seen," Reg said.

LeBlanc seemed surprised. "I was just now thinking how much they look like us." He ran his fingers over the seam at the center of the face. It made a clean vertical break from the middle of the forehead down to the middle of the amorphous chin. LeBlanc said it must be like the shell of an oyster or a giant clam. "But it's strange," he said, rolling it over once more. "If it's like a shell of the clam, where is the clam?"

He walked back to the pile and picked up a soft torso with one thin arm attached to it. He carried it back to Reg and tossed it on the ground. With a deft incision, he split the chest open and pulled back the dermal walls.

"You see? It's *très* bizarre. There are two different species." He used his knife to poke at the innards of his latest find. "These small animals, they have the internal organs. But the big ones, *pffft,* they are shells, they are empty."

Rahim and Guillaume had walked to the far end of the quarantine area, keeping well away from the alien corpses. Both of them were anxious to leave when they returned to where Reg was standing.

"The smell is horrible. I have seen enough," said the Frenchman.

"Yes, everything is under control," said the Saudi lieutenant. "Let us continue."

Reg nodded that he, too, was ready to leave this area and enter the ship. The penetrating ammonia vapors were heavy in the air, causing his eyes to water. If the air was contaminated with foreign pathogens, it was too late to do anything about it. Hundreds of men would have already been infected. But as the three of them started back to the truck, LeBlanc whistled sharply through his teeth and waved them over to where he was kneeling. He'd found something in the sand.

It was a greenish thing about an inch long and was squirming like a bristled caterpillar. LeBlanc said he thought it was some form of plant life. In the few minutes since he'd discovered it, he said, the wriggling, wormlike organism had nearly doubled in size.

"*Regardez,*" he said. "Look at this." He extended one of his gloved fingers and held it half an inch above the ground. The tiny creature lifted straight up, straining to reach the finger. When LeBlanc moved his hand slightly to the left, the tiny form bent in that direction.

"It senses your body heat," Reg said, "or maybe it smells you."

"Maybe," allowed the doctor. "I believe it wants something else. I think it feels the moisture." The doctor pulled his hand away, then watched as the small green shape turned and began wriggling toward the nearest source of moisture—the alien cadavers. When it had traveled a couple of inches, LeBlanc unscrewed the cap of his canteen and poured a small amount of water into the sand. The organism turned and immediately began burrowing into the wet spot, sucking the moisture out of the sand. As it did so, its body grew visibly, doubling in length.

"Interesting," said Guillaume, looking slightly queasy. "Where did you find it?"

"Here," LeBlanc said, "in the pile."

"Maybe there's more," Reg suggested. "There's plenty of moisture in these bodies." Thinking that Reg was probably right, LeBlanc began removing body pieces from the top of the heap and tossing them aside. He didn't have to dig very deeply before he found proof that Reg was right. The plants were growing at an exponential rate just below the surface of the heap. Thousands of slender, translucent tendrils many feet long had grown in thick bunches throughout the pile of biowreckage. They were glass-clear and writhed in protest to being exposed to the morning sun. Within moments, they changed color and began to turn green.

"This plant, it is very dangerous," LeBlanc said. "If it finds a lake or an ocean, maybe we cannot stop the growth. It must be contained here before it spreads."

"It might be a source of food for the aliens," Reg surmised. There was no way of knowing how many months or years or centuries they had been traveling through space. A fast-growing plant like this one would create an abundant source of nourishment. "The doctor's right," Reg said. "If this plant spreads, we could have an ecological nightmare on our hands."

Rahim immediately issued orders that no more bodies be brought out of the ship until the problem was better understood. Then he went to inspect one of the trucks that had been carrying the bodies to the quarantine site. First he checked the tires, then popped open the hood and looked into the engine compartment. Cursing in Arabic, he reached down and pulled away a handful of the vines. They had already overgrown the truck's radiator. Immediately, he regretted having touched them. He threw them aside and wiped his hand vigorously on the material of his robe. "Burn them," he shouted to the men off-loading the bodies, "burn everything, including the tracks."

After meeting with the officers in charge of the

quarantine area and making sure they understood the danger LeBlanc had found, the men returned to their own vehicle. After inspecting it for signs of the aggressive plant, the Peacekeepers piled in.

Rahim drove back toward the triangular breach in the wall of the destroyer and headed up the uneven ramp of debris. Although the path to the opening was treacherous and bumpy, Rahim drove fast. The soldiers riding in back were tossed around roughly, but they were eager to get inside and begin the work they had come to do. It was an ironic mission for a U.N. peacekeeping force: locate survivors of the battle and kill them.

They came to the top of the ramp and drove onto the smooth floor of the city destroyer's main deck. The gray walls that closed in around them were the color of graphite. They towered above the truck, smooth in some places and intricately worked in others, like large sections of circuit board. The ceilings of the first rooms they entered were low, but as they penetrated deeper, the domed roof climbed higher. Rahim was forced to slow the truck to a few miles per hour as he steered through the obstacle course of shattered walls and missing sections of floor. The first few hundred feet of the ship were a warren of collapsed passageways and work spaces extending both horizontally and vertically. Shafts of sunlight leaked in where the roof had torn away, but it was soon dark enough that Rahim switched on his headlights. Even though all of the internal walls were badly fractured, most of them appeared to be sturdy; others were teetering on the brink of collapse. It was like driving through a darkened house of cards that threatened to fall apart at any moment.

As he approached a narrow gap between two towering walls that had fallen against one another, Rahim honked his horn and flashed his headlights to alert oncoming drivers to his presence. Then he drove through the opening.

On the other side, they entered a curved hallway of monumental proportions. It was several hundred feet across and long enough that it disappeared around the bend of the ship in either direction. It was completely empty and reminded Reg of an underground flood channel he and his friends had played in when they were children, only this place was a thousand times larger. The truck suddenly felt like a small toy moving across the smooth floor of the chamber. A trail of burning flares marked the path to the far side of the space. Rahim hit the gas and sped into the darkness. He didn't slow down when they came to a soft spot in the road, a place where the floor hung limply into whatever open chamber lay below. It felt like driving across a swaying trampoline until they climbed up the other side and found solid footing once more.

As they approached the opposite wall, Reg looked up into the gloomy light and saw that there was a series of large rectangular openings, each one a doorway to a new level of the ship. On either side of the portals were massive, swollen structures that looked like the roots of some enormous tree. They were grayish white and stood out against the rest of the dark wall.

Rahim stopped the truck near the portal on the ground floor and everyone climbed out. The Peacekeepers switched on their flashlights and inspected the rootlike structures. It quickly became apparent that they were hollow inside and formed a natural staircase to the portal doors above.

"They are growing a lot of plants in here," Miriyam observed. Reg nodded as he studied the way the hollow structure twisted its way up the wall, but it looked as much like a thick vein as it did a root. He was quickly coming to realize that the ship was composed largely—if not completely—of organic materials. He and Miriyam walked past a group of Saudi soldiers who were standing near their trucks and smoking cigarettes, until they came to the place where the towering wall joined the floor. Reg knelt down and inspected the corner.

"What do you see?" Miriyam asked him.

"Look at the way the cracks ran through the floor and travel up the walls."

"What about it?"

"It means they're built from one piece of material. This whole room," he said, gesturing toward the massive hallway, "was cut from a single block. Unless..."

"Unless what?"

"Unless it was grown."

"If it was grown," Miriyam said, "it means we are inside a large animal. That the whole ship was living at some time."

"Not a very comforting thought, is it?" Reg moved his hand over the wall. Despite the hairline fractures running in all directions, the surface was smooth and hard. The texture was closer to leather than metal. It gave like soft wood when he drove his thumbnail into it and left a mark.

Some of the Peacekeepers had climbed up the hollow root-like structures and were beginning to investigate what lay behind the portal doors. Rahim yelled up at them that those areas had already been searched. They were identical in every detail to the room on the ground floor, the next stop on the tour he was giving them. As the Frenchmen began to climb down, Rahim led the way through the floor-level portal into an area he called the room of the barrels.

Inside, under a low ceiling, was another huge room. Battery-powered work lights were switched on to reveal a series of low walls that reached halfway to the ceiling and formed a kind of open maze. Rahim led the way to a hexagonal tank that was four feet deep and twelve feet across. The soldiers peered over the edge and saw themselves reflected in a shallow pool of silver liquid. Half-submerged in the shiny solution was a large pale body, an alien exoskeleton. It had long, powerfully built arms and legs. Instead of feet, it had a pair of hooked toes that curled forward like a ram's horns. The hands were similar to human hands. Each one had three bony fingers that reached lengths of up to twelve inches. But the part of the body that drew the most attention was the giant clamshell that composed the head and thorax region of the animal. It was split open along the seam running from the pointed crest of down to its abdomen. As LeBlanc had noted earlier, there were no internal organs. The interior walls of the shell were pinkish gray muscle. At the bottom of the tank, there was a piece of machinery that looked like a harness or mold. When the ship crashed, the body had torn free of the harness, and most of the fluid had sloshed out of the vat.

"This one, it is more smaller than the ones we found outside," LeBlanc pointed out. The body was about six feet long.

"Yes, yes," Rahim agreed. "It is still young, still growing. We believe this entire area is a farm to grow these creatures. They tell me this liquid is a growth culture. A preliminary chemical analysis shows a balanced pH and many hormones and nutrients."

"They're growing these bodies the same way our scientists culture cells?" Reg asked.

"Exactly," LeBlanc said, "but the level is very sophisticated, far beyond our ability."

"Is it alive?" Mohammed asked, peering down at the alien.

"No," Rahim answered definitively. "All of them are dead. We are certain of this." To prove his point, he took out a pistol and shot into the tank. The large body remained as lifeless as it had before.

"Remarkable," LeBlanc gasped. He shook his head in awe of the alien scientific accomplishments. "They have done what we cannot do: pluripotent cell differentiation.

This is something we humans cannot do. Maybe in one hundred years."

Miriyam was puzzled. "I don't understand how a species of animals can exist if they have to be grown like this. Don't they have sex?"

LeBlanc looked at her with his stray eye from the opposite side of the tank. "You have to understand that this one is not the real alien who drives the ship and fires the weapons. This one, it is only an armor, an empty body for the real aliens. They sit inside the shell like a little... how do you say?... the little man who rides the horse."

"Jockey?"

"Exactly. The real alien sits inside this empty body like a jockey. Without the little one inside, this one is without the life. *C'est brillant, n'est-cepas?*"

"Yeah," Miriyam replied sarcastically. "They're real geniuses."

Guillaume glanced curiously around the mazelike room of the barrels. "All of these pools have bodies in them?"

"Yes," Rahim said. "And the same on the floors above. There are thousands of these barrels."

As they talked, the long fingers of an exoskeletal hand lifted over the side of the tank and reached into the air. An "alien" voice called out, *"Aidez-moi! Je suis mort!"* It was Richaud, the same baby-faced soldier who had joked with Reg in the truck. He had found a severed arm lying nearby and was using it to put on a show for the others. No one found his impromptu puppet show particularly amusing. After a sharp word from Guillaume, Richaud tossed the arm away.

Rahim led the group through the labyrinth of half-wall partitions until they arrived at an open pit. It was as big around as a manhole leading down to a sewer. Turning to LeBlanc, he gestured toward the hole in the floor. "The plant you found outside is also here." When flashlights were pointed into the opening, they saw what he meant. The same glassy vines were clinging to the walls of the round shaft, writhing and wriggling in slow motion.

"Maybe there's water down there," Reg said, "or some other source of moisture."

"Perhaps," said the doctor, leaning over the opening with a flashlight and trying to measure the depth of the shaft. "Or perhaps there are more bodies."

"It's nice and dark down there," Miriyam said. "It's a place survivors would hide."

"We've got to find a way down to the lower levels," Reg said to Guillaume.

"I already thought of that." The Frenchman grunted. "My scouts have found an opening. Follow me."

Not far from the large door they'd stepped through to enter the room of the barrels, there was a long rip in the floor just wide enough for a large man to slip through. The floor of the next level was visible about twenty feet below. The Peacekeepers broke open their backpacks and began unpacking the gear they would need.

Lieutenant Rahim thought Reg and Guillaume were crazy for wanting to go belowdecks with such a small force, but he could see he wasn't going to be able to stop them. Reluctantly, he decided to join them.

Using ropes, the Peacekeepers were lowered through the opening two at a time. Guillaume ordered two of them to stay behind and keep an ear to the radio. Reg, Mohammed, and Miriyam were the last ones down. When they assembled on the lower level, they found themselves in a wide, rectangular passageway. The first thing Guillaume did was to order thermal and sonic scans, both of which came back negative. The weak light filtering down through the shaft cast a dim glow on the floor. Otherwise, they had only their flashlights. The floor felt spongy under their feet. Both it and the walls appeared to be made of muscle or some other living tissue. Thick bundles of the sinuous, fleshy material were coiled around one another, the color of granite and as flat as a brick wall. The material looked as if it had been pressed and compacted. But as LeBlanc pointed out, the walls had probably been grown that way, through the use of molds. As the group set off, Reg had the uneasy feeling he was moving through the bowels of some enormous living creature.

"I think you were right," he said quietly to Miriam, who was walking beside him.

"About what?"

"If there's anything still alive in this ship, this is where we'll find it."

"I felt much braver about all of this ten minutes ago," she said.

"Too late to turn back now. Where's the kid?"

"Leading the way, I think."

Moving in a loose line behind Guillaume and his two advance men, they walked fifty yards before they came to an opening in the wall. It looked like a sphincter muscle and stood three times as tall as a man. A thick lip of tissue lined the opening, floor to ceiling. The advance men went forward to inspect it, moving the last few feet on their stomachs and peering over the bottom of the lip. After a moment, they stood up and went into the chamber beyond. When they waved the others forward, they found a large, roughly oval chamber. The walls were made of the same material as in the passageway, with one conspicuous difference: They were full of small, rough-hewn caves that looked as if they'd been chopped, or eaten, out of the walls. Some were twenty feet long and had two doorways. Others were shallow depressions in the face of the wall. The soldiers found matting and shreds of dried vegetation in the deeper caves, which led them to conclude they had discovered sleeping quarters. But there were no bodies, no physical trace of the aliens they were hunting, so they moved on.

Farther down the passageway, they found a similar chamber, and then another. Their progress was slow because Guillaume insisted that each chamber be approached and examined with caution. Mohammed and Rahim both grew impatient. Mohammed because he was eager to find something that was still alive, and Rahim because he wasn't. He was anxious to get back to his own work, and pointed out the obvious: The passageway gave onto only one sort of room. Since there were no signs of survivors, he suggested they return to the surface.

"No. They are here," Mohammed said. "We must find them." He turned and led a hurried march toward the next opening. Along the way, they found a place where the wall had torn away from the floor, opening a gap to the next floor down. Reg had a claustrophobic moment when he saw that the gap was wide enough to slip through. He knew they were going to descend to the next level.

"Are there any signs of life?" Guillaume asked the first man through the crack. When he replied in the negative, the leader of the Peacekeepers looked at Reg. "Maybe we have gone far enough."

The last thing Reg wanted to do was wriggle into the hole and descend yet another level, but he shook his head. "We have to keep going," he said. "King Ibrahim and several hundred civilians are heading out here from At-Ta'if. We've got to make sure there won't be any surprises."

"And quickly," Rahim added. "There are many preparations still to be made before the king's arrival."

"Let's go then." Guillaume ordered two of his men to stay behind and maintain radio contact with the outside. Within minutes, the others had squeezed through the opening to the floor below. The new passageway was not straight and square like the one above. The walls were rough and curved like a mine tunnel and left only enough room for two people to walk abreast. The tunnel showed signs of use. The lower half of it, including the floor, had been worn smooth, and there were grooves and dents running continuously about three feet above the ground. The crack they had lowered themselves through was on the ceiling now, and it narrowed as they followed it a short distance to a door that blocked their path. It was a heavy, rounded shell that closed against a bulkhead partition. At the center of the door was a battered, copper-colored medallion about the size of a dinner plate. At one time, there must have been a flowerlike design etched into the metallic substance, but only traces of it remained around the edges.

"Open it," Guillaume said to one of his scouts.

The man reached out and touched the medallion with one finger. The door flew open and slammed against the wall. Flashlights explored the next part of the tunnel until the door slowly began to move closed again. When Guillaume touched the medallion, it shot open again. He stepped across the threshold and waved the others to follow him.

"Wait," Reg said. "Does that door open from the other side?" Guillaume, Mohammed, and the others who had stepped through turned and examined the door for a moment before it sealed behind them.

"That is a very good question," Guillaume called back. His voice came through the crack in the ceiling that extended a few feet into the far part of the tunnel before ending. "Don't touch the door. I will examine it." A moment later, he shouted through the crack that there was no way to open it from the other side.

After warning Guillaume to step away, Reg reached up and put his hand on the medallion. He felt a small electrical shock as the door swung open and smashed against the wall again.

"This is a one-way street," Miriyam observed.

"We'll need to leave someone here to open it," Reg said.

Guillaume posted two more guards and continued into the darkness of the next segment of the tunnel, Soon, they found a differently shaped door built into the sidewall of the tunnel. It was wider than the first one and slightly lower, but had the same copper medallion set outside it. Mohammed reached it first, but when he touched it, nothing happened. Others tried with the same result. They tried to force it open, but soon realized it was futile and continued to advance. They found several more of the side doors, none of which would open, before they arrived at another bulkhead. After posting another pair of guards to keep the door open, the remaining fourteen people stepped through.

Part of the ceiling had collapsed in the next segment of the tunnel. Without opening to the upper level, it drooped into their path. Two of the Peacekeepers ducked their heads and moved under it. They called out that one of the side doors had been forced ajar.

"See what is behind it," Guillaume ordered.

"A side tunnel," they reported.

"Check the first fifty meters."

After a tense moment of waiting, the two men came out from under the sagging ceiling and said the tunnel led to a cavelike room. There were no signs of survivors.

"We are going very slowly," Mohammed complained. "We have to find them fast and kill them."

Guillaume snapped at him to shut up and keep out of the way. Mohammed was in no mood to back down. He took a menacing step toward the rough-looking Frenchman, but Reg caught him by his skinny arm before he could do anything foolish. He pulled the young Iraqi past Guillaume, ducked under the low part of the roof, and entered the side tunnel.

After only a few steps, the walls opened around them, and they were standing in a cave. It was more like an underground cavern, full of stalactites and stalagmites. There was a forest of them, hanging from the ceiling and rising out of the floor at regularly spaced intervals. The columns looked as if they had been built little by little, by accretion, the way coral grows or the way wax builds up at the bottom of a candlestick. But the precise distances between them made it obvious that they were not naturally occurring. Scattered around on the floor were small objects that appeared to be hand tools, and larger ones that looked like water troughs. The space felt more like a factory than a cave, and there were a million places to hide.

When thermal and sonic scans came back negative, LeBlanc broke away from the others and rushed up to examine the nearest column. It was a stalagmite about four feet tall, jade green, and composed of a crystalline substance. It showed signs of having been scraped, chiseled, and hacked at.

"Look at this," the doctor said eagerly. He had his flashlight pointed at the top of the tapering stump. "Growth rings, the same that you have inside a tree." He looked up at Reg with his stray eye and nodded admiringly. "They were good farmers, these aliens."

"I recognize that color," Miriyam said.

"So do I," Reg nodded. "The color of the light surrounding the firing cone."

"Maybe they use this crystal as a power source."

"Yes," said LeBlanc. He took out a knife and used it to scrape off a layer of the material, then raked it into a sample bag. The others began to wander deeper into the chamber, finding various tools on the floor: rasps, chisels, machete-like blades—all of them smaller than human tools. The large objects that looked like water troughs were filled with small sacks made of a hard, flexible skin. When LeBlanc opened one of them up with his knife, he found it was filled with powder of the same jade green color. The doctor was convinced that the crystalline residue provided the aliens with a renewable, self-sustaining fuel that could be converted into enormous amounts of power. He pointed out that the sides of the trough matched the groove marks worn into the walls in the passageway outside. "So if we follow the marks on the walls, eventually…"

"Eventually, we'll get to the engine room," Reg finished the thought.

"We can learn how they converted this stuff"—he pointed to his sample of powder—"into such a great explosive. Maybe we will learn something good from them."

One of the Peacekeepers shouted and dropped his rifle, batting at something in front of his face. Instantly, a dozen rifles were pointed in his direction. It was the baby-faced soldier, Richaud. He spit on the floor and turned to the others, explaining that he'd run into something that felt like a spiderweb. He cracked a joke in French that brought a nervous chuckle from a few of the Peacekeepers, but Guillaume was not amused.

"Stay quiet and watch what you're doing," he told the soldier, then motioned for the doctor to go and have a look at him. But before LeBlanc could get to him, Richaud made a noise, and his body tensed up like a bird dog. He pointed toward a section of the room near the entrance where the ceiling had sagged almost to the floor.

"What is it?" Guillaume demanded.

"Can't you hear that?" Richaud asked. No one breathed as they listened for whatever it was that had spooked the Frenchman. "It's alive," he said.

"What is?"

"No," Richaud said, "no, no, NO!" He reached up and clutched the sides of his head and screamed. The others ran to Richaud's aid. He fell to the floor in the grip of a painful seizure and began to convulse. Reg and some others helped pin the soldier's flailing body to the floor so that LeBlanc could have a look at him, but there was nothing the doctor could do. Blood began to stream out of Richaud's nostrils and ears. His eyes, wide with terror, went pink, and then bright red. He continued to struggle and shout incoherently until his body went limp.

"He's dead," LeBlanc said in amazement.

"He said he ran into a spiderweb. Maybe it's poison," Miriyam suggested.

Every flashlight in the room turned toward the ceiling, but there was no sign of anything that looked like a spiderweb, only the carefully arranged rows of stalactites. As Reg scanned the chamber, a strange feeling came over him. At first he thought it was a powerful sense of déjà vu. But he quickly realized it was more than that. He was thinking in a way he didn't recognize at all. It was another presence inside of him, a mind thinking inside his own.

Miriyam noticed that Reg had gone still and silent. "What's the matter?"

He turned and looked at her, but couldn't answer. As his mouth moved, struggling to form words, a sharp pain gripped his neck and spiked upward into his brain. He screamed and grabbed his head as Richaud had done. As he collapsed to the floor, he felt a tremendous weight crushing down on his skull and tried frantically to push it away with his hands. He forced his eyes open and looked at the ceiling above him. At the same time, he saw himself lying on the floor, surrounded by people trying to help him. This second point of view, which overlapped his normal vision, came from low on ground, from the area below the collapsed ceiling, the same place Richaud had pointed to a moment before. Whatever the thing was that had invaded his brain, Reg realized it was there, nearby on the floor. The already-unbearable pain ratcheted upward in intensity, and he felt himself beginning to black out. His assailant, whatever it was, was reaching across the room with its mind, infiltrating his nervous system and working him like a puppet. With the last of his strength, he struggled to turn and lash out at his attacker, but there wasn't much he could do. His body went limp. But Reg didn't lose consciousness completely, and the pain did not leave him. He understood that there was only one way to relieve his suffering: He had to answer a question.

The question was not put to him in words, but in the form of images and an urgent sensation of need. He found himself standing in a huge, dark, cathedral space hiding from a band of filthy, vile creatures that had him surrounded. He knew somehow that these creatures were an enemy army, and he could feel the intense hatred and loathing they had for him. He sensed the presence of others, his own kind, hiding in the darkness.

Reg realized that he was inside a group mind—hundreds of individuals thinking together as if all tuned to the same radio frequency and able to communicate instantaneously by means of shorthand image/thought/impulses. Two overpowering sensations coursed through this group mind: a burning physical hunger and an intense loathing for the army of humans. Then the interrogation began. There was a great gash in the wall of the cathedral, a towering triangular opening. Beyond it, a bright sun beat down on the sands of a hostile alien planet. Outside, in the distance, a caravan of enemy vehicles was approaching across a barren plateau. The mind ordered him to divulge everything he knew about this approaching force. Reg recognized that they were limousines and armored military vehicles, being seen through the eyes of the aliens. To his horror, he was being asked to act as a spy for the aliens, to help them prepare an attack. But such was his fear and confusion that he complied without the slightest hesitation. In a rapid-fire sequence of half thoughts, he communicated everything he knew about the group and their plans, then begged for the excruciating pain to end. But the response from the mind was an order to die instead. It reached into him and forced his heart to stop beating, his lungs to stop breathing.

As Reg slipped toward death, he realized that he could resist, that the power of the group mind was not absolute. In some way he couldn't fully understand, he realized that the aliens couldn't control him without his consent. For a moment, his will struggled against the Will that was controlling him. He felt himself regaining some control, but when the pain intensified, he lay back and obeyed the command to die. Darkness.

There was a series of quick explosions, and then someone was speaking to him in a language he didn't understand. Reg's eyes shot open without being able to focus, and he gasped for air. An indistinct figure hovered over him, preparing to inject him with a hypodermic needle. In a daze, Reg swatted his hand at the needle and knocked it away. Slowly, he realized the strange language was French and the figure leaning over him was LeBlanc.

"You are not dead," the doctor said with surprise.

"Over there," Reg groaned, pointing in the direction of his attacker. "An alien. It's alive." He turned his head in that direction and saw Miriyam inspecting something under the collapsed ceiling with a machine gun in her hands.

"It's not alive anymore," she told him. "I killed it."

"How? How did you know?" Reg asked.

"You told us," said the doctor with the stray eye. "Don't you remember? We had no idea, but then you pointed to where it was hiding."

"It must have been trapped there when the ceiling fell on it," surmised Guillaume. "Are you okay? Can you walk?"

"We have to get out of here, have to run." Reg pulled himself into a sitting position and tried to shake the cobwebs out of his head. The attack had left him disoriented and slightly dizzy. "They're coming."

A shock of fear ran through everyone in the room. "Who's coming?"

"The others, the aliens. They know where we are," Reg said, struggling to find his feet. "We have to get outside and warn them."

LeBlanc prevented Reg from standing up. "What are you talking about? Tell us what happened."

"It used its mind. Some kind of telepathy," Reg explained, sorting through the experience, trying to make sense of it. "They were asking me things, torturing me."

"They? How many?"

Reg shook his head. He didn't know. "Many."

Guillaume knelt down beside him and spoke in an urgent whisper. "We found only one of them. Where are the others? How do you know they are coming?"

"Oh, my God," Reg gasped when he realized he'd given the aliens information they could use to attack the people in the royal entourage. "Let me up. They're going to attack. We've got to warn them."

Guillaume grabbed him by the collar, shook him roughly, and held him in place. "You're talking nonsense. Tell us what happened!" The Frenchman's scarred face was close to his, illuminated in the glow of the flashlights.

"This one," Reg began, pointing to the creature Miriyam had shot, "invaded my mind, attacked me with its mind. But there were others, other minds. They communicate... I don't know how to describe it... they think together, as a single mind. When this one reached inside of me, I was also inside of it. There was a melding, and I saw through its eyes, but I also saw through the eyes of the others. I saw what they were seeing. They're at the entrance to the ship, looking out of the same opening we drove through when we came in. Right now, the king and his people are arriving outside. The aliens are going to ambush them. They're going to kill the king."

Guillaume was alarmed, but remained skeptical. Reg had been through a traumatic experience and was badly shaken. The pain could have caused him to hallucinate. He had one more question. "How do the aliens know it is the king?"

"Because I told them," Reg answered. He shook free of Guillaume's grip, stood up, and began moving unsteadily toward the exit. Mohammed took Reg by the arm and assisted him.

"I think he is right," Rahim said, checking his watch. "King Ibrahim is scheduled to arrive exactly now. We must warn him at once."

The Peacekeepers followed Reg, Mohammed, and Miriyam through the side tunnel and into the main passageway. They turned and hurried toward the first bulkhead door. The Peacekeepers radioed to the men on the far side of the door to open it but received no reply.

Guillaume had given them orders to keep it open at all times.

Reg took the machine gun Miriyam was carrying and smashed the butt of it against the door, signaling to the men on the other side. When there was no response he threw down the gun and wedged his fingertips into the thin gap between the door and the bulkhead. "Help me!" he yelled over his shoulder. First Miriyam and then a few of the Peacekeepers stepped forward to try and pry the door open, but they did so reluctantly. If the men on the other side touched the copper medallion, the door would fly open and crush them against the wall. The bayonets the Peacekeepers had on their rifles provided them with the leverage they needed, but it took the full strength of six men and one woman to pull the door open twelve inches.

"Movement behind us. Something is coming," one of the soldiers standing farther back yelled to Guillaume.

"Pull harder!" Guillaume shouted.

When Rahim came forward to lend his strength to the effort, Miriyam turned and grunted at him. "You are skinny. Reach through. Touch the medallion."

"But the door will open too fast."

"Do it!"

The rail-thin Saudi lieutenant pushed his way past the soldiers straining against the strength of the door and reached his arm into the next chamber. "I will count to three," he told them. But he never got the chance to start counting. Something grabbed his arm and pulled hard enough to break his neck when it slammed against the side of the door. The others backed away, startled, and let the door smash closed on his limp body. A moment later, a tentacle the size of a python slid through the opening and began slashing through the air, searching for another victim.

The group retreated from the door and started in the other direction, but soon realized they were surrounded. The collapsed section of the ceiling that sagged into the passageway was moving. Although it weighed several tons, something was walking below it, lifting it out of the way as easily as if it were a bedsheet hanging on a clothesline. One of the soldiers moved closer and lay on his stomach, peering ahead with his flashlight.

"Two pairs of feet," he called back to the others.

As they braced themselves for the attack, there was an explosion in the passageway behind them. The door had been opened. They wheeled around to see a gruesome and terrifying sight: a ghost gray stump of a face jutting toward them from the center of a wide, flaring shell. The creature was an eight-foot-tall exoskeleton, one of the biomechanical suits of armor they'd discovered lying in the vats of liquid two floors above. It filled the doorway. The multiple pairs of tentacles on its back waved through the air like the hypnotic, ophidian locks of Medusa's hair, and the sight of the creature turned the humans momentarily to stone.

All except Mohammed. He was carrying the machine gun Miriyam had tossed to the floor. As soon as the hissing, many-armed beast revealed itself, Mohammed lowered the gun and charged ahead, firing and screaming as he went. His bullets bounced off the hard shell, but their collective impact began to crack it apart. When he was almost to the bulkhead, the pointed tip of the skeletal head shattered completely and broke away. It made no difference. With alarming agility and speed, the hideous creature darted through the bulkhead and speared the young Saudi in the chest with a tentacle, spraying blood everywhere. As Mohammed's body dropped to the floor, the Peacekeepers opened fire and hit the monster with hundreds of rounds of ammunition, knocking it a few steps backwards. Each bullet chipped away another piece of bone, but only little by little. It took several seconds of sustained firing until the thing died.

"Go! Go! Back to the entrance!"

The team broke into a sprint down the hallway, stepping over and around the fallen alien. When they were through the bulkhead, they stumbled on the bodies of the Peacekeepers who had been guarding the door. A moment later, the first of the two aliens behind them stepped clear of the fallen ceiling. The soldier bringing up the rear of the retreat didn't notice until it was too late. The big creature raced down the tunnel twice as fast as the humans and quickly caught them. One by one, the men running at the end of the line realized they were lost and turned to make their last stands. Each one blasted the alien with as many shells as he could before being trampled, killed, and tossed aside. Reg was running just behind Miriyam and Guillaume. Like the others, he was terrified out of his mind and desperate to climb out of the tunnel. But when he realized what was happening behind him, he stopped running and wrested the machine gun away from the

Peacekeeper who had taken it from the dead Mohammed.

"Keep going," Reg told the man, then pressed himself against the side of the tunnel and watched the flashlights of the last two men running toward him. He had decided to help them slow the aliens down in order to give Miriyam and the others time to escape. But the men didn't see him waiting and when he pushed away from the wall and began running alongside of them, he startled them so badly that they tripped over one another and went down in a heap. Reg fell with them and watched the flashlights break free and go rolling across the floor. As the men scrambled to collect their guns, the sound of rushing feet came toward them. They turned and fired into the darkness. They fired until their ammunition was nearly spent.

When they picked up their flashlights and looked behind them, fragments of an exoskeleton were spread across the floor of the tunnel, the bulk of it lying only a few paces away. Despite having been torn to pieces, the body was struggling slowly forward, determined to complete the hunt. Reg and the two men turned away from it and ran as fast as they could. Far ahead, they saw the bobbing flashlights of the main group. Then they heard gunfire and screaming.

"Stop," one of the Peacekeepers beside Reg said. "Back the other way."

"No, keep going." But the man had already turned and headed back in the other direction. Reg and the remaining soldier continued to run, but they slowed their pace because everything had gone silent and still ahead of them. A pair of rifles lay on the ground, the flashlights attached to them creating a dim pool of light on the floor.

"Maybe we *should* go the other way," the Frenchman said.

"No, there's another one back there."

"Yes, but only one. How many are up ahead?"

"Switch off your light. Let's keep going." The two men walked at a fast march through the pitch-darkness, feeling their way along the curving, uneven walls and keeping their fingers tight against the triggers of their guns. They walked for a long time before they heard a sound.

"Psst. Over here." The voice belonged to Guillaume. He told them not to turn on their lights, but he turned on his, keeping the palm of his hand closed over the bulb. Reg felt his way along the wall until he reached the spot. He could feel people huddled low against the wall, but couldn't immediately tell how many. Clumsily, he made his way close to Guillaume.

"Another one just ahead, twenty meters," he told Reg.

LeBlanc's voice whispered out of the inky blackness. "Put all your bullets to the face of the shell. We must kill the little one inside."

There was another report of gunfire, this time far down the narrow passageway. The man who had turned back had obviously found something. When the firing ceased abruptly, everyone could imagine what had happened. "We've got to do something," Reg said. "We're going to have company in a minute."

Miriyam said, "Better to take them one at a time."

And a moment later they heard the scraping of footsteps ahead. Guillaume switched on his flashlight, and the group opened fire. But the skeletal warrior quickly retreated behind the first curve in the tunnel.

Reg knew immediately that the creature was stalling, waiting for the one that was coming from behind so they could work together. Reg snapped a fresh cartridge of shells into the machine gun. "We can't wait any longer," he said, and started forward.

"Remember to aim for the head," Miriyam said, joining him.

The creature retreated no farther. When the team came

around the bend in the tunnel and began blasting away, it charged forward. The head-thorax shell dipped forward slightly, as if the alien wanted to gore them with the blunt tip of the pointed head. The team's decision to concentrate their firepower on the face led to mixed results. The hard material quickly fractured and then broke apart, but before the alien inside the suit could be killed, the exoskeleton turned away from the gunfire, scampering backward toward them, tentacles first. Guillaume fired until his ammunition was spent, then moved forward to use the tip of his gun as a spike. Before he could do so, one of the flailing tentacle arms connected and sent him sprawling against the wall. Guillaume was down but not out. As the exoskeleton stepped past him, he sprang to his feet and attacked it with his hands. He reached through the shattered face of the shell and grabbed hold of the squirming alien within. When he did so, the biomechanical suit of armor lost its coordination. The tentacles went limp, and the knees buckled. As the suit clattered to the ground, Guillaume was left holding a slender gray body about three and a half feet tall. It thrashed violently, trying to escape, but the Frenchman had his powerful hand wrapped tight around its tiny throat. Guillaume screamed out in pain when the alien attacked him mentally. He reached up to his own throat as if he were being strangled by an invisible hand. Reg and the others ran forward to give help, but before they reached him, Guillaume had smashed the creature's head open against the floor. Behind a set of delicate, almost-human facial features, the alien's brain was a swollen disk extending off the back of the skull. A thin membrane was all that protected the brain, and it split open easily under the force of Guillaume's strength. The small gray body was slathered in a layer of clear gelatin and smelled powerfully of ammonia.

Miriyam stepped over the fallen body armor and led the

way down the tunnel to the final door. They shouted at the top of their lungs to the men on the far side, but received no reply. On the ceiling, a small part of the crack the team had descended through extended past the door. It was no more than eight inches wide, too small to fit through.

"Open the door!" Miriyam screamed toward the opening. Although she assumed the two men stationed in the tunnel were dead, she hoped the men on the floor above would hear. Reg brushed past her and wedged the bayonet on a rifle he took from one of the soldiers into the crevice between the door and the bulkhead. The blade bent out of shape.

"He is coming. He is behind us," LeBlanc warned.

Reg took a flashlight from the soldier whose rifle he had and used it to examine the door. There was a thick band of ligament running down one side of it, acting as a hinge. With the bayonet, he stabbed into the tough, sinewy material and sliced away a small piece. But there wasn't time to cut through it by hand.

"Stand back!" he warned the others, then sent a spray of carefully aimed bullets into the hinge. When Miriyam saw what he was doing, she picked up the machine gun and joined in, the two of them firing until their ammunition was gone.

Behind them, the rest of the team opened fire on the armored warrior stalking them through the tunnel. While the others held the creature at bay, Reg and Miriyam attacked the remaining part of the hinge, and the door soon gave way. There was barely time to get clear of its path before it crashed to the ground. Without looking back, the two of them stepped over the door and raced into the next segment of the tunnel.

"Ladies first," Miriyam said, when they reached the tear in the ceiling. Reg obliged by lacing his fingers together and boosting her up to the opening. As she wriggled through the gap, the others arrived where Reg was standing, and he began lifting them toward the opening one by one. After the second soldier escaped, Miriyam dropped a pair of fresh assault rifles, taken from the Peacekeepers above, into the opening. They arrived just in time. LeBlanc and Guillaume picked them up and sent a volley of shells flying at the skeletal attacker, momentarily arresting its progress.

"Doctor, you're next," Reg said, waiting to boost the man up.

"No," Guillaume shouted, "you go." He positioned himself so that Reg could climb his body like a ladder and grab the hands reaching down through the hole. The men above quickly lifted Reg out to safety. Then he turned to do the same for LeBlanc.

A rope was tossed down to Guillaume, who grabbed it with one hand and fired with the other. As Guillaume wriggled through the hole and rolled away, a tentacle shot through the gap, trying to catch him. It wound around LeBlanc's leg instead and yanked him roughly toward the opening. Reg reacted quickly and caught the terrified doctor under the arms, helping to resist the strength of the tentacle. Before the others could help, another snakelike appendage darted out and grabbed Reg by the ankle. Screaming in pain, LeBlanc was torn from Reg's grasp and disappeared into the hole. Reg would have gone in behind him if Miriyam hadn't opened fire and severed the tentacle.

They heard the doctor screaming in pain on the floor below as more tentacles reached up and searched for more victims. When Reg hesitated, unwilling to leave LeBlanc behind, Miriyam pulled him away from the opening.

"We can't help him," she said. "Let's go."

The handful of survivors took off running down the rectangular passageway until they found the first opening, the one that led to the main deck of the alien ship.

8

A GOOD OLD-FASHIONED TURKEY SHOOT

"Allah preserve us, it looks a lot bigger than it did on TV."

King Ibrahim stepped from the back of his limousine at about nine in the morning and gaped at the staggering size of the wrecked fragment of alien airship. The rest of the royal motorcade, a mile-long line of limousines, rocket-launching vehicles, and M1A1 tanks, rolled past him and parked in no particular order near the collection of tents and the scaffolded stage set up near the edge of a bluff. The king's advance team had selected this site, a mere three hundred yards from the edge of the ship, primarily for the backdrop it offered: a view of the triangular opening half a mile away and, beyond that, the mysterious obsidian tower leaning above the curve of the dome. It had all the makings of a surreal media event: The small stage was dressed in the Saudi national colors of green, black, and white. Sprays of flowers lay in the sand around it Waiters poured out of the kitchen tent as the king's entourage continued to arrive, circulating among the cars with drink trays. Workmen were putting the finishing touches on the bright pink bridal tent, where the wedding ceremony would be held. There was a Sikh bartender, dressed in turban and tuxedo, offering nonalcoholic champagne to the guests. Musicians had been hired, and red carpets had been rolled out.

Mr. Roeder jogged up to the king's limousine to begin

briefing him on the preparations, but King Ibrahim had only one question on his mind. "Did you find me an alien or not?"

The American pointed to a jeep parked a safe distance away and the gray skeletal carcass tied across its hood. Patiently, he explained the details of the predatory green plant and the high risk of infection involved in using a corpse for the photo session. He urged the king to stay away from it.

"I came here to kill an alien. Couldn't you find me one that was still alive? Half-alive?"

"I'm afraid they're all dead, Your Majesty."

Frustrated, the king grabbed a pistol and took off down the hill, chased by a flock of camera crews. While he was gone, the crew of pilot heroes was ushered up onto the platform for group pictures. In addition to the foreign and Saudi pilots who had flown with Faisal from his camp in the desert, there were dozens of others who had answered to America's call to attack. In all, there were more than a hundred men representing nineteen different countries. Conspicuously absent were English major Reginald Cummins and the lone female pilot, Israeli captain Miriyam Marx. The pilots were in high spirits, but it took them quite a while to work out the question of who would stand next to whom. Victory had warmed them to one another personally, but the photographs would be lasting documents, and no one wanted to look like he was cozying up to the enemy.

"Say cheese!" the photographer yelled.

He took a series of shots—looking serious, looking happy, shaking their fists angrily—or, in Tye's case, flipping the bird at the wreckage that dominated the skyline behind them. The whole group beamed with pride. They had accomplished a hugely heroic deed, and their faces showed it. When they stepped off the podium, each pilot was handed a yellow rose and an envelope full of cash by one of the royal grandchildren. They were mingling with high-ranking Saudis when a shot rang out. In the distance, the king had fired a single bullet at the dead alien.

He rode back up the hill in a jeep, and, when he arrived, unsettling news awaited him. An assistant pulled him aside and handed him a phone. One of his field generals was on the line. He said a Frenchman had stormed into the headquarters tent only moments before, claiming to have been attacked inside the ship. According to the man's story, he'd ventured down into the bowels of the city destroyer with eighteen men and lost most of them to a handful of aliens.

"How many of these stories have you heard?" the king asked.

"This is the first one."

"Do you believe him?"

"Yes, sir, yes."

After inspecting the extraterrestrial cadaver, the king had lost his appetite for confrontations with any living members of the species. Hie size and strength of the body he'd seen were alarming. He wondered if the ammonia fumes he'd breathed might be poisonous. The idea of coming out here was beginning to feel like a huge mistake. "General, send search parties inside to check this man's story. Call me the moment you have news." The patriarch scanned the curved dome of the ship for a moment before making an announcement. "This isn't what I was expecting! It isn't right. We are going back to At-Ta'if."

"What about the wedding?" asked an advisor.

Ibrahim growled. He'd forgotten about that. He marched off in a new direction, this time to find Faisal.

The groom-to-be had slipped a gold-trimmed robe over his uniform and was surrounded by a group of fawning well-wishers, who parted for the king when he approached.

"*Faisal,*" the old man said, "I have changed my mind. Let's return to the palace and hold the ceremony in my gardens."

Faisal was mortified at the idea. A ceremony in the desert was the final brilliant element of the story he was constructing for himself. When future generations recounted his heroic deeds, he wanted it to end with the storybook flourish of a battlefield wedding. ...*Then, after laying low the enemies of God, the warrior knelt before the site of his victory and took as his reward the most beautiful bride in all the land. The king himself performed the marriage, whereupon Faisal, in his wisdom and mercy, freed the bride's brother after lecturing him sternly before the people*... Thinking fast, Faisal proposed the compromise of dispensing with the formal ceremony. All that was necessary was for the king to stand over the couple and declare them man and wife.

King Ibrahim wasn't happy with the proposal, but he agreed. "Bring that Yamani girl up here," he shouted, "so we can finish this business and go home."

When the bride's chauffeur opened the door, the shrouded figure that stepped out wasn't Fadeela. It was Faisal's wife, Hajami. She was five years older than her husband and, under normal circumstances, a timid personality. She had been rich when she married the ambitious young Saudi Air Force lieutenant from a penniless family who had promised her that she would always be his only wife. She had given him her fortune and three male children. The night before, when she learned of Fadeela's marriage proposal, she had argued savagely with her husband. Then, after Fadeela's friends decided to boycott the wedding, Faisal added insult to Hajami's injury by commanding her, under threat of divorce, to help prepare the body of his new bride. This was intimate work that required hours to accomplish: All of Fadeela's hair, except head hair and eyebrows, had to be removed; she was bathed, powdered, and perfumed, before intricate designs were painted on her hands and feet with henna dye. The whole time the two women worked together, Hajami maintained an icy silence.

Drums began to beat when the bride showed herself. She stepped out of the car wearing a simple white dress and flowers woven into the long braid that trailed down her back. Her face was uncovered and her feet were bare. If she was embarrassed about being seen this way, or distraught about marrying Faisal, she didn't show it. She moved in a businesslike manner past the gawking soldiers, grinning princes, and admiring foreigners. As she passed a gray Mercedes sedan, she paused long enough to tap her fingertips against the tinted glass of the rear window. A pair of manacled hands pressed against the inside of the pane. They belonged to Khalid. Faisal had promised Fadeela that her brother would be released immediately following the ceremony.

A few more strides brought her to her father's car, a blue Rolls-Royce. Mr. Yamani was indignant about being forced to trade his daughter for his son and made no attempt to disguise his newfound disgust with Faisal, a man he had counted among his friends. At the same time, he was choking with fear. Despite constant reassurances that there were no alien survivors, the sight of the destroyer awakened the sense of doom that had nearly driven him insane during the previous days. When Fadeela came within reach, he clutched the sides of her face tenderly and put his forehead against hers, apologizing with tears in his eyes for failing her. Reluctantly, he began to lead her to the place where Faisal and the king were waiting.

They had only gone a few steps when shouting erupted among the soldiers. A battered truck was climbing onto the bluff and speeding directly toward them. Warning shots failed to slow it down. Just as the soldiers took deadly aim, the driver slammed on the brakes and jumped out. It was Reg. His uniform spattered with blood, he came running toward the entourage, shouting like a wild man. Miriyam was right behind him. They'd dropped Guillaume at the Saudi army's headquarters tent on their way past. The pilots who recognized them ran forward to hear their news. Reg shouldered his way past the men, screaming at everyone to run for their lives.

"You've got to get out of here! Turn around and go!" In his fury to make them understand, he manhandled a prince or two, physically pushing them toward their vehicles. "Where's the king? Let me talk to the king!"

Instead of the king, he was confronted by half a dozen muscular Saudis, who blocked his path. Reg knocked two of them over and kept going. But a moment later he was tackled from behind and subdued by many pairs of hands. With both arms twisted to the breaking point behind his back, Reg was led through the murmuring crowd and then roughly thrown facefirst to the ground.

"Major Cummins, I've been expecting you." Faisal was grinning down at him, as unruffled and smugly confident as ever.

"Listen to me," Reg snarled, his heart still pounding, "I've been inside the ship. They're alive, many of them, hundreds, maybe thousands. They're going to attack." He pointed toward the breach. "They're going to ambush us."

Faisal wasn't buying it. He figured Reg had ulterior motives for disrupting the marriage. "They must be very friendly, these aliens of yours. How nice of them to explain all their terrible plans to you." His easy smile changed to an expression of disgust, and he ordered his men to take Reg away. Before they could, the king intervened.

"Major, what happened to you?" he asked.

Faisal yelled. "It is a trick. He only wants to interrupt our celebration."

"Silence! Let him answer."

Reg shook free of the guards and began telling his

story, The bloodstains on his uniform were still moist, and there was a wild urgency in his voice. It didn't take long for him to convince the king he was telling the truth. Before he had told everything, the king had ordered his assistants to begin turning the caravan around.

"One more thing, Your Majesty," Reg said. "They know you are here. When they attack, they'll look for you first."

Faisal snorted at Reg's melodramatics. "He's making this up! How can he possibly know these things?"

But King Ibrahim was already on the move. He hurried back to his limousine, got in, and screamed at the driver to take him away at once. Faisal walked over to Reg and leaned in, menacingly close. "You're a dead man, Major,"

"And you're a lying coward, Commander."

Shots rang out in the distance. Screams spread through the entourage as everyone turned to face the destroyer. The first alien had come out of the ship.

The lumbering, top-heavy beast pushed through a narrow opening near the triangular breach, moved a few strides out into the sand, and stopped. Ignoring the machine-gun fire, it made a 360-degree scan of the area. The flaring shell of its upper body rose to a pointed tip, and its heavily muscled arms reached almost to the ground. The bullets nicked away pieces of the exoskeleton until the shell cracked and caved in. A moment later, the whole wretched mass toppled over facefirst.

Soldiers and civilians stopped in place and looked on in stunned silence. As the king's limousine sped away, they watched foot soldiers move toward the fallen alien, guns at the ready.

While they were examining it, a second creature emerged. This one never hesitated. It hit the ground running and sprinted across the sand. Hugging the curve of the ship, its path took it directly in front of the royal entourage. It moved awkwardly across the sand and rocks, having evolved in some very different environment. The feet were hooked forward in such a way that the creature moved along standing atop its toe knuckles. The effect was something like a circus bear mincing forward on its hind legs. Still, the beast scurried along at surprising speed, twice as fast as a man.

A cheer went up when the machine-gun fire snapped the creature in half. Its waist was nothing but an exposed spinal column. When it broke, the torso went flying in one direction while the legs went in another. But the thing didn't die. The alien riding inside this suit of armor commanded the arms and tentacles to dig. Within seconds, it built itself a shallow foxhole.

New aliens began appearing every few seconds. Some ran zigzag patterns through the open desert until they were gunned down and killed, but most of them sprinted between the entourage and the massive outer wall of the destroyer, like ducks in a shooting gallery, trying to reach the foxhole. Almost none of them made it. The soldiers at the edge of the bluff began firing larger weapons, and the crowd cheered each time one of the skeletal bodies exploded. Some of the limousines began leaving. Many more were pinned in by parked cars and couldn't move. Drivers leaned on their horns, adding to the noise of the gunfire.

As the alien death toll climbed, the sense of panic abated. They had seemed invincible in the air but appeared helpless on the ground. It looked like the tables had turned. Some people climbed atop their vehicles to watch as others wandered closer to the action. Everyone wanted to see the monsters pay for the atrocities they had committed against humanity.

Faisal smelled another opportunity. Although he was an Air Force officer, he used his status as the man who had saved the Arab world to seize control of the ground army. He called forward a division of tanks and ordered his soldiers to follow them to the front of the conflict. He would join them as soon as he could find a camera crew. They moved off, leaving Reg to his own devices.

He retreated through the tangle of parked cars and found Mrs. Roeder. She was standing on the hood of limousine, talking into her headset radio. Reg jumped up onto the car and urged her to help evacuate the area. The American woman blinked at him in confusion. "Major, I admit you were right about there being survivors, but look around. This thing is shaping up into a good old-fashioned turkey shoot."

Indeed, the aliens were being killed almost as soon as they showed themselves. Most of them, at least. The handful that survived the sprint past the entourage joined their legless companion in the foxhole. It was now a long deep trench, and growing by the moment.

Not far from where Reg was standing, Tye checked his watch, then announced dryly, "I'd say it's time to run like hell."

Remi couldn't have agreed more. "But our driver is stuck. We need transportation." Like the other pilots, he trusted Reg and Miriyam's assessment of the danger. He called a huddle with some of the other pilots and quickly formed a plan. They would escape in the old truck Reg had commandeered earlier. Miriyam had thought to take the keys. Yossi slipped in behind the wheel and turned over the engine. Edward and Sutton were next to him in the cab.

"What are you waiting for? Let's go."

"What about Cummins?" Yossi asked. "We can't leave him."

Sutton wasn't sure Reg was worth the trouble, but volunteered to go get him. He dashed off, leaving Edward and Yossi, Palestinian and Israeli, together in the cab of the truck. There was an uncomfortable, dangerous silence between them. Looking for an excuse to step outside,

Edward studied the mayhem surrounding them and noticed a nearby truck with dozens of rifles lying in the back. He hurried over and grabbed an armful of them along with several boxes of ammunition. He jogged back to the truck and was loading them into the cab when a face appeared at the driver's side window. It was the burly Saudi captain from the camp. He grinned at Yossi and popped open a switchblade.

"*Get lost, you talking donkey*," Edward said in Arabic. "*This is our truck now.*"

"*Shut your mouth, filthy Palestinian dog, or I'll cut your Jewish boyfriend's throat.*" Pleased with himself for foiling the Zionist plot, the muscular captain opened the door and prepared to pull Yossi outside. Before he could do so, he felt the barrel of a gun pressing against the small of his back. A quick hand reached around and lifted his pistol from its holster.

"Drop the knife," came a voice from behind him. It was Miriyam. "If you cooperate, you live. If you make a noise, you die."

The Saudi knew she meant business. What was more, she'd probably get away with it. The sea of noise surrounding them would easily mask the sound of a bullet. His options, it seemed, were limited. Miriyam hustled him to the back of the truck, which was covered by a canvas roof, and made him climb inside. She told him to lie on his stomach, then sat on his back with her pistol pressed to his skull. The truck ground into low gear and started to move.

A few yards away, Sutton spotted Reg. "Cummins, let's get out of here," he yelled. "A group of us are taking that truck of yours and leaving." Reg hesitated. Mrs. Roeder was picking up the first reports of trouble coming from inside the ship, and Reg wanted to know what was happening. Sutton didn't wait. As soon as he'd delivered the message, he turned and left.

Saudi jets were gathering in the sky, and a pair of helicopters thwacked at the air overhead, moving toward the alien foxhole to finish off the survivors. Through the mayhem, Reg spotted Fadeela. Her father had spirited her away from the shooting and was shouting instructions to the driver of the car in which Khalid was being held prisoner. When she glanced in his direction, Reg waved his arms in the air and caught her attention. Their eyes met for a moment before Mr. Yamani dragged her by the wrist toward his own blue Rolls-Royce limousine. They piled inside and took off across the open desert at the head of a four-car caravan. It took Reg a while to realize that Sutton had gone. He was already climbing into the rear of the truck, which was turning around, preparing to leave.

The next ten seconds changed everything. Pulses of white light, energy bursts like the ones they'd faced during the dogfights, flew out of the triangular breach and struck the helicopters, destroying them instantly. Until that moment, the aliens had shown no signs of being armed. More pulse blasts sailed upward and began picking off the Saudi jets high above. Others whizzed toward the tents and the tangle of cars parked on the plateau. A limousine not far from Reg took one of the sizzling, fist-sized projectiles. The front end was turned into shrapnel and the entire vehicle tossed sideways. A separate flurry of shots came from the foxhole. Screaming and panic erupted on the plateau as the entourage was caught in the cross fire.

And their troubles were only beginning. Seconds after the shooting began, the alien ground army started pouring out of the destroyer. Hundreds of aliens, clad in their eight-foot-tall exoskeleton suits of armor, raced down the ramp of debris, firing as they came. Marching out behind them were scores of strange-looking chariots. These vehicles looked like oversize dark brown toboggans that had sprouted short sticklike legs. Each chariot carried a pair of aliens sitting side by side. The chariots looked too flimsy to handle the weight of their bulky passengers, but they raced down the sloping ramp with ease and, when they reached the desert floor, fanned out in several directions to surround the humans. It was the same type of blitzkrieg strategy their attacker planes had used the day before. Within seconds, the chariots had outpaced the alien foot soldiers. While some of the chariots trotted onto the plateau, others raced around the perimeter and began chasing down the cars that were trying to escape.

Reg turned and broke into a dead run, trying to catch up to his friends in the battered truck. Everything was chaos around him. Cars and people were smashing into one another, desperate to get away in time. The truck was just gathering speed when Reg raced up alongside it. Edward threw open his door and helped Reg pull himself inside.

With bullets and enemy pulse blasts flying through the air, Yossi stomped on the accelerator pedal and flew down a steep embankment, nearly rolling the truck. "Which way? Which way do I go?"

"That way," Reg said without hesitation, pointing east. In the distance, he could see the line of cars carrying the Yamani family. One of the alien chariots was following them. Unaware that they were being pursued, the Yamani caravan was bumping along slowly through a shallow valley. Yossi floored it and made up some ground, but they were still far behind when the aliens fired their first shot.

The car at the rear of the caravan exploded and flipped in the air. Once the other limousine drivers realized the danger behind them, they gunned their engines and tried to get away. They stayed together and raced along the bottom of a wide, shallow wadi. In his haste, the lead driver failed to notice the walls of the gully slowly closing in around him. Instead of steering toward the open, high ground, he drove into a shallow canyon, following its twists and turns.

The wadi walls were only four feet tall in some places, but they were too steep for the limousines to climb. The many-legged chariot chased after them, closing in.

Reg and Edward told Yossi to follow the cars into the wadi, but he swerved away and climbed a small embankment instead. It turned out to be the right decision. Keeping to higher ground, he raced along the top edge of the wadi, catching occasional glimpses of the aliens ahead. The difference in terrain allowed them to close the gap until they came within firing range.

Edward passed the rifles he'd taken to the soldiers riding in back. Miriyam had let the Saudi captain up, but she continued to keep an eye on him.

"What about him?" Remi shouted to her. "Give him a gun?" The Israeli woman and the Saudi man stared one another down. It was a long, steely stare, during which neither of them blinked. Remi watched them until he began to laugh. "You guys are too tough! You're scaring me."

Miriyam blinked first. She took a rifle from the African, then called across the truck to the Arab. "What's your name," she asked him.

"Ali Hassan."

"Ali, my name is Miriyam." She tossed him the rifle. "From now on, we fight together."

Ali couldn't help but grin. Needless to say, he'd never met a woman quite like this Jewish warrior. "Okay, sounds good to me."

Tye and Sutton were already in position. They had cut away the canvas tarp covering on the left side of the truck and were waiting for a clear shot at the alien chariot, but they were only getting occasional glimpses. Each time they sighted on the aliens, the aliens' pointed skeleton heads disappeared again behind the banks of the wadi.

"Faster, man, let's go," Edward screamed at Yossi. "You drive like my grandmother."

Behind the wheel, Yossi was driving as close to the soft edge of the wadi as he dared. "Who are these people we're chasing?" he wanted to know.

"Friends of mine," Reg said.

"Your Arab girl?"

Before Reg could answer, they drove downslope and saw the alien chariot right beside them, not twenty feet from the driver's door, speeding along a parallel course. The oversize aliens were crouched forward behind the chariot's front wall as the skinny legs of the sledlike vehicle pumped furiously in the sand. No steering controls or instrumentation of any kind was visible. The chariot seemed to guide itself around the obstacles in its path. A moment after gunfire started raining down on them, the big shell head of the creature closest to them turned to look up at the truck. Then it raised its arm and pointed one of its elongated bone fingers at Yossi. A pulse blast shot toward them and tore through the roof of the cab, inches above the driver's head.

Cursing in Hebrew, Yossi turned away and slowed down.

"What are you doing? Chase them!" Reg yelled.

"What are you, crazy? I'm not killing myself to save a bunch of rich Arabs."

That was the wrong thing to say. Edward took out a pistol and pointed it at the driver's head. "Drive, asshole, or I'll kill you and follow them myself." When Yossi hesitated, Edward squeezed the trigger until the hammer cocked into position.

"Okay, hold on tight." He slammed the gas pedal down and headed after them. Before they could catch up, a pulse blast toasted the third vehicle, and shots were whizzing past the gray Mercedes carrying Khalid.

Remi shouted forward to the men riding in the cab. "We need more ammunition."

"Make it count," Edward told him, handing him a few

twenty-four-round magazines. "This is the last we have."

An explosion flashed up out of the wadi, and, a second later, they caught sight of the car in which Khalid was being held a prisoner. It was turned upside down and burning. The soldiers in the back quickly used up their remaining bullets.

The chauffeur of the last car, the blue Rolls-Royce, slid open the glass partition and called back to his passengers. "Around the next turn, I'm going to stop. When I do, get out fast. I'm going to back up and ram them." The earthen walls were closing in on them, leaving only a few feet of clearance on either side, and the alien chariot was gaining on them. This was their last hope. "Hold on!"

After crashing through a barrier of acacia bushes and fishtailing around a bend, the driver slammed on the brakes. Fadeela threw open her door and pulled her elderly father into the sand. When they were clear of the door, the tires spun, and the Rolls started moving in reverse. The aliens' chariot came speeding around the corner right on cue, moving too fast to swerve out of the way. But as the chauffeur bore down on them, the thin insectile legs of the chariot sprang into the air and clattered over the roof of the Rolls as it passed underneath. The chariot settled smoothly to the ground and rushed past Fadeela and her father before it could slow down and stop. Then it turned in place and began marching back for the kill.

Fadeela heard a rumbling sound in the air as the chariot trotted closer, and one of the aliens leisurely raised a pointed finger in her direction. But both the creatures turned their heads in a new direction when a large shape came flying over the edge of the embankment. The battered Saudi army truck soared through the air and landed on top of the aliens and their chariot with a loud, splintering crack.

The people inside the truck were thrown forward like a collection of rag dolls. But none was seriously injured, and they came staggering outside to inspect the damage. The aliens, their exoskeleton armor, and their transport had all been mashed into an indistinguishable pulp. A few of the chariot's stick legs continued to twitch weakly as the smell of ammonia wafted into the air.

Reg jogged down the wadi to where Fadeela was holding her badly shaken father. When he got there, she stood up and threw her arms around him and squeezed him tightly, burying her face in his chest. When Mr. Yamani saw this, he snapped out of his teary-eyed stupor, stood up, and moved toward them. Reg assumed the old man was angry, when he was only grateful. He threw his arms around the both of them and held them while he cried.

As the others inspected the bodies under the truck, Miriyam warned everyone that the aliens could attack without touching, but that didn't stop Tye from climbing halfway under the truck when he noticed something moving. He was, after all, a mechanic. "Somebody come and have a look at this," he yelled. When the others came around to where he was, all they could see were his long legs lying in the sand. "Down here, look at this!" They squatted and saw him only inches away from an undamaged bony hand. There were four spiky gray fingers opening and closing very slowly.

"Don't touch it," Miriyam screamed at him. "It's still alive."

"Do I look insane? Of course I'm not going to touch it. But look at this gizmo on the hand. It's some kind of light display." He pointed to an amber-colored circular disk set into the back of the hand. It was blinking out a message or a picture—he couldn't tell which—composed of tiny diamond shapes.

Miriyam wasn't much concerned with his discovery. She understood the danger he was in, so she ducked underneath the foul-smelling truck and pumped a few slugs into the broken chest of the armor, making sure the little one inside was dead.

"Okay I think you killed it," Tye called. "The blinking stopped." He pried the disk out of the bone with a pocketknife and brought it out into the sunlight wrapped in a handkerchief. The top of it was like a thin sheet of amber-colored glass. It wasn't glass, though, because there were veins running through it. When he flipped it over, Miriyam recognized the coppery material lining the bottom—it was the same substance she'd seen on the doors in the bowels of the destroyer. She suggested showing it to Reg.

Yossi lit a cigarette and blew the smoke at Edward as he walked past. "You still think I drive like your grandmother?"

"No, you proved me wrong. You're a very fine driver," said the Palestinian as he reached into the breast pocket of Yossi's shirt, took the last cigarette out of the pack and lit it. "Probably you could have done even better if it was Jews inside the cars, instead of a worthless bunch of Arabs." He wadded up the empty package and tossed it at Yossi's feet.

No one was quite sure which direction they should go from there, but everyone agreed it should be *away* from the downed alien destroyer. The Yamanis' driver knew the area well and said there was an oasis town not far away. The truck was damaged but still operable. They found a place where it could be driven out of the wadi, then towed the limousine out as well. As they were preparing to drive away, a pair of men came walking toward them: Khalid, still in his handcuffs, and his jailer. They'd climbed out of their burning Mercedes seconds before it exploded. Mr. Yamani howled with joy at the sight of his son still alive. Fadeela ran forward to greet him. When they came closer, Reg told the jailer to unlock Khalid's handcuffs, but he refused.

"The instructions of Commander Faisal were clear,"

he announced in an official tone of voice. "Khalid Yamani will be freed only when the wedding has been completed."

The pilots exchanged glances with one another and without a word being spoken, they fanned out to surround the man. They might have been enemies in the past, but they were slowly forging themselves into a coherent unit. The jailer became visibly nervous when he realized what he was up against.

"Listen to me, little man." Miriyam started toward him, ready to settle the matter in her less-than-delicate way when a big hand fell on her shoulder and arrested her progress. It was Ali.

"Let me." He walked up to the guard and stood over him menacingly. "Do you know who I am?"

"You are Ali Hassan."

"That's right." He snatched away the jailer's keys and unshackled Khalid's hands. "I am Ali Hassan, and from now on I will fight with these people."

9

AN OASIS TOWN

About noon, the freshly dented Rolls-Royce and the equally battered old truck came to the oasis town of Qal'at Buqum. It was no more than a cluster of swaying green palm trees in the middle of an arid valley baking in the sun. From a distance, it looked an all-too-perfect mirage, except for the twenty-story-tall steel radio tower that rose from the center of town. Under normal circumstances, it was a dusty village with two hundred permanent residents. That day, there were almost a thousand people within its limits, down from the three thousand that had slept there the night before. You could walk from one end to the other in ten minutes. Brightly painted shops and houses with crumbling mud-plaster walls lined the road, standing shoulder to shoulder with the prefab commercial buildings built since the oil boom. On the eastern horizon stood the Asir mountains, the great barrier between Qal'at Buqum and the sea.

The town's central square was an asphalt parking lot overgrown with weeds around the edges. The Saudi military had established a command post there, retreating into the shade of the nearest building, the post office, to escape the intense midday heat. Some of the soldiers had been on the plateau with the royal family and their guests when the ambush took place.

As Reg and his crew were piling out of their truck, they were surrounded by children trying to sell them things.

Yossi pushed them aside as he moved past on his way to the Saudi headquarters. The others did the same. The last ones out of the truck were Tye and Sutton.

Sutton hesitated before wading into the mob of dirty children. He looked back and saw that Tye had taken out the amber medallion and was examining it for the umpteenth time.

"Will you quit fiddling with that blasted thing and let's go?" He jumped to the ground, and the children immediately swarmed around him, showing him wristwatches and sunglasses for sale. They tugged on his clothing, shouting, "This very good, this very cheap." Sutton roared angrily at them to get away, and they shrank from him in fear.

"For Pete's sake, man, they're just kids." Tye hopped out of the truck and waved hello. In a flash, the little salesmen were on him, pushing and shouting and shoving their wares into his face.

"My name Mohammed," said the tallest boy. He had dark eyes and the wispy beginnings of a mustache. His skin was as dark as Remi's. He slid an arm around Tye's waist. "I am your friend. You come with me the shop my cousin. Very good merchandise, very good price."

"I've got a friend named Mohammed. Did anyhow. Sorry, boys," he announced. "I'm broke. *Me no money.*" Of course, that wasn't quite true. He had a thick wad of Saudi riyals, the equivalent of five thousand American dollars, stuffed into his undershorts.

Even though the kids were pushy, Tye couldn't help feeling sorry for them. They were scrawny and dirty and looked like they didn't live anywhere in particular. One boy caught the tall Englishman's attention. All he had to sell were some old magazines. He opened one of them for Tye's inspection and held it toward his face. Just when they were letting Tye go his way, Sutton bolted back toward them and grabbed one of the oldest boys by the scruff of the neck, then shook him. "Sutton, what are you doing?"

"You little sneak," Sutton yelled at the kid, walking him roughly over to Tye. "Give it back to him." The boy, Mohammed, was terrified, crying and pleading with Sutton in Arabic.

"You're scaring the hell out him, man. Let him go."

"He's faking it," Sutton said. He shook the boy again and told him to quit crying or he'd call the Saudi soldiers over. "Thief get hand chop chop." Realizing Sutton wasn't going to fall for his act, Mohammed snapped out of it and straightened up.

"I no t'ief. You drop this one." He opened his hand and showed Tye the amber medallion he'd taken from Tye's pocket.

"Well that's interesting," Tye said, bending over to study the disk. "It's working again. Can I have my handkerchief, please."

"I no take—" When he began to protest, Sutton twisted the collar tighter around his throat. Mohammed pulled out the handkerchief and handed it over. Tye lifted the disk away from the boy's palm and it went blank again. He put it back down, and it lit up again.

"Isn't that queer?" Deciding it probably wasn't dangerous, he set it in his own palm. It worked again. He looked up at the pickpocket and smiled. "Thanks. I think you figured it out." Sutton turned him loose, but only after planting a hard kick in the seat of his pants. The boys all cursed them as they walked away to join the other pilots.

They found the rest of the squad standing around the village's post office, directly under the radio tower. Lookouts had climbed to the top of the twenty-story structure to keep a watch for any unwanted visitors. The soldiers who had escaped from the ill-fated photo session at the crash site had a grim tale to tell. Nearly everyone had been killed. The aliens took a number of additional casualties, but the battle had been a one-sided rout. After surrounding them, the chariots had moved in and systematically hunted the humans down. There had been several cases of "brain torture," an interrogation technique. Reg knew exactly what they were talking about, having suffered through it himself. The tanks had done almost no damage because the alien pulse blasts shorted out their electrical systems, and the Saudi Air Force couldn't get close enough to give effective air support. It was, in short, a slaughter.

Ali and Khalid were given assault rifles, but the soldiers refused to issue weapons or ammunition to any non-Saudis. They did, however, introduce Khalid to the town's leading merchant, an old woman in a traditional Bedouin dress and a black cloth wrapped around her leathery brown face. When Khalid asked if she had any ammunition, she squinted at his weapon.

"What is that?" she asked. "A Kalashnikov? I think I can help you. Do you have any money?"

Remi took out the envelope he'd been handed during the ceremony and tossed it to Khalid. "Buy the store," he said.

Khalid Yamani was used to handing out large sums of cash, not receiving them. He chuckled and said he'd bring Remi plenty of change, then started following the old woman toward her store.

"Always go in groups," Miriyam said. She pointed at Sutton and told him to go with Khalid.

Sutton didn't appreciate her tone of voice. "Yes, sir!" he said, and gave her a sarcastic salute before leaving.

"Why did you bring that guy?" Yossi asked when Sutton was gone. "He is a pain in the ass."

"You noticed that, too, eh?"

After a while, the heat drove them toward the shade

of the oasis's palm grove, where the temperature was twenty degrees cooler. As in many oasis towns, the actual springs at Qal'at Buqum were buried under concrete and surrounded by barbed wire. The pools of dark water babbling beneath the trees were all man-made and supplied by underground pipe. There were picnic benches, trash cans, and brick ovens for family barbecues. Scores of refugees from the cities had taken up residence in this shady park, living mostly out of the backs of their cars. Some of them wandered over to speak with the multinational squad of pilots when the sound of automatic gunfire came from overhead. The men perched in the radio tower were firing at something and shouting to the soldiers standing in the square below. The white flashes of an alien pulse weapon tore through the air and smashed into the radio tower, sending the lookouts plummeting to their deaths. The civilians hit the deck as Reg and his crew ran back toward the square. The destructive pulse bursts were coming from inside a walled compound just across the town's only road.

Reg found the ranking Saudi officer hiding in the bushes beside the post office. He and his men had already devised a plan to surround the compound. Before Reg could talk to them, they took off, running in crouches.

"Don't these bastards have anything better to do than follow us around?" Sutton asked, gesturing toward the alien hiding place. He and Khalid were back from their shopping spree and started passing out magazines full of cartridges.

"We should follow them," Khalid said, watching the soldiers advance. They had reached the edge of the road without incident. Making it across was going to be another matter.

When Miriyam stood up to survey the situation, a pulse blast tore into the front wall of the post office, only inches from her head. It didn't seem to bother her much. She squatted and conferred with Reg. "It looks like there's only two of them over there."

"They like to start small," Reg said, "then rush in and hit you from all sides."

She turned around and looked into the parklike oasis, thinking the same thing Reg was thinking. "If they get into these trees," she said, "they'll be able to drive us out into the open."

"We've got to split up and defend the perimeter."

"You're right. Three groups of three." She pointed at Tye and Ali. "You and you, follow me." Then she turned and hurried along the wall, leading the group toward the rear of the post-office building. From there, they headed off in different directions.

Reg, Remi, and Khalid ended up together. They jogged through the trees, keeping alert for signs of danger. As they passed campsites, Khalid shouted to the people in Arabic, warning them of the possible danger. Reg stopped and took a long look around.

"If you were an alien," he asked, "which way would you come?"

"Wherever there's no people to shoot at me," Remi answered.

Khalid disagreed. "They are hunters. They will go where they can kill."

Through the trees they spotted the shell of a long, narrow, abandoned building. The doors, roof, and windows were all missing. It had become a temporary home to several families of refugees. There was laundry hanging on the bushes nearby and the smoke of a cooking fire, but otherwise no signs of life.

"That's it," said Reg, and the three of them ran to reach the spot, splashing through a knee-deep pond that stood in their path. They could feel the presence of the enemy before they heard the moaning that came from inside the walls of the structure.

"Look over there in the bushes," Remi said. Two bodies, a man and a woman, lay flat on their backs with blood coming from their ears, eyes, and noses. Their eyes were wide-open, as if the last thing they'd seen had surprised them.

Reg heard a gasping, shuddering noise that sounded like someone being electrocuted. He led the way to the building, put his back against the wall, and edged toward an open window. Reg grabbed Khalid's arm and gave him a piece of advice. "Let's don't do anything crazy here. We've got to stay alive if we're going to kill them." He knew his friend sometimes couldn't distinguish between bravery and recklessness. But the warning fell on deaf ears. Khalid went straight to the window and looked inside. What he saw made him recoil in horror.

One of the aliens was kneeling in a doorway with the tentacles of his biomechanical suit holding three separate victims pinned to the floor. There were two children and a woman, their bodies convulsing in pain as the alien interrogated them mentally. Khalid screamed at the thing and opened fire. He sent a sustained volley of gunfire in through the window. The creature reacted by shuffling backwards into the next room, dragging one of the children with it. Khalid leapt inside and ran to the doorway. A pulse blast sliced through it and exploded against the far wall, nearly taking Khalid's handsome face with it.

The inside of the structure was a labyrinth of decayed walls and leaning doorways. By the time Reg and Remi climbed inside, the creature had retreated deeper into the building, dragging the child with it. Khalid bolted through the doorway into the next room and was immediately surrounded by pulse blasts. Despite the danger, Reg and Remi followed him in.

Dodging the explosions, they followed the sounds of

the alien through two more doorways. Khalid was about to step through the third when Remi held him back. They listened. The sound of sporadic gunfire was coming from several places in the oasis. During the spaces of silence, they could hear the child's labored breathing on the other side of the nearest wall. Remi pointed into the next room. It was waiting for them.

When Khalid peeked around the corner, there was a loud crunch, then something flew out of the doorway. It was the child's body, a girl about nine years old. She slid down a wall and landed in a broken heap. Reg thought Khalid would rush into the room, looking for revenge. Instead, he kept his cool. "There's a window behind him. You keep him busy, and I'll surprise him from outside." The men nodded as Khalid hurried back the way they'd come.

Reg and Remi kept their weapons trained on the doorway as the harsh sun beat down on them through the open roof. Then Reg pulled Remi closer to the wall and pointed up. He could give the murderous invader something else to think about by firing a few shells over the top. But as Remi was boosting him up, Reg lost his sense of balance. A strange sensation moved through him, a sensation he recognized as the presence of an alien mind.

As his Ethiopian comrade looked on in confusion, Reg sank to the floor, grimacing in anguish. The creature was reaching through the wall to infiltrate Reg's mind. A cramping pain shot through him, as if his body was a pincushion pierced by freezing cold needles. As quickly as it began, Reg knew there was only one way to make it stop. He had to tell everything he knew, had to open his memory to the intelligent presence inside him. And he did. At the alien's command, he conjured up the mental image of the post office and the Saudi soldiers trying to get across the road, then he "remembered" something he'd never seen before: a view from inside the compound, looking out at the post office and the radio tower, and as fast as he could think it, he was identifying the directions the soldiers would come from, then he was huddled in the bushes listening to Miriyam say, "three groups of three," and running toward the back of the building and splitting up. The pain and the rapid series of images running through his mind confused him, made him feel the need to show the alien everything it wanted to see. And then he was showing himself, sending an image of him and Remi huddled at the base of the wall. *And the third one, where is the third one?* It wanted to know about Khalid, and, for the first time, Reg resisted the thing's power, tried to deny it, but the memory-images were coming out of him in an unstoppable stream. He pictured Khalid running back through the tangle of walls toward the empty window frame. He tried to stop thinking, tried to take back control of his mind, desperate not to betray his friend, but found himself imagining Khalid running along the outside wall toward the alien's hiding place. Then he found a way to resist. With all the concentration he could muster, he steered his image of Khalid away from the wall and toward trees of the oasis. It was like guiding a dream while he was having it. To sustain his concentration, he made the image of Khalid start doing the first crazy things that came to mind. Khalid began to skip, then jumped into the air, grabbed the branch of a tree, and flipped himself impossibly high in the air like a gymnast.

The alien mind flared with anger inside his own, realizing Reg wasn't cooperating. The painful seizure intensified, and the wordless question rang through him: *Where is the third one?* But Reg was learning quickly. In his imagination, Khalid was suddenly dressed in top hat and tails, dancing through the oasis like Fred Astaire in the old movie Reg had seen a week earlier. The pain began to subside as Reg began to understand how he could control the confrontation with the invisible presence. The idea occurred to him that he might even be able to turn the tables and attack his attacker. At that point, the alien presence quickly withdrew.

A second later, the real Khalid leaned in a window and blasted away at the bioarmor until it collapsed, and the alien was torn to shreds.

In another part of the oasis, Tye had injured himself twice before his team had spotted any of the invaders. First he cut his hand tripping over a garbage can, then twisted an ankle trying to run backwards. For his own safety, Miriyam assigned him to stay where he was and "guard" the center of the oasis. Then she and Ali disappeared into a thicket of tall ferns and densely clustered palms.

The twigs and dried leaves on the ground crunched under their boots as they prowled forward, glancing at one another through the vegetation. The pair of them were about as different as two people could possibly be, but they shared soldiering skills in common and were able to move ahead efficiently and quietly, coordinating their movements with subtle gestures and facial expressions. Miriyam froze in mid-stride when she heard Ali tap his finger against the side of his assault rifle. He had seen something. She followed his gaze until she saw it, too. Far ahead, one of the tentacled gray giants was coming toward them. It was following a trickling stream of runoff water into the oasis.

Speaking only with his hands, Ali suggested they put themselves in the predator's path and lie in wait. Miriyam agreed and followed him toward a little clearing where the water ran close to a set of picnic tables. After selecting their hiding places, they settled in to wait. Between occasional bursts of gunfire coming from the battle near the post office, they could hear it rustling closer.

Ali couldn't see it from where he was, so he relied on Miriyam to monitor the thing's progress. She was hiding behind a tree and peeked around it every so often, then nodded in his direction. Then she looked around the oasis as if she were just realizing where she was. She shook her head and smiled at the absurdity of the situation. Ali smiled back at her, agreeing wholeheartedly. Silently, she asked if he was scared. He looked back at her with an expression that said of course not. But a moment later, he changed his mind and nodded that yes, he was. Terrified, in fact. They both smiled again until Miriyam realized the rustling had stopped.

She peeked out and saw something repulsive. The creature had stopped and lowered itself into a squatting position over the water. The large skull-thorax opened slowly, like the halves of a clamshell, to reveal the smaller body tucked inside under a layer of clear gelatin. It was an indistinct mass of tissue except for the bulging eyes. They stood out like a pair of polished-silver goose eggs. Ali snapped his fingers to get Miriyam's attention, but she waved him off without looking away from the gruesome sight. The alien lifted itself partially out of the body cavity and reached down to the water with its two-fingered hands. Although it made no attempt to scoop the water up or lower its mouthless face to the surface, it appeared to be drinking, absorbing the water through its skin.

Miriyam put her fingers to her lips, slid away from her tree, and began snaking silently closer. To get the shot she needed, she had to get down into the streambed away from intervening obstacles. She would be vulnerable, away from cover, but she wanted to pick the enemy off with one shot rather than risk a prolonged firefight. She crawled forward on her stomach until there was nothing between her and her target. Before she could kill it, the sound of an automatic weapon erupted in another part of the oasis. The alien darted back into its burrow and the bioarmor snapped closed. It started marching forward, fast. Miriyam had nowhere to run.

Ali reacted quickly when he saw she was trapped. "Here I am!" he cried. He stood up and showed himself in the clearing, waving his arms. He taunted the creature with choice Arab-style insults. "Come get me, you son of a jackal; come close so I can spit in your mouth."

A twelve-inch-long finger pointed at him, and a pulse blast sizzled between the trees, exploding into the picnic table beside Ali, tearing it to pieces. Running in a crouch, he got out of the clearing and into the trees, where he figured he was safe. "You missed me, you scab on a monkey's ass."

Miriyam bolted out of the streambed and ran for the nearest cover. She ducked behind a thick palm just as a white flash ripped into the other side of the trunk and broke the tree in half. It crashed down, pinning her to the ground. Ali made it over to her and tried to lift the tree away.

"Get me out of here!" She winced.

"I will," he said. Then he slipped out of view.

"Ali. don't leave me here, you bastard."

The exoskeleton's head was in sight, bobbing above the vegetation as it moved steadily forward. Miriyam didn't have a clear line, but she took aim the best she could and began to blast away. Ali hurried back with a thick plank of wood from the ruined picnic table and wedged it under the fallen trunk for leverage. The powerfully built soldier lifted the tree away as Miriyam continued to fire. The alien was almost on top of them. Its shell was cracking under the barrage of Miriyam's bullets, but not giving way. It was too late to run. The creature stepped out of the streambed and pointed its curving spike of a finger down at Miriyam.

Before it could fire, a series of gun blasts came from a new direction and hit the side of the shell. This distracted the creature just long enough for Ali to swing the wooden plank. With a loud cracking noise, the alien's hand broke off and hit the ground. Squealing in pain, the alien sent a tentacle forward to impale Ali, but he dodged it and jabbed the end of the plank into the thing's face. The shell wall collapsed, and when he pulled the wood away, Miriyam pumped bullets into the opening he had created.

The eight-foot-tall body wilted into a heap on the ground.

Miriyam and Ali breathed a sigh of relief, then looked to see where the mysterious salvo of shots had come from. Tye jogged up to them and looked down at the dead alien. "There's got to be a better way of killing these things," he said.

In another area of the oasis town, Yossi, Sutton, and Edward were about to discover a better way. The three of them were pinned down behind a low stone wall, with bullets whizzing over their heads in one direction and alien pulse blasts going in the other.

The land was higher at one end of the oasis, ending in a set of hills. The slope had been graded into a series of terraces, three-foot-tall walls made of stone. A large group of Saudi civilians, members of the same clan, had been living there since the invasion started. When they heard the shooting begin, they grabbed their weapons and rushed out to the stone walls, using them as barricades. They opened fire when a pair of tentacled killers came marching down the slope. When the Brit, the Palestinian, and the Israeli rushed up the slope to help them, a second pair of aliens appeared at the top of the hill and began blasting away. After slaughtering the defenders near the top, the aliens began picking off humans one at a time with their pulse weapons. The members of the clan hid themselves at the base of the slope, doing their best to keep the alien invaders at bay.

But their numbers were dwindling quickly. The day before, in the air, the pulse blasts coming from the alien attack planes had been only marginally accurate, connecting with their targets about ten percent of the time. But in their bioarmor, the aliens were much more lethal. Every thirty seconds, it seemed, the humans sustained another casualty, especially those trapped on the terraced hillside. The pulses couldn't reach them behind the walls, but almost everyone who broke into the open and dashed for the bottom of the hill was picked off.

Edward was desperate to get off the hill. "We've got to create a diversion and get down into the trees."

"Go ahead," Yossi sneered. "You'll never make it. We've got to wait for them to come to us."

"We're dead. We're definitely dead," Sutton moaned.

A couple of kids bolted into the open, running together. While everyone else was trying to get *off* the slope, these two came out of the trees and started advancing up the hill. The sound of clanking bottles came from the cardboard box they carried between them. They crouched a little as they ran, but otherwise failed to appreciate the danger they were in.

"I don't believe it," Sutton said. "Those are two of the little punks who pickpocketed Tye."

"What are they doing?"

"Sounds like they've got bottles," the Englishman said. "Maybe they're going to try selling us some sodas."

The men cringed as they watched the boys zigzag their way up the hill, waiting for the inevitable flash of the alien weapons that would tear their bodies apart. But somehow, miraculously, they made it all the way up and joined the others behind the wall.

"What the hell are you doing?"

"We kill dem," said the younger boy.

"We have many bombs we make," announced

Mohammed. He tipped the box and showed them what was inside: bottles filled with gasoline. Rags had been stuffed into the openings to act as wicks. Mohammed pulled out an engraved silver lighter and pretended to light the gas-soaked rag, then pantomimed throwing the bottle at his young friend, who summed up their strategy in three words.

"I am boom."

"Yes, we know. Molotov cocktails," Sutton said, shaking his head sadly. "The problem is that these creatures are wearing armor. They're protected. We need bazookas, not these rinky-dink little bottle bombs." The boys didn't understand a word he'd said.

"I am boom," repeated the younger boy.

"How much?" Sutton asked sardonically, assuming the boys were there to make a sale.

"Very good merchandise, very good price," Mohammed said with a grin. "For you, my friend, price is free." He offered one of the homemade weapons to Sutton, who refused it.

"I'll stick to bullets, thank you."

"They're coming," Yossi announced. The others peeked over the top of the wall and saw the four exoskeletons moving closer, one terrace at a time, peppering the area with pulse blasts as they came. When they noticed the human heads peeking over the top of the wall, they changed direction, moving in for a quick kill before continuing down into the trees.

The younger boy lit a bottle, stood up, and threw it as hard as he could. Rather than duck back down, he watched its flight through the air. Before it hit anything, he was dead. A pulse blast hit him square in the solar plexus and knocked him twenty paces down the slope. The alien energy bursts caused different kinds of damage depending on the material they interacted with. They twisted the heavy steel girders of the radio tower out of shape, but didn't explode human flesh. The boy's body was smashed, blackened, and bloody, but still in one piece. Mohammed's first reaction was to run to his friend, but Sutton pulled him back and pinned him against the wall, holding him there until he stopped struggling. An angry roar of gunshots came out of the trees, but the aliens continued to advance.

Yossi lit one of the gasoline-soaked wicks, sneaked a quick look over the wall, then threw as best he could, grenade-style, protecting himself from the counterfire. The bottle landed without exploding.

"That was terrible," Edward said. "You throw like my grandmother."

"You think you can do better?" He handed over a lit Molotov cocktail. "Show me." Edward measured the weight of the bottle in his hand before setting it aside and picking up a heavy stone.

"I know you Palestinians like to throw rocks," Yossi said, "but these guys aren't Jewish soldiers with rubber bullets."

"Just watch," Edward said. He lobbed the heavy stone high into the air in the direction of the aliens. As it reached the top of its arc, he stood up and tomahawked the bottle thirty-five feet on a straight line. As he hoped, the aliens were distracted by stone falling toward them. The bottle shattered against the blunt bone face of the closest creature and spread fire over the surface of the bioarmor. Edward ducked behind the wall again before a single pulse blast was fired.

Behind the wall, the men heard squealing and thrashing. They peeked over the edge and saw the creature staggering around, swatting at the flames with its tentacles. The walls of the big skull-thorax shell opened, and the fragile, skinny creature riding inside jumped out of the suit. Before it could scramble into the nearest bushes, a barrage of bullets came from the trees at the base of the slope and ripped it to shreds.

"Incredible! It worked!" Sutton shouted. He patted

Mohammed on the shoulder. "He went boom!"

"Don't be too happy," Edward cautioned. "There are three more, and they're coming this way."

Sutton stole a glance over the wall and realized he was right. "Don't these things learn?"

"Let's hope not," Edward said. Then he turned to Yossi, who was staring at him, impressed, and explained his skill with Molotov cocktails. "I got some practice during the Intifada."

The Israeli lit a couple more of the wicks. "This time, I won't throw like your grandmother. I'll pretend I'm throwing at Yasir Arafat."

The attack continued. The aliens followed their strategy of trying to surround the soldiers, but it wasn't enough. The men spread out and torched the creatures wherever they tried to cross the wall.

Half an hour later, all the aliens in Qal'at Buqum were dead. Those who had defended the oasis gathered near the post office, comparing notes and carrying the wounded to an infirmary at the end of town. Despite their victory and the fact that they'd found a reliable way of killing the invaders, there was only a guarded optimism. The officer in charge of the Saudi forces, fearing another sneak attack, sent dozens of men to stand sentry duty around the perimeter of the oasis.

In the strategy session that ensued, much of the discussion centered on acquiring the right weapons—flamethrowers. The Saudis had them, of course, but not many. None of the men milling around the center of town had ever trained with one. Locating them and getting them to where they were needed was going to take time.

Reg went to the Rolls-Royce and found Mr. Yamani exactly where he'd been since they arrived in Qal'at Buqum an hour before. He was curled up on the backseat with his arms wrapped around his head. Reg ducked inside to try and reassure the old man that he was safe, at least for the time being, but couldn't get a response out of him. He was trembling and mumbling to himself in Arabic. Khalid came up behind Reg and was angry that Fadeela had left her father in such a state.

Someone told them she had gone to the infirmary, and Reg volunteered to go and look for her. He walked down the road to the edge of town until he found the building. It was a dilapidated doctor's office that was ill equipped to handle the dozens of injuries sustained during the battle. He found the doctor in charge, a man who wore slacks and a silk shirt instead of the more traditional Saudi garments. He spoke English with a Scottish accent.

"She said her father was uncontrollably nervous and wanted something to calm him down. I kicked her out and told her not to come back until she was decently covered." Then he looked Reg over disapprovingly. "Why do you want to find her?" Reg didn't answer the man, just turned and left. As soon as he was on the street again, he saw the old truck coming in his direction. Miriyam and Remi were riding up front with Ali, who was driving.

"Hurry up and get in," Miriyam said. "We're going to a place where we can get some weapons."

"What's the big hurry?" Reg asked, glancing toward the center of town. A large convoy of military vehicles had begun to arrive.

"It's Faisal. He has taken Khalid prisoner again, and he's looking for you. Get in."

There didn't seem to be much choice, so Reg jumped in the rear compartment and watched the oasis town slowly recede from view. When he finally sat down, he noticed there was a man he didn't recognize riding along with them. It was a Saudi soldier with his *keffiyeh* pushed down to cover his face. There was something oddly fragile about the soldier, and when "he" finally looked up and smiled, Reg saw that it wasn't a man after all. It was Fadeela.

10

UGLY WEAPONS

As they motored east along a lonely stretch of highway, the only traffic they encountered was a convoy of military jeeps heading in the opposite direction and a Saudi army helicopter that buzzed up behind them before shooting ahead. It was about three in the afternoon, and the sun was at its most punishing. In the back of the truck, the breeze kept skin temperatures down, but the metal floor and walls were hot to the touch.

Tye hardly noticed. He had spread some rags on the floor near the tailgate and was busy examining his growing collection of alien biohardware. In the aftermath of the battle, he'd dislodged two more medallions from the backs of alien hands. But his concentration was centered on the examination of something that looked like a slightly warped piece of half-inch pipe. It was one of the pulse weapons.

Using a heavy stone, he'd broken open an exoskeleton forearm and dug the thing out. It lay just below the shell, nestled in the ropy white meat. Although it was the color and consistency of tooth enamel, the tube had soft flanges attached to its sides. He had found them wrapped around the muscles in the arm, and they had to be peeled away one by one before the weapon could be lifted out of its resting place. These flanges were about three inches long and one inch wide. They were flat and resembled the rubbery leaves of seaweed, but were the color of copper and composed of the same material found on the backs of the medallions. The pulse weapon looked more like a skinny prehistoric fish than any kind of gun he'd ever seen. It was hollow and open at the end where the ball of condensed energy was expelled. The other end was swollen and green—the same shade of green he'd seen flying along the underside of the city destroyer. The same green, Reg told him, as the crystalline pillars growing in the bowels of the ship.

"That thing is disgusting," Sutton told him. "Don't touch it. It's probably full of germs."

"I wiped it off," Tye said. "It's not like it's rotting meat or anything. It's some kind of machine." The other passengers had a hard time buying that. It didn't look like a machine.

"I don't like it," Edward said. "Remember when the Americans brought back rocks from Mars? The newspapers talked about the danger of germs or bacteria that we can't defend against. And that was only rocks; this thing came out of a body."

For once Yossi agreed with something Edward had to say. "I think we should get rid of it. It could be poison. Why take the risk?"

"If it's true," Fadeela said, "that the aliens have some strange diseases, it's already too late. Thousands of people throughout the country must have already been exposed to them. And we don't even know about the rest of the world."

The debate ended when Tye reached down and picked the thing up with his bare hand. The coppery flanges came to life and wrapped themselves around his arm, strapping the machine to his forearm. Startled by the rapid movement, the others recoiled, but Tye was more fascinated than afraid. He lifted his forearm close to his face and examined it closely before turning to the others. "I think it likes me."

"See if you can make it fire," Reg said.

Since there was nothing that looked like a trigger, Tye did as he'd seen the aliens do. He pointed his arm out the back of the truck and extended his finger. Nothing happened. He picked up one of the medallions and touched the coppery side to various parts of the device. He peeled it off and allowed it to reattach to his other arm. He flexed his muscles and shouted, "Fire!" but couldn't get the weapon to work. He turned to the others and shrugged. "Maybe you have to be eight feet tall and really, really ugly for it to work."

"If that's the case," Sutton joked, "you're our best candidate."

"Let me try it," Reg said, moving closer and reaching for the device.

Tye pulled away, not ready to relinquish control of the object. "This one's mine. You'll have to go out and find your own." He was only half kidding.

Reg explained his theory that the way to trigger the firing mechanism might involve some sort of telepathy or mental suggestion. "I've been thinking about these suits of armor they wear. How do they control them? It can't be that the suits are imitating the movements of the little guy operating them. For one thing, there's no room to move inside those chest cavities. And besides, the aliens don't have tentacles, but their suits do. It might be a simple matter of willing it to work. Let me see it for a minute."

Again, Tye pulled it away from Reg. "I've got plenty of mental control. I'll try it." He raised his arm and pointed his finger, this time with more ceremony. Speaking like a medium conducting a seance, he said, "I command you to fire a pulse blast. I am visualizing a pulse blast firing out of you. I command you to fire!" He was perfectly sincere, but some of the others began laughing at him.

"Oh ferchrissake, man, give me that thing."

Fadeela spoke on Reg's behalf. "Michael, let Reg try it.

He has been inside their minds twice already. Perhaps he can make it work."

Sutton was enjoying the show. "Do you have any idea how ridiculous you people look? May I remind you that this thing is from another galaxy, designed by an intelligence we don't understand?"

"Oh, go ahead," Tye said, holding his arm out so Reg could peel the rubbery flippers away from his skin. The instant Reg's fingertips came into contact with the device, there was a blinding flash. An energy pulse sailed into the sky for a mile or so before dissipating.

"Okay, you win." Tye peeled the tube off his arm, set it on the floor of the truck, and pushed it toward Reg. "Whatever you got from those aliens, it works."

Reg held the thing over his arm and allowed it to cling to him. His sweat quickly collected in pools under the flippers, which clung to his arm like clammy leaves. He willed the device to fire again, but had no more luck than Tye.

He continued fiddling with the strange device until Fadeela finally solved the riddle. She moved down to the end of the truck and told Reg to point the gun down at the shoulder of the road rushing away behind them. Then she touched the tip of her finger to one of the coppery flippers and, a second later, a pulse ripped out of the gun and exploded in the dirt.

"Now aim over there, at those rocks," she said. And again the gun went off a second after she touched it. The pulse flew in the direction of the rock formation he'd pointed at, but didn't connect. After some experimentation, the operating principles of the weapon became clear to them. Getting the weapon to fire required two or more people making contact with it and mentally commanding it to send out a pulse. Aiming it was just as easy. If both shooters agreed where they wanted the pulse to go, it went there.

It was an awesome weapon: lightweight, powerful, accurate, and didn't seem to need reloading. By force of will alone, it could be made to deliver one pulse per second. The team began to have fun with it, imagining they were blasting away at tentacled exoskeletons. They passed it around, and everyone learned to use it. Everyone except Sutton. He was waiting to be asked, but the invitation never came. Eventually, he moved toward the cab of the truck and pretended to take a nap.

"It makes sense," Reg said. "They think together, as one mind. But we're all separate. This little gizmo seems to need the go-ahead from more that one mind before it will fire. They must have built that function in, designed it that way."

"If we could build guns that worked the same way, it would solve a lot of our problems in the world," Edward mused. "If it always took more than one person to squeeze a trigger, we'd have less violence, especially killings. There would be no more lone gunmen going on killing sprees."

"Can you describe what it's like?" Yossi asked Reg. "What is this telepathic interrogation they do?"

"You mean the mind-lock?" Reg asked.

"Yeah, what does it feel like?"

"And how did you know there was more than one mind?"

Reg wasn't sure he could describe the sensation. He tried. At first he fumbled for the words, but then started talking more freely. He was still telling them about it when the truck pulled off the road and approached the gates of an isolated military facility.

Ali got out of the truck and talked to the soldiers in the guardhouse for several minutes before he convinced them to roll the gates open and allow the truck to pass.

They drove into what looked at first to be an ordinary

Saudi military base: jeeps, trucks, Quonset hut military barracks, and a few hangars alongside a poorly maintained landing strip.

Almost at once, the international crew realized something was amiss. The base was large enough to require several hundred personnel. But even in the middle of the afternoon, there was not a single person outside. The tires on the jeeps and trucks were flat, as if they hadn't been moved for a long time. The curtains and blinds were all drawn. None of the buildings seemed to have any air-conditioning units. Obviously, the entire base was some sort of decoy. They asked Ali about it, but he waved them off, telling them he didn't know anything about the place.

Farther on, they came into a well-tended part of the facility and were surprised to see a series of greenhouses surrounding a large one-story building. A sign in front identified it as the Al-Sayyid Agricultural Research Facility. The helicopter that had passed them earlier was parked on a patch of lawn between the greenhouses and the main building. The pilot of the craft saluted them as they drove past.

"Don't you think that's a little odd?" Reg asked. "There's not a farm within a hundred miles of here." No one knew quite what to make of the place, but they all had other issues on their minds.

"Maybe they want to make their desert bloom," Yossi suggested, and they left it at that.

Ali drove past the last set of buildings to the end of the paved road and headed out onto a dusty, rutted trail that took them into a field of weeds and tall bushes. When they'd driven half a mile, he stopped the truck and turned off the engine.

"This is it," he announced to his bewildered passengers. He left the trail and walked toward a dense clump of thorny bushes, which he kicked aside to clear a path.

At the center of the weed patch, they found themselves standing on a slab of concrete. Ali stomped on the ground with his boot until he heard a hollow sound. He then brushed away a layer of sand and dirt to reveal an iron door. Further searching led him to an electric switch box. He flipped it open and entered a sequence of numbers on the keypad hidden inside. There was a sharp click when the door unlocked automatically.

"I thought you didn't know anything about this place," Reg said.

Ali shrugged. "I lied." He lifted the door and led the way down a set of stairs.

The bunker was roughly the size of a basement for a house that was never built above. Its concrete walls were lined with steel shelving stocked with cardboard and metal boxes. Everything was coated in a layer of fine dust. When they wiped away the dust and read the packing labels, Edward and Ali were disappointed with what they saw.

"What does it say?" Miriyam asked.

"Gas masks," Edward told her. "Nothing but gas masks."

There were also rubber suits, medical supplies, and oxygen canisters—things you'd need in the event of chemical warfare. Ali was unfazed. He said they should keep looking, that there were flamethrowers down there somewhere.

Eventually, he found what he was looking for. A pair of antique flamethrowers that looked like thick-barreled field guns from World War I. He carried them out into the light and laid them on the ground.

"We came all the way out here for these?" Tye asked. "I'll be surprised if they still work."

"They work," Ali assured him, lifting several canisters of fuel out of the bunker. The Cyrillic lettering stenciled onto the tanks indicated that they had come from the former Soviet Union. Ali also found a pair of rotting leather harnesses that allowed the tanks to be strapped to the back of the soldiers using the weapons.

Edward volunteered to act as the guinea pig and test them. After connecting a tank to a flamethrower, he strapped the equipment on and lit the small pilot light at the tip of the gun. Then he pointed it out into the sand and squeezed the trigger. A roaring gush of flame spewed out and shot more than a hundred feet through the air. Alarmed, Edward quickly released the trigger, but the flame continued to flare out of the gun until the canister was empty. When it was finished, there was a trail of fire burning on the desert floor.

"It still works," Edward observed.

A few minutes later, as they were loading their supplies into the truck, they heard the sound of gunfire in the distance. It came from the agricultural facility. The team quickly piled into the truck and raced toward the greenhouses to see what was going on. They were still a mile away when they saw the helicopter parked on the lawn explode under the impact of an alien pulse weapon.

"Whoa! Stop the truck!"

Ali had the accelerator jammed down on the floor. The engine screamed in second gear before he shifted into third and raced forward. He gave every indication that he was going to drive right up to the front doors, whether the aliens were there or not. The passengers yelled at him to slow down, that he was going to get them all killed. Through the dingy glass of the greenhouses that surrounded the research building, they could see the movement of large shapes, aliens in their biomechanical armor. The only person the driver would listen to was Miriyam. She directed him to steer a course between two of the greenhouses and then to stop along a blank wall on the main building. Everyone grabbed weapons and jumped out of the truck, taking cover behind it.

Miriyam whispered some orders to Yossi in Hebrew.

He took off running, following the wall until he got to the corner of the building, and peered around it.

"What the hell are we doing?" Sutton asked nervously. "This place looks like a plant nursery. Let them take it." Yossi looked back and flashed a signal to Miriyam.

"He sees them," she told the others. "Stay close behind me. We're going in."

"Like hell we are." The other soldiers glanced behind them at Sutton. "I'm staying right here. It's stupid chasing them inside. Better to burn the place down and kill them as they come out." His idea would have carried more weight if not for the sound of gunshots coming from the interior of the building. Someone was in there defending the place, and, from the sound of things, needed help fast.

Miriyam didn't stay to argue. She pointed a finger at Tye. "You. You stay here with him." Then she hurried forward, scanning the area with her assault rifle, to join Yossi.

Reg told Fadeela to stay behind and keep an eye on his mates, but she ignored him. Gripping her rifle clumsily, she chased after the others. By the time she and Reg reached the corner, both Israelis were advancing along the wall of one of the greenhouses. They stopped and waved the others forward. When the group assembled, they were near the ruined helicopter. Miriyam signaled for silence, then pointed through the smudged glass of the greenhouse at an armored alien standing on the other side, its tentacles waving idly in the air as it kept watch over the building's entrance. Two of the many-legged chariots stood beside him.

"I'll take care of this one," Edward said, prowling forward with the flamethrower. Once he reached the corner of the greenhouse, he would be able to torch the alien in the back. Ali grabbed him by the arm and said not to use the flamethrower, that they couldn't risk setting fire to the building.

"Why?" Edward asked. "What's inside the building?"

The muscular Saudi captain declined to say, but obviously had his reasons. He led Edward back around the greenhouse to a safer angle. The alien sentry noticed them too late. Another roaring jet of fire spit from the barrel of the antique weapon, overwhelming the creature and one of the chariots. Within seconds, the exoskeleton toppled over and split open. The goo-slathered creature inside climbed out and tried to run. Remi killed it with a single shot.

"Let's move." Miriyam waved the others toward the building, and they darted for the open doors.

The team ran up the steps and hustled inside. Edward and Ali, coming from a different angle, were a few steps behind the others. As they reached the bottom step, gun blasts sounded from inside, and the team came scrambling back through the entrance with an alien warrior right behind them. As they scattered in all directions the skeletal figure lifted its powerful arm and took aim with its bony finger.

Edward, standing only ten feet away, closed his eyes and squeezed down on the handgrip of his flamethrower. When the canister was empty, the huge gray skeleton came crashing out of the fire and tumbled down the stairs. When the sides of the great shell head retracted and the delicately built creature within fell squirming and screeching to the ground, Yossi put a bullet into its head.

"We must go inside," Ali yelled. "There are... we cannot let what is inside burn. It is very dangerous." Edward's flamethrower had set the building on fire.

'Tell us what is inside," Miriyam demanded.

The captain hesitated, but finally blurted out the truth. "Biological weapons, chemical weapons. I don't know. But they are very dangerous, very dangerous. We must not let them escape into the air."

"Biological weapons?" Miriyam yelled. "Why do you have such filthy things? It is illegal!"

"There is no time to argue," Ali told her. "We must not let these weapons be captured."

Afraid of what might happen if he waited a moment longer, Ali rushed up the stairs and plunged through the fire-engulfed entrance room. The others followed him in. Stumbling and groping their way through the flames, they broke though into an adjoining hallway. With Ali and Miriyam in the lead, they began moving through the building, throwing open the first few doors they found. Behind the doors were private offices crowded with bookshelves and tables full of blueprints.

"Let's go! We've got to hurry," Miriyam yelled. She turned a corner in the hallway without checking first and took a pulse blast in the face. She flew backwards, slamming against the opposite wall. A second later, two aliens came screeching around the corner. The one in front was squeezing off pulse blasts to clear the way while the one behind him carried a silver box in his arms.

Reg opened one of the office doors and pulled Fadeela inside. Those who couldn't get out of the hallway rolled into the corners. They fired their weapons as the huge creatures trotted past them, but the aliens, seeing the fire ahead, ignored them. Afraid of the fire, the lead alien lowered its shoulder and crashed through one of the office doors. The other one followed him inside, and, a second later, there was a crash of breaking glass. They had escaped through one of the windows.

"They're getting away," Edward yelled, chasing into the office after them. When he reached the window frame, he took aim at the fleeing figures and prepared to blast them with liquid fire. Ali rushed in, grabbed the barrel of the flamethrower, and pointed it at the ceiling.

"Don't do it," he said in Arabic. "You'll kill all of us." In one motion, the creatures threw themselves into their chariot and began to race away. There was no possibility of catching them. "Come," Ali said, "we have to hurry." He pulled Edward back into the hallway, and they moved to where Fadeela and Remi were examining Miriyam. The pulse blast had turned her head into a blackened gourd with a few ringlet curls still hanging off the back.

"She's dead," Ali said sadly, "but we have to keep moving." He led the way down the twisting hallway, staying a few steps ahead of the others. They came to a set of glass security doors that required an electronic key. They'd been rammed open just wide enough to allow an eight-foot-tall body with a flaring head shell to slip between them. Ali raced through and into the next room, which was a laboratory full of sophisticated equipment arranged into several workstations. The bright white walls were splattered with blood. Four mangled bodies, men in lab coats, lay sprawled on the floor. Ali stepped over them and went to a steel door that looked like a walk-in safe. He got into position, then gave Yossi the nod to tear the door open. When he did, smoky wisps of chilled air floated out. The door led to another room, a refrigerated laboratory. Overturned tables and broken glass were strewn on the floor. Ali inched through the doorway. Yossi, close on his heels, scanned the frosty interior with the barrel of his assault rifle and halted when he saw something move. Ali stopped short when he felt Yossi's hand on his back. Without a word, Yossi reached past him and pointed toward the danger. Hiding in the corner, behind a set of rolling shelves, something twitched about three feet above the floor. To Ali it looked like the end of a tentacle. But as he moved closer and leveled his weapon, he saw that it was a human hand.

A man in a white lab coat was cowering in the corner, arms wrapped around his head. He was shaking with fear and with cold. He screamed when he heard the footsteps, and tried to burrow deeper into the corner. When they lifted him to his feet, there were trickles of blood coming from both nostrils, and the whites of his eyes had gone bright red. Ali picked him up and dragged him out of the cold room into the main laboratory.

"Where are the chemicals? We have to get them out of here."

The man looked at Ali blankly, then turned and stared around him at the bloodstained walls and the bodies on the floor. He didn't seem to recognize where he was, but his eyes focused when he noticed Edward's uniform. He snapped out of his daze and smiled weakly at the man with the flamethrower.

"*You're Jordanian? Me too,*" he said in Arabic, then immediately burst into tears.

"Where are the weapons?" Ali insisted. "Where are the chemicals?"

The man ignored the question, sinking to his knees and apologizing desperately to Edward in Arabic. Ali reached down and shook him. "The building is on fire," he shouted. "Where are the chemicals?"

The man continued to whimper as if he were begging for forgiveness. Reg got to his knees so he could talk to the man face-to-face. "It was inside you, wasn't it? Inside your head, hurting you and demanding to know things. And you told it everything it wanted to know so the pain would go away." The man's eyes opened wide in a new kind of terror, but Reg quickly moved to put him at ease. "They did the same thing to me. They're doing it to a lot of people. There's no reason to be ashamed. But right now the building is on fire, and you have chemical weapons in here. Where are they?"

"Not chemical," the man said softly. "Biological. We culture biological weapons, and they're gone. They took everything. We were evacuating and had packed everything we didn't destroy. There is a helicopter waiting outside."

"So there's nothing left?"

"Nothing," the man said. "The alien monsters took everything that was still here.

When Reg was convinced the building was clear of bioweapons, he picked the man up. "Is there another way out of here?"

The scientist was unsteady on his feet but walked under his own power to a side exit and led them outside. He sat down against one of the greenhouses while Ali went back inside to retrieve Miriyam's body. He carried her out on his shoulder and looked around for the best place to leave her. He decided on the greenhouse and carried her inside. Yossi found a shovel and dug a grave while the others talked to the scientist.

Reg didn't know much about biological weapons; none of them did. He knew they were meant to take advantage of human susceptibility to disease, that they were universally despised and widely manufactured. He knew that they were unstable weapons, difficult to control once they had been deployed.

"What were you making in there?"

"Too much." The scientist sobbed. "I told the Saudis we were producing too much, that it was dangerous." He looked up at the pilots, hoping for sympathy, but found only stern, impatient expressions. As he realized that they would force him to reveal the lab's secrets, his tone swung from apologetic to defensive. "I want to say, first of all, that most of our work here does not involve biological warfare."

"I hear you," Reg said evenly. "Go on."

He said that the lab's *research* required the production of many infectious cultures including smallpox, encephalitis, cholera, typhoid, and influenza. But the two agents they harvested in the greatest quantities were the bacterium anthrax and ebola, a virus. While insisting that the lab served only "experimental purposes," the scientist explained how the two agents were mixed to weapons-grade strength and stored inside glass tubes. If released into the environment, the two substances would create a highly lethal one-two punch. Anthrax, he said, strikes quickly, manifests as bloody lesions on the skin, and is lethal in fifty percent of cases. Ebola, the scientist explained, takes slightly longer, but kills ninety percent of the time. Within days, it would bring on high fever and internal hemorrhaging. In the final stages of death, the carrier would thrash about, spilling contaminated blood. The infection had the potential of spreading widely before symptoms could arise.

"And you created these things?" Fadeela asked. The scientist didn't answer.

Edward spit in the dirt where the man was sitting.

"Can the aliens use them?" Reg asked. "Aren't they hard to deploy?"

"I'm sorry. They know to use them; I told them several different ways. They forced me to tell them."

"What's the most efficient way to use them?" Tye asked. "Assuming, of course, that you're bent on world domination and want to kill as many humans as you possibly can."

The man was sure of his answer. "In aerosol form, during the early morning, so they can create droplets and spread along the ground, and best if sprayed from a high elevation over a population center."

"This stuff the aliens took, how many people could it kill?"

The scientist shrugged and said the question was impossible to answer.

"How many?" Fadeela insisted.

"Theoretically, several times the population of Earth. But realistically, only a few million."

When she heard those words come out of his mouth, Fadeela raised her rifle and almost shot him. "Don't say *only* a few million."

"They were never meant to be used!"

"How did they take the stuff?" Reg asked. "Did they just come in and raid the refrigerators?"

"As I told you, we were preparing to leave," the scientist said. "We had orders to relocate to the national facility in Riyadh. We had all the toxins packed for transport."

"Packed how?"

"Padded containers, this big," he said, miming a one-foot-square box with his hands, "with a handle."

"How many?"

'Two. The other one went out this morning."

"So all they took was one container?'

"Yes."

"Was it silver?" Reg asked, remembering seeing it in the alien's arms.

The scientist nodded and broke down in tears when they were finished questioning him. They left him sitting there and went inside the greenhouse, where they stood around in silence for a while, looking at the ground where they'd buried Miriyam. Everyone in the room realized how serious the situation had become. Even though a mere fraction of the alien population had survived the downing of their ship, it was beginning to look as if they were still strong enough and smart enough to win the war on the ground. Not only had the aliens carefully researched the Earth's ability to defend itself before arriving, they were also capable of gathering sensitive information at will. Tye walked outside and studied the workings of the amber medallion until the others were ready to leave. Obviously, they had celebrated their victory prematurely.

11

A ROADSIDE ENCOUNTER

The drive back toward the oasis was silent and slow. Despite the urgency of their errand—warning the Saudi Air Force not to bomb the alien ship for fear of dispersing the biological weapons—they traveled along at only thirty miles an hour. The truck's engine was threatening to mutiny. The needle on the temperature gauge was in the red. The oil light was flashing, and they were low on fuel. But there was another reason for their slow progress. Miriyam's death had stunned all of them, made them feel that their efforts at resistance were doomed to failure. No one felt the loss more acutely than Ali. The first time he'd met her, they had almost punched each other's lights out, but since then, he'd learned to admire and rely on her.

It was late afternoon, and the sun was a bright orange ball hanging over the Asir mountains, directly ahead of them. Ali squinted as he drove, doing his best to steer wide of the places where tongues of sand had licked up onto the highway. For miles around, the terrain was a flat wasteland of sand and stony hillocks, with a few patches of withered scrub brush.

Twenty miles from Qal'at Buqum, they spotted a metallic glimmer in the distance. It was coming from the solar panels mounted on the roof of an isolated gas station they'd passed on the way out. The main building was a modern box of glass and steel that looked like it had fallen off the back of a truck headed for a more civilized part of the world. Ali pulled in to the station, planning to stop just long enough to fill the tank and let the engine cool.

The station was open for business and attended by two older Saudi men who sat outside leaning against the wall of the convenience store. They were listening to loud, whining Arabic music and smoking tobacco from a *hookah,* a water pipe. Neither of the men gave any indication that the extraordinary events of the last three days had changed their lives in any way. When Ali skidded to a halt at the pumps, one of them went inside to tend the store, while the other slipped his shoes on and sauntered over to pump the gas. Fadeela was the first one out of the truck. She asked the attendant whether the station had a phone or a radio. Of course he had a phone, he answered, but it required a satellite uplink and hadn't been working since the trouble began.

"We have information for the army at Qal'at Buqum," she said, "an important message."

The man shrugged and pointed down the road. The only way to contact the army would be to go there in person. He didn't seem at all surprised to be conversing with a beautiful Saudi woman dressed in combat fatigues. Nor did he bat an eyelash when her traveling companions turned out to be three Brits, an Ethiopian, a Jordanian, an Israeli, and a powerfully built Saudi who was content to stay behind the wheel, looking crumpled and lost in contemplation. As he'd done ten thousand times before, the old man lifted the nozzle out of its cradle and began filling the gas tank while the passersby stretched their legs and wandered inside the store.

There wasn't much of anything on the shelves, and some of what there was looked as if it had been there for years. The pilots picked up everything that looked edible and as much bottled water as they could carry. Sutton was at the counter negotiating the price of dried dates. He picked up the entire display and set it down in front of the shopkeeper.

"How much?"

The man, who spoke not a word of English, calmly picked up a pencil and wrote the price on a slip of paper. When he pushed it across the counter, Sutton realized the Saudis didn't use Arabic numbers. Realizing he'd need help, he called Edward over, and a price was quickly established.

"We must look pretty strange to you," Edward said to the old man in his own language. "I bet you don't get many groups like us." The man flicked his hand lazily through the air as if batting the question away.

"You'd be surprised," he said. "If you stay in one spot long enough, eventually you see everything. Believe it or not, the whole world comes down this road, little by little." He gave the impression that nothing could surprise him, but his world-weary eyes widened slightly when the pilots began pulling huge amounts of cash from their envelopes to pay for their purchases.

Yossi bought two packs of cigarettes and tossed one at Edward before heading outside and walking across the asphalt toward the bathrooms, which were in a separate building, closer to the road. A moment after the convenience store's door closed behind Yossi, it swung open again. Tye rushed inside, agitated and out of breath.

"Look at this," he yelled, pushing his way up to the cash register. "I think I've found something." He had one of the amber medallions resting on the palm of his hand and put the other two on the counter.

"Will you stop playing with those things," Sutton said. "Has it ever occurred to you that you might be giving away our position every time you start fiddling with them?"

"That's exactly what I want to show you. Take a look." As he had shown them before, when the device came into contact with skin, hundreds of tiny diamond shapes appeared, seeming to float just below the transparent surface. Although they assumed the slowly pulsating shapes formed an intelligible pattern, they were unable to determine what it was.

"Help me," Edward said. "I can't read alien."

Tye grabbed for the first stray hand he could find. It turned out to be Fadeela's. He held it down on the counter and dropped the medallion into her palm. Using a pencil he found on the counter, he pointed at one of the tiny shapes near the periphery of the display surface. "Keep your eyes on this dot," he said. Then he put a second medallion in the shopkeeper's hand. When he did, the diamond shape in question doubled. When he picked up the third medallion in his own hand, it tripled.

"That's us," Reg said, figuring it out. "We're on their screens."

"I knew it. You're showing them where we are," Sutton said.

"Pretty interesting, don't you think?" Tye asked.

"Maybe too interesting," Fadeela said. She took the pencil from Tye and pointed to a double diamond moving slowly across the screen. "It looks like this one is coming in our direction." After watching for a moment, the others could see she was right.

"It looks like they're coming from the north," Reg said. "Try moving your hand to a new angle." Fadeela did, and the diamonds on the screen adjusted to her new position. "It works like a compass."

"More like a global positioning device."

"Well, whatever it is, let's go out and have a look."

They hurried out of the store and ran around the back side of the building. Far to the north, something was moving across the open desert fast enough to kick twin trails of dust high into the air.

"Are all of you dense?" Sutton demanded. He slapped the medallion out of Tye's hand and sent it skittering across the asphalt with a kick. "You're leading them straight to us. We've got to make ourselves scarce. I'll get Yossi. The rest of you get the truck started."

"Hold on there," Reg said, still staring across the sand. "I've got another idea."

Five minutes later, a pair of alien chariots trotted out of the desert and parked themselves on opposite sides of the restroom building. Their passengers dismounted and took a long look around. After a moment, the two that had stopped closer to the store turned and marched toward the men's bathroom. Except for their hideous, otherworldly appearance, they could have been just two more motorists who had stopped to use the facilities before continuing on their journey. Most of the pilots were hiding inside the store, along with the two men who ran the station.

"Okay. *Now* I have seen everything," one of the old men said in Arabic.

A heartbeat after the first alien walked through the bathroom door, he was blown back outside by the jet of fire shooting from Edward's flamethrower. His startled companion backed away, but didn't get too far before Remi stepped outside and unleashed a second torrent of flames. Both skeletal bodies staggered through the flames, slapping at themselves with hands and tentacles until the walls of their suits opened and the creatures inside squirmed out and tried to run. One of them collapsed in the fire. Edward polished the other one off with a single shot from his pistol.

Even before they saw the flare of the flamethrowers, the other two aliens knew there was trouble. One of them came sprinting around the corner, moving too fast to maintain its balance. The knuckles of its curved toes slid out from under it, and it spilled sideways to the ground. As it fell, it fired a series of quick shots that sent Edward and Remi scrambling back into the men's room for cover. The creature used its tentacles to lift itself to its feet, then began marching deliberately toward the rest room, firing one pulse blast after another. The blasts tore into the wall, tearing it down a few bricks at a time. The remaining alien brought the chariot around to offer backup. Maintaining a cautious distance from the building, the alien brought it to a stop in the middle of the highway. Its comrade continued to pulverize the front wall of the restroom building, moving closer each time it fired.

"They're in trouble," Yossi said. "Let's help them."

"Where's that alien gun?" Reg asked Tye. "Time to give it a test." The men rushed toward the exit doors, leaving Fadeela with the dumbstruck shopkeepers. She was about to follow them outside when she had an idea. She picked up one of the amber medallions and pressed the coppery side against the back of her hand. As soon as she did so, the alien firing the pulse blasts froze for a moment and swiveled its magnificent shell head around to look in her direction. Then it pointed its finger straight toward her.

"Get down!" she yelled. The old men hit the deck a split second before a white flash shattered the window and tore into the store.

This momentary distraction was all the opportunity Remi needed. He popped out of the men's room and discharged another spike of liquefied fire. It splattered against the alien's back. As the creature screeched and fell to the ground, the other soldiers opened fire on the alien sitting in his chariot. Before their bullets could do more than ding against his armor, the creature ducked behind the protective front wall of the vehicle. Under a hailstorm of bullets, the sled broke into a backwards sprint, moving just as smoothly as it did when running forward.

"Come back here, you bloody wanker," Sutton shouted after the retreating vehicle.

"That's the first time we've chased one off," Tye observed.

"We've got him outnumbered and outgunned," Reg

said. "He's the first one to show any sense."

But the creature's retreat was only temporary. After stopping a safe distance out in the desert to survey the scene, it charged to the attack once more. The alien kept low behind the superhard material of the chariot's front wall and fired blindly as it came.

Tye was amazed. "It's like a pit bull with a bone in its mouth. It just doesn't know when to give up." A moment later, a pulse zinged past him and ripped into the front wall of the station house.

"Keep him pinned down," Reg yelled to Sutton and Yossi. "We'll move up and get the angle on him." Then he and Tye hustled forward to the edge of the road and took cover behind a stack of discarded tires. Tye unwrapped the pulse weapon and let it climb onto his arm. Then he stole a glance over the tires and was alarmed to see the chariot heading directly toward them. He was nervous and breathing hard.

"What if it doesn't work this time?" he asked, looking down at the thing on his arm. Reg patted him on the shoulder and tried to reassure him.

"Remember: It's all mental. If we both tell it to fire, it'll fire. All we have to do is concentrate. Aim right at the head, and we'll be okay."

While bullets and pulse blasts ripped by in opposite directions overhead, Reg and Tye hunkered down and waited. The next time they peeked out, the front wall of the chariot was nearly on top of them. It was about to pass well within a tentacle's reach.

"One shot," Reg said. "Make it count."

Tye extended his arm like a rifle, and Reg gripped the copper-colored flippers. When the front end of the chariot brushed past, they came face-to-face with the crouching exoskeleton. The eight-foot-tall beast recoiled when it saw the humans. Reg mentally willed the gun to fire, but nothing happened. The sight of the hideous beast so close to them had distracted Tye from his purpose. With a screech, the startled alien lifted a tentacle to lash at the men.

"Fire!" Reg yelled, visualizing the pulse leaving the end of the weapon. It worked. The shell face blew apart just as the tentacle came across the side of Tye's head; it connected with the force of a heavyweight's punch and sent Tye flying. Reg pulled out a pistol and stood over the still-quivering body. A pair of reflective eyes stared up at him through the jagged opening in the armor. He pointed the pistol and prepared to kill it, but hesitated. *Would it be possible*, he wondered, *to take the thing prisoner? Could I interrogate it the same way they did to me?* He could feel it trying to attack telepathically, but its mental energy was very weak. Reg knew it was dying. He was still standing there thinking when Sutton ran up and pumped twenty shells into the opening, turning the alien's head into a lumpy liquid paste. Sutton could have gone on firing, but Reg stopped him.

"First the Israeli woman, and now Tye." Sutton was trembling with anger. "He wasn't much of a soldier, but one hell of a nice kid."

"I'm not quite dead yet," came a voice from behind them, "just resting."

Blood was streaming down the side of Tye's head. He'd lost a chunk of his left ear, but was otherwise uninjured. With help from the others, he got to his feet and slowly regained his balance. "I'm fine," he said. "I've taken harder hits during rugby matches."

Once he saw that Tye was going to pull through, Sutton regretted sounding like a mollycoddler and changed his tune. "It's your own fault, you know. You ever hear of a thing called ducking?" Then he took one of his friend's arms and led him back toward the damaged service station.

Yossi had gone to check on Edward and Remi. They

came out of the destroyed rest room and extinguished their flamethrowers. The three men walked over to the alien chariot and took their first unhurried look at the inside of the vehicle. Like the other alien technologies they'd seen, it looked like the shell of a living thing. The riding area was shaped like a shallow bowl coated with a thick slathering of the same clear jelly lining the inside of the bioarmor cavities. Sand, dust, and twigs covered this sticky substance everywhere except where the aliens had recently been kneeling. There were no steering controls, knobs, or dials. There wasn't even anything to hold on to.

"Should we burn it?" Edward asked.

"No," Yossi told him. "Maybe we can use it." He whistled Reg over to take a look, then used a pocketknife to scrape away the layer of gelatin until he reached the layer of tough gray meat lining the inside of the shell. "Watch out, it might jump," he warned the others before stabbing down at the meat with his knife. Nothing happened. Although the surface of the flesh gave when he touched it with his blade, he couldn't tear it open.

"He wants to steal their car," Edward said when Reg walked up.

"Maybe it works the same way as the pulse weapon," Yossi said. "I think we should try it."

Reg looked down at the sand-soaked goop lining the inside of the chariot. "It'd be nice if we could run it through a car wash and clean it up first." But he agreed that they should experiment. He used Yossi's knife to clear the gunk away from a second area, then pressed a finger down onto the shell's spongy lining. Nothing happened until Yossi did the same thing. With both of them touching it simultaneously, the joints in the stick-figure legs flexed and bristled. "Make it walk," Reg said.

Yossi looked at him uncertainly. "How?"

"Just imagine it. Try to picture in your—"

"Agh!" Yossi yanked his hand away when he felt the thing begin to step forward. The legs quit walking the moment he broke the contact. He looked at Reg. "It is very disgusting."

"I agree. Let's try it again."

Within a few minutes the two men were walking the chariot around the grounds of the filling station like a clumsy, obedient dog. Using nothing more than their fingertips, they learned to make it stand in place, turn in a slow circle, and move in any direction they ordered. It was easy once they got the hang of it, simply a matter of will. But they couldn't get it to move as gracefully as the aliens had. The legs became confused whenever the men gave it conflicting mental signals. They also learned that the gelatin material was an essential part of the operating system. When they cleaned it completely from an area, the vehicle didn't register their skin contact.

It was Fadeela who stopped them. "It's time to go," she said, reminding everyone they had an important message to deliver to the army at the oasis.

"I think we should take this thing with us," Yossi said. "It could be useful."

"It's too big," Fadeela told him. "There isn't room in the truck."

But Reg knew what he had in mind. He grimaced down at the chariot's bed of slime and then up at his Israeli ally. "All right. But it's going to be a long, sticky ride."

A few minutes later, after saying good-bye to the elderly gas-station keepers, the truck rolled out onto the road and turned in the direction of Qal'at Buqum. A few car lengths behind, Reg and Yossi sat cross-legged in the alien chariot, their rear ends sunk into the layer of extraterrestrial ooze. They looked like characters in a futuristic version of *A Thousand and One Nights*, riding a strange-looking magic carpet across the desert.

12

BACK TO THE OASIS

The sky was black, except for a streak of violet hanging over the western horizon when the old truck grumbled to the top of a rise in the road overlooking what still remained of Qal'at Buqum. The only lights in the oasis came from the scattered fires burning the last of its buildings. Ali pulled onto the shoulder and steered toward a cluster of civilians who had gathered on a bluff above the ruined village.

When they saw the alien chariot skulking through the darkness behind the truck, the civilians panicked. Shots rang out. Fortunately, neither Reg nor Yossi was hit. Word of the captured vehicle spread fast, and soon there were a hundred people crowded around the sled-shaped craft. The human charioteers brought it around to the front of the truck and parked in the one remaining headlight to give everyone a chance to examine it. Some of them used the opportunity to throw stones and kick at the sticklike legs. When Reg made no move to stop them, neither did the others. These people had every right to be angry. Angry not only with the armor-clad alien warriors who had decimated their town, but with Faisal's army, which had allowed it to happen.

Soon after Reg's group had stolen away to the east, Faisal and his advisors had concocted a plan which they quickly put into motion. After dumping poison into the outdoor pools and burying a few land mines, they withdrew their forces toward the mountains and established a camp. The townspeople were left to their own devices. As the old woman who had sold them ammunition earlier that day put it, they were left as bait. Most residents had loaded their possessions into their cars and driven into the mountains, taking the road toward Dawqah on the coast. Others, the people standing around them, had retreated a few thousand yards into the desert, onto the bluff. A handful of desperate men, with only a few weapons among them, had stayed behind to defend the oasis.

Late in the afternoon, the people on the bluff had watched the chariots come across the desert and spread out around the oasis before entering en masse. The men and boys who had stayed behind were counting on Molotov cocktails as much as on guns to repel the attack. Apparently, it didn't work very well because the aliens used very few pulse blasts to subdue the human defenders. One group of survivors made it to the edge of the oasis, but when they tried to run across the open desert, a chariot followed them out and caught them one by one. As it began to get dark, the fires started, and the oasis village was burned to the ground. Some of the chariots had left again in the direction of their crashed airship, but no one could agree on how many.

Reg stared down the hill as the last of Qal'at Buqum's fires burned down. A pair of headlights came over the distant horizon, headed along the road that would take them through the center of the village. Everyone on the bluff watched quietly as the headlights entered the town, paused for a few moments near the central post office, then continued up the hill in their direction. Reg and the others ran out into the road to meet whoever was coming up the hill, which turned out to be a pair of Saudi soldiers in a jeep. The civilians surrounded their car, asking questions about their village. The soldiers said they'd seen nothing but a few dead humans and burning buildings. They said they were on an important errand and couldn't answer any more questions. The driver put the jeep in gear and began plowing slowly through the crowd until Ali Hassan stepped into their headlights. When they saw him, the soldiers killed the engine and got out of the car. Ali told the crowd to stay back, then held a short conference with the pair. The three of them talked for a few minutes before returning to the jeep. Ali sat in the driver's seat and spoke on the radio, shouting angrily into the handset. When he was finished, he began arguing with the soldiers, who drove away only after Ali threatened them at gunpoint.

"What was that all about?" Reg asked, when Ali came striding toward him a moment later.

"We need to talk," the Saudi captain said, clapping one of his powerful hands onto Reg's shoulders and escorting him toward the truck. When they were inside, he told Reg to roll up his window, then looked around to make sure no one was lurking nearby.

"What the hell is going on?" Reg asked. He didn't know what Ali had learned from the passing soldiers, but clearly it wasn't good news.

"It's Faisal. He's moved his army into the mountains. They are about six miles up the road that leads to the town of Dawqah. I know the place. It is easy to defend. If the aliens attack him there, he will make them pay."

"Then let's hope they do attack. But not until *after* we've convinced Faisal not to bomb the destroyer." Reg stayed quiet for a moment or two, waiting to hear the reason for the private conference. But Ali only stared straight ahead, gripping the steering wheel as if he meant to strangle it.

Eventually, Reg broke the silence. "How long will it take to reach Faisal's camp?"

"There is a problem."

"Yes, I was beginning to suspect as much."

After glancing around once more, Ali explained. "Faisal has given an order. The order is to kill Reg Cummins. There is a reward for the man who does it."

"I see. Well, I'm sure it's a large reward," Reg said, pretending to be flattered by the attention.

Ali looked him in the eyes and nodded seriously. "Very large."

"Interesting," Reg said calmly, as he began to think about the fastest way out of the truck. "Obviously, you learned about this from those soldiers in the jeep."

Ali shook his head. "I spoke to Faisal on the radio. He told me that if I didn't kill you myself, I can never come back."

"And you'd like to go back?"

"Naturally."

Reg casually slid his hand close to the door handle, preparing to escape if Ali reached for his pistol. "That puts you in a bit of a predicament. Have you decided what you're going to do?"

Ali smiled. "Yes, I have. I told Faisal something I learned from American movies. I said, 'go screw yourself!'" Ali laughed, and Reg joined in, uneasily. "And then I said something else, something stupid maybe."

"What was that?"

"I told him to call off the order. I said that I'm going to kill him if anything happens to you."

Reg stared at him for a minute without blinking. "You really said that?"

Ali sighed and nodded, indicating that the decision hadn't been an easy one.

Reg was impressed. The first words he could remember coming from Ali's mouth were a chauvinistic warning to the Israeli pilots that no Jews were allowed in Saudi Arabia. But now he'd made an irreversible decision to join a group that included a Jew, an ill-behaved Saudi woman, a Palestinian, and three Westerners—one of whom had a price on his head. Reg knew it was one thing for him, a foreigner, to cast his lot with this ragtag, international group, but was quite another for a Saudi officer to do the same thing, especially on his home soil. It took real guts. Or insanity. Or both.

"Did you tell Faisal about the biological weapons?"

"He already knew about them," Ali said. "He said there is a plan to attack the ship by air and land. I told him that we believe the germ canisters are inside the ship. Will that stop him from going ahead with his plan? I don't know."

"Well, after your conversation, I don't think you should be the one to go up there and try to talk him out of it."

"I don't think Faisal would be happy to see either one of us."

"Still, we ought to send someone up there to try to convince him." Neither one of them said it, but they knew that Fadeela would be the most logical candidate for the job. She had bargaining chips at her disposal that no man could possess.

"Good," Ali agreed, and opened his door. "But first we have to get out of this area. These people will soon hear of the reward on your head. Probably, they will not try to harm you. But they have lost their homes and everything else. They are desperate. We should find another place." He stepped out of the truck to begin collecting the rest of the team.

"One more thing," Reg said. "Just in case I don't get a chance to say this later: Thanks."

Ali smiled. "No problem."

A few minutes later, they were on the road again. The civilians of Qal'at Buqum, emboldened by what they'd heard from the soldiers in the jeep, started marching down the hill in a group to see what remained of their homes and shops. Reg and the team decided to escort them in case they ran into any trouble. If the town was clear, they would proceed with the task of stopping Faisal from bombing the downed destroyer.

Only one of the truck's headlights had survived when Yossi had driven it over the embankment that morning and smashed down on the alien chariot. Like a growling cyclops, the battered vehicle rolled down the middle of Qal'at Buqum's only road at five miles per hour. Walking alongside and behind it were a group of Saudis, some of them carrying guns, some of them armed only with sticks and stones. Edward and Remi protected the truck's flanks with their flamethrowers. Reg and Yossi knelt in the alien chariot, one hundred feet behind, resting the barrels of their assault rifles on the curving front wall. Tye and Fadeela were ready with the pulse weapon.

Lying in the road were the remains of several of the men who had tried to fend off the alien attack. Some of the corpses were blackened by pulse blasts, others showed signs of having succumbed to the pain of mental interrogation. It wasn't until they were approaching the post office at the center of town that they realized why the place felt so empty: The trees were gone. The two thousand palms and tamarind trees that had provided a lush canopy of green on either side of the road were missing. When they turned the headlight of the truck into the park, they saw what remained: felled and twisted trees, many of them broken off at the roots, others left standing but stripped of their foliage. The floor of the oasis had been swept clean of the ferns and ground-cover plants that had been there only hours before. Even the bark had been peeled away from the tree trunks.

The trees had been damaged in two ways: Some had been broken, probably by the strength of the biomechanical armor. On other trees, the baric and leaves had been stripped away in furrows, almost as if they'd been cleaned with a large potato peeler. The furrows were continuous, traveling in spirals up the length of the trunks. It looked as if they'd been eaten, but there was no evidence that either teeth or blades had been used.

Yossi returned from a quick foray deeper into the oasis and said he'd found an undamaged glade of trees surrounding one of the larger artificial ponds. The team decided to investigate, and Ali ran the truck over a curb and entered the park. The moon, the truck's remaining headlight, and the small flames licking from the barrels of the flamethrowers all combined to cast eerie, crisscrossing shadows through the broken, denuded trees.

When they came to the glade Yossi had described, it didn't take long to discover that the aliens had left something behind. Dozens of white globules glistened in the glare of the headlight. Roughly the size of basketballs, some of them sat on the ground lining the banks of the pool, others drooped from the tree trunks.

"What the hell?" Sutton asked, leading the rest of the team close to one of them. It clung to the yellowish base of a tamarind tree, dangling about a foot above the ground.

"It looks like a ball of phlegm," remarked Tye.

"Or a cocoon," Fadeela said.

"I'm going to see what's inside," Reg said, pulling out a pocket-knife. "Do me a favor, will you? If anything jumps out at me, kill it before it can do anything nasty."

Then he reached out and sliced through the membrane. It was hollow inside, like a pouch. When the incision was long enough, the membrane tore open and a lump of flesh spilled onto the ground: an alien embryo. It was alive.

"Get out of the light," Reg said, leaning down for a closer look at the thing. Its tiny platelike head was translucent and fully formed. There was no skull, so Reg could see the brain working like a muscle just below the skin. Its pulpy limbs were still incipient little stubs that writhed through the air like the antennae on a garden snail.

"It wants to be cuddled," Tye joked grimly. "He thinks you're his daddy."

"Well, let's see if baby's hungry," Reg said. He reached up and pulled off a handful of the tamarind's red-and-yellow-striped flowers and sprinkled them onto the young alien's body. Within seconds, they began to break down and dissolve.

"It's digesting them."

"I'm officially disgusted now," Sutton remarked.

"That explains the damage to the other trees," Fadeela said. "The spiral markings. If they feed by dissolving their food and absorbing it through their skins, they could have crawled up the trees, eating as they moved. There doesn't seem to be any mouth." The fetus's eyelids opened a crack, and the fetus looked up at the humans. Its silvery eyes reflected like mirrors in the light. Reg looked up suddenly and scanned the area as if he'd heard something.

"What is it? What's the matter?"

"I'm not sure," he said, "but I don't think we're alone. Let's fan out and see what we can find."

"What do we do about Junior?" Tye asked.

"Leave it," Reg said. "We'll have to burn the glade before we leave."

Suddenly, there was a rush of movement in the bushes on the other side of the lake. The group hurried toward the source of the noise, letting the flamethrowers lead the way. By the time they arrived, whatever had made the noise was gone.

"Look at this," Yossi said. There was a fresh splash of water on the ground near some bushes. "Something was hiding here, watching us."

"Found a footprint," Sutton announced. "Only two toes on it. Headed that direction." The team moved where he'd pointed, toward an area thick with ground cover. They fanned out and beat the bushes as they advanced.

They'd traveled less than fifty paces when Fadeela stopped.

"There it is," she whispered. "There it is." The others didn't know where she was pointing them. Then she muttered something in Arabic, buckled at the knees, and fell to the ground. When the others reached her, she was clutching the sides of her head and moaning in pain.

"It's close by," Reg shouted. "Find it before it kills her." The others scattered in all directions, kicking the bushes and checking behind every tree. Reg got down on his knees and forced Fadeela into a sitting position. "Where is it?" he asked, shaking her. "Show me where it is! Point to it!"

Desperate to help her, he picked her up in his arms and began to carry her out of the area. Only then did she extend her arm and point toward her attacker. She pointed straight up into the trees. Reg looked up and saw a pair of silver eyes amid the fronds of a palm. He reached for his pistol, took aim, and squeezed off several rounds. A moment later, the alien body came plunging through the air and hit the ground.

Fadeela's body, which had been rigid and trembling, relaxed into Reg's arms. A moment later, she opened her eyes and looked up at him. When she realized what had happened, she tried to smile but ended up crying. Sutton was the first one to reach them.

"You need to get her out of here," he said. "We'll destroy the rest of these egg sacs and meet you out on the road."

Reg nodded gratefully and carried Fadeela out of the trees.

After carrying her out to the trees, Reg had set Fadeela down near the edge of the road and rocked her in his arms while she cried. The encounter with the alien hadn't done her any lasting physical damage, but she was badly shaken. Between sobs, she tried to explain the fierce, overwhelming malice she'd felt from the alien mind.

"I never imagined there could be such a hatred," she said. "They only want one thing. They want us dead and out of their way." Her eyes had widened as she came to the dread realization of how focused the aliens were on annihilating the human race. When a fresh tear had run down her cheek, he reached out to catch it on his finger. He had only been attempting to comfort her when he leaned down and whispered to her, "I know, I know," he'd said, "but you're going to be all right now. I'll see to that."

As soon as those words had left his mouth, Fadeela changed. Her body began to stiffen, and she pulled away from him." I can take care of myself. Take your hands off of me and get away."

It had been nearly an hour since then, and they hadn't spoken a word to each other since. They rode in the back of the truck along with Sutton, Remi, and Tye. All five of them sat facing in separate directions, lost in their private ruminations. They had managed to avoid being killed thus far, but they were beginning to think it was only temporary. Although they tried not to, they couldn't help sniffing at the air every now and again, wondering if they'd be able to tell when the deadly pathogens would surround them, let loose from the vials the aliens had stolen.

Eventually, Ali slowed the truck, pulled off the road, and parked behind a stand of tall brush that would hide them from any passing vehicles. They had come within a mile of the turnoff to Dawqah, the road that led to Faisal's hiding place in the mountains. Dried twigs and branches were strewn around on the ground, and everyone wanted to build a fire, but it was too dangerous. The flames might be spotted by a roving band of alien chariots. Or they might attract soldiers with orders to kill Reg.

A brief meeting was held at the tailgate of the truck, during which two goals were agreed upon. First, someone had to go to Faisal's camp and make sure he understood that attacking the downed destroyer meant exposing the entire country to anthrax and ebola contagion. Second, Reg and Ali had to leave the country as soon as possible. The team would have to split up, something none of them wanted.

"I'll go up there and speak to Faisal. I'm the logical choice," Edward said. Remi and Yossi volunteered to go with him.

"He'll be surprised to see me again," Yossi said. "We'll be able to convince him."

Ali endorsed the plan and began working out some of the particulars, when Fadeela broke her silence and made an announcement.

"No," Fadeela said. "I am the one who must go to speak with Faisal. The rest of you will put yourselves in grave danger by showing your faces there. You probably wouldn't be able to get close to him. But I am certain I can convince him. I will make him listen."

"The woman is right," Ali said. "Edward can drive her. Is everyone agreed?"

"I will go alone," Fadeela said. "You can drive me to the turnoff, and we will find someone who is driving to the camp. I will go with them while the rest of you escape."

Reg was about to raise an objection when Fadeela shot him a determined look. Obviously, she had made up her mind to go.

"No, no objections," he said.

"Fine," Ali announced. "We will rest for half an hour and then set out."

Reg wandered away from the others and found a place to sit where he could watch the highway. Every few minutes, a lone truck or a fleet of jeeps would rumble past. After a few minutes, Fadeela walked over and stood near him. She looked at Reg in the dim light of the moon and smiled.

"I'm glad to see you're feeling better," he told her.

"Actually, I'm worse, but thank you. I came to say

good-bye, and to apologize for the way I spoke to you before."

"Totally unnecessary," he said, hanging his head. When Fadeela laughed out loud, Reg looked up, wondering why.

"You're acting like a wounded puppy. I don't think you understand why I was upset, and before I leave I wanted you to know why."

"I'm all ears, princess," Reg said, looking at her expectantly. The moment the nickname princess had come out of his mouth, he regretted using it. He called her that only because he was feeling betrayed by her decision to go to Faisal's camp. It made sense that she should be the one to go, but he couldn't help feeling that she was somehow choosing Faisal over him.

"My wish is to be attacked by another alien," she said.

"Huh?"

"Yes. I hope it happens again, because the next time, I will be stronger. I am going to control it, just as you did in the oasis. I think I understand now what you meant about being able to resist them."

Reg scowled at this ludicrous idea. "I, for one, hope you don't run across any more of them. I hope none of us do."

"You don't think I'll be able to resist? You think I'm too weak?"

"Not at all."

"Yes, you do. You said it just now. You called me princess again."

"Look, I don't really think you're a princess. I was just… I'm sorry I said that. You've been fighting like a banshee all day, and you deserve some credit."

"What is a banshee?"

"A jinn. You've been fighting like a jinn. You saved Edward and Remi's lives at that petrol station this afternoon. That whole wall would have collapsed if you hadn't worked that trick with the medallion. You bought them the time they needed to stay alive."

"But as you point out, it was only a trick. Now that I understand what the enemy is, I know that tricks are not enough. I want to be taken seriously. I don't want to be treated like a helpless little girl." She imitated the way Reg had spoken to her earlier:

"*It's going to be all right. I'll take care of you. Don't worry.*' I want to be like that Jewish woman. What was her name?"

"Miriyam."

"Yes, Miriyam. She was *useful*. She was a real soldier. Let me ask you something about her. Did you like her?"

"Yes, I did. She was a brave woman."

"As I suspected. And what about me, do you like me?"

Reg looked up at her, surprised by the question. "Yes," he said after a moment. "I like you very much."

"Why?"

"Why do I like you?"

"Yes, why?"

"There are lots of reasons," he said vaguely. But after thinking it over for a moment, he decided on an answer. "I like that you hate being called a princess. I like your bravery and the fact that you want to be braver still. Most of all, I like that you haven't given up."

Fadeela smiled broadly. "An excellent answer," she said, "a very correct answer. I have not given up. In fact, I have an idea to discuss with you. It's a plan that may strike you as too bold, but I've been thinking about—"

"Whoa! Hold on." Reg held up his hands. "Turnabout is fair play. What about me?

"What about you?"

"I think you're attracted to me. I think you like me," Reg said, going out on a limb. "Am I right?"

Fadeela grimaced and looked impatient. "Of course I'm attracted to you. You're handsome, brave, intelligent, moderately well educated, young, strong, and a good listener. I've practically been throwing myself at you since the moment we met, but right now I have something more important to discuss with you. May I go on?"

"Please do."

"I've come up with a plan, and I want you to tell me what you think of it. What time is it now?"

He checked his watch. "Quarter to one."

"That leaves only a few hours until morning. If the aliens are planning to use the germ weapons they took today, won't they do so early in the morning?"

"I don't know. That scientist we met seemed to think that would be the best time. The most lethal time."

"After the hate I felt coming from the alien that attacked me, I would expect them to try and maximize the killing power. We have to go to their ship and find those weapons before they can be used."

Reg thought she was joking, but quickly realized she was completely serious. "That's madness. We can't waltz in there, grab the stuff, and run."

"Why not?"

"Well, there must be a thousand reasons, but the main one is that they'd kill us before we got inside. Secondly, if we did manage to make it inside, they'd kill us there. And don't forget, we don't *know* the canisters are inside the ship. That's nothing but a hunch. But let's say they *are* inside. You must have noticed that the ship is a rather large place. We could wander around in there for weeks without finding what we were looking for. Furthermore, if we show up and start shooting, what's to prevent them from using the weapons immediately? I could go on and on, but I hope that gives you the idea."

"We have to try," she said, then began to address his concerns one by one. "We have proven we can fight against them. If we move quickly, we can break past them and get inside. The germ canisters must be inside the ship, since they have nowhere else to go. We will find them in the black tower because these are important weapons and they would be taken to the control center of the ship. Since we are a small group, we will rely on stealth more than on our guns. If we move quietly and strike quickly, we can find the weapons before they are used. I think it's worth a try."

"You left out something important. Once we've rushed in there and gathered up enough poison to wipe out the entire planet, how do we get out again without releasing it into the atmosphere?"

"I leave that part to you. A chance to prove yourself." She smiled.

"Utter madness. As bad as the American plan to bring down the shields," he said, shaking his head. But Fadeela could see that he was thinking it over, walking through it step by step. And the longer he thought about it, the more he became convinced that it had a chance—an infinitesimally tiny chance—of actually working.

"It would take an incredible amount of good luck, and we wouldn't be able to do it alone. But I admit that in theory, at least, it could work if we had help from someone with an army at his personal disposal. Someone like Faisal. Without him, there's no way." As far as Reg was concerned, the question was closed. Fadeela took an oblique approach to opening it again.

"Reg," she said quietly. "Your pain is showing again. Your fear. If there is ever to be a future for us, you must tell me. What happened to you during the Gulf War?"

He felt the doors to his heart start to slam closed inside his chest, but managed to keep them ajar long enough to ask, "Your brother never told you?"

"I know there was an accident. But I want *you* to tell me. Please. I think it is relevant."

He didn't see how it could be, but trusted her enough

to go on. Once he started talking, he realized that despite having thought about it every single day, he hadn't talked about it out loud for a long time. "Not much to tell really. I was flying a bombing run out of Dhahran. It was the second day of the war. We'd been out the day before and had some good success. Hit most of our targets without losing anyone, so we were all feeling good. Confident. Especially my group. We were more than confident. We were so damned cocky we were getting reprimanded right and left by our superiors. I remember that before we went up that morning, there was a briefing session where they showed us photographs with the latest target information. You know, hit this building, don't hit that one, watch out for anti-aircraft positions at points X, Y, and Z. And I'm sorry to say that I hardly paid any attention. I was just so anxious to get on with it.

"When we came in over Baghdad, their guns started pumping more flak into the air than I thought possible. It was an incredible fireworks show. I was certain our group leader was going to turn back, but he didn't. He set us loose, and we flew right into the middle of the firestorm. This might sound childish, but once I was over the city, I felt like I was playing a video game. I was dodging shells like mad and hunting down my targets at the same time. I didn't care how dangerous it was. Back in those days, I thought I was immortal, and nothing could scare me. I was having fun. And getting the job done. I hit a warehouse next to some railroad tracks, then an electrical station. Then, as I was making a turn, I saw a building I recognized from the briefing session. It wasn't on my list, but there it was right in front of me, so I said why not and dropped one of my smart bombs. I can still see it as if it were yesterday. It was a reddish brown round building and my bomb hit the bull's-eye. Went through the roof exactly in the center. I was pretty proud of that shot, especially since I hadn't even taken any time to line it up.

"I didn't realize there was a problem until I landed. The reason they'd showed us the picture of the round building was to tell us *not* to hit it. That previous intelligence had been updated. It was a college gymnasium that was being used to house the people who'd been bombed out of their houses. And I'd had a merry old time killing and injuring them. The final toll was somewhere around a hundred and eighty people.

"A few years later I came back to teach air combat to young Arab hotshots like your brother. You can believe I make sure they learn to do things carefully. I'm the RAF's poster boy in the fight against carelessness." He looked over a Fadeela. Her expression hadn't changed at all. "Does that answer your question?"

She spoke quietly. "You feel guilty, and you've come back to our country to redeem yourself."

Reg shrugged.

"Then, Reg, this is your chance. When you were over Baghdad, you were playing a game, and you killed a hundred and eighty nameless, faceless Arabs. I think you're different now. You understand that we Arabs aren't merely pieces moving across your game board. You can never bring those Iraqi people back to life, but you can save others. Millions of others."

He knew she was right. The plan she'd outlined was dangerous to the point of absurdity, but he had to give it a try. He owed the families of his Iraqi victims at least that much. And even if he'd never made that horrible mistake, he would have gone through with the plan for the sake of the woman sitting next to him. Remembering something important, he suddenly sprang to his feet.

"What is it?" Fadeela asked.

"The other day Faisal said something to Yossi and Miriyam. He said that even though they were Jewish, and he didn't like them, they had the right to stay with him for three days. Was he just making that up?"

"Not at all. It is a very old tradition of ours. If a stranger enters your camp, you must offer him comfort for three days."

"You think Faisal would honor the custom if he saw me?" Fadeela thought for a minute. "If there are others around him, witnesses, then he would have no choice." Reg stood up and looked around. He spotted Ali standing near the truck and started walking toward him.

"Where are you going?" Fadeela asked him.

"I'm going to pay your fiancé a visit. But I'll need that uniform you're wearing before I go."

13

TO THE CAMP

"He's a dead man," Sutton droned, as Reg and Fadeela climbed into the rear area of the battered truck.

Yossi reluctantly agreed. "Faisal's going to kill him the minute he shows his face."

"If he gets that far," Tye chimed in.

When Reg had explained that he was going to disguise himself and sneak into the army's camp in the hills, they had tried to talk him out of it. But Reg wanted to do more than merely warn against bombarding the ship while there were bioweapons inside. He also wanted to enlist Faisal's help. Without it, they would have no chance of pulling off Fadeela's plan.

"I'll see you all in a couple of hours," Reg said, as Ali slipped behind the wheel and started the engine. "Then we'll have some real fun."

"We'll be here waiting for you. Be careful," the others called back, waving and smiling as if they were optimistic about his chances. Faisal seemed to get whatever he wanted from his troops, and at that point he wanted Reg Cummins's head. Under those circumstances, visiting his camp armed with nothing more substantial to protect himself than some ancient Bedouin custom seemed, at best, recklessly dangerous.

"See you soon," Sutton called, as the truck drove away. "In the next life, that is."

Driving with the headlights off, Ali prowled up the

highway and reached the Dawqah turnoff without incident. After parking the truck at the isolated crossroads, he came around the back to discover that Reg and Fadeela had switched uniforms along the way. She was now dressed as a British flight instructor and he as a Saudi infantryman.

"How do I look?" Reg asked.

Ali wanted to answer that he looked like an English pilot wearing a Saudi uniform. The olive green fatigues, which had been baggy on Fadeela, fit Reg snugly. His wrists and ankles protruded awkwardly beyond the cuffs, and the shirt would barely button closed over his chest. Three days of exposure to the sun had darkened his skin to the point where he might be able to pass, in the darkness of night, as an Arab, but his whiskers had bleached blond.

"You look fine," Ali lied without hesitation, "but take this." He took off his *keffiyeh* and set it on Reg's head, pulling it down until it covered his eyes. "That's better."

"Someone is coming." Fadeela said, looking down the highway. The three of them waited tensely as the headlights came toward them through the warm night, then turned up the mountain road. It was a convoy of sand-stained Toyota trucks carrying steel water drums. Ali stood in the road and waved them to a stop. After a brief conversation with the driver of each vehicle, he came to where Reg and Fadeela had hidden themselves.

"You can ride with these men," Ali told Reg. "They are delivering water to the camp."

Reg tilted his head back so he could see the line of trucks. "Good enough," he said, staring toward the road. "I'll ride in back with the barrels."

"Wait!" Fadeela stopped him.

"What is it?"

She looked him over, worried about his appearance.

She made a quick adjustment to his uniform. "Let me hear what you are going to say when someone asks you a question."

Reg grunted inarticulately.

"Perfect." She smiled.

"Guess I should go," Reg said without moving. He lifted the edge of his *keffiyeh* so he could see Fadeela's face.

She looked up at him, concerned. "And remember: Get yourself as close to Faisal as you can before you speak to him, preferably when there are many people around him. If you can put a hand on him—"

"I know. I know." They'd already gone over the best way to approach Faisal several times. "But before I go…"

"Yes?"

"Don't you wish to wish me good luck? In England, it would be appropriate to give me a kiss right about now. It's sort of a tradition." Although it was dark, he saw that his words had startled her. Nevertheless, her lips parted slowly into a warm smile.

"I'm always interested in trying new things," she said softly. She moved toward him until her lips were only inches from his. "If and when you make it back alive, we should discuss this subject at length." Then she stepped back and offered him a military salute.

Reg let his *keffiyeh* fall again to the bridge of his nose. "I'll definitely take you up on that," he said, then began shuffling his way toward the idling Toyotas. As he wandered half-blind into the headlights, the men in the trucks all noticed his strange behavior and the fact that his uniform was too small. Reg groped the air until his hands found the tailgate. With Ali's help, he climbed on and perched atop the stack of steel water drums.

"How long should we wait for you?" Ali whispered.

"Not long. If I'm not back in a couple of hours, move on to Plan B without me."

Ali was confused. "Plan B? What is that?"

"You'll think of something."

Ali grinned and stepped away, motioning the convoy to continue. But the driver of the lead vehicle waved him over for a word. He was concerned.

"Who is this lunatic you're putting on my truck?" the man asked. "What's the matter with him?"

Ali leaned in close and stared menacingly at the driver. "Can you keep a secret?"

Intimidated by Ali's size and strength, the man nodded vigorously that he could.

"He's royal. One of the king's favorite nephews. He went crazy under all the pressure, so I'd stay out of his way if I were you. Don't even talk to him."

"Yes, yes, I understand," the man stammered. "Thank you, sir." Then he shifted into gear and started up the twisting mountain road. The higher the road climbed, the more treacherous the turns became. Steep canyon walls rose on either side, and Reg quickly understood why Faisal had chosen to retreat to this place: It was safe and easy to defend. Dirt service roads ran along the clifftops, allowing troops and weapons to be moved into place. In the moonlight, Reg could see the silhouettes of field cannons, mortars, and rocket launchers overlooking the road. If the aliens tried to force their way through the pass, it would be like shooting fish in a barrel. The obvious difference, of course, would be that the fish would be shooting back.

When they'd traveled four or five miles, the first trees began to appear, and soon they reached the army's main staging area: a large, level field on the south side of the road. Hundreds of soldiers, their weapons, equipment, and vehicles were located in the dried grass. The noise of gasoline-powered generators jackhammered the air, and high-intensity lamps flooded the field with a glaring light.

* * *

The water trucks turned off the road and, moving slowly, followed the tire tracks that led to the center of the camp. Just as Reg was about to slip over the side and make his way to the nearest shadows, the convoy was stopped for an inspection.

Reg pushed the *keffiyeh* even lower over his eyes and slouched against the water drums. One of the soldiers walked around behind the truck. When the man spoke, Reg shrugged his shoulders and grunted noncommittally. Apparently, this answer was not satisfactory because the guard repeated the question, testily this time. Reg knew he'd have to try something else. After hesitating for a moment, he imitated something he'd seen his student-pilots do a thousand times: He waved a hand at the heavens, and said, *"Insha'allah!"* It was an all-purpose phrase meaning; *Who knows?* Or *It's in God's hands.* It was the thing people said when they didn't know what else to say. Luckily, it seemed to amuse the soldier. He chuckled and waved the trucks forward.

As they moved deeper into the camp, Reg waited for an opportune moment to slip away. Despite the late hour, everyone was wide-awake and buzzing with energy. Groups of soldiers were everywhere: Most of them were moving from place to place, preparing for the next confrontation. They drove past a cluster of utility vans that had been outfitted to act as mobile field-communications centers and on toward the loudest, brightest, noisiest part of the camp: the mess tent. Reg jumped to the ground, walked alongside the truck for a few paces, then turned away as if he knew exactly where he was headed. Some soldiers spoke to him, but he kept his head down and brushed past them without drawing much attention. Or so he hoped. As he moved away from the lights, he began to breathe easier until someone came up from behind and grabbed his arm.

"You are the Englishman, the Teacher. I know you."

Reg wheeled around to find himself face-to-face with a tall man in a well-tailored blue suit caked with dust. He looked like a commercial airline pilot. He had wavy hair combed straight back, a small goatee, and bright teeth that he displayed in an ear-to-ear smile. Reg recognized him as the Yamanis' chauffeur.

"My name is Abdul. What happened to your uniform?"

"Happy to see you again," Reg whispered. He clamped a friendly arm around Abdul's shoulders, then forced him to walk. "Listen, I'm looking for someone, and I want you to help me find him." Abdul nodded. He was a little confused about where Reg was leading him, but he agreed to help.

Not far away, a tent flap pushed open, and a clutch of Saudi officers stepped out of the command tent. When Faisal ducked outside and strode past them, they hurried to keep pace. He was on his way to the radio vans with a message he wanted relayed to his advance troops, the men stationed closest to the fallen destroyer. It was important enough that he wanted to explain it himself. When they saw him coming, the communications technicians snapped to attention and saluted. Faisal ordered them to ease and asked for the latest reports. It was evident from their faces that his soldiers regarded Faisal with a type of respect akin to awe. He had already defeated the aliens once, and they believed he could do it a second time. They would have followed any order he gave them.

"The message shall say exactly this: King Ibrahim is hiding here in the mountain pass to Dawqah with an army of less than one hundred men to protect him."

"But, sir, we just monitored one of the king's communiqués. He is in At-Ta'if."

"Can our advance troops hear those same broadcasts?"

"No, sir."

"Then deliver the message as I gave it to you. Say that if the king is killed, the army will surrender. Tell them to remain in their positions but intercept any enemy forces that advance in this direction."

"He is setting a trap, a very intelligent trap," one of the radiomen told the others enthusiastically. They quickly joined him in loud praise of the strategy. By that point, all of them knew the aliens were interrogating the humans they caught, and the information they gleaned gave them a powerful advantage, By planting the false information in the minds of his men, Faisal was trusting that it would eventually make its way into the alien consciousness. It might have been the first interspecies disinformation campaign. After basking in the adulation of his troops, Faisal and his officers turned to go, but a strange-looking soldier stepped into their path and lifted his *keffiyeh*.

"Good evening, Commander," Reg said with a level stare. When Faisal saw who it was, he nearly tripped over his own feet trying to back up. He glared at Reg and reached for his pistol. Very loudly, Reg invoked the Bedouin custom of hospitality. "I ask to be accepted as a guest in your camp!" he shouted.

There was a moment of tense silence. From the murderous looks he was getting, Reg thought every man in the camp must know about the price Faisal had put on his head. But the next moment, the commander regained his composure and relaxed. He even forced himself to chuckle. The others followed his lead.

"Major Cummins, you startled me."

"I am asking to be accepted as your guest," Reg said again, just as loudly.

"Gentlemen," Faisal said, turning to the others, "this is one of the pilots who assisted me in destroying the enemy over Mecca. Everyone will treat him as a brother while he remains here with us." He spoke to them with a broad smile that disappeared the moment he turned back to face Reg. "What do you want?"

"I was at your base in Al-Sayyid today when your stockpile of biological agents was taken by the aliens."

Before he could go on, Faisal interrupted him, saying that Reg was mistaken. "Saudi Arabia has no biological-weapons program." Then he sent his radio operators back to work and led Reg several paces away so they could speak without being overheard. His officers followed. "There is no need for my men to know about the weapons you are talking about," he said angrily.

"I disagree. We're all in danger of being exposed to some very lethal diseases. If the aliens can figure out a way to deploy those poisons, everyone from here to Sweden is in danger."

"Yes, I know," Faisal shot back. "But I don't think you came here to criticize us for having developed these weapons."

"You're right. I came here because I've got a plan to get them back. Actually, it's Fadeela's plan." When they heard her name mentioned, Faisal's officers tensed up and looked as if they might come at Reg all at once. On the day that should have been his coronation as a major hero, Faisal had suffered the pain of having his bride-to-be "kidnapped" by a band of foreigners. The men surrounding him seemed anxious to avenge their hero's suffering.

"Where is Fadeela now?" Faisal asked.

"Safe," was all Reg would say.

"Women are so unpredictable, so full of surprises, don't you agree, Major?"

Reg didn't return the smile he was offered. "Fadeela's no ordinary woman."

Faisal only shrugged, then ordered his officers to leave

them. Reg wasn't happy to see the men leave. Although they were hostile, they were also witnesses that would make it difficult for Faisal to go back on his promise of hospitality. Faisal walked to the front of the command tent and invited Reg inside. He smiled that smug smile of his when Reg thought twice before heading into the tent.

"Major, you would not have come here unless you needed my help with your plan. I think you have no choice but to trust me."

Realizing he was right, Reg went inside, and the two antagonists talked for the next half hour. Outside, a dozen men held their ears close to the tent, trying to eavesdrop on the conversation. They heard Faisal laugh when Reg explained what he wanted to do. "It would be suicide," the commander said loudly. But Reg doggedly continued to explain how the plan could work in a voice that was too low for the men outside to hear. They argued about the dangers of the biological weapons, air support, and the equipment Reg and his team would need for their raid. The men listening knew Faisal was seriously considering lending his help when he poked his head outside and asked for one of his lieutenants, a man who had climbed the first few stories of the tower at the front of the alien ship.

When the two men finally emerged from the tent, they synchronized their watches, looking somber but optimistic. Faisal carried a handwritten list which he turned over to one of his supply sergeants. "Major Cummins will be traveling to Dawqah with a fragile cargo," he announced, gesturing past the hilltops toward the Red Sea. "Give him one of our best trucks and all the supplies on this list. Make sure it is organized and ready for him in ten minutes." Then he leaned in close to Reg, and whispered. "Your plan is dangerous, but I believe it can work. I expect to see you and your people back here within a few hours. With Fadeela Yamani, of course," he added.

"If we're lucky, *and* we get the air support we need," Reg said, "you'll see her."

"Good luck," he said, smiling. The two men shook hands before Faisal turned away to attend to other business. Despite his encouraging tone, he was certain he would never see Reg Cummins again. Or Fadeela Yamani. They would both be killed before they ever set a foot inside the ruined city destroyer. He was resigned to the fact that the legend he was creating for himself would take on a bittersweet twist at the end: *But before they could be wed, his lovely bride was carried into the desert and slain by the savage infidels.* It wasn't the ending he'd imagined, but it was one he could live with.

When Faisal was gone, the Yamanis' chauffeur, Abdul, approached Reg enthusiastically. "Dawqah? Why are you going there? Mr. Yamani and I will go with you."

"Abdul, where is Khalid? I have to talk to him."

"Impossible," Abdul said, pointing to the surrounding hilltops. "He is somewhere up there, a prisoner. No one may speak to him, only his father."

"Well, let's talk to his father, then." They went to the Yamanis' Rolls-Royce and, when they opened the back door of the limousine, found Mr. Yamani disheveled, sitting bolt upright, yelling into a cellular phone. He appeared to be midway through an argumentative strategy session with the Saudi king. Although he seemed in better spirits than the last time Reg had seen him, there was a manic quality to the way he spoke into the receiver and slashed his free hand through the air. Abdul, like an orderly in a psychiatric ward, reached into the car and took the phone away from the old man, gently but firmly.

"I told you, sir, the telephone is not working. But look who is here. You have a visitor. Do you remember Major Cummins? He is going to Dawqah."

Yamani looked up, confused. He stared at Reg

for a moment without recognizing him. Then his expression changed.

"The Teacher! Come in, come in." Warmly, he waved Reg inside and offered him the seat facing his own. He seemed all at once to regain control of himself. "Do you have any news about my daughter? They tell me she was killed today, but I don't believe them."

Reg assured him that Fadeela was alive and well. Then, looking into the old man's eyes, he asked a series of questions in order to determine the man's mental state. Yamani recognized the patronizing tone in his voice.

"I have not completely lost my mind, Major Cummins, and I will thank you not to speak to me as if I have. The telephone, it is simply a game. A way of thinking out loud while I sit here with nothing to do. Now, tell me, what is this about going to Dawqah?"

We're not actually going to Dawqah," Reg explained. "That's just the cover story."

"I don't want to hear a story. I want to hear the truth."

As quickly as he could, Reg outlined the plan, leaving out one important detail. He didn't say that Fadeela would be joining the raiding party. There wasn't any point in adding to the man's burden. Mr. Yamani appeared to follow Reg's explanation, nodding and grunting at the appropriate moments. But when he was finished, Yamani seemed lost again.

"Dawqah is a nasty little town," he said. "The beaches are polluted with oil, and there is absolutely nothing to do there. I suggest we rendezvous in Jeddah instead. Have you ever been to Jeddah?" Reg could see he was wasting valuable time.

"Take care of yourself, sir. It's time for me to go." He started out of the car, but Yamani grabbed his sleeve and held fast. He seemed to be having another painful moment of clarity, but it was impossible to be sure. Tears welled up and poured down his cheeks.

"I am grateful, very grateful to you. Tell Fadeela that her old father is joining the war, that he is going to fight from now on."

"I'll tell her," Reg promised. But the once-great man didn't hear him. His mind had darted off in a new direction, and he began shouting angrily at his chauffeur.

"Abdul, coffee! Where are you? Bring me some coffee. Don't you realize we are at war? You know I can't fight without my coffee!"

It looked like the last war Mr. Yamani would ever fight was the one for control of his mind. Reg figured the chances of him winning were somewhere between slim and none. Then again, he reminded himself, the old man had a better chance of making a full recovery than he and his ragtag unit had of living past sunrise.

He didn't check to see if the supply sergeant had given him all the items on the list. He got in the truck and drove away at once, wondering if he could trust Faisal. A couple of miles down the road, he pulled off the road after a blind curve to make sure he wasn't being followed, then continued down the hill.

1 4

THE RAID

When Reg pulled an armored Mercedes truck off the road and drove toward the stand of scrub brush, everyone's mood changed dramatically. The fact that he was back made it seem like anything was possible. Sutton and Yossi ran out to meet the truck and jumped on the running boards.

"Cummins," said Sutton, "you're the luckiest son of a bitch I've ever met. I'm beginning to think I ought to stick close to you. Maybe some of that luck will rub off."

"Luck?" Reg asked with a cockeyed grin. "Maybe. But also a lot of skill."

"More like a lot of chutzpah." Yossi laughed.

Once Reg pulled the truck to a stop, the others bombarded him with questions about what Faisal's reaction had been, the size of the army in the hills, and the dangers he had faced.

"Faisal's got over a thousand men up there. I asked him to give me half of them for an assault on the spaceship's tower."

"What'd he say?"

"After he stopped laughing, he said no. He wasn't taking me seriously at all until I played my trump card." He broke off and looked at Fadeela. "I told him who came up with the idea of raiding the ship. And I told him we were going ahead with it whether he helped us or not. That got his attention. Suddenly, he couldn't help me enough. He started pulling out maps, ordering supplies, calling soldiers into his tent to give us scouting reports. And he promised we'd have air cover. A group of Saudi jets will be waiting for us when we get to the city destroyer."

"But no troops?" Fadeela asked.

"No troops," Reg said.

"In other words, he refused to help us."

Reg shrugged. "He gave us these supplies," he said, gesturing to the cargo bed of the truck, "and he didn't kill me. Didn't even send anyone to follow me."

"What do you make of it?" Edward asked.

"He wants us to go to the tower," Ali said. "He doesn't think we'll survive."

"Exactly," Reg said. "The only reason he gave me these weapons and let me go was so we'd all go into the destroyer." He shot another look at Fadeela for her reaction before asking, "Who knows what time it is?"

"Two a.m.," Yossi said, "which leaves only about three hours until dawn."

"Then we've got to hurry," Reg said. "Everyone pull these supplies off the truck and pick out a weapon or two. The more the merrier. We can discuss the rest along the way."

But before Reg could contemplate loading himself down with firearms, there was a pressing piece of business. He grabbed Fadeela and pulled her to the front of the truck. "Take off those clothes," he said. "This uniform is too tight. It's killing me." He leaned against the battering ram that extended off the front of the chassis, pulled off his shoes, then began unbuttoning his shirt.

"What else did Faisal say?" she asked, beginning to unlace her own boots.

"He had a message for you."

"What was it?"

"He said for you to be careful. Isn't that a classic? After I explained what we're proposing to do, he turns to me with a perfectly serious expression on his face and says, *'Tell her to be careful.'*"

"We are going to be married soon. Naturally, he is concerned," she said facetiously, trying to laugh it off. *But not concerned enough to try to stop me,* she thought. As much as she despised Faisal, the fact that he hadn't tried to keep her away from the spacecraft hurt her. By giving Reg the weapons, he was actually encouraging her to go and probably get killed.

"Hurry up with those pants," Reg said, slipping out of the ones she had lent him. "Faisal also said he wouldn't have given me any help at all if it hadn't been your plan. He said you were a brave woman, and he's looking forward to seeing you again soon. Or something along those lines. I don't think he meant a word of it." Waiting for Fadeela to get undressed, Reg stood there in nothing but his jockey shorts and a pair of dirty white socks as easily and unselfconsciously as if he were in a preflight locker room talking with a fellow pilot. Earlier, when he and Fadeela had exchanged uniforms in the back of the moving truck, they'd modestly turned their backs to one another. But now he stood in plain view of her, too focused on the details of the plan and the danger that lay ahead to feel the slightest twinge of embarrassment.

Fadeela hesitated. "Please turn around."

He did, and changed the subject. "I spoke to your father. He seems fine, in better spirits. That chauffeur of yours, Abdul, is taking good care of him. Your father had a message for you, too: 'Tell my daughter I've joined the fight.'"

"What about Khalid?"

"I wasn't able to talk to him, but I think he's fine. Faisal's got him posted to a gunnery battalion on the canyon cliffs. Ah, that's a thousand times better," Reg said as he zipped himself into his own trousers again. "I don't know where you found that uniform, but it rides awfully high in the crotch."

"I plan on having it altered as soon as I can make an appointment with my family's tailor," she shot back.

"Smart aleck." Reg grinned. "Let's go pick you out a weapon. Maybe a rolling pin." He led the way to the back of the truck, where the others were outfitting themselves. Ali had found a five-foot-long field gun that fired rounds the size of Cuban cigars. It was designed as a stationary weapon, but the broad-chested soldier took his *keffiyeh* back from Reg and tied it around the gun to create a shoulder sling. Edward strapped a flamethrower harness onto his back. A far cry from the antique weapon he had used the previous afternoon, this new flamethrower featured a lightweight ceramic canister that carried double the fuel, had adjustable settings, and didn't require a constantly burning pilot—a major asset during a sneak attack. Remi, who along with Sutton was going to stay outside and guard the entrance while the others entered the ship, had chosen a bazooka-style, shoulder-mounted rocket launcher. Reg picked up a fully automatic machine gun and offered it to Fadeela. "Think you can handle one of these, or would you rather help Tye operate the alien pulse gun?"

She accepted the machine gun, but then muscled past Reg and picked up the only remaining flamethrower. "I'll take this one, too. Fire is what they hate the most. Fire is what I'm going to give them." She slipped her arms into the harness assembly, then moved off to discuss the weapon with Edward.

"I don't like it," Ali whispered to Reg. "She's not a soldier; she's a woman, and she doesn't know what she's doing."

Reg glanced over his shoulder. "I'd be careful about saying that to her face," he told Ali. "She's liable to barbecue you."

Fadeela must have heard them talking. "Is there a problem?" she asked, moving closer and holding the nozzle of her weapon menacingly in Reg and Ali's direction.

Ali glared at her for a minute before backing down. "No, there is no problem."

"Good." She turned around and fired a test shot at a set of nearby rocks. Night turned to bright day as the powerful jet of fire shot fifty feet and splattered against the stones. Because the fuel was laced with generous amounts of napalm, the fire continued to burn long after it hit the ground.

Ali's anger flared as hotly as the flames. "What are you doing, stupid woman? You're showing the aliens where we are."

Fadeela mocked him. "Why are you so afraid? Don't worry. If the big bad aliens come, I'll protect you." Edward laughed at her joke, but Ali was far from amused.

As the napalm-enhanced fire burned and dripped down the rocks, Reg called everyone together for a final strategy session. "Listen up. Even with Faisal's help, this isn't going to be easy. Everything within ten miles of the ship is heavily patrolled. The aliens move in pairs on their chariots. Hopefully, we'll see them before they see us. But according to Faisal, they've got another trick: They bury themselves in the sand like land mines and pop up when humans come too close. Keep your eyes open. Faisal will be sending jets to bomb the northern edge of the ship. We'll approach from the south and slip into the tower during the distraction."

"If we can get past the patrols," said Ali.

"Right. We won't know if we can do that until we're out there. We may have to turn back."

"No turning back," Fadeela said matter-of-factly.

"She's right," Yossi said. "If they release those weapons into the air at dawn, we're dead just the same. Better to go down fighting."

Reg squatted and drew a picture of the tower in the dirt. "I've been told there's no way to enter the tower directly from the outside, so we'll have to enter here, where the right side of the tower meets the front of the ship. The Saudi army was exploring this opening when the aliens began their attack."

"What did they find out?" Remi asked.

Reg shrugged. "There weren't any survivors." He looked at the anxious faces around him. "Hopefully, we'll have better luck."

"Let's climb to the top of those rocks so we can have a look around."

Tye and Yossi, who were riding next to Reg in the chariot, looked at the almost vertical stone cliff in front of them, then at one another, then finally at Reg. It would have been safer to dismount and climb up the slope under their own power, but neither of them objected. Instead they concentrated on moving toward the top of the stone wall and, through the magic of alien bioengineering, the chariot began to pick its way up the craggy cliff. The angle was so steep that they would have slid off the back of the chariot if it hadn't been for the ingenious harness Tye had made by fastening several lengths of nylon rope around the body of the sled-shaped alien construct to keep them in.

"Don't try to steer," Reg insisted. "Don't tell it which way to go; just focus on getting to the top. It's like a horse—it knows the best way."

When the chariot stopped at the top of the rocks, Reg lifted himself out of the layer of foul-smelling ooze that coated the seating area and surveyed the valley ahead through a pair of binoculars. He looked nothing like the unassuming man who had entered Faisal's camp earlier that night. Now he was heavily armed with an automatic machine gun on his back, a belt of grenades slung over his shoulder, and a holster on each hip. One holster held a .357 Magnum loaded with armor-piercing shells. In the other was a flare gun.

Only a couple of miles ahead, the mountain-sized remains of the alien city destroyer loomed in the darkness. The light of the moon glimmered across what remained of the domed roof, and there was just enough light for them to see their objective: the tower rising from the front of the ruined spacecraft. Far to his right, Reg looked out on the plateau that was to have been the site of Faisal's wedding. It was littered with destroyed and abandoned vehicles. The flags and bunting decorating the photo platform fluttered in a warm breeze blowing across the desert from the south. Everything was perfectly quiet except for the idling engines of the two trucks nearby.

"Something is very wrong with this picture," Reg said as he searched for signs of alien activity through the binoculars. At the base of the tower, he spotted the large opening Faisal's men had told him about. It was big enough to drive a truck through. "We should have run into some resistance by now. We should have seen them at least."

"Don't sound so disappointed," Yossi said. "After all, we're trying to avoid them, remember?"

The agreement Reg had made with Faisal was simple enough. It called for the team to elude as many of the alien patrols as possible until they were within ten miles of the fallen ship. At that point, they would send up flares to signal the Saudi Air Force to begin bombing the far side of the ship as a diversionary tactic. Despite the high loss rates the Saudis had sustained each time they had tried to make bombing runs on the remains of the destroyer, Faisal had assured Reg that air cover would be waiting for him by the time he arrived at the ten-mile perimeter. Since the aliens were mysteriously absent, it didn't appear they needed any help to make it inside. But what about on the way out, assuming they lived that long? If they managed to find and recapture the case of biological pathogens, the aliens weren't likely to let them escape without sending chariots to chase them. In that scenario, a few well-placed bombs dropped in the path of their pursuers would make a world of difference.

"You think those Saudi jets will show up?"

Reg shrugged and came back to the chariot. When he sat down, the conductive goop accepted him with a slurping noise. "Faisal promised they would, but obviously that's no guarantee. If we're going in, we have to assume there won't be any help."

Yossi nodded and thought the situation over. "Who needs them? The aliens have gone away and left the front door wide-open. Maybe we can sneak in and out before they come back."

Tye couldn't believe it was going to be that easy. "Maybe they're *not* gone," he said. "Maybe they're hiding just inside that opening waiting to zap us when we step through. Or maybe they're sleeping and when they hear us—"

Reg interrupted him. "That's the risk we have to take."

"And we better do it soon," Yossi said. "Only a couple of hours until dawn."

Tye unwrapped a couple of the amber-colored medallions and laid them on his forearm. He fiddled with them for a moment, but could find none of the black diamonds that signaled alien proximity. "The coast is clear," he said. "In fact, it's empty."

"Let's get back to the trucks," Reg said.

The chariot obeyed immediately and bolted down the steep, uneven slope. The skinny, bone white legs took them bouncing, bucking, and stumbling forward until they reached the desert floor once again, then whisked them smoothly up to the driver's side window of the lead truck, where Sutton was behind the wheel. Edward sat next to him in the cab, monitoring the reports coming over the radio in Arabic. Remi and Fadeela were in the cargo area, keeping their eyes peeled for the enemy, while Ali drove the other, older truck.

"You smell that?" Sutton asked, sniffing the air with ferretlike intensity. "Something smells funny, like mildew or something." Like the rest of them, he was hyperalert to signs that the biological weapons had already been released. In addition to noticing odd smells in the air, they'd imagined burning sensations in their noses and lungs and spotted ominous-looking clouds on the horizon, only to have them turn out to be bushes or stands of rock.

"Smells like you're imagining something," Remi called down to the driver.

Reg said, "It doesn't look like Faisal's boys are going to show. But we don't need them. Actually, it's better this way; gives us the element of surprise."

"Yeah, but on the way out?"

"That's a lifetime from now," Fadeela said.

Reg grinned at her choice of words.

Then Sutton surprised them all by yelling, "If we meet any damned resistance on the way out, we'll blow their bloody heads off! Let's go. Let's rock and roll."

"Wait a second. Listen to this." Edward, who had been listening to radio reports, leaned past Sutton so he could make eye contact with Reg, sitting in the alien chariot outside. "I think I found out where our spacemen are. They've sent an army to At-Ta'if. Right now, they're attacking the southern outskirts of the city." Sutton asked, "So they're gone?"

"If they are," Reg said, grinning, "that would make it a whole lot easier to sneak in, wouldn't it? Turn toward the ship," he said aloud. When he, Yossi, and Tye simultaneously willed it to happen, it did. The chariot turned sharply and began trotting forward, awkwardly at first, until the men mentally agreed on the speed they wanted. With a clear set of mental commands steering it, the chariot moved across the sand smoothly and gracefully.

"It's like a magic carpet," Tye said, as they picked up speed. The pace they settled on was fast—as fast as the bioengineered dune buggy would carry them, which turned out to be forty miles per hour. They slowed down only once, as they came to the last earthen barrier and looked across the wide-open no-man's-land in front of them. Ali parked the battered old truck there, leaving it as an emergency backup, then jumped into the back of the Mercedes. Now the only obstacles standing between them and the unbelievably large mass of the city destroyer were the destroyed vehicles left behind by the Saudi army. Once they were out in the open terrain, the Mercedes quickly outpaced the chariot. Sutton kept the pedal to the metal and shot ahead, literally leaving Reg and his fellow drivers in the dust.

As they raced closer, the staggeringly large tower seemed poised to topple over and crush them like fleas, its great height creating the optical illusion that it was about to fall forward. The three men crouched behind the front wall of the chariot expected pulse blasts to begin raining down at them at any moment. Sensing their fear, the chariot veered sharply away from the tower and started across the open desert.

Reg choked down the fear that was rising in his chest and sounded an order. "Concentrate on following the truck!" And a moment later, the vehicle did exactly that. But it wasn't the last misstep. Each time one of the men glanced up at the darkened, blank face of the tower, the chariot responded to his terror and tried to steer away. Then, to add to their problems, they noticed something new and truly alarming. There was a massive tubular form crawling down the front face of the tower, like a ten-foot-diameter snake, something that definitely hadn't been there during the daylight hours. The chariot balked under the confusion of conflicting mental signals it received from its drivers, then came to a dead halt.

"What the hell is that?"

Switching on their flashlights, they saw what appeared to be an enormous root or section of pipe. Growing up the wall of the tower, it rose beyond the limits of their vision and appeared to be growing right before their eyes, causing the tower to undulate and move.

"I don't like the looks of that," Tye said, his voice full of jitters. "They've planted their magic beans, and this is the beanstalk we're supposed to climb up, right?" But as they watched the slow movements, they realized that it wasn't growing out of the ground. It was growing *down*, burrowing deeper by the moment.

"Better to take our chances on the inside," Yossi said, and the chariot moved off. They turned the corner of the tower and raced to where the others were preparing to enter the break in the destroyer's wall. Ali had already broken open several flares and tossed them inside the ground-level opening, determining that the first few yards at least were safe. He and Fadeela stood at the ragged opening, impatient to slip inside.

"Did you see that thing climbing up the tower?" Edward asked in a harsh whisper, bringing a pair of lightweight thermal blankets to the chariot.

"It's not climbing," Tye answered him. "It's digging itself into the ground."

Edward spread the blankets under the rope harness at the back of the chariot to create a "passenger area." Most of the gelatin coating had already been scraped away. The blankets were to prevent any further contact with the goop. Getting three people to cooperate in the driving was tough enough. They didn't need six people steering.

"Hop on," Reg told Edward. He did, and the chariot jogged forward to where Ali was standing guard over the opening. Sutton ran up behind them before they went inside. 'Tye," he whisper-shouted, "leave us one of those disk things of yours. And don't you people be in there forever. Remi and I can't sit around picking our noses out here past sunup." Tye tossed him one of the medallions. "And one more thing," Sutton called. "Good luck."

Ali and Fadeela stepped through the opening, made a quick inspection, and waved for the chariot to follow them.

Inside, the team found themselves facing a tangle of collapsed walls. What had once been a series of rooms and passageways was now utterly smashed to pieces. They quickly found a path through the charred, broken debris and arrived at the sidewall of the tower, which extended deep into the body of the ship. This wall was made of a different material and had sustained no visible damage.

"Wait here," Ali told the men in the chariot as he moved to inspect the wall. "You too," he told Fadeela when she followed him. She ignored him and accompanied him into the long, partially collapsed corridor that ran along the edge of the wall.

"It's thin," Ali said, rapping his knuckles against the wall.

Fadeela pushed against it. It didn't give. It felt like a razor-thin sheet of rough-cut glass. She told Ali to shoot his way through it, and both of them backed away. Ali fired a single shot and, when the wall held, went to inspect the damage. Not even a nick. He and Fadeela waded a few paces into the darkness of the corridor, trying to find the end of it with their flashlights, but it was too long. They ran back to the chariot, jumped on the back, and took hold of the harness ropes like bull riders at a rodeo.

"Straight ahead," Reg commanded, and the chariot bolted forward, carrying the six heavily armed humans with ease. They set out at a cautious trot, but soon increased their speed by urging the chariot to move faster. The trip over the uneven floor felt like riding a rickety roller coaster. They were tossed one way, then the other, straining the whole while to spot signs of danger. They sped forward for a long time until they reached the end of the tower and turned the corner.

"Stop!"

The chariot legs went stiff and stopped short. Ahead, dim round lights glowed out of the jet blackness, weakly illuminating the floor and walls.

"Back up," someone hissed. The chariot shuddered but stayed put.

"No, don't," Reg countered. "They're not moving."

"What is it?" Tye whispered, extending his arm over the front rail of the chariot so Yossi could help him fire the alien pulse weapon if need be.

"They're not moving," Reg said again. "Let's go for a look." After a moment of hesitation, the stick legs began moving forward again, but slowly and reluctantly now. As they came closer, it became apparent that they were not the first humans to enter the tower. The lights were coming from a cluster of Saudi jeeps that must have been parked there since the alien ambush almost twenty-four hours earlier. There must have been fresh batteries to keep the headlights lit up for all that time. A ghostly rustle of static came from the radio of the closest vehicle. There was no trace of any soldiers, but they could see where the last man had been and what he'd been doing. His rifle was leaning against the inside of the open door and his water bottle was balanced on the narrow dashboard. He'd been talking on the radio and writing something down when the trouble began, probably very suddenly. His clipboard lay nearby on the ground. Edward picked it up and began studying it. There were no signs of the physical struggle everyone knew must have taken place.

The jeeps were parked outside the opening to the tower. Where once there had been a great, towering wall, there was now only a confusion of bent structural bars and shreds of fire-blackened sheeting. The first several stories of the tower were exposed to view where the wall had torn away. They were ruined completely, blasted to pieces by explosions and the crash. The rear cargo areas of the jeeps were loaded with recovered artifacts, most of them tagged and labeled. Mostly, they were pieces of shattered machinery, and all were composed of organic matter.

"You still think we're going to find that silver case?" Reg asked Fadeela.

"Or die trying," she said, lifting her gaze and flashlight up to explore the massive, shredded wall of the tower. "If it's here, that's where we'll find it."

Edward found something that helped confirm her suspicions.

"This is not good news." He came toward them, reading from the clipboard. "The men in these jeeps were climbing the tower and searching for survivors. Then, on the level thirteen, something happened."

Reg and Fadeela spoke at the same time. "What does it say?"

Edward shook his head. "That something grabbed them. Then it says control room."

Reg arched an eyebrow. "Control room? On the thirteenth floor?"

Edward took the report off the clipboard and stuffed it in his pocket. "That's what it says."

"Well, what are we waiting for? Let's go have a look around." Reg had already estimated that the height of each of the exposed floors was sixty feet. Getting to the thirteenth floor would be the equivalent of climbing a fifty-story building.

"Check this out," Tye called softly. He'd found a platter-sized object in one of the jeeps. "It's the granddaddy of all medallions." It was the color of liquid amber and had the same hair-thin veins running through it as the disks he'd been carrying with him. "Watch. It lights up when you touch it." Tye rested his palm on it and a fuzzy, fast-moving image formed on the surface. The image was too indistinct to recognize, but it seemed to be shifting and changing at a chaotic speed.

Reg leaned in for a better look. "What's it doing?"

"Beats me," Tye said, "but it looks like a broadcast, doesn't it?"

"Check your medallions. See if we're still alone in here."

When Tye pulled them out of his pocket, he got two surprises. First, the complex, shifting pattern of diamonds was gone and in its place was a flower design that covered the entire face of the disk. It was the same rigidly symmetrical "daisy" pattern found on the bottom of the city destroyer. Second, he could feel the small medallion drawn to the larger slab like a magnet. It gave him an idea. "These two pieces are attracting one another," he told Reg. "That must be the basis of their tracking system."

"That's fascinating," Reg said impatiently. "Are there any aliens around?"

"That I can't tell you," Tye admitted. "But if I see any, you'll be the first to know."

Reg whistled through his teeth and waved everyone toward the tower. Seeing that the lower floors had been decimated beyond use, he moved directly to one of the X-shaped structural beams and began to climb. Each girder was as tall as he was, and there were about ten of them between floors. They were made of bone, or something very similar to it, and were encrusted with a brittle moss that flaked apart under their hands. As they climbed the first several stories of the mile-high tower, they saw that the floors were made of the same razor-thin material as the exterior walls. The loose edges fluttered like pieces of tissue paper in the breeze Reg made as he climbed past. Despite its seeming fragility, the material was strong enough to withstand the powerful explosions that had obliterated most of the ship.

They continued to climb up the girders until they were dripping with sweat, and their arms began to tire. Young, lanky, and unencumbered by heavy weaponry, Tye scaled the support beams more easily than the others. Still, he was the first to suggest looking for a different way up. "This is taking too long," he called down to the others. "There must be a better way to the top."

"Keep moving," Ali grunted from below, and the team continued to climb, painfully, floor by floor, up the stack of X-shaped girders. Eventually, they reached a place where the damage was less severe. A ceiling of the ultrathin material prevented them from climbing higher. They left the girders and moved deeper into the tower.

With Reg in the lead, they moved at a fast march through the piles of twisted debris. The enormous room had been turned into an empty box by the force of the explosions. They walked uphill through the leaning skyscraper, then broke into a jog until the front wall of the tower came into view. The destruction was less complete here, and it was possible to imagine what the interior must have looked like before the crash.

Sections of transparent wall still stood in places, or hung from the ceiling like ragged sheets of ice. They had once divided the floor into smaller rooms, workstations of some kind. When Ali rapped on one of the walls with his knuckles, the vibrations caused it to make a humming noise.

"Look at this," Tye called from the far side of the glassy barrier. He'd found a room that was only slightly damaged. It was the size of a small auditorium, and there were low black benches arranged in rows. Hanging on the forward wall was a flat, squared-off sheet of material that looked like a modified tortoiseshell. "Looks like a really uncomfortable movie theater," he mused, sitting down on one of the benches. The seat of his pants was still wet with the thick gel that lined the floor of the chariot. It made a rude noise as he sat down. "Aaagh!" Tye jumped up immediately when the bench moved beneath him. "What in the—"

He reached down and touched it again, with his hand this time. The surface of the bench was as hard and as smooth as polished marble. But when activated by the galvanic charge coursing through his fingertips, it bubbled to life, its surface rising into a series of inch-tall welts. Struggling against the impulse to tear his hand away, Tye held it in place and watched in horrified fascination as the transformation of the stonelike material continued. Tiny lines of light appeared in the surface, first as a dull glow, but then brightening to form a complex grid. Within moments, the entire length of the bench lit up with a visual display, showing an unintelligible, highly complicated blueprint: half anatomical drawing and half engineering schematic. They realized it wasn't a bench but a table designed to be used by a creature half his size.

Reg had forged ahead to the front wall of the tower. When the others followed him, they saw bands of blotchy light leaking through a network of narrow "windows." A series of thin geometric lines ran the entire height and length of the huge wall, each one emitting an uneven greenish glow. Reg stared up at the strange green lines, trying to understand the significance of the pattern they made. When he brought his face close to one of them, he saw that the large plates covering the outside of the tower were connected to one another by some sort of dense, stringy ligament. In some places, all that stood between Reg and the outside world was the same ultrathin material that was used in the construction of the rest of the tower. This time it was more than semitransparent. Reg could see through it to the desert outside, which was brightly lit in a sickly, green-tinted glare.

"What is it?" hadeela asked.

"They're windows," Reg said. "They seem to be amplifying the light outside. Take a look." The others pressed close to the spy holes and stared through them.

"Fantastic!" Tye said.

"It's like looking through night-vision goggles," Edward said.

"And a magnifying glass."

The scene was almost too bright for their eyes. The rocky hills and wadis of the desert floor were illuminated in a harsh glare, as if enclosed in a giant copying machine. At the same time that it amplified the light, the material acted as a telescope. When Edward spotted a shape moving across a dune top far in the distance, the image quickly focused and enlarged until he could see that it was a lone alien soldier out on patrol in a chariot. The magnification continued until he could make out the individual tentacles on the armored creature's shoulder blades and the glowing three-inch medallion on the back of his bony hand. He stepped back, blinked his eyes, and his vision returned to normal.

"Very strange," he said. "Someday I'm going to build a house with windows like this."

"I can see Sutton and Remi," Yossi said, pressing his forehead against the surface and looking straight down. "They look nervous."

"Now we understand why we are losing so many planes

when we try to attack them here," Ali said, pondering the windows. "They can see us coming from a great distance."

"Which means," said Edward, pointing out the obvious, "that if there are any survivors in this tower, they probably watched us drive up."

"Doesn't matter now," Reg said, checking his watch under the beam of his flashlight. "We're not climbing fast enough. We've been inside almost an hour and we're just past halfway up. We've got to find a faster route."

"Yeah, but where?" They scanned the ruined monumental space with their flashlights but saw nothing that looked remotely like a staircase. In the distance, near the center of the tower, rubble was piled high around a set of columns that reached to the ceiling. They headed in that direction.

Along the way, they passed an overturned set of the black worktables. When they came close to them, Yossi stopped short, froze in his tracks, and swung his machine gun into position. Holding his flashlight steady, he stared straight ahead with all the concentration of a bird dog, while the others fanned out to surround the spot. When he gave the signal, they began closing in from all sides, aware that if it was an alien they'd cornered, a telepathic attack was imminent.

Everyone held their breath and stepped closer, their weapons trained where Yossi was pointing. There was a rustling sound and then a flash of movement as a small gray body leapt from its hiding place and darted in one direction, then another, looking for a way past the humans.

Ali and Yossi both shot at the thing, but missed. Their bullets ricocheted into the distance. With surprising speed and agility, the creature bolted forward and would have gotten away if Reg hadn't pounced and knocked it to the floor. He grabbed it around the neck and felt his fingers sink into the spongy flesh.

When the shock wave of pain tore through his body, Reg was ready. He lifted the creature off the ground and slammed it against one of the touch-activated tabletops.

The pain's not real, he told himself. *You can resist it.*

Once more, Reg lifted the homuncular body with his half-paralyzed arm and brought it crashing down against the stone-solid surface of the table, sending a telepathic message of his own: *Obey or die.* But the alien continued to resist. Reg continued to pound it against the tabletop until its body went as limp as a rag doll and it fell into a stunned submission. Then he leaned over it and saw himself reflected in the surface of the alien's silvery eyes. Reg had been waiting for a moment like this: He tried to read the alien's mind. He conjured up the image of the silver box from his memory and attempted to "send" the image to the alien.

"Where is it?" he demanded loudly. "Where's the box?"

When he received no answer, Reg fed the creature another mouthful of tabletop.

"It's dead," Edward told him.

"No," Reg said. He could feel the thing's consciousness. It was monitoring him, playing possum. But he didn't know how to access its thoughts. Telepathy was, after all, an alien skill, not a human one.

"What should we do with it?" Fadeela asked.

"Kill it," Reg said, searching the bulging silvery eyes for signs of fear. The only thing he felt in return was a hateful defiance. Ali stepped up to the table, lifted the butt end of his heavy, five-foot-long gun, and held it over the alien's enlarged brainpan.

"Should I?"

Last chance, Reg warned the creature. Its eyes closed calmly a moment before Ali slammed his weapon down and split open its skull. Reg felt the life slip out of the little body in his grip. He backed away, wiping his hands clean on his uniform and breathing hard.

"I really hate those little bastards," he said.

The team regrouped and continued the search, marching quickly through the monumental darkness. They had only gone a short distance when they saw the flash of an alien pulse weapon and heard a startled scream that sounded like Tye. The others hit the deck and prepared to fire in the direction of the noise, assuming the bioarmored aliens had finally shown up to defend the tower.

"Sorry!" Tye called through the darkness. "That was only us." He and Yossi had gone ahead of the others and found something that had startled them.

"Come this way," Yossi called, signaling with his flashlight. "We found something." The others raced forward and saw the two men investigating a deep recess in the wall.

"What is it? What did you find?"

Tye was down on his knees leaning into an opening, shining his light straight down. "It's a shaft of some kind."

"Ugh! What are those things on the walls?" Fadeela asked, disgusted by what she saw. The inside of the shaft was lined with sickly-looking white strands.

"I don't know, but I just lost my appetite," Ali said. The vertical tube seemed to travel the entire height of the tower, and its walls were overgrown with slender white tendrils that hung limply in tangled masses. Reg thought the tendrils looked like relatives of the vines he'd seen growing in other parts of the ship.

"There's that horrible smell again," Edward said, backing away. "Ammonia."

Tye turned to face the group. "That smell could be a good thing. Think about it. The pulse gun, the chariot, their bioarmor."

Reg understood instantly. "Of course. This is another one of their machines. But what?"

"I think it's a lift," Tye said. "It's got to be." He cautiously leaned over the edge and peered once more into the bottomless pit. "All of their technology is basically ripped off from other species or cultures. They must be zipping around the universe, conquering one planet after another and adapting the technologies and life-forms they find to serve their own purposes. You know what I think this shaft must have been?"

The others didn't have a clue.

"A giant esophagus," he announced with a dramatic expression. "The aliens probably found some poor brontosaurus-sized slob, cut his throat out, put it in one of those liquid growing vats of theirs and—*voila!*— instant elevator. These stringy white things hanging down the sides are cilia, just like you find in the human windpipe. I'll wager ten quid that if we touch them, they'll do something." He glanced around at the others. "Any takers?"

"Maybe they have stairs," Yossi offered.

When no one volunteered, Tye took matters into his own hands, literally. He reached out and grabbed one of the gooey white strands. Instantly, the entire shaft erupted to life. Tens of thousands of white tendrils began to whip around the interior of the shaft in a writhing frenzy. Pleased with himself, Tye smiled an I-told-you-so smile, not noticing that the strands were crawling up his arm. By the time he realized what was happening, the stringy tendrils had wound themselves around his shoulder and pulled him inside.

The group had just enough time to recoil in horror and level their guns at the man-eating tendrils before Tye came flying out and landed, ass over teakettle, in a heap ten feet away. The tentacles all dropped limp, and the shaft went quiet again.

"Michael, are you all right?" Fadeela asked.

Tye sat up and spit out an oily piece of tendril. "It wasn't exactly a Riviera holiday, but yeah, I'm okay." He was covered head to foot in a fine layer of the foul-smelling slime.

"There goes your elevator theory," Yossi smirked.

"Not at all," he said, getting to his feet. "I got a little nervous is all. Once I was inside, the only thing I was thinking about was *getting out*, not *going up*. It did what I asked. Maybe I'll have one more go. I don't think it's dangerous." Before the others could dissuade him, he marched back and jumped inside. The long strands flared to life again, whipping back and forth like overcaffeinated sea snakes, and caught him. He screamed suddenly and was carried off. A moment later, the movement stopped suddenly, and the tendrils all fell dormant.

Carefully, Reg leaned a few inches into the shaft and looked up, then down. 'Tye! Can you hear me?" He backed away from the opening when he heard something coming toward him from above. Tye's helmet flew past, falling to the bottom. 'Tye!" Reg shouted again, then, straining to hear a response. He was about to give up when the millions of thin white strands whipped into a frenzy of movement once more. Reg leapt back from the opening and, a second later, Tye came flying out of the shaft and landed once more in a heap.

"Gotta work on the landing, but I think I'm getting the hang of it," he said.

"We thought this thing ate you for breakfast," Reg said. "Where'd you go?"

"Up. How far up, I'm not exactly sure." He looked at Yossi through the darkness. "I told you it was a lift," he said. "And guess what it turns out to be?"

"A lift?"

"Precisely. This time, when I went inside, I thought about moving upward. Just like with the chariot. Next thing I knew, *whoosh,* I was going up."

"See any shiny metallic cases up there?" Reg asked, glancing at his watch.

"I didn't stay long enough to look around," Tye answered.

"Wait a second," Edward said. "The report on that clipboard, it said something grabbed them, remember? Then it said control room. The case is up there, it has to be."

"That's what I've been saying all along," Fadeela pointed out. "Let's ride this thing to the top."

Tye lectured the group. "Don't be distracted once you get inside. Think about traveling up, concentrate on getting to the top." He reached his arm inside and brought the stringy white cilia to life once more. They wrapped themselves around his lanky frame and dragged him inside. "Can you see me in here?" Tye called through the storm of movement.

He was fully engulfed, but the others caught occasional glimpses of him—a kneecap here, an elbow there. They watched Tye think himself up a few feet then back down again until he was hovering in front of them again. Without leaving the shaft, he called through the rustling cilia, "Everybody clear on the concept?" Then, without waiting for an answer, "Good. See you at the top."

Yossi was the first to follow. He took a deep breath and stepped bravely to the threshold of the shaft, but lost his resolve and hesitated, staring into the grasping tendrils, overwhelmed by the strangeness of what he was about to do.

"This is *not* why I joined the Air Force," he moaned, closing his eyes tight and leaning forward until he felt the moist strands begin to lash softly across his face and chest. The next thing he knew, they had wrapped themselves around him and dragged him inside. It was an odd, terrifying sensation. He suddenly found himself floating in a zero-gravity environment. The moist white strands came at him from every angle and buoyed him up, each one lifting a tiny fraction of his weight. When he opened his mouth to yell, the strands darted into his mouth. He batted at them with his arms and kicked with his legs, but felt no resistance. It was like fighting against the air. Individually, the tendrils had very little strength, but they were wickedly quick and adjusted to changes in his position as fast as he could make them. It took a second or two for Yossi to realize that although he was floating inside the shaft, he wasn't moving. *I need to move up*, he remembered. The mere thought wasn't enough, it had to be a positive act of will. *Up, up, I want to move up!* Sensing his desire through the conductive medium of the gelatin, the tendrils obeyed. Yossi shot upward, tumbling end over end. Once he stopped struggling, the ride was surprisingly comfortable. Then it came to an abrupt end. He was spit out of the shaft and crashed to the floor. When he looked up, Tye was looking down at him.

"Weird, isn't it? Come on, get out of the way before the next person comes through." Still slightly disoriented from the experience, Yossi allowed Tye to drag him to one side a moment before Edward came crashing out of the esophageal bioelevator. One by one, the others followed until the group had reassembled on the new, higher stage of the tower.

"That was disgusting." Fadeela winced, wiping the film of clear gelatin off her face. "Are we at the top?"

"Doesn't look like it," Reg said with a sinking feeling. He moved a few strides into the cavernous space. It was a virtual replica of the floors below, full of the same shattered walls and pieces of broken equipment. In the distance, the false daylight filtered through the gaps between the exterior plates. "It looks like there's at least one more floor above."

Through the semitransparent ceiling, they could see

what appeared to be an open chamber above. It looked completely empty. The team marched toward the front of the tower, keeping their eyes open for a way up to the next story.

"I just realized something," Reg announced. "This floor above us, it has to be the exit bay for their attacker planes."

"Yeah, I think you're right," Tye said, nodding. He was the only one who had been with Reg during the first attack over Jerusalem, when hundreds of the disk-shaped attackers had come swarming out of an opening about three-quarters of the way up the face of the tower. "This is the tunnel they flew out of. It's as wide as the tower itself."

Ali cursed in Arabic, then said, "There's got to be a way around it."

"Maybe along the sides," Fadeela suggested, and started to walk in that direction.

"Sounds logical," Ali grudgingly agreed, and began to follow.

Just then the walls began to quake violently, followed by a booming explosion. The floor shifted sideways beneath their feet, powerfully enough to knock all of them to the ground. With a shudder, the tower leaned another degree off center. The entire structure teetered back and forth as the support beams on the lower levels decided whether to give way and collapse. When it seemed as if they would hold for a while longer, Fadeela was the first to break the silence. "And what exactly was that?"

"I think your fiancé's planes have decided to show up after all."

"Just when we need them least," Edward observed. "They're going to knock the tower over before we can get outside."

"It's getting close to sunup," Reg announced. "We've got to find these bioweapons."

"No, seriously," Edward said, "they're going to knock

the tower over. Isn't it time to get out of here?"

"Plenty of time left." Reg smiled. His expression changed suddenly as an idea occurred to him. He broke into a jog, searching the ceiling with his flashlight.

"What is it?"

"This way." The others followed, weaving through the obstacle course of ruined workstations and collapsed walls. A hundred yards before they reached the sidewall of the tower, Reg stopped and pointed his flashlight up at the ceiling. "There it is."

Lying massively on the floor above was the titanic taproot they'd seen as they entered the ship. It looked like an oil pipeline stretching away toward the front of the ship. If it were still growing and burrowing into the earth, there were no signs of it. The thing lay motionless.

Ali stared up at the giant organic tube, stunned by a horrible epiphany. "They're not going to put the biological weapons into the air. They're going to put them into the ground."

Tye was confused. "Uh, wouldn't that be a good thing? To bury the poisons?"

"Into the water, the groundwater," Ali explained. "This is the desert, but there is water. An underground river, one of the largest in the world. It supplies the cities in the north with their water." He shook his head thinking how many people would be infected if the water supply were contaminated, and how quickly the carriers would infect others.

"Look up there," Yossi said, pointing his flashlight at the ceiling. Dimly visible through the ceiling were the bottoms of alien feet. Three sets of them came padding alongside the taproot until they were directly overhead. Yossi followed them with his flashlight.

'Turn that thing off, you jackass," Edward hissed. "You're showing them where we are."

But the aliens already knew where the humans were. They lingered for a moment, looking down through the semitransparent material before heading off in a new direction. Fadeela raised her flamethrower to take a shot, but Reg stopped her.

"Let's follow them."

He bolted into the darkness, blazing a trail over and around the piles of debris lying in his path. He used the flashlight attached to his machine gun to keep track of the alien feet, unconcerned that he was giving away his own position. He chased them a couple of hundred yards until they disappeared. The others followed as best they could. By the time they caught up to him, Reg was climbing a sort of trellis composed of thick diagonal bars. He was already halfway to the top and didn't look back to see if the others were following.

Out of breath by the time he climbed to the top, he found himself in the long, low corridor of the attacker exit bay. He took a few strides into the empty space and strained to hear the sound of the retreating aliens over the pounding of his own heart. But the only noise came from the rest of the team struggling up the trellis. As they stepped away from the trellis, he switched on his flashlight briefly and scanned the new room. In the distance, there was the ten-foot-tall taproot running past a set of columns, but otherwise the space was vacant. It was just tall enough to accommodate one of the sixty-foot-long attacker ships. The floor and ceiling were covered with skid marks where the wobbling airships had brushed against them.

There was no sign of the aliens.

"Did you see which way they went?" Yossi asked. He and Tye had their forearms locked together, ready to fire the alien pulse gun.

"No," Reg answered. "But I've got a feeling they're still nearby."

"Listen," Fadeela said. "Outside. You can hear the bombers." The tunnel was open at one end. The sound of the distant jet engines echoed down the corridor, and there was a slight breeze.

"First things first," Ali said. "We've got to destroy that root before they can use it to poison the water supply." The taproot was more than a hundred yards away.

"You're right," Reg said uneasily. He had the sense that the team was being watched. "Let's head in that direction, but not in a bunch. We're making ourselves an easy target. Edward, you and I will go first. The rest of you follow in pairs."

Reg took off, running in a crouch, but stopped suddenly after only a few steps.

"What is it?" Edward asked.

ZAP! A fist-sized ball of light sliced through the darkness. As Edward twisted and ducked out of the way, he raised his free hand instinctively to shield himself. The green pulse streaked past his hand, removing four of his fingers and leaving a burn mark across his forehead as it went. He screamed in pain and hit the floor as a second blast sailed over his head.

Reg and Ali opened up with their guns, blasting away in the direction of the attack. Tye and Yossi sent a pulse blast of their own skittering away into the darkness. But it was Fadeela who put the aliens on the defensive. She charged toward the source of the enemy fire, squeezing out a long arc of flame as she ran. The fire lit up the gloomy corridor and exposed their attackers.

There were three aliens—two of them in exoskeletal armor. The warriors were marching inexorably forward with their fingers extended in the firing position until the fire overwhelmed them. They recoiled from the flames and, in their panic, tripped over their biomechanical legs and crashed to the ground.

"Hold your fire," Reg screamed. Fadeela was in the way, charging forward without a thought for her own safety. Before the lumbering giants could regain their feet and escape, she sprayed them with a heavy dose of thick liquid fire. By the time their thorax shells popped open and the creatures within wriggled into the open, Reg and Ali had come forward and were in position to finish them off.

"There's one more," Ali shouted as he ran past the smoldering bodies, "this way." They chased the fleeing alien into the shadows of the exit bay, moving toward the open front of the tower and leaving the light of the flames behind them.

"More fire," Reg yelled when it seemed the alien would escape.

Fadeela raised her flamethrower and was about to send out another plume of fire when she realized there was no need. She knew exactly where the alien was standing. It was to her right, not far away, cowering against the tower's sidewall. Without a word being exchanged, all of the humans turned in the same direction and slowly raised their weapons toward the spot. They knew what they were going to see: a tall, unarmed alien with opalescent white skin. And when they aimed their flashlights in that direction, that is exactly what they saw. The alien moved very slowly away from the wall, its huge eyes squinting into the glare of the flashlights, and raised its hands above its head.

It told them it wanted to surrender.

15

A VERY CLOSE ENCOUNTER

Another bomb rocked into the downed spacecraft. The tower absorbed the shock wave without tilting any farther off center, but as it swayed and shook beneath their feet, Reg and the others were reminded that time was running short. Dawn was quickly approaching and the Saudi jets outside were threatening to fell the tower like a tall tree.

The alien stood perfectly still, its goose-egg eyes reflecting the beams of the flashlights. The only movements it made occurred inside its body. Beneath the translucent membrane of its skin, knots of tissue clutched and released in peristaltic motion. This creature was not like the others the team had encountered. It stood a full head taller, and its skin glistened a nacreous white. Its emaciated limbs looked long and graceful in comparison to its smaller, grayer brethren, but, like them, its face was nothing more than a blunt spot on the front of its neck. Its large brain hung off the back of the skull like a meaty, pie-sized tumor.

The frail captive had ample reason not to move. It had a large-caliber field gun, two flamethrowers, two fully automatic machine guns, a pistol, and an alien pulse weapon pointed its way. The humans who held these weapons were waiting for the creature to make the slightest of false moves, anything that would give them the excuse they wanted to blow it to bits. They were nervous, frightened, and thirsty for revenge, but something told them it would be a mistake to squeeze their triggers. The alien lifted its white, two-fingered hands in the air as a sign of its surrender and "spoke" to Reg.

In a single, sustained, telepathic thought, it communicated several ideas at once. It told Reg: that there were no more bio-armored soldiers nearby; that it was personally incapable of violence; that it would cooperate fully if the humans gave it a chance; and that killing a potentially useful prisoner would be a grave tactical error.

It took a long, confusing moment for Reg to sort out the multilayered mental message the alien was sending. It came to him as a *feeling* rather than in the symbolic language he was accustomed to using. The communication was both a physical sensation that tingled through his nervous system and a recognizable emotion. There were no words, no need for interpretation, no possibility of misunderstanding. But the ideas were piled on top of one another, strung together in a way that took some getting used to. Once he began to understand the telepathy, the ideas resonated with a strange familiarity through some long-unused section of his brain. And there was a rationality to the communication that caught Reg off guard. All the aliens he'd faced previously had sprung at him mentally with the same ferocious energy they used in their physical attacks. This "Tall One," on the other hand, was serene, intelligent and—more importantly— afraid to die.

Without lifting his eyes away from his prisoner, Reg began to explain to the others what the alien had told him. There was no need. The rest of the team could also *hear* the alien thinking.

"It's reading our minds," Ali said nervously. "We should kill it."

"No. *We* are reading *its* mind," Tye said. "Aren't we?"

"Don't kill it!" Edward demanded. "There's no need. It's not going to hurt us, and we need its help."

"Not going to hurt us?" Yossi asked. "What about your hand?"

Edward had his mangled left hand tucked under his right arm to staunch the bleeding, but kept his flamethrower in the ready position. He and the alien answered Yossi's question simultaneously, one silently, the other aloud. "It's the others ones who shot me," Edward insisted, "the ones in the suits of armor. This one is different. Can't you feel what it's telling us?"

"I think he's right," Tye said. "Maybe it knows where the biological weapons are."

Reg tightened his grip on his .357 Magnum, walked forward until he was standing within an arm's length of the five-foot-tall ghostlike figure, and pointed the gun at its forehead. The alien didn't flinch, but everyone sensed its panic level rising. As calmly as he could manage, Reg spoke to it. "I'm going to put a big, messy hole through your ugly face unless you help us. Understand?"

It understood.

"We're looking for a silver case. It's full of little glass test tubes, and we want you to…" Reg didn't need to finish putting the idea into words. The alien was already answering. It pointed one of its hands, a set of banana-sized pincers, toward the horizon of the ceiling, then "spoke" once more. In one mental stroke, it told them, in no particular order: that the silver case would be found on the floor immediately above; that it would gladly lead them to the spot; and that the biological poisons were still safely inside their sealed tubes. There was no question about what the alien wanted. It was trying to exchange cooperation for survival.

"I don't like it," Ali grumbled after *listening* to the alien. He turned and swept the darkened exit bay with his flashlight. "I've got a bad feeling. He wants to trap us. Why are the weapons upstairs? Why aren't they over there?" He pointed the flashlight in the direction of the distant taproot. "It doesn't make sense."

"Why don't we ask him," Fadeela said. She walked angrily to where Reg was standing, gave the alien a sharp thump on the chest with the warm tip of her flamethrower, and spoke to it in heated Arabic. She wanted to know what the taproot was for.

The Tall One was remarkably forthcoming in its reply. Without words or images, it answered Fadeela's question in surprising detail: The massive root, nearly two miles long from end to end, customarily served as a food source for the aliens and had been grown from a tiny seed; the one growing down the side of the tower had been altered to grow in such a way that it would serve as a powerful pump; the tip of the plant had already penetrated to the level of the groundwater; the test tubes were to have been snugged into a specially designed insertion, a cartridge chamber, and then forced downward under explosive pressure; the first anthrax deaths in the northern population centers would have occurred within seventy-two hours. The alien understood, and began to explain, the geometric progression of infection among the human population. The lethal efficiency of the plan seemed to please the creature.

"That's enough!" Fadeela shouted. She felt like punching the balloon-headed creature right between its bulging chrome-colored eyes. Before she could, Reg made a decision.

"This is our best bet," he announced. "We'll follow our little friend upstairs. If he leads us to the silver case, we'll let him live. If not, he's vapor, and we'll come down here and destroy that big root." He started the alien marching with a shove.

He knew Ali was probably right. Chances were good that it was leading them into an ambush. There was no way to know for sure. Even though the individual they'd captured seemed to be cooperating, Reg knew the aliens worked together as seamlessly as bees from the same hive and that they had descended on Earth intent on exterminating humanity. They were colonizers, and cold-blooded killers. It made sense that there would be a trap waiting for them on the floor above, and that's exactly what Reg was hoping for. If the silver case was the bait, there was always a chance of getting away with it before the trap was sprung.

As they walked, Yossi tore off his shirt and used it to make bandages and a tourniquet for Edward's wound. "Listen, I know you don't like to take advice from Jews," he told Edward, "but next time, don't try to *catch* the bullet. *Try getting out of the way.*"

Tye took off his belt, looped it, and slipped it over the alien's head to create a choker leash, which he promptly handed to Reg. The alien's head bobbed heavily atop its thin neck as it shuffled across the floor. Its movements were stiff and wobbly at the same time, somewhat like an old man's.

Very quickly, they came to a trellis of diagonal bars like the one they'd found earlier. Reg kept the alien tightly tethered with the belt leash as they began to climb. Ali and Yossi helped Edward up the bars. Fadeela shot ahead and reached the new level first. By the time the others caught up to her, she had already wandered beyond the short entrance hall and out into the open, exposing herself to the danger of being picked off by a sniper's pulse blast.

She was standing in a room that was as wide as a prairie and of incredible height. It had once been full of tall crystalline spires, towers within towers, most of which were now reduced to a jagged rubble. The architecture was stark and utilitarian. In many places, the spires were still connected to one another by horizontal footbridges. There were plenty of places left to hide; enough to hold a small army. But it would only take a sniper or two to finish the team off. They stopped at the end of the low hallway and crouched at the threshold.

"Woman," Ali hissed at her quietly, "come back here before you get all of us killed."

"Quiet, dog breath," Fadeela answered at normal volume. She was staring straight up, lost in contemplation of the vast ceiling, which was composed of thousands of diamond-shaped panes of the light-amplifying, telescoping glass. Light from the outside world poured in through the panes as if it were midday, but only through a few at a time. Circular clusters of them lit up to create a moving pattern across the ceiling, like a half dozen spotlights sliding across the skies over a destroyed city. Reg leaned out of the hallway far enough to follow Fadeela's gaze. He looked up at the hazy blob of light she seemed to be following as it traveled, a few panes at a time, across the ceiling. The moment he focused his eyes on it, it began to change. Suddenly, the windows showed him a fighter jet streaking silently through the predawn sky at a high altitude. A moment later, the image magnified and refocused until he could see that it was an American-built F-15. The image magnified again, and he could read the serial numbers stenciled onto the undersides of the plane's wings. He blinked and looked away, slightly disoriented.

Tye stared out into the open space ahead with a combination of awe and dread. "What drives such small creatures," he asked, "to build on such a gigantic scale?" As if the proportions of the room were too grand to contemplate, he turned his attention to something small. The floor was covered with pieces of debris, some of which looked like tools or machine pieces. Tye stretched one of his long arms through the doorway and picked one of them up. It looked like an ordinary ball bearing, but stung his fingertips when he squeezed it. An inspection under his flashlight showed him that it was covered with bristles, a stiff metallic fuzz. He put it in his pocket and was about to back away from the opening when the alien *spoke* again.

This time, no one could feel the thoughts except Tye. It "suggested" that he pick up one more, and it forcibly steered his attention to something that looked like a half-melted black pen. The alien told him it was a medical tool that could be used to treat Edward's wounds. When Tye retrieved it, the alien communicated to the rest of the group what the wand could do: stem Edward's bleeding; repair the shattered bone; clear and cauterize the wound; and accelerate the regrowth of the skin.

"It could be a weapon," Tye pointed out, looking down at the lightweight object. One end of it flattened out into a dull blade.

"Give it to him. Let him try," Edward said urgently. The bandages Yossi had made for him were already saturated and dripping with blood. If the bleeding didn't stop soon, he wouldn't be able to keep pace with the others.

After a nod from Reg, Tye held the instrument out and let the alien's thick awkward fingers take it from him. The creature fumbled with the tool for only a moment, then tossed it aside before Edward could finish unbandaging his mutilated hand. By the time he did, the bleeding had already stopped. A moment later, he realized the pain was gone, too.

"That's a good start," he said. "But can you grow my fingers back?" The alien no longer seemed interested. It turned away and began walking toward the open room. It stopped when it came to the end of the leash and felt the belt tug at his throat. After a moment of hesitation, Reg followed the alien out of the hallway.

The dimly lit space around them was quadruple the size of the largest domed sports arena on Earth and was filled with softly pulsating light. In addition to the spotlights of false daylight coming from the ceiling, there was a strobing, flashing light coming off the floor. As they walked farther into the room, they discovered the source of this strange light.

Huge slabs of the same amber-colored substance had been set into the sloping, bowl-shaped floor in the shape of a flower. Each petal was the size of a soccer field and was glowing a warm orange color through the darkness. A few strides brought them to the end of the nearest petal. It was cracked and broken. In places, large chunks were missing after being damaged during the ship's crash. There was evidence that something or someone had been collecting the missing sections and setting them back into place like the pieces of a mammoth jigsaw puzzle. As with the plate of the same material Tye had found in the back of the jeeps, the glassy "petals" were emitting a shifting pattern of light. Blurred, fast-moving images streaked across the surface, but were unintelligible to the humans. A long walk from where they were standing, down at the eye of the flower, there was an amber lump that stood on a pedestal several inches above the floor.

"Okay, we're here," Reg told the alien. "Where's the box?"

Still eager to help, the creature communicated another cluster of associated ideas. The box, it told them, lay open on top of a worktable in one of the laboratory rooms at the far side of the tower; it gave them the exact location and showed them the best path to take. The instructions were so clear that any one of the humans could have drawn a map. The alien began to shuffle its feet, prepared to lead them to the spot.

"We don't need that thing anymore," Ali said, gesturing toward their alien guide with his weapon. He was more convinced than ever that they were being led into a trap. Telepathic assurances aside, the crumbling spires that rose on both sides of the path they would take offered the perfect hiding places for snipers. "We know where we're headed. We can go by ourselves. Edward and Yossi, you come with me. The rest of you wait here for us. We'll be back soon. I hope."

The three men jogged off without any further discussion and quickly began to fade from view behind the screen of eerily pulsating light. Reg pulled the Tall One back toward the shelter of the entrance hall and maintained a watchful attitude, while Tye and Fadeela moved deeper into the room and explored the erratically flashing light of the flower.

"It's the mother of all medallions," Tye said, "the heart of their tracking system." He pulled one of the small medallions out of his pocket and felt it drawn toward the floor, like iron to a magnet. When the small disk touched his skin and activated, the pattern it showed was a representation of the huge flower-shape that lay stretched out below him. "Hmmm. I wonder what happened to all those little diamond shapes."

"I think I know," Fadeela told him, pointing toward the amber blob at the center of the flower. "There they are."

Cautiously, the two of them walked down toward the spot where the petals came together and examined the glowing lump set on the pedestal. It seemed to be made of the same material as the broken amber slabs around them, but it was definitely alive. It was a foot-tall mass of semiliquid biomatter contained within thin membrane walls. Its body produced a phosphorescent light from within, except on one side, where the skin was black.

"Looks like an octopus," Fadeela said, her lip curling in disgust.

"Looks like a big brain to me."

"A brain with legs?"

A series of thin arms grew from the bottom of the transparent blob and reached out to connect with each of the eight gigantic petals. Where they attached to the blob, these arms looked as moist and frail as a snail's body, but solidified as they fused with the surface of the amber material. Beads of an oily liquid ran down the organism's sides like sap leaking from a tree.

"There are your diamonds," Fadeela said, pointing toward the black spot on the blob's flank.

Tye squatted for a closer look and realized she was right. Except for a very few strays, all of the tiny diamonds had clustered in one spot on the side of the bloblike body. He thought it over for a minute before asking a question. "At-Ta'if is to the north, isn't it?"

"The northwest. Why?"

Tye glanced around the interior of the tower to get his bearings. "So northwest is that direction," he said, pointing. Fadeela understood what he was getting at. The dark diamonds had all clustered on the northwest wall of the gelatinous body.

"So, this octopus is keeping track of where all the aliens are. And Edward was right about the radio reports. They're attacking At-Ta'if." They noticed that the petal extending in the direction of the battle was flashing and pulsing much more rapidly than the others.

"That must be how it works," Tye said. "Now, if each of these petals functions like a giant medallion, they won't work unless they're being touched by some living thing. We could royally screw the alien army by killing this brain-thing. Their whole tracking and guidance system would shut down." Tye pulled a knife from the leg pocket of his uniform and was about to plunge it into the soft body when the alien "spoke" urgently from the distance, offering some insights into the flower-shaped apparatus.

This time, the interconnected telepathic ideas were embedded in a background sensation of painful loss. Although it was not a human emotion, both Tye and

Fadeela winced with sadness the moment they felt it. It was a deep feeling of separation and the aching wish to be reunited. They quickly realized that these feelings were coming from the lump of biomatter that sat sweating on the pedestal. Somehow, the alien was making it possible for them to feel what the simple organism was feeling: an intense chronic sadness, the same traumatic sense of loss a mother feels for her stolen children.

The emotion suddenly vanished and the Tall One *explained* to them: that every piece of the amber material, down to the tiniest sliver, *knew* where all the other pieces were; that the magnetic attraction between the fragments was a result of a desire to be rejoined; and that the amber-oozing creature at the center of the device was, in many respects, like a human—filthy with excrement, semi-intelligent, and wallowing in base emotions.

When the explanation was over, Tye backed away from the blob remorsefully. "I can't do it," he said, reaching into his pocket and pulling out his last two medallions. "Go on, be free," he said to the disks, as he tossed them toward their parent. "Go keep Big Mama company."

"Michael, you were right!" Fadeela said. "We have to kill this thing. Their whole navigation system will crash."

Tye knew she was right, but hesitated and stared down at his shoes. The Tall One had left him with a deep sympathy for the tortured creature, which the aliens had been holding as a prisoner for who-knew-how-long. He turned the knife over and over in his hand, trying to gather the strength to murder the poor animal, when he noticed something moving between his feet. Something was on the story below, on the floor of the exit bay.

He dropped to his knees, pressed his face close to the semitransparent flooring material, and cupped his hands around his eyes to block out the strobing light. He saw what looked like a trio of small manta rays swimming through murky water, but quickly realized they were three alien skulls seen from above. They were making their way toward the taproot, and one of them was holding a square silver object in its arms.

"What are you doing, praying?" Fadeela asked. When Tye didn't answer, she turned away to deal with the blob animal herself.

As carefully and quietly as possible, Tye stood up and began to walk back toward the spot where Reg was standing guard over the captive alien. He realized that the Tall One had deceived them. Instead of luring them into a trap, it had led them up here on a wild-goose chase in order to give the others time to complete their plan of poisoning the region's water supply.

"Where are you going now?" Fadeela demanded.

"Back in a minute," he answered as casually as he could manage. He thought he could hide his thoughts from the alien. "Just need to talk to Reg for a moment." To distract himself from what he'd learned, he began to whistle as he walked. But he was too nervous to carry a tune. The closer he came to Reg, the stronger became his desire to turn around and walk the other way. He didn't realize what was happening at first and pushed himself forward. His pace grew slower and slower, as a paralysis fell over his limbs. Then he stopped moving altogether. Only then did he realize that the Tall One, standing beside Reg like a docile house pet, was exerting a form of telepathic control over him. He opened his mouth to shout out a warning, but found he couldn't speak. He tried to turn around, but his feet were rooted to the floor. Trapped inside his uncooperative body, he waited in the darkness for Reg or Fadeela to notice that something was wrong. Then a strange idea infiltrated his consciousness: *The way to solve this problem is to kill myself.* He looked down and realized he was still holding the knife. The blade slowly tilted upward. Tye, knowing what was about to happen, struggled desperately to regain control of his arm, but couldn't. The knife jerked upward and stabbed into his left shoulder, where it lodged deep in the muscle and ligament. As if in a dream, he worked the blade free, then immediately plunged it into the softer tissue of his stomach. Although stupefied by what he was doing to himself, he felt no pain and was unable to make any sound. He pulled the knife free once more and prepared to stab into his heart when a shot rang out.

Tye collapsed to the floor and howled in pain. The next thing he knew, Reg was kneeling beside him, checking his wounds.

"Am I dead?" Tye asked.

"No. But our little helper is. He made you do this, didn't he?" Tye nodded. "Listen, they're down there, right below us. And they've got the case." He quickly explained what he'd seen through the floor, then lifted his head and looked at his wounds. "I'm not going to die or anything like that, am I?"

"Wait here for the others," Reg said, then turned and sprinted away just as Fadeela ran up to the spot.

"Reg, wait," she called. "Where are you going?"

He didn't answer. He tore into the dark hallway and flew down the trellis ladder. A few seconds later, he was running headlong through the darkness of the exit bay with his machine gun gripped tightly between his hands. He didn't switch on his flashlight for fear of showing the aliens where he was. Instead, he took his best guess about where the taproot was and plunged blindly ahead. To his right, the first violet-blue light of morning showed the outline of the rectangular opening at the front of the tower. In a few minutes, there would be enough light to see where he was headed. But he didn't have a few minutes to spare. He continued moving forward, all of his senses on alert, searching for the aliens Tye had seen. When he heard a noise in the distance, he stopped running and stood stock-still. Above the sound of his labored breathing and furiously pounding heart, he heard it again. It was the sound of the clasps being opened on the silver case. He aimed his machine gun at the sound, then switched on his flashlight.

A pair of bulging silver eyes looked back at him from beside the taproot, only a few strides away. It was another Tall One, awkwardly manipulating the metallic suitcase that Reg had been chasing ever since he first saw it at Al-Sayyid. One of the three clasps was still fastened. He'd arrived just in time.

"Back away, handsome," Reg growled at the alien, trying hard to sound cool, composed, and in control, when the truth was that he was terrified. When the alien didn't obey, Reg gathered himself and started moving forward, ready to blast through the alien's scrawny chest if it made a sudden movement. There were two more Tall Ones standing nearby, but they seemed unconcerned with Reg's presence. They turned their backs to him and resumed the tasks they'd been performing before he'd interrupted them. Although Reg didn't look in their direction, he found that he knew precisely what they were doing: going ahead with the deployment of the biological weapons. They were breaking open the membrane that covered the fourteen slotted cartridges that would accommodate the test tubes.

Just give me the box and I won't hurt any of you, Reg told them without a sound escaping his lips, but he was also thinking, *As soon as I have it I'll kill all three of you.* He edged forward until, face-to-face with the nearest Tall One, he extended a shaking hand and grabbed the handle of the silver case. When at last he had the thing safely in his grasp, a nervous smile crossed his lips. He breathed a huge sigh of relief and wiped the sweat from his eyes with the sleeve of his uniform. Now that he was holding all the cards, he could relax. *Three quick bullets*, he thought, *one for each of these ghouls, and then I can leave.* But before he could finish the job, the machine gun began to feel heavy in his right hand, and he let it rest on his hip. *Three quick shots,* he told himself.

Then again, he thought, there was no real need to kill them. The Tall Ones didn't seem to be violent like the smaller aliens. They were, in fact, a rather admirable species. Reg began more and more to see the situation from their perspective and had soon developed second thoughts about taking the biological weapons away from them. After all, they were only doing what was necessary. Their invasion of the Earth was a matter of their own survival, not some random act of cruelty. Compared to humans, they were kinder, cleaner, better organized, more peaceful, and, ultimately, wiser. They were, in short, the far superior species and deserved to inherit the Earth, even if they planned to stay only a short while.

It was a horrible idea, but it continued to unfold in his mind with an undeniable logic, like the blossoming of a sweet, poisonous flower. He suddenly saw humanity through the eyes of the aliens: a race of filthy and sadistic animals, the equivalent of cockroaches with guns. Suddenly, he regretted having killed the Tall One who had led him upstairs. The gentle creature had only been trying to help, keeping the humans out of the way while the final preparations were made to inject the microbes deep into the earth. Instead of being thankful, Reg had blown its brains out, murdered it execution-style.

The hatred and contempt the Tall Ones felt for him awakened all of his own self-hatred and brought him crashing back to the event that had shattered his life several years before: his ill-fated bombing run during the Gulf War. He remembered walking into that postflight debriefing room feeling like he was the king of the world, then the next moment wanting to curl up and die when they told him what he'd done. The whole gruesome scene replayed itself as if it were happening again for the first time. He remembered standing in front of a television watching rescue workers pull the dead, the maimed, and the burned out of the rubble of the gymnasium his missile had destroyed, and he wanted nothing more than to end his own miserable life.

He set the silver case on the floor and backed away, lost in the miasma of his guilt and self-loathing. Then he swung his machine gun over his shoulder and began to walk toward the opening at the end of the exit bay. Reg knew what he had to do: throw himself into the air and fly down to the desert floor!

As these thoughts dominated his mind and controlled his actions, another part of Reg was kicking and screaming with the desperation of a drowning man. Trapped inside his own mind and disconnected from his body, he struggled to regain control and shake off the effects of the telepathic haze the Tall Ones had cast over him. But thrash and struggle as he might, he continued to march toward the precipice. In his anxiety, his mind flashed back to the question he'd asked himself after surviving that first catastrophic encounter with the alien attackers: *Had he lived to fight again or only saved himself for a more horrible death later on?*

Now he knew. He was doomed as certainly as a man in a canoe speeding toward a waterfall without a paddle. And he told himself he'd been right all along: The people of Earth were too divided among themselves to answer the challenge of the highly disciplined alien forces. They'd come close with their too crazy plan, they'd shot the city destroyers out of the air. But that was cold comfort for a man marching toward his own unwilling suicide. He thought again of what he'd told the pilots gathered around the radio tent in the desert: that the only sane thing was to try something crazy.

In the sky beyond the exit-bay door, Reg heard a familiar sound: the screaming turbines of a jet as it dropped into a bombing run. He watched the plane rocket toward him out of the distance, hoping it would destroy the tower before the biological poisons could be released. But long before it came within firing range, it disintegrated in the green flash of a pulse burst.

"Reg! Reg!" He heard Fadeela's voice over his shoulder. Part of him wanted to turn around, if only to see her one last time before he died, but the other part thought she'd try to stop him from doing what needed to be done. He broke into a jog.

DO SOMETHING! Reg screamed inwardly, but the nightmare continued to sweep him toward the opening. The southeastern horizon appeared before him like a pastel landscape painting, framed by the monumental rectangle of the exit bay. Only a few seconds before he would have stepped off the edge, he remembered how he'd tricked the alien behind the wall in the oasis, how he'd used his imagination to make Khalid, like a character in a dream, begin doing all sorts of improbable things: turning somersaults and flipping himself through the trees like a gymnast.

DO SOMETHING! DO SOMETHING CRAZY! Instead of toying to resist his forward momentum, Reg willed himself to run even faster. To his surprise, it worked. Then he imagined himself skipping like a carefree schoolboy, and his body responded again. He pictured himself moving side to side, sliding his feet like an ice-skater. Soon his body responded, but he was still moving forward. He needed something crazier and needed it fast. So he did the first thing that came into his head: He danced. He broke into a very bad imitation of the dancing he knew from old musicals, a sliding athletic dance like Gene Kelly used to do.

Even though his feet wanted to carry him straight ahead, he steered them into a sidestep shuffle. He was almost at the edge of the precipice. *Keep dancing!* he told himself. It took all his energy to maintain his concentration. He tried everything he could think of: spinning, leaping, tumbling, stomping his feet. Each of these strange gyrations worked for only a few seconds until the impulse to jump reasserted itself and carried him another step forward. Desperate to save himself, Reg started shucking and jiving, jitterbugging and hoofing, flailing around spastically, doing whatever odd movement came to mind. He kept it up until Fadeela's voice broke the spell.

"Reg! What are you doing?!" she yelled as she came running toward him down the immense corridor.

He backed away from the opening and, horrified at what he had been about to do, turned around to see her emerging from the shadows. "Over here," he yelled to her. "I'm all right now. I almost jumped."

She ran toward him without slowing down. "Come on, we've got to hurry. Let's jump together." She grabbed him by the arm and tried to tug him into the open air. When he resisted, she was angry and confused. "What are you doing?" she demanded. "We've got to jump. They're waiting!"

Reg wrapped his arms around her waist and lifted her off the ground. "Sorry, princess, you're coming with me." She thrashed from side to side and kicked savagely as Reg turned and started back into the exit bay. Less than halfway back to the spot where the aliens were readying the biological poisons, Ali, Edward, and Yossi came jogging up from the opposite direction.

"Help me!" Fadeela shrieked. "He's gone insane. Help!"

The three men stopped running and looked on in bewilderment as Reg explained the situation. "She's trying to jump out of the tower," Reg told them. "The aliens, they're controlling her. Help me hold her."

"Why are you doing this?" Ali asked. "You understand what we have to do." He gestured Yossi and Edward to move in from the sides, while he moved cautiously forward, speaking in a soothing voice as he prepared to spring at Reg. "Let her go, Reg. Put her on the ground."

Reg tightened his grip around Fadeela's waist and whispered into her ear. "Princess, I know you're in there. I know you can hear me. I want you to pretend you're riding a bicycle. Start kicking your legs."

She replied by butting the back of her skull against the bridge of his nose. Just as Yossi and Edward closed in from either side and prepared to grab him, Reg tried one last time. "Kick, Princess." Then he lifted her even higher off the ground and charged at Ali.

"I am not a princess!" she screamed. And her legs began churning in front of her like the blades on a threshing machine. Ali was standing in the way as Fadeela, legs pumping, came flying toward him. Reg threw her on top of the Saudi captain and, as the two of them crashed to the floor, he lowered his head and bulled his way past them, narrowly escaping the grasping hands of the other two men.

Running as fast as he could, Reg raised his machine gun in one hand and his pistol in the other and began blasting. As he came closer to the place where the aliens were working, he felt a numbness spread through his limbs and his pace slow to a trot. As the paralysis continued to spread, Reg gritted his teeth and pushed himself forward. He could feel the Tall Ones watching him from the darkness, trying to force their way back into his mind. Struggling with all his might against the invisible power, he dragged himself as close to the aliens as he could. Then he stopped and went perfectly still. His left hand went slack, and the pistol dropped to the floor. He appeared to be dead on his feet. He closed his eyes and felt/listened to the telepathic bombardment coming at him from three separate directions. Something like a smile flickered faintly across Reg's lips when he realized that he knew exactly where each alien was standing. *Three quick bullets*. Reg snapped his machine gun into position and fired three shots into the darkness.

There was a crash as the silver case hit the ground and glass test tubes bounced on the floor. The silent screaming in his head went quiet, and the strength returned to his arms. He was sure the Tall Ones were dead. He moved forward a few steps until he felt the hardness of a test tube under his boot and stopped short. He backed up and squatted down, feeling for the vial with his hand, hoping it wasn't broken. If it was, he would be dead in a matter of days, perhaps hours. Luckily, it seemed to be in one piece, and he slipped it into his shirt pocket. He set the gun aside and moved around the floor on his hands and knees, groping for test tubes as he listened to the shouts of Fadeela and Ali as they ran toward him.

"Over here!" he called to them. "But watch your step. There are test tubes all over the floor."

By the time Reg killed the aliens, the four of them had run to the edge of the tower and were about to throw themselves off the side. Their flashlights lit up the area. Everything was riddled with bullet holes: the bodies of the three Tall Ones, the side of the taproot, and even the silver case.

"Oh, no. If any of the tubes are broken..." Edward began.

"...we might as well go back and jump," Yossi finished the thought. They began searching the floor and quickly found half of the fourteen test tubes, all of them with their seals in place. Five more were discovered inside the taproot, already loaded into the slots that had been grown for them. The meat of the root was wet and orange, like the flesh of a ripe mango. Ali reached inside and gingerly worked them free one at a time, then handed them to

Edward, who used his good hand to place them, ever so carefully, back into the battered case.

"I've got another one right here," Reg said. "Give me some light." He reached into his shirt pocket and pulled out the tube he'd stepped on with his boot. It was cracked from top to bottom, but not all the way through. The structural integrity of the tube hadn't been violated. The honey-colored liquid inside looked harmless enough, like a sample of clean motor oil. Reg gazed nervously at the deadly nectar, which was enough, in theory, to send the entire human species into extinction. "Hey, Edward," he said with a slight quiver in his voice, "I think you'd better get over here with that case before I drop this thing." His fingers were trembling and continued to do so until the fragile beaker was resting peacefully in its foam channel.

"We need one more," Edward announced. "Be careful where you step."

As the team searched the floor on hands and knees, a pair of explosions shook the tower. A handful of Saudi jets were still in the sky, intent on toppling the tower. The massive structure groaned loudly and tipped even farther. All the equipment the Tall Ones had left scattered on the floor began sliding. Shouting filled the exit bay.

"Time to get out!"

"Let's go! Back down to the shaft!"

"Not yet!" Reg yelled. "Listen!" Cutting through the rest of the noise was the high-pitched tinkle of rolling glass. The final test tube was skittering downslope with the rest of the debris.

"Hurry! Before it breaks."

They chased the sound of the tube through the darkness.

"I've got it!" Yossi shouted. He carried it to Edward, using both hands. When it was finally locked inside the damaged case, he took off his glasses and wiped the sweat from his forehead.

"Now can we please get the hell out of here?"

They ran to the trellis and began to climb down, Edward hugging the case to his chest. They were almost to the floor of the lower story when Fadeela stopped and looked around.

"We're missing someone. Where's Michael?" she asked. In all the confusion, they'd left him behind.

"I'm right behind you!" came a voice from above. They turned their flashlight upward and saw him climbing down the bars. His uniform was soaked in blood from his wounds, and it looked like his stomach was severely distended. When he caught up to the rest of the team, Yossi turned a flashlight on his swollen belly.

"What, did they make you pregnant up there?"

"Oh, that?" Tye asked, patting the front of his uniform. "I decided to bring Big Mama along with me. She's practically human."

"No!" Fadeela said. "You've got to leave it here. If you bring it, they'll know where we are. We can't let them get the bioweapons back."

"We'll talk about it outside," Reg said. He knew Tye had saved the strange creature for "humanitarian" reasons, but he suddenly realized it might serve another purpose. The six of them rushed across the floor, threw themselves into the esophageal elevator, then climbed down the several flights of X-shaped girders. Bomb blasts continued to rock the tower. As quickly as their feet would carry them, the team was on ground level once more. They hurried out of the tower, looking for the chariot they'd left near the abandoned jeeps.

Tye lagged behind the others. He had made the first part of the trip down without any assistance, but his stab wounds began to take their toll as he climbed down the last few stories. He couldn't use his left arm, and his stomach was cramping. Reg and Ali stayed behind the others to help him. As they brought him down, the entire tower groaned and leaned, threatening to collapse at any moment. When they came running out of the tower and into the area where the jeeps were parked, they learned that the chariot was gone. Yossi, Edward, and Fadeela were laboring to push-start one of the jeeps.

"Get in," Yossi yelled, as soon as the engine kicked to life. Ali and Reg tossed Tye into the passenger seat and jumped aboard a second before Yossi slammed his foot down on the pedal and went careening around the corner. He took them bumping and swerving along the side of the tower until they saw daylight filtering in through the gash in the exterior wall. There was no way to make the jeep climb over the debris that the chariot had crossed on the way inside, so they left it behind and exited the city destroyer on foot.

It was murky dawn outside. There was a roar of jets in the air and the screeching death throes of the tower behind them. Reg loaded the flare gun he'd been carrying and shot one flare after another into the air as they ran into the desert, trying to put as much distance as possible between themselves and the ship.

"Where's Sutton?" Edward yelled, carrying the case with great care. Despite all the mayhem surrounding him, he kept his attention focused on making certain the case wasn't jostled or dropped. As they hurried away from the tower, Fadeela ran up alongside Reg.

"Okay, that was my part of the plan," she told him. "I got us into the ship and outside with the silver box. The rest is up to you."

Right on cue, a growling noise came rumbling toward them, and soon they saw the headlights of the Mercedes truck. Sutton pulled up and skidded to a stop.

"We're being bombed!" he screamed. "Whose idea was this?" Reg helped Tye climb into the front seat, then jumped in himself. Remi helped the others pile into the back. When they were all aboard, they shouted in one voice at the driver: "Go!"

Sutton was spitting mad. "This is Faisal's doing, isn't it? If I get my hands on that bastard, I'll tear him apart. Here we are trying to save his damnable country, and he starts bombing us. Remi and I were nearly blown to bits out here while you lot were lolly-gagging inside. And what happened to you?" he asked Tye. "What's that under your shirt?"

'Trouble ahead!" Reg called, pointing out the front window. Straight in front of them, standing atop a sand dune, was a fully armored alien warrior. It raised its arm into the firing position and pointed its finger at the truck. Everyone ducked, but there was no blast of light. The creature merely stood there watching the truck come closer. After a moment of hesitation, it lowered its head and charged the Mercedes. Remi, riding on top of the cab, fired his rocket launcher, and the warrior's bioarmor blew apart a half second before Sutton smashed into it with the truck's battering ram. The tires trampled over the body. Turning an alien into roadkill did wonders for Sutton's mood.

"Take that, you ugly piece of crap," he bellowed. He turned to his passengers with an exhilarated smile on his face. "That felt rather good."

"I'm glad you think so because here comes another one!" Tye said. As before, one of the exoskeletal beasts had them dead to rights. It pointed its long finger at the grille of the speeding truck, but did nothing.

"They're not firing at us," Reg noticed. "They must be afraid of hitting this." He patted the lump under Tye's shirt. Ali opened up with his field gun as Remi launched another bazooka shell. The creature was torn to pieces. Sutton steered around it.

"You're right," Tye realized. "That's exactly it. They're afraid to hit Big Mama. And they all know where she is. They can feel her."

"What the hell are you talking about? Who is Big

Mama?" Sutton asked. Tye tore open his shirt and introduced them. When he saw the gelatinous lump of biomatter throbbing and glowing phosphorescent against Tye's bleeding stomach, Sutton nearly jumped out of the moving vehicle.

"Oh my God, what is that thing?"

"Big Mama is sort of like a brain. She directs traffic for the aliens, lets them know where they're at."

Sutton was disgusted. "It's a *brain*? You *took* a brain? Get rid of it!"

"Watch out!" Another alien stepped into the truck's path. It didn't hesitate as the others had done, but charged immediately toward the Mercedes's headlights.

"Bring it on, bug boy!" Sutton yelled. Instead of trying to steer around the creature, he veered directly toward it, spoiling for another head-on collision. He was expecting Remi to use his rocket launcher again, but there hadn't been time to reload. The creature lowered its head like a bull, and there was a thunderous crack when it collided with the steel bar of the truck's battering ram. Fragments of the head-thorax shell flew high into the air, but they didn't feel the creature's body under their tires.

"It's hanging on," Remi shouted from his perch. The big Ethiopian scooted himself to the driver's side of the cab to get a clear shot at the thing. Before he could, the front left tire exploded and the truck lurched to the side. A second later, the first tentacle threw itself over the hood and stabbed through the sheet metal. Sutton kept the accelerator pedal crushed against the floorboard as a second tentacle reached up and wound itself around the side mirror.

"Steer," he told Tye. He took out a pistol and started to open the door, ready to polish the creature off with a bullet or two. But the third tentacle was deadly. It broke through the windshield and smashed Sutton's head against the back wall. Another long arm snaked in through the open door and wrapped itself around the driver's body. Remi fired at last, and all the tentacles fell limp at the same time. The alien fell to the sand, dragging Sutton outside with it.

Reg slid past Tye, took the wheel, and accelerated. "Check your medallion," he said. "See if there are more of them ahead of us."

Tye's mind was blank, still processing what had just happened. "Sutton's dead," he said meekly.

"The medallion. Check it," Reg yelled.

Absently, Tye searched through his pockets until he remembered he'd left his last medallion in the tower. But the one he'd given Sutton was sitting on the dashboard, folded into a paper napkin. He unwrapped it and put it against his skin.

"Not working," he told Reg. "Still getting the flower design."

"What about that thing?" Reg pointed to the brainlike blob resting on Tye's lap. "Does it show where the aliens are?"

Tye studied the warm lump's transparent skin and the mass of diamond shapes that were all gathered on one side of the body. He experimented with it for a moment before figuring it out.

"What does it say?" Reg asked.

"It looks like we've got several hundred aliens moving in this direction." He looked up at Reg. "They're leaving At-Ta'if, and I think they're coming after us."

"Perfect," Reg said. "How far away are they?"

"How should I know? I guess we're just going to leave him back there?" he said, glancing into the side mirror and watching Sutton's body recede from view.

Reg kept his eyes focused on the rough terrain ahead of him, driving as fast as he could. It was a long way back to Faisal's camp.

16

INTO THE HILLS

The fifth day of the invasion began in worse fashion than any of the others. Reg found the road a mile before the Dawqah turnoff. He stayed off the asphalt, driving along the rough shoulder at forty-five miles per hour in order to keep the flat tire on the rim as long as possible. When they reached the isolated crossroads, the sun was lifting in the east. Several miles behind them, a massive dust cloud indicated pursuit by the alien army. The flat tire made the truck difficult to steer. Reg muscled it onto the pavement and pulled hard to make the turn into the hills.

"Can't we go any faster?" Tye asked, glancing behind them nervously. "They're definitely catching up."

"Only a few more miles," Reg said. "Faisal's got enough firepower up on those cliffs ahead of us to sink a battleship. We're almost home." Reg started up the winding incline at an average speed of thirty miles per hour. But a mile up the road, there was a sharp left-hand turn that pulled the tire off the rim and nearly sent the truck and its lethal cargo sailing over the embankment.

After that, Reg drove in a shower of sparks. The unprotected rim scraped against the road, wearing away by the moment and leaving a continuous scar in the surface of the road. There was no choice except to keep going. The rocky canyon walls rose up to enclose them, and Tye scoured them with his eyes, desperate for some sign of the well-equipped army Reg had described.

"Where are they? There's no one here."

"They're here. Just a little farther." The mountain pass looked like a completely different universe now that it was daylight, but Reg began to suspect that Tye was right. They should have seen some of the larger guns by now. The rim continued to grind away on the roadway, and each turn was more difficult than the last. Ali climbed along the outside of the truck and slipped in behind the wheel to relieve Reg when he had exhausted the strength in his arms. They were six miles up the road, and the rim was nearly down to the brake shoes.

"There they are!" Tye shouted. "We made it."

Standing in the middle of the road ahead of them were a handful of Saudi soldiers manning a roadblock. To the left, Reg recognized the field that had been occupied by Faisal's army only hours before. It was empty. On the cliffs to the right were some jeeps with turret guns, but no heavy artillery.

"That stinking bastard!" Reg shouted. He assumed Faisal had double-crossed him, that he'd evacuated the canyon and left him to die as a twisted form of revenge. But when the soldiers came forward, they explained what had happened.

"The aliens left their ship and marched against At-Ta'if. The king ordered our commander to defend the city." They claimed not to know anything about Reg or biological weapons or a raid on the ship. Faisal was so sure that Reg, Fadeela, and the others would be killed, he hadn't even bothered to tell his men about it.

"Where are your vehicles?" Ali asked.

The man said they'd been left with two jeeps, both of which were up on the cliffs keeping a lookout. When Ali had explained about the biological weapons they were carrying and that the alien army was chasing them, the leader got on his radio and called the jeeps down. Ali held a brief strategy session with the soldiers while the jeeps came bumping down the dirt trail along the face of the cliffs above them. When they'd agreed on a plan of action, Ali found Reg.

"There is a road that follows the crest of the mountains," he explained, pointing uphill. "It is about one mile from here. They have two jeeps. One will carry the weapons down to Dawqah. I will take the other jeep and lead them along the mountains. I will need the thing Tye took from the ship. They will follow it."

"Good idea," Reg said, "but I'm the one who should lead them into the hills. You know the area. You've got to—"

Before he could finish his sentence, a streak of light ripped across the sky and smashed into one of the jeeps moving along the trail, demolishing it. It rolled off the trail and tumbled down the hillside, breaking apart on road. The soldiers in the other jeep stopped and took cover behind their vehicle. A moment later, they suffered the same fate. A pulse blast tore into the side of the vehicle and flipped it over. A few hundred yards downhill, a pair of aliens had climbed one of the cliffs with their chariot and were firing into the clearing.

Edward and Reg raced back to the truck. Reg climbed in the back, grabbed the silver box, and tossed it out to Edward, whose heart almost stopped beating when he saw the deadly microbes flying through the air. He caught it as gently as he could, then took off running uphill. Reg strapped on a flamethrower and came around to the passenger door. The translucent amber creature was lying on the front seat. Reg unfastened a couple of shirt buttons, pressed the organism to his stomach, then buttoned back up. A few seconds after he left the truck, it was destroyed when one of the alien projectiles smashed into it. Edward was already a hundred yards closer to the crest of the hill, running as fast as he could and not turning back.

"Ali," Reg yelled, "you follow Edward; make sure he gets away." He patted the lump under his shirt. "I'll lead them up onto those rocks to buy you some time."

Ali nodded and started to run. Reg crossed the road and headed across the field that had been Faisal's headquarters. Above the far end of it was a steep outcropping of rocky hills. It would be difficult for the aliens to follow there. The Saudis on the hilltops began firing into the canyon. They were answered by flurries of pulse blasts. Halfway across the field, Reg heard someone calling his name. He looked back at the road. Fadeela was waving good-bye, half a step ahead of Ali, who was urging her forward. Reg gave her a farewell smile and a crisp salute before continuing on his way.

The rocky ground was treacherous and steep. Reg ran blindly, letting the topography dictate the path he took. Weaving around boulders and leaping over ditches, he ran until he found himself hemmed in by sheer walls of crumbling rock. He tried to climb, but with one hand holding the flamethrower, he could only make it halfway up the wall. He turned to check behind him and saw an alien chariot coming over the rocks in the distance. He slid his arms out of the harness and tossed the flamethrower, canisters and all, onto the shelf of rock above him. Even with both hands free, it was a difficult to reach the top. The rocks crumbled to gravel when he tried to pull himself up. When he finally squirmed over the side, he found himself stranded on an isolated stone shelf, a flat rock fifty feet across. If he was going to continue moving, Reg had only two choices: Go back the way he'd come, or scale another crumbling rock face.

He glanced around the shelf and judged it as good a place as any to die. He still had two canisters of fuel for the flamethrower, enough to buy Edward a few more minutes of time. He pulled the brain-shaped amber lump out of his shirt and set it in the sun, then retreated behind a boulder to wait. He could hear the aliens moving closer, stumbling over the rocks in their cumbersome biomechanical suits of armor. It sounded like there were hundreds of them. The waiting seemed eternal. He fought back the urge to spring out into the open and blast a few of them with fire, knowing that every second he could stall them increased the chances of Fadeela and the others being able to escape. He imagined they must already be past the summit and starting down the other side of the mountain. As he pictured them running, he suddenly realized he couldn't let the aliens take him alive. If so, they would learn where the biological weapons were. He checked his pistol and found he had two bullets left, which was one more than he needed.

The aliens arrived and surrounded the shelf. Reg listened to their tentacles scraping at the rock walls as they tried to climb. Then the first one lifted its enormous shell head over the lip of the rock. Reg swung his flamethrower around, waiting for it to show itself fully before he fired.

Machine-gun fire came from the cliffs above. The bullets chipped away at the alien's exoskeletal armor and knocked it back over the side. Reg looked up and saw a white barrier fence, the type that lines the curves of mountain roads to keep careless motorists from driving off the sides. He could see people shouting and running. They looked like civilians. One of them stood at the edge, a man who took off his *keffiyeh* and waved it through the air as he shouted down the hill. Reg signaled for the guy to stop making a target of himself before he was picked off by a pulse weapon. Before he could make the man understand, a dozen blasts of light flew up the canyon and exploded where the man had been standing. When the dust began to clear, the man was gone, and Reg thought he must be dead. A moment later, however, he was standing there waving and shouting again. He was shouting in English and seemed to know Reg's name. More pulse blasts ripped into the cliffs on which he stood. At the same time, two of the aliens came over the edge of Reg's shelf and started toward the amber homing device.

"Over here, boys." The shell heads swiveled on their thin waists to face Reg, who blasted them with a burst of his flamethrower. The burning skeletons staggered off the edge of the shelf and fell onto the rocks. That left Reg with one canister of fuel. He decided he would let them get to the organism next time and give them a chance to pick it up before he toasted them.

Once again, the man on the cliffs was yelling down to Reg. *Who is this fool?* Reg wondered. And then he recognized the voice. It was Thomson!

Reg darted into the open, picked up the organism, then returned to the edge of the stone shelf and looked over the side. Dozens of aliens were massed just below him. They were climbing over one another to reach the top. They looked up at Reg, who held the organism out in front of him.

"Looking for this?" he asked before spraying them with the final burst of his flamethrower. As they writhed, he looked up and saw that there were several hundred aliens swarming toward him through the canyon. Arms lifted toward him from every direction, but none of them fired. Either they'd been trained not to risk damage to the brainlike creature, or it disabled their weapons, Reg couldn't tell which. He ran to the base of the next cliff, stuffed the organism back into his shirt, and began climbing. Before he'd gone very far, there were aliens climbing after him. They would have caught him easily except for the bullets coming from above. Each time one of them got close to Reg, it was knocked off the rock by a hail of small-arms fire.

Arab voices cheered him on from the road above,

urging him to keep climbing. A strong hand reached over the last ledge and pulled Reg up to safety. It belonged to a wrinkled, elderly woman who looked old enough to be Reg's grandmother. But she was large and strong, and it hurt when she slapped Reg on the back to welcome him. He rolled away from the edge and surveyed the situation. The defenders of the clifftop were a motley group indeed. Half of them were women and many of them were elderly. By the way they were dressed, he recognized them as Yemenis. The women wore a distinctive, beaked sort of veil, and the men all had broad daggers, *djambiyas*, tucked into their belts. Crouching behind their barricades, they looked more like a crowd rioting for better retirement benefits than an army capable of repulsing the brunt of the alien attack. Thomson ran forward in a crouch.

"I'm beginning to wonder about you, Cummins. You pissed off everyone out in the desert, and now you've done something to make the aliens mad. They seem to be following you."

Reg was incredulous. "What are you doing here?"

The colonel rolled his eyes. "I could write a book. Come on, follow me." He led the way to the opposite side of the road, where they would be out of the line of fire. Parked along the shoulder was the Yemeni caravan's transportation: horses, camels, bicycles, motorcycles, and a few passenger cars.

Thomson explained that after the city destroyer was shot down, some rough-looking customers showed up in the desert asking about Reg. He'd hidden himself in the dunes until they flew away, then accepted a ride in a helicopter to Khamis Moushayt. From there, he'd gone to the town of Abha in Yemen, where he'd enlisted in this civilian army that was coming to join the war in the desert.

"We've been traveling since yesterday noon, and just when we got to our turnoff road, I recognized that

Ethiopian chap from the camp. He told me you'd gone this way."

As Thomson spoke, Reg looked down the other side of the mountain. As he'd seen many times from the air, one side was a collection of desolate stone canyons leading down to the inhospitable desert, while the other was moist, green, and overgrown with trees. The verdant western slope was steep. It plunged dramatically down to a narrow coastal plane. Beyond that was the Red Sea. The smokestacks of the oil refinery at Dawqah glinted back at him in the sun, as if trying to catch his attention. Reg remembered what Mr. Yamani had said about Dawqah being a "nasty little town." But from where he stood, it sparkled like the promised land. He interrupted what the colonel was saying.

"Thomson, I need a car. I have to get to the coast." He lifted the amber-colored organism out of his shirt and showed it to him. "They're chasing me because of this."

"Oh, Lord," Thomson said, recoiling from the pulsating mass. "What is it?"

"No time to explain. But they can sense where it is. I want to lead them down the coast. If I stay here, all these people will be slaughtered."

"Come with me."

They jogged down the road until Thomson found someone he recognized, a young man in tight slacks and a silk dress shirt. He looked like he was dressed for an evening of disco dancing except for the *djambiya* tucked into his wide leather belt. Whipping out his trusty phrase book, Thomson said a few words to him in pidgin Arabic.

"*Mish mumkin,*" the man said. *Impossible.* His car keys made a visible lump in the tight fabric of his pants pocket.

"Show him," Thomson said. Reg obliged. When the man saw the brainlike blob he took out his keys without another word and tossed them to Reg. Thomson led him to a battered Ford sedan. Reg jumped in and started the engine.

"You coming?" he asked Thomson.

"I'll take my chances here."

"Get these people out of the way if you can. They're not going to make much difference."

"Good luck."

"See you around." Reg had shifted into drive and put his foot on the gas, when Thomson remembered something and called to him.

"I almost forgot. Here's that tape recording you wanted." From his breast pocket, he pulled out a cassette tape and handed it through the window. "I wouldn't play it in front of Faisal if I were you. He comes off smelling pretty rotten."

"You're a good man, Colonel."

"Tally-ho and all that rot," he shot back, as Reg hit the gas and sped away.

When he came to the road leading down to the coast, he saw Remi among the men firing at the advancing aliens. He honked the horn until the big Ethiopian turned around and ran to the car. He jumped in and they took off down the hill, driving slowly and honking their horn. Reg thought the rest of the team might be moving through the trees and wanted to draw their attention. It worked. About two miles from the turnoff, they encountered a beanpole of a man with bright red hair standing in the middle of the road with his legs spread wide and a rifle pointed at them. It was Tye.

When Reg rolled to a stop, the others came running out of the trees and crammed themselves and their weapons into the two-door sedan. Edward was the last one standing outside.

"Too many big people and too many guns," he said. Reg, Ali, and Tye were already crowded into the front seat, with Ali's field gun stretching from one door to the other. Edward handed the silver case delicately to a pair of hands in the backseat before climbing inside to join Fadeela, Remi, and Yossi. Before the doors were closed, Reg put his foot through the floor and sent them hurtling down the road.

"Where are we going?" Ali asked, then quickly changed his mind. "Don't tell me. I probably don't want to know." After a couple of miles, the team convinced Reg to slow down. They had a large start on the aliens, and as long as they kept the pace above fifty miles per hour, the chariots couldn't gain on them.

As the others watched out the rear window for signs of danger, Fadeela was developing another plan. "When we reach the coastal road, there is an airport a few miles north of Dawqah. We can take a plane from there to Jeddah, where someone will know how to dispose of these horrible weapons."

Reg kept his eyes on the road and said that was a good idea. When they came out of the trees and saw the coast road in front of them, everyone breathed a sigh of relief. They were almost home free. They turned north onto the highway and increased their speed. There was traffic on the highway, but not much. Many of the cars they passed were loaded down with families and as many personal possessions as they could carry. The faces behind the windows looked tired and frightened. Hardly anyone gave Reg or the overcrowded Ford a second glance. For a few moments, it felt almost like an ordinary day. The other drivers were observing the speed limit and the rules of the road. Some of them flashed dirty looks at Reg as he sped past them, not suspecting the car with the Yemeni license plates contained enough weapons-grade poison to kill everyone in the Middle East. Even though it was still a few miles ahead of them, Reg could smell the gaseous stench of the refinery.

"I don't believe it," Yossi said from the backseat.

"What's that?" Tye asked.

"They're coming through the trees. All of them." They all turned to see what he was talking about and could hardly believe their eyes. It looked like an avalanche moving diagonally down the mountainside, shaking the trees as it came. The alien army had left the winding road to take a more efficient angle of pursuit. They crashed down the slope at a phenomenal rate of speed, weaving around some trees, knocking the others to the ground.

A blaring horn brought Reg's attention back to his driving. He swerved back into his lane a second before colliding head-on with a semi. Ali had already figured out what Reg had in mind and pointed him toward the exit he wanted. Then he turned around and told the others what he thought the crazed Englishman behind the wheel had in mind. When he was finished Reg looked at him, impressed.

"I thought the only mind readers around here were the ones from outer space."

They sped toward the front gates of the refinery and the guards who stepped out of their kiosk to question them. The car crashed through a fence and charged into the facility. They followed the road between a pair of gigantic storage tanks, then past the separating station with its open construction and vertical spires rising like stainless-steel minarets. Soon they came to a round, heavily fortified building that looked like it must be the refinery's control room. When the Ford skidded to a halt, a half dozen men who had been standing around drinking coffee and talking scattered in all directions, thinking they were under attack by terrorists.

Ali caught one of them and dragged him back to the car, explaining, as politely as he could under the circumstances, that they needed access to the refinery's computer system. When the man asked why, Ali told him.

"We need to spill all the oil on the ground and set the place on fire."

"Are you crazy?"

"That has nothing to do with it! Show us the computers!"

The man scoffed and refused to cooperate. The team did what they could to convince him. Fadeela told him that several hundred, perhaps thousands, of aliens would be arriving at the refinery within the next few minutes, and Reg showed him the amber-colored organism. Still the man refused. But he changed his mind when Yossi shot him in the forearm, then pushed the man's nose flat with the hot end of his pistol.

"I'll count to three," said the Israeli. "One, two—"

"Don't shoot!" shouted the injured man. "I will take you inside!"

He led them up a set of steel stairs and entered a numerical code into the keypad next to the door. It opened, and Ali shoved the man through the doorway. Tye, Fadeela, and Remi followed him.

"What about the case?" Edward asked. "We have to get these biological weapons out of the area."

"We'll burn them," Reg said, "along with everything else."

"That's too dangerous. There's still time to get them out of here."

Reg tossed the keys to Yossi. "Go with him." And after wishing both men luck, he entered the control room.

At first, the technicians inside resisted. They said it was impossible to spill the oil intentionally, that the computers weren't designed to do such things. The only way to accomplish what the team was asking would be to physically destroy the pipelines one by one. The whole time they talked, Tye leaned over the main routing screen, studying it. When Reg came to look over his shoulder, he saw a complicated diagram showing a tangle of lines and a confusing galaxy of blinking lights. The display was no more comprehensible to him than the designs he'd seen on the tops of the black tables inside the tower.

"It looks simple enough," Tye said. "This board controls the movement of oil through the entire refinery. It allows them to pump it out of one tank and into another. See how the pipelines are all numbered to correspond with the switches here at the bottom. Then you've got your pressure gauges and automatic shut-offs at intervals along each pipe." He pointed to various spots on the schematic, assuming Reg was following along.

"So how do we spill the oil?"

"Easy. We close down all the lines and start all the pumps at the same time. Then we sit back and wait for the pipes to burst under the pressure." He started throwing switches with both hands, activating some and deactivating others, while Reg looked on skeptically. It couldn't be that easy, could it? For a minute, it seemed to work. Red lights started flashing and warning buzzers sounded. But then everything returned to normal. Tye scratched his chin, thinking. "The system senses the pressure buildup and shuts down the pumps."

"How do we circumvent the shutoff system?" he asked the technicians.

"*Mish mumkin*," one of them said. "We cannot override the fail-safe. It's all automatic."

"Yossi and Edward are coming back. And they've got company," Fadeela announced, looking out a window. Reg knew what she was talking about and dragged one of the technicians across the room to show him. The man looked outside and couldn't believe his eyes. Less than a hundred yards from him, a pair of ugly gray creatures with heads that looked rather like overgrown oyster shells were riding a walking sled and firing blasts of white light out of their fingertips. He stared at this startling scene for a moment or two, then ran to the switchboard and began pulling wires from the underside of the console. He shouted to his colleagues, who joined him at the control boards. Within seconds, the red lights and warning buzzers came back to life. The muffled sound of explosions came through the walls. All around the refinery, pipes began splitting open. Oil sprayed high into the air in some places and flowed out in dark rivers in others.

"We have done what you asked," said the man who had torn out the wires. "Now let us leave. We have helicopters. You can go with us."

"Wait. We're not finished. How can we light the oil? We have to set it on fire."

The man tossed Reg a book of matches and turned for the door. Almost as soon as it sealed behind him, something slammed against the outside wall on the opposite side of the room. Four armored aliens, sensing the presence of the amber organism, were trying to break in to retrieve it.

"Everybody outside!" Leaving the brain inside, the team raced out the door and made sure it was sealed behind them. They ran to take cover behind the next building and saw the Ford parked there. Ali found his field gun in the backseat and strapped it over his shoulder. A moment later, Edward came around the corner carrying the silver case. Yossi was right behind him.

"What happened?"

"We couldn't find our way back to the front gates until it was too late. They're all crossing the highway," Yossi said. "More than a thousand of them."

"We should have destroyed the weapons before," Edward said. "I'm going to do it now."

"How?"

"Give me those matches and I'll climb up there." He

pointed to the ladder rising up the side of one of the ten-story-tall storage tanks. "When I'm inside, I'll set the whole thing on fire."

"My God," Tye said, impressed with the man's conviction.

"I'll go with you," Yossi said, "I've got a lighter. And besides, you can't trust a Palestinian with a big job." It was Yossi's idea of a joke. For the first time since they'd known him, he smiled.

Edward shook his head and appealed to the others. "Now do you see why we can't stand the Jews?" But he returned Yossi's grin, and said, "Come on, madman, let's go." The two men ran toward the nearest storage tank and began climbing the vertical steel ladder as fast as they could, bickering as they went.

Remi tipped over a trash can and found a discarded newspaper to use as kindling. "Let's get started," he said, and led the way toward the nearest lake of freshly spilled oil. They lit the newspaper and dropped it onto the oil, expecting it to erupt immediately into flames. Instead, the oil soaked into the paper until the fire went out. They tried again, this time using more paper to make a hotter fire.

"It's supposed to burn," Reg said.

A car came speeding around a corner not far away and turned toward the main gate. Before it got very far, a pulse blast ripped into its side. The vehicle flipped over and burst into flame. When they saw this, the team turned toward Tye.

"One step ahead of you," he said, pulling out the alien weapon and unfolding the cloth he used to carry it. He let the flipperlike protrusions wind themselves around his forearm, then invited Reg to help him. "What do we hit?"

"Anything that will blow up."

But the pulse weapon proved no more useful than the burning newspapers. They used it to blow open the side of an oil tank, to tear a gaping hole in the side of a building, and to dig craters in the ground where the oil was pooling. But they couldn't start a fire.

They did, however, attract the attention of a squad of aliens, who came away from the control room to investigate. Ali knocked them backwards with a few blasts from his field gun while Reg and Tye picked them off one by one with the pulse gun. But more of them started coming around the corner. They came by the dozens, fearless behind their armor, and advanced on the four troublesome earthlings.

"We have to fall back," Ali said.

But Reg disagreed. He pointed to Edward and Yossi, who were only halfway to the top of the ladder. They were shielded from view of the aliens by the curve of the tank. "We've got to hold them here until those two are inside. Then we'll fall back."

"By then it will be too late," Fadeela said. "They're surrounding us."

There was no choice but to stay and defend their position. The best they could hope for was a fiery death, that once the two men were inside the tank, they would be successful in blowing it up and that the fire would spread. If not, all they would have accomplished was leading the aliens out of the desert and into the more densely populated coastal plain. And there was still a chance of the anthrax spores and ebola virus being spread.

When Edward reached the top, he handed the case to Yossi, lifted the cap door at the side of the roof, and lowered himself inside. After taking the case back, he started down the ladder that ran along the inside of the tank. Then, as Yossi was climbing in after him, a series of loud explosions came from the far end of the refinery.

"Sounds like bombs," Remi remarked.

"Yes, and helicopters," Ali added.

"It must be the men from the control room," Fadeela said. "They said they had helicopters."

But a moment later, they saw a squadron of Apache helicopters rising over the oil field, firing missiles down at the alien army and starting a massive fire in the oil, a fire which quickly began rolling toward them. When pulse blasts began zipping toward the helicopters, they ducked behind the outlying buildings. Then another group of the fearsome gunships appeared on the opposite horizon and fired another volley of shells down onto the oil-soaked grounds.

"They're starting fires around the perimeter," Reg observed. "Smart boys."

As soon as the aliens turned to fire on the second group of helicopters, the Apaches lowered out of view, and a third group lifted from the direction of the highway. When their shells slammed into the ground, a wall of fire cut off the team's only means of escape. They were boxed in.

Reg looked around and nodded approvingly, thinking, *Now that's the way you run an aerial assault.* He didn't know if any of the men piloting the helicopters had been his students, but that didn't stop him from feeling proud of the way they were conducting the operation. They were achieving their objectives without taking unnecessary risks and were displaying extraordinary teamwork.

"Where in the hell did these guys come from?" Tye wondered.

"They must be Faisal's men," Reg said.

The aliens panicked when they found themselves surrounded by fire. They ran in crazed circles, firing their weapons into the flames. Some of them opened their shells and jumped out. The ones who had been firing at the team forgot about them and rushed off to join the mayhem.

Yossi climbed back to the opening in the top of the tank. Reg noticed him because he was waving his arms and shouting, but he wasn't shouting to Reg or the others. A helicopter came from the direction of the highway, broke through the wall of flame, and hovered over the tower long enough to allow Yossi and Edward to climb in. It wasn't one of the Apaches, but a civilian helicopter.

"Hey, what about us?" Tye shouted. He and Remi ran to the nearest ladder and began to climb. Ali slung his gun over his back and followed them. Reg and Fadeela found another ladder, and they, too, began to climb. The helicopter disappeared only moments after they started up the ladders, but they all continued climbing. The steel rungs were hard on their hands, especially Fadeela's. The harsh metal rubbed through the skin on her palms, and she was bleeding before they were halfway up. At the three-quarters mark, her arms were so tired they began to shake.

"I know you're going to think I'm a princess, but I don't know if I can make it to the top. Let me stay here and rest. You can go around me."

"I'll help you."

"No. Let me do it myself. I just need to rest for a while."

Reg stared up at her, watching to make sure she didn't lose her grip when he noticed something strange. Although neither of them was moving, he could feel movement in the ladder. He looked down and saw an armored alien climbing up behind them. It was moving fast, taking the rungs two at a time and using all twelve of its limbs to pull itself upward.

"I hope you're ready for this," Reg said. He climbed another step and shocked Fadeela by wedging his head between her legs and lifting her backside onto his shoulders. Before she could protest, he started climbing as fast as he could. There was no need to look down to see if the alien was getting closer. Reg could feel it gaining on them through the vibrations in the ladder. When they got to the top, Reg fired his last bullet at their pursuer, then he and Fadeela ran onto the curving roof of the tank. From their new vantage point, they could see the Apache helicopters surrounding the refinery. They were keeping low to the ground, well away from the fires they'd started. The civilian helicopter they'd seen pick up their comrades was coming in for another pass, but the alien was already at the top of the ladder. It stepped onto the roof and let the humans regard it in all its horrible glory. The tentacles sprouting from its back waved in the air like a gruesome peacock spreading its tail feathers. As the helicopter came closer, the creature ignored it and marched toward Reg and Fadeela. As it stepped onto the crest of the roof, a pulse blast whizzed past Reg's ear and struck the exoskeleton square in the face, shattering the armor and knocking it over the side of the tank. When Reg spun around, he saw Tye and Remi waving to him, the alien tube gun sandwiched between their arms.

"I don't believe it," Fadeela muttered when she saw the royal crest painted on the door of the helicopter. "It's the king's private helicopter." But that surprise was nothing compared to the one she got a moment later when a disheveled old man leaned his head out of the cargo door and waved them inside. It was her father, Karmal Yamani.

Fadeela allowed Reg to help lift her over the landing bars, then reached back to help pull him inside. She sprang into her father's arms as the chopper began to lift away. The old man winked at Reg over his daughter's shoulder.

"I told you I had joined the fight."

"You did this? I thought it must be Faisal."

King Ibrahim turned around to face them from the copilot's seat. "Faisal is still driving in circles in the desert wondering where the aliens went."

As the pilot lifted the chopper away from the roof of the storage tank and turned to head away, the ship listed violently toward the copilot's side. Something heavy had grabbed onto the landing gear, and everyone inside knew immediately what it had to be. Before anyone had a chance to reach for a gun, a tentacle reached into the rear passenger area and began to slash through the air. Reg, closest to the door, picked up the first heavy object he could lay his hands on, a fire extinguisher. Ignoring the tentacle, he rushed toward the open door and leaned outside. The mangled exoskeleton was only a few feet below him. Its huge head-thorax shell had been shattered, but its many limbs were wrapped tightly around the landing bars. Reg used the extinguisher to deliver a hard blow to the center of the cracked shell, knocking a large section of it away. The alien hidden below the shell was now exposed to view, but before Reg could deliver a second blow, the tentacle clipped him hard on the back of the head. He felt himself go light-headed, then collapse. The fleshy arm wound itself around his neck and began pulling him outside. Fadeela caught him by the feet and struggled for a moment against the more powerful alien. Her resistance bought just enough time for the king to open the copilot's door and peer down into the hideous confusion of limbs and broken shell. Staring up at him were a pair of bulging, reflective eyes. He drew a pistol from the folds of his robes and put a single bullet into the alien's head. As it died, all the life went out of the biomechanical suit of armor. The tentacles, including the one around Reg's neck, went limp, and the creature plunged to the ground.

"*Allah-u akbar,*" cried the king, shaking a fist at the alien as it fell away. "You see? Finally, I got my wish to kill one of them! I did it! I killed him." The aging monarch continued to celebrate as his pilot swooped to the next storage tanker and set down long enough for Ali, Remi, and Tye to climb aboard. Reg was beginning to recover his senses by the time they all stepped inside. "Did you see?" King Ibrahim asked the new passengers. "I killed one of them!"

As the helicopter lifted away from the refinery, there was a series of powerful explosions that sent fire roaring high into the air. The intense heat began exploding the holding tanks, feeding the already-raging fire with ton after ton of additional fuel. Soon, every square inch of the refinery was fully engulfed. The helicopter gunships patrolled the perimeter of the blaze in case any of the aliens escaped, but none did.

The king ordered the helicopter to hover nearby as the inferno consumed the enemy forces, then told his pilot to take them to Jeddah.

Ali leaned forward and spoke bluntly to the king. "We cannot leave without our friends, the two men who were picked up first."

King Ibrahim turned around in his chair and arched an eyebrow. "One of them is a Palestinian masquerading as a Jordanian, and the other is a Jew. You call these men your friends?"

"Yes," Ali answered without hesitation. "Good friends."

Mr. Yamani assured the muscular captain there was no reason to worry about Yossi and Edward. "They are in good hands. My son, Khalid, is with them. He will escort them back to At-Ta'if, where the biological weapons will be destroyed."

"Khalid has been released?" Fadeela asked her father. She was on the floor of the helicopter, sitting next to the still-woozy Reg.

"Yes, Faisal let him go this morning before he retreated from the mountains. I think he expected your brother to die at the hands of the aliens."

"Speaking of Ghalil Faisal," said the king, unbuckling

himself from his chair and moving aft to join the others, "I spoke to him by radio earlier today. He had many interesting things to say about you, Major Cummins. Not very positive things, I am afraid."

"That doesn't really surprise me," Reg said. "Faisal and I haven't really hit it off during the past few days."

"In fact," the king continued, "he would like to see you arrested. According to him, you have committed several criminal acts since the invasion began." Fadeela sat bolt upright, ready to defend Reg against Faisal's accusations. Before she could say a word, both her father and the king spoke to her sternly, telling her to let Reg answer for himself.

The king outlined the most serious of Faisal's allegations: that Reg had shot down an Egyptian pilot over whom he had no authority because the man had refused to obey his orders; that he had urged Saudi pilots to disobey their orders during an engagement with the enemy; that he had kidnapped a Saudi woman, Fadeela, on what should have been her wedding day; that he had trespassed on the grounds of the Saudi military facility at Al-Sayyid; and that he had stolen weapons and ammunition from that same facility. Considering that all these acts had been committed within a span of less than four days, it was quite an impressive list. When the king was finished, he asked Reg to answer the charges.

"They're all true," Reg said without batting an eyelid. "And if I had to do it all again, I'd make the exactly the same decisions."

It wasn't the answer the king had been expecting.

"I was never kidnapped," Fadeela couldn't help interjecting. "It was my choice to go with these people." The king ignored her and stared intently at Reg, waiting for him to go on.

First, Reg explained the circumstances under which he had "shot down" the Egyptian pilot who refused to turn away from Khamis Moushayt. King Ibrahim listened carefully, running his fingers through his beard until Reg was finished.

"If what you say is true, and I believe that it is, you must be quite a fine pilot."

"He's the best," Tye interjected.

King Ibrahim nodded. "So I have been told. But do you also admit that you urged our pilots to disobey Faisal's orders over Mecca?"

Tye, Remi, Ali, and Fadeela all broke into the conversation at once, insisting that Reg had acted with good cause. Reg quieted them with a gesture and continued speaking to the king.

"I did what I thought was right," he said. "I knew Faisal was making a horrible mistake, that he was sending those men to their deaths."

"*Knew* or *believed?*" the king asked.

Reg hesitated for a moment before answering. "I believed so."

"In other words, your assessment of the situation differed from Commander Faisal's?" In only a few moments, the king had cut to the quick of the matter.

"Yes, it was my assessment against his. But before you have me arrested, there's something I think you should listen to." He pulled out of his pocket the audiocassette Thomson had given him. "Have you got a tape deck in this copter?"

The question stung the monarch. "Major Cummins, this is the royal helicopter. Of course there is a cassette player." He took the tape from Reg and plugged it in. A moment later, the sounds of the air battle over Mecca filled the helicopter's passenger compartment. King Ibrahim turned the volume up loud, and for the rest of the flight to Jeddah, hardly a word was spoken.

When they arrived at King Abdul Aziz International

Airport at about four in the afternoon, the helicopter swept past the large tent-shaped *hajj* terminal built especially to accommodate pilgrims en route to Mecca. The pilot landed the craft on a helipad outside the terminal reserved for the exclusive use of the royal family. There was a large contingent of soldiers and servants waiting there to greet them. One of the faces in the crowd was familiar. It was Faisal. He stood about a hundred feet from the helicopter, his olive green uniform encrusted with the sweat and dust accumulated during a long day of chasing the alien army across the desert. He smiled menacingly at Reg when the two of them made eye contact, then sent some of his soldiers to surround the king's chopper, just in case Reg tried to make a run for it.

But Reg had no intention of running. When he saw Faisal, he jumped out of the helicopter and marched directly toward him. Fadeela and the others followed him outside, leaving the king still listening to the recording. "Where the hell were you?" Reg demanded loudly as he marched threateningly toward Faisal.

The Saudi commander retained his customary poise, refusing to return Reg's hostile tone. As his soldiers stepped into Reg's path, he smiled easily and shook his head in disbelief. "I was absolutely correct, wasn't I? You are a difficult man to kill."

"Where were you?" Reg repeated fiercely. "We agreed we would work together."

"So we did," Faisal said, moving closer. "I ordered the air strike against the alien ship, just as we planned. But my pilots told me you never came outside."

"That's a lie. I fired a dozen flares into the air when we came out. Those jets were supposed to follow us to your camp in the hills. They didn't. But we made it into the hills without them, only to find you gone."

"A matter of priorities, Major. The city of At-Ta'if came

under attack during the night. I was forced to relocate my forces before you returned. In doing so, praise be to Allah, I saved thousands, perhaps hundreds of thousands of lives." Faisal and the men around him realized that this was a lie. By the time his forces arrived at At-Ta'if, the aliens had already left to chase Reg and his team across the desert. But he was accustomed to taking credit for more than he actually accomplished. "In any case," he went on, "we were successful in removing the biological agents from the alien ship before my planes destroyed it completely. You have been very helpful. And what is more, you have brought Fadeela back to me without a scratch on her pretty face."

Before Faisal could protect himself, Reg swung at him and connected. The blow landed squarely on the tip of Faisal's chin and sent him sprawling to the ground. A pair of soldiers grabbed Reg and pinned his arms behind his back while others leveled their guns at Remi, Ali, and Tye.

Faisal picked himself off the ground, rubbing his jaw, and gave Reg a deadly stare. He paused for a moment deciding how best to hurt him before issuing a command to his men. "Take the girl inside and wait for me." A pair of soldiers each grabbed one of Fadeela's arms and forced her toward the terminal building. Held at gunpoint, Ali and the others were powerless to stop them.

Faisal moved uncomfortably close to Reg, until they were practically nose to nose. "When my pilots first told me you'd come out of the ship alive," he hissed, "I was disappointed. But now I see that this way is better. Not only will I be able to enjoy the sweet fruit of this woman, but I will also have the pleasure of attending your public execution." Reg struggled to free his arms for another swing, but the soldiers held them fast. Instead, Faisal delivered a crushing punch that connected with Reg's rib cage. He was preparing to hit him again when the loudspeakers mounted to the exterior of the terminal building came to life and began blaring out a recorded conversation.

REG: "I repeat: Saudi commander, you have broken formation. You are currently running in the wrong direction."

FAISAL: "Do not interfere!... I'm afraid you are mistaken, major. You must be watching the wrong plane."

REG: "Negative, Faisal. I'm directly above you. Close enough to read your wing markings. You are running away from the engagement."

FAISAL: "Stay out of this, Cummins! I am not running. I am... I am positioning myself to observe the attack."

REG: "Admit it, Faisal, you're saving yourself because you know what's going to happen to those men. Order them to it break off."

FAISAL: "Damn you, Cummins, stay quiet! Cooperate with me and you will be rewarded."

REG: "And if I don't?"

FAISAL: "Then I will personally shoot you out of the sky."

REG: "I wouldn't advise it. You'd only be wasting another one of your king's planes."

FAISAL: "King Ibrahim is no longer a factor. The Saudi Air Force is now completely under my command and it is my will that—"

As Faisal listened, horrified, he forgot completely about punishing Reg and looked around desperately for the source of the embarrassing transmission. He soon spotted King Ibrahim staring at him sternly from the shadowy recesses of the royal helicopter. Brushing past Reg, Faisal ran to the helipad. "Stop this recording at once!" he shouted.

"Why should I?" the king asked.

Faisal stammered out an answer. "Because this is not... this was... you are exposing military secrets. You are... people may misunderstand."

"I don't understand," said the king, feigning confusion. "You said before the tape would prove Khalid Yamani's guilt and establish your bravery in the battle. This tape doesn't match the story you told everyone after the battle. In fact, it sounds as if you turned and ran."

Faisal glanced around helplessly at the loudspeakers, which continued to broadcast the sounds of the battle to the entire airport. "There is no need to continue playing the tape. I will explain everything," he told the king. "After all, you need me."

"How so?"

"I am the Saudi hero who saved Mecca!" he shouted. "Do you want to give the credit to a bunch of Western infidels and Jews? I can be very useful to you and your family. Without me, you will appear weak. As if you needed help from outside to protect the Holy City."

"I'm not so sure," said King Ibrahim, stroking his beard. "It seems to me Khalid Yamani acted quite bravely during the battle. Perhaps he will be accepted as our country's hero during the battle. But as I say, I'm not certain. That is why I am broadcasting the tape right now over several military frequencies to all parts of the country. This time, we can let the people decide who they consider their hero."

When Faisal learned that the entire nation was listening to the recording, he realized at once that he was finished. There would be no way to explain why he had flown away from that first bombing run, or why he had muscled the others out of the way to get the first shot for himself. It was all there on the tape, and he knew it. He backed away from the helicopter, then turned and ran toward a jeep that had been left unattended.

King Ibrahim made no move to stop him. Instead, he watched as Faisal jumped into the vehicle and drove away, burning with humiliation. A moment later, he picked up the handset on his radio and spoke to someone inside the terminal building. He ordered that Fadeela Yamani be found and brought outside again as soon as she was decently covered. Then he called to Reg.

"Major Cummins, come here please. We have not finished all of our business together. There is still the matter of your reward."

"Don't forget about your friends," Tye joked, as Reg began moving back to the royal helicopter.

Reg seemed in a great hurry to speak to the king. He hurried along for a few paces, then broke into a full run. It wasn't that he was eager to collect his reward; he was concerned about Fadeela. He informed the king that their chat would have to wait until he was positive Fadeela was safe. The old man laughed at his earnest concern and assured him he had already taken care of the matter. Then he invited Reg inside the helicopter, where the two men sat face-to-face for the next several minutes, negotiating. After some time, Mr. Yamani was called in to join them. The three of them were still talking when Fadeela reemerged from the terminal, escorted by a different set of soldiers. Somewhere, they had found a spare *abaya* and given it to her so she could cover herself. Reg happened to glance up from his conversation long enough to take in the strange sight of her: a battle-tested woman warrior wearing dusty combat fatigues beneath a long skein of black fabric that reached nearly to her ankles. Her boots, stained with oil and blood, protruded from below the cloth. She came striding out of the terminal in an unladylike fashion and joined Tye, Remi, and Ali. The three men pointed toward the helicopter, explaining the situation to her. When she learned what Reg and her father were discussing with the king, she put her hands on her hips and shook her veiled head back and forth to express her displeasure.

A few moments later, the three men stepped out of the helicopter and moved to join the others. Reg trailed along behind the two older men, who chatted amiably with each other as they doddered slowly across the landing pad, ignoring the last hour of the day's punishing heat. They smiled broadly, as if they were both pleased with the arrangement that had been hammered out. Reg's expression, on the other hand, gave no indication of how the negotiations had gone. When at last they reached the place where Fadeela and the others were waiting, the king's mood suddenly changed.

"I do not understand these Englishmen," he began loudly. "For his role in protecting our nation, I promised to give Major Cummins anything it was within my power to grant him. I offered him millions of dollars, my properties in Hawaii, one of my personal jets. But he insisted on asking for something else," he said, glancing toward Fadeela, "something that is not mine to give. The most I was able to do was to speak on his behalf to my old friend Karmal Yamani. Perhaps to save me from appearing ungenerous, Mr. Yamani has consented to the major's request." Then he turned to face the shrouded figure of Fadeela. "You must be quite an extraordinary young woman. The only thing he asks for is for you."

Fadeela's anger boiled over. "And you, the ruler of Saudi Arabia, custodian of the holy cities of Mecca and Medina, appear quite willing to oblige him. You give a Saudi woman to a Western man like you were handing over a cow." The king took a step backward, startled by the woman's outburst. He was trying to deliver the good news that she was going to get what she wanted, and was unprepared to face her wrath.

"I think you don't understand," King Ibrahim said.

"I understand that you men believe you can control me like a piece of property, trade me to one another like an old car. And in this case, you can't claim it is the will of Allah because he's not even a Muslim." Although her face was covered, Reg could feel Fadeela's green eyes staring at him like a pair of burning X-ray beams.

"She thinks I've asked to marry her," Reg said, explaining Fadeela's reaction.

"Haven't you?" she asked in a smaller voice.

Reg shook his head no.

"The very opposite," the king told her. "He has asked that you be given the power to choose your own husband. Accordingly, your engagement to Ghalil Faisal is officially canceled. Of course, if you still wish to marry Faisal, you may. Or anyone else for that matter."

"Is it true?" Fadeela asked her father.

He nodded that it was. "And if you wish to continue your education, either here or abroad, you are free to do so. I am not sure how many universities are left standing, but this time I will not interfere with your studies. It is up to you to decide."

"So, if I want to marry this man," Fadeela said, taking Remi by the arm, "I may do so without asking anyone's permission?" The king and her father nodded, but Remi warned her that his wife probably wouldn't like the idea. Fadeela, enjoying the idea of her new freedom, moved to Ali and took him by the arm. "Or this man?" Again, the answer was yes. Nodding, she turned, and as she began moving toward Reg, Tye couldn't resist clearing his throat ostentatiously.

"Aren't you forgetting someone?" he asked, pretending to be hurt.

"Forgive me." Fadeela laughed. She took hold of Tye's aim as she had with the other men, and asked, "Or this one?"

King Ibrahim and Mr. Yamani both made the same joke. "No, not that one!"

When Tye had recovered from his momentary

heartbreak, Fadeela walked over and stood in front of Reg. "Thank you. This is a wonderful gift."

"It's the least I could do. After all, you gave me what I needed most: something worth fighting for."

"I'm smiling."

"I'm glad."

"But I hope you don't expect me to act like a foolish girl and ask you to marry me."

"That thought never crossed my mind, princess."

"Liar. But tell me, is it true you turned down all the riches King Ibrahim offered you?" When Reg said it was, Fadeela shook her head in disappointment. "You could have made the rest of your life relatively comfortable. Isn't that the goal of all Westerners? But now, I'm afraid you've made things difficult for yourself." Again, she shook her head sadly.

"I'd appreciate any advice you could give me on the subject," Reg said.

"Actually, I've already come up with a few ideas. Shall we walk?"

The two of them strolled away from the others, past the helicopter, and out into the late-afternoon sun. They walked up and down the apron of the nearest runway for a long while, making decisions about the future.